STAND BY,
STAND BY

Chris Ryan

STAND BY, STAND BY

ZERO OPTION

ARROW

This edition published by Arrow in 2002,
an imprint of The Random Group,
20 Vauxhall Bridge Road, London SW1V 2SA

Papers used by Random House UK Ltd are natural
recyclable products made from wood grown in
sustainable forests. The manufacturing processes
conform to the environment regulations of the
country of origin.

A catalogue record for this book is available
from the British Library

Printed and bound in Great Britain by
Cox & Wyman Ltd, Reading, Berkshire

ISBN 0 09 188544 2

For my mother

ACKNOWLEDGEMENTS

I wish to give special thanks to someone who shall remain anonymous but without whose editorial help I would never have finished this. To all my family and friends for their patience and understanding. Also to Mark Booth, Liz Rowlinson, Tracey Jennings and Nicky Eaton at Century.

The Castle

As the knights fight in the hall, people stand by the wall.
Jokers joke whilst people poke at one another.
Shrieking sounds down below where cellars glow.
The King sits on his throne when people groan.
The Lady who wears silver threads lives in dread of the
    spider and the dead.

by Sarah Ryan, aged 7, 1996

GLOSSARY

ASU	IRA Active Service Unit
Basha	Sleeping shelter
Bergen	Rucksack
BG	Bodyguard (noun or verb)
Blue-on-blue	Accidental strike on own forces
Box	General name for intelligence services
Casevac	Casualty evacuation
CAT	Counter-attack team
Comms	Communications
CTR	Close target reconnaissance
DET	Intelligence gathering organization
DAS	Colombian Police
DF	Direction finding
Dicker	IRA scout
Director	Officer commanding special forces, generally a brigadier
DOP	Drop-off point
DPMs	Disruptive pattern material camouflage garments
DZ	Drop zone
EMOE	Explosive method of entry
ERV	Emergency rendezvous
EMU	Encryption device
FMB	Forward mounting base
FOB	Forward operating base
GPS	Global positioning system (navigation aid)
Head-Shed	Headquarters
Incoming	Incoming fire
Int	Intelligence
IO	Intelligence officer
LO	Liaison officer

LUP	Lying-up point
LZ	Landing zone
Magellan	Brand name of GPS
OP	Observation post
PE	Plastic explosive
Phys	Physical exercise
PIRA	Provisional IRA
Player	Terrorist
PNGs	Passive night goggles
PUP	Pick-up point
QRF	Quick reaction force
RTU	Return to unit
Rupert	Officer
SAM	Surface-to-air missile
Satcom	Telephone using satellite transmission
SEAL	Sea, Air and Land – American special forces unit
Shreddies	Army-issue underpants
SOCO	Scene of Crimes Officer
SP	Special Projects
SSM	Squadron sergeant major
RUC	Royal Ulster Constabulary
TACBE	Emergency radio
TCG	Tactical Control Group
Tout	Informer
UCBT	Under-car booby trap
US	Unserviceable
VCP	Vehicle control point
319	VHF radio

WEAPONS

AK 47	Soviet-design 7.62mm short rifle
203	Combination of 5.56mm automatic rifle (top barrel) and 40mm grenade launcher (below)
HK 53	5.56mm automatic rifle
Galil	Israeli-made 7.62mm automatic rifle
G3	7.62mm automatic rifle
Long	Any rifle
L2	Hand grenade
MP 5	9mm sub-machine-gun
RPG7	Soviet-made rocket launcher
SA80	5.56mm rifle
Short	Any pistol
Sig	Sigsauer 9mm pistol

ONE

That night the dream came again. As usual I was being swept forward, unable to control my speed. I felt as though I was on a roller-coaster at a fairground, accelerating bumpily through the cold, dark air. But why were no other passengers riding with me? Why was I alone in this freezing night?

The ride was very rough. OK, I thought, the track's buckled, but I can handle it – and I clung tight to the side-rails to stop myself being flung out. Then something began to drag at my left arm, holding it back, as if that side of the carriage was being left behind. Let go, dickhead! I told myself, but my fingers wouldn't unclamp from the rail. Pain ripped through me. I thought, I'm going down here. I'm going to get torn in half.

The cold was horrendous. The air pouring past me was so frozen it was searing my skin. When I opened my mouth to yell, it drove a fierce pain into the roots of my teeth, so that I had to clamp my lips shut. Then over the black horizon ahead came a gleam of light. I was hurtling towards that bright rim, the rim of the world. All too well I knew what I'd see beyond it. Up and on I went, faster than ever, my arm being torn in half at the elbow.

Then in a split second I was over the top and into the light, diving towards an operating theatre as big as an airport. A wall of heat rushed up to meet me, so that in an instant I was pouring sweat, like down in the sands of Abu Dhabi. Brilliant lamps blazed on to the table, and life-support equipment was ranged alongside: drips, oxygen cylinders, white dishes full of instruments. Attendants in green gowns and masks were waiting, ready – and in the centre stood a tall surgeon with a hypodermic syringe the length of an AK 47, the point of its gleaming needle levelled at my eye. I longed for a gun so I could drop him at a distance, but no: I was going in close. 'BASTARDS!' I roared as I hurtled down towards him. 'BASTARDS! BASTARDS!'

I woke up. Kath stood in the doorway, the light from the landing shining on her straight fair hair. In the background Tim was crying.

'Geordie,' she said quietly. 'Are you all right?'

'Yeah, yeah.' I tried to turn over, but I found I'd got the bedclothes wound around me so I was trussed like an oven-ready chicken.

Kath came across and put her hand on my forehead. 'You're soaking. Better change the sheets. I'll get you a clean pair.'

'I'll be OK, thanks. What time is it?'

'Just after three.' She sat down on the edge of the bed, silhouetted against the light. With one hand she drew her dressing-gown tight around her neck, and with the other she smoothed out the top sheet. 'What time did you get to bed?'

'Not sure. Maybe half one.'

'How much did you drink?'

'Not a lot. Two or three more Scotches.'

She knew perfectly well that I'd been hitting the booze far worse than I admitted, and going to ridiculous lengths to cover up. She knew that alcohol was becoming a serious problem for me, and several times she'd pleaded with me to seek professional advice.

Now she asked, 'What happened? Was it the dream again?'

'Yeah. Was I making a noise?'

'I thought someone was killing you. You were yelling at the top of your voice. It woke Tim.'

'I'm sorry.'

'It's all right. I meant to ask – did you hear any news about when Tony's coming over to do selection?'

'He'll be here in June, I think. Why?'

'Just wondered.'

I knew what she was thinking: that Tony had been my salvation in Iraq, and might again act as a stabilizing influence when he arrived in England. He might help me get the whole spring came. Under her direction I did the heavy digging, but it was she who planned and planted everything. She was thrilled to find that several of the trees in the spinney were rowans, or mountain ash – her favourites – which put on a tremendous show of bright-red berries in the autumn. The place and its associations reminded me of my childhood home in the north, where as a boy I was forever ferreting rabbits and walking the hedgerows.

In KC we were as happy as anybody could have been. It was the first time that either of us had lived in a house without a number – in our eyes a big plus, as it made us feel we had the edge over our friends living in towns. The house and rooms were exactly the right size for us, neither too big nor too small. The place was so private that in summer we could sunbathe stark naked on the lawn. Kath got a vegetable patch going, and grew some cracking beans, peas, potatoes and lettuces, and herbs galore. We ate so many fresh salads that our ears started turning green. In winter we were snug as squirrels, because I got permission from the neighbouring farmer to collect firewood from the spinney, and in the living room we kept a Norwegian log-burner on the go day and night. The stove had a back-boiler for boosting the hot water; if I opened up the draught, I could get the tank boiling.

The footpaths and woodland tracks were ideal for running, and I could do my phys – physical training – at home just as well as round the camp. Soon I had two circuits worked out – one of six miles, one of eight. Kath talked of getting a horse . . . if we could persuade the farmer to rent us a paddock, and after the baby had arrived.

Tim was born, on time, in the County Hospital in Hereford. I watched him come into the world, holding Kath's hand and trying to share her pain. He weighed 8 lbs 2 oz, and once he was cleaned up we could see he was going to have hair even fairer and eyes even bluer than his mother's. Kath's parents were so chuffed with their first grandchild that they came straight over from Belfast to see him; they stayed in the cottage, and Meg helped with the baby for a few days, until Kath got her strength back. Den, a retired doctor, didn't do much except offer medical tips – and I don't think he did much at home either, except watch television.

So we carried on, happy with each other. In the summer of 1990 I went to Africa with the squadron, on team training. We were away two months, but I got back to find everything just the same, and Kath and I carried on where we'd left off. It was only when Saddam invaded Kuwait, and D Squadron was deployed to the Gulf, that things began to go belly-up.

Leaving was tough. Before we flew out from Brize Norton at the start of January '91, Kath and I had some emotional moments trying to plan a future for her and Tim, in case I didn't come back. The house would be hers, of course, and she would be free to sell it if she wanted. But I told her it would be my wish that she should marry again, and that the kid should be educated as well as she could afford, at some fee-paying school if no good state school was available. Such thoughts brought with them many tears, but we did our best to look the future in the face.

Next day we were gone. Before the war started I was able to phone Kath from time to time, from the R & R centres established in the desert, and everything was OK. The satellite connections were perfect, and it was like talking to her in the room next door. But once we deployed across the border into Iraq at the end of January there was no chance of further communication, and it wasn't until the ninth of April, when members of D Squadron were reunited in Cyprus on our way home, that I spoke to her again. And as it turned out, during those ten weeks – in the desert, in hospital, in prison – I'd been through quite a bit.

On the line to Akrotiri, Kath sounded very much herself – worried about me, lively, loving, full of news about Tim. It was I who had changed.

Like everyone else I looked forward to getting home; for weeks I'd yearned to be back in England. Yet when I reached Hereford, there was something wrong. I didn't go straight home. I didn't want to – couldn't face it. To my shame, I went out on the piss with a couple of the single lads who lived on the block. All *they* wanted was to have a few beers and go downtown to see if they could pick up a girl for the night. For me, things weren't so simple.

By the time I reached the cottage I wasn't making much sense. Kath looked terrific – I could see that in an objective sort of way – but she also looked shocked that I had arrived back in such a state. Tim had grown inches and was starting to talk. She'd taught him to say 'Dad', and he brought the word out on cue. I should have been bowled over. Instead I felt nothing. It was extraordinary, but I didn't even feel randy. By then the other guys would have been randy as hell; during the flight they hadn't been able to stop talking about how they were going to screw their bollocks off the moment the Herc touched the tarmac. I should have been the same, but I didn't seem to fancy Kath any more. I couldn't make love to her; I could hardly kiss her on the cheek, or even look her in the eye. As for telling her what had happened to me – I just explained a bit about my arm, and skirted round the rest.

She was hurt, of course. Although she played it down, she couldn't conceal her worry and unhappiness. I think she hoped that time would heal the trouble between us, whatever it was, and after a while things would return to normal.

All along I knew that the fault lay with me, not her, and I tried to say so. But then began the nightmares and the headaches started. I started on the booze – something I'd never much bothered with before – and instead of mending, our relationship went further downhill, until we were making space round each other as we moved about the house, and hardly speaking.

When I went to the Med Centre in camp for checks on my arm I should have told the doc what was happening. But naturally I didn't want to reveal what seemed to be weaknesses. Like everyone in the Regiment, I wanted to get sent on operations: that was the whole point of life. To admit one had psychological problems was the surest way of missing some good trip, or even of blighting one's career completely and being put on the back burner. When the head-shed offered us the services of a shrink, nobody wanted to go near him.

The Paracetamol was starting to take effect. Slowly my head eased and some of the anxieties fell away. I heard the clock in the living room strike four, and that was all.

Next day was bright and brilliant, a glorious May morning. When I came into the kitchen, sunlight was already streaming across the table, and Tim's face, plastered with porridge, was such a sight I couldn't help smiling. But I felt terrible, hung over from the mixture of drinks that I'd poured down myself the night before.

As always, Kath had made proper coffee, and, as I got myself a cup, I announced, 'I've come to a decision. I'm going to see the doc.'

'Great!' Kath's face lit up. 'See what he says. It can't do any harm.'

'That's right. If I don't like it, I don't need to take any notice.'

I was soon away, driving into town. She'd gone back to her job at the bank in the mornings, and was putting Tim into a tots' playschool. At lunchtime a friend gave them both a lift home, so all I had to do was drop them off on my way to the camp.

At Stirling Lines – named after David Stirling, who founded the SAS as a long-range desert group in Africa during World War Two – the usual two MoD Plods in uniform were on the gate. As I drove towards them they recognized me, waved and raised the barrier. In the car-park I found myself next to a mate from D Squadron, Pat Martin, who was just locking his Scorpio.

'Hi, Pat,' I said. 'Listen, will you tell Tom that I'm going to the Med Centre? I'll be up the Squadron later.'

'No bother. Something the matter?'

'Just checking my arm.'

It was coming up to 8.30. The rest of the guys would already be assembling in the Squadron Interest Room for Prayers – properly, roll-call and morning briefing. I knew that Tom Dawson, the sergeant major, would accept my message, and that I could square him later. One of the Old and Bold, he'd done more than fifteen years in the Regiment, and had seen it all – the tail-end of the Dhofar campaign, the Falklands, the Gulf. In the Falklands he'd been one of the few who survived the Sea King crash. Seventeen members of D and G Squadrons and half a dozen others were killed when the chopper went down in the sea on a cross-decking sortie. He'd told me he too suffered nightmares. He'd been unable to sleep in a dark room with the door shut; if ever he woke to find the door closed he'd leap up in a frenzy. His own experiences had made him sympathetic, and I knew he'd support me.

I headed straight for the Med Centre, hoping that Tracy Jordan would be on duty. There were two girls who took turns at the front desk, week on, week off. Sheila was small and dumpy, about as lively as a suet pudding, but Tracy was something else. Nearly six feet in her socks, with wild coppery curls tied in a top-knot that made her look even taller, she was all arms and legs, and at twenty-three or -four, still seemed like an overgrown filly. She was quite a well-known figure about camp because she was athletic, and was often to be seen running with a girl friend in the lunch hour. Rumour had it that she was a demon at squash; apart from being fit, she could stand in the centre of the court and scoop the ball out of the corners without having to move very far.

I knew practically nothing else about her. But I'd often noticed that her eyes carried a hint of suppressed merriment; this, combined with a tendency to make mildly piss-taking remarks, made a lot of the guys fancy her. But she had rumbled the bonk-and-be-off tactics of the Regiment long ago, and stuck to a boyfriend from outside. All the same, reporting sick was less of a drag if Tracy was on duty.

My luck was in. There she sat at her desk, in a snowy sweatshirt and pale blue jeans. Today the ribbon holding her top-knot was emerald green. Did her eyebrows go up as she saw me come in?

'Sergeant Geordie Sharp!' she announced in that faintly mocking voice. 'What can I do for you today?'

'Watch yourself,' I told her.

9

'What do you mean?' She wriggled her slim little behind around on her chair in mock indignation.

'Just that,' I said. 'I need to see Doc Anderson.'

'Major Anderson's off. It's Captain Lester.'

'OK then.'

'There's only one ahead of you. Take a seat. Shouldn't be long.'

She rummaged in a filing cupboard for my documents, and handed me the brown manila packet. It didn't worry me that Anderson was away – I'd never got much change out of him. Maybe this new guy would be better.

I waited a couple of minutes, then the light above the door changed from red to green and I went in to find a young, fit-looking man with prematurely grey hair cut very short. He took a quick look at the outside of my packet and said, 'Hello, George.'

'It's Geordie,' I told him. 'My Christian name's George, but I never use it. Everyone calls me Geordie. My accent and all.'

'OK.' He gave a twitch of a grin, opened the packet and began to read the papers. 'Injury to your left arm,' he said. 'Compound fractures of the humerus. Pinned and plated in an Iraqi hospital.'

He pulled out an X-ray, fitted it into the front of a light-box on the wall, and studied it for a moment.

'Is that what's giving you trouble?'

'No, no. My arm's fine.'

'Can I have a look?'

'Sure.' I pulled up the sleeve of my sweater and laid my arm on the desk. He felt it carefully along the line of the scar and looked back at the X-ray.

'Tender?'

'Not too bad.'

'Can you use it all right?'

'No bother.'

'Turn your hand back and forth . . . open and close your fingers . . . . Weights?'

'I've started again with light ones. Just building up.'

10

'I see. How did you do it?'

'Came off my motor bike.'

'Ah!' He took my wrist and sat silent for a moment, counting my pulse rate. I liked his direct, no-nonsense manner. Then he asked, 'What's the matter, then?'

'Headaches,' I said. 'They're getting really bad. And I'm having nightmares that scare the shit out of me.'

'Did you hit your head in the crash?'

'No – not that I know of. My head never gave any trouble at the time. This only started recently.'

'Have you been taking anything?'

'Only the odd aspirin and Paracetamol.'

'You're sure you haven't been concocting things out of your med pack? Some of you fellows are buggers for self-help, I know.'

'No, no. I don't touch any of that.'

'What about booze?'

'Well . . .'

'Are you drinking a lot?'

'A bit.'

'How much?'

'Too much.'

'OK.'

He put me on the couch, brought out his stethoscope and listened to my heart. Then he took my blood pressure with the old arm clamp, looked into my ears and shone lights in my eyes. As he was working he said casually, 'How did you come to fall off the bike?'

'It was at night. We were 150 kilometres inside Iraq, behind enemy lines, hitting the comms towers and blowing up fibre-optic lines. And we were on the lookout for mobile Scud launchers. That night the squadron was tasked to move up and find a new lying-up position in which to hide the following day. I was recceing forward on a motorbike. The ground was very rough – a lot of rocks and loose gravel, with sudden deep ditches. We started to see lights in the distance ahead – vehicles moving – and we accelerated to cut them off. I dropped into a bloody great hole – never saw it – and the

11

bike came down on top of me. Smashed my arm against a rock.'

'Then what?'

'If you're interested?'

'Sure.'

'The guys picked me up and splinted the arm as best they could. Not a pretty sight. One end of the bone was sticking out through the muscle. They put me in the back of a Land Rover and called for a medevac. The head-shed in Saudi was co-ordinating rescue efforts with the Americans. They sent a message to say that a joint operation would be diverted to pick me up. A chopper would come in the following night, to lift me out along with two American casualties.'

I paused and looked sideways at the doctor. He still seemed to be interested, so I went on. 'That worked fine. We spent the day lying up in a wadi, and soon after dark the heli picked us up on time, with some SEAL guys riding security. But we'd been flying for no more than ten minutes when we were targeted by a SAM. One moment we were cruising steadily, then suddenly everything went crazy. Sirens blasted off, the chopper began to dive and twist in violent evasive manoeuvres, the pilot fired off his chaff in the hope of decoying the missile – but no luck. Suddenly there was this almighty bang. It felt as if the chopper had been hit sideways like a tennis ball. The next thing I knew there was another terrific impact, and we were on the ground. Tony, one of the SEALs, was dragging me out of the wreckage. When we made a check, we found we were the only two alive. The co-pilot had been decapitated. The pilot had lost both arms. What we couldn't understand was how the chopper hadn't caught fire. Soon we saw lights coming at us. Before we could get ourselves together we'd been surrounded by fifty or sixty Iraqis. We could have dropped one or two, but not dozens. So that was us captured.'

I stopped. I was still lying on my back on the couch, talking up to the ceiling. I seemed to be out of breath. I realized that I'd been speaking faster and faster. I turned my head to the right and looked at the doc again. He was watching me carefully.

12

'Carry on,' he said.

I looked back at the ceiling.

'I don't remember too much about the next bit. I already had a fever – must have got dirt into my arm, the wound was infected. Also I'd banged one of my morphine syrettes into my leg, and got some more from other guys, so I was quite dopey. They threw us into the back of a truck and drove for the rest of that night. We got to some military camp. They tried to interrogate me – I got slapped around the head a bit – but they could see I wasn't making much sense, and I didn't give them anything but my name and number. I stuck to my pre-arranged cover-story – that I was a medic, and I'd come out as part of a joint Anglo-US team to recover downed air-crew.

'Then we were rolling again, in some other wagon. That part's even hazier. I think I was delirious by that stage. The next thing I remember is lying on an operating table, with guys in green gowns and masks standing round. Jesus! I thought. What are they going to do to me? I tried to get up, but couldn't. I seemed to be strapped to the table. I was fucking terrified.

'Then this tall guy appeared beside me. He had no mask on, so I could see he had a thick, black moustache, just like Saddam. Under it he was smiling – a nasty, thin kind of smile. When he started to talk I was amazed, because he spoke fluent English.

'"I'm going to operate on your injured arm," he said. "But don't worry. I know what I am doing. I was trained in England at one of your best hospitals – the John Radcliffe, in Oxford."

'For a moment I was reassured. I knew the Radcliffe, and I reckoned the Iraqi must have been there; he couldn't have invented that name out of the blue. I think I said, "Great!".

'"Your English medical system is very good," he went on. "What is not so good is that you tell us lies about yourself. It is important for us to know which unit you belong to, Sergeant Sharp. Come now – we need to know."

'I repeated my spiel about being a medic belonging to 22 Para Field Ambulance, the unit I'd invented. I could see he didn't believe me, and after a few other questions he asked

13

sarcastically, "Where is it based, this famous unit?"

'"Wroughton," I replied, referring to the tri-service hospital in Wiltshire.

'He'd heard of Wroughton, because he'd been there while at Oxford. It made him pause, but not for long. All this time the lights were blazing down into my face. I was shuddering and sweating with the fever. Then with a sudden movement the Iraqi picked something up from a trolley beside him and held it over me.

'"You see this?" he said, and the half-smile had died from under his black moustache. "This is a hypodermic syringe, full of anaesthetic. If I plunge the needle into your arm, it will put you out. But if I touch your eyeball with it, you will never see again."

'"Bastard!" I told him.

'"So, what is your real unit, please?"

'"Bastard!" I shouted again.

'"Sergeant Sharp, this needle is very sharp. You like my little joke? You should laugh, to show you appreciate Iraqi humour. We are a very humorous people. Now – if the needle goes into your eye, you will not feel much. But afterwards, I promise you, you will not see anything at all. Which is your master eye?"

'I knew what was coming next, so I held my mouth shut.

'"You don't know? Or you won't say? It doesn't matter. We'll assume your right eye is master, and start with that. Perhaps when that is gone, you will see sense with your left."

'He held the syringe so close in front of my face that I couldn't focus on it any more. I struggled and fought to free my good arm and my legs. I think I shat myself. I yelled at the top of my voice, "BASTARDS! The whole fucking lot of you are BASTARDS!"'

A noise somewhere close to me brought me back to Hereford. A loud knock had sounded on the door, which now burst open. Tracy's head appeared in the gap. The saucy look had gone from her face, and she was looking quite scared. 'You lot all right in here?' she asked. 'I thought the doc was getting attacked.'

'It's OK.' Doc Lester smiled. 'The devils are coming out of him.'

Tracy withdrew, and I apologized for making such a noise. Once again I was soaked in sweat.

'Go on,' the doctor said again.

'He did it three or four times. I don't know what happened in the end – whether I passed out, or whether he stuck the needle in my arm. I came round to find the operation done, and my arm in plaster.'

'Whoever he was, he did a good job,' said the doc. 'Plated it, too. The X-rays show a perfect union.'

'If ever I see him again I'll make the shit fly out of him.'

Doc Lester took my wrist again and counted. 'Your pulse-rate's gone from 64 to 180,' he remarked. He looked once more at the X-ray. 'And then you were in gaol?'

'Yes. Two weeks or so in the hospital, then five weeks in one prison or another, eating crap and feeling like death.'

'But no torture?'

'It depends what you mean by torture. There was no systematic interrogation, but every now and then the guards would give us a kicking or a beating. And they'd hit us around with whips. There was one who'd come and tap on my plaster cast with a wooden stick, harder and harder, until I yelled. The worst thing was that we hadn't a clue about what was happening – in the war or anywhere else. The Iraqis kept giving us a load of shit about how the Coalition was losing, but we never heard any proper news.'

'Who's "we"?'

'Myself and Tony Lopez, the American SEAL on the medevac chopper that got shot down. His cover story was similar to mine, and when he stuck to it, the Iraqis eventually put us together. He's a great guy, Tony. Bags of guts. As it happens, he's coming here on selection any time now.'

The doctor thought for a minute, then asked, 'So now you're getting headaches? When did they start?'

'A couple of weeks ago. Also, I started getting this recurrent nightmare. It's always more or less the same – a version of that scene in the hospital.'

'I'm not surprised.' The doc got up and walked to the window, looking out. 'I think you're suffering from delayed shock. It's stress brought on by what you went through. People in our profession are starting to talk about something called post-traumatic stress. It's to do with the after-effects of wounds and captivity – though nobody knows much about it yet. Have you seen a shrink?'

'No. They offered us one, but none of the guys fancied it.'

'How about taking your troubles home? Have you talked to your mum, for instance?'

'I don't have one.'

'Or your dad?'

'No. I'm an orphan.'

'Oh.' He picked up a sheet of paper from the desk and looked at it again. 'I see. I'm sorry.'

'No sweat.'

'What about your wife?'

'That's the trouble.' I sat up. 'This is it, Doc. I can't talk to her.'

'Why not?'

'I don't know. It's not her fault, it's mine. She hasn't changed, but I have. Could they have given me something in the prison?'

'Like what?'

'Something that would put me off her . . . that would kill my sex drive? Bromide or something?'

The doctor laughed, but not unkindly. 'If they did they've got drugs the West has never heard of.'

'So what's happened, then? I don't even fancy her any more. She gets on my nerves. Everything she says or does seems to jar. I used to love her, but I don't now.'

'As I said, it's all down to delayed shock. The stress is catching up on you.'

'So what can I do about it? The worst of it is, she's busting herself to look after me, but that only seems to make things worse. I don't want her around the place.'

'You need a break. Do you have any children?'

'One. Tim – he's coming up for three.'

16

'Does your wife have a family?'

'Yes. They're across the water, near Belfast.'

'Could she go and stay with them for a while?'

'Well, I suppose so.' I thought about it for a moment, and asked, 'You mean, we have a trial separation?'

'That would make it into a bit of a drama. I wouldn't call it that. Just call it a break. You could try it for two or three weeks. It would give you a chance to sort yourself out. Meanwhile, I'll give you something to take. Two a day.' He scribbled out a prescription and handed me the chit. 'Take it easy,' he said. 'You'll be OK in a while. Try and ease off the booze, as well. That'll help.'

'Thanks, Doc. Thanks for listening.'

'It was a pleasure,' he said. 'I enjoyed hearing your story.'

I stood up and headed for the door.

'That'll be £57.50,' Tracy said as I came out.

'I'll send a cheque.'

'Seriously, are you OK?' She uncrossed her long legs and stood up. She was almost as tall as me.

'More or less. I've been getting these headaches.'

She came and stood close to me, looking into my face. 'It's what happened over there, isn't it?'

'I guess so.'

'Well – I'm sorry. I hope you're better soon. You probably need time to get over it.'

'That's what the doc said.'

'Good luck, then.'

'Thanks, Tracy. Your medicine's as good as anybody's.' I was going to give her a peck on the cheek, but at that instant the telephone rang.

After so much emotion, my Spanish course seemed deadlier than ever. There were eight of us studying, and the bait was the possibility that a team job might come up in Colombia, where the forces of law and order were fighting the drug barons in the war against cocaine. The thought of a trip to South America was certainly an incentive, but when it came down to the nitty-gritty – Jesus Christ! (Or, as they would say

17

down there, *¡Jesu-Cristo!*) There I sat, struggling to concentrate on the strange words and pronunciation, while all the time my mind was on Kath and what I was going to tell her. What would my mates in the Squadron say if she went home? Would they write me off as a wanker? I supposed we could invent some problem – it was true that her mother was soon going into hospital for a hip replacement, and would need looking after for a while afterwards . . .

Our instructor was a flabby-looking major from the Education Corps, with thin, fair hair and a poncified accent. He could speak Spanish all right, but it was *quiero hablar* this and *más desfacio, por favor* that, until my headache was worse than ever, in spite of Doc Lester's magic pills. I stuck out the day, but only because the thought of facing Kath was worse.

When I got home that evening, I didn't say much at first. I repeated what the doc had told me about delayed reaction and the after-effects of stress, but I waited till Kath had tucked Tim up in bed before I nerved myself to put the knife in.

I was just going to get another Scotch, but stopped myself. She was standing at one of the units in the kitchen, chopping vegetables on a wooden board. I sat down at the table behind her and said, 'Kath, I've had an idea.'

'Oh yes?'

I told her what the doc had suggested. For a while she continued chopping. Then the movement of her hand ceased, but she didn't turn round. I thought she was crying. I knew I should go over and comfort her, take her by the shoulders, but the great block that had stifled my emotions wouldn't allow it. I sat there in agony until suddenly she turned on me, eyes blazing.

'So, it's a separation you want,' she said bitterly.

'No, no. Just a break.'

'A trial separation is what they call it.'

'Well – whatever.'

'There's only one thing I want to know.'

'What's that?'

'Is there someone else?'

I was so taken aback I hesitated before answering and,

18

naturally, that made things worse. 'No, no!' I insisted. 'There's nobody.'

'Are you sure?'

'Of course. For God's sake!'

I can't deny that my mind flew straight to Tracy – but nevertheless what I'd said was true.

Kath waited a moment, chopping away again at her vegetables, before she asked, 'How do I know Mum will have us? You realize she's going into the Musgrave any moment? She can't put it off – she's been waiting for years.'

'Of course. I know. I thought maybe it would be a good idea if you were there to give her a hand when she comes out.'

'Big deal! How long am I supposed to go for?'

'It depends. Maybe a month.'

'What's everyone going to say?'

'We'll put it round that your mum needs help after her operation.'

'I can see you've thought it all out.'

'Kath – it's my fault, I know. I'm not blaming you. It's all down to me.'

She gave me a strange look. I think she was more scared than angry.

'I'll have to hand in my notice at the bank.'

'I know. But that's not the end of the world. I'll be able to send money.'

'Who'll look after you if I go?'

'I'll manage. I can get most meals in camp.'

When she looked round again, her eyes were full of tears, and she said, half in pity, half in contempt, 'You poor old thing!'

The bank took her resignation in good part, and we arranged for her to go the following Saturday. Her mother positively welcomed the plan, although she didn't know what was behind it, of course. The movements clerk in camp booked air tickets – two out of my allocation of three – so that there was no cost to us. Kath didn't take much luggage – one suitcase for herself and a holdall for Tim. As for Tim, if he'd cried as they were leaving, I think I'd have cracked up; thank God he didn't. We'd told him he was going for a holiday with his Gran, and that chuffed him no end. He began packing his favourite teddies and telling everyone how the aeroplane would lift them up over the water and come down in Gran's house.

We left KC at 6.30 on another lovely morning. Both of us were holding emotion at bay by keeping up a strictly practical front. As Kath got into the car she said, 'Don't forget to single the carrots when they're big enough, in about a week. Leave them spaced at one every couple of inches, and push the earth well down afterwards. Otherwise carrot fly will get in.'

As we headed for Birmingham, our side of the motorway was almost empty; at the weekend, most people were going south. We didn't talk much, and when I set the two of them down at the departure door of the terminal building, it was just a quick kiss on the cheek and, 'We'll speak soon, then.' As I drove away I turned my head and saw little Tim waving.

TWO

Tony was due in from the SEAL base in Florida one evening towards the end of June. The US military flight was scheduled to arrive at RAF Lyneham at 1630, so I borrowed a car from the MT section and drove up the A40 to give him a lift to Hereford. When it turned out that the plane was an hour late, I sat around in the arrivals lounge and had plenty of time to reflect on our conversations in the Iraqi gaol.

Born in Puerto Rico, the son of an electrician, he had one brother. When he was five, his father had decided to take the family to America, in search of a better life for them all. As they were leaving, the father said they were going because America was the land of opportunity. But things didn't work out well for them. They ended up living in a Hispanic area of New York, and after a couple of years Tony's father died, so his mother was left to bring up the two boys on her own. By the time Tony left school he'd been stabbed twice and shot once, all in casual muggings. Prospects of civilian work were zero, so as soon as he was old enough he joined the US Marine Corps, and after two or maybe three years went on into the Navy SEALs.

In 1989 he'd taken part in Operation Just Cause, aimed at removing President Noriega from Panama. A team of four divers was to put explosive charges on Noriega's 65-foot patrol boat, the *Presidente Porras*, so that the vessel couldn't be used to escape. Having left their own ship in two Gemini inflatables, they slipped into the harbour in wetsuits with enough oxygen to give them four hours underwater. Once they'd identified the boat, they hung 24-lb timed charges of plastic explosive over the propellers before returning undetected to their mother ship.

As they were leaving, they heard the explosives go off, and

knew the patrol boat was out of action for the duration, if not for ever. The success put them on a high as they flew off by helicopter for their second task – to capture Paitilla airfield, not far from Panama City, and to disable a Lear jet owned by Noriega.

The platoon were so confident about their plan that they saw no need to take heavy weapons; they thought they could accomplish the task by stealth – sneak in, take out a few guards, and have the airfield under their command. But as their choppers approached they started to take incoming fire. Too late they realized that the place was full of Noriega's troops, armed with heavy weapons. The SEALs eventually managed to capture the field, but only at severe cost. In the firefights, which were fearsome, they suffered eleven casualties, four of them dead. Among those four were three of Tony's good mates. And so he learnt how easily an operation can go tits-up, ending in a bag of shit.

At last the tannoy announced the arrival of the flight, and in came the C-141 from Florida. A few minutes later Tony burst out of the Customs exit, with a pack on his back and a big holdall in his left hand. When he saw me waiting, his face lit up. 'Well, I'll be damned!' he exclaimed, hammering me on the shoulder with his free fist.

'You're looking good!' I said.

'You too.'

He'd put on weight – which was hardly a surprise, considering he'd been half-starved the last time I saw him. Now he was fit and bronzed, altogether in great shape. His tan accentuated the Puerto Rican elements in his appearance. With his jet-black hair and thick, arched eyebrows he was very dark anyway, almost swarthy; now his skin was even darker, and his teeth, when he grinned, shone even whiter. His hard New York accent was just as I remembered it: 'work' came out as 'woik', 'person' as 'poyson'.

The OC had asked me to help him settle in, so on his first night I showed him round the camp before leaving him to have a shower and get his head down until the jet-lag wore off. On the second evening I drove him out to Keeper's Cottage,

22

and on the way I decided to break the news about me and Kath. I could have kept up the pretence that she'd gone home to look after her mother, but I'd got to know Tony so well that I didn't feel like trying to deceive him. Of course he'd never seen her, but I'd talked so much about her while we were guests of Saddam that he must have felt he knew her well.

'Hey,' he said when he heard. 'That's too bad. But you'll get her back over.'

It was a statement, rather than a question.

'Maybe,' I said. 'I've chilled out a good bit since she went away.'

'You'll want to see the kid, anyway.'

Again I knew he was right.

The rain was pissing down, so KC didn't look its best, but Tony fell for it, drenched as it was. He kept saying, 'This is real neat!' and started on about the possibilities of hunting. He seemed surprised I hadn't been out blasting the local wildlife. 'Why, I bet you could hunt squirrels right in back here,' he said, looking up at the oak spinney.

'Oh, yeah. There's plenty of them. Rabbits too.'

'Who's the gardener?' he asked, surveying the unkempt forest of vegetables.

'Kath. I haven't a clue. Every time we speak on the phone she tells me to do this or that – earth up the spuds or thin out the lettuces – but I just don't have the time.'

Indoors, the first thing Tony saw was a photo of her and Tim, taken recently in fine weather on the shore of Strangford Lough, with a background of water and smooth green islands. Kath was wearing a blue check dress and Tim, in a pale blue T-shirt and grey shorts, was standing on a stone wall, so his head was nearly level with hers. The picture had arrived only the day before, and I'd stuck it on the mantelpiece in the living room.

'But she's beautiful!' said Tony. 'And so's he. Some kid, that. What is he now? Three?'

'And a bit.'

'You sure must be proud of them.'

I made some noncommittal noise and went into the kitchen

23

to open a window. The whole cottage smelt stuffy. Tony realized the place was in a mess – I watched his dark eyes checking things, saw him run a finger through the dust on the table-top – but he was too tactful to say anything about it. I poured a couple of Scotches and we settled down for some crack.

'So how's things?' he asked.

'Improving. I had a low patch when I couldn't get myself together at all. I was getting bad headaches and recurring nightmares about Iraq. I went on the piss – but I was so zonked I couldn't even bring myself to go downtown with the guys. Instead I was buying cans of Stella, twenty-four at a time, and drinking them here on my own with Scotches in between. But I'm over that now. No more headaches. Nightmares gone. Everything's fine, except for this damned course.'

'What's that?'

'This language course. There's a possibility of a team job in Colombia, so there's ten of us learning Spanish.'

'No kidding! You realize Spanish is my first language?'

'I knew you spoke it.'

'Sure do. My mom and dad always talked Spanish at home, and I grew up with it. I expect it would sound like shit to people in Madrid, but it's Spanish all the same.'

Looking out of the window, he fired off a rapid sentence. 'Get that?'

'Only that it was something about the weather.'

'Correct. I asked if it always pisses with rain during the British summer.'

'¡Siempre!' I had to think. '¡Sin falta!'

'Boy! You got it!'

'I fucking haven't, Tony. That's the trouble. I'm finding it a real hassle. Our final tests are coming up in a couple of weeks, too.'

'Well. You just gotta fight and get through them. I guess I've been fighting to survive ever since I was a kid.'

Soon we made a plan. Tony was already very fit; on the initial stages of the selection course, over the Welsh

24

mountains, he would have little trouble in purely physical terms. But I knew what a help it would be to him if he learnt the routes over the Brecon Beacons in advance: that way, he would have a big advantage if the weather turned bad or fog came down. So I offered to walk some of the ground with him, and in return, while we were tabbing, he would give me informal Spanish lessons, to increase my fluency and confidence. The deal suited us both.

We were still talking as dusk set in, and I began to wish I'd done something about supper. Over the past few weeks I'd been picking up takeaways on my run home, or else making do with a jacket potato baked in the microwave. Now I remembered that in Iraq, as we ate shitty rice and lusted after our favourite dishes, Tony had described how he liked to cook.

'You hungry?' I asked.

'Sure.'

'Want to try your hand in the kitchen? I don't know what there is, but have a look.'

A search in the cupboards revealed nothing but a few tins of baked beans and a packet of spaghetti. Fuelled by the Scotch, Tony launched a tirade against my housekeeping.

'Jesus!' he exclaimed. 'There ain't enough here to feed a goddam mouse! You can't have been shopping in decades. No garlic. No tomato paste. No chilli. No nothing.'

'Our prospects improved when he found a bottle of olive oil and a tin of anchovies in the larder. He went into the garden with a torch and returned with a bucket full of spinach, the dark green leaves glistening with rain. Soon we were eating fishy, oily, peppery spaghetti, which we pretended was a traditional Puerto Rican recipe, and spinach pureed with butter, salt and pepper, which I had to admit was outstanding. Tomorrow, Tony promised, we would pay a joint visit to the supermarket and put the kitchen in order.

Three days later we drove out to the Beacons. In his regular training Tony had started to hump loads in his bergen: he hadn't been used to it, but I told him it was essential to build up slowly to the 55 lbs that he would have to carry during the four weeks of hill-walking which formed the first part of the selection course. For our first recce, however, we took only light day-sacks containing a couple of sandwiches and a waterbottle apiece.

Needless to say, rain was falling, and the clouds were touching the tops of the mountains. I parked the car in a lay-by on the B-road that runs along the side of the Talybont reservoir, so that we could get a look at the map while we were still in the dry. Tony had a hell of a pair of boots – high-leg, black leather Matterhorns lined with Goretex – and as he was lacing them up I twisted the map round until it was aligned with the compass.

'On test week you'll be walking all round this area,' I told him, pointing with the blade of my clasp-knife. 'We'll start off up the side of the wood here, and get on to these ridges. This is the first part of the Endurance route, and you do it at night, starting out at 0300. Once you get on to the high ground the going's easy. It's just a matter of snaking round the ridges. You're aiming for the summit of Pen-y-Fan . . . here. Highest point in the Beacons, and the centre of our universe. It's said that every guy in the Regiment has the outline of the Fan graven on his heart.

'What we'll do is come round the ridge here, across the feature known as the Windy Gap, then up a horrendous climb known as Jacob's Ladder. You almost have to use your hands to go up. The path's been eroded out of the clay and you're on the edge of some jagged rocks, which fall away to your right. On Endurance you're supposed to average four ks an hour, but on the ladder you come to a grinding halt. That's why you have to run down the hills. In fact, the guys start jogging the moment they get on to any downward slope.

'Anyway, the ladder takes us up the back of the Fan to the summit. Then we drop down here, skirt round the flank of Corn Du and head for the obelisk . . . here. After that we swing away on this path, and come down to the Storey Arms on the main road. Used to be a pub, but now it's an outdoor education centre. Cross the road, and we'll climb up on to Fan Fawr. The spot height there's one of your check-points, and it's quite difficult to find. The course then takes you right away to the Cray Reservoir, in the distance to the west, but we haven't got time for that today.

'This last stretch before the Cray is bloody horrible. First there's miles of moon grass, all tussocks. Then there's this sod of a wood.' I pointed to a triangular plantation cradled in a bowl of steep slopes. 'It's a hell of a long way round the wood, but going through it's a bugger because of all the drainage ditches. So either way you're in the shit. But, as I say, we won't get that far today. What we'll do is cross the road again at the AA box, here, and climb back over. Then we'll go down through the woods to the reservoir, and the dam on which the route ends.'

'Looks like some hike,' said Tony.

'It is. Even with our light loads it'll take all day.'

We sorted our gear, locked the car and set off. As I expected, Tony moved easily, economically. He could have left me on the climbs, but that day we weren't racing. Going up the steep lower flank of the Fan, we had no breath to spare for talking; Tony's only utterance was one sudden, good-humoured outburst: 'Nothing but rain, stone walls and goddam sheep!'

But then, as we came out on to the ridges, the weather began to break. The rain stopped, the clouds parted, and we started to see great green slopes sweeping away below us on either side. Our spirits lifted, and Tony set in to talk Spanish, slowly and methodically, asking questions about the landscape, describing things we could see. To my surprise, I found I could understand him pretty well, and answers came more easily than I'd expected. Alone with a good friend, and having no reason to feel embarrassed, I found that my confidence built quickly. All the lessons of the past few weeks began to fall into place, and at last the language was making sense. More than that, I found it a pleasure to use.

By the time we'd scrabbled our way up Jacob's Ladder and reached the summit of the Fan the sun had come out, so we sat by the trig stone to eat our sandwiches. When Tony described the scenery as 'real pretty' I didn't argue. I realized

27

that, to him, used to the huge open spaces of America, the whole environment seemed dinky and small-scale – and on that hazy summer's day the Brecons were looking their most serene. This, the highest point, might be only 3,000 feet above sea-level, but I knew what the hills could be like when they showed their teeth in the wind and sleet of a winter night. 'The obelisk's a memorial to a little boy who died up there one August,' I said. 'It was in 1900, and he was trying to cross from one farm to another when the fog came down. Tommy Jones, he was called. It was twenty-nine days before they found him, curled up in a hollow where the pillar now stands.'

From our vantage-point I explained how important it was to try to maintain our height on the way back across Fan Fawr, before the inevitable steep descent to the checkpoint by the AA box on the main road. 'Thereafter, the route to trig-point 642 is really tough, an absolute ball-breaker: whichever way you go, you can't avoid fierce climbs and drops.'

We could just make out 642 in the distance to the south. I told Tony that the stone bears a brass plaque in memory of Tony Swerzy, a member of the SAS killed on the Everest expedition of 1984.

And so we went on again, and kept going for the rest of that hazy summer afternoon.

Tony had been allotted a room in camp, but I suggested he might like to spend some nights in the cottage – an offer which he took up with alacrity. Apart from providing cheerful company, he raised culinary standards no end, as baked beans on toast gave way to steaming paella and chilli con carne. He had a heavy hand with the Tabasco, but that suited me fine, and one evening I was inspired to retaliate with the one sure weapon in my armoury, a curry as hot as Hades.

We went up to the Brecons several more times, and spent a couple of weekends walking some of the other routes, including Point-to-Point and Pipeline. We also went over the course for the Heavy Carry day – and with every outing I was improving my fluency in conversational Spanish.

28

The language course was a tough one, especially for guys like us who were used to a mainly physical existence. Our facilities were good – we had videos, audio-tapes and a separate audio-lab for making tapes of our own if we wanted – but the hours were long, and the lessons demanded a high level of concentration. We kicked off at 9.00 a.m., with the desks in the classroom set out in a horseshoe shape. Round the walls were big posters illustrating various weapons and armoured vehicles, with captions and statistics in Spanish. The poncified major in the Education Corps taught us grammar, and later in the mornings a Colombian professor would come up from Cardiff University to give us conversation. She'd chat to each of us in turn, starting off with '*Buenos dios. ¿Tiene hora?*' and we'd answer, '*Si, señora, son las doce menos cuatro,*' or whatever. The woman was a fearsome age, and knee-high to a piss-pot, but she had a great sense of humour, and generally turned the conversation into areas of interest to us: '*¿Hay un bar por aquí?*' and so on.

By 12.30 everyone would be desperate to clear their heads, so it was into shorts, singlets and trainers and away for a run, five or six miles round the lanes at the back of the camp. On wet days some of the guys preferred a session on the weights in the gym. Then a quick shower, into DPMs again, and a dash down to the NAAFI for a sandwich or a pie, before being back into the classroom for 2 o'clock. By about 3.30 I'd see some of the guys dozing off. They'd have their heads propped in their hands, ostensibly concentrating like hell on their books, but then suddenly a hand would slip and a head would lurch downwards, and the owner would wake up with a start. By the time classes ended at 4.30, we'd all had enough – but then we had a pile of homework to take back with us.

Several months previously I'd applied to go on the Northern Ireland course, and now, one morning after Prayers in the Squadron Interest Room, the SSM said, 'Right, as soon as we're finished here, I want to see the following in my office.' He read out a list of names, and mine was on it.

In we went, one at a time. Tom was sitting at his desk in one corner of the little room, and the squadron clerk was pattering away at his word-processor in the other.

'OK, Geordie,' the SSM began. 'You want to go to the NI Troop?'

'Right.'

'We've got you down for troop training, starting July twentieth. You OK with that?'

'Yep. That's fine.'

'Good. You want to get yourself down to see Johnny Hopton, who's running the course. Find out if there's any particular preparation you can do beforehand. Are you happy with that?'

'That's fine.'

'Right, then. You start on the twentieth.'

I went out feeling chuffed to bollocks. Everyone wanted to get on the NI course, because a posting to Ulster meant live operations, rather than the endless training which otherwise was the Regiment's lot in peacetime. Ulster meant danger, excitement and the chance to take on a real enemy. I knew that the posting was partly a question of seniority – the head-shed probably needed a couple of sergeants on the course – but I also knew they must have got together and talked about possible candidates, and I was glad to know they hadn't been put off by my low patch after the Gulf.

The idea of a tour in Northern Ireland naturally made me think more than ever of Kath and Tim. What would happen if they were in Belfast and I got posted there? Would I be able to go and visit them, or would they be out of bounds? The possibility was way off, but I checked – and the answer was that, yes; guys in the troop were allowed to make social visits, provided the area was safe.

The training course would last four months. As I thought of my family, that suddenly began to seem a long time. I found I was missing them, and began to wonder if I should ask Kath to come back. Her mother had had her hip operation in the Musgrave, and it had been a success. The hospital had sent her home after only a week, and Kath's presence had turned out to be a bit of a godsend. But now that Meg was almost fully mobile again, and out of pain, there was no reason from her point of view why Kath shouldn't come home.

I would have to admit to everyone – Kath, her parents, and above all myself – that I'd made a big mistake. It wasn't exactly a question of swallowing my pride; I didn't feel proud at all – anything but. Rather, it was a question of being certain that I wasn't going to make things worse by dragging Kath and Tim home. If they did come back, and I got posted across the water, we'd be separated again anyway for the whole year of the tour . . . . The permutations went round and round in my mind. Take action? Or wait some more?

When we sat our final test on the Spanish course, my confidence had built up to a new high, largely because of Tony. Thanks to our conversations, not even the prospect of giving a lecture to the rest of the course could faze me. I stood up and talked for three minutes about the relative merits of Real Madrid and Arsenal as if I was the greatest soccer pundit on the Costa. Besides the talk, we had to answer questions about a video we'd been shown, act as interpreter in a conversation between a Colombian woman and a third party, and write a description of our favourite holiday resort. I chose Corfu, and gave it the works. Next morning, I was amazed to see my name at the top of the list of passes.

That night I phoned Kath and told her the news. She sounded bright and lively, full of the joys of summer. They'd been out somewhere along the coast, and Tim had been paddling in the sea. He was talking a lot now, and he'd been asking where his dad was.

As she talked, the idea I'd been holding back for weeks swept over me. On impulse I said, 'Listen, Kath. How about coming back?'

I heard her draw in her breath. There was a pause.

'Why not try it?' I urged.

Then she said, 'Geordie! You mean it?'

'Of course. I'm a whole lot better. I'm back to normal. Off the booze altogether. Things don't seem right without you.'

31

She must have burst into tears. Half a minute passed, and I could hear snuffling sounds.

'Kath – are you there?'

'Yes. Geordie?'

'What?'

'I'm dying to see you.'

'Great! Come on over, then.'

'Of course I'll come. But listen.'

'What?'

I heard her blow her nose. 'Mum's had to go back into hospital. She's been getting pain down her leg. We're hoping it's nothing serious, but the implant could have shifted, and they want her in for a few days' observation. I've told her I'll be here to look after her when she comes out. I won't be able to make it for a couple of weeks.'

'Not to worry. I can wait. As long as I know you're on your way.'

'Have you pinched the tops off the beans yet?'

'Yes,' I said, telling a white lie. 'I did that.'

'Brilliant,' she said. 'Lots of love, Geordie.'

'Same to you.'

As soon as I put the phone down, I whipped out into the vegetable patch. Jesus, I thought, I've boobed here. The fucking beans were nearly up to my shoulder and covered with big white flowers! The smell was enough to stop you in your tracks. What was I supposed to do? Pick the flowers off? No – that would take forever. 'Pinch the tops off,' she'd said. But where did the top begin? What was top and what was stalk? There seemed to be bunches of buds all the way up. In the end I thought, To hell with it, and went along the rows nipping four or five inches off the top of each plant, and hoping the damn things would survive.

THREE

The NI course was an eye-opener to all twelve of us who took it. Most of it happened at the Llangwern Army Training Area, known as LATA, just a few miles into Wales. Because it was so close, we carried on living where we were, in and around camp, and drove there and back every day.

On the first morning we went down in a coach, and spent the day getting issued with all manner of fancy kit, not least cars. There was a pool of cars which lived at LATA, and they were handed out to us like toys – one to every two or three of us – for the duration of the course. I was given the keys of a dark-blue Cavalier, which I shared with Pat Martin. Like all the other cars, it was quite a sporty beast but inconspicuous; that was the point – it was fast enough to get us out of trouble but didn't stand out or attract attention. The guy who handed it over told me I would be responsible for maintaining it in good nick, and for bringing it into the MT section if any problem needed sorting out. Then he added, 'This one goes all right – but wait till you get across the water and try the intercept cars. They're something else.'

The other goodies we got on day one included our waistcoats – one operational, one for civilian clothes. The ops waistcoat was designed to keep everything off the wearer's legs: it had pockets for radio, spare magazines and grenades, and a built-in holder for a secondary weapon, the handgun. There were also places for plasticuffs and torches – all the little knick-knacks – and inside pockets to hold your orange armband and baseball cap with ARMY written on it, so that in any contact you could instantly turn yourself into a member of the security forces.

The civilian waistcoat had a place for a covert radio, which you worked with a small earpiece, a mike taped to your chest, and a pressel switch in one pocket, so that you could communicate without appearing to move. The drill was to carry a pistol – probably a Walther PPK, generally known as your disco gun – about your person. If you wore a T-shirt next to the skin and another shirt over it, a bit loose, nobody would spot anything.

Most of LATA lay on one side of a main road, shielded from passing traffic by a high wire fence and an evergreen hedge. As somebody gleefully pointed out, the designers of the fence had screwed up, tilting the two-foot overhang of barbed wire inwards rather than outwards, as if its function was to stop people getting out, rather than vice-versa. 'It's like it used to be in East Fucking Germany,' said Pat as he surveyed it contemptuously. 'Anything to stop the bastards getting out.'

Pat was like that. A big, solidly built fellow, much into weight-lifting, he had ruddy cheeks and brown eyes as shiny as horse-chestnuts. He was forever laughing and joking, and never failed to come up with some cheerfully obscene comment – a typical Cockney, always ready with a blast of effing-this and effing-that, enough to startle strangers. Whenever faced with a surprise or setback, his verbal reaction was so explosive that people who didn't know him thought he was volatile and highly-strung. But really that was just his way of letting off steam, and underneath he was as solid as a rock.

His bulk was deceptive, too. At your first sight of him you might think he was muscle-bound. Far from it – he could do 100 metres in 11 seconds, as well as being able to throw small guys over walls and suchlike – a very useful attribute when you're on the counter-terrorist team and things get physical. He and I hadn't had much to do with each other before the course, but at LATA we teamed up and found we could work well as a pair.

The training area itself consisted largely of rough fields running up to meet Prescott's Wood, a big stand of trees that covered the sides and top of a rounded hill, with a road winding through it, ideal for ambushes and illegal VCPs (vehicle control points). The fields looked more or less like neglected farmland, but they included a few surprises. There were several ranges, outdoors and in. The Garaback, for instance, was a two-storey building which had the walls of its rooms lined with steel sheets and rubber matting, so that live rounds would go through the rubber and drop down without ricocheting.

The course began gently with sessions on lock-picking. These took place in a special room packed with locks of every kind – doorlocks, padlocks, everything – plus a key-cutting machine, for us to use to manufacture our own. Outside we learnt to open cars with a slim jim, a long sliver of metal like a ruler, with hooks on it and small sections cut out.

Something else new to me was photography. We were taught to use cameras with short-focus lenses, for recording serial numbers of weapons and suchlike, and also telephoto monsters, for taking covert long-range pictures of people who might be players. We developed, printed and blew up our own shots in the darkroom on site.

At the same time, we did exercises like Kim's game, in which we were each given a bunch of mug-shots to study, and then, in a live parade, asked to identify any of the faces we'd been looking at. It was drummed into us that our lives might depend on recognizing a key player at a key moment.

A more active pursuit was fast driving, for which the police came down and took us out one-to-one. Most of us were already pretty competent, but we all got sharpened up. We put in big mileage on narrow country roads, such as we'd be using in Ireland, and learned to drive fast but safely. Then they took us to a big municipal car-park, empty in the early hours of the morning, where we used vehicles fitted with a special attachment – a frame which was mounted under the car, like a cradle on small wheels, with hydraulic controls that enabled the instructor to take most of the weight off the tyres. My teacher had a dial with a scale of one to five, and at five the Cavalier became like a turd on black ice, spinning at the slightest provocation. Here we learnt J-turns, yanking on the handbrake to spin the car in its own length.

The best session, though, was on the morning the police

took us to a breaker's yard and we bought a load of old bangers for about £50 apiece, to practise ramming. To get out of an illegal VCP or knock a hostile vehicle off the road you need to know what you're doing, and for half a day we behaved like lunatics in full-sized dodgems, hammering the shit out of each other.

Another big issue was weaponry, principally the G3s, the Heckler & Koch 7.62mm rifles which are the standard weapon in Northern Ireland. With a magazine holding twenty rounds, and an excellent mechanism that hardly gives any stoppages, the G3 is ideal for firing into cars, since its penetration is far greater than that of the lower-powered Armalite. The longs (rifles are known as 'longs', pistols as 'shorts') at LATA were numbered with white paint on the butt, and I got No. 7, which I always reckon is lucky for me. Each of us also got an HK 53, a smaller, neater rifle, .556 calibre, good for tucking under the front seat of a car; and a Sig – properly a Sigsauer P 226 – a 9mm pistol, accurate and reliable, and not prone to stoppages. We were told to carry weapons on exercises, just to get used to them, but at night they went into a lock-up in a classroom, and it was the duty-sergeant's job to make certain they were secure.

At that time the situation in Ulster was pretty bad, and almost every day there was news on TV or in the papers of another atrocity. One afternoon not long into the course the daily programme billed a brief on the political background in Northern Ireland, and the way special forces fitted into the fight against terrorism. Before the lecture, nobody seemed to rate the importance of this topic very highly; the afternoon was fine and hot – definitely not the sort of conditions for sitting in a Portakabin classroom – and a couple of the lads tried to skive off on some pretence. But the moment the talk started, everybody was hooked.

The speaker introduced himself as Chief Superintendent James Morrison of the Royal Ulster Constabulary. He was quite an elderly guy, grey haired, grey faced, grey suited, grey all over. Even his voice was grey: a monotone so quiet it was difficult to hear. He perched his arse on the front of the table and spoke without props, notes or gestures; yet what he said had us leaning forward in our seats.

'It's war you're going to,' he began. 'It's war and nothing else, so it is. It's been going on for twenty-five years, and I've been in it all that time. I still don't understand Northern Ireland, and I never will. But I do believe we'd be doing a lot better if we'd dropped more of the enemy on operations. I wouldn't send somebody out just to shoot three or four of them; but on specific operations, of which we've had knowledge, it would have put a heck of a lot of fear into them if we'd killed a few more. I shouldn't be saying this to yous fellers but, flip, I am.'

That had us fairly hooked, and nobody moved as he went on to outline the way special forces fitted into the campaign against terrorism, in combination with the green army, the RUC, Special Branch and various other intelligence organizations. He then sketched in the nature and behaviour of the IRA. He described how the original IRA, known as the Stickies, had turned away from violence and become doves. Today's hawks were the Provisional IRA, or PIRA (in his accent, 'Payra'). He sketched their organization: at the top, the Army Council, and under that the Northern and Southern Commands – one for Ulster, one for the Republic. The task of the Southern Command was to organize terrorist attacks on the mainland. In the north there were three brigades, sub-divided into small cells known as ASUs, or Active Service Units, which formed the core of IRA activity.

Fragmentation was the name of their game, he said. Each cell probably consisted of only three or four people: a bomber, a shooter, a driver, and maybe one other. Very often they did not know each other; they didn't even know their colleagues' names. The intention was that if anyone was caught, it was impossible for him to give anyone else away. Fragmentation also made life more difficult for the informers – or touts – who might squeal on one phase of a job, but would rarely be able to find out about the operation as a whole.

Morrison told us how the players spent their lives targeting policemen, endlessly trying to pick them up as they left work

37

and follow them back to their homes. 'I tell you – just the other day they targeted one of my officers. I'll call him John. The man came home from work at eleven o'clock at night. He hadn't been indoors a minute before a call came from a friend in Special Branch. "Look, John," says the caller, "close your curtains. There's somebody in your back garden. Don't worry – they're ours. If anyone comes to your front door in the next few minutes, let them in, and they'll look after you."

'Sure enough, more people came. They stayed the night. They told John that some form of attack on him was imminent. They expected it to be a UCBT – an under-car booby trap – and they had people outside ready to grab the bomber. They waited all night, and no one came. Something had spooked them. All the same, John had to move house . . .'

On and on went the hypnotic voice, telling us about deep hides, concreted over or sealed into houses behind false walls, where quartermasters would store weapons and ammunition for months or even years. We heard of transit hides, less elaborate caches, where one man would deposit a weapon and another would collect it to do a particular shooting. He told us how the IRA staged burglaries to decoy the police into killing areas, and how they themselves would never risk firing a rifle or a rocket from a position that didn't afford them a clear escape route.

'There's another thing as well now: they're into drugs. I know this won't really concern yous guys – it's the business of other agencies – but you'd better be aware of it. The PIRA always needs money, for weapons and explosives and whatever, and, as you know, there's tremendous money in drugs. So they're into narcotics too, bringing in drugs from the south, and distributing them on.'

The chief paused, looking round at all of us, and then said by way of summing up: 'Oh yes, they're the most cunning bastards on earth. They're good bastards in their way and, flip, you underestimate those feckers at your peril.'

He stopped, and everyone sat silent. Then a voice from the floor asked, 'Do you hate them?'

'Hate them?' The speaker seemed to reflect for a moment,

then his voice grew suddenly louder. 'Yes, I truly hate them, the murdering, treacherous, lying bastards. I've seen one of my young officers cut down by them in the prime of his life. I've heard his little boy asking when his daddy's coming home, and somebody telling him his daddy won't be getting up anymore, because he's there in his coffin. When that happens to a family, it's terrible, and you don't ever forget it.'

The speaker was staying that night in the officers' mess in camp, and after the talk he was invited there for a drink. We drove back to Hereford, showered, changed, and piled into the mess for a couple of beers and some polite conversation. With no particular motive – merely to socialize – I asked the chief if by any chance he'd met my father-in-law, who was quite well-known as a GP around his area of East Belfast. It turned out that the two hadn't come across each other, and there was no connection; but in the long-term that chance contact was to have far-reaching effects.

The brief on Northern Ireland had brought the course into sharp focus, and when we began doing car-drills for VCPs and ambushes, the guys went into everything with new fervour. Reg Brown, our new instructor (himself from the Regiment), drummed into us the fact that when we drove towards a normal VCP, dressed in civilian clothes and in a civilian car, the green soldiers manning the barrier would naturally take us for Irishmen. It was therefore necessary to have all weapons stowed well out of sight, and to let the guys know covertly that we were from the security forces. The way to do this was to keep our ID cards inside our Northern Ireland driving licences, so that when a driver showed his licence the guard would open it up and see the card. Then, if he was properly trained, he would chat for a minute, say, 'Fine,' and hand the licence back, and we'd be smoothly on our way. Anyone watching would take us for normal punters.

That was the drill for a normal VCP. But it was also likely, Reg told us, that we would come across illegal check-points, set up by the players in Catholic areas as shows of strength, to demonstrate to the locals that they were in charge. 'If you see it early enough,' he told us, 'spin out and disappear. If you're already into it, keep calm, drive on, but slow down as if you're going to stop. Stay in low gear, and make sure your pistol's to hand in the right-hand door-well. As the guy comes towards you, to ask who you are, wind the window down, grab the pistol and whack him. Then, if there's no barrier ahead, accelerate hard and use the car as a weapon to hit any other players who may be on the road.

'If the road's blocked, start off the same. The driver drops the first guy, but at the same time the passenger starts putting down a massive amount of fire on his side. The two guys in the back debus, go wide, and put down more fire. The front two jump out, move back through the others, and put down rounds themselves. All four of you pepperpot back into a line, and then assess the situation. If you've taken out two or three of the players, and there are only four or five altogether, the commander may take the decision to move forward and finish them off. Also, of course, you've got your radios, and by now you will have called for assistance . . .'

Much of our training took place in Prescott's Wood, where everything was pretty realistic. We built OPs by digging in, carefully disposing of the soil, and meticulously roofing the hides with branches, turf, dead grass and leaves so that no sign of disturbance was visible. From those vantage points we had to keep watch on spots like culverts, in which (according to one scenario) a bomb had been hidden, and report any activity that had taken place in the area. We also had to fight our way out of ambushes laid on by guys from the Regiment, who would open the proceedings by throwing a petrol bomb into the road in front of our car.

Often we were out in the countryside, away from LATA altogether. Many of the farmers round Hereford were really on side, and were glad to let us use their land and buildings. Once an arrangement was in place, someone would tell them that if they saw movement round an outlying barn, or in one of their hedges, on a particular day, not to worry; they were to carry on with their normal activities. Our scenario would lay down that some players were using the barn as a transit hide; we'd build an OP in a spot overlooking it, and go to ground there, watching for business to develop. Since much of the land was similar to the ground in Northern Ireland – undulating fields divided by thick hedges – it was ideal for training.

On top of all this there was a good deal of physical activity. The guys went for their normal daily runs or sessions in the gym, and twice a week an instructor from the Bodyguard Wing took us for unarmed combat. Although quite a small guy, he had a reputation for being able to deck even the biggest lads, and he taught us the holds for disabling people or taking them out. 'It's easy enough to kill someone,' he said cheerily. 'All you need do is use your hand to push their nose-bone up into their brain. Or you can rip their wind-pipe out. But the best thing in a life-threatening situation is just to break the neck.' He instructed us to take each other on and learn the moves in slow time, encouraging us to fight dirty by gouging eyes, going for the crotch and so on.

All in all, the course was pretty demanding, but good fun. I felt I was putting a lot into it, but also getting a lot out of it, learning all the time.

Then one morning everything went to rat-shit. We were firing pistols at about ten o'clock when a call came through to the range house, and someone shouted, 'Geordie, you're wanted on the phone.' Puzzled, I went in and picked up the receiver. There on the line was the adjutant's clerk, calling from camp.

'Is that Geordie Sharp?'

'Yep.'

'There's a bit of an emergency. The adjutant needs to see you urgently.'

'What's it about?'

'I'm afraid I don't know. That's the only message: you've got to get right back.'

Christ! I thought, now what have I done? I must be in for a fearsome bollocking.

I looked round for someone to take charge of my weapons, and the nearest guy was Pat Martin. 'Hey, Pat, I've got to

41

head back to the Lines. Will you make sure my weapons and kit-bag go back in the locker?'

'No problem,' he answered. 'What's the matter? Have you dropped a bollock?'

'Not that I know of.' I shrugged and I handed him my pistol, told him my HK 53 was in the hut, and said I'd take the grey admin Sierra.

I drove fast, unable to think of anything I'd done wrong. In a few minutes I was back at camp, parked up and hurrying to the adjutant's office. When I saw the SSM standing in the room, by the Rupert's desk, and also John Stone, who'd been best man at my wedding, I knew something was very wrong.

The adjutant stood up awkwardly as I came in: another sign of big trouble. In that warm weather he was wearing his DPMs, with the sleeves of his shirt rolled up.

'Sit down, Geordie,' he said, waving at a chair, and then: 'Listen, I'm afraid I've got bad news for you. Your wife's been killed.'

'Oh no!' I remember I sat forward with my elbows on my thighs, my hands clasped tight together.

'Yes. We got a signal an hour ago. A bomb went off in a shopping centre in Belfast this morning. It seems to have been an own-goal; the bomber was blown to pieces, but he took out five civilians as well.'

My ears heard the words the adjutant was saying, but my brain hardly seemed to take them in. My mind and body had gone numb. I could not move or speak. I sat and stared at the front of the desk, just ahead of me, as if I had turned to stone.

'The rest of the course is being informed,' he went on. 'We want you to take a couple of days off, to make up your mind what you'd like to do.'

My voice came back in a kind of croak. 'What happened?'

'She'd gone shopping. That's all the information we have so far. She was outside, on the pavement, when the explosion occurred. She was killed instantly. Can't have known anything.'

'What time was it?'

'Just after 9.30.'

42

'What about the kid?'

'He was at playschool.'

'Thank God for that.' I put my face in my hands.

'You'll need time to chill out,' the adjutant was saying. 'There's no pressure on you to complete the NI course. After this, you may not want to go over there at all. If that's what you decide, everyone will understand. You don't have to go on the operational tour. If you'd prefer it, you can go back to the squadron, and we can look for a posting elsewhere. See how you feel in a couple of days.'

'She was coming back!' I said bitterly. And then again, before I could stop myself, I almost shouted, *'She was coming back!'*

'I know, Geordie. Everyone knows that. Everyone's with you.' He cleared his throat and went on, 'As I say, take a couple of days off. If there's anything you need – help with organizing the funeral – come and tell us. Get it sorted out with the boss and SSM. Now – John can give you a lift home.'

I took a deep breath to get hold of myself, then stood up and nodded to the adjutant. John put a hand on my shoulder and steered me towards the door. Outside, he said, 'Will I take you back?' I nodded again, and walked blindly to his car. As he drove I noticed how tanned he was and asked where he'd been. 'Africa,' was the answer. 'Just come back from an exercise in Botswana.'

'What was it like?'

He began to answer, but I could hardly listen. I realized I'd only asked the question in an attempt to keep my mind off my private horror. I seemed to be short of breath, and had to inhale deeply to steady myself.

At the cottage John came into the kitchen with me and said loudly, 'Let's have a brew. Where's the kettle?'

'There.' I pointed. 'There's milk in the fridge.' Then I sat down at the table, staring out of the window, straight into the vegetable garden, mind in a whirl of guilt and remorse. The kettle began to sing, and presently I heard John say something.

'What was that?'

43

'I see you've got a bottle of Scotch. Would a quick one help?'

'No, no. Tea'll be fine.'

I shivered with cold. When John handed me a mug, I piled three spoonfuls of sugar into it, and as I drank it, I felt a hot flush rising through me.

'Jesus Christ!' I said. 'Why her? Why did it have to be her?'

John shook his head and looked down into his tea. Then, noticing the strange kit in one corner, he said, 'Whose is that?'

'It belongs to Tony Lopez, the SEAL guy who's trying to join the squadron. He's been staying here.'

'Oh – that's the guy who was in the nick with you?'

'That's him.'

'How's he doing?'

'Terrific. One of the best.'

'Will he pass selection?'

'He'll walk it. He's fitter than the rest put together, and he's got most of the necessary skills already. Been in the jungle, for instance.'

'He must be crazy to leave the SEALs. Train in the sun . . . all the assets you want . . . Does he realize what hard work he's letting himself in for?'

'I don't know. It's only for a couple of years.'

'Rather him than me. I dread the thought of walking over those hills with a fifty-five-pound bergen.' John looked at me and said, 'You'd better phone Kath's parents.'

'In a minute.'

My mind flew to the spacious house in Helen's Bay – a safe and smart residental resort a few miles north-east of Belfast, on the shore of Belfast Lough – with its big gardens and handsome trees and stunning views of the sea. Kath's mother always kept the family home immaculate: never a speck of dust, never a cushion out of place. I'd always supposed that this obsession with cleanliness had something to do with the fact that Kath's father, Den, had been a doctor. Often in the past few weeks I'd wondered what Tim had made of it, dropping bits of food and scattering his toys about the fitted Wilton carpets.

I nerved myself to make the call. Then I said, 'Better do it,' and went to the telephone.

A strange voice answered: a man, with a strong Belfast accent.

'Who's that?'

'Sergeant Harris, RUC.'

'Can I speak to Mrs O'Brien?'

'I'm sorry. She's not very well just now.'

'Doctor O'Brien, then.'

'Who's calling?'

'His son-in-law.'

There was a pause before Den came on, sounding very shaken. 'We can't believe it,' he said. 'We just can't take it in.'

'Me neither. How's Mum?'

'She's in shock. We've given her some sedation.'

'Look, I'll come over as soon as I can. Tomorrow, probably.'

'Thanks, Geordie.'

'Den – where is she?'

'Who?'

'Kath.'

'Browns are collecting her from the hospital.'

'Browns?'

'The funeral directors.'

'Have you seen her?'

'No. She was . . . she was . . . . The damage was pretty bad. They identified her from her credit cards and driving licence.'

'Oh God! What about Tim?'

'He doesn't know yet. Geordie, are you all right?'

'More or less. I've a friend with me here at the cottage. I'll be there tomorrow. Give my love to Mum.'

'So I will.'

I rang off.

Little by little I felt anger starting to burn inside me. Once again I heard old Morrison, the RUC chief, saying, 'I hate those bastards. I truly do,' and suddenly I too felt hatred for the IRA, furious personal hatred for the man who had sent the bomber on his murderous errand.

45

'Fuck them!' I said, so loudly that it made John start.

'Who?'

'The IRA. Whoever killed her. I'll get that bastard somehow, if it's the last thing I do.'

The next two days were a nightmare, and I stumbled through them as though I was half awake. The only mercy was that delayed shock seemed to be numbing my sensibilities and keeping grief at bay.

Early on the Tuesday morning I drove up the M5 to Birmingham Airport, exactly as I had on the day I sent Kath off. The head-shed had fixed me up with an open return to Belfast, but I had yet to collect the ticket. Moving on autopilot, I put the car in the long-term park, walked to the terminal building, found the ticket desk and checked in, all in a mechanical, unfeeling way. It was only when I reached the security check and some dickhead challenged me about where I was going that I really came round. There must have been something about my face that made him pick me out. Suddenly he was demanding to know my name and address in Belfast. When he asked the purpose of my visit, I gave it to him straight, in the most hostile voice I could manage: 'I'm . . . going . . . to . . . bury . . . my . . . wife.' That stopped him in his tracks – but he was such a turd that he didn't have the grace to apologize. He just said, 'All right,' and motioned me on.

The plane was only half full, and the flight seemed incredibly short. Nevertheless, it gave me time to think through the security implications of my visit. Kath and I were married in Hereford; the wedding had never been reported in the Northern Ireland papers, and nobody over there knew that she had been associated with the British forces. In the list of bomb victims, her name had been given as Mrs Sharp, a Belfast housewife – again, there had been no mention of her husband. If anyone asked my profession, I would tell them I was an aircraft fitter, working in Bristol. Provided I didn't stray into the hard areas of West Belfast there should be no trouble.

46

In forty minutes we had landed at Belfast City Airport, and I was walking out through the funny, old-fashioned building which looked as though it dated from the fifties. I grabbed a taxi and gave the driver the address, dreading the moment of arrival and yet wanting to be there quickly.

It was Tim who saved the day from being a disaster. Too young to know what had happened, he was carrying on as normal. When he saw me come in the door, he took one look and ran at me with a yell of 'Dad!' I held him up against me – a hefty, warm, live bundle, bigger than I remembered – and found that dealing with him defused the tension of seeing Kath's parents again. All the same, I was upset by their appearance. They had both put on ten years. Meg in particular looked very frail, and when I went to kiss her on the cheek, she was all bones. She was still limping a little, but in a different way from before her operation, and claimed that her hip was now fine; it was just the leg muscles that needed strengthening.

Tim apart, the best thing was their attitude to me. They could easily have blamed me for the tragedy. In fact they went out of their way to show that they understood the problems our marriage had been through, and that they didn't hold it against me for behaving as I had. Whenever I made attempts to apologize they brushed them gently aside.

In the evening, after tea, Den asked about Kath's financial arrangements – whether she'd made a will or had any life insurance. I couldn't answer his questions, because she had always been the family banker – and I'd been so stunned by the news of her death that I hadn't had time to check.

That afternoon he and I went to Browns, the undertakers, to make arrangements. The middle-aged man on duty did his best to put us at our ease, but he threw me completely when he asked how we proposed to carry Kath's coffin out of the church after the service. 'I take it you'll be one of the bearer party,' he said.

'What? Me? I thought your people took care of that.'

'No, sir. It's the custom here for the family to provide the bearers.'

47

'That's right,' said Den gently. 'Most people do that.'

'Well . . .' I was left struggling. I couldn't face the thought of being so close to her, of carrying her remains. 'I'm sorry,' I said. 'I don't think I can do that.'

'It's all right.' Den raised a hand as if signalling to the undertaker that he would deal with the point in a moment, and went on to ask about the service at the crematorium. I felt terrible, burning with shame that I couldn't do the decent, normal thing.

Then I heard the kindly voice asking if I would like to have a tree for her.

'Where?'

'In the cemetery at Roselawn. Many people do have trees as memorials, rather than a stone. We can arrange to have one for you.'

I thought for a moment. I'd never liked big, heavy gravestones. A living memorial seemed a better idea. So I said, 'Yes, please.'

'What kind of tree? We have beech and ash saplings newly planted.'

I was going to ask for an ash, but at the last moment I remembered the trees that she had loved in the spinney behind KC. 'Could it be a rowan, a mountain ash?'

'Yes, of course. We can arrange a rowan. And would you like to have a plaque at the foot?'

'Yes, please.'

'What wording would you like on the plaque?'

I closed my eyes to concentrate, and cleared my throat. 'In loving memory of Kathleen Sharp. From George.' Then I added hurriedly, 'No: "From George and Tim." '

The day of the funeral was as tough as any I could remember. After breakfast I drove Meg and Tim to the playschool he'd been attending, and we dropped him there. All he'd been told about his mum, so far, was that she had gone away for a few days. At some point we would have to break the news to him, but it seemed better to wait until we had all had a chance to get hold of ourselves.

The church service was set for 11.30 in the morning, but

members of the family began arriving at the house an hour before that. Meg and Kath's younger sister Angela were busy in the kitchen, preparing sandwiches and rolls for the wake; and as they wouldn't let other mourners come in there, I had to hold the fort with Den in the living room. Some of the people I knew, some I didn't. I forced myself to make small talk with all of them. The saving grace was the picture window which took up most of one wall and looked straight down over the sea. Birds were busy about the rocks, and every now and then a boat would come into sight, providing a blessed distraction and a new subject for conversation. For a few wonderful moments a fishing trawler, on its way out, appeared to have caught fire. Black smoke poured from its funnel, and the little ship steamed round in a circle, and everyone became quite excited by its apparent distress; but then suddenly the smoke was doused and the boat went on its way.

At last it was time to go. Two big, black Daimlers took the main family party, with the rest following in vehicles of their own. At the church the coffin, covered with flowers, was already in place on trestles at the head of the aisle. I found myself consciously trying not to think of what lay inside it. Suddenly I saw the bodies of the pilot and co-pilot of the helicopter that came down in the Iraqi desert, their limbs twisted and ripped off. I told myself to remember what she'd been like, but I found that small things were irritating me: the church was much too big for a congregation this size, we filled only the middle of the first few pews; the minister was young and nervous and kept stumbling over his words; the first hymn was one I'd never heard of. But then, in what seemed like no time at all we'd sung 'Oh God Our Help In Ages Past', and the bearers were lifting the coffin on to their shoulders, to carry it down the aisle. To my shame, I didn't even know them. Cousins? Friends of the family? Whoever they were, Den had recruited them, and they all looked fairly young. Along with everyone else, I stood and waited till they had cleared the church door. Then we were back into the funeral car and following the hearse out of the city, up to the Roselawn

49

cemetery, high on a rounded hill. We drove through an impressive pair of gates and into the biggest graveyard I'd ever seen – hundreds upon hundreds of tombstones and other memorials, set in straight lines over the hillsides, with neatly mown grass all round, and the road sweeping back and forth between. There were also thousands of trees, mostly young, planted in copses and bigger stands, the ground beneath them covered in wood-chips to keep down the weeds. I saw several places where I would like Kath's rowan to be.

At the top of the hill we came to the crematorium, a low, brick building set among sculpted grass banks and beds of flowers. The fact that everything was so perfectly kept seemed to make it more of an ordeal, rather than lessen it. There was a short delay while we waited for the party ahead of us to clear. Then it was our turn to file into the plain little chapel. As if from a great distance, I heard the priest say, 'Man that is born of woman hath but a short time to live, and is full of misery. He cometh up, and is cut down like a flower; he fleeth as it were a shadow, and never continueth in one stay.' It was all I could do to endure until the end, the dreadful moment when the coffin descended through a hole in the floor and Kath was gone.

Outside again, looking down, I realized that the cemetery had a huge view over Belfast, lying below us to the north-west. At the back of my mind I felt it was wrong that my thoughts should be turning so swiftly from the past to the future, but that is what they were doing. 'Whoever he is, he's down there somewhere,' I told myself. 'And wherever he is, I'll get him.'

FOUR

There was no question of my quitting the course. On the contrary, I couldn't wait to rejoin it. Early on Friday morning I nipped into camp and left a message for the adjutant saying I was back on side, then got myself straight down to LATA, determined to make up whatever ground I had lost through being away.

For the first couple of days the guys treated me rather strangely. There was none of the usual banter and piss-taking; instead, their attitude was respectful. Were they anxious not to hurt my feelings? Looking back, I can see that they expected me to be in pieces and were trying to handle me gently. But at the time I found it annoying. Outside the course I had one or two close mates – Tony and John Stone – who knew how hard I had been hit, and I was glad of their help; Pat Martin was another bulwark for me. The rest of the course may well have thought I was an unfeeling bastard, and didn't care much about what had happened. If that was the score, all the better, because I didn't want anyone to know what I had in mind. What nobody realized was that the agony of losing Kath had transformed itself into a ferocious desire for revenge. Grief had turned into anger, despair into steely determination. Far from being in distress, I came back on fire with new motivation.

I'd read in some newspaper that the own-goal bomber had been given a full-scale military funeral in West Belfast. Never mind that his incompetence had led to the deaths of five innocent civilians, or that a Protestant riot had broken out while he was being buried, with thousands of pounds' worth of damage caused. In the twisted minds of the IRA he had died in active service, and was a martyr, a hero. Brilliant!

To focus my animosity, I had given my target a name.

51

Because he was obviously a leading player, I had called him Gary, after Gary Player, the golfer. In my mind's eye Gary had reddish hair and beard, and sly, pig-like eyes. He was of medium height, and sloppily dressed – altogether a scruffy individual, dirty and slovenly – but cunning, and bigoted as hell, a dirty fighter and a dangerous customer. Trying to work out the position he might occupy in the IRA hierarchy, I had done my best to reconstruct events. The bomber had been an unemployed twenty-two-year-old. No doubt he had been a member of some ASU, which also included a shooter and a driver. Probably the bomber had been given orders to pick up from Point A the device which was to kill him, and deposit it at Point B. But who had given the orders? That was the key question. According to our instructor Reg Brown, who'd already done a tour in Northern Ireland, it would almost certainly have been an ops officer or a quartermaster in the Belfast brigade.

Maybe I was deluding myself, but I felt sure that fate was pointing me in the direction of my enemy. Already we were into August. Provided I got through the rest of the course OK, I would be posted to Belfast in October, only two months off; and then, for a year, I would be on the man's doorstep, trained, armed, and furnished with every pretext for taking terrorists out. When, in the middle of August, Loyalist gunmen killed seven people in eight days, and the IRA responded in kind, I persuaded myself that nobody would notice one more apparently sectarian killing.

On the domestic front, things were under control, if not great. After a family discussion we had agreed that it would be best for me to leave Tim with his Gran. Meg had pulled up again after her operation, and said she could manage. When I came across in the autumn, at least I'd be able to see something of the kid. In England there was no one to look after him.

At Keeper's Cottage I'd left Kath's things exactly as they were – clothes, shoes, hats, a few bits of jewellery. I could have given everything to Oxfam but somehow I didn't want to, so I shut the wardrobe doors, left her dressing table as it was, and deferred action indefinitely.

At the end of August a 1,000lb bomb went off outside the RUC station at Markethill in County Armagh. Miraculously, no one was hurt, but the explosion further sharpened our eagerness to get across the water. Down at LATA we were into the most fascinating part of the course: surveillance, or the art of following a target, either on foot or by car, without being seen. In this, for the first time, we became fully aware of the role that was going to be played in our lives by the shadowy organization known as the 'Det'. Short for 'Detachment', the name referred to the undercover intelligence-gathering unit that worked alongside our guys across the water. Whereas our role was reactive, theirs was passive: watching, spotting faces, gathering information, learning about the enemy.

The Det was made up of guys drawn from all corners of the forces; within the SAS they were known as 'Walts'. Some had come from the Regiment, but others were from all sections of the British services, and as far as work went, the whole lot kept themselves very much to themselves. In Belfast our guys shared a canteen and bar with them, and we were told that they were friendly enough off-duty; at LATA, whenever I saw some of them, I noticed how totally unremarkable they looked. I'm sure they'd been picked partly for their anonymous appearance, and for the fact that they had no distinguishing features. They were neither too tall nor too short, neither too fat nor spectacularly thin. None of them was particularly good-looking, but no one was all that ugly either. They all seemed to be uniform and neutral, so that they would blend effortlessly into a crowd anywhere in Northern Europe, and if you saw a couple of them in a car you wouldn't look twice. But we soon realized that they were highly trained, and an indispensable weapon in the fight againt terrorism.

Until we tried it, I don't think any of us had realized what an elaborate business surveillance was – a team of eight or ten men or women tracking a single target, all in immediate touch with each other by covert radio, all speaking a special language. The radios were secure, and scrambling devices made it impossible for outsiders to listen in. The jargon wasn't designed to baffle anyone; rather, its aim was to achieve economy and precision – to cut down time on the air and eliminate misunderstandings. Thus 'Bravo' was any man, 'Echo' any woman, 'Charlie' any car. 'Foxtrot' meant on the move on foot, 'Mobile' in a car. 'Complete' signified that a person had gone into a house or a car. 'Getting a trigger' meant getting your eyes on the target or the place where he was last seen.

To give us an idea, the instructor set up a scenario on the magic board – the big sheet of white-enamelled metal that covered most of the front wall of the classroom. Switching on a projector, he put a blown-up street-plan on the board and placed a few magnetic counters on it. One was black – the target – and the others white. Also on the plan were some coloured spots – red, green and blue, with numbers on them. Each of these, he explained, was used to identify a particular area. It was far easier and quicker to say 'Green One' than 'The crossroads at the intersection of River Street and Upper Richmond Way,' or give the place's grid-reference.

'Now,' he began, 'the most important guy in any surveillance operation is the one running it from the ops room. He's sat there with all his radios on, a couple of helpers, and a blown-up map of the area you're in. One big plus about this part of your training is that it gets you shit-hot on the radio. You've got to be really slick in reporting the target's movements. If you're slow, you're too late – he's gone round a corner and you've lost him.

'Now, what happens if the target goes to ground in a house? Well, it's up to the controller to bring people in to box the site.' He moved four white counters on to street junctions around the black blob. 'There you are. You sit on corners, in cafés or bars, waiting for the target to reappear. If you do your job properly, he can't get out of the box without one of you seeing him.

'If you think he's seen you, the golden rule is: peel off. Tell everyone else and get lost. Things go tits-up when somebody *thinks* he's OK and carries on. If you do that, all you manage to do is confirm to the target that surveillance is on him, and he may go to ground for weeks. OK, then, listen to this.'

He switched on an audio-tape – a hissing, crackly recording of a live operation. Every time a new voice came in he moved the corresponding white counter, and after every report he shifted the black target to a new position, all the time throwing in explanations of his own.

'I've got the trigger on Bravo One's house,' said the first voice. 'At the moment he's complete.'

'In other words, he's indoors,' said the instructor.

Then, a moment later, the voice said, 'Stand by, stand by. The door's open. Oh no. Nothing. It's his wife going to the bins.' Another pause. Then, 'Stand by, stand by. That's Bravo One leaving. He's foxtrot northwards.'

'He's walking up this street here,' the instructor explained, sliding the black counter upwards.

The voice came in again. 'He's wearing black on blue. Heading for the Drover's Arms on the corner. Now he's turning right . . .'

Another voice, a Scottish accent: 'Yeah, I've got him. I can take him down Commercial Street. He's foxtrot eastwards. Now he's joined up with Bravo Two. They've both gone complete in Charlie One, a bronze Escort. Can't get the number.'

'Both targets are in the car,' said the instructor, placing a yellow disc on the board.

A few seconds passed, and the Scots voice returned: 'Charlie One mobile eastwards towards Green Three.'

Then came another voice, measured, authoritative, the controller: 'Steve, are you covering Green Three?'

'On Green Three, facing north.'

'Prepare to take over Charlie One . . .'

As I listened, I felt the hairs on my neck rise up. The process was fascinating in itself, but in my mind's eye I was part of a team in West Belfast, tracking two players through the seedy Nationalist areas – maybe the Falls Road or Andersontown. The guys in the car were leading us towards Gary Player and a major contact. Any moment I might set eyes on my No. 1 enemy.

The soundtrack fell silent. 'If you're driving,' the instructor said, 'the one place you don't want to be is in the car behind the target. Keep two or three cars back. If people are doing something they didn't ought to be doing, they're forever looking behind them in their mirrors. If you do find yourself behind, for Christ's sake peel off at the first opportunity and get someone else to take over.'

'Stop, stop, stop!' called a new voice from the tape. 'Charlie One has pulled up in a lay-by at 489346. Bravo Two is foxtrot towards a telephone kiosk . . .'

The lads were getting excited by the idea of going across the water, and enthusiasm rose still higher whenever guys came back with stories of live operations. Several concerned the ace sniper who was doing shoots in the border area and in Belfast, taking soldiers out with a .50 rifle – a fearsome weapon which could put a round straight through a man's chest, flak jacket and all, at five or six hundred metres. The sniper was highly skilled and well organized. From the way he operated, the Det concluded that he had been trained in America. He had a lot of dickers – lookouts – who would check that an area was clear before he ventured forth. Then, if all was well, he'd come out and do a shoot on an army patrol. The only man known to have survived an attack from him was a soldier who'd been on patrol in West Belfast. The incoming round hit his SA 80, which he was holding across his chest. The weapon disintegrated, and parts of it (or of the .50 bullet) flew upwards, ripping chunks out of his face; but at least he wasn't killed.

The Regiment had set out to get the sniper by staging a come-on, posing as a green army patrol. The idea was to egg him on and keep him on the air so that the radio specialists could DF him and find out where he was based. It was dicey as hell, but it nearly worked. A few of the Regiment guys dressed up as ordinary soldiers and went through the motions of mounting a patrol. As they came into the target area, through their earpieces they could hear a dicker commentating on their progress.

'OK,' said this Ulster voice, 'there's a patrol coming down

56

the road. They'll be in your field of view in about thirty seconds.'

The sniper did not answer. There was a pause, then a sudden change of emphasis. 'Jaysus!' said the Ulster voice. 'There's something wrong here. They've got the wrong fecking weapons. They've got G3s, not SA 80s. The fellers are older, as well. They don't look like squaddies at all.'

The sniper realized immediately that the patrol was an SAS one. All he said was, 'I'm pulling off.' With that he fell silent, and the attempt at DF-ing him failed.

That wasn't the end of it, though. The Regiment tried again; this time they went to the lengths of taking a black fellow over, to make the patrol look still more realistic. They carried SA 80s, so that everything seemed pukka. It was quite an elaborate operation, with some guys airborne in a chopper and others deployed on the ground around the periphery, to block the sniper in if they got a line on where he was set up.

Again the patrol was listening out as the dickers commentated on their approach, but this time, to their consternation, they heard the shooter say, 'Right, I'm ready to fire. I'll take the second fecker from the front.' At that they did a bomb-burst, and every man hit the deck in a different direction. Then they upped and ran like stags, all over the place. They didn't collect back at the emergency rendezvous for more than an hour, and by then the gunman had once again melted into the night.

Of all our training, it was the range practices that I enjoyed most. Partly it was because I had become quite good with a pistol; but beyond that, in putting down live rounds I felt I was getting closer to my objective than on any of the rest of our activities, realistic though they were.

For pistol training we'd head out to the range at 0900. A couple of the guys were detailed to collect ammunition from the stores and lug the heavy metal boxes to the range hut. One man would go round putting up the red flags, to show that live firing was in progress, and the rest of us would sort out the targets.

The range had high stop-banks of soil thrown up in a horseshoe shape, so that you could fire at targets round three sides of it. Old railway sleepers were set into the ground, with holes drilled into them so that targets could easily be set up. We'd start by firing off two or three magazines just to get comfortable. Everyone had used pistols earlier in their training, so they all knew which their master eye was and how to take up a proper, easy stance: semi-crouching, with – for a right-hander – the left hand cupped round the outside of the right, supporting it.

If rounds started going low, you knew you were snatching at the trigger – and the instructors had a special drill for correcting that fault. One of them would say, 'Hey, try doing the old ball and dummy with me.' Then he'd stand behind the shooter and load his pistol for him, sometimes putting live rounds in the magazine, sometimes leaving it empty, so that the man pulling the trigger didn't know if it was going to go off or not. That way, if he *was* flinching and snatching, the instructor could see the end of the barrel dip, and try to rectify the fault.

After the guys had sorted themselves out and got their eyes in, everyone would have a brew from the urn by the target shed. Then the instructor would move on to drawing from holsters. He'd line up the lads in front of the targets and call, 'UP!' Everyone would draw, fire a quick double-tap, then re-holster the pistol. Then we'd turn through ninety degrees to the right or left, and at the second command we'd draw, swivel and fire. Next we'd turn the other way, shoot from that position, and finally face backwards, so that we had to spin through 180 degrees.

Then we'd do some walking practice – maybe four of us at a time. The aim was to get everybody nice and confident, walking with their hands at their sides, in a relaxed attitude. Then at the command 'UP!' we'd stop, draw, whip round and fire, all in a split second. If the targets were numbered, and we were walking in pairs, the instructor might yell 'ONE AND FOUR!' whereupon we'd have to engage those two targets. When each practice finished, the instructor would say, 'OK, guys, paste up,' and we'd go forward to stick coloured patches over the bullet holes.

At some stage, as we were firing, he'd yell 'Stoppage!' and we'd go down on one knee, hitting the release button of the magazine as we went; we'd whip the magazine out, slot another in, and be firing again as we came back up. In a contact, our lives might depend on the speed with which we reacted, and I practised until I could do the change in less than three seconds.

Speed and accuracy were everything. With the Hun's Head targets – the silhouette of a German soldier's head and trunk – it was always the head we aimed at, and up to twenty paces I reckoned I could put a double-tap straight through the middle of the forehead ten times out of ten. With the bigger Figure 11 targets we stuck on small white patches to give us precise aiming marks.

I found it odd that the lads who weren't actually firing would show little interest in what was going on. They'd sit on the bench outside the hut, chit-chatting away – the young ones would be on about the old trout they'd been humping the night before, the older guys about the extensions they were putting on their houses. As for me, I couldn't get enough of it. I had grown fanatically determined that if ever my chance came across the water, I wasn't going to flunk it. I'm sure some of the guys thought I was becoming obsessive, and I suppose I was – but only for a reason about which I couldn't enlighten them.

All our training emphasized the need for restraint and split-second timing. Many times in the past (we heard), our predecessors had had to wait until players were actually levelling weapons in front of them before they themselves could fire; if they'd shot sooner, before they were under immediate threat, they could have ended up in court charged with murder. It seemed ridiculous that the dice should be so heavily loaded in the terrorists' favour – yet that was the way things stood.

I recalled part of old Morrison's tirade, in which he had

lambasted the excessive restraints under which the security forces had to work: 'When we've brought a murderer into the station,' he'd said, 'if I so much as cuff him on the ear, that'll guarantee to put me in court. If I kick the chair from under him, that's an assault. Even if I lean over the table to emphasize a point, that's threatening him, and the interview's stopped because it's being monitored by the chief inspector sitting in the back.'

In some irrational way, I felt that the normal restrictions did not apply to me. Gary Player had already committed murder, and that was sufficient justification for my taking him out, never mind any further crimes he might commit. At the back of my mind I realized that in planning a personal vendetta I was stepping out of line. The essence of any SAS operation is teamwork, and here I was, trying to crack something on my own.

Working solo, without mates to cover my movements, would expose me to a far greater risk of getting shot or captured. Normally, working in pairs, you cover each other, and you can shoot your way out of trouble. Alone, without a partner, I could easily end up in the shit. I never really faced up to the thought of what might happen if I was captured. Very few of the guys ever did. Deep down, they knew perfectly well that if the IRA got them, they would be whipped south of the border and would probably never see the light of day again. They would die – but not before they had suffered unspeakable tortures. For this reason, some of them privately admitted that if things looked really bad they'd shoot themselves; but most preferred to believe they would come out fighting. I was one of that majority.

Apart from survival, there was also the little matter of identifying my victim. How in hell was I to find out who he was? And even if I did discover his name, how was I to track him down? Such was the force of my anger that I had no doubt I would find him somehow.

One morning a couple of weeks before the end of the course, I was due to have my arm checked by a specialist in the tri-service hospital at Wroughton. By then I was so hyped up that the thought of losing half a day's training quite pissed me off – but I scented possible compensation in the fact that Tracy might be on duty when I clocked in at the camp Med Centre to pick up my X-rays.

She was. When I appeared, she was on the phone, but before I'd taken two steps into the room she banged down the receiver with a loud cry of 'SHIT!'

'Something the matter?'

'It's our effing landlord. He's throwing us out.'

'That's tough. What happened?'

She told me she'd been living with a friend, Susan, in a flat on the outskirts of town. They had no proper security of tenure, and now the owner of the house was going abroad and wanted to let the whole place as a single unit. He had given the girls a fortnight to pack their bags.

Listening to Tracy talk, watching her, I thought she had changed. Her face was lit up with indignation, but she seemed more mature, less wild and tarty than I remembered her. Maybe I was influenced by the fact that she'd been very sweet about Kath the first time I'd seen her after the disaster. In any case, *I* now felt sorry for *her*.

Even so, it wasn't until I was in the minibus, half-way to Wroughton, that the idea hit me. For some time I'd been worrying what would happen to Keeper's Cottage when I went to Belfast. Tony was about to go off on the jungle phase of his selection course; in any case, he wouldn't want to live out in the country on his own while I was away. I could simply lock the door and go, but I didn't want the place to stand empty for months on end.

So why not offer the house to Tracy and Susan? I didn't know whether or not Susan had a car, but Tracy certainly had one, and could easily commute in and out. As long as being out in the wilds didn't spook them, they could live in the cottage rent-free, look after things till I got back, and give themselves time to find permanent accommodation elsewhere.

At Wroughton there was the usual delay. A backlog of

patients had built up, and I was told I'd have to wait half an hour; so I went down the corridor to the pay-phone and called the Med Centre's reception.

'Hi,' I began. 'It's me, Geordie.'

'What's happened now? Left your head behind?'

'Listen – I've had an idea about a place for you and Susan. You can have my house. It's going to be empty from the end of the month, for the best part of a year.'

'Where is it?'

'Off the Madley road, about four miles out.'

'How much d'you want for it?'

'Nothing. I just need to have it looked after.'

'Well . . .'

I could practically see her squirming her neat little arse about on her chair.

'Tell you what – I could pick you up tonight and take you out to have a look. Susan as well; you'd better both see it. It's pretty much out in the wilds, on its own. What do you think?'

'Are you sure?'

'Of course. I wouldn't be ringing otherwise.'

'What time, then?'

'Wait one. I'll be back up from LATA about half-seven. Say half-eight. What's your address?'

She gave it, and then said, 'There's no strings attached to this, are there?'

'Of course not.'

I was there five minutes early, showered and changed. Naturally I'd said nothing to the guys on the course, but all day I'd been haunted by a peculiar feeling, half guilt, half anticipation. Was I being disloyal to Kath's memory? There was no denying that I found Tracy attractive. But then I told myself, hell – I'm just trying to fix up a business arrangement, of mutual benefit.

Or so I thought – until she came flying down the steps of the house, all legs and arms.

'Where's Susan?' I asked.

'She had a date already. But she likes the idea, and she's

62

given me power of attorney to do what I think fit. Anyway, her job means she is away a lot, travelling.'

'Let's go, then.'

She was wearing a silver-grey track suit, and had a small bag hung over one shoulder. From the scent that wafted off her in the car I didn't think she'd been running. I had a good look at her profile for the first time, and saw that it matched her manner exactly, being rather pert and perky. On our way out she asked about Tim, and I explained he was with his Gran in Belfast.

'Is he OK?'

I turned to look at her, and saw her looking steadily, seriously, back at me.

'I think so. Lucky he's so young.'

'That's right.'

She fell silent for a couple of minutes. But then, as I turned down the lane to the cottage, she exclaimed, 'Gawd! You said it!'

'What?'

'Buried away.'

'D'you mind that?'

'I dunno. I've never lived in a place like this.'

When we got out of the car she shuddered and said in an aggrieved voice, 'It's dark!'

'What did you expect? It's night-time.'

'I mean, there are no lights anywhere.'

'This is the country. You don't have lights in the country. Don't need any. If you eat plenty of carrots, you can see in the dark.'

'You're kidding.'

'Honest!'

'There could be people lurking about out here.'

'What sort of people?'

'Rapists. Homicidal maniacs.'

'There are far more of them in towns. This isn't the environment for people like that.'

For a few seconds I thought she was going to throw a wobbly, especially when an owl sounded off close by. But in fact things went the other way. Once inside, she responded strongly to the place. She was a city kid all right, but her mind was open, and she was prepared to learn and adapt. She loved the house, saw the mess, gave me a mild bollocking, said she'd take over, and set straight in to clear up the kitchen.

'Eh,' I said, 'You can't do that.'

'Stop me.'

'You'd better have a drink, then. Glass of wine?'

'Thanks.'

One thing very soon led to another. She offered to cook something for supper. I suggested that we go out to the pub in the village, which served a reasonable evening meal. She said, 'No, that would be a waste of money.' Suddenly I heard myself say, 'You mean the waste of an opportunity?' The next thing I knew, we were in the bedroom, and I saw an immensely long flash of thigh as she pulled off her jogging pants.

'Jesus!' I cried. 'This is crazy. I haven't any – er . . .'

'I have!' She made a grab for the little bag she'd brought with her. 'Isn't that the Boy Scouts' motto "Be prepared"?'

In the morning, as we sat having a cup of coffee in the kitchen, I said, 'I should never have brought you here like this.'

'I'm glad you did.'

'I feel guilty.'

'Why? You're on your own. You've no one else.'

'No – but it's so soon after Kath.'

'You never messed about when she was alive.'

'No.'

'I've been worrying about you for weeks.'

'You didn't show it much.'

'How could I?'

'I know.'

She shook her head and put her hand over mine. I looked up into her face and said, 'Somehow, with you, I feel myself. I feel normal – comfortable, like.'

'Same here.' She smiled, producing tiny creases down her cheeks.

'What will people think, though?' I asked.

'They won't think anything. They needn't know I've spent the night here. As long as we don't walk into work wrapped round each other.'

'Jesus, no! I'll run you home round the back way, and go in on my own.'

'And then –' Tracy went on with her own line of thought – 'when Susan and I move in, it'll look like a straightforward business arrangement.'

'What about when I come back?'

'Tonight, you mean?'

'No, no – from across the water.'

'I'll be waiting here for you.'

'You mean that?'

'If you want me.'

The course ended with two big exercises, one out in the country and one mainly in town. In the first, we were told that a bomb had been planted in a certain culvert, under a country lane, out in the middle of a large estate. According to the scenario, command wires had been spotted running up a hedge to a firing point in the corner of an old quarry. Good intelligence had been received to the effect that terrorists were coming back at night to detonate the bomb when a vehicle patrol went past. I was detailed to command an operation to take them out.

There was no time for an on-site recce. For an hour we pored over the 1:50,000 map, planning covert approaches to the spot marked as the target. Then, as dark was coming on, we bussed out to a drop-off point, tabbed in across country, over the back of a hill, and prepared to lie up in wait. In the last of the light we found the command wires and traced the top end of them to a drain beside a gate-post, where the fence coming up from the culvert reached one corner of the quarry.

It was a filthy night, pissing with rain. The gate-post was nearly at the summit of the hill, and from it we could look down on the lane, which ran along the contour below us, across our front. Having set the rest of the patrol to cover us,

Pat and I worked our way down the command wires, to make sure they were connected to the device. Crafty bastards, the terrorists had coupled them up to the barbed wire, so that for most of the run the fence itself would act as a conductor: that way, no extra wires were needed, and there was nothing unusual to be seen. At the bottom end we picked up the special circuit again and followed it to an old milk churn under the little bridge.

That was good enough. Back near the firing-point, I deployed two pairs of guys left and right, as cut-offs, in case Pat and I – the killer group – missed the players and they tried to run out sideways. Then we settled into a small hollow thirty metres from the gate-post. There were a couple of more obvious hiding places, closer to the target; but the depression was just deep enough to cover us, especially in the dark, and it wasn't the kind of feature that would attract anyone's attention. I set the bipod of the G3 on the front of the dip, and wriggled around until it was at a comfortable height.

As the night wore on our hollow gradually filled with water, until we were lying in a couple of inches of liquid mud. The moon was three-quarters full, but because of the clouds its light was very faint, and I wished we'd had time to set out ambush lights. In the event, I had to keep switching on the kite-sight of my G3 to get a good view of the culvert area. In the grey-green glow of the sight the fence posts along the road showed up clearly, but when I looked with the naked eye I could scarcely make them out.

I was finding it hard to concentrate. Half the time my mind was slipping away to Tracy, and the way she'd wrapped her great long legs round me, first round my waist, then round my neck. What a night! And how fantastic that she was hell-bent on taking root in the cottage. To bring myself back to earth, I tried to imagine that I was no longer in the safe, soft Herefordshire countryside, but in some godforsaken corner of Ulster, with fanatical murderers lurking behind every hedge, and Gary Player himself coming to detonate the bomb.

Our magazines might have been loaded with blanks, but all the other details of the exercise were as real as could be. We knew the Det trainees were out as well, tracking the alleged players, but apart from occasional checks on the comms net, nothing happened until about 2.30 a.m. By then the rain had cleared and the night had gone very quiet. Suddenly, a gun-shot cracked off in the woods on the slopes opposite, and echoes rolled away down the valley to our right.

I had my radio in the special pocket of my ops waistcoat, down the left side of my chest. Two small throat-mikes were held in position either side of my Adam's apple by a choker of elastic. The pressel-switch, or transmission button, was a small rubber dome clipped on to the front of my windproof smock. If ever I found myself so close to the enemy that I couldn't speak, Control would interrogate me through my earpiece, and I would answer by using different numbers of presses – one for no, two for yes – which came across at the other end as quick bursts of static.

Now I gave it one blip to alert Control.

'Zero Alpha,' came the voice of the boss, who I knew was in a command vehicle a couple of miles down the road.

'Bravo Five-One,' I said quietly. 'There's been a shot fired approximately five hundred metres north of our location.'

'Roger. Checking. Wait out.'

Before I could say anything else, two more shots rang out. Pat, a yard to my left, came out with, 'Fucking hell! It's Arma-fucking-geddon!' Then, way off in the distance, torches began to flash. A pair of headlights flicked on, and a vehicle went haring along a woodland ride, the beams whipping wildly up and down. Men shouted, and a big dog, maybe a German Shepherd, barked. The sounds were all faint with distance, but clearly coming towards us.

'Bravo Five-One to all callsigns,' I said. 'I think it's poachers at the squire's pheasants. Nothing to do with us. But it could be a come-on. Just sit tight.'

Gradually the commotion died down. The vehicle drove off and silence returned. A few minutes later I picked up some movement below. I nudged Pat and brought the butt of the G3 up to my shoulder. But all the kite-sight revealed was a fox, padding up the hedge towards us. The animal came right to the firing-point, stopped, sniffed and cocked its leg against the gate-post. Then it turned through the gate and disappeared to our left.

'Well I'm buggered!' muttered Pat. 'One fox foxtrot towards target!'

At last, soon after three, the Det came on the air. 'Two X-rays, foxtrot towards your location, nearing zero six zero,' said a Scottish voice. 'Three hundred metres from firing-point.'

'Bravo Five-One, roger.'

My neck crawled. The baddies were not doing anything as straightforward as coming along the lane to the culvert and up the hedge towards us; rather, they were moving in across country, from behind our left shoulders. The slope of the ground meant that we wouldn't be able to see them until the last moment.

'X-rays still foxtrot,' said the Det Scot. 'Two hundred metres.'

A couple of minutes ticked by. Then, 'Zero Alpha,' came the boss's voice in my ear. 'Have you got eyes on the X-rays?'

By then they could have been almost on top of us, too close for me to speak. I gave a single punch on my pressel to signify 'No.'

I lay like a stone, holding my breath, listening. A minute passed, then another. The boss called again and asked the same question. Again I gave him one press.

Where the hell were they? With the utmost caution I turned my head until it was facing backwards like an owl's. Nobody in sight. Obviously they were waiting out, somewhere very close. We knew that they were there, and they knew that we were there. They were trying to wind us up and push us into making a mistake.

Sod them. On the net I heard the boss asking the Det to check the bearing-to-target they had given. The answer came back confirming it. Still no movement near us.

Then Pat reached out and touched my left arm.

There they were – two black heads and torsos showing against the sky, a few yards off to our left. The pair moved

68

forward in a crouching attitude, so close I could hear the rustle of their clothes.

Gently I raised the butt of the G3 to my shoulder and looked through the kite-sight. The figures showed up in every detail. One was carrying a weapon, a long, and the other had a box-like object slung from his left hand. As I watched they went to ground by the gate-post.

I gave a touch on the pressel.

'Zero Alpha,' said the boss. 'Have you got X-rays on target?'

Two presses.

'Are they armed?'

Two presses.

'How far off are they? Less than thirty metres?'

Two presses.

'Twenty metres?'

Two presses.

'Three patrol Charlies mobile, direction target,' said the Det voice. 'Have you got eyes on them?'

One press. But a moment later I saw them – three Land Rovers driving on sidelights up the lane. This, for me, was the moment of decision. Yes, I told myself, these two guys were definitely a threat. The patrol was within seconds of passing over the culvert. The terrorists were on the firing-point. If we didn't drop them immediately they'd detonate their bomb, possibly with disastrous results.

'Stand by, stand by,' I whispered to Pat. I sensed, rather than saw, him bring the butt of his weapon up into his shoulder. My own rifle sat steady on its bipod. I pushed the safety catch forward to 'Automatic'. Then at the top of my voice I yelled, 'ARMY! ARMY! ARMY! HALT OR I FIRE!'

Instantly the pair split, one running right, one left. At the first movement I let rip at the right-hand figure with three short bursts. Pat did the same at the left (I was aware of flame spurting from the muzzle of his rifle). Both players went down and lay still. I gave mine another burst, on the ground, to make sure of him, waited a few seconds, and got back on the radio.

'Bravo Five-One. Contact! Two terrorists dead. No casualties ourselves. Checking the area. Wait out.'

We had a quick look round, made sure none of the other guys had seen anyone. Then I reported, 'No other terrorists on target,' and asked for the QRF – a green army team – to move up to the prearranged rendezvous. I deputed Pat to meet them and explain exactly what had happened. Then I saw that the rest of my team got the hell out; the instructors had hammered into us the fact that in Northern Ireland a crowd gathers immediately at the scene of any incident, and it is bad news if locals see the faces of members of the special forces.

Soon we were away back to base in a couple of the Land Rovers that had acted as the threatened patrol. Behind, on the ground, the alleged terrorists would still be lying where they had fallen, until a photographer had taken pictures of them. Also on the scene would be one of the Regiment acting as the LO (or Liaison Officer) – he'd be directing the QRF, who would cordon off the whole area. Nobody else would be allowed until the arrival of the SOCO, the Scene of Crimes Officer, who was from the RUC. He would measure distances and angles, collect up the cartridge cases and make notes for his report.

After a wash-up, we got our heads down, but not for long, because the exercise continued in the morning with a full-scale inquiry. Not only did a proper judge preside in court, with real-life barristers holding forth; the Regiment brought down about sixty cooks and bottle-washers from the squadron, to act as audience and sit there heckling. We'd been told how easy it would be to let ourselves down by getting details wrong when we gave our accounts of what had happened, or by giving away more information than necessary; so we briefed ourselves carefully beforehand, and in the event got the whole incident well squared away. The best bit of the morning came when one of the cooks, Jimmy Bell, went way over the top. We didn't know whether he'd had a couple of pints on the way down or what, but he became so obnoxious with his heckling and his shouts of 'Order!

70

Order!' that the judge ordered him removed from the court, and it was all we could do to sit there with straight faces.

Maybe because of my upbringing in the country, I felt more at home operating out on farms and in the woods than in towns. But the next event on our programme was a four-day spell in Lydd and Hythe, the mock village on the Kent coast purpose-built for training. That is an eye-opener, because there are video cameras set up on every corner, and after a house assault you could run the tape and see exactly what everyone had done. If someone had behaved like a prat it was useless for him to deny it, because there he was on the video, pissing about for all to see.

Our final exercise – a joint one with the MI5 – was mostly urban. The scenario was that two major players had just come across the water and gone to ground in Birmingham. MI5 trainees followed them to a house in Solihull, where they were supposed to have secreted some weapons in a garage. It fell to Pat and myself to do a CTR, and exercise our newly acquired skills as lock-pickers by breaking into the garage at night to verify the information. Sure enough, we found a cache of two dummy AK 47s and some bomb-making equipment. We reported the find and pulled off, taking care to remove all traces of our entry, and left a couple of guys in an OP that covered both house and garage.

MI5, meanwhile, was continuing its own surveillance, boxing the area to make sure that the villains didn't slip away unobserved. But it was our guys in the OP who saw the players loading their weapons into a car next morning. By then we were all pretty professional at keeping up a running commentary, and this one came over without hesitation: 'OK. Bravos One and Two are in garage. They've got the weapons. Now they're loading them into Charlie One. Weapons definitely in boot of car. Stand by, stand by. Bravos One and Two mobile towards Blue Three.'

Seconds later the MI5 boys came up with, 'OK, I have Charlie One at Blue Three mobile towards Blue Two.'

So it went on. Charlie One, a battered old blue Montego estate, was followed to a deserted farmhouse in the hills outside Kidderminster. This was the base from which they were going to mount their operation. Again our troop went in at night to put an OP on the farm, and when the baddies turned up to collect their weapons we ambushed them, in theory killing the lot. In fact (according to the scenario) one escaped, and moved north to join an ASU in Wolverhampton – so the exercise continued in pursuit of him, and the action moved up there.

When the course ended, we had a couple of beers at the bar in LATA, then went back for a Chinese meal in Hereford. After that we felt we'd taken enough fried rice and crispy noodles on board to soak up a few more beers, so we went on to the Falcon, one of the Regiment's regular haunts. By then we'd all grown our hair fairly long, as part of our preparation for Northern Ireland, but we were all of much the same age, size and physique, and it wasn't difficult for outsiders to tell where we came from.

As usual we stood around together, occupying what we regarded as our own territory, at one end of the main bar, and before long we began to get aggro from a gang of town lads in the opposite corner. At first they were just making the odd sarcastic remark, more or less loud enough for us to hear. Then one of them, as he came past on his way to the bar, deliberately barged into me with his shoulder. He was quite a big lad, with straw-coloured hair shaved flat at the top to make an Elvis-type quiff.

'Hey,' I said. 'What's the matter with you? Bog off, before you get hurt.'

He mouthed some obscenity, then turned to the barman. I could see that he was drunk enough to behave stupidly, but not so drunk that he couldn't do somebody serious damage. When he came back with two pints of lager, I stood well aside. Apart from anything else, Fred, the landlord, had recently installed closed-circuit TV, so that if anything did start he would have the evidence on tape – and in the event of trouble, he'd be straight up the camp next morning.

Nothing more happened for a while; but when I went for a

slash, out of the corner of my eye I saw the fellow get up and start after me. Then, as I stood at the communal urinal, he came and took up position right beside me, not having a piss himself, but peering down at my midriff in the most offensive fashion.

'Look,' I said, 'I told you to fuck off.'

'Not much to bloody write home about, is it?' he said contemptuously. 'Can't think what she sees in it.'

I saw his right hand moving down towards his pocket, so I didn't wait any longer, but dropped him where he stood. He slid down the enamel face and finished up lying on his left side with his head in the trough. Just the place for him. I made a quick grab into his trouser pocket. Sure enough, he had a flick-knife. In a second I had lifted the lid of the flushing cistern and dropped it in. Maybe in a few years' time, if rusty water started coming down the system, somebody would have a look and discover its corroded remains.

Back in the bar I muttered, 'Time to thin out, lads. We could have a problem. I'll see you.'

'Where's your admirer?' asked Pat.

'Just having a little nap.'

With that I said good-night to Fred and moved off casually. On the way home I tried to make sense of the yobbo's aggression. Tracy had said something about recently breaking up with a boyfriend . . . but no – she would never have been friends with a turd like that. And anyway, how could he possibly associate me with her? She and I had never been seen together in town. I decided that there was no connection; it was just normal jealousy of the Regiment coming out. All the same, the incident made me realize how much the girl was on my mind.

FIVE

A few days before we left, at the start of December, we heard on the grapevine that 500 men of the First Glosters had been sent to Ulster in response to the latest upsurge of violence. It certainly sounded as though we were going to get some action.

Several of the lads went berserk over their packing, insisting that they take almost every single object they possessed. We knew that our accommodation was going to be basic – no more than a series of Portakabins inside a warehouse – yet they seemed hell-bent on having their fridges, TV sets, microwaves and God-knows-what with them. There was no limit on what we were allowed to take – the bulk items went ahead by road and ferry, leaving us with only our ops kit – all the same, I didn't go in for much heavy stuff; for one thing, I didn't think I'd need it, and for another, I didn't want to strip the cottage just as the girls moved in. In the end all I took was my Technics stereo system, minus the speakers, because I reckoned they'd piss off my neighbours in a close-quarter environment, and in any case I'd recently invested in a pair of Stax headphones whose sound quality put the speakers in the shade.

A Puma came into camp on the Monday afternoon, and lifted the twelve of us away over the Welsh mountains. Looking across the cabin, I was glad to see the grizzled, close-cropped head of Tom Dawson, the sergeant major, who was coming as our second-in-command on the final posting of his career. I suppose that in a way he was a father figure to us all, and, maybe because I had no parents of my own, I'd benefited more than most of the guys from his wisdom and long experience.

We put down to refuel in a shit-hole of a depot on the coast, and then did a flit across the sea. The crossing gave me time to reflect on the set-up at home. Tracy and Susan had moved their things in the day before, and we'd piled Kath's clothes into the small spare bedroom. The three of us had spent that night in separate rooms, as proper as could be. In the morning I'd shown the girls how to work the central heating system and how to manage the wood-burning stove. I'd amassed a big store of logs, so they had plenty of fuel. 'For God's sake don't burn the place down,' I told Tracy. 'That's the only rule.'

At that stage I don't think she'd said anything to Susan about her long-term plans; all Susan knew was that they had somewhere to live for the next few months. But when we were alone for a moment Tracy said again, 'When you come back, I'll be waiting for you.' That gave me a big kick, of course, but I was still disturbed by the speed at which everything had happened. Kath had been killed on 28 July, and we were now only just into December. Four months. I kept telling myself that it wasn't me who had written Kath off. I hadn't done anything to get rid of her. Fate, or whatever, had snatched her.

My soul-searching didn't last long. Soon we were over the coast and landing in the camp on the outskirts of Belfast. Inside the warehouse, the first thing we saw was a man with pink hair. 'For fuck's sake!' cried Pat. 'What's this? A poofters' convention?' But an old SAS hand, who'd been there for a couple of months already, assured us that it was only one of the Det guys who'd tried to dye his fair hair brown but had got the mixture wrong. The senior wrangler explained that it was perfectly legitimate for members of the Det to change their appearance for cover purposes. This fellow, however, was going to have to stay out of sight for a few days, until he got himself sorted.

Apart from the pink head, our immediate surroundings weren't that cheerful, but Pat and I got cabins next to each other and soon settled ourselves in. Some previous occupant of mine must have been a freak for Pirelli calendars, because it was tits and bums on every wall. Rather than rip them down and have bare cream-coloured panels all round, I left them where they were, gradually persuading myself that in some respects the June bird looked remarkably like Tracy.

The best that could be said for our set-up was that everything was under one roof: not only our cabins, but also the briefing room, armoury, MT depot, canteen, bar, showers and bogs were situated within the warehouse. To me it had a claustrophobic air, but the guys who handed over to us assured us that you soon got used to it. One feature nobody had warned us about was the rats. That first evening a sudden yell of outrage went up, and we ran out of our cabins to see a guy called Ginger Norris pointing up into the roof.

'Look at that!' he roared. 'The biggest fucking rat you've ever seen!'

Sure enough, there on one of the girders perched a vast rat, a real monster, and, when a volley of trainers went up at it, all it did was move a tier higher and sit there polishing its whiskers, cool as a pint of Stella. 'Jesus Christ!' cried Ginger. 'Never mind the PIRA or anybody else, the next thing'll be we'll all go down with lepto–fucking–spirosis.' He was all for taking out the rat with his Sig, until somebody pointed out that we'd be even worse off if he shot the roof full of holes and let the rain through.

'It's those wankers of cooks,' explained one of the old hands. 'They sling all the leftover food in open bins out the back of the cookhouse, and the rats eat themselves stupid. It's like giving them a free run of the menu at the Dorchester.'

'Why don't we get some cats?' I suggested.

'Cats?' said Ginger derisively. 'Cats? Rats this size would have them for breakfast.'

Our first couple of days were spent on orientation, getting to know Belfast itself. Even though I'd made several visits to my in-laws in Helen's Bay, and had come into the city centre from the east, I'd never been in West Belfast, and now I was appalled by the sheer squalor of the place. I'd seen endless pictures of it on television, of course, and I was familiar with the crude murals of black-hooded figures painted on the sides of buildings; but nothing had quite prepared me for the pure grot – the scruffiness, the meanness, the ugliness, the filth.

Our own senior guys drove us around the softer areas of the city in unmarked cars; but the hard areas were out of bounds to such vehicles, and the only way we could get a look at them was by courtesy of the RUC, who gave us tours, two at a time, in the back of their armoured Land Rovers.

That meant, first of all, getting infiltrated into one of the fortified police stations – an experience in itself. The one Pat and I went to was defended like Fort Knox with high, anti-rocket wire-mesh screens, mortar-proof walls of reinforced concrete, and closed-circuit television cameras bristling from every rooftop. Driving in, we passed through three separate manned gateways; then, to enter the building, we went round a couple of corners – thick walls set at right-angles to each other to cut down the chance of blast penetration.

Inside, a sergeant gave us a quick tour, mainly of the ops room, where radios crackled and the walls were covered with large-scale maps dotted with coloured pins. This station, said our guide, had been attacked more than a hundred times, with rockets, mortars, sniper fire and coffee-jar devices, or petrol bombs. 'They fired an RPG7 from the distilleries into the canteen, so they did,' he told us. 'There were no fatalities, but quite a few people were injured. Then they tried to float a bomb down the stream which passes under the station in a tunnel. We have a cage on either end, and cameras, but still they were going to try it. Luckily the Special Branch got wind of what was happening, and they aborted the attempt.'

From one of the sangars – high, fortified towers – we had a great view over the city. Everything looked peaceful enough, yet still our guide could speak of nothing but attacks. One great merit of the station's position, he explained, was that it had a school and a housing estate right behind it. These made the PIRA reluctant to fire mortars in that direction, because the weapons were notoriously unreliable, and an overshoot that caused civilian casualties would create very bad publicity.

We ventured out on patrol in a police Land Rover. A constable drove, and a sergeant called Martin kept up a running commentary from the passenger seat. We crouched in the back, craning forward to peer out through the armoured glass of the windscreen, with a third RUC man scanning through the small aperture in one of the rear doors.

Here, on this corner, a rocket attack on a police Land Rover had cut an RUC sergeant nearly in half. Here a lad had tried to throw a bomb over the wall into a police station, but he'd dropped it, and it blew off his arm. Here, on the Falls Road, was the infamous Rock Bar, where members of the PIRA would meet for a pint. Here they had staged a burglary on a library, and as a policeman approached to investigate they'd opened up on him with an M 60 machine-gun. Here was Rose Cottage, inhabited by a harmless old pensioner. Under the pretence of befriending him, IRA men had offered to decorate a room for him, and in the course of doing so they had built a false wall, shortening the room by about five feet and creating a major weapons hide, later discovered by the Royal Marines.

We were patrolling as a pair, in company with a second vehicle, never far from it, in case one or other suddenly needed help. Martin was frequently on his radio: 'Six Five, roger. We're just going to Sebastopol. . . We're passing Berlin.' Every now and then our partner vehicle would drive past in the opposite direction, as the pair wove intricate patterns through the sordid, run-down streets. Again and again Martin said, 'The whole of this road is divided, Green Nationalists on one side, Orange Protestants on the other.' But he kept emphasizing that most of the population was perfectly normal: 'There's so many decent people here. The proportion of bad ones is very small.' Nevertheless, he agreed that he was constantly on the lookout for familiar faces, trying to spot known players and work out their patterns of movement, and after an hour I felt the entire place was poisoned by hatred.

Back in the station, Pat and I went off to have a piss. The nearest gents was tucked away on the floor below, and Martin came down to show us the route, leaving us to find our own way back. As we emerged, a man in civvies was coming along the corridor towards us – quite an old guy, with grey hair – and as I glanced at him I felt a prickle of recognition. In the same instant his face gave a flicker as he recognized me.

'Hello,' he said. 'I know you, surely.'

'Yes – we met in Hereford.'

It was Chief Superintendent Morrison, the RUC man who'd talked to our course at LATA.

'Geordie Sharp,' I said, 'and this is a colleague, Pat.'

We all shook hands, and Morrison said, 'Have you a moment for a chat? This is my office, right here.'

He pointed at a door beside us. Instinctively I said, 'D'you want to go on up, Pat? I'll be with you in a couple of minutes.'

Pat got the message and thinned out. The chief ushered me into his office, large but bare, and gestured at a chair in front of the desk. 'Take a seat. Just come over?'

'That's right.'

'Well, I hope you have a successful tour.'

I wasn't quite sure what he meant by that. Was it just innocent good wishes? I said, 'Thanks.'

He started fiddling with a glass paperweight. Then, looking steadily at me across the desk, he said, 'I believe you lost your wife in the Queensfield bomb.'

'That's right.'

'I'm so sorry. I know it was an own-goal, but there's no consolation in that. Very likely the device would have killed even more people if it had gone off where they meant it to. I think I told you over in England, we're up against real bastards here, evil bastards. What I didn't say to your course was that I've lost my own brother to them, and his son, my nephew. So I can imagine how you feel.'

'Thanks,' I repeated.

'Sympathy's not much use. I've learnt that over the years. But you have mine, and if there's anything I can do to help, you'll let me know.'

Even as he spoke, an idea was opening up in my mind.

'That's very good of you,' I said, and then I added casually, 'I don't suppose you know who did it – who was responsible for the bomb?'

'I'd have to check. Why?' His lined, grey face softened into a smile. 'D'you fancy going after them or something?'

79

'No, no.' I forced a smile in return. 'I just thought it might help somehow, to know.'

'Of course. And if I did find out any information, what would I do with it?'

'Maybe you could send it care of my father-in-law. That would be the safest.' I gave him the address in Helen's Bay.

'Good enough. And now maybe you'd better rejoin your colleague. I'm pleased to have seen you again.'

I went back to the ops room feeling like a conspirator, busy with my own thoughts – only to find that the others were talking about a subject of intense interest to me: the way in which leading players protected their houses. Many had closed-circuit TV cover front and back, Martin was saying, and most reinforced their front doors with steel plates and big, heavy, old-fashioned iron bars which could be swung or slotted into place at night, making it impossible to force an entry. Often they'd have an inner door as well, with an air-lock between the two in which they could scrutinize visitors. Then, at the bottom of the stairs, they'd have a cage or grille of heavyweight weldmesh, so that they could seal off the upper floor. That way, they were safe from all but the most determined attacks.

The troop's eight intercept cars were monsters in disguise. They looked quite ordinary, but under their sedate exterior lurked mighty engines and any number of refinements. Some of the engines had merely been hotted-up, but others had been replaced by more powerful units altogether. The extra punch was needed because the cars were carrying a huge amount of weight in the form of armour – at the front, along the side-panels, and behind the two back seats. To manage all this, as well as four blokes and their gear, rifles, shotguns, assault kits, door-charges and so on, the springs and shock-absorbers had been uprated. Even so, the belly-plates were liable to ground when you went over bumps like sleeping policemen, sending out showers of sparks.

Inside each car there was a comprehensive comms system, with the radio tucked away in the glove compartment, a pressel-switch down by the handbrake, and a microphone slotted into the sun visor. For normal covert operations we'd listen through our earpieces, but there was also a loudspeaker fitted into the glove compartment for when the shit hit the fan. 'If you get into a chase, and the villains know you're after them, there's no point in trying to stay covert, so you switch to the speaker,' somebody explained. 'Equally, if you start to take incoming, and the windscreen goes, your earpieces are the last thing you need.'

I didn't appreciate quite what the cars would do until I went out for a familiarization drive. The one I had was an old Rover 2000 known as the Bluesmobile. It looked drab and decrepit, as if it was well past its scrap-by date, and when we started out I thought I was driving a tank, so heavy did it feel. But as soon as I got out on to the ring road and put my foot down – that was something else. In a few seconds we were doing 150 m.p.h., with a good bit in hand, and only a build-up of traffic far ahead made me ease off. Thereafter I took things more steadily and concentrated on getting familiar with the radio system. One lesson I learnt from the run is that a G3 is a brute of a weapon to take in a car: too long to fit down neatly beside the driver's seat, and difficult to bring up quickly. I'd already heard of an occasion when a G3 had slipped so that the muzzle landed on the accelerator pedal, and the driver suddenly found himself heading off into the sunset at a great rate of knots. Now I saw the wisdom of bringing an HK 53, which would fit comfortably under the seat.

Our familiarization was supposed to last for the first couple of weeks, but in the event things turned out less leisurely. One evening I was in my cabin, with Eric Clapton keeping the world at bay, when through the music I heard a call on the tannoy: 'Standby team into the briefing room.'

In half a minute all ten of us had assembled.

Tom Dawson, the second-in-command, was in charge. 'Right, lads,' he began. 'We've got a fast ball. Operation Eggshell. It's a babysitting job, with a few strings attached.

81

There's a hit going down on a senior political figure, timed for 2230 tonight. The boss is at TCG, getting details. Basically it's a city job, in East Belfast. We need four guys to babysit and six to deploy in the intercept cars.'

He turned to me. 'Geordie, you're to command the house party. The address is Knocklofty Park. There's no time for an on-site recce, so you'll need to take a good look at the map and get your arses down there a.s.a.p. Covert approach from wasteground behind. If you want to grab something to eat you've got twenty minutes. Final briefing at 2000, and roll immediately after.'

Because I'd already eaten, I had plenty of time to sort and check my kit: HK 53, side-arm, magazines for both, torch, knife, wire-cutters, covert radio. We'd go in wearing civilian clothes, but with our ops waistcoats on. I told all my guys to bring a pair of clean trainers for when we got inside the house; even if the people you're looking after are about to be blown to kingdom come, they don't take it kindly if you mess up their carpets. I also packed a roll of heavy-duty polythene and one of lightweight black cloth, for doctoring up a lookout room when we established ourselves in the target. (With film slanted across a room from ceiling to floor and the back wall blacked out, you can move around without somebody outside being able to see you.) Then I thought, if the old people are going to be in the house, we'd better take flak-jackets for them, just in case shrapnel comes through the floor or one of the doors. Also we needed a couple of big medical packs.

At 2000 the boss, Captain John Mason, was still down at TCG, so our final briefing came from Tom.

'Just to confirm details,' he began. 'The PIRA's target is Freddy Quinlan, the Unionist MP. He's already at home with his wife. He's been offered the chance to leave, but he's declined. He's that way: doesn't rate the opposition, stupid bugger. Normally he has no security on the house whatsoever, not even any cameras. But that's his lookout.

'Our information is that the PIRA are planning a rocket attack. Probably a drive-past. They'll launch an RPG7 to take out the front door, then follow up on foot to finish off anyone who has survived. That means your guys, Geordie, will want to be upstairs with the family. At the same time, it's vital that you preserve an impression of normal activity. The curtains will be drawn, but we want people to move around the house naturally for as long as possible. OK?'

I nodded, and he went on, pushing a large-scale town plan across the table towards me, 'Your covert approach will be through wasteland behind the house. It's the former grounds of a mansion, gone to seed. We'll get you dropped off here' – he pointed with a pencil – 'and it'll only be a short walk in, three hundred metres at the outside. Between the edge of the park and the back garden is a wooden panel fence. Don't go over that, in case the players have eyes-on from behind one of the adjacent properties. Get under it, or through the bottom. The back door of the house will be open for you. OK?'

Again I nodded. 'How do we recognize the house and garden from the back?'

'There's a World Wildlife Fund panda symbol hung over the outside of the fence.'

'What about the telephone? Is the line bugged?'

'Possibly. Special Branch have told Quinlan to carry on taking normal calls, but obviously not to mention the operation.'

'Fair enough.'

'Anything else?'

'A rocket will probably blow the hell out of the electrics and leave the house dark. We'd better take some ambush lights as an emergency back-up.'

'Good thinking.'

Tom went on to brief the car-teams and the QRF. I listened with half an ear, studying the map. The old park or garden showed up as a sizeable green blob in the middle of massed streets and houses, but there was nothing to be learnt about it from where we were. The drop-off point was on the far side of the park from our destination, so all we needed to do was cross the wasteground in an easterly direction.

As soon as Tom finished, the signals corporal went through his own plan. The boss's callsign for the night was Zero

Alpha, and our house team was designated Hotel One. We were also assigned a chatter-net on a different frequency, so that if necessary we could talk to each other without cluttering up the main channel. Our car units were Mobile One, Mobile Two and so on. The house was designated 'the target', the back door was 'Red' and the front door 'White'. Some of our guys were to mount an OP in a garden across the road – that party had the callsign Whisky. The Det, with various Delta numbers, were already out on surveillance.

A few minutes after eight a grey van pulled into the warehouse. The legend on the panel said, 'NORTHERN IRELAND ELECTRICITY VAN – Engineering Department', and the vehicle had a big sliding side door, excellent for an unobtrusive exit. My house team piled in and set off. With the pair of ambush lights and power-pack, my bergen was going to be quite a burden, even though we were going on such a short operation. I'm sure Pat spoke for all of us when he said, 'I don't like the thought of this fucking rocket coming in.'

'Neither do I,' I told him. 'But as long as the house is reasonably substantial we'll be OK upstairs.'

Peering forward through the windscreen, I said to Titch, the driver, 'You will bring us in with the door on the kerb-side, won't you?'

'No sweat.'

Twenty minutes of twisting and turning through the city brought us to our objective.

'Here's the park now,' said Titch. 'I'm just running down the side of it. The lay-by's a couple of hundred yards farther on. Stand by to debus.'

The moment he stopped I hit the handle, slid the door and was outside, landing in a shallow puddle. I took a quick look round. It was pretty good: a smallish recess at the edge of the suburban road, screened by bushes. Some traffic was passing, but none very close. Immediately behind us were the old iron railings of the mansion's grounds, topped by two strands of barbed wire. Rather than risk getting hung up I cut through them, peeled them back and went over the railings, quickly followed by the other three. Titch had got out and opened the bonnet of the van. I saw him peering about under it with a torch, tugging at electric leads as if checking for a fault. As soon as we were clear he slammed the bonnet shut and drove off. I was pretty sure nobody had seen us.

Inside the park it was like being on an island, dark and peaceful, with the city traffic roaring and grinding round in the distance outside. As I waited for my eyes to acclimatize, one of the Det guys came up on the radio with, 'Delta Two, a dicker's just walked down the street past White.'

'Sounds like the job's going down OK,' I whispered. 'We'd better get in there.'

Round the perimeter of the park ran a belt of mature trees, some of them pines. The air was full of the smell of evergreens and ivy. Once through the trees, we came out on to open grass. At the edge of the cover I paused for a look round. Away to our left, a couple of hundred yards off on the crest of a rise, stood the old mansion, dark as dark, a heavy-looking Victorian building with turrets and pointed eaves. The grass we were on must once have been the lawn. Some lawn! Three or four acres, at least. We moved swiftly across it, towards more high trees on the far side. Ahead of us, between the trunks, lights were showing – the backs of the houses in our target road.

The ground beneath the second belt of trees was choked by undergrowth – diabolical bramble bushes, five or six feet high, interlaced with elder. Rather than crash through the thicket, we tried to pick a way between, only to find ourselves on the edge of a flooded area, perhaps an old pond. Pulling off, we made another approach, and soon came to a six-foot wooden fence along the backs of the gardens. A quick cast to the right brought us face-to-face with the reassuring black-and-white shape of the panda badge.

'Pity to carve this up,' I whispered, feeling the wooden panels.

'It's OK,' answered Jimmy Adair. 'There's a drain running under it.'

He'd found a kind of culvert, and with a few jabs from our collapsible shovel we enlarged it enough for us to wriggle through. The back of the house was only ten metres off: whitewashed walls, several windows, the back-door conveniently screened by a projecting outhouse. A light was showing upstairs, but the curtains of that room were drawn.

We stood in the shadows by the fence. I held in my pressel-switch and said softly, 'Hotel One. On Red now.'

'Zero Alpha, roger,' answered the boss.

As promised, the door was open. We slipped into a short corridor and locked up behind us, shooting home the bolts at the top and bottom. A smell of cooking hung in the air. We took off our boots, stacked them in a neat heap and put on our clean trainers. Then, leaving the others to cover me, I went quietly forward, HK 53 at the ready, past the kitchen and into the hall.

The TV was on in one of the front rooms. I knocked on the door, pushed it open a foot or so and showed myself in the gap. The woman saw me first – a small, elderly person with white hair swept back in a bun. She gave a bit of a cry and stood up.

'It's all right,' I said. 'We're here to look after you.'

The husband was a fierce-looking little fellow, with curly silver hair, dark eyebrows, and thick-rimmed glasses; he was wearing a fawn cardigan and matching slippers, like any retired professional. As soon as I saw him, I recognized his face from news bulletins and the papers.

From the darkness of the hall I asked him if the front curtains were fully drawn.

'Sure they are,' he said testily. 'That was the first thing your people told us. We've got the old blackout blind pulled down as well.' As he came towards me he said, 'This is ridiculous,' but not in a voice that carried much conviction. I caught a trace of whisky on his breath. He was easily old enough to be my father, so I didn't feel I could give him too many orders, still less pull him around physically if he became difficult. I was glad to find that his irritation was only bluff; when I assured him that the threat was not only real but imminent, he agreed to move upstairs.

'What I don't understand is this,' he said. 'If you know

they're coming, why the heck can't you intercept them before they get here?'

'The trouble is, we don't know where they're coming from. We have other units outside, and with a bit of luck, they may get to the villains before they do any damage to the house. But we can't take chances with your safety.'

Before I could stop her, his wife switched off the television.

'Sorry,' I said. 'We'd better leave that on.'

She gave me a look, but went back to the channel they'd been on.

It turned out that the couple slept at the back of the house – the room in which we'd seen the light – and had another set in their bedroom. As quickly as we could, we got them safely in there, and told them that if they needed to go to the bathroom they mustn't switch on any more lights.

'Here,' I said, getting out the flak-jackets. 'If you don't mind, put these on. They're a bit heavy and uncomfortable, but they could just save your lives.' Then I took the medical packs into the bathroom and opened them up so that the IV kits were immediately to hand.

Next we took a look round downstairs. The house was solidly built, with floors that didn't bounce, and walls which felt good when you hit them. The whole place was tidy as could be. I found it hard to believe that the shit was about to be blown out of it. The front door was locked and bolted, but only medium-strong, and it had a half-moon of frosted glass above it. The thought of an RPG7 rocket coming through it was not amusing. The weapon was developed by the Russians more than thirty years ago, in the depths of the Cold War, for the express purpose of taking out British or American tanks; though extremely simple, it was capable of destroying any armoured vehicle, let alone an ordinary car or somebody's front door. The chances were that if one came through into the hall, it would blow out the back wall of the house as well.

The only firefighting equipment was one ancient-looking extinguisher, but I put this ready, just inside the kitchen. Luckily the stairs started from the back of the hall and came forward towards the front, so that if we did get a rocket through the door, the main blast would be directed through the kitchen and out of the back door, rather than upwards. 'Let's get our boots out of the line of fire, anyway,' said Pat, and we shifted them into a scullery.

Upstairs again, I saw that the landing ran across the back of the stairwell. Kneeling behind the white-painted wooden banisters, we could cover the whole of the hall. If any assault party tried to follow up a rocket, we could take them out from there, no bother.

I checked all the doors, and once I'd got the layout I detailed Jimmy to remain in the back bedroom with our hosts, in case anyone started trying to come through the rear window. In the front bedroom on the left, facing forwards, we slung a sheet of polythene at a forty-five degree angle, fixing it to the walls with drawing-pins brought for the purpose, so that we could look through the window without being visible from outside. To complete the optical illusion, we pinned our thin black cloth over the rear wall, cutting out background reflection.

Hardly had we done that when Pat, who was looking out, said, 'Hey, there's someone coming past.'

In the patchy illumination of the street-lamps we saw a young man in what looked like jeans and a black donkey jacket walk past from right to left. He was trying to maintain a nonchalant appearance, but we saw him take a sideways glance at the target.

'One of their dickers, I bet,' said Jimmy.

Sure enough, a moment later the Det came up with 'Delta Two. That same dicker's gone back the other way.'

'Hotel One,' I called. 'Established on target.'

'Roger,' answered the boss. 'Stand by.'

I was still new enough to the game to be surprised by the immediacy with which our team's voices jumped out of the night. I knew that the boss was miles away, at the desk, and that the Det guys were spread out all over town. But from the speed with which people came up on the air, they might have been in a tight ring round the target.

I decided that when, or if, the attack came, we'd go to

ground in the blacked-out bedroom and close the door. Then, immediately after the explosion, we'd whip out on to the landing so that we could drop anyone who came into the hall below. We therefore constructed a kind of shelter out of the two single beds, tipping them on edge and tilting the tops inwards against each other, like a tent, with the mattresses on the floor to give some protection from below, and room for us to crawl in so that we had cover in case the ceiling came down. Then I set the two ambush lights out, one on either side of the landing, so that if anyone fired up at them, the rounds would go well clear of our own position. I ran the wires round the landing so that the switch was at the point where I intended to be.

Waiting was no joke. We'd turned up the sound of the TV a bit, so that we could hear it burbling away, and the ever-changing light from the screen flickered out into the hall. Occasionally one of us went down to open or close the living-room door a bit, so that any watcher would see a change in the light showing through the frosted glass over the front door, and conclude that Quinlan and his wife were in or out of the room. When I went down for the last time I left the door shut, as if they were both in the room. Each of those trips downstairs made my hair crawl. What if the players had given the Det the slip, and were lining their rocket-launcher up at that very moment?

In fact, we had plenty of radio chat to keep us abreast of the situation. At 2215 the same dicker made a third pass. He'd taken the trouble to go round in a big circle, so that he came by in the same direction as on his earlier appearance, and gave the casual impression of being another walker going the same way. But the Det knew him too well, and reported a definite sighting. After that, though, no other pedestrians showed, and we guessed the strike was coming up. Our intercept cars had taken up strategic positions in surrounding streets, in case the hit-car escaped immediate ambush, and they too came on the air occasionally, with callsigns India One, India Two and so on.

From time to time I briefed our landlord on the latest

situation. At 2220 the lady of the house offered us a brew, made from an upstairs kettle, which we gratefully accepted, one at a time. 'So long as you don't damage anything,' she kept repeating. I promised her that we'd be as careful as we could, but said that I couldn't vouch for our friends on the other side.

Minute by minute, the time ticked on. My mind was flying round in circles: Kath, Tim, Tracy, Gary Player . . . It was too much to hope that he would have been assigned to carry out tonight's hit. Almost certainly he was too senior to take part at the front: he'd be sitting back safely in some command post. But by God, if *any* player appeared down there in the hall, there was only one way he'd ever leave the building, and that was feet first, in a bag.

Then at 2235, came the call we'd been expecting. 'Delta Three. Suspect black Volvo mobile towards target. Sun roof is open, so anticipate drive-past rocket attack. Estimate time to target one minute.'

'Roger,' answered Delta Control.

Then it was our boss: 'Zero Alpha. Assault imminent. Confirm prepared.'

'Hotel One,' I answered. 'Roger.'

'Delta Two,' came a Welsh voice. 'Confirm Volvo mobile to target. Westwards down Craven Avenue. Estimate thirty seconds.'

'Zero Alpha to Hotel One,' said the boss. 'Stand by, stand by.'

'Hotel One, roger.'

I nipped into the back bedroom. 'On the floor, please,' I said. 'They're coming.'

There was something pathetic about seeing the old couple go stiffly down on their knees on their double mattress, then lie flat, tucking themselves in against the flank of their own bed. Jimmy yanked another mattress off the bed so that it covered them, then lay down on the outside of the pair, a human wall.

I dived into the front bedroom, closed the door and laid my HK 53 along the wainscoting, where I could put my hand on it in the dark. The other two guys were already on their backs in the makeshift sangar.

I don't know how many seconds passed. I imagined the rocketeer climbing to his feet in the passenger seat, head through the sun-roof opening, bracing himself as the wagon swung round a corner. In my mind I saw him bring up the awkwardly long launcher and settle it into his shoulder. Suddenly I thought of a German friend who loathed all Volvos, and, whenever he saw one, shouted, '*SCHEISS-AUTO!*' This one was a shit-car, all right.

I caught one more Det report, calling the Volvo into the start of our road. Then I closed my eyes and clamped my hands over my ears.

I just heard the car engine, screaming at high revs in some low gear. Then came the *whoosh* of a rocket being fired, and an almighty, earth-moving *BANG!* I felt the floor flex beneath me. The door of our room flew open and smacked back against the end of one bed. From hall and landing came the sound of plaster falling. My instinct was to yell at the top of my voice, to let out the tension, but I fought down the impulse.

The lights had gone out. The television had been silenced. In a second all three of us were at the banister rail, weapons trained on the hall. The air down there was full of smoke or dust or both. Through it I saw that the front door had gone, and street-lights were showing through an open rectangle. I had my hand on the switch of the ambush lights, but something made me hesitate. If there were any rats incoming, I wanted them well in the trap. But were there any? From outside came a sudden hammer of rounds going down, then more, and more. Then a screech of tyres followed by a heavy impact. We'd got the car, for sure.

From somewhere under us at the back of the hall came a flicker of ruddy light. Fire. Nothing serious as yet; just enough to give useful illumination. But already I'd come down a notch or two from my peak of tension. The shots outside, and the noise of the crash – everything suggested that the gunmen had gone under.

Not at all. Movement in the doorway. Two dark, hooded

figures ran in, kicked the door of the living room wide and opened up through the gap with sub-machine-guns, spraying the room with uncontrolled bursts. In the confines of the house the noise was shattering, and the players themselves were adding to it. No silence for them. High on adrenalin, they were roaring obscenities fit to bust: fecking this and fecking that. When one of them flashed a torch round the room and found there was nobody in it, they yelled even louder.

All this had taken maybe four seconds. By the time they ran back into the hall, the flames below us were bigger and giving better light. They illuminated our targets just enough. The range was point blank, and they never even looked up. Two short bursts from each of us, and down they went. In the flickering light I'd gone for the mass of their upper chests, but one of them caught it in the head as well when he fell forward. I saw the armour-piercing rounds rip his balaclava open, and pieces of skull fly out.

Another volley of rounds spurted from the other man's weapon, but only because in going down he'd pulled the trigger inadvertently, and the rounds smacked harmlessly into the wall at floor level. As he crumpled on to the carpet, I gave him a quick double-tap in the head. The body gave a couple of violent jerks, then lay still.

For several seconds we didn't move. We were safe in the smoky darkness, and in a brilliant position. If fifty players had followed the first two in we could have dropped them all. The reek of cordite filled the air. Suddenly there was noise and movement above us – a creak, a snap, a rustle, a tearing sound. I faced upwards to see a big chunk of plasterboard fall away from the ceiling and plummet on to the stairs, where it burst and bounced down in smaller pieces, raising another cloud of dust, as if a shell had landed.

'Jimmy!' I yelled.

'Aye,' he called from the back bedroom.

'Your people all right?'

'Fine.'

'Keep them there a minute.'

Now I did turn on the ambush lights, so that they illuminated the hall and caught the smoke, which was rising in clouds. Through it I could see the two bodies lying hunched against the wainscoting, one either side, and the blood seeping out over the pale carpet. Both men had fallen on their weapons, which were buried beneath them. I felt for my pressel with shaking fingers.

'Hotel One. Two X-rays dead on target. White demolished. No home casualties. Get the QRF up!' I knew I was shouting, but I couldn't help it.

The leader of the fire-party was also shouting. Everyone was trying to get on the air at once.

'Zero Alpha,' said the boss firmly. 'EVERYBODY WAIT OUT! Now. Hotel One. Is your area secure?'

'Hotel One, roger. Area secure.'

'Roger. Hotel Two. Is *your* area secure?'

'Hotel Two. Two dead X-rays. One RPG. One side-arm. This area is now secure.'

'Zero Alpha. Inform all stations. QRF coming in now. Stand by for pick-up.'

Covered by the other two, I stepped cautiously down the stairs. The shreds of the front door hung from its hinges, but the centre of it had been blown clean out. Cold air was wafting in through the hole, and carrying with it the rising wail of an ambulance or fire engine.

My immediate concern was to stop the house burning down. Luckily it turned out that the only things on fire were some old newspapers and magazines, and the extinguisher, ancient as it was, soon put them out.

The Quinlans were amazingly resilient. They stumbled out of their bedroom looking like startled owls, white-faced, hair on end, eyes wide. 'So long as you don't damage anything,' the old girl had said. Now their hall and everything in it had been destroyed. Pictures had been torn from the walls and blown into a heap of shattered frames and glass at the far end. The grandfather clock had been reduced to matchwood. Two chairs and a table were fit only for the fire. Plaster and paper had been ripped out of the walls in horizontal strips. The kitchen, also, was a wreck. I suppose the old people were in shock, but they seemed incredibly philosophical about the damage.

With their directions, using our torches, we found the fuse boxes and trip switches in the kitchen, but the system must have suffered major damage because it wouldn't come alive again. Perhaps it was just as well.

All of a sudden Pat began to laugh. 'No fucking damage!' he gasped. 'Fucking roll on!' He was laughing so much he had to sit down. In a couple of seconds I was helpless as well, doubled up, in hysterics. I knew it was a reaction to release of tension, caused by an excess of adrenalin, but that didn't help me stop. I realized that the Quinlans must think us incredibly callous, or crazy, or both – but again, that was no deterrent. Only when an RUC officer stuck his head round the door and said, 'What's so bloody funny, then?' did we manage to pull ourselves together.

The QRF arrived, cleared the street and cordoned it off. Suddenly the house was full of people, among them a couple of firemen, and the Scene of Crimes Officer, who began taking measurements and statements, and chalking on to the landing carpet the positions from which we'd fired. A photographer took pictures of the bodies. They weren't looking all that pretty. One had the skull split clean down the middle, over the cranium. The armour-piercing rounds had opened up his head like a melon. Grey brain was showing through the gap, and the scalp had slid over to one side, crumpling the face into folds. The eyeballs were bulging out of their sockets. Brain and blood were spattered over the wall behind. Both terrorists looked very young. As the bodies were being bundled into bags I asked the RUC man if he knew who they were, but he shook his head. 'From the Lisburn ASU, by all accounts,' he said, 'but beyond that, I've no idea.'

Back in the warehouse we held a big debriefing. It turned out that our own reactive OP had nailed the Volvo, killing both the driver and the guy who fired the rocket. They'd captured not only the rocket launcher, but two AK 47s and a couple of side-arms as well.

At first we were baffled about how the two-man assault party had escaped detection, and where they'd come from. The car had not stopped or even slowed down, so they couldn't have been in it. The mystery was solved by a search of the front garden, which revealed that they'd lain up in the shrubs either side of the front path. They must have slipped in there immediately after dark, before our surveillance was in place, and stuck it out for nearly five hours.

In any case, the bag for the night was four, and everyone was really chuffed that the operation had gone down. After the wash-up we all got in the bar together – RUC, the Det and us – for a few celebratory beers. By then the Det and the RUC between them had identified the dead terrorists, but the names meant nothing to me.

Among those celebrating was the guy with pink hair. When I got close to him, I began to think I'd seen him somewhere before.

'Listen,' I said, 'I'm sure I know you. Where could it have been?'

'Two Para,' he said immediately, with a grin. 'Aldershot.'

'Right, right!'

Suddenly we were on net. His name was Mike Grigson, and though we'd never really met we'd been in the same company for a brief spell. We began to exchange chit-chat, and hit it off well. He'd done a year with the Det already, and obviously knew the score. For the past few days he'd been taken off outside duties and given some role in the head-shed, until he was fit to appear in public again.

'What went wrong?' I asked.

'Duffed up the fucking mixture, didn't I?' he said cheerfully. 'That's the trouble with being fair-haired – I stand out in a bloody crowd. I was trying to do something about it.'

As for myself, I couldn't make out whether I was on a high or a low. One moment everything seemed terrific, because it had all gone according to the book; the next, I felt terrible at having killed, or helped to kill, two people. Yet perhaps the worst thing was the realization of how difficult my self-appointed task was going to be. A major operation, with all the

95

stops out, had accounted for four lowly paddies. How was I ever going to get near Mr Big on my own?

A couple of pints later I bought Pink Mike a drink and asked casually, 'So, who were those players tonight?'

'Nobody much. Rank and file from the Lisburn ASU.'

'Had you seen them before?'

'The two in the car, yes. The driver and the rocketeer. Not the others.'

'How d'you recognize them?'

'We're out looking for them all the time. That's our job. Besides, we've got dozens of mug-shots in the ops room. Covert pictures, but some of them pretty good.'

'Could I have a look at them sometime?'

'You're not supposed to, really. But maybe we could fix it. Why?'

'Just curious, that's all.'

SIX

Ten days or so after that, just before Christmas, I had the evening off, and drove out to Helen's Bay to see the family. It was easy enough to get away – all I had to do was clock myself out and enter my business as 'Socializing'. I booked out one of the admin cars on the wall-chart in the ops room – a dark-blue, two-litre Sierra with the callsign Tango Four – and marked up my destination and time out, which was 1735. The car had normal covert comms; in the event of an emergency while I was out in the vehicle, the head-shed would still have the means to recall me, in the form of a bleeper which I carried in my trouser pocket. If that went off, I was to contact base immediately. The device had a switch that could be put on to 'Pulse', so that if a call came in a tight situation you could feel it rather than hear it, and no one else's attention would be attracted. As an extra precaution I took along my Walther PPK; there seemed practically no chance that I would need it, but out there you can never tell.

It was already dark when I pulled out of the base and set off north-eastwards. The rush-hour traffic was heavy, and to make matters worse the bypass had been closed; at the time I assumed it was the result of an accident, but later I heard that there had been a punishment shooting incident which had left vehicles strewn all over the main road. Rather than be late, I took a risk and cut through a hard area which I knew was out of bounds. I realized this was a stupid thing to do, but I thought I could get away with it for once.

My luck was out. Travelling down the Falls Road, I saw a street protest ahead. Twenty or thirty people with placards were demanding political status for prisoners. I didn't fancy the look of the crowd, or the thought of the dickers who might be hanging round its fringes, so I took a right into

Beechmount Drive and Ballymurphy Street, across Beechmount Avenue ('RPG Avenue' to its fans), and so back into the Falls and Divis Street, before making my way out to the Sydenham bypass and the Bangor road.

As I drove, my mind was on recent events. Operation Eggshell had been followed by an inquest, very similar to the one staged at LATA, at which we'd given evidence from behind a screen. Our training had stood us in good stead. The terrorists had been caught fair and square; three had actually fired weapons, and the fourth had had an AK 47 in his possession, as well as a Browning pistol. So we had no trouble justifying the action we took. Oddly enough, the stress of the operation had brought on a recurrence of my nightmare, but the dream came only once, and in a less frightening form than before. All through it I remained aware that it *was* only a dream, and at the back of my mind I knew I was in control.

Tango Four was quite speedy when it got going, but none too quick off the mark. On the floor in front of the passenger seat I had a present for Tim – a box-kit of solid wooden figures, pieces and blocks with sockets cut out of them which built up into a fire engine, with a crew riding on top and a ladder perched above them. The smooth solidity of the kit appealed to me, and I felt sure he'd like it too. My only worry was that it might be a bit young for him, he was growing up that fast. I'd managed to go over several times, and I could see him changing from week to week.

Maybe I was thinking too much about him, or about the procedures in court. Maybe I had just dropped my guard because I was off duty. Either way, I had reached Holywood, only a few miles short of my destination, before I became aware that I was being followed. For some time I'd been half-noticing an odd pair of headlights behind me, the left-hand or kerb light showing much yellower than the right. Sometimes they were one car behind, sometimes two. Suddenly I realized that they had been there for an unhealthy length of time.

I thought, Shit – I should never have taken that short-cut. Whoever they are, they must have picked me up in West Belfast. Ahead on my left I saw the bright lights of a line of shops, facing on to the main drag but set back from it in a small road of its own. I flipped on the indicator, pulled in and cruised slowly along, peering out sideways as if in search of some particular shop. Several had closed already, but a few were still open.

The uneven lights copied my move. The car came into the lay-by and crawled along, hanging back. Out on the main road again I accelerated hard, only to see a big roundabout ahead. I went into it fast, using gears and engine to brake. As I decelerated, the lights closed rapidly from behind. Instead of going straight on – as I'd been planning – or turning off, I held the gear-lever in second and kept the car in a tight right-hand turn, tyres squealing, all the way round. Glancing to my right across the mound of the roundabout, I caught a side-on glimpse of my tail. Under the street lights it looked a sickly mid-green, and pretty much beaten up – an old banger. It could have been a Cortina, but I wasn't sure. There were two guys in the front.

As I popped out on the Bangor road again, the lights were still behind me. No doubt about it now. Bloody hell! My neck began to crawl. I was after them – or rather, one of them – but they were also after me.

What were they trying to achieve? The simplest explanation was that they hoped to find out where I was going. That ditched my evening's programme, for a start. Maybe the registration number had been blown, and they'd picked me up from that. Like all the troop's cars, this one had five or six sets of plates for use in different areas. But still they could have recognized the number I had on that day. Another possibility was that I'd been spotted as I came close to the demo in the Falls Road. Or maybe these were just two dickers at large, up to their usual bullying tricks. If they spotted a car which they thought was new to an area, they might easily harass it, purely to annoy the driver. They might also try to overtake and stop me, just for the pleasure of telling me to fuck off. The worst scenario was that they were organized players, with colleagues up ahead, and that they were already trying to position a second car for an ambush.

I felt for the pressel-switch of the radio, down by the gear-lever, and called, 'Tango Four.'

'Zero Alpha,' the desk answered.

'Tango Four. I'm out past Holywood and getting a hard follow. Can you help with a back-up?'

'Roger. What's your location?'

'On the A2, inland from Helen's Bay. Heading eastwards for Red Seven. Just past Craigavad.'

'Roger. Stand by.' Then, a moment later, 'I have two Indians on orientation training not far south of you. Are you sure you've got a tail?'

'Absolutely. I've just done a 360 round a roundabout, and they're still behind me. I don't know if they're trying to lift me or what, but I can't get rid of them.'

'Roger. Keep heading for Red Seven, and whatever you do, stay on the main.'

'Roger.' Red Seven was the next big junction ahead, on the outskirts of Bangor, the seaside town. I could either carry on into the town or hang a right, heading south for New-townards. My instinct was to keep out of built-up areas until I got help. The Indians were our intercept cars, and once they were in support, things would be different. On my own I didn't fancy getting lost in a maze of side-streets. Even to be held up at traffic lights would be bad news. Above all, I didn't want to get caught in a cul-de-sac.

For the time being I drove steadily, to show no sign of panic. A few seconds later I called, 'Tango Four. Proposing to turn right at Red Seven.'

'Zero Alpha,' replied the desk. 'Affirmative. Turn right, and right again at Red Eight.'

'Roger.'

'Confirm two Indians mobile towards you. What make of car are we looking for?'

'It's a crappy old banger. Mid-green. Could be a Cortina, but I'm not sure. I'm identifying it from its uneven lights. The kerb-side headlight's yellow, the outer one white. You can't mistake it if you get ahead.'

'Roger.'

100

As I drove with one hand, I was holding the map over the wheel with the other and trying to check my route. It was dangerous and difficult, because the interior light tended to dazzle one and reduce forward visibility.

Still, in the mirror, I could see the lights two vehicles back. I thought I'd better stand down my in-laws before things got any hotter. I felt for my mobile phone, dialled, waited, and got Den.

'Hi, Den. It's me, Geordie. I'm sorry, but I've had a call-out. I'm going to have to postpone my visit.'

'Oh, that's too bad. Tim was really looking forward to it.'

'I know. So was I. Tomorrow, maybe?'

'Everything all right?'

'Yeah, yeah. Everything's fine.'

'You in a car?'

'That's right. Why?'

'It sounds noisy.'

'It is. Look, I'll speak to you soon. Sorry about this. Give Tim a hug from me.'

Everything was far from all right. I came to Red Eight, another big roundabout, and took the main road to the right. The lights stayed with me.

'Tango Four,' I called. 'Passing Red Eight now.'

'Roger,' came the answer. 'You've got Red Nine a mile ahead. Hang another right there, for Newtownards. Confirm two Indians closing on your location.'

'Roger, and thanks.'

So far I hadn't heard the desk talking to the intercepts, who must have been on a different net. But suddenly they switched over and came through loud and clear. The first thing I heard was India One calling his location as Red One Six. I recognized the voice: it was Matt Matthews, a long, thin Yorkshireman. I couldn't get a proper look at the map, but as far as I remembered, that was the junction in Comber, a small place five miles south of Newtownards. Then he confirmed, 'India One mobile towards Red-One-Five.' That was in the centre of Newtownards. They were heading straight towards me. I thought of them as a pair of cheetahs, coming up country in immense bounds.

I managed a quick glance at the map, and saw that a left turn in Newtownards would take me out towards the shore of Strangford Lough, away from civilization.

'Tango Four to India One,' I called. 'I'm mobile southwards towards Red-One-Two. Proposing turn left there, on to the shore road. Can you get something planned down there soonest?'

'India One,' said Matt. 'Wait out.'

'Tango Four. Now passing Conlig. I still have the tail, but they don't seem to be trying to close.'

'India One. Roger. If you can, slow down. We need to get ahead of you.'

Slow down! Hell! I eased off the accelerator until I was doing only forty-five. The crazy lights came surging up behind. Reaching across with my right hand, I drew my PPK from its shoulder holster. Some guys, when driving off-duty, would sit on their pistols or keep them stuffed down between their legs. But I always thought that if I got rammed or had a crash the gun might fly forward off the seat and disappear under it or beneath the pedals. A shoulder holster was safer. With the PPK in my hand, I brought a round into the breech and slipped the pistol into the pocket on the inside of the driver's door.

To my amazement I heard India One call, 'Red-One-Five now.' Jesus! I thought. He's in Newtownards already. He must have been going like shit off a shovel. Seconds later he called, 'Red-One-Four,' and I knew he was safely through ahead of me, turning on to the lough road.

The lights had dropped back again. Already I could see the beginning of the town ahead.

'Tango Four. Hitting the outskirts of Newtownards.'

'Zero Alpha, carry on to Red-One-Four. Left there.'

'Roger.'

The Indians and the desk began an urgent discussion – something about a parking place. I couldn't look at the map long enough to pick up the one they were talking about. At the 30 m.p.h. limit I eased down to about thirty-five. More cars were heading north out of town than going in.

Then I saw traffic lights in the distance ahead. Shit! I did *not* want to stop. Timing was critical. As I approached, the lights were green; now, if I got it right, I might be able to shoot them as yellow changed to red and cut off the pursuit.

I hung back, hung back, then at the last instant slammed into second and hit the accelerator. Done it! I thought. I should have known better. From behind came a squeal of brakes and angry hooting. The lights swerved wildly, left and right, then steadied again. Bastards – they'd got across on the red.

'Tango Four. Approaching Red-One-Four.'

'India One. Roger. One k and a bit past it, you'll come out beside the lough, on your right. The road's right by the water. Another k and there's a parking place on the right, between the road and the water. We're complete at the far end of the parking place. Dive in here at the last minute, and give us a flash as you come in. Over.'

'Tango Four. Roger.'

'India One. If the baddies follow you in, drive straight through, out the other end and back on to the highway. Then we'll follow and take them out. If they go past, all the better. We'll take them out anyway.'

'Roger.'

At the T-junction a left-hand filter let me through without stopping, and I accelerated away.

As I did so, India One called the desk. 'Intercept imminent. Permission to proceed on own initiative.'

'Zero Alpha. Roger. At your discretion. If the situation's life-threatening, go ahead.'

In a few seconds I had the water of the lough on my right. I pushed my speed up to sixty, then to sixty-five.

'Tango Four,' I called. 'Beside the water.'

'India One. Keep coming.'

'Estimate fifty seconds to park-place. Forty, thirty . . .'

'India One, we've got you. And the tail. Keep coming.'

'Tango Four. Twenty seconds. I've got the sign. Turning in . . . NOW!'

Thank God there was nothing coming the other way. At

the last instant, without giving any signal or braking, I wrenched the wheel hard to the right. The Sierra heeled and slewed with a screech of tyres. Rocking and twitching, I shot into the parking area, a long strip just above the water, with a low stone wall along its outer edge.

The manoeuvre took the tail by surprise. Before the driver could react he had passed the opening. I saw his brake-lights flash for an instant, then the car speed up again. At the far end of the park two cars sat waiting. Both were dark, but I had no doubt that they were hot to trot, with engines running. Sure enough, as the tail car went by the exit, both leapt forward and out on to the highway.

Headlights blazed up as they gave chase. Oncoming drivers flashed at them in vain. Everything had happened so fast that I had never stopped, never even slowed down much. I simply put my foot down again, came back on to the road and joined the pursuit.

The dickers (or whoever they were) must have realized something was wrong. They must have known they were in the shit, because they began to drive like hell. Eighty was about the most their wagon would do, but they held that speed through some fearsome bends, and it was all I could do to keep the Sierra on the road.

The lead Indian was our big Audi Quattro, with its crab-like grip of the road transmitted through all four wheels, and its engine souped up to give it the acceleration of a Ferrari. There was no way the dickers could escape it. But equally, for the moment, there was no way it could get past them.

'India One,' called Matt. 'Taking command of the intercept. We're mobile behind the target towards Yellow Eight. We'll grab the first chance to overtake.'

'India Two,' came a new voice. 'The road widens out below the park at Mount Stewart, three ks ahead. That's your best chance.'

'India One. Roger. We'll try it.'

Suddenly everything slowed dramatically. The target had come up behind another car, an innocent red Mini. Oncoming traffic was preventing anyone overtaking. Now the target was well illuminated by the Audi's lights and sure enough, it was an old Cortina.

India One was crowding up behind it, hoping to unnerve the driver with the blaze of light. But then, as the oncoming traffic cleared, the Cortina whipped out and overtook the dawdling Mini.

'Stand by, stand by,' called Matt. 'Going . . . NOW!'

The Cortina driver made the mistake of hanging over on the right-hand side of the road after he'd overtaken. With a fierce surge of power the Audi was past the Mini and pulling up on the left-hand side of the target. The second intercept car, a Rover, was there too, a couple of feet from the Cortina's back bumper.

From my tail-end-Charlie position I saw it all as if in slow motion. The Audi cut in hard across the Cortina's left front wing. The dicker driver stood on his brakes, but the big car hit his front end a glancing blow that threw the vehicle sideways against a stone wall, stopping it dead. A second later the driver of the Rover deliberately rammed into the back of it, to shock the inhabitants for a couple of seconds while the team from the Audi jumped out. In an instant the road was full of our guys, all crouching behind their own cars with weapons levelled over the roofs and bonnets.

I slid the Sierra to a halt and leapt out. Somehow the red Mini had squeezed through the gap behind the Audi's tail, but it had come to rest a hundred metres down the road, as if the driver was busy having a heart attack.

'OUT!' yelled Matt. 'Out! Hands on the roof! Move!'

This was a dicey moment. If the villains had weapons, they might be desperate enough to use them. But because we didn't know for sure that they were armed, we couldn't open fire.

At last the passenger door of the Cortina opened, and a shaven-headed youth looked out, blinking.

'Fucking OUT!' roared Matt.

The youth struggled out. A second later he was spreadeagled over the bonnet of the Cortina, face down. A rapid body-search, and he was flat on his face in the road with a knee in his back, his driver the same. The driver had a cut on his right temple, where his head had hit the door in the crash, but it was nothing serious.

A preliminary search of the car revealed no weapons, but while it was going on I vaulted over the wall to have a look beyond. From my position behind the Cortina at the moment of the crash, I thought I'd seen a flash as something flew out of the driver's window and over the wall. Sure enough, my foot now hit something heavy – and up came a Luger 9mm automatic. I was about to yell out that I'd found it, but a sixth sense made me hold my tongue. In that instant I realized that the weapon could come in handy. I'd already worked out that if I did manage to close in on Gary Player and drop him, I must make it look like a sectarian killing. Therefore it would be brilliant to use a weapon that was common among the players. If the forensic boys managed to establish what kind of pistol had fired the fatal round, there'd be no chance of them tracing it back to me. On the contrary, if it had been used in previous shootings, it would probably be traced back to the IRA, and the police would conclude that the latest murder was the result of internecine feuding. And so, instead of crowing about my discovery, I stuffed the Luger down inside my waistband and hopped back over the wall.

Matt was taking no chances. Through the head-shed he called out not only the RUC and the Liaison Officer, but also a flatbed truck, so that the car could be taken away for forensic examination and a thorough search. At the least it would yield fingerprints; at best, it might turn out to have secret compartments, with weapons, traces of explosive or other incriminating evidence in them. In any case, the Cortina was undrivable, as its right front wheel had buckled under the impact with the wall. The Audi, in contrast, had suffered nothing but superficial dents.

We drove back to base in a discreet, well-spaced convoy, with the Sierra in the middle and the intercept cars fore and aft. That was the last journey the Sierra would make for the troop. Now it had been blown, it would have to be binned, at any rate from Ulster. The only future for it was to be sent back to England and used as a range car. The intercept cars would probably go in for a paint job.

The entire incident had lasted less than an hour. We reached base without further trouble, but I found that in the warehouse the atmosphere wasn't very sweet. 'Hey, Geordie,' one of the senior guys said as I was going to dump kit in my room, 'you want to watch yourself. This place has been in fucking uproar since you sent the balloon up. You sure you haven't been somewhere you had no business to be? Better get your story right, or you'll be deep in it.'

The wash-up was pretty hostile. The sergeant major couldn't make out how I'd been picked up. As far as anyone knew, the Sierra hadn't been blown before I took it out. There was a strong suspicion that I'd been somewhere out of bounds, but I denied it strenuously, inventing a fictitious route round the edges of the city. I think I got away with it, but the debrief left me with the feeling that I'd almost dropped a colossal bollock. It also left me disturbed by the fact that I'd been forced into telling lies – something that I never like doing, least of all to my mates. Yet another worry was the sheer number of the enemy. The bastards seemed to be everywhere, with nothing to do but lurk about and look for targets. The one big consolation was that I hadn't led them to my in-laws' home. To have done that would have been a disaster of the first magnitude.

As soon as things had settled, I phoned them and got Meg.

'I'm really sorry about that,' I began.

'What happened?'

'It was just that a job came up suddenly.'

'Well – it's a bit late now. Tim's asleep already.'

'No, no – I wasn't meaning I'd come out now. I only called to apologize. I had a present for Tim, too.'

'You couldn't help it, I'm sure. There's always another day. But you ought to come and see him more often. He's getting to be a bit of a handful.'

'Oh, like what?'

'He doesn't always want to do what I tell him. He's inclined to lose his temper, too. I'm not saying I can't manage him, but the more he sees of his father the better it will be.' She broke off for a moment and then added, 'By the way, a letter came for you.'

'Really? What is it?'

'I don't know. It doesn't look very exciting. A small brown envelope, typed – that's all.'

A prickle went up my neck. Maybe Chief Superintendent Morrison had surfaced.

'It can't be anything important,' I said casually. 'Why not open it and tell me what it says?'

'All right, then. Hold on while I get it.'

There was a pause. Then I heard rustling, ripping noises.

'Well!' said Meg in her most superior voice. 'It's nothing much at all. Just one typed line, in fact.'

'What does it say?'

' "Your man is Declan Farrell." '

'What? Say that again. At least, no – wait one while I get a pencil. Hold on.'

I was in the public phone booth outside the canteen, and had to make a dash for the ops room to borrow paper and pencil from the duty clerk. Back at the booth, I grabbed the receiver and said, 'Hello? Yes?'

'What's the matter with you?' said Meg. 'You sound all flustered.'

'No, no. I'm fine. Just had to grab a pencil. What's the name again?'

She repeated it, and spelt it out.

'Fine. Got it.'

'Does it mean anything to you?'

'Not a lot. But I'll work it out. Thanks anyway.'

In the morning I phoned Morrison on his direct line to ask if I could go and see him.

'You got my note, then?'

'That's right.'

'D'you know a pub called the Old Bell, out on the Comber road?'

'I'll find it.'

'Fine. It's on your right going out. I'll meet you there at seven-thirty tonight.'

Settled in a quiet corner, the chief could have been any old businessman having a pint on his way home after work. But what he had to say related to business far beyond most ordinary people. Basically, he was trying to warn me not to tangle with Farrell, because of the sheer nastiness of the character.

'You'd be the better for leaving him alone,' he said, 'For instance, when two harmless young lads were caught trying to nick his car for joyriding, he had them brought to him, and rather than crippling them in the traditional way, using an electric drill, he had them held down while he himself used a hand drill to perforate their kneecaps. So pleased was he with this arbitrary sentence that he went straight out and gave himself a lavish dinner.'

Morrison took a swig from his pint of stout and went on in his quiet, tired voice, 'And did you hear about the young woman they battered to death this time last year? You remember that one? No? Well, Farrell thought she was a Protestant informer, or working for us. So they grabbed her. Of course she couldn't tell them anything, because she didn't know anything. She was perfectly innocent, not involved at all. First she was raped, then they took her out behind a pub and beat her to a pulp with hammers. When they found they couldn't kill her by stamping on her, they finished her off by hurling a breeze-block down on her head. That's Farrell for you. There's nothing subtle about IRA torture; it's just the most basic and brutal thuggery.'

He went on to say that Farrell was one of the IRA's chief extortionists, and that he raised many thousands of pounds a year from running protection rackets. 'He'll go to the manager of a big building site and say, "Look, if you don't want your machinery to go missing, or you don't want your walls to fall down, it'll cost you a couple of hundred a week." Security firms – that's another racket. The IRA charge for seven or eight men to guard a factory, when in fact there are only two working. The irony is that, with the IRA on the scene, the place isn't going to get raided anyway; one thing thieves can do without is getting kneecapped.

'The same thing with drug-dealers. The PIRA limit the number who are allowed to operate, either on the streets or in clubs, and they take a percentage of their profits.'

Morrison stopped, giving me a steady look. 'Your man Farrell has his finger in every fecking pie – and if anyone else tries to get a hand in, he doesn't hesitate to cut it off.'

SEVEN

In the morning I happened to see Pink Mike crossing the warehouse on his way back from the bog. He was looking pleased with himself, as if he'd had a monumental shit. His hair was on the mend, too – it had gone a kind of rich auburn.

'Hey,' I called, 'got a minute?'

'Sure. What is it?'

'Have you heard of a player called Declan Farrell?'

'Christ, have I!'

'What d'you mean?'

'It's like asking if I've heard of the Pope. He's one of the big bastards.'

'Really! D'you have any info about him?'

'There's a bloody great file that lists all his villainies. What do you want to know?'

'Anything about him – what he looks like, where he hangs out.'

'What's your interest?'

'I heard someone talking about him. He sounds a vicious sod.'

'He is. I'll sort you out something. Where will you be?'

'I'm on standby, so unless something breaks I'll be around the warehouse. I'm going to the gym now for an hour. Then I'll be in my cabin.'

'I'll be over, then.'

Never had the weights seemed lighter. I suppose it was the flow of adrenalin that pepped me up, but I found myself going through the lifts with incredible ease. It was my day for back and chest. Before the injury to my arm I'd been a member of the 220 Club, bench-pressing four big 55-lb Olympic discs on the bar – and even though that was no big deal in real weight-lifting terms, I'd only recently climbed back to it. Some days

111

I still found it a strain, but that morning an hour flew past. Then I did twenty minutes on one of the stationary bikes, and after a shower and a dhobi session in the laundromat, I was bouncing around the cabin when Mike reappeared.

Under one arm he was carrying a rolled-up towel, out of which he produced a big brown envelope. 'For Christ's sake be careful,' he said, handing it over. 'This stuff is highly classified. It's not supposed to leave our ops room. The most up-to-date sheet is missing, because Box have borrowed it, but everything else is there. I'll come back for it after lunch.'

With him gone, I closed the door and pushed a wedge under the inside, silently praying that we didn't get a call-out in the next hour. Then I opened the envelope.

The first things I saw were two photographs, mug-shots, taken with a telephoto lens but well focused – good, clear pictures. I stared at them in consternation. I'd been seeing Gary Player in my mind so clearly that I had his likeness firmly in my head – and this wasn't him. It took me a few moments to sweep away the figment of my imagination and concentrate on reality.

In place of the scruffy, tousled, sandy-haired fellow I'd invented for myself, here was someone dark and definitely good-looking, in his thirties. Far from having thuggish, Neanderthal features, the face was rather distinguished: high forehead, thick eyebrows, dark hair well cut and neatly brushed back, and a strong, square jaw. The eyes were dark as well, and, even in those unflattering photos, lively. At some stage the nose had been broken and left with a slight flattening at the bridge, but that only added to the appeal of the face.

If the man's appearance disconcerted me, the notes on his career and character gave me still more of a shock.

TERRORIST SUSPECT NO. 608

Name:	FARRELL, Declan Ambrose
Date of Birth:	1958
Place:	Fruithill Park, Andersonstown Road, Belfast.

Education:	Christian Brothers' School, Glen Road, Belfast.
	8 O levels.
	3 A levels B B B.
	Queen's University Belfast.
	2nd Class degree, Mechanical Engineering, 1979.
	Rugby, trial for University XV. Wing forward.
Religion:	Catholic.
Height:	6' 2"
Build:	Broad shoulders, good figure.
Appearance:	Tends to dress well. Wears suits.
Weight:	210 lbs approx.
Distinguishing Features:	Nose broken while boxing as boy. Flattening at bridge. Limps slightly on left foot as a result of car accident.
Politics:	Fanatical nationalist.
Cover Occupations:	Has sometimes posed as Consulting Engineer.
Finances:	No special sources known.
Aliases:	Seamus Malone. Has also used the name Fearn.

I had to read these details several times to make them sink in. No moron, this. On the contrary, he was far better educated than me, with three A levels and a university degree. Bigger, too – an inch taller, and a lot heavier. A physical sort of guy, he'd played rugger almost at university standard. A boxer as well. A big, strong fellow, and aggressive by the sound of it. Sure enough, the accompanying notes described him as 'aggressive, assertive, likes to throw his weight about. In his youth, much given to fighting in public.' (In the margin somebody had added in pencil, 'Still likes a fight. The Black Barrel brawl, 1988'.) He was said to have a sadistic streak, and to favour torturing prisoners. Once, it was reputed, he had tied an enemy up and cut him to pieces with a chain-saw. At home he kept dogs, generally big ones – Rottweilers, Rhodesian Ridgebacks or Pit Bulls.

His career in terrorism was poorly charted, because he had always been too clever to be caught, or even to leave clear traces of his activity. His involvement in incidents was usually recorded as 'suspected' rather than 'confirmed'. For a time he had been active around South Armagh, near the Border, and it seemed that he preferred rural operations to those in towns. But later he had concentrated on Belfast, and now, at the latest entry on the sheets, he was down as the adjutant of the PIRA's West Belfast Brigade. Although the dossier listed several specific incidents which he was thought to have orchestrated, it did not mention the Queensfield bomb; this, I assumed, was because the incident had taken place after my last sheet had run out, and it would appear on the page which Mike had said was missing. I didn't stop to think why Box – our name for MI5 – should have borrowed it. I just assumed they were investigating some aspect of Farrell's career.

Alongside the heading 'Address', several lines had been entered and crossed out. Evidently he had moved around a good deal. The latest entry said simply, 'Ballyconvil'. It looked as though that was where he had last been heard of. Altogether, he seemed to be in the same category as many IRA suspects: the authorities knew who he was, and where he was, but so far hadn't been able to pin anything major on him. I remembered Chief Superintendent Morrison saying, 'We know who the feckers are, so we do – if only we could just go and get them.'

Ballyconvil was the only name on any of the sheets that I needed to remember. I made a note of it on a slip of paper, and sat staring at the photograph until the face had burned into my mind. Yes – on more thorough inspection, the mouth was thin and cruel. The eyes could well be the same. But why in hell had a man of such intelligence chosen to become a scumbag? What had turned him into a terrorist?

My study of the dossier left me feeling personally threatened. Inadvertently, I had chosen to take on a hell of an opponent. Farrell sounded a powerful man in all senses of the word. Yet in a way all his attributes only strengthened my feeling of enmity. Before I'd known anything about him I'd hated him. Now I felt jealous of him, too. It was a useful combination.

I got the file back to Mike without incident, and went straight to the big gazetteer in our ops room. It gave several Ballyconvils, but there was one which stood out from all others as the most likely: a village on the back of the hills just to the north of West Belfast. From there anyone could drop on to the motorway, and in less than ten minutes be safe in the Republican fastnesses of the Falls or the Ardoyne.

Before I could do any more research, another operation came up. Once again, through a tout, the Det got wind of an attempt to shoot a prominent Unionist, this one a farmer who served as a part-time volunteer in the Ulster Defence Force. Like Quinlan, he had openly defied the PIRA for years, and lived in his isolated farmhouse with very little security. Now, when the tip-off came, it was clear that he urgently needed a team of babysitters.

At the same time, we got word that the weapons for the shoot would be deposited in a transit hide some ten kilometres from the target. The hide was in an old barn, part of a property that had been on the market for a year or more. Because we didn't have a precise date or time for the shoot, the head-shed decided to put an OP on the barn, so that we could keep an eye on what was happening, and warn the babysitters when the villains were on their way. There was also the chance that we might catch them in possession of weapons when they returned from their hit.

Guess who was detailed to man the OP? Yours truly. It didn't worry me, because I enjoy that sort of job. What did worry me a bit was when I heard that I'd got to take a Det guy in with me, because the head-shed wanted some experienced observer to get a good look at this particular bunch of terrorists, to see if he could identify any of them. Some of the Det boys could be real tossers when it came to any sort of hardship, so when I learnt that my companion was to be Mike

Grigson I was relieved. Having been in the Paras, he knew how to carry on in an OP, and could look after himself.

At the preliminary briefing, the boss detailed Pat Martin and myself to carry out a preliminary recce of the place. It turned out that the property consisted of a semi-derelict cottage as well as the barn, and ran to some six acres. It was out in the hills south-west of the city, and as we pored over the map on the ops room table, I found myself thinking that a shitehawk could fly over the mountains from there to Ballyconvil in five minutes or less.

'One pass only,' the boss was saying. 'There's so little traffic down that road it's not worth risking a second look. There could easily be eyes on. Just a straight drive past. Don't even slow down.'

'Right,' I said. 'What do we know about the house?'

'It's up for sale. The agents say it's empty, but we're not sure. Somebody could be using it.'

'If we want to do a thorough recce,' said Pat, 'why doesn't one of us put on a suit and pose as a potential buyer? Get the keys from the agents and go along all pukka?'

'Good suggestion,' said the boss, 'but again, it's not worth the risk. If there is a player inside, he'll probably have a video lined up on the entrance. There's iron gates across the approach, secured with a padlock and chain. While you're tinkering with that they'll get a nice film of you, from which they can take mug-shots for their files.'

'Normal OP, then,' I said. 'What's this? Looks like a wall or hedge round the farmyard.' I pointed to a faint mark on the 1:25,000 map, a dotted line which seemed to define the property. 'It could be a ditch as well. The best thing might be to dig in out in the field – here – and then to move in close at night. Where's the hide supposed to be?'

The boss consulted a note. 'As you face the barn, in the right-hand back corner. A 45-gallon polythene water-butt has been dug into the ground, top flush with the floor, and covered with straw.'

'So, to get a view of anyone putting a weapon into it, or taking one out, we'll need to be about . . . here.' I picked a spot in the hedge or ditch that looked as though it should give a view into the barn.

'That's right.' The boss straightened up with a muttered curse. He'd hurt his back parachuting a few months before, and it was still giving him gyp. 'You'd be very close to the action there – have to take it easy. Well, there's not much more we can tell from the map. You might as well be on your way.'

'Fine. We should be back by four.'

Operation Deadlock was under way. Pat and I took the scruffiest, least remarkable of the ops cars, a green Marina covered with dust and grime, and set off by a roundabout route for the high country to the south-west. Our target, Ballyduff, had been advertised by the selling agents as 'in need of refurbishment'. It sounded just the sort of place that players would use as a transit hide: well isolated and out in the country, yet only twenty minutes from the IRA heartlands of West Belfast.

Pat drove while I read the map. 'Hang a left here,' I said as we came over a shallow crest. 'Then it's straight down.'

Up there on the hills the farmland was rough as rough could be. The hairy-looking fields sprouted clumps of rushes, and rocks poked up through the coarse grass. In the depths of winter the whole landscape was dun-coloured and dead-looking. Rusty barbed-wire fences sagged, and in the hedgerows a few stunted trees were all bent in the same direction by the prevailing west wind. Puddles of water glistened in every depression of that upland bog. It was the exact equivalent of West Belfast in rural terms – scruffy, clapped out, a shit-heap, ideally matched to the mentality and habits of the PIRA.

'Glad I'm not a bloody cow up here,' said Pat.

'You'd need to be able to live on pure grot. Look out, now – the house'll be down here on our right.'

We were on a minor road, marked yellow on the map, which ran gently downhill. Though straight as a ruler, it wouldn't be any use for overtaking in a chase because it was about seven feet wide, with ditches on either side.

'You'd never get past,' said Pat, reading my thoughts.

'Not a chance. Here we are, now. Ease off a touch, but keep rolling.'

For moments like this, when there wasn't much time, I had trained myself to concentrate intently, so that my mind took a series of snapshots. Now in quick succession I got the following: along the back of the property, a line of bare trees; a long, low, whitewashed bungalow facing away from us, downhill; rusting corrugated iron roof, no windows in the back; beyond it, farther from the road and to our right, a sizeable barn, set at right-angles to the house, corrugated iron walls as well as roof; barn thirty metres from the far end of cottage; front of cottage decrepit, some window panes broken and boarded; pale blue door, same colour as wrought-iron entrance gates; gates chained together – old chain, but shiny new padlock; grounds gone to seed.

Ten metres out from the front of house, and parallel to it, a line of ash trees ran along an overgrown ditch – the feature I'd picked out on the map. Outside the ditch, rough pasture sloped down into the distance. Maybe there was a stream across the bottom.

In four or five seconds we were past.

'Notice anything particular?' I asked.

'Brand-new padlock. I bet they've put it on there until they've done the job.'

'Looks like it.'

'No mains electricity.'

'I don't reckon it's got mains water, either. See that hand-pump outside the door?'

'Yep. Good place for a CTR, that ditch under the trees.'

'Perfect. I'll come in up that field.'

'The front door of the house wasn't properly shut,' Pat added. 'I reckon someone's been using it.' Then he mimicked a la-di-da estate agent's voice as he quoted derisively, ' "In need of refurbishment". I should fucking well think so! The place'd fall down if you farted.'

Two miles further on we came to a small crossroads and turned right. Already the short winter afternoon was dying,

118

and in the dusk the fields looked even wilder.

'Anywhere here would do for the drop–off,' I said. 'We've got a junction coming up, a lane in from the left. Let's make it there.' I took a note of the grid reference, and we headed for base.

Back in the warehouse, the babysitting party were getting their kit sorted. They'd done a recce of their own, and had picked a drop-off point from which they could infiltrate over fields and slip into the target's house through the back garden.

Mike and I had no arguments about what kit we would take. He was well equipped anyway, with his own G3 and kite-sight. The only item he needed to borrow was an all-in-one sniper suit, Goretex-lined and covered in DPM material. Those things are great for keeping you warm and dry; the only trouble is that you can't run in them. But it didn't look to me as though we were going to do much running. The important thing was to make sure we had everything we might need for a stay of several days: food, obviously, and water, but also such extras as cling-film to crap into, and plastic bags in which to seal the said crap. Also a spare water bottle for pissing into. You might think that to piss a couple of times in the middle of a boggy field would make no difference, but you'd be surprised how it starts to stink. The point was, nobody could be sure how long we might have to spend in the OP. Also it was vitally important to write WATER clearly on water bottles and PISS clearly on the others.

Apart from those basics, we needed food – mainly boil-in-the-bag rations, which could be eaten cold – spare shirt, sleeping-bag, torch, collapsible shovel, wire netting for the roof of the OP, spotter-scope, and so on. It all made up into a considerable load.

At 1800 we held a final briefing. The Det would be out in force with six or eight cars. Four of our own intercept cars would be deployed, but they would hang well back so as not to arouse suspicion. Our callsigns for the night were all Sierras. Sierra One was the babysitter group, Sierra Two ourselves, and the rest of our cars Sierras with higher numbers. The main locations were designated Black: Black One was the target house, Black Two the hide, Black Three the babysitters' drop-off point, Black Four ours. The last two doubled as emergency rendezvous points, in case anything went wrong.

Pat drove us out to Black Four. As we approached, he flipped the switch which cut out the brake-lights. At the instant he pulled up for the major road, Mike and I whipped open our doors and slipped out to right and left. The car carried on without stopping, to turn left and disappear over the hill.

We gave it five minutes, listening, watching. The night was soft and still. No other traffic was moving. Reassured, we crossed the road, climbed a barbed-wire fence, and set off uphill across the field on a bearing of 160 mils, moving slowly over the damp grass, with myself in front and Mike watching the rear.

All around us, at ground level, the night was completely dark, not a gleam from house or car. Only in the sky to the north-east was there a faint glow, rising from the lights of Belfast. But as our eyes slowly adjusted to night vision, we could see well enough.

In three-quarters of a mile we crossed six fences or hedges, the last of them on a slight rise. From there, I calculated, the cottage should be in view, across a shallow depression. No problem. The kite-sight picked it out well, the house and barn showing through a line of trees. I waited to check the wind: a breath fanned against our faces, wafting down from the north-east, taking our scent back the way we had come.

My aim was to approach within two hundred metres of the perimeter fence, and establish our OP in a suitable hollow out in the field. Three hundred metres off, I whispered to Mike to wait and cover me while I recced forward. There was no shortage of possible locations. The field was exceedingly rough, and I found plenty of holes three or four feet deep where the peaty soil had been eroded away and rock was showing through. I chose a depression with a front wall of rock some two feet high, topped with peaty soil and tussocks of grass, and went back to bring Mike up. The site was almost a natural slit-trench. Working as silently as we could, we pitched a sloping roof of wire netting, anchored it with pins top and bottom, and covered it with sods of turf sliced out of a nearby hollow. Some handfuls of long dead grass scattered over the top completed our roof, which tapered down almost to ground level at one side, leaving room at the other so that we could roll out sideways. At the top of the front wall, in the centre, I cut out a notch of turf to make a lookout aperture.

'Safe as Fort Knox,' I told Mike. 'We'll call the place that.' Then I went through to the desk: 'Sierra Two, OP established. Going forward to choose site for CTR.'

We peeled off our sniper suits and left everything we didn't immediately need packed in our bergens, in case anything happened and we had to run for it. The night was reasonably warm, so it was no hardship, and we moved forward wearing only our ops waistcoats and windproofs on top of ordinary DPMs.

The field was so uneven that walking over it in the dark was awkward. We kept stumbling into holes, and we had to take it slowly. A couple of times I heard scuttling noises just in front of us, but I assumed that they were being made by rabbits. A sweep with the kite-sight revealed that the field was full of them.

Remembering the position of the barn door, and the angle I needed, I made a cautious approach to the hedge right opposite the front door of the cottage. A dry ditch, some brambles and the trunks of a couple of ash trees gave us all the cover we needed. With careful movements I cleared a space round us, cutting away any bramble shoots that might snag our clothes, and settled down to wait.

The cottage door was ten metres away, the barn door about thirty. The time was 2130. According to our tout, the delivery of arms was planned for 2300. As close in to the target as that, I didn't want to speak, so I waited for the desk to come up and ask if we were in position, and replied with a couple of jabs on my pressel.

121

The minutes ticked slowly past. I heard the reports of the Det guys moving around, but there seemed to be no enemy activity. Then at 2210 Delta Four, who was somewhere down the lanes behind us, came up with, 'Stand by. There's a vehicle mobile towards Black Two.' Soon its headlights appeared, but they went straight past the gates at speed.

A moment later I froze. Until then I had thought the place was deserted. Now, through the kite-sight, I saw a figure standing in the door of the barn. Evidently the man had been alerted by the car; he'd come out, maybe thinking this was his delivery. I was disconcerted to think that he'd been there all the time without my realizing it. Luckily our discipline had been good, and we hadn't made a sound. I nudged Mike, pointing at the barn. As if reading my thoughts, the desk came up with, 'Sierra Two, do you have X-rays on target?' and I gave him another double touch on the pressel.

'How many? More than one?'

A single press.

The desk began to ask more questions. It was impossible to answer them by buzzes. I reckoned the barn was far enough away for it to be safe to speak softly, so I got my head right down in the ditch and pulled the hood of my windproof round so that it was covering my face. That way, my throat mikes were unimpeded but my voice wouldn't carry any distance. I explained what was happening, and was told to stand by.

The drop-off time came and went. 'As usual, the Paddy Factor's operating,' Mike whispered.

Yes – the Paddy Factor. The sheer unreliability of the players made our job even more difficult. Clever and cunning as the bastards were, they could also be totally undisciplined. Already, in my short time in the Province, I'd heard of one case in which two men were on their way to murder a policeman, but decided to drop in at a pub for a pint to stiffen their morale. Six pints apiece later they were still in the bar, pissed as owls, their mission forgotten. Another time two fellows heading for a shoot had an argument with each other; they ended up fighting each other to a standstill, and again the mission went by the board. So tonight maybe our crowd wouldn't come at all.

Well past midnight, the man in the barn emerged for a stroll. He walked right past us, three metres away, and on to the gates, where he took a piss. The night was so still that we could hear every drop falling. Then he fiddled with the padlock – whoever might have put the new lock on, he had the right key – dropped the chain, and pulled the gates open one at a time. Hinges squealed and metal scraped over the gravel of the drive. That done, the man came sauntering back to pass us again and return to the barn. I guessed he was a guard, a kind of dicker, stationed there to make sure nobody else approached the place. I reckoned he was quite dedicated, as he'd been hanging around for hours in the dark, and had never showed so much as a gleam of light.

As if his little promenade had stirred the weather, the wind began to blow, drifting down the hill into our faces, and swirling round the cottage. In a few minutes it had become quite gusty, and I was glad because the noise of it made me feel less exposed.

At last, at about 0130, the Det reported another vehicle heading our way. Again the headlights came up from behind us, but this time they swung in through the gates, illuminating the cottage for a second before the driver snapped them off. He came past us on sidelights only – a van – and rolled on until he was almost inside the barn. Two men jumped out and called a quiet greeting to their waiting colleague. The kite-sight gave me a clear picture of all three.

I gave a jab on the pressel-switch.

'Zero Alpha. Have you X-rays on target?'

Talking into my hood, I whispered, 'Sierra Two, affirmative. Two X-rays arrived by van. Just about to unload into the barn. Wait one. Yes – one man has two longs. So has the other. Four longs into the barn. Can't see much in there. Wait one – better now. They have a torch on in the back right-hand corner. Longs being lowered into hole below ground level. There's straw round it. All four longs complete in hide . . . X-rays returning to rear of vehicle. Lifting out a heavy box. Two – two boxes. They look like ammunition, from the weight. Two boxes into barn, into cache. Ammo also complete.'

They didn't hang about. I saw them lowering some form of lid and raking loose straw back into position; then all three came out and boarded the van. It looked as though there was a partition between front and back, because they had to put one man in through the rear doors and close him in. At the gates, one of them got out to fasten the padlock and chain behind them.

'X-rays complete in van and mobile northwards,' I reported. 'Propose making CTR of barn itself.'

'Zero Alpha,' answered the desk. 'Are you certain it's clear?'

'Looks good.'

'At your discretion, then.'

'Roger. Wait out.'

'Did you get a look at any faces?' I asked Mike.

'Not really. Not enough light. But I wasn't expecting anything much from tonight. These guys who move the weapons around are only minor players. It's the shooters I'd like to see.'

'Well, hang on here and cover me while I suss out the barn. If anything happens, start putting rounds through the roof. Then RV back at Fort Knox. Switch to the chatter-net for the time being.'

I was pretty confident that everyone had gone, but I took no chances. I stood at the barn door and listened for a while before I went in. Then I switched on my infra-red torch, invisible to the naked eye. Through my passive night goggles the interior of the barn showed up as light as day.

There was a good deal of loose straw piled in the far right-hand corner, and a low stack of bales to the right, only a couple of layers high. From the indentation on top of them, I could see that someone had been sleeping there. The floor was beaten earth. In the middle of it stood a wooden trestle table, with a frying pan and some plates on it, all dirty with old grease. There were also two tin-openers and an intact can of

124

Pal dog-food. Jesus, I thought, these must be some low-level Paddies if that's what they're living on. The rest of the stuff in the barn was junk: a pile of old sacks; an ancient hay-cutter, rusted to hell; a couple of buckets, full of holes, with twisted handles; a ruined armchair with springs and stuffing bursting through dark-red upholstery.

I picked up a broken pitch-fork handle and began sounding the floor beneath the straw. At the fourth or fifth prod I got a hollow thump. Down on one knee, I drew the straw aside to reveal a circular sheet of heavy marine plywood, like the end of a beer barrel, with a piece of two-by-two nailed to the middle of it to form a makeshift handle. Fingers under one edge, fiddle around, lift gently. I couldn't see or feel any booby-trap device.

Up came the board. Beneath it, the lid of a black plastic dustbin. Up came that too – and there, glinting in the torch-light, were four AK 47s, standing on their butts, muzzles uppermost. Beside them, two black ammunition boxes were stacked end on end. Holding the barrel carefully with a gloved hand, I lifted one of the rifles, and saw it had had plenty of use – the metal was scratched, and the woodwork of the butt and fore-end was chipped and scraped. The PNGs didn't give enough clarity for me to see fine detail, so I pushed them up on to my forehead, whipped out my pencil torch and shone the fine beam on to the lettering beside the breech. The script was Chinese – no doubt that was where the weapon had come from. I lowered it carefully into place and flipped up the lid of one ammunition box. It was filled to the top with loose live rounds, but through them I saw something green and glinting. A quick rummage revealed two L2 hand-grenades, smooth green spheres about the size of a fist with a yellow band round them, and the inscription L2–A2. How the hell had the bastards got *them* – standard British Army issue?

Having checked the cache mentally, I replaced the box, the lid, the board, the straw, and withdrew, making sure not to step in any bare patch that might take a footprint. At the door of the barn I searched with my kite-sight for our OP in the ditch, and was glad to find that I couldn't see any sign of Mike. But he was there all right – and once we'd reported to the desk that the hide was complete, we pulled off to our basha in the field.

All through the next day we lay low, sharing stags, two hours on and two off. We had the spotter scope trained on the cottage, and at that range the field of view took in the gates as well. Apart from the odd car passing up and down the road, the only event was the arrival of a party of potential buyers to look at the house in the middle of the morning.

Mike was having a kip, but I woke him up. 'Now,' I said, 'watch this. If it was the dickers who put that new lock on the gates, they've fucked up. They obviously weren't expecting any customers.'

A middle-aged gent in a dark suit got out of the car and went to undo the padlock. He tried for a couple of minutes, gave it a big shake, scratched his head, looked back at the car and tried again. Finally he turned and said something through the car window. Out got a young-looking couple, the bird a not-bad-looking blonde in a tight, short skirt. There was no way they could approach the home of their dreams except by climbing over the stone wall beside the gate. Fatty Estate Agent went first, and reached back to give the blonde a hand. Up she came, arse-on to us, with her skirt riding halfway up her kidneys, and displaying a pair of outrageous mauve knickers.

'Phworrrhh!' went Mike.

'What's the matter? You desperate?'

'You haven't been out here for a fucking year, mate.'

The clients straightened themselves out, walked up the drive and in through the front door. As Pat had noticed on our initial recce, it wasn't locked, and the agent pushed it straight open. The visit wasn't a success. In about thirty seconds the party was out again and off back towards the car; they never went behind the house or anywhere near the barn. One look at the cottage was enough for them. Then it was back over the wall, a repeat flash of the royal purple, and another dying groan from Mike. 'Phworrrhh!' he went again, as if someone had stuck a knife in his guts. The agent took one final,

126

disgusted look at the padlock and drove off.

Somewhere, sometime, I'd seen knickers that colour before. Suddenly I got it: Singapore, on an exercise. We'd done a drop into Changhi airfield, and afterwards we were invited into the RAF officers' mess for a drink. There in a glass-fronted showcase on the wall was a pair of purple satin pants, exactly the colour of the ones we'd just seen, and underneath, the legend: 'SUPERSONIC KNICKERS. These knickers were wrested from GLORIA in the JACARANDA NIGHT CLUB on 14 January 1976, and flown at Mach 1.5 in a Mk 3 Phantom of 43 Squadron, by Squadron Leader Jeremy Turner, the following morning. RIP.'

I told Mike the story, and he struck back with one about how a colleague of his in the Det had started going out with this slapper from Belfast. Everyone knew that her brother was in the PIRA, and told him for Christ's sake to be careful. His only concession was to ask a couple of his mates to follow him in a second vehicle when he went to pick her up. He'd hardly got her on board when they saw something fly out of the passenger's window. Afterwards, when they asked him what it was, he explained, 'I said to her, "Ey – last time you weren't wearing any knickers. What you got some on now for?" Whereupon she made a grab and *rrrippp*, away they went, and there's her saying, "Not any more, I haven't!"'

Talk of knickers whiled away an enjoyable few minutes, but still we had six more hours of daylight to get through. All day long rain had threatened but held off. It was lucky for us that there were no cattle on the ground, either in our field or in any of the ones adjoining. That meant there was no reason for the local farmer to come out and look around. A shepherd with a collie would have been the worst, but there were no sheep either. With the wind blowing steadily from the cottage and away down the open country behind us, it was safe to have the occasional brew, and to boil up a couple of hot meals. As I'd expected, Mike's manners in the OP were pretty good; once the stink of his aftershave had worn off – no joke, a potential danger – there wasn't a lot I could criticize.

As always on that kind of job, the prime enemy was

boredom. After a couple of hours with no activity or movement, I was bored out of my mind. My thoughts went round and round in circles, but kept coming back to two subjects. The nice one was Tracy, the less pleasant was the edginess in my mother-in-law's voice. It wasn't like her to be as sharp as that.

At least, when Mike and I were both awake, we could chat. As casually as possible, I brought up the subject of Declan Farrell. I'd pretended I'd heard about the chain-saw incident earlier, from someone else, and wondered what sort of a man he might be. 'He must be a right hard bugger, to do a thing like that.'

'He is,' Mike agreed. 'He's supposed to have a filthy temper. I don't know how many people he's kneecapped.'

'What drives him? I mean, what makes him do it?'

'What makes any of them do it? It's bred into them from infancy. You've heard those street kids of three and four effing and blinding. You've seen them throwing stones at the patrols. It's in their blood. They grow up knowing nothing else.'

'Have you ever seen Farrell?'

'A couple of times. He's quite an impressive-looking guy, I have to admit.'

'But he'd never actually do an operation now? Too senior?'

'I dunno. They've lost a lot of lower-grade operators lately. They may be thin on the ground. Besides, he likes getting involved. Also, he's that arrogant, he might come out just to show the lads how things should be done. If they've fucked up on the last couple of jobs – as they have – he might fancy giving a lead himself.'

'You don't think he'll come tonight?'

'Could do. Why – you scared?'

I forced myself to laugh. 'No, just curious.' Suddenly I realized I'd used that expression before, and disciplined myself never to use it again.

There was no change of plan during the day. Every time the desk came through the message was the same: 'NTR –

128

Nothing to Report.' In the absence of any more news from the touts, we assumed that the shoot would go down at 2200 that night.

On that dull winter afternoon, soon after five, we moved forward again to take up the same position in the ditch. I noticed that the wind was dropping and the temperature falling, but paid no particular attention.

From the net we knew that the babysitting team had stayed *in situ*, like us, and that the Det were moving out into the country again. So were our intercept cars. Across a wide area of the countryside, the trap was being set.

This time the players were early – and where they came from, nobody could say. We got no warning; somehow, they eluded the Det. Suddenly, at only 2120, there were lights coming up the road from behind us. I managed to put a call through while the vehicle was still at the gate and somebody was undoing the lock, but then, as it cruised in past us, we had to go quiet.

This time it was a car – an old two-litre Rover, superficially similar to our own Interceptor. The driver swung round to the right beside the end of the cottage, then backed out and came forward again, to stop, facing the road, almost in front of us. Close as we were, we couldn't see the registration number, which looked as if it had been deliberately caked with cowshit. Four men got out and slammed the doors, not bothering to keep the noise down. I guessed they'd all had a couple of pints. Then one opened the boot, lifted out a bundle, and all four walked across to the barn. Seconds later somebody struck a match and a gas pressure-lamp hissed into action.

A harsh yellow glare flooded the inside of the building. One of the men seemed to realize that they were being careless, because he came back to the threshold, looking to right and left, and said loudly, 'This fecking barn's supposed to have doors on it, too. Whatever happened to them?'

'Bollocks to the doors,' said another voice. 'Get fecking changed.'

From the bundle somebody sorted out long black garments, and all four began to pull them on.

129

In Mike's ear I whispered, 'Recognize anyone?'

He nodded twice, staring intently.

'Farrell?'

He shook his head.

In a minute or so the four men were encased in black from head to foot. One of them had opened up the hide, and was handing out the rifles and loaded magazines. I heard magazines clicking home.

I felt my heart going like a hammer, and took a couple of deep breaths. Jesus! I had the G3 set on automatic, and levelled at the group, thirty metres off. I could wallop them all.

One man, the shortest in the group, walked round the other three, giving them a cursory inspection. Then he doused the lamp, and all four walked to the car.

The moment they were rolling, I got on the radio. 'Sierra Two. Four X-rays have collected weapons and ammunition from Black Two. Four AK 47s. Now complete in dark-green Rover 2000. Mobile northwards from my location.'

'Zero Alpha,' answered the desk. 'Roger.'

'Fuck it!' I gasped. 'Why didn't we drop the bastards?'

'I know. It drives you up the bloody wall.'

Mike stood up and shook himself, as if to throw off the weight of frustration. Then he called, 'Delta Eight. Those four X-rays – two unknown to me, but the others are Eamonn O'Reilly and Jonty Best. Over.'

For the next half-hour all we could do was listen as the hit team moved in erratically on its target. We heard the Det cars reporting the Rover forward, from Green Five to Green Four and Green Three. From there it was only four or five hundred metres to the target, but for some reason the players veered off into open country and disappeared for twenty minutes. Then at last they were picked up again, heading back to Green Three. This time we reckoned the raid would go down within the next few seconds. But then came an unexpected twist: instead of stopping at the farmhouse, the assault vehicle went straight past. One of the intercept teams requested permission to take it out, but the head-shed refused. The desk wanted to let things develop and see what was going to happen.

Mike and I waited tensely, wound up on full alert. I imagined all our people being in the same state – some in the farmhouse, as I'd been a few days back, some in an OP outside the house; most in cars, all poised to react. Had something spooked the players? Time and again a job collapsed when they took fright at the last moment. Maybe they'd spotted one of our cars lurking in a strange place. Maybe they'd seen something at the house itself. We listened out, expecting to hear a report from the agency monitoring CB radio, which normally caught what the players were saying to each other.

Half an hour went by. Then suddenly somebody picked up the Rover again, incoming towards the farmhouse, apparently making another run. This time the desk decided on action, and scrambled two intercept teams to take it out before it reached the target. After a quick manoeuvre they trapped it, by the simple expedient of placing one car to block the lane ahead of it, and sending another up behind.

Then came another twist. The trapped Rover wasn't carrying the hit team. The two men in it were unarmed, dressed in ordinary clothes, and claimed to be on their way home from a session in the pub. A preliminary search of the car revealed no weapons. The vehicle seemed to be completely clean.

Consternation. Was this the hit car, emptied out? Or was it a look-alike decoy? Suddenly, as I listened to the exchanges, I realized that the desk was calling me, asking again if I'd got the number of the car we'd reported.

'Sierra Two, negative,' I replied.

The desk ordered the two men to be brought in for questioning, and the car detained for forensic examination. Was that it for the night, then?

Not for us. It was Mike who saw the lights coming at high speed from the north.

'Look out!' he said. 'They're back.'

The car came screaming down the narrow road. The driver was in either a great hurry or a great rage. He flung the Rover right-handed through the gates, roared past us and scorched

131

to a halt with the nose of the car in the barn doorway and the headlights still on. The illumination was so good that binoculars were more use than kite-sights. The same four men leapt out, all effing and blinding at the tops of their voices, and began to unload their weapons. One kicked the straw away from the top of the hide and lifted the cover, but they were all furious for a few moments and stood arguing.

'Sierra Two,' I reported urgently. 'Four X-rays back at Black Two. They still have their weapons. We could smack them all. Permission to open fire. Over.'

'Zero Alpha,' the desk answered. 'Roger. Wait one.' Then, 'Zero Alpha to Sierra Two. Negative – no permission. Don't do anything. Let them go. Over.'

'Sierra Two, roger.'

'Oh for fuck's sake!' whispered Mike in my ear.

Such was the commotion that until the very last moment the players didn't realize another car had arrived. Nor did we. It must have come very quietly, maybe without headlights. All at once it was in through the gate and sliding past us, to stop behind the Rover. Two men got out, leaving the doors open, and strode towards the shemozzle in the barn. Something made me focus on the driver, a big man with a slight limp. As he advanced he called out in a deep voice, 'What the feck's going on here? Cunts! Get a hold of yourselves.'

The instant he reached the light and I saw his face, I knew.

So did Mike. 'Fucking Farrell!' he exclaimed. 'There he is!'

'Sierra Two,' I called again. 'Two more X-rays now on location. One is Declan Farrell, repeat Farrell. Request permission to fire. Over.'

Again the answer was negative. I couldn't believe it. I had the cross-hairs of the sight steady on the side of the bastard's head. My finger was on the trigger. One touch, and Kath's death would be avenged. Between the two of us, Mike and I could have dropped all six terrorists where they stood. Not one of them would even have got out of the barn.

Then suddenly we found we had an urgent problem of our own. As I lowered my G3, I noticed Farrell's car rock on its springs, as if someone was shifting around inside it. The car rocked again. Against the dim light I saw something leap over the back of the front seat, and out of the driver's door came not another player, but a bloody great dog, a Rotty.

'Jesus!' I breathed. 'Now we're in it.'

The blessed north wind of the day had died away, and odd puffs were coming from all directions. The dog trotted across to the front of the cottage and lifted his leg against the door-post. Then he began sniffing along the front wall. If we moved we'd be bound to attract his attention, but if we lay still he'd get us anyway. It would only be a matter of seconds before he picked up our scent.

'Come on,' I hissed at Mike, 'we've got to pull out.'

Too late. The dog stopped, lifted his head and stood staring in our direction. Then he let fly a volley of barks and lunged forward. We lay flat. He pulled up two feet away, dancing high on his toes, barking and snarling like hell.

'BUSTER!' yelled Farrell from the barn. 'Quiet, you bastard! Come here!'

The dog's only response was to bark even louder. He began really doing his nut. Gobs of spit were flying out of his chops and landing on us. His barks would have wakened the dead. We were in an impossible position. If we kept still, someone would be over to see what he was going mad about (perhaps even Farrell himself – this at least could provide me with an excuse to take him out). But then again, if we shifted, the dog would go for us.

All this went through my mind in about half a second. I tried to slide my right hand down my side to bring my knife out of its sheath, but even that slight movement was enough to trigger an attack. With a thump like a sack of cement landing, the dog was on top of us, gnashing viciously. His jaws closed on Mike's right forearm, and he was growling thunderously. Still I wanted to get the knife into him, but the instant I moved he let go and bit again, this time Mike's shoulder. The dog was bracing his rear legs and twitching his arse about as he got pressure on and tried to drag backwards. There was only one thing for it. I rammed the muzzle of the

G3 against the dog's ribs and put one round through his chest. The report was slightly muffled, but still there was a loud, dull *boom*.

The impact of the shot lifted the creature clean off us and threw his body on to the bank, where he lay twitching, with a few last noises, half-barks, half-grunts, choking out of his mouth.

'Run!' I hissed.

We scrambled backwards out of the ditch and stumbled into the boggy field. For a second the voices in the barn had fallen silent. Then the men began to yell. We ran as best we could, tripping over the tussocks. Through the screen of trees we saw figures pour out of the barn. A moment later there came a rattle of automatic fire, and rounds went cracking over our heads. We dropped into a hole, about fifty metres back from the ditch. In the dark we were reasonably safe. A second rifle opened up. We heard rounds smacking into the ground away to our right. Obviously the players thought we had come in from the road and were going back that way. They fired wildly, whole magazines full, in that direction.

As soon as they stopped, we ran again, aiming for Fort Knox. In the confusion we lost our markers, and had to cast out, right and left, to find it. In the shelter of the rock bank at last, we stopped to get our breath.

'How's the arm?'

'I can feel it's bleeding, but not too bad. Hand's working OK.'

'Sierra Two,' I called. 'We've been compromised. No casualties, but we need an urgent pick-up. We'll be at Black-Four-One five minutes from now.'

'Zero Alpha,' the desk answered. 'Roger.'

'Sierra Two. We've stirred up a hornet's nest at Black Two, so I recommend all units steer clear of it.'

Still the villains were convinced that we'd come in from the road. They were poncing down the drive with flashlights, loosing off into the dark. I thought of the purple knickers going over that wall.

It took us about a minute to collect all our gear and destroy the OP. Once we'd recovered the ground-pegs and dragged off the wire-netting, the turf-and-grass roof collapsed in a heap, leaving little sign that anybody had been there. As a final touch, I kicked away the edges of the observation notch that we'd cut in the bank so that it would look like a natural hollow.

Ten minutes later we were back at our dropping-off point, lurking behind a convenient stone wall. We'd hardly got into position when Pat came up on the radio to say that he was closing on the location. I acknowledged, and we emerged into the road. Almost at once we saw headlights coming up the hill, and within seconds we were safe in the back of the car, heading for home.

EIGHT

After that fiasco it took me three or four days to chill out. My big disappointment was not so much that the PIRA had pulled out of their operation; what pissed me off was the fact that I'd missed – or rather, been deprived of – a golden chance of settling my personal score. The whole business could have been squared away. If Mike and I had opened fire, we'd have had little trouble afterwards establishing that we'd used reasonable force; having been faced with four armed men, we would have had no difficulty in maintaining that our lives had been in jeopardy.

The wash-up didn't provide any clues as to why the players had quit, but it did reveal why the desk had forbidden us to shoot. We learnt that one of the four gunmen was a key tout, and that his continued existence was considered of paramount importance. Better him alive than Farrell dead – at least, that was what we were told at the time. Later, I came to wonder if that was the whole truth.

This setback made me do some hard thinking. Farrell had lost his dog, but he probably thought Buster had saved his life. There was no way he could pinpoint the identity of the would-be assassin who'd tried to nail him, but he would certainly guess that it had been a member of the security forces. After such a close shave, he surely wouldn't risk himself in the field again for a while. My own time in Ulster was rapidly ticking away. It followed that, if I was going to get Farrell, I must go after him on my own.

The idea excited me, because I knew how dangerous a solo mission would be. Of course I'd just had another illustration of how vital it was to work in pairs. If that dog had got hold of me on my own I could easily have ended up getting captured. The risks of a one-man operation were all too obvious. But there was something about Farrell's arrogance that goaded me on: the way he'd yelled at his own guys as he arrived at the barn – even those few words had made him sound a real bully-boy.

Already I'd formed the outline of a plan. I'd find out where he lived, set up an OP on his house, observe his movements in and out, and then, once I had him sussed, take him out with my secretly confiscated 9mm Luger. I'd fired so many thousands of rounds on the range that I was confident I could put a double-tap into his head from fifteen or twenty metres – and that would be the end of him. My main difficulty was to get enough time off. To find the house might take several recces; to establish the pattern of his movements would need several more. I could take the odd evening off and pretend to be socializing with my in-laws, but sooner or later I would surely get caught by some emergency – a call would go out, pulling all the guys back, and I wouldn't be there to answer it. Instead, I'd be stuck out in the middle of some godforsaken bog, waiting for Mr Big-Boy to come home.

The next time I visited Kath's parents was for Christmas lunch. We had a fine meal with all the trimmings, and then the traditional handing-out of presents from under the decorated tree. Tim, being easily the youngest person present, got the job of messenger, taking each package to the right person. As long as he was the centre of attention he behaved perfectly, but later he threw a tantrum for no visible reason, and I could see he was becoming too much for his gran. I think he was reacting to the loss of his mother and the break-up of his home. Apparently these rages were becoming quite frequent. Suddenly he'd let fly with a scream and refuse to co-operate. No wonder he was getting on Meg's nerves – and on mine.

Lying in my cabin one night, unable to sleep, I started thinking about Tracy (as usual). I'd been phoning her most evenings, and had sent an expensive silver bracelet as a Christmas present. Our relationship was going great guns – as far as it could while we were a few hundred miles apart. I had no doubt we were going to stick together when I got home, and I was pretty sure she'd take Tim over, as if he were her own. She had only ever seen him as a baby, when he'd been brought into the Med Centre in Hereford, but that didn't seem to worry her.

Now I had a brainwave. Partly because I'd volunteered to work over Christmas, I had a week's leave coming up, and I'd been planning to go home. But if I did the opposite, bringing Tracy over, I could take local leave, and have a chance to pursue my own devious plans in the Province. At the same time, she could start getting to know Tim. Furthermore – my mind ran on – we could have a kind of premature honeymoon at my in-laws' holiday cottage on the north coast. The place was standing empty, and it was in a safe enough area. We'd take Tim with us, and at the very least give Meg a break. Afterwards, if all had gone well, Tracy might take him back with her to Keeper's Cottage and start getting our family settled there – maybe not after this first visit, but some time later.

For once the tide seemed to be running in my favour. Three phone calls fixed everything: one to Tracy, one to Meg, one to the airline. The great thing about Tracy – or one of the great things about her – was the positive way she reacted to new ideas. I can't stand people with negative attitudes, who reject suggestions on principle before they've even thought about them. Tracy's outlook was the opposite of that: everything new was fun, or likely to be – and so it turned out when I suggested that she might come over. 'Great!' was her reaction. Susan could hold the fort at KC. She herself could take a week off work any time, she said. Her only question was, 'When?'

Meg was almost equally enthusiastic. I put over the idea that Tracy was a trained nurse, and fully capable of looking after a young child. I said, truthfully enough, that her elder sister had two young boys of her own, and that Tracy had helped look after them. I'm sure my in-laws must have seen the way things were going. They'd known that I'd left Tracy in possession of the house in England, and when I said she was coming over, no doubt they put two and two together; but they were too sensible to criticize my arrangements. As for the troop – instead of having to creep out on surreptitious expeditions, I merely said that I was proposing to spend my leave in a holiday cottage on the north coast.

After its last little dust-up the Sierra had been smartly retired from our stable of cars, and in its place I had a Cavalier. This time I drove with one eye permanently on the rear mirror, and once I'd come off the M2 at Junction Four, I made a couple of unnecessary stops – one at a garage to buy some peppermints, one in a lay-by to check under the bonnet for some imaginary engine fault. Satisfied that I had no tail, I headed up round the edge of the hills towards the village of Ballyconvil.

The place was so small that when I saw it my heart sank. Four, five, six little houses straggling along the road – and that was it. One, with 'LIAM'S' painted white-on-green above the door, was a bar cum general store, and the others were ordinary dwellings, so poor and mean I couldn't imagine Farrell setting foot inside any of them, let alone living there. If the village had been anywhere at home, I'd have gone into the pub for a pint and made casual inquiries about the neighbourhood; but here, I knew, the appearance of a stranger speaking with an English accent would immediately raise an alert. Word would go round in a flash; everybody would be talking and on the lookout.

All I could do was drive straight through the place and on up the hill. But as I glanced back to my left, I realized that there was one more house, set apart from the rest of the hamlet on higher ground. It was hidden from the road directly below it by the fact that it stood back on a ledge, and remained out of view until anybody passing was clear of the other houses. The place looked like a farm, with a couple of barns set round a yard, but even a fleeting glimpse gave the impression that it wasn't a run-of-the-mill ramshackle farmhouse. The old buildings had been renovated in the past year or two: the roofs were tidy and straight, the windows in the house new. The set-up looked too smart to be a working farm. Right, I thought, that can only be him.

I drove on for twenty minutes, stopped in a lay-by and watched the mirror for ten minutes between intervals of studying my 1:50,000 map. Very few cars passed, and none gave me any cause to worry. Obviously I wouldn't be able to park in the village when I did my CTRs; I needed somewhere secure to leave the car. My eye fastened on some blocks of forestry, green on the map. The one nearest to Ballyconvil was round the back of the hill from the farm, but only one kilometre or so away across country. It was worth a look, anyway.

A short drive brought me into sight of it. As I expected, it was a dense conifer plantation which climbed the hillside and swept round into a big bowl. The public road followed the contour-line below it, and a barbed-wire fence bounded its lower edge. After a few hundred metres I came to the entrance, a gravelled drive leading up into the trees and turning left. Following the road, I came to a barrier in the form of a heavy wooden pole, hinged on a pivot at one end and padlocked with a chain to a post at the other. No supersonic knickers here – only a sign saying: 'FORESTRY COMMISSION. NO ADMISSION TO UNAUTHORIZED PERSONS.'

I got out and had a look round. The gates were nicely out of sight of the main road. The gravel was clean and hard, so that tyres left no mark on it. A careful check of the chain, the padlock and the ground showed that the entrance had not been opened for some time. Evidently there was no work going on in the wood, no thinning or felling. The set-up seemed ideal for my purposes. After my lock-picking course at LATA, the barrier would present no problem. Once inside, I could drive up to a convenient point in the forest, hide the car, and go in round the shoulder of the hill on foot. If, by ill chance, someone came across the vehicle while I was away and reported it, I'd say that it had been nicked, and must have been dumped up there by the villains.

With that settled, I turned round and drove back along the same road. My second pass through Ballyconvil confirmed earlier impressions. The farmhouse came into view as I approached the village, and I saw that its walls had been freshly painted white. The window frames were new and made of dark wood. The roof was as it should be – traditional slate. At the back, a stretch of high-wire fence was showing. Somebody had spent a lot of money on the place. But there was no car outside the door, and no sign of any activity.

That second pass also gave me a chance to look at the background. Behind the house, rough grass fields sloped away up the flank of the hill, with much the same texture as the one in which Mike and I made our OP; but after only one field's width the farmland gave out and the mountain proper began. The cut-off was a fence running horizontally round the contour; above it, thickets of gorse grew among the bracken, and higher still the bracken gave way to heather. It looked as though the gorse would be perfect for an OP – prickly, but brilliant cover, within less than two hundred yards of the target.

On the morning Tracy was due in, I got Pat to lift me out to the City Airport, and I was there in time to pick up a hire-car before the flight from Birmingham landed. When the car-hire girl told me all she had left was a red Datsun I nearly flipped. Red! That was the last colour I wanted. Especially in the forest – it would show for miles. But then I told myself, 'Come on, you're a civvy tourist for the week. Behave like one.' So I paid with my Visa card, gave my in-laws' address, and signed for the Datsun.

When Tracy appeared in the scruffy arrival area, we ran straight to each other and held on tight without speaking. I think other people could feel the high current of emotion flowing between us, because they kept away and didn't even look in our direction. Through her shiny blue shell-suit she felt slim and fit.

'You've lost weight,' she said.

'I know. Things are pretty tense over here.'

'It suits you, though.'

'Good!'

This was her first visit to Belfast, and as we headed out for Helen's Bay I explained that we were already on the north-

141

eastern edge of the city, well away from all the nasties in the West. The holiday cottage, I said, was even farther from the centre of the troubles, so that there was no need to worry.

Tracy went over big with both my in-laws – she said all the right things, and made an immediate hit. Den told her she was too thin, and said she should eat more; in particular, he insisted she should have another piece of the lemon cake which Meg had made and put out with the coffee. As for Tim – Tracy started straight in, playing with his train set and talking to him as if he was an adult. I couldn't believe it. After about thirty seconds they were having a serious discussion about why the signals went green for go and red for stop.

It didn't seem the right moment for a talk about long-term plans, so we packed up and got going, on the basis that all three of us would be away for the week. Den had bought Tim a new car-seat because he'd outgrown his old one, and we fixed that in the back of the Datsun. As we drove off I realized what great cover it was to look like a regular family on holiday in a hire-car, innocent and harmless as could be. Only I knew that the Luger was in the boot. We stopped once to stock up from a little supermarket in a village, and the entire journey took not much more than an hour.

The cottage wasn't quite what I'd been expecting. I'd been imagining something tucked away on its own – but I hadn't known the address: No. 1 Coastguard Row. It was one of four, built for the local coastguards, and stood at the end of a little terrace overlooking the sea, perched above the road so that you had to leave the car down below and walk up a flight of stone steps to the front garden. I immediately thought, Ah, this is handy, because the houses were out of sight of the road, and nobody would spot a car coming or going at odd hours of the night or early morning.

Inside everything was fine. Meg had phoned a friendly neighbour, who kept a spare key, and got her to switch on the underfloor heating, so that the place was warm and welcoming. Tim had been there before, so of course he considered himself an expert on the house's layout, and showed us which rooms were which.

142

It was a good job we had him with us, otherwise we'd have spent all day in bed, as well as all night.

With a fire going in the front room the house became a cocoon, cradling our little family, and there wasn't much temptation to go outside. All the same, that first afternoon we walked along the shingly beach. The tide was coming in, and the sea was flat and calm, with only the tiniest waves turning over as they hit the shore. I showed Tim how to choose flat stones and give them an underarm flick so that they did ducks-and-drakes across the water. At that stage he wasn't much good at throwing, and he spun himself round in circles with his efforts to get more leverage on to his arm. I noticed that there was plenty of driftwood on the high-tide line, so on the way back I collected an armful for the store in the shed behind the cottage.

All the time I was thinking of the white farmhouse at Ballyconvil and the dark forest on the hill. How was I going to account for my need to be absent for hours at a time? Why should I want to disappear in the middle of what was, in effect, our honeymoon?

I'd already tried to explain to Tracy that guys in the Regiment habitually told their wives and girlfriends as little as possible about what they were doing. It was plain good sense and good security, I said, to restrict knowledge to a minimum. With her knack of going straight to the point, she'd come back with, 'Well, *that* doesn't sound great. If you're not coming clean about your work, how am I to know what else you may be covering up?' She was right, of course. Secrecy breeds distrust – and now, with our relationship hardly started, I was going to have to start deceiving her.

I said nothing that day. While she was getting supper on the go I walked down to the pub at the other end of the village. Den had told me that out there, in tourist country, it was safe enough, especially as he and Meg were well known locally. The place was called the Spanish Galleon, and the walls were covered with mementoes of the Armada, mostly pictures of fantastic gold jewellery recovered from the *Girona*, which was wrecked off the coast in the autumn of 1588. I bought myself

143

a pint of stout and explained to the landlord that we'd come to the cottage for the week. I couldn't tell whether or not he knew about Kath, so we just had a general chat, mostly about fishing. A fellow about my age, who was already at the bar, said he had a friend who owned a fishing boat at some place nearby. After a while I bought a bottle of plonk for supper and set off home.

In the morning, before it was fully light, Tim came bursting into our room in his pyjamas. 'Why are the beds pushed together?' he demanded.

'So we can have a cuddle,' said Tracy.

'Gran and Grandad don't have them like that.'

'Well – come on in and have a cuddle anyway.'

Next thing, he was in between us, wriggling like a ferret.

'Why are you bare?' he asked accusingly.

Jesus! I couldn't help laughing.

'This duvet's nice and warm,' said Tracy. 'We don't need pyjamas.'

So it went on. She was brilliant with him, especially when he started on about God.

'Who's God?' he wanted to know.

'He's like a big father, up there in heaven.'

'Why can't I see him, then?'

'He's like the wind. You can feel the wind, but you can't see it. You know? God's like that.'

'What does he feel like?'

'Sort of warm. Like if someone's kind to you. He feels good.'

'Is Mummy in heaven?'

'Yes. I'm sure she is.'

'Why did she have to go there?'

'I expect God wanted her.'

'What did he want her *for*?'

'Because she was a very good person.'

'Can I go and see her?'

'Not really. . .'

The inquisition was relentless, but Tracy was equal to it; she never lost her cool or cut Tim short with an

144

unsympathetic answer. By the end of breakfast there was a terrific bond between the two of them. Altogether we were a happy family that morning.

It was all the harder, then, to break the news that I had to go off in the afternoon to do a job of work. Tracy looked really pissed off. 'But I thought you were on leave,' she said. 'That's the whole point of my being here.'

'I know,' I prevaricated, 'But there were a couple of things outstanding. I promised the lads I'd get them done.'

She knew I was being deliberately evasive, but because of the earlier conversations we'd had about security she didn't press for more information. When I said I'd be back after dark, she just said, 'Take care. You'll find supper waiting.'

It was less than an hour's drive to Ballyconvil. But I didn't go to the village at all. Navigating with the help of the big-scale map, I took a swing out right-handed, to the west, and came up to the forestry plantation from the opposite direction. Once again the entrance was deserted. A quick check confirmed that nobody had moved it since my last visit. Pulling on a pair of thin silk gloves, I brought out my little collection of bent levers and spikes, and in a minute I had the padlock open. The barrier-pole swung up easily, with the lump of concrete on its end acting as a counterweight. With the car through, I closed the gates and put the padlock back in position.

Inside the plantation, the road climbed to the left in a wide curve. The spruces on either side were quite large – maybe thirty years old and fifty feet tall – and they'd never been thinned, so that they were growing in a solid mass. Nobody could look into the forest from a distance and see a car moving. Half a kilometre up, I reached a fork and took the left, along the contour, in the direction I wanted. Round a corner the road suddenly came to an end in an apron of gravel, a spread big enough for timber-trucks to turn. Uphill, above it, was a small patch of bare ground under the first rows of trees; I got out and checked that it was firm, then backed the car as far under the branches as it would go, out of sight of any passing helicopter. I'd thought about cutting branches and covering it completely, but decided that, if I did, it would be too obvious that somebody had tried to hide it. Instead, I relied on an element of bluff. On the front passenger seat I left a book that I'd sent away for: *Field Guide to the Birds of the British Isles*. (I'd taken some stick when that arrived in the warehouse and was opened by Security in case it was a bomb – 'Fucking hell, there's only one kind of bird that Geordie's interested in,' and so on. Very witty.) Now, I hoped, it might come into its own.

I locked up, settled my day-sack on my back and set off along a fire-break that continued the line of the hard road. It felt odd to be moving operationally in the open without a G3 or a covert radio. It felt even odder to be on my own, without at least one partner in immediate contact. All I had in the way of equipment, apart from the Luger and the kite-sight, was my knife, wire-cutters, secateurs, a torch and a pair of binoculars. While planning the sortie I'd thought hard about borrowing one of the troop cameras, so that I could take pictures of Farrell, develop them myself, and make certain I had the right man. After a while, though, I'd abandoned the idea. One problem was that I couldn't take a camera away for a whole week without its absence being noticed – and in any case, I knew well enough what Farrell looked like. What with Pink Mike's photos and our live sighting at the transit hide, there was no chance I could mistake him.

Heather and rough grass had grown across the ride, but along the middle a narrow path had remained open, and the going was easy. About two hundred metres from the turning-place it bent to the right. As soon as I was out of sight of the car I dropped down and crawled into the wood, coming round in a half-circle under the trees and putting in a few minutes' covert observation to make sure nobody had followed me up.

That was easier said than done. The lower branches of the trees had all died from lack of light, but they were still stiff and spiky, the lowest of them growing to within a couple of feet of the ground. Even when I tried to crawl along the smooth carpet of old pine needles; my day-sack kept catching. In most places the only remedy was to belly-crawl, right down flat. Even as I was worming my way back to the path I thought how impossible it would be to make any speed through a plantation as dense as this.

Like a snake, I wriggled carefully up to the edge of the ride, and for fifteen minutes I lay there watching the car through binoculars. Nothing moved, and gradually I relaxed. Maybe I was being excessively cautious – but you never know.

Emerging again, I shook the spruce needles out of my shirt collar and went on along the track. In a few minutes I came to the boundary fence – a two-metre-high barrier of squared wire – and looked cautiously out. Ahead was the slope of the open hill, falling from right to left: wide stretches of heather, patches of dead-looking grass, clumps of gorse. Unless there was somebody up on the hill itself, which seemed unlikely, I felt confident no one would see me, because the nearest farmland and houses were way down over the brow. In any case, I had done my best to dress up as a hiker or bird-watcher, in a dull-coloured windproof and thick grey Norwegian stockings pulled up to the knees over my jeans, like plus fours.

Take it easy, though, I told myself. Don't rush it. I gave myself a couple of minutes inside the fence, then climbed over and took another look round. Somehow I needed to mark my entry-point, for when I came back in the dark. To have tied a handkerchief to the fence would have been too obvious. Looking back into the wood, I saw a bare dead branch, stripped of its bark and nearly white. I climbed back in, threaded it into the mesh near the top of the wire at an angle, as if it had blown there, and climbed out again.

On the move in the open, I worked my way round the contour. Only ten minutes later I stuck my head cautiously over a rise and found I could see down to the farm. A short belly-crawl brought me into a dry stream-bed, and that in turn led down to a clump of gorse just above the highest field. Having crept round the edge of the bushes, I cut away some of the lower branches and scraped the ground beneath them clear of prickles to make a comfortable nest. With minimum effort I'd fashioned myself a perfect OP.

The farmhouse and its outbuildings were less than 200 metres below me. The house – to the right as I looked – was long and low, and ranged with its back to the hill, which rose in a mown grass bank immediately behind, so that the top of the bank was only a few feet from the gutter of the slate roof. House and bank were separated by a path no more than a yard wide. There were only two windows in the back of the house, and both were small – lavatories or bathrooms, I guessed. The left-hand end of the house jutted forward, away from the hill, like the foot of a blunt L, and there, in the middle of the end wall, in my full view, was the front door, with a little pitched roof over a porch.

To me, the house was of secondary interest. Far more important was the high mesh fence which bounded the property and abutted the ends of the farm buildings, so that the entire establishment was enclosed by wire or stone; it took me a few moments to work out that the area surrounding the house was one huge dog-run. The drive came in through gates a couple of metres high on the side farthest from me. Any doubt about this being Farrell's place was dispelled when a dog suddenly came into view, sniffing along the perimeter fence. The animal was a hefty-looking Rottweiler, no doubt the partner of the late and unlamented Buster.

Scanning for details, I spotted a video camera on one corner of the house, covering the approach, and what looked like a security light high on the wall. At first I imagined that the light would be activated by infra-red sensors, but then I realized that if a dog was loose in the compound outside, the system would drive people crazy by popping on and off all night.

There appeared to be nobody at home; certainly there was no car standing outside. Then, as I lay watching, I heard a cow bellow, and I realized that at least one of the barns was still in use for its original purpose. That was a surprise. From the high standard to which the outbuildings had been renovated, I'd assumed that farming had gone out of the window. Then

I thought, Maybe keeping cattle is a form of cover, a pretence of normality designed to draw attention away from other activities.

The afternoon passed slowly. At about 3.30 light rain began to fall, so I pulled on my waterproof. The temptation to doze off was strong, especially after our energetic sessions during the night. To stay awake, I kept trying to work out how I would drop Farrell if or when he came home. By far the easiest would be to get him with a G3 or a hunting rifle from up the hill, above the compound and outside it. But since I couldn't sneak a G3 out of the warehouse (or lay my hands on a hunting rifle), I was going to have to go in close and use the Luger. Because the dog was constantly on the move around its patch, that was going to be difficult. I tried to measure the distance between the porch, where Farrell would probably get out of his car, and the nearest point of the top fence from which I'd have a clear view of him: twenty-five metres at least. I'd want to be closer than that to make sure.

At least the Luger was in good shape. When I first got it, I saw that it was old but in immaculate order, as we generally found with PIRA weapons. Someone had really looked after it – but all the same I'd stripped it down, cleaned it thoroughly and given it a good oiling. One afternoon, when a gale was blowing and the noise of the wind was enough to cover the shots, I'd managed to take it out into an old gravel pit and put twenty or thirty rounds through it, so I knew it wouldn't let me down.

Just after four o'clock there came a surprise. Up the drive wandered an old crone, a real bog peasant, with a black scarf round her head, an ancient overcoat nearly down to her ankles, buttoned-up boots, and smoking a pipe. The dog ran to meet her, and as she let herself in through the gates it jumped up with its paws on her shoulders. She gave it a kiss and slipped it some tit-bit, after which it went with her as she headed into the farmyard. Through the binoculars I watched her take the pipe from her mouth and put it down on what looked like an old stand for milk-churns. Then she disappeared into one of the sheds and came out with a bucket.

A steel gate clanged as she went into the open-fronted barn, presumably feeding the cattle in there. Later she brought an armful of hay across the yard and dumped that in the same area. All the time the dog was at her heels, clearly glad of her company. Then she picked up her pipe and vanished round the far side of the house, where I guessed she was feeding the dog. Finally she went back out through the gates. This time I saw that they opened automatically, presumably worked by pressure pads under the road.

Darkness fell soon after the old girl had disappeared down the hill. I wanted to move in closer, but the wind was dangerous; I could feel what there was of it eddying past me from above – and after our experience at the transit hide, I didn't want to blow things by stirring up the dog. So I stayed where I was and waited.

My reward arrived just after six o'clock. Headlights came blazing up the hill and a car swept in towards the gates, which opened in front of it. I saw the Rotty rush out and leap around as the car cruised forward and pulled up outside the door. On went the security light, and out got three men. I saw straight away that the driver was Farrell, but I could make nothing of the other two. The car was a Mercedes estate, and before any of the men entered the house they opened the tail-gate, took out some heavy-looking suitcases, two apiece, and staggered across to the nearest outbuilding. From the way they were buckling at the knees I could tell they had a fair weight on board. When they reached the outhouse Farrell produced a bunch of keys, with which he unlocked a door. Once the suitcases were stashed inside, the men went over to the house, and soon several lights were showing as they settled down inside.

That was enough for day one of my campaign. I'd established that the farmhouse was Farrell's, and that he was using it. All I had to do now was devise some means of getting in close. As I walked back up the hill in the dark, my mind was already working on it.

At the forest gate I put on my gloves again to close the padlock, once again leaving it cocked at a particular angle, so when I returned I would see if anyone else had been through.

In bed that night we were still lying entwined, with Tracy's back towards me, when she said, 'Geordie, what are you doing?'

I was half asleep, and muttered, 'What?'

'Out there, with that gun.'

'What gun?'

'The pistol. I found it under that pile of clothes.'

'Oh, that. I need it for self-protection. That's all.'

She went quiet for a minute, then said, 'You're going after someone, aren't you?'

I tried to keep myself relaxed. If I let myself tense up, she'd be bound to feel it. I was in a real spot. If I tried to bluff it out, she'd know I was lying – she had a tremendous sense for that. And if I did start telling lies, I'd undermine our relationship right at the beginning.

'Don't worry,' I said. 'It'll be all right.'

'It's the person who killed Kath, isn't it?'

'Trace!' Now I did tense and pull away from her. 'How the hell did you know that?'

'I guessed it. I've had the whole afternoon to think about it. I reckoned, Either he's on leave, or he isn't. He can't be half-working. I know you lot don't work alone. It's always in pairs, isn't it?'

I nodded. My forehead was still against the back of her head, and, although she couldn't see me she could feel the movement.

'Well? You're trying to kill him?'

I nodded again.

'Why?'

'He killed Kath. That's why.'

'I don't suppose he meant to.'

'He sent the bomber to kill *some*body. He's killed plenty of others, too. He's a murdering bastard.'

'An eye for an eye.'

'That's right.'

'Why not just leave him?'

151

'Trace, this is nothing to do with you.'

'Of course it is!' She suddenly turned over to face me and said angrily, 'If we're going together, I'm part of everything you do.'

I wanted to tell her gently that she couldn't be, that my profession made any such arrangement impossible. But I sidestepped, and said I'd reconsider things when we were fresh in the morning.

'The trouble with you,' she said, 'is that you're a loner. You know that, don't you? You're always wanting to do things on your own.'

Next day, Tuesday, the weather gave me a breathing space. A westerly gale brought in tremendous rainstorms, which continued on and off until dark, and made it no sort of a day for lying out in the open. After lunch we went for a drive up the coast and walked along part of the Giant's Causeway. Tim loved the amazing formations of rock, like chopped-off pillars, and jumped tirelessly from one to another until another storm drove us back into the car. I suspected Tracy thought she'd won the argument – although I hadn't made any definite promise to lay off, I didn't seem to be taking any further action.

In fact my mind was working full-time on the problem of how to get in close on Ballyconvil farmhouse. Wire-cutters would see to the perimeter fence all right, and if I came along the back of the house, between the grass bank and the building, I could position myself at the corner, only two or three metres from where Farrell had got out of the Merc. But what about the ruddy dog? If I bought a pound of steak, or liver, and doctored it up, there was little doubt that the Rotty would wolf it down. But if I put the dog under before Farrell returned home, he would immediately notice something was wrong if the beast didn't run out to greet him. Worse still, it might freak out in front of the house, where he'd be bound to see it. And what if he arrived back with a couple of other guys, as he had before? Would I have to take them out as well to make my getaway?

When Wednesday dawned fine, I decided I would have to have another go. Tracy was upset, of course, and we had our first real row; but I limited the damage by promising that I was only going on another recce – which was true up to a point. I needed to check Farrell's movements at least once more before committing myself.

This time I started later, and didn't reach the forestry gates until 1600. I took a careful look at the padlock, decided it hadn't moved since my last visit, drove through and up to the same parking place. Once again I saw nobody on my way to the OP, and I was there in time to watch the old peasant-lady going about her evening business. The dog was loose as before; it followed her about, and from the pattern of their movements I reckoned she fed it at the same place, out of my sight. That could be a problem: after its meal, it would be less hungry.

With the clear sky, the light was hanging on for a few extra minutes, and full dark didn't come down until after five. By then the wind had turned to the north, straight in my face, and I reckoned it was safe to move down to a position only fifty metres above the wire. There I lay down behind a solitary gorse bush, studying the farmyard with the kite-sight. The dog must have laid up somewhere, because I couldn't see it, and in the hour that followed I had nothing to do but think. In particular I thought about the amazing contrast between being cocooned in the light and warmth of the family one minute, and lying alone on a cold, black hill the next, trying to fight the forces of darkness single-handed. Maybe Tracy was right? Maybe I was a loner?

The Merc came up the drive at almost exactly the same time as before, just after six. Was this another delivery of weapons or whatever? Once again the dog raced out to meet the car and danced attendance as it moved up to the front door, but this time only two people got out: Farrell and a woman. Through my binoculars she looked young and smartly dressed, in a pale jacket and skirt and carrying a handbag that must have been made of patent leather, because it flashed in the security lights. This time I got a good sight of

153

him, too. He'd put on weight since those photographs; I could see it about the jowls. There was his limp again, too – a small dip on the left foot – but still he moved quite sharply. I watched him unlock the door and hold it open for his companion. Then the house came to life as the interior lights went on one by one and the security lamps were doused.

'You think you're safe in there,' I said quietly. I held in an imaginary pressel-switch and said, 'Tango One, target complete in house. Permission to proceed. Over.' Then I told myself to stop pissing about, and set off for the car.

I was back at the cottage by eight o'clock. Tim was already asleep, and a good smell of supper filled the air. I sat down at the kitchen table, preparing to relax, but Tracy pulled me up sharp. 'A man called to see you,' she said.

'Jesus! What sort of a man?'

'I dunno. About your age. Quite scruffy.'

'Irish?'

'Yes, of course.'

'What did he want?'

'He said, were you the man who's mad after the fishing?' She put on an Ulster accent, rather well.

'Oh – right. It was that guy from the pub, then.' I remembered I'd talked to a man in the Spanish Galleon about the possibility of going out in one of the local boats – but I hadn't made any arrangement.

'He was wearing earrings,' Tracy said.

'Not my fellow, then. Someone else.'

'Don't look so worried.'

'Listen!' I stood up. 'We've got to get out of here.'

'What – now?'

'Yes, right away.'

'Why? You keep telling me this is a safe area.'

'Yes, but now the bastards have found me.'

'Oh, Geordie – come on! Your imagination's running away from you. The man was friendly enough. Relax. Sit down and have a drink.'

I sat down again, and took a sip from the glass of red wine

154

she'd poured for me. But I wasn't feeling relaxed in the slightest.

'What did he say?'

'He asked how long we were staying.'

'What did you tell him?'

'To the end of the week.'

'Then what?'

'He said he'd call back tomorrow.'

'Hell!'

The inquiry could have been genuine, but the conversation in the pub had been so casual it didn't seem likely. Or was Tracy right? Was I becoming the victim of my own fantasies, seeing enemies everywhere?

Once you're in that state of mind, getting out of it is very difficult, and I couldn't shake it off. I did settle enough to decide we'd stay in the cottage that night, but first I took two of the wooden chairs from the kitchen and jammed one at an angle under the handle of the front door, the other at the back. I also dug the Luger out of my day-sack and kept it handy, wherever I was. Tracy thought I was overreacting, I know, but she saw how serious I was, and didn't say much.

After supper I said, 'Look – I've got a plan. You don't have to go along with it. It's up to you.'

'Go on, then.'

'They've seen me here. They've seen you with me. Someone has. Therefore, the quicker we get you back to England, the better. In the morning we'll pull out of here, back to Belfast, and I'll put you on the plane.'

She reached across the corner of the table and put her hand over mine. Her eyes were swimming.

'I'm sorry, love.' I said, 'But that's the safest.'

Still she looked at me.

'There's something else,' I went on. 'I think you should take Tim with you. If you will.'

That was too much. She burst into tears, head down on the table. I held on tightly to her hand.

'Don't cry. As I said, you don't have to.'

'No, no!' she said fiercely, sitting bolt upright. 'It isn't that.

It's the opposite. I want to have Tim with me. But I want you too. I want all of us to be together, somewhere safe.'

The night passed without incident, but in the morning I inspected the car with the utmost care, checking the wheels for any sign of a trigger device, and lying flat on my back in the road to wriggle underneath and scan for booby traps. When I found nothing, I wondered again whether I wasn't creating a drama about nothing.

We closed down the cottage and handed the key back to the neighbour, making up some excuse for leaving early. Then, from a call-box in the next village, I phoned my in-laws to warn them that we were on our way back. I didn't try to explain that Tracy was going to take Tim to England with her – better to leave that one until we could talk it through in person. Over the phone, our decision might have sounded like an insult – as though we didn't trust Meg to look after the boy properly.

As soon as we knew we'd got tickets on the afternoon plane, Tracy packed up Tim's kit and stuck it out in the hall. Then we all had a cheerful lunch, with everybody in good spirits. Far from there being any tears, Tim was thrilled by the prospect of another flight, and of going back to Keeper's Cottage. Looking at him, and thinking how like Kath he was becoming, I reckoned he had inherited something of her steady nature: as long as people were kind to him, he didn't seem to mind who he was with. And of course Tracy had been wonderful with him from the start. It may have been wishful thinking, but I honestly felt that he was already seeing her as his mother.

With only three days of leave left, it was hardly worth my going to England. On my way to the airport I promised not to go chasing after personal enemies any more. From now on, I said, I'd just keep my head down.

It was two-thirty when we reached the terminal, for the three-fifteen flight. I helped them check in, and waved good-bye as they disappeared into the security area, with promises I'd phone that evening to make sure they were safe home.

156

As soon as they had gone, I hustled back to the short-term car-park. I'm afraid I'd told Tracy that I was going to turn the hire-car in and get one of the guys in the troop to come out and lift me back to camp. In fact I never went near the car-hire office. I drove the red Datsun out of the airport and headed straight for Ballyconvil.

NINE

I reached the forestry gate without incident. This was later than either of my previous visits, and by the time I'd parked the car in its usual spot dusk had thickened among the trees which didn't worry me – if Farrell ran true to form, he wouldn't be home for at least another hour and a half. On the way over I'd bought a big steak from a village supermarket and stopped in a lay-by to doctor it. I slit it open to form a sandwich and gave it a good filling of barbiturate powder.

I'd decided the best option was to wait for full darkness, then cut through the wire on the bank behind the house. Once into the compound, I'd lie up by the back corner of the building, within four or five yards of where the Merc should come to rest. If the wind direction made it possible, I'd leave the dog alone. If he detected my presence I'd have to throw him the meat. When I fired the shots to drop Farrell, the dog might come for me, but if necessary I could drop him too.

I just hoped that the boss didn't come back with a whole troop of admirers. The snag about the Luger was that I only had a single magazine, holding eight rounds. Once I'd fired them, it would take maybe twenty seconds to reload. If Farrell had that bird with him it would be tough on her, but that was just too bad. With the shooting over, I'd be back through the fence and away.

If the dog came for me at that point, I could still try the meat – and if he ignored it I could whack him with a bullet.

All this was going through my head as I locked up the car and did a mental check: pistol, spare rounds, knife, torch, binoculars, wire-cutters, meat. With everything either about my person or in my day-sack, there was no reason to wait any longer. But at the last moment I realized I was shivering with excitement or anticipation, or both. I said to myself, 'Chill out.'

Taking a deep breath, I set off along the forest track between the high, dark trees. The wind was light and in my face; as far as I could tell from this distance, that meant it should be blowing from the house to the hill. That was good.

I was nearly at the forestry fence before I sensed something wrong. Suddenly I got a strong feeling I wasn't alone. I stopped. I hadn't heard or seen anything, but a message had reached me somehow. I stood still, the blood pounding in my ears. Sniffing the air, I smelt nothing except the clean breath of the spruce. My normal senses produced no evidence of trouble, but my sixth sense was saying 'Look out!' loud and clear.

I took one step closer to the edge of the ride and again stood still, invisible in the blackness, waiting to see if anything moved. The wind stirred faintly through the tops of the spruce, but that was the only sound. What the hell was wrong? Normally I never get spooked. I regard the night as a friend, not as a foe or anything to be frightened of. But here something was definitely amiss.

I gave it a couple of minutes, struggling to get hold of myself. I could pull out, obviously – but that would be pitsville, an almighty waste. All day, all week, I'd been psyching myself up to get the job over and done with, and this was my best chance. I knew that if I quit now, I'd never forgive myself.

Gradually, as I stood there, I got the feeling that there was somebody ahead of me on the ride, between me and the forest boundary. Again I had no physical evidence, just the feeling. Then I thought that maybe it was a poacher. There were probably fallow deer in the wood, and some local could easily be after them. He might have seen my car come up, and be waiting for the coast to clear. Well, if we did have a clash, it needn't be anything serious.

Time was passing. I couldn't hang about much longer, or Farrell would be back and safely inside before I reached my firing position. Nor could I see much future in trying to work round to my objective some other way. I hadn't checked out the other tracks inside the forest, and if I started trying to work them out now, I might easily finish up getting lost.

159

I gave a shudder, half involuntary, half deliberate, as if a good shake would throw off my doubts. Then I went forward.

Fifty yards farther on, I knew too late that my instinct had been right. All at once there *was* somebody on the track ahead – and not one person, but two. Two dark figures, blacker than the night. For a split second I still thought they might be poachers. Then, from the way they came at me, I knew they couldn't be.

I turned back and started to run, only to see a torch flash on ahead of me. I'd been followed as well. Cut off. There was only one way to go: sideways, downhill, straight into the trees. I dived to my right, aiming to plunge under the lowest branches and slither or crawl down the smooth carpet of needles on the ground. But it didn't work. Immediately a branch snagged on my day-sack. Another jabbed into my left temple, ripping my skin. Behind me I heard the bark of a big, heavy dog.

I found myself in a bit of a clearing. Two more dark figures loomed in front of me. I lowered my head, charged forward and nutted the left-hand one properly, dropping him in his tracks. The second took a dive at my legs and brought me down. I kneed him in the crotch and hit out with my left fist, struggling to get at the Luger with my right hand. Then a heavy animal came crashing through the trees and a second later jaws closed on my right ankle.

Suddenly there were men all round me, hammering at me with sticks. I tried to shield my head, but took some damaging blows about the neck. My shoulders and kidneys got a battering, and I couldn't get up because of the dog. I started to feel sick. Then a torch blazed down into my face and a voice said, 'OK, come on out of it!' I tried to get up and run, but somebody else crashed into me from the side, knocking me back to the ground. Next second I was face-down in the pine needles with a knee in my back and another guy sitting on my head.

For a few horrible moments I was shitting myself. I thought I'd been grabbed by the PIRA. In the gleams of torchlight I saw that my attackers were dressed darkly and wearing ski-masks. Fucking hell, I thought, Farrell's got wind of my movements. I really thought I was going down.

Then I realized that the voices I could hear were relatively cultured. Somebody dragged my arms back and snapped a pair of cuffs round my wrists. The guy who'd sat on my head stood up and said, 'On your feet!' The dog had let go of me, but it was still jumping around. Then someone tied a cord to my wrists, and two of them hustled me back through the stiff lower branches of the trees to the open ride.

By then a whole load of torches were bobbing about. There seemed to be guys everywhere. When I moved my feet a couple of inches, one of them snapped, 'If you don't want a big clog stuck on yer, stand still.'

The next thing was a body search, expertly carried out. Two men shone torches in my face while a third ran his hands over me. He soon found the Luger and my sheath-knife; of course my day-sack wouldn't slip off with my hands locked together, so he had to undo its straps.

Then a different man came up in front of me – some sort of boss, I guessed – and said, 'What the hell d'you think you're doing up here?'

From the odd glint of metal about his shoulders I got the impression that this figure was in uniform. But, not knowing who he was, I reckoned it best to keep quiet. Then, behind him, I saw something white, and a second later two fellows dragged a big bag down over my head. At the top end was a hood with an elasticated drawstring, which settled tight round my face, leaving my vision clear. The bottom end was pulled in close round my knees, with my arms and hands inside. I felt humiliated to be trussed and bundled like that, but it gave me a clue about the identity of my captors. Those white bags are what the RUC use to cocoon prisoners, so that traces of explosives or gunpowder or blood or any other tell-tale substance aren't rubbed or washed off on the way to the station. I'd been lifted not by the PIRA, but by some arm of the security forces, probably HMSU, the Headquarters Mobile Support Unit, the RUC's equivalent of the SAS.

'Look,' I said to nobody in particular. 'I don't know who you guys are, but I'm SAS.'

161

'SAS?' said an Ulster voice incredulously. 'With a fucking Luger? Bollocks. Think of something better – and get moving.'

A shove in the back started me off along the ride towards where I'd left the car. A man with a torch lit the way, but on the uneven track, and with my hands behind me, it was difficult to balance, and I kept stumbling. Ahead, I saw headlights sweeping up the hard road, and by the time we reached the turning-place several vehicles had assembled, the gargle of radios burbling out of them.

At the back of a long-wheel-base Land Rover someone yanked open the door and propelled me in, telling me to lie on the floor. Two other guys climbed in and sat on the side-benches, one with his boots right in my face. The door slammed, and immediately we set off downhill.

That was one hell of a journey. I was getting my right shoulder, elbow, hip and ankle well battered on the bare steel of the floor as we went over bumps; but more agonizing was the mental torture I was suffering. In the space of a few minutes, my whole life and career had gone tits-up. That was me finished in the SAS, I felt certain – it was inevitable I'd be RTU'd. Probably that was me finished with Tracy, too. When she found I'd gone straight back on the job after promising to lay off, she might well ditch me.

Almost worse of all, that was the end of my attempt to level the score with Farrell. I couldn't imagine I'd ever get another chance. And how in hell had these people cottoned on to me? Perhaps someone had seen the Datsun going up into the forest and reported it?

I wasn't going to show weakness by asking more questions; in any case, I was sure nobody would answer if I did speak. I felt certain we were heading back into Belfast, and after half an hour I began to see orange street-lamps above us as I peered up through the back window. There was a good deal of stopping and starting at traffic-lights. Then we went slowly through three successive pairs of high mesh gates into what I guessed must be a police station.

The driver backed fast up some sort of ramp and came to

an abrupt halt. The back door was opened from outside, my two escorts scrambled out and dragged me after them. I got a quick impression of high brick walls forming a narrow cul-de-sac, before being bundled in through a door at the end.

Inside a brightly lit office an RUC sergeant was sitting at a desk.

'I'm Sergeant West,' announced one of the men holding me. 'We've arrested this man under Section Fourteen. He was found in possession of a weapon in suspicious circumstances in the forest above Ballyconvil, suspected of being a terrorist.'

'Fine,' said the custody sergeant. 'Put him in there, and get the bag off him.'

He nodded towards the first room across the corridor, which was a cell, bare but clean and smelling of disinfectant.

In there, with the door securely shut, my two attendants pulled the white bag over my head and one of them released the handcuffs. 'Right,' he said. 'Get your clothes off.'

'Wait a minute . . .'

'Get 'em off. Everything except socks and pants.' The door opened, and someone handed in a grey track suit. The sergeant who'd arrested me dropped it on to the bed, which was a raised concrete bench. 'You can put that on afterwards.'

'Look,' I snapped. 'I'm not a fucking criminal. I'm in the SAS.'

'Yes,' said the sergeant, equably enough. 'And I'm the Colonel-in-Chief of the Coldstream Guards. So just do as I say, and put your clothes in there.'

He held out a black plastic bin-liner and reluctantly I started to strip off.

I saw the sergeant staring at me. 'What happened to your face?' he asked.

'Nothing – why?'

'You've blood all down your right side, looks like a cut on your forehead.'

I put my hand up and felt a matt surface down my cheek. Until that moment I'd felt nothing. 'Oh, that. I ran into a tree.'

'Nobody hit you, then?'

'No.' I dropped my clothes into the bag and pulled on the track suit, which stank of mothballs.

The sergeant left the bag on the floor and went out saying, 'The Scene of Crimes Officer will be with you in a moment.'

I sat down on the bed feeling stunned. I knew I'd be deep in the shit with the Regiment. But all the same, my overwhelming desire was to get out of this gaol and back to the troop, among my own people, as soon as possible.

The door of the cell opened, and in came not the SOCO, but the custody sergeant holding a paste-board and a biro. 'I've given you the custody number one-oh-two,' he said. 'What's your name?'

'Sharp. Geordie Sharp. Sergeant in 22nd SAS.'

He gave me a hard look and said, 'Are you suffering from any illness?'

'No.'

'Do you need any medication?'

'No.'

'Are you injured in any way?'

'Only this cut.' I pointed at my head. 'And I got a load of bruises. And a bite in the ankle from a dog. But I don't think it's serious.'

'Do you want anyone informed of your arrest?'

'Yes, I do.' I gave him the name and number of Tom Dawson, the sergeant major, troop second-in-command, and asked if I could speak to him.

'No,' was the answer. 'I'll speak to him myself.'

The custody sergeant went out, and the cell door clanged shut again. Next man in was the SOCO, a thin, lugubrious-looking fellow with a ferrety face, carrying a white tray with instruments on it.

'I need to take some samples,' he said.

'What for?'

'It's routine.'

'Bloody hell!'

'Nothing to worry about. Hold out your hands, one at a time.'

164

Like a robot, I did as I was told, watching with a mixture of fascination and revulsion as he wiped swabs of cotton wool carefully over my fingers and palms, then used a flat-ended gouge to dig out minute scrapings of dirt from under my fingernails. Finally he took a pair of scissors and cut some hair from my forelock, which was short enough anyway.

As he worked, I felt myself getting more and more steamed up. In the end I came out with, 'This is bloody ridiculous! I haven't done anything.'

'I've heard that before,' said the SOCO mildly. 'None of them has ever done anything. They're all as innocent as lambs, so they are.'

Just as he was finishing, the custody sergeant reappeared and said, 'Right, you're wanted for questioning.'

He took me across the corridor into an interview room, where a table was set out with one chair on the far side of it and several in front. We sat down briefly, waiting for someone. I'd already decided to say as little as possible until one of my own people turned up; but suddenly an idea occurred to me.

'What station is this?' I asked.

'I'm not allowed to tell you.'

'Does Chief Superintendent Morrison work here?'

'Morrison?' The sergeant was obviously surprised that I knew the name. I'd scored a point. But he said, 'No. Not here.'

'Well, can you get a message to him? Tell him I'm here?'

The sergeant looked at his watch. 'He's probably off duty now. It's after eight.'

'How about calling him at home, then?'

'I don't think he'd welcome being disturbed. He's probably at his tea.'

'At least he could authenticate who I am . . .'

The door opened, and in came a chief superintendent, a small, neat, sandy-haired man, who sat down on the far side of the table and said, 'Now, I need to ask you a few questions.'

He was quietly spoken and courteous, but I knew that every word I said was being recorded, so I said as few as possible. I tried to give away nothing beyond my name, rank and number, and kept repeating that I was a member of the SAS. But when the chief asked, 'Are you saying that you were taking part in some official operation?' I had to answer, 'No.'

'What *were* you doing, then?'

'I can't say.'

'Where did you get the Luger?'

'Pass.'

'It's not one of your unit's normal weapons.'

'No.'

All the time my mind was in the warehouse, in the ops room. I kept thinking of the consternation that news of my arrest must be causing, the acute embarrassment at having one of the guys go off his trolley. I hoped to hell that someone was already on his way across to rescue me. Further, I hoped it would be Tom, rather than Peter Ailles, the troop boss, whom I hardly knew. That wasn't his fault; it was just that he spent so much time at TCG, liaising, that the guys in the troop saw very little of him.

After a while the chief ran out of questions, so I asked a couple myself.

'What's happened to the hire-car?'

'Don't worry. It'll be taken care of.'

'The keys were in the pocket of my windproof.'

'Yes. We found them.'

'Have you informed my people that I'm here?'

He picked up a telephone and spoke briefly. 'Yes,' he said, 'they know. There's someone on the way over. Meanwhile, we'll get the doctor to clean up that cut. When did you last have anything to eat?'

I stared at him. Was he offering me food? What was this place? A fucking hotel with cells? I had to think back. Of course – we'd had lunch with my in-laws. 'About one o'clock.'

'Do you want something now?'

I shook my head. I couldn't have eaten a thing. 'No, thanks.'

The custody sergeant took me along to the medical room, where a doctor cleaned the rip on my temple, declared that it

166

didn't need stitching, sprayed it with disinfectant, and put a dressing over it. He also took a look at the puncture-marks on my ankle and gave them similar treatment.

'I don't think you'll get rabies,' he said, 'but you'd better have an anti-tet.' When he saw the bruises on my shoulders he said, 'You may be glad to know that you've got one broken police nose to your credit.'

Back in the cell, I sat on the bed with my mind spinning. There was no way I could start telling lies within the Regiment. The only thing to do would be to admit the truth. But, Jesus – the humiliation of it! Not only had I broken all the rules and tried to take out a target on my own, but I'd failed to carry out the operation efficiently. I'd failed to recce the ground properly, failed to notice that I was under surveillance, failed in everything.

The minutes crawled past, and I felt sick with remorse. Nine o'clock. Tracy would be home by now. Suddenly I wanted contact with her. I'd promised to call.

I pressed the button beside the door, to sound the buzzer. Presently the hatch opened and a face appeared outside the grille.

'Is it possible to make a telephone call?'

'Afraid not.'

'Can you make a call on my behalf?'

'Only to inform someone that you're in custody.'

Bloody hell! That was the last thing I wanted her to hear. So I said, 'Forget it, then,' and tried to settle down.

At last, about 9.30, there was a stir out in the corridor, and I heard several pairs of boots on the floor. The door of the cell swung open, and my heart jumped. There was Tom, a bit haggard and drawn, but big and reassuring all the same. I could have embraced the old bugger, I was so glad to see him.

'Is this him?' asked the custody sergeant.

'It is.'

'D'you want to have a word with him?'

'Sure.'

They ushered Tom into the cell and closed the door. For a

167

few seconds he stood looking at me as if I was a ghost. Then he said, 'For fuck's sake, Geordie, what's this about?'

I glanced round the shiny yellow walls. 'Tom, I can't talk in here. I'm sure the place is bugged. For Christ's sake get me out.'

'Yes, but what the bloody hell have you been doing? You've dropped a king-sized bollock, I can tell you. The shit's hit the fan in a big way. You're a fucking disgrace to the Regiment.'

That was the nearest I'd ever heard Tom come to shouting. Then he calmed down a bit and said, 'Don't worry. We're going. You're not under arrest. But what the hell have you done?'

'Nothing. I haven't killed anybody. I haven't threatened anybody. I haven't damaged any property. Nothing.'

'What's the problem, then?'

'I'll tell you when we get out of here. There's one thing, though.'

'What's that?'

'The bastards here have entered me in their records. I saw them doing it. We'll need to get the entry erased.'

'Don't worry. That's in hand. This has gone right to the head-shed in Hereford.'

'Already?'

'Yep. They're closing everything down in double time. If any mention of it gets out, you'll really be in it. Meanwhile, I've got to take responsibility for you. Let's get you out of those fucking pyjamas, for a start.'

Tom banged on the door until someone opened it, then called for my kit to be returned. While I was dressing he went out to deal with the chief superintendent. I don't know what arrangement he made, but somehow he got things well enough squared away to take me with him. The hire-car was still on my mind; I felt in the pocket of my windproof, and found that the keys had gone. I had visions of the Datsun sitting in the wood for weeks, and a phenomenal bill from the hire company winging in my direction. But when I mentioned the problem to the custody sergeant, he said the same thing as before: the car had been dealt with.

Tom had brought two vehicles, for mutual back-up, but as I rode back across the city in his company we couldn't talk, because the driver was from the pool and possibly insecure. Only when we reached the ops room was it possible to open up.

By then it was eleven o'clock. The boss had come in, or stayed up, specially to see me. He sat at a desk, with me in front of him and Tom beside me, together with a clerk to take notes and work the tape recorder. I was relieved to find the atmosphere reasonably sympathetic; everybody was puzzled and worried, but not too hostile.

'You look knackered, Geordie,' the boss began. 'Have you had anything to eat?'

'Not since lunch.'

'What about a cup of tea?'

'Great.'

'And a sandwich? Yes.' He called through the open door, 'Get us a sandwich and a cup of tea, will you?'

As somebody went off to the canteen, he said, 'By rights I should be sending you down to Lisburn, but there's something big on there and they can't deal with you. I can't deal with you either, but I've been told to take down a preliminary statement. So – what happened?'

I told them everything – that I'd found out that Farrell was behind the bomb that killed Kath, and that I'd tracked him down and stalked him. When the boss asked how I'd got my information, I just said, 'From the RUC.' Then Tom asked where the Luger had come from, and I had to admit that I'd nicked it after the car hit. Everything I said seemed to sound flat and ordinary. There was nothing impressive about my performance, and I finished up lamely by saying, 'I suppose I got a bit obsessed.'

'You can say that again.' Tom scratched his grizzled head. 'You went off your bloody rocker.'

Somebody brought the sandwich and mug of tea, and I got them down me. I felt curiously calm, as if everything was now over and done with. I said, 'Can I ask something?'

'Go ahead.'

'How was it I got lifted?'

The boss gave a wry smile. 'I checked with the Det, and it appears you weren't the only person chasing that target. People have been watching him for a couple of months. You're right that he's one of the leading players, and now he's getting into drugs. Apparently our little plans are maturing nicely – so the last thing they wanted was to have Farrell topped just as he was about to lead them on to something hot. When you came on the scene, they weren't very pleased.'

I sat silent as this information sank in, remembering how, on my first CTR, Farrell and his two companions had staggered from the Mercedes to the barn with those heavy cases. I thought, Should I mention that now? Then I decided not to, as I didn't want to start being cross-examined by RUC agents. The boss jolted me back to the present by saying, 'Well, I don't know what's going to happen. All I can say is that you're off back to Hereford first thing in the morning.'

I looked at Tom, as if to question the ruling, but he only said, 'That's you finished in Northern Ireland, right enough. You'd better shift your arse and get packed, because the chopper's coming in at nine o'clock.'

It felt extraordinary to be back in camp so suddenly, so far ahead of expectations. People I knew were surprised to see me, and asked what was up. I took refuge in simple evasions – 'Just back for a few days,' and so on. In theory I could have been on leave, as guys from the troop got a week's leave every month. But if I was on leave, why was I hanging around the Lines?

By the end of my first day back I'd had bollockings aplenty. But on the whole the mood was sombre rather than angry; there was no screaming and shouting, more puzzlement. When I went in on CO's orders, I was sat down and told how stupid I'd been. 'Surely you realize by now that we do things in small teams,' the colonel said. 'That's the whole basis of the Regiment.' He had very clear, pale blue eyes that penetrated like lasers, and now I was getting the full glare.

'What we do not do is bugger off and try to carry out idiotic missions on our own. For all you knew – for all the checking you'd done – we could have been running an operation of our own against Farrell. You could have ended up shooting some of your own mates, or vice versa. It's bad enough to have fallen foul of the HMSU. It makes us look a load of pricks. An own-goal would have been that much worse.'

I nodded. There was nothing I could say.

The CO leafed through some papers on his desk. 'The pity of it is, you were doing very well until then. I've got some positive reports here. You were making an excellent comeback after your various problems. Now you've gone and blown it.'

He put his thumbs to his cheekbones and his fingers to his temples, staring down at the desk-top as though his head was aching. 'If I RTU'd you, you wouldn't have a leg to stand on. Would you?'

I shook my head.

'By rights, you should be RTU'd. If a thing like this got out it could do tremendous damage to the Regiment. But in view of what you went through in the Gulf, and losing your wife, we're prepared to give you another chance. At the same time, to show I'm not condoning what you did, I'm putting you on a three months' warning. As you know, any slip-ups during that period, and you'll be out.

'Also, I'm going to fine you heavily. I've discussed your case with the Director in London, and he's instructed me to fine you £2,500. I've got no alternative. Is there anything you want to say?'

Again I shook my head. The fine was fearsome – a whole month's pay, which I knew would be stopped at source. That month, there'd simply be nothing coming into my account.

'You're to take a week off, while things settle down,' the CO was saying. 'You live out, don't you? Well, keep out of camp for that time. The most important thing is that nobody else should know what has happened. If you have to say anything, say there was a personality clash, as a result of which you had to come home. If what you did leaks out, that'll constitute an offence under your three months' warning. Understood?'

171

'Fair enough.'

'Don't forget: the bottom line is that you've got to pull yourself together properly. From now on you're really going to be watched. If you want to survive, you'll have to get your finger out.'

By the time all that was over, it was early afternoon. I reckoned Tracy would already be back at Keeper's Cottage, so I phoned her there. She was amazed to hear that I was in Hereford. 'What's happened?' she asked. 'Come over for a day?'

'For good,' I said. 'Things have changed a bit. I'll tell you when I see you. I'm heading out now.'

'Why didn't you phone last night?'

'I couldn't. Tell you in a minute.'

It seemed incredible that I'd said goodbye to her at Belfast City Airport less than twenty-four hours earlier. Half my life seemed to have gone by since then.

I was going to call for a taxi. Then I thought about my fine and changed my mind. After a while I managed to press one of the cooks into making a diversion on his way home and giving me a lift. I even made him stop at a flower shop while I ran in. There I had to curb my natural extravagance again, and forgo the big bouquet that I fancied most. Hounded by the thought of my empty bank balance, I settled for six red roses.

The first thing Tracy said to me was, 'You went back after him, didn't you?'

'Yes.'

'And you got lifted.'

'How on earth d'you know that?'

'It's written all over your face.'

'It'd better not be. I've been sworn to silence about what happened.'

'You can tell me, anyway.'

I told her. The hardest thing was to admit that I'd deliberately deceived her about my intentions, that I'd been planning to go back on the attack even before she and Tim had left. Although I didn't say it, I felt it was nearly as bad as if I'd

172

gone off and screwed some other woman the second she was out of my sight. All I could do was apologize, and promise that that was the end of deception between us.

Tracy was fantastically forgiving – even if there was a touch of the schoolmarm in her when she said, 'Well, that'll teach you to mess about.' Then she took me to see Tim, who was playing in the sitting room. 'Look!' she called out cheerfully. 'Here's your dad come home. Isn't that lovely!'

TEN

All through the next week I was way up and way down. Part of the time I felt incredible relief at being clear of Northern Ireland, at having escaped from that cesspool of hatred and fear. It felt great to be away from the dark, horrible, underhand warfare practised by the scumbags of the PIRA.

At other times I was desolate at having let my mates down. I kept thinking of Pat, stuck over the water for another nine months, and Mike, no longer pink or punk, but still bearing the scars of Farrell's Rotty on his right shoulder.

The fact that the head-shed had been lenient with me didn't lessen my feeling of shame and degradation. Privately, I reckoned the mainspring of their attitude was fear that, if they did get rid of me, I would start mouthing off about the Regiment to outsiders. They'd calculated that it would be safer all round to keep me where I was.

The last thing I wanted was to go back to my parent unit, the Parachute Regiment. For a couple of days I seriously considered leaving the army altogether, and to test the water about civilian jobs I phoned two guys who'd got out the year before. Neither was particularly encouraging. Both had gone into forms of BG work – bodyguarding – but both said that, although the jobs were well paid, they were also boring as hell.

One was retained by an Arab sheikh, and although he spent most of his time twiddling his thumbs, he had to be prepared to take off for any corner of the globe the instant the phone rang. The other had signed up with a crazy Dutch family of millionaires who lived in mortal fear of having their two boys kidnapped. Father and mother were both nutty as fruitcakes, constantly feuding with each other, but it sounded as if the kids needed a shrink even worse than the parents. They refused to do what they were told, couldn't sleep in the dark, ate junk food at all hours of the day and night, and did nothing but lie around watching videos, the more violent the better. The idea of working for people like that turned me right off, and as I had no other ideas about what I could do, I decided I'd better stay put.

More than that, I realized how much the Regiment meant to me – how hard it had been to get in, how much I had put into the years of training, how much I'd lose if I left. Before I'd gone off the rails my prospects had been excellent – and now I became determined to do my best for myself, as well as repay the trust the Regiment had put in me. That meant ditching all thoughts of becoming a rogue warrior and consigning my idea of revenge to the past. Besides, what would I achieve if I did drop Farrell? I'd have a murder on my hands – and it wouldn't bring Kath back.

Two people in particular made me determined to soldier on. One was Tracy, who was emerging as more and more of a star with every day that passed. On the surface she carried on as if nothing had happened – going in to work at the Med Centre, taking Tim to the camp playschool, cooking for us in the evening – but underneath the surface she was giving me phenomenal moral support. I know it sounds stupid, but I was amazed that someone of such slender physique and sunny personality could have such resources of strength inside her. It made me feel humble, first that I had made such a boob myself, and second that I had underrated her.

My other saviour was Tony. As I'd predicted, he had sailed through selection, and was now a fully-fledged member of D Squadron. He immediately heard on the grapevine that I'd come back, and blew into the cottage for coffee on Sunday morning. There was no way I could conceal what had happened from him, so we went for a hike through the woods around one of my jogging circuits, and I told him the story.

His reaction was positive, to say the least. Far from criticizing what I'd done, he lamented the fact that I hadn't quite succeeded. 'Maybe I could go get him for you,' he suggested, when I described the layout of the forest, the OP in the gorse, the perimeter fence and the house. 'Now we know exactly where he is, maybe I should line up a deer-hunting trip over there. You said there are deer in those woods? OK. I get a hunting permit and go over. Then I have the right weapon to take him out from up the hill, without going near the house. What about that?'

But we agreed to let the idea of a hunting trip ride, meanwhile, and we resorted to the age-old SAS formula for sorting out personal troubles: we drove out to Talybont, parked in the lay-by, and tabbed it as hard as we could to the summit of Pen-y-Fan. No matter that it was a miserable day, with rainstorms sweeping across the bare mountains; the physical challenge and the grandeur of the hills wrought their usual magic, and I came home with my confidence at least partially restored. Of course I would carry on with the Regiment.

On the Monday morning when I went back to work, things took a turn for the better. At Morning Prayers in the Squadron Interest Room the sergeant major asked me to see him in his office immediately afterwards, and when I went in there he said, 'Geordie, I'm glad to say you're in luck. You don't fucking deserve it, but there's a slot come up for you. Geoff Hunt, who's been on the SP team, fell off a pissy little wall on Friday and broke his ankle. That means we need a guy to take his place. You're a trained assaulter, so in you go.'

'Fine,' I replied. 'How long will it be for?'

'There's six weeks of the squadron's tour left. After that, we'll find you something else.'

'Great!'

My enthusiasm wasn't just for show. I'd been dreading the possibility that they were going to make me ops sergeant – the worst job around, as it amounted to sitting on your backside in the ops room and being little more than tea-boy for the head-shed, with endless paperwork. I was genuinely glad to go back into the Special Projects (or Counter-Terrorist) Team for a spell. I'd already done one tour with them and enjoyed it, so it was no trouble to slip back into harness.

The task of the unit was to respond instantaneously to any

terrorist attack, such as the hijack of an aircraft or seizure of a building. Of the two teams, Red and Blue, one was always at thirty minutes' readiness, with vehicles loaded, ready to roll, and the other at three hours. In fact the first team was often capable of taking off within ten minutes of an alert.

Life on the SP team could be quite exciting. If a call-out came, you could never be sure whether it was an exercise or a genuine emergency. One of the Regiment's greatest ever hits – the siege at the Iranian Embassy in London in 1980 – began with just such uncertainty. On the morning of 30 May, a former member of the Regiment, Dusty Gray, phoned the head-shed from Heathrow Airport and tipped them off that all the Metropolitan Police's terrorist dogs had suddenly been whipped away to London.

It so happened that at that moment a major exercise was getting under way. According to the scenario, there'd been a hijack attempt at an airfield in the north-east, and the SP team was about to deploy in response. Then in came this call from Dusty Gray. At first the CO thought it was someone trying to take the piss and screw up the start of the exercise by feeding him duff information, but then he decided it was for real. Before any official notification came in, he said, 'Bugger the exercise,' and deployed the SP team to a holding location on the way to London. The result was that when the media later came and camped outside the gates to watch for warriors departing, they saw fuck-all – until six days later, when every television screen in the country showed our guys abseiling down from the Embassy roof in their black kit and taking the villains out. Twelve years on from that historic event, the terrorist threat remained much the same, and the head-shed often sprang an exercise without any warning to keep the guys on their toes.

In between, we were ceaselessly training. The thirty-minute team had to stay within easy range of camp and train locally, but the rest were free to go up country and do things like practise aircraft-entry and visit prominent buildings that might become targets for terrorist take-over.

Being on the team meant that I could carry on living at

home, because my address was easily within the thirty-minute limit. At night, when the roads were clear, I could be inside the warehouse within eleven minutes. Like everyone else, I carried a bleeper wherever I went. If all the numbers appearing on its screen were one, I knew it was a practice call-out; what we wanted was all the nines – the real thing.

There were sixteen of us assaulters on the Blue Team, and for me it was a bit of a comedown to be merely one of the pack. On my earlier tour I'd been Sniper Team Commander – in effect the third in command of the whole outfit, under the boss (a captain) and a staff sergeant. But any active employment was better than being stuck behind the desk in the ops room.

We usually began our day at 0830 with an hour's fitness training. Then we'd practise abseiling, fast-roping out of helicopters, climbing glass walls with suckers, entry into rooms – all pretty physical stuff. I enjoyed the challenge of getting really fit again, and put in extra hours at the gym; in that role you need all the strength you can muster – you're forever lifting people, pulling them about or restraining them. You're also carrying a lot of extra weight – apart from the MP 5 sub-machine-gun and pistol, there's the body armour, kevlar helmet and ops waistcoat (loaded with axe, stun grenades and ammunition). For all these reasons, upper-body strength is a real asset.

The other thing we did was fire pistols. We fired pistols until we were almost out of our minds. Hundreds of rounds a day. Sometimes at Hun's Head targets on the camp's own range, sometimes in the Killing House, sometimes in the Garaback down at LATA. It would have been easy to go stale, get bored of it, but I concentrated by imagining (still) that my target was Farrell, and telling myself that somewhere, sometime, all these practice rounds would pay off.

Inevitably, our training was repetitive. We fast-roped until we could do it in our sleep. We practised entry into rooms until it was second nature. I had an advantage, coming in towards the end of the tour – I hadn't been doing these things for such a long time. I could see that some of the guys were already bored witless. They'd begun to take outrageous risks,

178

like urging the chopper pilot to go in at a higher speed when we were about to fast-rope down to the top of the building, or even dispensing with the rope altogether, jumping instead. This, apparently, was where my predecessor had come unstuck: the head-shed had been led to believe he'd hurt himself jumping off a wall, but in fact he'd been attempting an unscheduled, ropeless descent from a helicopter.

With a month of the SP tour to go, a new buzz-word suddenly started circulating: Colombia. A fastball job had come up – the squadron had been tasked to send out a team at short notice to train the president's bodyguard.

'Colombia?' said Murdo McFarlane, the redheaded Jock, in the canteen one lunchtime. 'Is that in Canada?'

'Is it bollocks,' big Johnny Ellis said. 'That's Columbia with a U, twat. This one's in South America. It's a hotbed of drugs and fucking corruption. Cocaine pours out of it like water out of the Amazon. That's why El Presidente needs so much guarding: the drug barons spend their lives trying to top the bastard.'

'How d'you know so much about it?' I asked. 'Have you been out there?'

'No, I just saw a video.'

'Spanish-speaking, I suppose?'

'*Absolutamente.*'

The gossip set me thinking. Maybe, with my good result in the Spanish course, I would be in with a chance of getting on board.

A couple more days passed, then up went a list on the Orderly Room notice board, headed 'Operation Bluebird'. The ten-man bodyguard training team, it announced, would be commanded by Captain Peter Black; second in command would be Sergeant Geordie Sharp. Specially attached as interpreter and liaison officer would be Sergeant Tony Lopez (US SEAL, now of D Squadron). The team would deploy via RAF Brize Norton on 10 March 1992 – barely three weeks away. That meant we had to start sorting ourselves out straight away.

179

On the day after the announcement I had a preliminary meeting with the Rupert. I'd seen him about the camp – a tall, slim, fair-haired fellow, only twenty-five or so – but I hadn't had any real contact with him. Rumour reported that he'd been to Eton, and that he seemed only a little the worse for the experience; certainly he'd come from the Grenadier Guards. Whatever else, he was quite a physical sort of guy, and ran like the wind; he'd played as a winger for the squadron's Rugby XV, and had scored a good few tries. Anyone who could do that and survive had my admiration, because the methods used in those matches are horrendous – real caveman stuff. But I'd been warned about him by one of the sergeants in Training Wing, who'd described him as 'a flaming idiot', able to talk his way out of anything but lacking in any soldiering skills. On the range he'd proved positively dangerous. The safest place to be when he was firing a weapon was straight in front of him. Under the stress of using live rounds his command and control went out the window. On the other hand, when giving a briefing or appreciation, he could sound quite impressive. No doubt that was why he'd passed Officers' Week on selection.

So I had severe reservations about him. My antipathy was increased by a factor of which nobody in the head-shed could possibly be aware. At a Christmas party in the officers' mess, to which civilian staff from the camp had been invited, he'd come on strong with Tracy and tried to take her back to his room. When she refused he kept on at her, not just that evening but on several later occasions as well – so much so that I almost went round and briefed him up to keep away.

The result was that, when we met formally in the Squadron OC's office, I was fairly cool.

'Geordie,' the OC said, 'have you met Peter Black? He joined the squadron while you were away. He's going to command Air Troop.'

'Hi,' I said. 'Yeah – I've seen you around.' We shook hands and sat down in front of the OC's desk.

The boss then ran through the arrangements for the forthcoming team job. I was to be in command, and Black was to act as our liaison link between the British Embassy and the Colombians, for administrative purposes.

'Peter,' he said, 'Geordie's had plenty of experience, so if you have any problems, it'll be best to consult him first.'

'I expect we'll manage,' Black replied, but I could see the OC's remark had pissed him off.

There were a few more general points to be settled, and when the boss had finished, Black and I went into the Squadron Interest Room to work out details.

He certainly had a posh accent, and his eyes were set rather too close together in his narrow face.

'What do you know about Colombia?' he asked.

'Fuck-all, to put it bluntly.'

'That makes two of us.' He grinned. 'There's a briefing laid on for tomorrow, so we'll start learning then. You've been in the Regiment more years than I have months, and you know a hell of a lot more about it. So I'm going to be leaning on you for advice.'

'Fair enough.'

'Now. When we get out there, the team's going to be based at a Colombian army camp at a place called Santa Rosa, about 250 ks south of Bogotá. You'll be there – obviously – and Tony Lopez will be helping liaise with the Colombians locally. But it looks as though I'm going to be stuck mostly in Bogotá itself, liaising with the British Embassy . . .'

He went on to ask my opinion of the other guys nominated for the team, and we assigned each one a particular lesson that he would teach: personal security, residential security, hotel security, vehicle anti-ambush drill, counter-attack team drill, movement by helicopter and so on – about twenty in all.

'What about Ellis?' he asked. 'What's his special strength?'

'Johnny Ellis? His advantage is just that: strength. He's built like a bloody gorilla; a really hard man. He's the guy for the physical training and unarmed combat. He'll sort out the Colombians, no bother. Him and Murdo.'

'Is that McFarlane?'

'Right. If Johnny's a gorilla, Murdo's a yeti. The only

difference between them is their colour. One's got fair hair, the other red.'

'Is it Murdo who plays the pipes?'

'It is, and it's a fucking disaster. You can't stop him.'

Gradually, we got everyone sorted. Other key members of the team were Stewart McQuarrie (also a Jock) and Mel Scott, both in their mid-twenties and fairly new to the Regiment. Stew was another very physical guy, strong and quick on his feet – a free-fall specialist who liked walking out on to the wings of bi-planes and dropping off. We nominated him to take charge of the close-protection training, on which he'd done a lot of work and contributed some new ideas. Mel, who came from Liverpool, was small, and rather quiet, though given to occasional lightning repartee. He was also an excellent instructor with a gift for putting things over in a clear, amusing way – and off-duty he was one of the squadron's leading piss-artists.

I myself opted for weapon and demolition training, at which I'd had a good deal of experience. All of us, of course, were primarily fighting men, trained to kill, but we looked forward to sharing some of our skills with other people. Closer acquaintance with Black didn't improve my opinion of him. Just as his face was a little ferrety, with its close-set eyes and pointed nose, so there was something of the ferret in his approach to things. He kept asking quick, sharp questions, and seemed insatiable in his quest for information. Whether or not he was going to use it sensibly was another matter. I felt I was going to have to keep a close eye on him – I hoped he wouldn't do anything stupid while he was at the embassy. Ruperts on their own, away from the guys and with a captive audience, are notorious for adopting James Bond attitudes and telling tall stories about the Regiment.

One of the most important features of team jobs overseas is discretion. The SAS quietly trains special units in countries all over the world, and our guys depend on the British embassies for liaison with foreign governments. I'd seen this in practice in Africa, when one of the lads had a car accident. Because of the good relationship between the team and the embassy, everything was quickly sorted out, and the driver escaped a dose of prison. Instead of losing a member – which would have disrupted the training programme – the team remained intact.

I think there are a lot of misconceptions about the roles of officers and men within the SAS. In most Regiments the lower ranks automatically salute an officer as a form of respect. In the SAS nobody salutes. Respect is not necessarily accorded to rank: it has to be won. This doesn't mean that the other ranks look down on the officers. Far from it – there are plenty of first-class Ruperts. Unfortunately, there are also plenty of pricks; and now it looked as though I'd been landed with one of them.

Next day, in the evening, we had a briefing on Colombia and its problems, given by an Int officer who had come down from London. He was a good, articulate speaker, and knew his stuff, but a lot of the political complications he mentioned went over our heads. Naturally our main interest centred on drugs – to be precise, on cocaine.

'Now, it's not my job to tell you fellows how to carry on,' he began, 'but I do suggest very strongly that you don't get involved in drugs of any kind. You're bound to be offered them in towns, but for God's sake don't touch them. The vendors may easily be trying to set you up; they may even be plain-clothes police.

'As I'm sure you know, pure cocaine comes in the form of fine white powder. But in Colombia there's also stuff called *basuco*, the base from which cocaine is refined. It's coarser and greyer – looks a bit like granulated sugar. Another drug to be aware of is *burundanga*, which removes your will to resist. I know it sounds ridiculous, but that's just what it does. Villains put it into food or drinks, and then, when they ask for your wallet or your car keys, you just hand them over. As *burundanga* has no taste or smell, the only way to make sure you avoid it is to keep reasonable company.'

He paused, took a drink of water, and went on: 'Fortunately, you're going to be working with, and for, DAS,

183

the secret police. They're by far the most powerful official organization in the country. Everyone else lives in fear of them – they do what they want, and they can even order the army about. They're a bit like the Gestapo in Nazi Germany, or the Savak in Iran under the Shah.

'The sheer scale of the drug problem is difficult to grasp. If I say that Colombia controls eighty per cent of the world market in cocaine, it doesn't mean much. But look at it this way: the drug barons are so rich and powerful that they have their own ocean-going ships, their own jet aircraft, their own *islands*, even, for moving their products around the world. If they want to eliminate some enemy, they don't hesitate to blow up a civilian airliner in flight and kill everybody on board. A hundred and fifty innocent people murdered – that's nothing to them, provided they get their man. On the ground, by the way, a favourite method of dealing with an opponent is to give him the Colombian neck-tie: they cut his throat, and leave him with his tongue hanging out through the slit.'

That made all the guys pay attention. This was getting interesting. It reminded me of the day at LATA when Morrison began to talk about the PIRA and its methods.

The drug business, our visitor went on, was controlled by a few regional mafias, known as cartels. During the 1980s the strongest of these had been the Medellin cartel, centred round the city of that name to the north-west of Bogotá. When the government tried to take it on, the cartel responded with a long-running campaign, during which the Minister of Justice, the publisher of the leading newspaper *El Espectador*, and the Attorney General were all assassinated.

When the president declared all-out war in 1989, government forces seized nearly a thousand buildings and ranches, more than 350 aircraft, numerous boats, over a thousand weapons and 30,000 rounds of ammunition. The cartel retaliated by downing an aircraft belonging to the national airline Avianca on a scheduled flight from Bogotá to Cali, with the loss of everyone on board. They also blew up the newspaper offices and police headquarters in the capital. Eventually a colossal man-hunt ended with the death of one of the Medellin leaders, Gonzalo Rodriguez Gacha, known as 'El Mexicano'. Subsequently most of his former colleagues gave themselves up, including the notorious Pablo Escobar.

That name rang a loud bell for me. I remembered being fascinated by a newspaper picture of a sleek young guy with thick black wavy hair and a lazy right eye, described as the richest criminal in the world.

'As usual in Colombia,' said the speaker, 'it was a colossal fix. In effect the drug barons surrendered on their own terms. They were given token sentences, and allowed to serve them in a purpose-built prison at Envigado, Escobar's home town, where they're living in luxury.

'When they were put away, the power of the Medellin cartel declined, and narco-terrorism subsided for some time. But all that happened was that the Cali cartel came up in its place, and the drug trade kept on growing. Cocaine paste continued to pour in from Peru and Bolivia. The Colombians refined it at clandestine laboratories hidden deep in the jungle, and exported pure cocaine to countries all over the world, but mainly to North America.

'In the early days, couriers called *mulas* – mules – were used to smuggle the drug out in small quantities, but now that's all gone by the board. Today, it's big time. The Cali cartel has developed a system of flying planeloads out to islands in the Caribbean, then loading ships destined for Europe.

'As I said, the scale of it defies imagination. In the mid-eighties Escobar alone was reckoned to be worth two billion dollars. The funny thing is, he grew up the happiest kid you could imagine, in a strongly religious home. But then he got expelled from school and drifted into crime – stealing tombstones, stealing cars. Before he was twenty he was into contract killing. Then he started driving coca paste from the Andes to the laboratories in Medellin. He made so much money that by the time he was thirty he'd bought a *hacienda* for over sixty million dollars.

'The irony of it is that at the height of his criminality he was seen as a great philanthropist. He built hundreds of new houses for slum-dwellers in his area, and they all thought he

185

was a saint. A very complex guy, by the sound of it: with one hand he was building hospitals for the poor, and with the other he was having whole families assassinated. One of his favourite methods of killing a man was by forcing a red-hot spike into his brain.'

He paused, looking round at our group of ten. Then he added, 'That's Colombia for you. Of course, none of this is directly relevant to your mission. You're not going to be fighting the Cali cartel or chasing Escobar. At least, I hope not.' He laughed.

'Apart from the drug cartels, there are a number of terrorist organizations battling for purely political ends. In other words, Colombia is not an easy country to govern. The president, Cesar Gaviria, has just announced an entirely new constitution, but that doesn't by any means guarantee stability. In fact, he has every need of a highly efficient bodyguard – and no doubt that's why he's called upon your Regiment for assistance.'

The next couple of weeks were pretty hectic. I was still on the SP Team, of course, and still training every day, half-expecting a call-out. In the intervals, I was working out what we needed in the way of stores and equipment, and the other guys on the team were going up to the Team Tasks' Cell in camp to sort out the materials they would need for teaching the various lessons. Videos, slides, diagrams, paperwork – everything was stored in made-up packs, stacked in pigeon-holes that stretched from floor to ceiling. We also had a talk from the MO on the various filthy diseases to which we might be exposed: yellow fever, typhus, tetanus and rabies, to say nothing of AIDS.

In the evenings there was a special refresher course in Spanish, and the teacher from Cardiff who'd helped us earlier came up a couple of times to give us a flying start. In particular, she put us right on some of the ways in which Colombian Spanish differs from the language on the mainland – for instance, that *ll* is pronounced as *y*, rather than *ly*, and that a *c* before an *i* or an *e* sounds like *s* rather than *th*.

She also produced some cracking local expressions, like *carajo* (shit), *jincho* (pissed) and *cabron* (arsehole or jerk). Of course, Tony could have told us these and a lot more, but coming from old Maria, they made a great impression. I told everybody to get stuck into their Spanish, because I knew that an important element in Operation Bluebird would be winning the hearts and minds of the Colombians. If we could communicate with them properly on a person-to-person basis, and establish good relations, the chances of their government ordering British arms and equipment some time in the future would be that much greater.

We seemed to need a mountain of kit. For our personal weapons we took MP 5 Kurtzes – the short-barrelled version of the sub-machine-gun – as well as Beretta pistols, a couple of 53s and a couple of 203s – combination weapons with an automatic rifle in the top barrel and 40mm grenade launcher below. We also loaded up a terrific amount of ammunition, because we'd heard there was a shortage out there. Also, we'd heard that the Colombian *jundis* – the ordinary soldiers – couldn't shoot for pussy, and needed a lot of training purely in weapon skills. So I signed for pallets full of ammunition boxes – 7.62 rounds for their Galil rifles, and 9mm for the MP 5s and Berettas – as well as a load of PE4 plastic explosive, and saw it all packed into steel Lacon boxes along with hundreds of targets and our personal heavy gear. If we'd known what was going to happen we'd have taken jungle kit – but as far as we could tell at that point, we were merely going to spend six or seven weeks in a reasonably civilized camp. I don't know what it was that made me pack my Magellan GPS – the hand-held global positioning system that communicates with satellites and tells you your location on the face of the earth to within a few feet. Maybe I thought I would show off the miracles of western technology to our students in the jungle.

The best feature of our preparation was that each of us got an extra payment of £3,000 in travellers' cheques. Described as an overseas allowance, it was an addition to our normal pay – a kind of bonus for going abroad. For me it came just in time, as the loss of a month's pay had left me struggling, and

I put all but £500 straight into the bank. The money also consolidated the feeling that I was back in the fold.

Several of the other guys also stashed their unexpected loot, but a couple kept all the money on them, determined to blow it in the night-spots of Bogotá and buy emeralds, which were rumoured to be incredibly cheap. They were the financially incurables. As somebody remarked, 'Giving that amount of money to fucking Johnny's like giving whisky to an Indian.' When Johnny announced that in Bogotá night clubs the girls danced on the tables and didn't wear knickers, the place was in an uproar. What with the money, the promise of a hot climate, and the language, the lads were getting a bit above themselves. As they went about the camp I could hear the most outrageous greetings: '*Buenas tardes*, Shitface. *¿Como esta?*' and 'On your *bicicleta, cabron.*'

On the day we were due to fly, Tracy took the morning off so that we could spend some time together, and we had a scene uncomfortably like the one with Kath before I went to the Gulf.

'It's only for two months,' I said, 'and there's nothing dangerous about it. All the same, we'd better know were we stand. Don't get upset, but I've changed my will.'

'So?'

'If I'm run over by a bus in Bogotá, you get everything, including the house. Except for Tim's trust fund. That stays the same.'

'That's fantastic. But, Geordie?'

'What?' I saw Tracy looking at me in a peculiar way.

'Don't do anything stupid this time. It's not fair on me and Tim.'

'Of course I won't.'

Still she was looking at me with a strange expression. 'Geordie,' she said, 'I want you to have this.' She reached into the pocket of her jeans and brought out a blue velvet box.

I took it and opened it. Inside was a little silver figure on a chain, small, but heavy and solid for its size.

'Wear it round your neck,' she said.

'Who is it?'

'St Christopher. The patron saint of travellers. He'll bring you luck. He'll bring you back safe.'

'But where did you get it?'

'I bought it, stupid!'

'You shouldn't have bothered.'

'I wanted to. Put it on.'

I slipped it over my head and gave her a kiss.

'There's something I need to tell you,' she said.

'What's that, love?'

'It's just that I seem to be pregnant.'

ELEVEN

It's an old joke in the RAF that Lockheed, manufacturers of the Hercules C 130 transport, solved the aircraft's noise problem by putting it all inside. When you hear a Herc fly over it doesn't sound too bad, and even at close quarters the scream of the four turbo-props is tolerable. Inside the back, though, it's a different matter. The high, penetrating whine bores into your head, and after seven or eight hours even earplugs and defenders can't keep it out of your brain.

That was what we had to contend with – three consecutive marathon flights of eight, eight and five hours respectively. The pull-down seats along the sides of the fuselage are impossible to sit on for more than a few minutes, so the guys slung their parachute-silk hammocks and crashed out in them, swinging along to the rhythm of the aircraft. Most RAF crews would have gone ballistic at people taking such liberties with their aircraft, but our particular crew was dedicated to special forces missions, and we knew several of them personally, so more or less anything went. It was also possible to make the odd comfortable nest among our Lacon boxes. Looking at the steel trunks, all padlocked and labelled and held down by heavy-duty netting, I reflected on the weight of the kit we were taking. The boxes of ammunition were four-man carries, and many of the others weren't much lighter.

From Brize Norton the plane lumbered across the Atlantic to Gander, in Newfoundland, where it went tits-up on the runway, so that we had to kill time while its load was transferred to another. The next hop took us to Belize, north of Panama, where it was stinking hot. Finally we flew down to a military airfield somewhere in the west of Colombia, the flight being timed so that we came in at the dead of night, when nobody would see us.

After so many hours cooped up, the lads were pissed off to find that they weren't allowed to leave the aircraft. Instead, some immigration official came on board to stamp our passports. When we heard that we had to fly on for another couple of hours to a little-used military airfield way out in the country, the pilots were even more pissed off, as they'd never seen the place before, and it had no proper runway lights. But in the end there was no problem, and we finally staggered out into the warm tropical darkness at about 0400, just in time for a shower and a nap before breakfast.

Daylight revealed that the camp was built on level ground, and that the perimeter fence enclosed a large area of maybe fifty acres. Beyond the wire, scrub had been cleared back for another hundred yards or so, and then dense secondary jungle took over. In the far distance, above the trees, we could see bare rocky mountains. The buildings were all new, made of concrete, and reasonably well finished, with mosquito screens over the windows, doors that fitted, and showers that worked. The only trouble was, the place was alive with flies, big spiders and geckos; instead of rats, as in Belfast, it was lizards, going like smoke up and down the walls, racing across the walkways and disappearing into holes among the rocks.

We spent most of day one sorting ourselves out. We went for a run round the perimeter and did a bit of phys to get the flight out of our systems. The dry season, known as the *verrano*, was coming to an end, but the weather seemed to be holding up. Early morning was relatively cool, but by eleven or so the heat had built into the high eighties, even though we were 3,000 feet above sea-level, and for us, not yet acclimatized, the temperature was quite oppressive. That didn't stop the guys lying out after lunch and sunbathing in their shreddies. They'd immediately spotted the possibility of acquiring a serious tan; I also saw the possibility of getting seriously burnt, and I let it be known that if anyone was careless enough to roast himself, he'd be seriously fined. Because we didn't want to make ourselves conspicuous by wearing any kind of uniform, we'd decided to go for shorts and T-shirts, and that in itself presented a problem, as our necks and knees were glaringly white.

Another plus was the big swimming pool, which we could use whenever we wanted. The canteen, which we shared with the Colombians, was an attractive, airy place, but at first most of the guys couldn't take the food at all. It seemed to be beans and chillis with everything, and by the end of the day most of us were racing for the bog. As everyone was expressly ordered to put used paper into a bin, rather than down the pan, the shit-house was not a place in which to sit thinking fine thoughts.

Peter Black spent that day with us to see us in, and came with me and Tony to meet his opposite number, Captain Jaime Ortiga – a smooth guy, dark and Indian-looking, with a pencil-thin moustache. He was all smiles as he ushered us into his office. The room was bare, with whitewashed walls and a single big fan turning slowly overhead. The only decoration was a colour photograph, mounted and framed, on the wall behind the boss's desk. It showed a middle-aged guy in a peaked cap with a red band, and about three hundredweight of medals on his chest.

Have a go, I thought. Break the ice. So, summoning my best accent, I asked, '¿Hay el Presidente?'

Captain Jaime looked hellishly startled. He spun round as if someone had driven a pin into his arse, saw the photo, and suddenly realized what I had said. The moustache spread out in a wide smile.

'¡Si, si! El Presidente Gaviria! ¿Hablar castellano?'

'Un poco.'

'¡Muy bien!'

That little exchange put him in high good humour, and, with Tony interpreting, he gave us a very civil welcome to the base. I was pleased to find that I could understand almost everything he said, even if I got a bit tongue-tied when trying to answer questions. I heard him ask Tony how he came to have such fluent Spanish, and Tony kept out of trouble by saying that he'd learnt it as a child.

The captain told us that the group he wanted us to train

consisted of forty-two DAS officers. Some were new to bodyguard work, but others had already been partially trained by the Americans. Suddenly he broke into English to say: 'We no like Americans. British better! British tactic better!' No doubt he meant it as a compliment. I was watching Tony's face, and saw one eyebrow go up by about two millimetres.

It was agreed that we would start training next morning. With the preliminaries settled, Black set off for Bogotá in a Land Cruiser, together with his diplomatic bag, the radio codes and so on. The drive was said to take about four hours. He told us he was going to be based in the Hostal Bonavento, a small hotel near the British Embassy in the northern quarter of the city. He reckoned he'd be spending a good deal of time at the embassy, in the office of the defence attaché, which had a direct satellite link with the UK. Since we had a portable satcom set with us, keeping in touch with him would present no problem.

Training started on day two. Startled out of their wits by Murdo McFarlane's reveille, the home team shambled out on to the barrack square at 0630, all shapes and sizes in white T-shirts with little DAS logos on them and dark-blue trousers.

We formed them up in three ranks, comprising three groups of fifteen, fifteen and twelve. At my request, Tony put over a little spiel about the requirement for physical fitness and strength in BG work, and the need to be able to heave bodies around in quick time. I could see one or two of the Colombians looking fairly sick, and when we set them running round the perimeter wire, the fatties soon fell away behind. By the time we'd given them a dose of circuit-training they looked about done-for; but after a shower and breakfast they came out spruce enough for training proper. We were hoping to pass them all out in the end, so we wanted to nurse them along.

At an early stage we explained to them that the team which eventually emerged would have two elements: the bodyguard itself, which would surround the president and give him close protection, and the counter-attack squad, which would range out ahead of him whenever he was on the move, making a show of its weapons and letting everyone know that it had real teeth. I'd expected the majority of them to prefer the second option, and I was surprised to find that most of them thought it was the BG work that was really macho. They thought they were defending God, and all wanted to be the man who saved the president's life – i.e. in the bodyguard itself. The idea of going CAT really pissed them off. At a later stage we planned to split the course into two main streams, but for the time being we tried to teach all of them a bit of everything.

They certainly needed some instruction, most of all in the use of weapons. Some were OK with their pistols, but when it came to rifles and machine-guns they were useless. I could see that they were actually scared of the weapons, and sometimes shut their eyes when they pulled the trigger. They were also excitable, and inclined to be bloody dangerous. There was one short-arsed guy considered even by his mates to be a bit cracked in the head. His name was Alejandro, but they referred to him openly as 'El Loco' – the loony – so we did the same. One day I had him firing his Galil on automatic when suddenly he gave a yell and dropped the weapon, which went on blasting off of its own accord, leaping about on the ground and sending rounds winging away into sundry parts of Colombia. Fortunately there were only half a dozen rounds left in the magazine and nobody got hurt. When I tore into him for letting go, El Loco protested that the gun wouldn't stop firing when he released the trigger – and when we stripped it down, we found that the sear had indeed broken.

To sharpen up their powers of observation, we laid out a special lane through the jungle surrounding the camp, putting down things like compasses, small pieces of map, matchboxes and other objects that wouldn't normally have been there. We then made them walk down the lane, one at a time, taking notes of what they'd spotted. To keep them on the ball we made a few booby traps out of trip-wires connected to thunderflashes.

I also gingered them up with a few little explosives. The aim of working with plastic explosive was to make them aware of the damage a car-bomb could do, and to teach them what to look for when they were clearing an area – to keep eyes open for suspicious packages or anything out of the ordinary. They were fascinated when I broke some eight-ounce sticks of explosive out of their wrapping paper and started to knead them in my hands. When I proposed to set fire to a lump of the stuff they were poised for the off; and when I did ignite it, they disappeared like shit off a shovel into the jungle, because PE 4 burns with a merry roar and an intense orange flame. They weren't to know that it can't explode if ignited, unless it's in a bloody great lump of thirty pounds or more. Later we got the wreck of an old car out into an area surrounded by rocks, and, working on the principle of P for Plenty, I put a charge of nearly five pounds underneath the chassis. When the students saw the whole thing rise to the height of the tree-tops, they were chuffed to bollocks.

That helped bring them on side. But it was when we started on car drills that we really got a good spirit going. Until then the Colombians tended to feign indifference, especially the ones who'd already had some training from the Yanks. They thought they knew it all, and weren't interested in learning anything new. But when they heard what we were actually saying, and saw that our methods were far superior, they came over to us in a big way. For instance, the Americans had taught them that if they got attacked from one side, all they had to do was turn in that direction and assault the enemy. When we showed them how to pepperpot outwards, and come in from different angles under covering fire, they were mightily impressed.

The other thing that chuffed them was unarmed combat. At first they were laughing at Murdo because of the dark-red colour of his hair and moustache, and the tattoos which covered him from the neck down. (When he showed them the pair of eyes on his arse, they fell down laughing.) Soon they were calling him '*El Mono*' – the ape. But when he invited them to attack him, one after another, he decked the lot, or tied them in such knots that they were very soon crying for mercy. Then he started to divulge a few secrets of holds and so on, and their respect for him became enormous.

What they didn't realize was that Murdo was one of the few Jocks never known to take a drink; to him, fitness was a creed, and his obsession with it gave him a strong practical interest in medicine. On this trip he acted as our medic, treating several of the Colombians for minor injuries – most of which he'd inflicted himself. All this made him very popular with the locals.

Another cause of amazement to the Colombians was Marky Springer, generally known as Sparky because he was our principal signaller. Over six foot tall, thin as a piece of wire, and covered in dense black hair, Sparky looked like a bloody great spider. He didn't drink either, and, unlike Murdo, he was fanatically mean about money. Tight as a gnat's arsehole, he hoarded every penny, and never went out to celebrate. Yet he, too, was a first-class operator, able to turn his hand to many skills.

Driving techniques and range-work were taught by Stew McQuarrie, one of the ugliest members of D Squadron, and a renowned piss-artist, given to drowning his sorrows in case he should catch sight of himself in the mirror. With his wiry bleached hair and permanently wrinkled forehead, he looked a picture of misery. The great thing about Stew, though, was that even if he got smashed out of his mind one evening, he'd be there on the dot in the morning, ready to give his all. In spite of the beer he put away, he had the steadiest of hands, and was one of our best marksmen.

As I walked round watching the lads at work, and listening to them teaching, I felt pleased with the way things were going. But the experience also made me realize that, competent as they all were, there is no such thing as a typical SAS guy: they are all individuals, all very different.

As for the Colombians, they liked it best when we started showing them close-protection formations, such as the closed box (in which they formed tightly round the main man) or the open V (with two guys watching for any threat from the front, ready to stop anyone coming inside, and another guy always on the main man's shoulder).

By the end of the first week our guys had settled in well. Everyone was walking around saying '*¡Carajo!*' instead of 'Shit!' and '*Jodido*' in place of 'It's fucked'. At the start of a lesson they'd crack off with 'OK, *para bolas!*' rather than 'Pay attention', and they'd learnt that '*mamar gallo*' meant to take the piss out of somebody.

After work, the trainees talked endlessly about drugs. The fact that Escobar was in the nick had them well wound up, and they kept telling stories about him: how in his prime he'd been earning a million dollars a day; how he'd established a full-scale zoo, with rhinos and elephants, at his *estancia*; and how he'd mounted one of his early cocaine-running aircraft on top of an arch over the road leading to his house, as a kind of trophy.

The drug war was on everybody's mind, and one evening we had another brief, this time from an officer of the Colombian anti-narcotics unit. A lot of what he said was already familiar to us, but when he got down to the nitty-gritty he became much more interesting. Talking of Escobar, for instance, he described a telephone conversation in which the drug baron had been speaking to his wife. When she protested about screams she could hear in the background, Escobar shouted, 'Just keep that fellow quiet until I've finished my conversation.' It transpired that the man yelling was losing his fingers, one by one, to a pair of bolt-croppers, because he was suspected of having lifted a few thousand dollars from one of the bulk payments. If that fellow erred again, the narcotics officer told us, not only he, but his whole family, would be executed – children, wife, parents, the lot.

'Yes,' said the officer, in his fractured English, 'I am sorry, but life is a little cheap in Colombia. You know, last year the narcos want to kill one *sapo* – an informer, literally a toad. They hear he is in the police station. Next to it is some apartments. So what do they do? They bring a truck full of explosive. Park it outside. Big bang. End of police station. End of apartments. One informer dead. Also two hundred other persons dead. *¡Maravilloso!*'

He also said they'd recently caught a notorious torturer called Gonzales whose speciality was sawing off his victims' heads in front of their families. It wasn't that he wanted to conceal anybody's identity, just that he enjoyed dismemberment.

We didn't have much in the way of entertainment, but while everything was relatively new that hardly mattered. One advantage was that there seemed to be no threat from guerrillas or other nasties, so that security was totally relaxed. In the evenings we could stroll down the road to the nearest village, where there was a bar cum restaurant which served incredibly cheap meals. For the equivalent of about fifty pence we could eat to bursting point, and the local beer was about fifteen pence a bottle. We could tell from the label that the stuff was brewed just down the road, and it cleared your gut like paint-stripper; but you could get nicely wrecked on it just the same.

For our first few days we reckoned the national sport must be cycling. Every time we went out of camp we saw streams of *fanaticos* flying down the road like the clappers on racing bikes. Then one evening we went to the pub and found that a big soccer match was on. A huge television screen had gone up in one corner of the bar; the picture was diabolical, and so was the sound, which was turned up to about 2,000 decibels, but the place was packed with fans, roaring like lunatics. By the time the right team won, they were dancing on the tables. This led to our discovery that the nation was soccer-mad, and that Captain Jaime was a keen supporter of the team he called 'Espurs'. Unfortunately none of our lads could match his knowledge or answer his questions about the club's latest exploits, but soccer always made a good subject for casual conversation. At least we'd heard of Captain Jaime's hero 'Gary Leeneker', Spurs' skipper, and when the local radio station reported that his team had been defeated by Nottingham Forest in the semi-final of the Rumbelows' League Cup, we were able to sympathize.

It was at the end of our second week that we went up to

Bogotá. When work finished on Thursday night, we declared a long weekend and prepared to head for the bright lights. Many of our trainees came from the capital, and they couldn't wait to get back there, so they set off ahead of us in their own cars, promising to meet us at our hotel and show us the best places to buy emeralds and leather goods.

Peter Black had been down to see us once, but he'd called off a second visit on the pretext that the international situation was difficult, and that he needed to be in the embassy. He'd booked us into the Hostal Bonavento for the nights of Friday and Saturday.

We set off in two Land Cruisers early on Friday morning, with Colombian drivers, in high spirits and full of expectation. After two weeks on the edge of the jungle, everyone was ready for a bit of the old *vida regalada*, or, as some call it, high life. Everyone, that is, except Sparky Springer, who preferred to stay in camp on his own, eating shit, and refused to spend a single centavo if he could avoid it. Since he was easily the most proficient guy on the 319 radio, it was no bad thing that he stayed on site.

By third-world standards the road was pretty good, with only the odd mega pothole to double up the Toyota's springs, and the main obstacles to progress were pack-animals and buses. Donkeys and mules were plodding along under huge burdens, often with loads so wide that they took up as much space as a car. The peasants leading or riding them mostly wore dark-coloured hats like pork pies, with little turned-up rims, although some of the women had their heads swathed in black scarves.

The buses were going faster than the carts and donkeys, but not much. Just to look at, they were quite an eyeful, because every square inch of the bodywork was painted in brilliant colours, hot reds, yellows and blues. A lot of the decoration was in formal patterns, but often, in the middle of a panel, there'd be an elaborate picture – a view of mountains, a stretch of coastline, a church or a bridge. Every vehicle must have taken hundreds of hours to paint. They were grossly overloaded, stuffed to the gills with passengers, and most were leaning drunkenly to right or left, with half the suspension knackered. Black diesel smoke poured from their exhausts, and the slightest uphill incline dragged them down to about 20 m.p.h., if not to a halt.

Some of the hilly country we went through was farmed, but thousands of acres were still scrub. Beside the road peasants were selling fruit and bottled drinks from little shacks made of corrugated tin. Every village had a whitewashed church with a big cross above it, and all along the roadside were shrines to the Virgin Mary, with statues set in little arched recesses. As we progressed through a mountain pass, we saw that some of the shrines were hacked out of the living rock. Everything looked primitive and peaceful, and it was hard to imagine that the country was in the grip of narco-war.

As we trundled along I tried to think forward. The Colombians wanted the grand finale of our training to take place in Bogotá. The idea was that a team of our best recruits would show off their newly learnt skills by taking the president himself, or maybe his deputy, straight through the centre of the capital in a three-car motorcade, with a big, armoured limo in the centre, to the national stadium. Even though that great event was still a month or more ahead, I was keen to see some of the course over which it would take place.

For almost all our four-hour journey we were climbing, so the air became progressively cooler. Peter Black had warned us that we might feel faint at first, because the city's nearly 9,000 feet above sea-level, and if you go up to that height quickly you can suffer from lack of oxygen. Maybe the drive had been slow enough to allow us to acclimatize; whatever, we simply felt relieved to escape from the heat.

The run-in to Bogotá was across a level plain, with a haze of smog ahead of us, and big mountains dominating the eastern skyline. Our first sight of the city was a severe let-down. Along the sides of the road there was a straggle of tumbledown shacks, which gradually thickened up into a vast and incredibly sordid jumble. Corrugated tin, parts of old cars, wooden boards, inverted bathtubs, doors, canvas, sheets of metal, plywood and cardboard – you name it, the

Colombians had used it to run up their hovels. Mangy-looking dogs were nosing about the heaps of garbage. Tethered donkeys stood around, eyes shut, ears back. 'Shitsville!' cried someone – and so it was. These were the notorious *barrios*, or slums, that people had kept telling us about. Even passing through with the car windows closed, we got the impression that the place must stink to high heaven.

Soon, though, we were through the worst, and into an area that was still poor but at least had proper buildings. Our driver, Simon, who spoke a few words of English, had been proposing to head round the western outskirts to our destination in the northern quarter, but I told him to go right through the centre, so that we could get a look at it. Shiny high-rise blocks loomed ahead, and after a few more minutes we came to the centre itself. Another world. Suddenly we could have been in any prosperous European or American city – Frankfurt, Brussels, Chicago. Gleaming skyscrapers of glass and steel soared into the sky, and at street level the shops were as glossy as could be, full of expensive clothes, furniture, video cameras, hi-fi and other electronic equipment. Cafés, bars, restaurants and cinemas jostled in between. The contrast with the slums was incredible.

The city had been built on a grid system, with the main streets running north and south; but every one was jammed solid by cars and buses. With so many engines ticking over, the pollution was horrendous. The combination of smog and altitude made it difficult to breathe. Whenever lights changed and a mass of traffic surged forward, every driver clapped his hand on the horn and kept it there, so that the noise was outrageous as well.

'We'll need to watch ourselves here,' I said as an old woman narrowly escaped death under the wheels of a cement truck. 'They don't give a flying monkey's for pedestrians.'

'Sure don't,' Tony replied. 'And the other thing you need to watch out for is pickpockets. See all those kids – those street urchins? *Gamines*. They're partly beggars, partly thieves. While one's accosting you, another slides up and tries to snatch your wallet.'

Soon I realized that the system of street names, or rather numbers, could hardly have been simpler. All the big roads running north and south, parallel with the mountains, were called *carreras*, or avenues. The streets running across them at right-angles were *calles*. We were heading north on Carrera Septima, and the further we went, the higher the number of the *calles* became, rising from single figures in the centre. As we inched our way forward, Simon kept up a running commentary, pointing out sights of interest.

On one corner, where crowds of people were milling about among some stalls on the pavement, he pointed and said, 'These men selling *esmeralda*.'

'Emeralds in the street?'

'*Ciertamente*,' said Simon indignantly. 'Every day.'

I had a sudden vision of an emerald necklace flashing on Tracy's skin. Wouldn't green stones look fabulous on her freckled neck, framed by that chestnut hair?

The Calle numbers kept rising, through the twenties, into the thirties and forties. Our hotel, the Bonavento, was way out on Calle 93, but conveniently placed within a few blocks of the British Embassy on 98. The further north we drove, the ritzier the surroundings became; from the number of big houses set back inside walled compounds, it was clear that we were entering the smart residential area of the city. There were also fancy-looking restaurants by the dozen.

The Hostal Bonavento turned out to be smaller than I'd expected, and they tried to pack us in three to a room; but I insisted that we got four rooms altogether. That meant one lot of three and three pairs, and I went into a room with Tony. We dumped our kit, had a wash and went for a quick lunch. I'd already arranged to go round to the embassy at 2.30, and I wanted Tony to come with me; but I told everyone else that they could fix their own programmes, provided they were back at the hotel and fit to travel in time for our return journey at lunchtime on Sunday.

I think at the back of my mind I'd been hoping that the embassy would be a beautiful old colonial building, standing in the middle of a walled garden. Far from it. It was merely a suite of offices on the fourth floor of a modern tower block, with the amazing name the Torre Propaganda Sancho. Having sat on our arses for four hours we opted to walk round there rather than take a taxi.

The air was thin, all right. Even tabbing at a normal pace made us pant. Because we'd heard that the Colombians clocked visitors as they went into the embassy we'd decided not to turn up together; so a couple of blocks away we split and I went on ahead.

Inside the foyer of the propaganda tower a receptionist took my details, gave me a visitor's badge, and directed me into the lift. 'Embajada Británica' said the elaborate gold writing outside the door on the fourth-floor landing. I rang the bell and waited, not quite knowing what to expect. There was quite a long pause before anything happened, and I was on the point of ringing again when the security system clicked into life and a woman's voice said, 'Can I help you?'

'Sergeant Sharp to see Captain Black.'

A buzzer sounded and the door opened. Inside, waiting to receive me, stood an amazingly attractive woman, simply dressed in a white shirt and black skirt, with long, dark hair and a distinctly Spanish look about her oval face, olive skin and black eyes. She was older than me, I reckoned, but not much.

'Hello,' she said, smiling and holding out an elegant hand, 'I'm Luisa Bolton. I'm sorry to have kept you waiting, but our receptionist's off sick, and I'm having to double.'

Her English was perfect, but with a slight Spanish intonation. I introduced myself, and explained that Tony would be with us in a moment. Then I asked, 'What do you do normally, then?'

'Communications – that's my job. Come in, anyway. Peter's with the ambassador for the moment. Will you have some coffee?'

She led the way into an ultra-modern office, leaving a trail of some weird perfume behind her, and I perched awkwardly on a swivel chair among the fax-machines, teleprinters and word-processors while she went into a little annexe and set a coffee percolator on the go. A plate-glass window gave a dramatic view of the nearby mountains to the east, with expensive-looking properties clinging to their lower slopes. On the opposite wall the only decoration was a huge coloured print of a condor with its wings outstretched. The picture must have been ten feet wide, nearly life-size.

Soon, another delicious smell was mingling with the perfume: fresh, home-grown coffee. It was odd, but this woman was reminding me strongly of Tracy. Her colouring was quite different, and her legs weren't so long, but there was something about her movements and mannerisms that was familiar and enticing. I realized I was watching her with more than just professional interest. I gave myself a sharp mental bollocking. Hands off! For one thing, Tracy had been fantastic in taking on both my house and my child. For another, I knew that any involvement with a member of the embassy staff might lead to serious complications – especially as I was still on a warning order from the Regiment, and needed to play everything straight.

In a couple of minutes Tony arrived, and I introduced him. As Luisa organized cups and saucers, she asked questions about our journey up, and we answered politely. But all the time I was thinking, 'There's something going on here. It was that one word which had tipped me off: the way she'd referred to the Rupert simply as 'Peter'. In a flash of intuition I felt certain he was humping her. Why else would she refer to him in that familiar way, by his first name only? That was why he'd suddenly cancelled his second visit to the camp: he'd got straight into a legover engagement and was having too good a time in Bogotá.

I wondered if I ought to have a word with him straight away, tell him to screw the nut. This was his first team job. In the past, plenty of jobs had been ruined by one guy not being able to keep his pecker in his pants. I realized though that if I said anything, it might lead to a major confrontation to the detriment of the team. Already there was an atmosphere between us, and any criticism from me would be bound to make it worse.

As Luisa came back carrying the cups, I got a look at her left hand. No rings. I slipped a look at Tony. He was fancying her something torrid, but he hadn't heard what I had.

'Milk?' she asked.

'Thanks.'

'Sugar?'

'No, thank you.'

I stirred my cup and said innocently, 'Have you been out here long?'

'Most of my life.' She gave that dazzling smile again. 'My family settled here at the beginning of the century. They were Spanish. Then, in the fifties, my father came from England, married my mother, and settled down here. So I'm half Spanish, but have an English surname. And no "o" in my Luisa.'

'How are comms with the UK?' I asked.

'They're terrific now,' she answered. 'The telephone used to be terrible: The lines were always jammed, and if you did get through, the interference was impossible. But with satellites, it's fantastic. We can talk to London as if it were next door. And of course your own satellite phone is incredible.'

We made small talk for a few minutes. Then we heard movement outside, and a solid, stocky man appeared in the doorway, holding a sheaf of papers. He was in his early forties, I guessed, overweight, with neck bulging over collar and gut over waistband.

'Hello,' he said. 'I'm John Palmer, Defence Attaché.'

Black was with him, and all four of us went into Palmer's office. There was nothing difficult to discuss. I reported that everything was going fine down at the camp; apart from the odd attack of gut-rot, all our guys were well and enjoying themselves. There was no friction with the natives. On the contrary, the locals were friendly. Our trainees were responding well to a bit of pressure and would make up into a reasonable BG team. I could see no particular problems coming up.

The news from the other end was less promising. The DA

revealed that diplomatic relations between Britain and Colombia were under strain, after the arrest of a Colombian student at Essex University on charges of drug-smuggling. There had been verbal fisticuffs between the two governments, and threats to expel embassy staff at both ends. All this made our own position precarious; it was therefore essential that we did nothing to make the ill-feeling worse.

'Of course, your presence in the country is entirely unofficial,' the DA told me. 'Things might get very difficult if the media reported that you were here.'

'Don't worry,' I told him. 'Nobody's planning to sell his story to the *Espectador*. Our lads are all fairly sensible.' Privately I was thinking, What sort of a prick is this? What's he trying to tell me?

After half an hour of rather uneasy chat, we pulled out. As we were leaving, Luisa gave me a card with all the embassy phone numbers on it, including an emergency number, a home number for herself, and one for Major J.R. Palmer, Defence Attaché. On our way out Tony said, as a parting shot, 'No chance of your keeping us company at supper, I suppose? Show us the sights a bit?'

Again she nearly killed him with that smile, 'That would be wonderful,' she said. 'But as it happens we've got a reception on here. I'm on duty. That puts me out, I'm afraid.'

'Oh well – not to worry. Another time, perhaps.'

Black came down in the lift with us, and on the way I said, 'I presume you're invited to the party tonight.'

The light was rather dim, but I'm sure he blushed. 'Actually,' he said, 'I am.'

We'd decided not to piss about leaving the tower separately. As we started walking, Tony didn't make any comment for a moment, but then he said, 'He's screwing her.'

'I wondered if I should say something to him. He could fuck up the whole operation.'

'How did he get into the Regiment?' Tony asked.

'They must have been short of officers when he came along.'

It was the prospect of belly-dancing that made Tony and I choose the Four Seasons restaurant: authentic Colombian food, and a bit of entertainment thrown in. By seven-thirty we were definitely hungry, so we called up one of the black-and-yellow taxis and rode it into town. The other guys had long since disappeared like water into sand. I predicted that Mel, for one, would come back shit-faced and minus his wallet.

Our own idea was probably much the same as everyone else's: to have a good meal, suss out the belly-dancing and then head on for some of the hotter night-spots. Unfortunately it didn't work out.

The restaurant was fine. A couple of photos in the window had been unpromising – the dancer, Carmencita, looked more like a Michelin ad than a great seducer – but we had a beer in the bar, and then chose a table beside the small dance floor. We both had the same main course – *tamales*, maize pancakes with a terrific, spicy filling of chopped meat and vegetables. The filling was delicious, but so hot that we needed several more drinks to swill it down, and we hit the Carlsberg Specials.

We were just sitting back anticipating that action might soon start up, when the thunderbolt struck. Our table gave us a good view of everyone who came in and out, but I wasn't paying much attention. A party of four men sat down at the table next to ours. Then, looking straight past Tony, over his left shoulder, I froze.

'Hey!' Tony was leaning forward. 'What's the matter? You look as though you've seen a ghost.'

'I have. Let's get the hell out of here.'

Forcing myself to move my hand casually, I signalled a passing waiter and made motions for him to write out our bill. But when I picked up my glass to finish the beer, my hand was shaking – because there, barely ten feet away, sat Declan Farrell.

'What is it?' said Tony. 'You look real sick. You've gone white as paint.'

'Talk in Spanish,' I muttered. 'Talk about football. Anything.'

He looked at me as though I was crazy, but he started in. I hardly heard what he was saying, because I was desperately trying to collect my wits. It's OK, I kept telling myself. You're in no danger, because Farrell has never seen you. He's never set eyes on you. He hasn't a clue what you look like. If you don't do anything crazy, he can't possibly pick you out. Reason told me that Tony and I were not particularly conspicuous. Plenty of other people in the restaurant were dressed like us in casual shirts and jeans. Farrell, in contrast, was wearing a smart lightweight jacket and tie. One of his companions was the same; the other two had leather jackets and open-necked shirts. Without letting my eyes linger on them, I tried to assess who was who. All were dark haired, Farrell as dark as any. I guessed the second tie-wearer, who had pale skin, was Irish, and the other two Colombian.

With Tony still making the odd remark in Spanish, I got out my wallet and pushed it across the table. 'You pay,' I muttered. 'I'm going to use the phone.'

The telephone was round a corner and in a kind of cupboard on the way to the gents – private enough, provided nobody walked past. The equipment was modern, with one slot for cards and another for coins. I brought out a handful of change and surveyed it. The rate of exchange was about 1,000 pesos to the pound. A 100-peso coin seemed about right for a local call, so I lifted the receiver, fed one in and dialled Luisa's office number. I reckoned the reception would still be in progress, and I just hoped it was going on within earshot.

The number rang and rang, ten, twenty, thirty times, before at last someone answered, a man. '*¿Digame?*'

'Captain Black, *por favor.*'

'*¿Quién?*'

'Captain Black.'

'*No conocer.*'

'Major Palmer, then.'

'*Momento.*'

He put down the receiver, and through it I could hear faint

party noises. My mind was in overdrive. Farrell being watched in Ballyconvil because he was into drugs. Farrell staggering home to his outhouse with heavy suitcases. Farrell now in Bogotá. Morrison's story was that the PIRA was into Colombia in a big way. I'd known they had been taking percentages from dealers on the street in Belfast, but this was another league: their involvement could be world-wide, and might increase their power to buy weapons to a fantastic degree.

At last someone came to the phone.

'Palmer here. Who's that?'

'Geordie Sharp.'

'Who?'

I repeated my name.

'Sorry, old boy. I don't think I know you.'

Jesus! I thought. The guy's half-pissed. Taking care to keep my voice even, I said, 'We met this afternoon. Can I speak to Peter Black, please?'

'Good God yes, I know who you are. The SAS chappie. Up from the savannah. What did you want?'

'To speak to Peter Black. Urgently.'

'Black? Black? I'm not sure I can find him. Can't I deal with it? What time is it? Where are you, anyway?'

'*Please . . . find . . . him!*' I ground the words out as if I was speaking to a child.

'Oh, all right. Hang on then.'

The telephone began to beep. Feverishly I dredged up more coins and stuffed a couple into the slot. Somebody came along the passage and went past me: none of the Farrell party. I waited, shifting from one foot to the other, and hoping to hell that Black was more sober than the DA.

At last he came on the line. 'Yes?' he said. 'What's happening, Geordie? Have you got a problem?'

'Yes. A big one. The PIRA are in town.'

'Are you trying to take the piss out of me?'

'No I'm not. It's Farrell.'

'Bloody hell!'

'He's with some Colombians.'

209

'Where is he?'

'Where I'm speaking from. It's a restaurant called the Four Seasons. On Carrera 15, 84-22.'

'I know it. *Bloody hell!*'

'Exactly.'

'Who are you with?'

'Tony Lopez.'

'You'd better get out of there.'

'Don't worry. We're on our way back to the hotel.'

'OK. Where are the rest of the lads?'

'Christ knows. They've gone on the piss all over town.'

'You can't get them back?'

'Not a chance.'

'I want you all out of Bogotá as soon as possible.'

'Well, we can't go before tomorrow.'

'That'll have to do.'

'Will you alert Hereford about this?'

'Of course.'

'Great. I'll see you back at the hotel.'

I returned to our table slowly, loitering to see if I could overhear any conversation from our neighbours. Sure enough, one of Farrell's companions was speaking with an Ulster accent. 'That'll be fine,' was all I got, but the 'fine' came out as *fayeen*.

Tony had already settled the bill. 'Everything all right?' he asked.

'No. Let's get a taxi.'

'Where are we going?'

'Back to the hotel.'

'Don't you want to walk?'

'Not now.'

'What about the belly-dancer?'

'She can stuff herself.'

Knowing Farrell, I felt sure he would have dickers out on the street, watching his arse for him, and I didn't want one of them to spot me. Even in the taxi I thought it safer not to talk, in case the driver was a plant and could understand English. Not until we were back in our hotel room could I enlighten

210

Tony about what had happened.

'Sure it was him?' he asked.

'Absolutely. One hundred per cent. I'd know him any-where. He was the big guy right behind you.'

'You should have stuck a knife in his back there and then.'

'We would have been lynched.'

'What in hell's he doing here?'

'He's got to be trying to set up some big drugs deal. Or buying weapons. Or both. Both probably.'

'You don't think it's something to do with the fact that our guys are out here?'

'Can't be. There's no way he could know about us.'

'Well, what do we do?'

'Black said he'd come round here to make a plan.'

Black never came. Tony and I had arrived back in the hotel at 9.30, and by ten I was getting worried – the embassy was only five minutes' drive away. By 10.30 I knew something had gone seriously wrong.

The hotel had no phones in the bedrooms; the only thing to do was to call from the one in the foyer. Luckily, by then, there was nobody about.

I put 100 pesos in the slot and dialled. Again there was a long wait, and at last a Spanish voice. I handed the receiver to Tony. He listened, then said, '*Momento*,' and put his hand over the mouthpiece.

'They all went down to the restaurant.'

'Who?'

'The DA, Black and the woman.'

'All together?'

'Apparently.'

'What time?'

'Immediately after you'd called.'

'Jesus! What the hell were they doing?'

Tony shook his head. 'Maybe they wanted to check Farrell out.'

'They must have been crazy. You know what? I believe they've been lifted.'

Tony took his hand off the phone and said, '*Momento, por favor.*'

'We need to call Hereford,' I said. 'Immediately. We can't do it from here. We need the secure comms in the embassy. Ask if we can go in and use them.'

Tony began to parley, but the guy on the other end – the night caretaker – said he couldn't admit us without permission from the duty officer. Eventually, after a lot of haggling, Tony got the name of the second secretary, and his home number.

I took back the receiver and dialled again. By then it was after eleven. Probably the guy had gone to bed. But no – the call was answered immediately.

'Egerton,' said a crisp, youngish voice.

I apologized for disturbing him, then launched into an explanation, keeping everything as short as possible. Instead of asking stupid questions or prevaricating, he said, 'I'll meet you in the foyer of the embassy tower in ten minutes.'

'Thank God,' I said to Tony. 'Somebody's on the ball.'

Egerton. The name seemed vaguely familiar. I'd heard it before, but for the moment I couldn't place it.

Again I didn't fancy walking. I felt as if the black spirit of Ulster had followed me five thousand miles across the ocean and now infested the streets of the Colombian capital. So I got the night porter to call up a taxi, and asked Tony to stay where he was, in case the missing party turned up after all.

'Sure,' he agreed. 'But know what? First I'll take a cab back to the restaurant, just to make sure they didn't go in and have a meal.'

'If Farrell's still there, he'll see you.'

'I'll pretend I lost something, OK? I lost a book. My guide book to Bogotá. Maybe I left it there?'

'Take it easy, then, and call me at the embassy.'

Bill Egerton was tall, thin, bespectacled, and in his early thirties, a scholarly-looking fellow with a long, pale indoor face, but wonderfully quick to grasp the point.

'Yes,' he agreed immediately. 'You'd better call Hereford. England's five hours ahead of us, so it's 4.15 a.m. over there.

Is that all right?'

'It'll have to be.'

I was carrying the camp emergency number in my wallet, and I knew the orderly officer would be on duty in the guardroom. The call had hardly gone through before it was answered. Reception was perfect, and by a stroke of luck I recognized the voice.

'Chalky? It's Geordie Sharp.'

'Fucking hell! I wasn't expecting you just now.'

'Well, listen. We're in the shit. Who's the duty officer?'

'It's Bob Keeling.'

'OK. I need to speak to him.'

'Now? It's half past four in the morning.'

'I know. This is urgent.'

'OK. I'll wake him up.'

I waited a minute. In the pause I saw the guardroom, with all the lists pinned on the notice board and the bunches of keys on their hooks. Then, close at hand, I heard another phone ring. Egerton picked it up, said a few words and put it down. 'Your American colleague's checked the restaurant. They aren't there. The other party's gone as well.'

'Thanks.'

The secure circuit came alive again.

'Yes?' Bob Keeling sounded sleepy and slow.

'Geordie Sharp in Bogotá. There's been a lift. Two British diplomats and our own Rupert, Peter Black.'

'Say that again.'

I repeated it.

'Christ!' exclaimed Keeling, coming fully alert. 'When did this happen?'

'About half an hour ago.'

'I'll get the ops officer in right away.'

'Fine. You've got my number.'

'He'll call you back.'

I rang off and saw Egerton staring at me. 'Were you at the party?' I asked.

'Yes – but because I was on duty, I was only drinking orange juice.'

213

'I don't want to be offensive, but the DA sounded pissed.'

Egerton twitched. 'Yes. He overdoes it a bit.'

I sat thinking for a minute. Then I said, 'If this *is* drug-related, what will they do with them?'

'If they were only narcos, they'd demand a ransom. That happens all the time. But if the IRA's involved – I don't know. I've no experience of that organization.'

'Where are they likely to take them?'

'Out of town somewhere. Probably into the jungle.'

'How do we track them down, then?'

'Ah!' Egerton gave a very slight smile. 'Our sources of information are quite good. Unofficially, we're in touch with people known as *sapos*.'

'Toads,' I said.

'You've heard of them. For quite a small consideration from the slush fund – say 25,000 pesos – they produce very useful intelligence.' Then he added, 'Of course, it's nothing to what can be got from high-tech equipment.'

'Such as?'

'You know how they found the laboratories at Tranquilandia?'

He saw that I wasn't with him, and explained: 'The biggest cocaine factory there's ever been. It had a dozen laboratories turning out over three tons of the stuff every month. The narcos practically built a town there for their workers – houses, roads, a landing strip, everything, in the middle of the jungle. That was back a bit, in the eighties, when the Medellin cartel was at its height.

'The United States Drug Enforcement Agency found the place by putting tracking devices into a couple of drums of ether, which is one of the agents used in the manufacture of cocaine. Satellites tracked the drums right down into the Amazon basin.'

'You know a lot about this.'

'Well, I got interested.'

'Is it true that DAS really run the country?'

'You could say that. They're extremely powerful. Most people live in fear of them.'

'And you have contact with them?'

'Very much so. The Commander-in-Chief's a personal friend. Why?'

'I was thinking we may need their help.'

'You could get help from the DEA, I'm sure. They've got people here all the time. Also there's the Colombian Police's own anti-narcotics unit.'

'We need to keep this in the family. If some big organization goes in with guns blazing, the first thing the narcos will do is top their hostages. Our own speciality is covert approach and surprise.'

Minutes ticked away. Then the secure line rang and I grabbed the receiver.

'Geordie? You have a problem?' Far from sounding annoyed at having been dragged out of bed, Alan Andrews, the ops officer, was all lit up.

'Sorry to get you in,' I said.

'Not to worry. What is it?'

'I'm in Bogotá and we've got a fastball. Peter Black's been lifted by the PIRA, or by Colombians, or both.' I told him what had happened, cutting everything short.

'I'll inform the Director immediately,' he said. 'He'll be round to the Foreign Office as soon as they're in business. We'll get a squadron on standby.'

'Great. The question is, what do I do now? The earliest I can collect the guys together is tomorrow morning. I'd like to get everyone back to our training camp, but it's four hours out of town.'

'What time is it now?'

'Quarter to midnight. We're five hours behind you.'

'Wait one. I'll speak to the CO and call you back.'

Five minutes later he came on again. 'I've talked to the CO,' he said. 'Recovery of the personnel is the number one priority. Everything else has to give place to it. You'll have to suspend the training course, or cancel it if need be.'

'Roger. We'll keep this phone manned from now on. It's the best comms base by far.'

'Good. The other thing is, this whole saga needs to stay

215

under wraps. Officially, you aren't there. The diplomatic shit's already stirring over the guy at Essex University, so it's essential you keep your head down, if you can.'

'That's fine by me.'

I rang off. 'As I thought, they don't want the Colombians involved,' I told Egerton. 'Is that going to make things awkward for you?'

'We'll have to see what happens. If the DA doesn't reappear fairly soon, we'll have to report his absence. But we can give it a few hours anyway. The Ambassador's gone off for the weekend; if we can avoid having to drag him back, all the better.'

'Listen,' I said. 'This is really very good of you. Don't let me land you in it too.'

'That's all right. I had a brother in your Regiment, so it's a pleasure to help.'

TWELVE

Egerton announced that he was going to stay over, and called his wife to tell her. Then he revealed that there were a couple of bedrooms behind the offices, and offered me one of them. As this seemed a better option than returning to the hotel, I took it. Before I turned in, I phoned Tony again and brought him up to date. I said he should get his head down.

I tried to do the same, but couldn't. I was half-listening through the open door for the phone, half-cursing the way things had gone to ratshit. In a way it was my fault. If I hadn't recognized Farrell and reported his presence, nothing would have happened. On the other hand, I couldn't have ignored him and left him to carry on with whatever villainy he was engaged in. If the PIRA were into drug-running to the extent of sending him to Bogotá, it was really bad news for the Province, and something that ought to be tackled right away.

I think I lay awake most of the night, imagining various scenarios; but in fact I must have gone to sleep, because suddenly I became aware of Egerton standing over me with a brew of tea. It was 6 o'clock in the morning.

'Things are moving,' he said. 'We've had a police report of a disturbance outside your restaurant, so I guess that was it. Also, I made a couple of calls. They should produce results within an hour.'

'Brilliant. Is there a back way out of the building?'

'Certainly. If you carry on down to the lower garage level in the lift, you can walk out of the pedestrian exit.'

'Great. I want to nip back to the hotel to square things away. Now that this has happened, there's bound to be someone watching the embassy, and I don't want to be seen.'

'Fair enough.'

By then it was mid-morning in England. I called Hereford again, and was put straight on to the CO.

'No positive news yet?' he asked.

'No, but things are on the move. What do you advise about our location? I could send the team back to camp, but that's more than four hours out of town. I'd rather have them on hand in case we have to head off somewhere quickly.'

'I understand. Are they in a secure place?'

'Reasonably. The hotel think we're hydro engineers.'

'Keep them there for the moment, then. If you find out where the hostages have been taken, you'll need to set up a forward mounting base in the area, and get your people into it.'

'Fine.'

'We've been looking at ways of getting a squadron out to back you up. It's been to Defence Minister and Foreign Minister level. We're just waiting for clearance from the FO.'

'Good. We're OK for the moment. I'm getting first-class support in the embassy.' As Bill was temporarily out of earshot I asked, 'Do you know of a guy in the Regiment called Egerton?'

'Donald? Don Egerton. Of course. He was a star. Killed on an exercise in Africa four or five years ago.'

'Oh – right. I thought the name was familiar. It's his brother in charge here.'

'Glad to hear it.'

I hung up and glanced at my watch. I knew that, whatever might be said officially, ways would be found to get reinforcements out to us. Once the Regiment's involved in an operation of this kind, obstructions tend to fall away.

Then . . . there was a good chance that on this Saturday morning Tracy would be at home. Worth a try, anyway.

I dialled – and there she was.

'Geordie! What's happening?'

'Nothing. Everything's cool. I just got a chance to call.'

'Well, great. Where are you?'

'In Bogotá.'

'How's the weather?'

'All right. Not as hot as in camp. We're 9,000 feet above sea-level. What about there?'

'Typical March – cold and wet.'

'How's Tim?'

'On top form. He's got a friend here for the day – Alex Kirkby, from the village.'

'Oh, great. Everything all right, then?'

'Yes. Well . . . it was funny. A man rang last night.'

'What did he want?'

'He just asked how you were enjoying yourself in the sun.'

'Nothing else?'

'No. I asked what he meant, but he rang off.'

I felt a stab of anxiety. 'What sort of a voice did he have?'

'Nothing special. I couldn't place it.'

'Not Irish?'

'I wouldn't say so.'

'Listen. If it happens again, call the police. OK?'

'OK.'

'And don't worry. It was probably just some nutter.'

I said goodbye and rang off. Although I'd pretended to be nonchalant, I was disturbed. Outside the Regiment, nobody was supposed to know where we were. Who'd passed word around that I was in Colombia?

Before I had time to start worrying, Bill Egerton returned and showed me the way out via the fire-stairs, lending me a key so that I could come back in the same way.

I ran down to the lower garage floor and came out of the door cautiously. The car-park was three-quarters empty, and there was nobody in sight. The rear of the block was deserted, too. I turned to the right and set off, noticing for the first time that the building was flanked by a garden full of spectacularly bright flowers.

I walked the short leg to the hotel without picking up a tail. Tony had dragged everyone out of bed, and I got them all into the room he and I had been sharing. Most of them were looking rough. As I predicted, Mel had lost his money. He still had his wallet, but he'd got so smashed that someone had nicked all his cash from it without him noticing. The only things he had left were some emeralds he'd bought from a guy in the street and stashed in a pocket of his jeans. At least, he thought they were emeralds. The others reckoned they were bits of green glass.

'Listen,' I said. 'The shit's hit the fan.'

I told them the score, then said, 'We're to stay put for the moment. Then, if we find out where the hostages are, we'll go in and get them out. Meanwhile, I'm going to phone Captain Jaime and tell him the course is suspended for a couple of days. I'm heading back to the embassy now. Tony'll follow me, to man the secure phone. The rest of you are going to have to stick it out here in the hotel. OK?'

At the sniff of an operation their hangovers fell away, and everyone gladly ditched their plans to buy leather jackets. Those could wait. I had a shave and a shower and got some breakfast down me, then grabbed a taxi to the back of the embassy. Egerton was certainly well organized. His wife had come in, bringing his shaving kit and some weekend clothes.

'Progress,' he began. 'We've got a lead. Word is that the party's flown out to a brand-new refinery in the jungle on the Rio Caquetá.'

'Where's that?'

'Way down south, in the Amazonas, near the border with Peru.'

'How do you get there?'

'Not easy. There are no roads. The only way's to fly.'

'In that case we're definitely going to need help from your friends in DAS. Will your friend fix things for us?'

'I think so.' He picked up a telephone, dialled and began speaking rapidly in Spanish. He glanced at me a couple of times as he was talking, and ended with, '*Sí, sí. Muchas gracias.*'

He turned to me. 'He wants to see you.'

'When?'

'Now. A car will collect you in a few minutes.'

'Does he speak English?'

'Perfectly. He went to Harvard.'

'What's his name?'

'General Felipe Nariño.'

At that moment the door-buzzer sounded and Tony arrived. 'The guys are standing by to move,' he announced. 'I've called Captain Jaime at the camp and told him the course is suspended for the time being. Also, I spoke to Sparky and put him in the picture.'

'We'd better get our arses back down there,' I said.

Egerton cleared his throat. 'I think you'll find you've got air transport at your disposal. You'll need to go back to get your kit and presumably the camp you've been at has a landing strip?'

'Sure.'

'Then it might pay you not to send anyone off by road. Hang on until you've seen the general.'

Five minutes later I was in the back of an air-conditioned Mercedes 500 with smoked-out windows, sweeping through the outskirts of the city towards the palatial establishments perched on the slopes of the mountain. I didn't feel by any means secure. It wasn't beyond the bounds of possibility that I was being lifted. But no – surely DAS were on our side? Not only were we training the bodyguard for them; we'd now got caught up in the fight against the narcos, and so were in a position to give them help.

This was not a peaceful environment. Outside the big condos, all protected by high wire fences, bodyguards openly flaunted sub-machine-guns. My driver – young, swarthy, grey-uniformed – handled the car well but with amazing arrogance. Twice he went straight over red lights, and at every opportunity he blasted pedestrians out of the way with his horn. No doubt he was immune from prosecution.

Soon we arrived at a pair of high wire gates, set in a twelve-foot wall of concrete blocks topped with broken glass. Except that I couldn't see any closed-circuit TV cameras, the compound was unpleasantly similar to the RUC stations in Belfast. The gates were opened mechanically by some unseen person, and we drew up outside a brand-new office block. The Merc had hardly come to rest before a man stepped forward,

221

opened the door beside me and ushered me into the building.

In the passage he muttered, '*Disculpe*,' and ran his hands over me in a swift, skilled frisk, which instantly brought to light my Sig, which I was carrying in a pancake holster on my waist. '*Disculpe*,' he repeated as he removed the weapon. Then he led the way up a shallow flight of stairs and knocked on a door.

General Nariño was short and stocky, with a broad forehead, greying hair swept across it, and slightly hooded eyes. His appearance immediately made me think of Marlon Brando – a dangerously sleek version of the actor, but a look-alike all the same. He was wearing an expensive-looking sky-blue suit and a black tie with a lightning strike down the centre. As I came in he got up from behind his desk and came forward to greet me. His hand was soft and gentle.

'Sergeant Sharp? Pleased to meet you,' he said. 'Take a seat.'

'Thanks.'

As Egerton had said, the General's English – or rather, American – was perfect. But in spite of his superficial geniality I felt he was hard and cold.

Whatever else, he had a magnificent office. Because the building was perched high on the side of the mountain, the windows commanded a panoramic view of the city. His king-sized desk and long, oval conference table were both made from some fine, rich-coloured wood like mahogany, but not so dark. The floor was made of wood as well, with a couple of bright rugs to give colour. No linoleum or chrome or glass-topped tables here. As I sat down, a tray with a cup of coffee on it appeared at my elbow. Again it crossed my mind that the coffee could be laced with the drug we'd heard about in Hereford – *burundanga* – which removes your will to resist; but again I thought, No, this is all above board.

'You have a problem, I think,' the General began.

'That's right. These three people have been lifted.'

'And you think the IRA is involved?'

'I know it is.' I gave him a short run-down on Farrell, without explaining my personal connection. I simply said that

222

I'd worked in Belfast and seen him there.

'Well, it sounds as if your group has been flown to a site on the Rio Caquetá.'

'I gather that's very remote.'

'It sure is. Look.' He stood up and went over to the end wall, where he switched on a spotlight to illuminate a huge map of the country. Using a billiard cue, he began to point out details.

'We're here, in Bogotá, nearly in the centre of Colombia. Away down south is this vast area known as Los Amazonas. It's part of the Amazon basin. As you can see, it's one hell of a size. Eight hundred kilometres from here to here. No roads, just thousands of square kilometres of rainforest.

'Now, for some weeks past we've been getting rumours of a new laboratory on the bank of the Rio Caquetá – here.' He ran the tip of the billiard cue along a river flowing in a big curve towards the Amazon itself. 'It's here –' he drew a circle – 'downstream of a settlement called Puerto Pizarro. A few days ago, American satellites picked up a new construction site.'

He came back and sat down again. 'The reasons the narcos set up in places like that are simple. First, it gives them protection – we don't have the resources to find them. Second, they can bring in their raw supplies by boat upriver from the Amazon. Third, they're close to the Peruvian border, and in a few minutes they can flip across by light plane.

'In the past they built the labs right beside airstrips, but lately they've gotten more sophisticated. Now they put the buildings some distance from the strip, which makes them harder to find. Communication between the two may be by road, but it could also be by water. Say by a tributary of the main waterway.

'We expect Caquetá to conform to this new pattern. There's an army airstrip at Puerto Pizarro, fairly close by, and a military outpost. But we're not too struck on low-level air reconnaissance. First, the distances are very big. Second, if the facility's a few kilometres off the river, you're probably going to miss it on a single pass. Third, the narcos are more than capable of shooting down a low-flying aircraft. They have all modern weapons, including surface-to-air missiles.'

I nodded. An awkward silence followed. I wanted to propose a plan of action, but at the same time I didn't want this guy to think I was teaching him to suck eggs. In the end I said, 'Do you mind if I make a suggestion?'

'Go right ahead.'

'If a major assault went in on the facility – say by helicopter gunships – the narcos would top the hostages and throw them in the river before any incoming troops could get on the ground. Now in a way this problem is of our own making. If possible we'd like to crack it ourselves. I have a team of ten men, all highly trained. We're used to working together. We operate best as a self-contained unit, and our speciality is covert approach. We'd aim to infiltrate the area without being detected, find out the camp routine, and strike at whatever moment seemed most advantageous. We're most effective in that covert kind of role. If we can be sure the hostages have been taken to this place, and you can lift us to within a reasonable distance of it, we'll recover them on our own.'

The General looked at me steadily, as if he was sizing up my fighting potential. Then he said, 'Your men have won a lot of respect down at Santa Rosa.'

'We're jungle trained,' I said.

'We have helicopters – Hueys.'

'Where are they?'

'All over.'

'Could you get a couple down to Puerto . . . Puerto Pizarro today?'

'I expect so, yes.'

'We'll need some logistics back-up, too.'

'Such as?'

'Mosquito nets, hammocks, DPMs, medical packs. Ropes, in case we have to rope down out of a chopper. Inflatable boats, too, by the sound of it. Normally, we'd have all this as a matter of routine. But we didn't come equipped for an operation of this kind. Rations, also. We brought a small amount of food with us, for emergencies, but not enough to deploy with.'

'All that can be arranged.' Nariño had been making some notes, and now looked coolly at me.

'I'm sorry to break the training course. That's going well.'

'Too bad. Maybe you can pick it up again when this is over.'

Once more I nodded. Then I said, 'The immediate problem is, we left most of our stuff in the camp at Santa Rosa. We need to get back there fast to pick up our kit and weapons.'

'Of course. One moment.' He picked up a telephone, pressed a single button and began to speak, quietly but firmly. I could pick up the gist of it; he was giving orders for an aircraft to be made available. I sat looking at the big map, and the ocean of green, denoting jungle, that lay in the far south.

The General put his hand over the mouthpiece of the phone and asked, 'Where are your men now?'

'At the Hostal Bonavento.'

He spoke into the receiver again, then turned back to me and said, 'A truck will collect them at eleven o'clock and lift them out to the military airfield. The flight down will take less than an hour. The aircraft can refuel at Santa Rosa, and then fly you on to Puerto Pizarro.'

'Thank you,' I replied. 'I appreciate your quick response.' As soon as I'd said that, I thought it sounded phoney – but I didn't want to seem too effusive. To appear a bit warmer I added, 'Bill Egerton at the embassy asked me to give you his best wishes.'

For the first time a slight smile lit up the broad, impassive face. With his right elbow on the desk he held out his hand, palm down and fingers extended, and in a curious gesture rocked it slightly to right and left, as if to express that a certain amount of give-and-take went on between the DAS and the embassy. 'Yes,' he said. 'Bill is a good friend of ours.'

As I got up to go, he brought out a card, scribbled a number on the back, and handed it to me. 'This is my direct line, here or at home. You can call me any time,' he said. 'I'm glad to help.'

Back at the embassy I found Tony talking on the satcom telephone. He was giving, or checking, some coordinates. 'Yeah,' he said, 'that's seventy-three fifty west, zero degrees fifty south. OK.'

Seeing me come in, he turned and raised a thumb, then said into the mouthpiece, 'Call back when you've seen the next one. Fine. Thanks.'

He hung up and said, 'We got it!'

'What?'

'The hostage location.'

'How?'

'Satellites. I called my guys in Fort Worth, and they went right through to Langley, Virginia. One satellite or another is passing over here every twenty minutes. They checked their records and found that a new construction site's been growing during the past few weeks on a big bend of the Rio Caquetá –'

I held up a hand. 'Don't think I'm trying to take the piss, Tony, but I know all that already.'

I told what I'd heard from the general.

'OK,' he said equably. 'Anyway, the controllers are going for a high-resolution shot of it on one of the next passes.'

'Brilliant!'

Our only map was too small-scale to be much use, but Tony had marked a dot in the green area just north of the river, about eighty ks east of the settlement. No road of any kind approached the township, or whatever it was.

Already it was after 10.30. Time was zipping past. I phoned the hotel to warn the guys to be ready for the off at eleven. Then I called Hereford to update the boss on the situation. I said we were planning to set up a forward mounting base at Puerto Pizarro, and play it from there. I told him I'd leave Tony Lopez as anchor-man in the embassy, and report in on our portable satcom phone as soon as I got back to it.

I was on the point of leaving when Tony's mate in Langley came through again to say that the close-up satellite shot showed details of the new workings at the Caquetá site. There were now three buildings, as opposed to two a week ago, and the snap-shot, taken twenty minutes earlier, showed a twin-engined aircraft sitting on a strip carved out of the jungle alongside the river about one k away.

'That's got to be the aircraft which took our party in,' I said. 'That clinches it.'

Getting up to go, I tried to thank Bill Egerton for all he'd done. 'I'm sorry. This has wrecked your weekend.'

'Not a bit. If I wasn't here, I'd only be sitting in the garden reading *The Times* weekly edition. This is much more entertaining!'

Tony came down in the lift with me. 'Listen,' I said. 'I'm really sorry to be leaving you here.'

'No sweat, Geordie. I'm having a ball. Playing ambassadors is great.'

'Yep, but if there's some action, you'll want to be part of it.'

'Sure. But who knows where the action's gonna be? Take care, anyway.'

A battered army three-ton truck clattered up to the hotel a couple of minutes before eleven. I checked that all bills were paid and all rooms clear, then we bundled into the back and rode out to the airfield, a short run of less than fifteen minutes.

The military field proved to be one side of the El Dorado civilian airport. A Herc, painted drab olive green, without markings, stood on the pan. A military truck was parked beside the tail-ramp, and guys were loading stores into it like ants. Our driver drew up alongside it and we piled out. Inside the back of the plane there was already a fair stack of kit, and as we arrived some of the loadies were starting to lash it down.

The Colombian head-loadie came down from the flight-deck for a rapid conference with the boss of the logistic party, ticking items off a list. Then he turned to me with a cheerful grin and said, '*Por favor*', waving us to go aboard. He followed us in, checking that we'd all belted up into the canvas sling-seats along the sides. He said, 'Fly one hour.'

Then he spoke to the pilot on the intercom, and hit the button to raise the tail ramp. The engines began to turn, and that dreaded whine built up to full strength as the big aircraft lumbered forward.

The flight lasted no more than fifty minutes, but it gave me time to think. If we did manage to launch an operation against the new drugs complex, everything would depend on surprise. If the narcos got wind of a rescue attempt, or thought an attack was coming in, they'd top the hostages for sure. This meant that we had to get in covertly, establish an OP, discover the routine of the place, and take the defenders by surprise.

The pilot never bothered to gain any great altitude, and air currents coming off the mountains made the flight pretty rough. I was glad when the plane banged down hard on the dirt runway at Santa Rosa, and there was Sparky, waving like a lunatic from the edge of the strip. I thought he was taking the piss out of us for coming back early, and spending all our money while he'd been hoarding his. Not at all. He was frantic for me to get on the satcom link to Tony in Bogotá.

'But I've only just left the bugger,' I protested.

'I know, but there's been a development. He says you're to call immediately.'

'OK, guys.' I looked round. 'Leave the Colombian stores on board. Everyone get their personal kit packed up and ready for the off. We need to load all our ammunition and PE, as well. Make sure we don't leave anything behind.'

'Aren't we coming back?' somebody asked.

'Might be. Might not. It depends how things go. Anyway, we're off in a few minutes.'

Sparky had the spike of the little dish aerial stuck into the ground outside our accommodation block, but the satellite had wandered out of range, and for a couple of minutes we couldn't make any contact. Then, having checked with his compass and reset the elevation, he suddenly hit it spot-on. The call went through, the line clear as clear.

'Tony – hi. What's on?'

'The bastards have split the party. We got two separate

reports from the toads within a few minutes of your leaving. One party's gone to the Caquetá, all right. But the other's in Cartagena.'

'Jesus! Where's that?'

'It's a port on the north coast.'

'Fucking hell. Who's where?'

'One toad said that the *gringa* and four *gringos*, one old and three young, have been taken to the Rio Caquetá.'

'That sounds like our party, with a couple of PIRA in tow.'

'Yeah – but listen to this. The other toad said that a *gringo con cabellos rubios* had been put on board a ship at Cartagena.'

'Jesus Christ! Fair hair – that must mean Peter, the Rupert.'

'Exactly.'

'Do we know what ship it is?'

'Yep. It's a cargo vessel called the *Santa Maria de la Mar*. Nine thousand tons. Panamanian registered. It's making ready to sail for Amsterdam.'

'God almighty. They're trying to get him out of the country. The PIRA must have found out he's from the Regiment.'

'Right. They'll beat the shit out of him to make him talk.'

'Maybe they're aiming to get him back to Northern Ireland. Tony, we need to hit that ship. Maybe we'd better turn round and come back.' I thought for a moment. Then I realized that what we needed were the special skills of the Boat Troop. We could undertake more or less any operation on land, and a couple of us had trained for short periods with the boat guys. But if it came to a ship assault we were neither fully trained nor properly equipped.

I said as much to Tony, then added, 'We'll carry on with our own operation. But I'm going to call Hereford and get the Boat Troop put on standby.'

'Wait a bit. It's not that easy. If we're going to hit the ship we've got to hit the lab at the same time. And vice versa. We need two operations, co-ordinated down to the last few seconds. Otherwise the narcos will top the other half of the equation.'

'OK. Two operations. But, Christ – when's the ship due to sail?'

'Some time tomorrow. Our information is that she's heading for an offshore island, to trans-ship drugs. Our best tactic will be to hit her there, when the crew's not expecting anything. But we need to know where she's going. The toad said Amsterdam. That could be right, in the end, but it could be disinformation. She could head in any goddamn direction. What we've got to do is get a tracking device on board her before she sails.'

Even as he talked, in my mind I was seeing the guys in the Boat Troop. I knew several of them well: Steve, Roger, Merv – all first-class operators. This looked like an ideal task for them.

'The trouble is,' I said, 'our lot will never get here in time. They have to go round about four stops on the way, like we did, spread over several days.'

'No,' replied Tony. 'But mine will. The SEALs'll get there. There's a team on standby in Florida all the time. Your government will have to clear it from England, but I'm going to call my guys right away and give them advance warning that they're gonna go stick a device on the ship while she's still in port. A hit out at sea or at an island would be another matter. That would stir the diplomatic shit, and it might need clearance from the Pentagon. But we can get a bleeper in place without anyone knowing.'

'Great! Go ahead with that. I'll speak to the head-shed in Hereford and tell them the score.'

'Listen,' Tony said. 'You got a pencil and paper? I did a couple of calculations, based on the satellite information. On your jungle location, you need to chopper in towards the target without getting close enough to alert anybody. The best thing will be to cut straight across from the base at Puerto Pizarro to the north of the target. Aim for the tributary and come down that. That way, you won't fly closer to the laboratory than eight or nine ks, and nobody's going to hear you. If you head out from the base on zero–eight–seven degrees, you'll hit the Rio Cuemani ten ks north of the new airstrip.'

'OK,' I said. 'I got a note of that.'

'South of the big river,' he went on, 'there's a solitary mountain. I guess it'll stand right out of the flat jungle. Looks like it's got a conical peak. You're never going to be closer to it than fifty ks, but you'll see it away to your right. When you get level with it, you'll be coming to your tributary.'

He went on to describe the precise layout of the landing-strip, the link road (which didn't run straight, but wound through the forest) and the buildings of the laboratory itself. As he talked I wrote and sketched details in my note-book.

'Thanks, Tony. Zero-eight-seven will be our heading. I'll get on to Hereford now.'

I was about to line up the call when I saw Captain Jaime heading towards us. Pretending I felt happy, I said, '¡Hola, Capitán! Embarrada.' A big problem.

He seemed a bit disgruntled, and wanted some explanation. I gave it, itching to be on the move. 'How many days will you be away?' he asked.

'One or two,' I said casually. 'That should do it.'

Of course I hadn't a clue. But I could see that he was getting the shits worrying how to keep forty-odd men occupied.

Sparky tuned his dish again, and we got through to Hereford. Again they put me on to the CO. I briefed him on the situation, then said, 'Boss, this has the makings of a first-class international fuck-up.'

'Don't worry,' said the Colonel. 'We've got the diplomatic side well under control. I don't think there's going to be any attempt to stop you. We've already cleared the SEALs' involvement with the US government. It's great that Tony Lopez is there to liaise.'

'A big stroke of luck, I know.'

'Wait one,' said the CO. 'Straighten me out on the different locations. I've got a map in front of me.'

'OK. We're calling them Green One, Two, Three and Four. Green One's Tony, in Bogotá. I'm now on Green Two, at the training camp at Santa Rosa, about 250 ks south of Bogotá. But it's only a camp and a village, so probably it won't be on your map. The ship that we think Peter Black's been put

231

on is at Cartagena, on the north coast, about eleven o'clock from Bogotá. We're calling the ship Blue One.'

'Right,' went the boss. 'I have that.'

'Green Three is an army outpost at Puerto Pizarro, on the Rio Caquetá, about seven o'clock from Bogotá, 400 ks further south from my present location, and right out in the Amazon basin. Again, you probably haven't got that marked – it's pretty small. Green Four is the other hostage location, fifty ks east of Pizarro, on the north side of the river, where it swings round in a big bend.'

'Pizarro. Can't see that either. What's your plan, anyway?'

'There's a landing strip at the army outpost. DAS have put a Herc at our disposal, and we're off down there in a few minutes. We'll be there in a couple of hours. We'll make the camp our forward mounting base. Then we'll chopper out, establish an FOB, and put in an OP on the laboratory, to work out a recovery.'

'You're definitely going to need back-up.'

'That's right. We're short of all assets, weapons particularly. Apart from pistols, we've only got two G3s and two 203s. The trouble is, it'll take you bloody days to get here. It took us three days just to reach Colombia.'

'Don't worry. There's a mountain of war stores sitting in Belize. We can organize some of that down to you in a matter of hours. So – more 203s. More grenades. What else?'

'Basically, jungle gear for ten. Ponchos, mozzie nets, boots, hats. I think DAS have sorted some stuff out for us, but I don't know how good it is.'

'What about rations?'

'We've got a few with us, and DAS have given us some more. Christ knows what they are, but they're on board.'

'Boats?'

'Yep. They've lent us a few rubber dinghies. We haven't unpacked them yet.'

'OK, then. We'll try to line up a couple more. Happy landings. Report when you're on your new location.'

'Roger. We'll speak soon.'

Inside the accommodation block I threw my stuff into kit-bag and bergen. By the time I went out again, Captain Jaime had already organized the loading of our ammunition. In less than half an hour we had everything squared away on board the Herc. As I looked round the camp, with its pool and dusty football field, I felt sorry to be leaving so soon.

'*Adios, Capitán.*' Although I was hatless, I gave him a stylish salute. 'I hope we'll be back in a couple of days.'

Aboard the Herc, I went up on to the flight-deck to make sure we all agreed about where we were heading. There was no problem, but I stayed in the upper cabin to soak up a bit of Colombian geography. From down in the back you could see practically nothing, unless you stood up with your eye at one of the portholes; from up front there was a great view, as the ridges and spurs of the *Cordillera Oriental* fell away behind us and an endless vista of dark green spread out ahead, with bright silver veins of rivers running through it towards the east. The vast emptiness of the land was enough to scare the shit out of you. I felt for my little silver medallion, on its chain, and thought of home.

Compared with most hostage rescues, this one looked extremely dicey. For one thing, we were short of assets – we were certain to be out-numbered and out-gunned. On the SP team and in Northern Ireland we'd trained daily for house assault and hostage release but normally we had superior firepower, and major reinforcements at our disposal. Besides, the hostages were almost always close at hand. Here the opposite was true. Distances were immense, chances of reinforcement minimal. Our own firepower was strictly limited. We had no casevac facilities. We were going into the unknown, to a destination we hadn't even identified precisely. Basically, ten guys were attempting to do a job that would have taxed a squadron. Further, we knew from our various briefs how ruthless the enemy were – if any of us got captured, we could expect no mercy.

My mind kept returning to Black. Was he still alive? And if he was, how much had he already given away? We'd been trained, in the event of capture, to try to hold out for twenty-

233

four hours, and then, if possible, to fall back on controlled release, giving away only low-grade information. But everybody knew that this was easier said than done. What had Black told Farrell? What about the aminosity between Black, me and Tracy? Had he said anything about me? Had he revealed that I had been lifted from above Farrell's farm? I was speculating wildly, I knew, but it was impossible not to.

The pilot, a friendly guy, occasionally called out a name and pointed, but I wasn't concentrating too much on the scenery; all I could think about was how stretched we were going to be, how dependent we were on our satcom. If that freaked out, we'd have real problems. Then I became aware that the pilot was repeating some word insistently, and when I focused on him I realized he was saying, '*Caquetá, Caquetá.*'

There below us a vast river was snaking through the jungle, winding on for ever in coils through that terrific expanse of trees. For a whole half-hour we followed its course, and nothing below us changed. Occasionally, on the bank of a tributary, I saw a tiny cleared area of lighter green, with what looked like wooden huts along the edge. Obviously people were living there, and I wondered whether they were Indians. What a life! The isolation was something I could hardly imagine. The surface of the rainforest was never smooth and uniform, like that of a cultivated plantation; rather, it was rough and ragged, with trees of all different heights. There was something alien about the colour of it, too: the green wasn't anything like an English green, but darker and heavier.

At last, right on the nose, the outline of the mountain Tony had mentioned began to show through the haze ahead, and soon afterwards the pilot began his descent. As we came down, the river grew until it seemed as wide as the English Channel. From a high altitude it had shone dully like pewter, but at low level it turned muddy brown, with occasional swirls that showed the strength of the current. In the last couple of minutes we saw a huddle of shacks on the north bank, with a few more substantial buildings behind them, and a couple of boats moored alongside a jetty.

Then we were over the perimeter of the camp, which

looked much the same as the one we'd just left: a dirt strip, a high boundary fence, two lines of single-storey white buildings, one small warehouse, and goalposts with sagging crossbars at either end of a dusty football field. The best thing about it was the sight of a Huey helicopter parked on the pan outside the warehouse.

As we debussed, the heat hit us. Down at this level the air was ten times hotter and stickier. We were greeted by an army lieutenant, with circles of sweat spreading out from under the arms of his khaki fatigues, and wearing big shades. His English was even sketchier than my Spanish, so I had to make a real effort to communicate. After struggling for a while, and establishing that the chopper was out of action with a gearbox defect, I had an inspiration: call Tony and get him to interpret. I needed to speak to him anyway.

'We made it to Puerto Pizarro,' I told him.

'What's it like?'

'Hot as hell. Just a little camp surrounded by jungle. There's one Huey here, but it's gone US. Spare parts are supposed to be on the way. What news your end?'

'The SEALs are deploying. They're going in tonight to stick a tracking device on the *Santa Maria*. Then it doesn't matter where she sails – we can go get her to coincide with your operation.'

'Great!'

'Your Boat Troop guys are on their way, too. I don't know how he hacked it, but the CO's got an RAF TriStar held back, and they're flying direct to Belize tonight. One hop only. They'll be there at 0100 local time.' He paused, then said, 'Hey – I got you some pretty good detail from the satellite station. You have a pencil and paper?'

'Wait one.' I brought out the little notebook I always carry in the breast-pocket of my shirt, with a miniature pencil down the spine. 'OK. Fire away.'

'The new lab complex is near that big bend of the river, like we said. But it's four ks north of the Caquetá. The airstrip's confirmed along the bank of the tributary, and some kind of jetty's been built there, on the west bank. The buildings are

235

grouped round a small compound one k west of the airstrip. There's a road of sorts connecting the two, probably earth. It snakes around through the trees.'

As he talked, I was drawing a sketch. 'D'you have the layout of the building?'

'Sure. There's two rectangular structures that look finished, each about fifty metres long. They're set out in a line, running east–west. The third building, across the end of the compound, is still under construction.'

'Tony,' I said, 'I've been thinking the best way to make a covert approach would be to come down the tributary at night in a rubber dinghy, then slide in for a CTR. What about that?'

'Sounds good. I confirm. Chopper out of your present location on zero–eight–seven, dead straight for sixty ks. Then you hit the Cuemani, coming down from your left across your front. The alignment of the tributary's very nearly north–south. It's coming from three–five–zero and heading to one–seven–zero. Famous last words, but you really can't miss it. OK, Geordie? But for Pete's sake don't try swimming. Those rivers are full of crocs.'

'Right,' I said. 'I'm calling this Operation Crocodile. Op Croc. Listen, the lieutenant here doesn't speak much English. Could you run through the plan with him? Thanks.'

I handed the receiver over. Suddenly I began to feel rather good. We were within spitting distance of some action. Things were about to become interesting.

The lieutenant listened to Tony for a while, asked a few questions, and said, '*Si*,' a great many times. When he seemed to have finished, I beckoned for him to hand the receiver back. 'Tony,' I said, ' tell him for Christ's sake to get the Huey airworthy. I don't know what's wrong with it – I think it's a gearbox problem. He's supposed to be flying parts in, but I'm not too sure.'

The guys were humping the stores out of the Herc and loading them on to a trailer pulled by a Willys jeep, vintage about 1942. 'As you value your bollocks,' I told them, 'no swimming in the river. It's heaving with crocodiles.' I turned to the beshaded lieutenant and made extravagant jaw-snapping motions with my arms. '¡*Si, si!*' he confirmed. '¡*Cocodrilos –muchísimos!*'

'Fucking great!' said Murdo. 'That's all we want. If the Amazon's the arsehole of the world, I reckon we're about 5,000 ks up it.'

Murdo had a point. The facilities the Colombians offered us were as crappy as could be. They themselves looked to be fairly well set up in the better of the two barrack-blocks, with a generator, mozzie screens and fridges – and I didn't grudge them whatever comforts they'd been able to devise. If you had to spend any length of time in that hell-hole, you'd need everything you could get to stay sane. The block they gave us was another matter: no electricity, bare concrete rooms without doors, the iron bedsteads all rusted, no water in the showers, the bog an open hole in the floor.

When we unpacked the stores, things looked up a bit, because the General had done us well: there were four dinghy packs, two outboards, hammocks, mozzie nets, waterbottles, machetes and twenty sets of jungle DPMs. Once we'd sorted them out, everyone got a size that more or less fitted him, with another set in reserve. There were also four big boxes of MREs – US forces' standard-issue Meals Ready to Eat, or, as they'd been known in the Gulf, Meals Rejected by Ethiopians. In fact they were pretty good, especially the things like corned-beef hash and chilli con carne. The guys soon got brews going with their hexi cookers, and after some sort of a meal, spirits picked up.

In the usual way, we planned our tactics at an O-group that took the form of a Chinese parliament, with everyone sitting round in a circle on the ground. Obviously we weren't going anywhere that night, but there was no harm in having a plan ready. The sun was already sinking towards the jungle in a thick haze, and the temperature was dropping slightly. Even so, we were all still sweating like pigs.

Even if the Huey became airworthy, its maximum load, besides the pilot and navigator, would be three guys plus kit, one dinghy kit plus engine, and skeleton equipment and stores.

I offered to stay back, but everyone agreed I should lead from the front. That made me one of the three to fly. The second had to be Sparky Springer, as he was our radio specialist. For the third, I nominated Murdo McFarlane. Provided he left his blasted pipes behind, he'd be as good as anyone in the jungle.

The next wave – which would follow us in the next evening by the same route, provided the Huey was serviceable – would consist of Johnny Ellis, Stew McQuarrie and Mel Scott.

THIRTEEN

Author's Note
Because I was in the jungle at the time, I could not witness the SEALs' approach to the Santa Maria de la Mar, or the Boat Troop's assault on the island of Desierto. I have therefore built my account of the actions on the reports of men who took part. All were well known either to Tony Lopez or to me, and I am satisfied that the account is substantially accurate.

The SEAL team landed at a military airfield outside the old colonial town and port of Cartagena. The unmarked Herc which brought them from Florida touched down at 1600 local time, leaving them enough daylight for a quick scout round the port. As Tony later emphasized, they would normally have carried out a much more thorough reconnaissance, watching their target for several days to establish the routine on board and looking for weak spots; but this was a fastball, and left no time for niceties.

DAS had laid on two nondescript vans to transport the team and their gear. They also provided a local liaison officer to brief Master Sergeant Al Layton, the team leader. The Colombian informed him that the ship was lying in berth No. 7 on No. 1 Pier, the western of the two main arms at the *Terminal Maritimo* on Manga Island, at the north side of the bay. The dock gates were guarded by regular police, and there was no chance of gaining access through them, but the ship could be seen from the south side of the bay. Al therefore had the team driven to an observation point on the southern shore.

Casual clothes did much to disguise the physiques of the eight team members. Al was twenty-six, and although of only medium height he was extremely powerful, with particular strength in his upper body. His colleagues were all much the same, built up by years of swimming, running and work in the gym. Had they all stripped off on the beach they would have started a riot.

The vans parked on the south-east side of the bay, on a stretch of the shore that nobody had yet got around to developing. Other vehicles were already scattered along it, so that the new arrivals attracted no attention, and Al's guys were able to carry out covert observation without hindrance. The Old Town, out on the point beyond the harbour, did not interest them. Nor did the new, high-rise blocks in the smart suburb of Bocagrande, away to their left. They wasted no time looking at the tourist boats drifting in and out of the harbour as they plied to the coral reefs offshore. Their attention was focused exclusively on the *Santa Maria*.

The ship was a fair distance across the bay, but through binoculars and a 30-power telescope they were able to make out useful details. She was moored with her bow facing the bay and her starboard side to the quay, so that they were looking at her port bow. She was second in line on that side of the harbour, with other ships moored close up fore and aft. Her hull was black and her upperworks white, but showing rusty patches, and she was flying the Panamanian flag. She looked scruffy, at least twenty years old. As Al and his men watched, she was still being loaded; two tall dock cranes were swinging nets over her deck and lowering them into the forward hold. According to DAS information, her cargo was officially coffee, but almost certainly included cocaine, probably several tons of it. With a street value in the United States of $35,000 a kilo, the illicit element in her holds could well have been worth over a hundred million.

For the SEAL team, the position of the ship was ideal. From where they were, they could swim straight to her without coming close to any other vessel or the dockside. At their normal average speed of a hundred metres in three minutes, it would take them just under half an hour to cross the bay. They decided that their best access point was forward of the accommodation, and beside the third hold; the hatch-cover stood three or four feet proud of the deck, and would

240

help conceal them as they came over the rail. Having sized things up, Al opted for a midnight departure; because she was still loading, it was clear that the *Santa Maria* wasn't on the point of sailing, and if they reached her well after midnight there was a good chance that all the crew except the gangplank guard would be in their bunks.

During the interval, the team repaired to an empty warehouse which DAS had taken over. There they had plenty of room to lay their gear out and check it through. As usual, Al split his party into two four-man teams, A and B, each of two pairs. Team A would do the swim and place the device, with Team B in reserve, keeping a lookout and ready to go after them or stage a diversion, should the need arise.

By 2345 both teams were back on the dockside at their launch point, clad in their black Spandex wetsuits. Working in pairs, each man checking his buddy, they squeezed out all the excess air and breathed themselves down until the suits were clinging to their bodies. Over the neoprene suits went their ops waistcoats, loaded with weapons and ammunition. Each man had an MP 5 and three spare magazines, besides a Browning and two spare mags for that. The weapons had all been soaked in Silverspeed and thoroughly oiled; immersion in water would make no difference to them. For safety's sake each man clipped his shooters to him with nylon lanyards and small karabiners.

Working with his buddy, Gus Ford, Al breathed down all his equipment to clear the air from it, then lashed a hooligan bar – an angled jemmy with a spike on one end – to the middle of Gus's back. Each man checked the other off:

'MP 5?'

'Yep.'

'Magazines?'

'Three.'

'Lanyard?'

'Yep.'

'Hooligan bar?'

'Yep.'

'Respirator?'

241

'OK.'

Al was also carrying the transponder, sealed in polythene and attached by a lanyard to a ring on his waist. Normally, in salt water, he needed eight kilograms of extra weight to stop him bobbing on the surface. The transponder, together with its magnetic fastener, weighed one kilo, so he loaded one more kilo weight into a spare pocket. Finally the men pulled on their Drega rebreathing kits – cumbersome, heavy outfits incorporating mask, hood and oxygen bottle, that use a sealed circuit so that they let out no bubbles. Again each buddy checked his partner, then the supervisor said, 'OK, guys. Go on gas.'

To purge his lungs of extra nitrogen, Al took three deep breaths of oxygen, in through the mouth, out through the nose. His mask misted up immediately, and he was uncomfortably aware that he had thirty ks of equipment slung round his neck. Even though he'd been diving for ten years, he still hated this moment. If he was going to get an O_2 hit, this was when it would come. He himself had never gone down with oxygen poisoning, but he'd seen other guys go into spasm and then arc back, rigid. The cure was plenty of fresh air, quickly – but the experience was one he could do without.

Once in the water, everything changed. He felt comfortable and secure in a world with which he was completely familiar. After one last check to make sure his three companions were ready he set off, swimming on a bearing of 305 degrees.

The night was very dark. There was no moon, and hazy cloud was blocking the starlight. The water of the bay lay still as black ink, with the distant lights of the harbour and the town reflected in it. For the first half of the journey Al judged it safe to remain on the surface. He swam gently, keeping well within his capabilities, and watching the compass, depth-gauge and timer on the swim board held out ahead of him.

After fifteen minutes, with the party out in the middle of the bay, an offshore breeze started up, putting a ripple on the water. Then Al heard a speedboat approaching from behind his left shoulder. It could have been narcos, running a consignment of drugs across from Bocagrande to one of the ships in the harbour. It could have been late-night revellers taking a short-cut home. Whatever, he was taking no chances, so he and the others dived – and the speedboat passed harmlessly above them.

Thereafter he swam at a depth of four metres, coming up at the end of every three minutes to check his position. At twenty-one minutes the harbour lights were much closer, but still it was impossible to tell which ship was which, and he had to rely on the compass bearing to keep him oriented. All the time Gus was one man's length behind him, guided by the phosphorescence which Al's passage through the water was creating. The other two followed at similar intervals behind.

At twenty-seven minutes he slowed, and when Gus came alongside he gave him one squeeze on the arm to indicate that he was surfacing for another observe. This time he found a big hulk of ship right in front of him, but he could tell by the outline of her bow against the sky that she was the first in the line. They had drifted slightly to the left of their target. The tide must have been going out faster than they'd expected. Sinking back, he gave Gus two squeezes to indicate that they were approaching the target, then swam on, heading right. Three minutes later he surfaced again. This time he was just off the bow of the *Santa Maria*. The big white letters of her name stood out boldly from the sweep of the black hull.

Diving again, he gave Gus three presses to tell him they'd arrived. Gus passed the message back to the other pair. All four men surfaced and swam gently to their right, observing from a distance. Apart from one light showing through an open doorway in the accommodation block, and one naked bulb dangling from a cargo derrick, the ship was dark.

Satisfied that their plan was good, Al swam in and clamped himself to the side with two magnets. Now he was close, a faint hum of generators told him that the ship was alive. There was also the usual background noise of water slapping gently against the hull. Four presses, passed back through the team, confirmed that they were at the entry point. Al pulled off his rebreathing kit and magneted it on to the side, out of the way, and the others did the same. If anything went wrong

243

while they were on board, they could jump over the rail and recover the sets from this temporary storage. Peering up, Al was glad to see that the curve of the hull put them out of sight – and range – of anyone looking down.

It took Gus only a few seconds to assemble the telescopic pole which had travelled strapped to his back. As he fitted the lengths together, the No. 3 swimmer, Jack Ashby, was unrolling the thirty-foot kevlar ladder. Then, with two of the others holding him steady on short ropes, Gus swam out a few feet, hoisted the pole and hooked the ladder over the ship's rail.

Al was the first up. His jungle boots made only faint scuffling sounds on the ship's side. When his head reached deck level he paused, listening. Then with a quick scramble he was over the rail and against the hatch cover, Browning in hand. A moment later he holstered the pistol and brought his MP 5 to the ready. A tug on the ladder: two up. Another tug: three up. The fourth man, Sonny Mitchell, came up and took station to secure their entry point.

The other three moved cautiously aft, keeping in the deep shadows thrown by the single light high on the derrick. Al was thinking to himself, 'Now we've got this far, why don't we go in and rescue the hostage?' The trouble was, they didn't know which part of the ship the poor bastard was in – he could have been down in one of the holds – and in any case, he was bound to be guarded.

The night air was hot and moist. Inside his suit Al was sweating freely. Creeping aft, he came level with the start of the accommodation block. The first doorway stood open. Beyond it was a porthole, also open. Through it Al could hear the hiss of water moving through pipes. The john. Just the place, except that he wanted somewhere higher, on an upper deck. It was odds on that all the plumbing systems were stacked on top of each other.

A metal companionway led upwards. Leaving Jack to guard the base of it, Al and Gus went up. Another open doorway. Another porthole in a similar position. There was one more deck above them, but there was no more external companionway, and this was the highest they could go without penetrating into the heart of the accommodation.

Al pointed to the porthole and stuck up a thumb, meaning 'This will do'. Gus stood guard with his MP 5 at the ready while he stepped carefully over the sill. The metal door of the john was ajar. He applied pressure very gently, in case it squeaked, but the hinges gave silently. With the door open, there was enough light for him to see all he needed: a cistern above the twin urinals on the outside bulkhead.

The metal lid was held in place by small bolts with wing-nuts on them, one at either end. The threads of the bolts had been painted over, and he couldn't shift the nuts with finger and thumb. Pulling out a pair of pliers, he unclipped them from their lanyard, reached up, and got the nuts moving. In a few more seconds he had lifted off the metal lid and laid it carefully on the floor. Then he drew his knife from its sheath, slit the wrappings of the transponder, pulled out the pin to activate the device and held it firmly to prevent any sudden jerk as its powerful circular plate-magnet clamped itself to the underside of the lid. A moment later he had the lid back in position. It was fractionally tilted forward by the aerial wire leading out over the rim and propping the back up, but no Colombian seaman was going to notice that. He screwed the wing-nuts back down by hand, leaving the upper threads of the bolts bare of paint. Nothing he could do about that – but again, it was highly unlikely that anyone would notice so small a change. Providentially, a metal pipe ran up and down the bulkhead behind the cistern, giving him an ideal conductor. He wound the naked end of the wire round it, and pushed the rest of the coil down out of sight.

Out in the open again, he faced in the direction of the rear party, onshore across the bay, and turned on an infra-red torch, invisible to the naked eye, but instantly detectable to someone with the correct receiver. Seconds later a voice in his earpiece said, 'OK, Al. We're just going to check your signal strength with base. Stand by.'

He waited, thinking of the satellites passing overhead, and reflecting on how extraordinary it was that the little device he'd just stuck in the john could communicate with them. Then came the voice from the shore again. 'OK, Al. They have you loud and clear. Signal strength six. That's as good as you're gonna get.'

He doused the torch and raised a thumb to Gus. The two of them checked each other in whispers:

'Pliers?'

'Yeah.'

'Knife?'

'Yeah.'

'All screws back in position?'

'Two screws back.'

Both knew full well that the slightest trace of their presence, the smallest alien object, could destroy the secrecy of their visit. Satisfied that all was well, they crept down the companionway to the main deck. Back at their entry point, they unhooked the ladder and secured it temporarily with long lines of paracord tied in slip-knots, which would fall away when pulled from below. Al saw the other three down, then went over the side. Two tugs on the cords brought the ladder splashing softly down on them. With their rebreathing kits back on, they sank away into the black depths of the harbour, and the *Santa Maria* bore no more trace of their entry than if she had been visited by a ghost.

FOURTEEN

Most of the time I was worrying about Peter Black. The poor bastard was going to get skinned alive by the PIRA. I tried to stop myself thinking of all the things they'd do to him to make him talk.

It was good to hear that the SEALs had successfully planted the transponder, and that satellites were picking up its signals. Then Tony came through to say that the ship had sailed from Cartagena at 0830, and that she was heading north into the Caribbean. The head-shed in Hereford told us that a consignment of stores was on its way down to us from Belize, and that a quick-reaction force put together from B and G Squadrons was standing by to fly in.

We unpacked the dinghies and inflated them to make sure they weren't punctured. All day, on and off, I nagged the local boss about the Huey spares, and he made radio calls about them. But it wasn't till 1500 that at last an aged Dakota came droning in from the west, bringing the parts and a couple of mechanics. We watched from a distance as they went to work, and we could hardly believe it when, around 1630, they announced that they'd cured the problem. The pilot and navigator walked out, started up, and took the Huey for a test flight around the area. Back on the deck, they reported that everything was fine.

At 1700 I held a final O-group to confirm details. By then I'd drawn out a bigger plan on the side of a cardboard ration box, and I used it for reference. Also we had a fairly good map that the DAS had provided. 'Operation Crocodile,' I began. 'Voice comms out of the forward operating base will be insecure, so we'll refer to locations by call-signs only. OK? Our locations are as follows. The Bogotá Embassy is Green One. The training camp at Santa Rosa's Green Two. This forward mounting base

247

here is Green Three. And finally, the FOB, close to or on the target, is Green Four. It's easy to remember, because the locations are numbered in the order we've been through them, or will be through them.'

'Green!' exclaimed Murdo sarcastically. 'Everything's fucking green, as far as the eye can fucking see.'

'OK,' I went on. 'So it's the four greens. Now, personnel. Murdo, Sparky and I will chopper in to a point approximately here.' I indicated a spot on the bank of the Cuemani. 'If the Huey can land, so much the better. Otherwise we'll fast-rope down. We'll identify the spot by displaying the cloth, either pegged down in the open or tied to a tree. Then we'll launch the boat, proceed downriver and get ourselves in position for a CTR. During tomorrow, the second wave of three will chopper out to the same point and come downriver to join us. After that, we'll have to play things by ear.'

A few questions, and everything was wrapped up. By 1720 we were hot to trot. We took one G3, two 203s and three pistols, plus ammunition and a box of PE. Luckily I'd thrown an ops waistcoat into my Lacon box before leaving the UK, so that accommodated a lot of my personal kit, including the Magellan.

The pilot, Pedro, and his navigator were both young fellows with short, spiky black hair. Neither spoke more than a few words of English, so I went through everything several times, making certain they'd got the right bearing – zero-eight-seven – firmly in their heads. I also impressed on the pilot that it was essential he memorize the spot at which he put us down, so that he could find it again next day. Also, after he'd dropped us, he had to swing out to the north and return to base in a wide arc, as though he was searching the jungle for lost persons.

He started up and took off without fuss, and in a few seconds we were over the forest-sea, skimming through the hot dusk just clear of the highest trees. I caught an occasional flash of emerald, red or yellow as some brilliantly coloured bird took off in fright, but otherwise our whole world was drab grey-green. Looking forward over the pilot's shoulder, I watched the needle of the compass sitting steadily on the correct heading.

Apprehension crept up on me. Why were we going in on this crazy operation? Because my first loyalty was to the Regiment, I'd far rather have been in on the plan to rescue Peter Black. Maybe we should have devoted all our resources to that. Then again, I thought, even if we'd turned around at Santa Rosa and headed back north, so that we could go in to storm the boat in harbour at Cartagena, the narcos would probably have topped their captive before we could reach him. Better leave things there to the SEALs or the Boat Troop. Meanwhile, down here in the jungle . . . I had no strong feelings about the DA. I didn't care too much about what happened to him. But Luisa was a different matter. The idea of a beautiful, intelligent woman getting roughly handled, maybe raped or killed, through no fault of her own, was difficult to live with. Maybe it sounds sexist, but for me at any rate she was the main reason for going in.

The navigator and I had calculated that, cruising at 120 knots, we would reach the Cuemani in twenty-three minutes. Twenty-one minutes into the flight, the pilot began to lift up to gain a wider view of our surroundings. Already the light was going, and the forest beneath us had turned from grey-green to nearly black. Then suddenly ahead was the gleam of the river, across our line of approach.

In seconds we were over the near bank. I motioned to Pedro to slow down and turn right, over the water. I was prepared to fly about two ks downstream, towards the airstrip, but no nearer. Within that distance we'd have to find a landing zone of some sort.

As he hovered, we searched in vain for an opening in the cover. The forest grew right to the bank of the river, the trees overhanging the stream. I'd started to think we would have to fast-rope through the canopy when suddenly I spotted a slight rise in the ground, an outcrop of rock, which formed a little cliff. The chopper could have landed on it, but for a single tree growing out of a cleft.

I gave a shout and pointed down. Pedro went straight in

and hovered at a good height. We lowered the pack containing the dinghy, and then our three bergens in a single bundle. Finally we ourselves slid down individual ropes and signalled we were clear. Up went the Huey with our lines trailing from its belly. It swung off to the north as instructed, and in a minute the noise of its engine had died away.

The occasional bird was still calling, perhaps stirred up by the aircraft, and frogs were croaking; but apart from those natural noises, there wasn't a sound. In the last of the light we took stock of our surroundings. On three sides the jungle stretched away unbroken. On the fourth, right below us, ran the river. We were on top of the small cliff, maybe thirty feet high, but the face of it was not vertical: it had enough of a slope and enough hand-holds for us to scramble down. I pulled out the strip of pale-coloured cloth which I'd borrowed from the Colombians, spread it over the rock and weighted it down with three or four loose stones.

I took out my Magellan, set it up, and waited for it to lock on to a passing satellite. When I got an accurate reading, I wrote it in my notebook, so that we could pass back the precise location of the landing zone when Sparky got his 319 going. Then we broke out the rubber dinghy from its pack, inflated it with the hand-pump and lowered it over the cliff, followed by the outboard on a separate tether. Within ten minutes of landing, we were drifting downriver, steering with the paddles and letting our eyes become accustomed to the gathering dusk.

Except where there was a rock-face similar to the one we had come down, the jungle pressed in to the very edge of the banks, overhanging the water. The river was at least two hundred yards wide, and I could see from the bare face of the banks that it was below its highest level. Because we were out in mid-stream, and the forest was so uniform, with few landmarks, we found it hard to tell what speed we were making; but when we augmented the current by paddling, we reckoned we were doing at least three knots, or about five k.p.h. At that rate, we'd be at the airstrip within two hours.

Occasionally a loud slap and a splash would sound from the

stream. In fact I think most of the disturbances came from fish, but several times I felt the hair come up on my neck just from the thought of crocodiles. The pilot of the Herc had told me that the Caquetá was over two thousand kilometres long. Even though we were only on a tributary, our own river was big enough – and here we were, going down it in a tiny rubber boat to an unknown destination in the heart of the biggest rainforest on earth.

We must have been travelling faster than we thought, because after only one hour forty I suddenly realized that there was no longer a wall of jungle on the right bank. We had come to a place where the trees had been cut away. Further downstream I made out a long, grey shape which could only be the landing jetty.

'Look out!' I whispered. 'Back up! Paddle for the bank.'

Murdo and Sparky spun the dinghy and headed across the current for the shore. A few trees still clung to the edge of the water, and we came in under them among a mass of roots. Standing up in the back of the little rubber boat, I got hold of an overhanging branch and pulled us in.

The roots, over which we had to scramble ashore, were treacherous in the extreme: invisible, uneven, and slippery as ice. Getting wet up to mid-thigh hardly mattered, though as the night was so warm; more serious was the noise we made floundering about. We tethered the boat temporarily to a branch and scrabbled up the steep earth bank, to find ourselves on the edge of a flat, clear space: the new airstrip. Away to our left, glimmering like a big, white moth, was a twin-engined plane, a square-bodied Islander.

Immediately we had a problem: what to do with the boat? To drag it ashore, through the mat of roots and branches, would be impossible. An alternative was to climb back on board and let it drift downstream, bringing it ashore on the new wharf. The trouble with that one was that the jetty might be guarded – and if we got the dinghy on land, what would we do with it then? A third alternative was to head back upstream and cache the boat on the edge of the virgin jungle; but, given the strength of the current, I doubted we'd make any headway

251

with paddles alone, and I didn't want to risk starting up the outboard. In the end, after a rapid Chinese parliament, we decided to leave the dinghy where it was. It was well hidden from boats passing on the river by overhanging branches, and the chances of anyone searching the bank along the perimeter of the airstrip seemed infinitesimal. Once on the airfield, we took a note of the boat's position by reference to a single tree that stood taller than the rest.

Pepperpotting was the order of the night. By luck we'd come ashore near the northern end of the landing strip. The plane was parked at the south end, about six hundred metres away. While one of us went forward to check our immediate surroundings, the other two covered him from a distance. Then, at a low whistle, they moved up, and one of them took over the lead. We stalked the aircraft with extreme care, moving silently over the raw, scraped earth of the runway. We expected to find at least one guard stationed by it, or in it, and we were surprised to find the Islander deserted. The temptation to booby-trap it was almost overwhelming: we had the explosive and detonators. But I had to keep reminding myself that our mission was one of covert approach and extraction, not one of sabotage.

In the dark it was difficult to tell whether or not we were leaving any tracks; but as we moved round the plane in single file, Murdo, at the back, was swishing a branch of big leaves back and forth across our trail.

Leaving the plane, we headed for the wall of forest to the west, aiming for the corner of the field. Sure enough, there was the road, leading off into the jungle, a pale strip just visible. Dark as the night was out in the open, it was still blacker under the trees, and I paused before entering the tunnel.

'Give us your branch, Murdo,' I said quietly. 'It looks to me as though security's very lax. They're so far from civilization that they don't reckon there's any threat. They're relying on the isolation to protect them. But I'm not taking any chances.'

I stripped the leaves and side-shoots off the branch, until I was left with a springy stick about four feet long, and I moved down the road with this held out at an angle in front of me, in case we came on a trip wire connected to an alarm. But the track was clear.

As Tony had described, the track wound in curves between the trees. It could have been made like that for reasons of camouflage – to preserve as much tree-cover as possible – or for reasons of economy, to save shifting obstructions unnecessarily. Probably the engineers had chosen the easiest route, which involved the minimum of clearing.

We moved in bursts. I'd go on a hundred steps, then stop in the middle of the road. The other two waited a couple of minutes, then closed on me. The darkness was such that twice they went past me, only a few feet away, without seeing me, and I had to hiss at them to stop.

At that erratic pace it took us half an hour to cover a kilometre. Several times I froze, hearing movements on the edge of the jungle to right or left, but after a while I realized that the disturbances were caused by animals, possibly jaguars, more likely snakes.

By about 10.30 the moon was rising. The sky was growing lighter, and we could see the tree canopy silhouetted in black against it. Then we began to hear the hum of a machine – probably a generator – in the distance ahead. Finally we made out lights showing through the trees.

It was after 11 p.m. when we reached the edge of the clearing, and from the lack of movement we reckoned the place had settled down for the night. Hanging back under the trees, we scanned the new settlement. The approach road opened out into a clearing perhaps seventy metres wide and two hundred long. On the left-hand side, as we looked, two long, low buildings were laid out end to end, running away from us and continuing the line of the road. Beyond them, at right-angles across the far end of the clearing, a third building was still under construction, the skeleton of its roof showing up white in the moonlight. In front of it several vehicles were parked: a couple of bulldozer diggers, two or three dump-trucks, and two jeeps.

The nearest building looked like the accommodation block. It had doors and windows, and the walls went right up to the eaves of the corrugated iron roof. The second building was not much more than a roof on pillars – part of the side we could see had a wall about head-high, but the rest of it was open. That, I guessed, was the laboratory. Somewhere at the back of that a generator was drumming, and a couple of bare electric bulbs flickered erratically.

'How the fuck did they get the stuff here to build all this?' whispered Sparky.

'By water,' I told him. 'A boat comes upriver. An army of guys with power-saws goes ashore. Next they land a bulldozer to clear the road, and the site. Then some trucks to carry concrete blocks, cement and so on. In about a week, it's cocaine city.'

Skirting the open ground, we moved forward and to our right to get a closer view. I wished to hell we had PNGs or kite-sights. As it was, we had to make do with one pair of binoculars, which gathered light well but was no substitute for real night-vision equipment.

On the right-hand side of the clearing we found a high rampart of logs, roots and earth. Everything bulldozed off the site had been pushed up into a heap about twenty feet tall and over a hundred yards long. Immediately behind it was a tangle of virgin forest. In fact, all the debris had been pushed back and piled up into and around the first of the standing trees, so that when we tried to creep round the back of it, we found it impossible to make progress. But when we scrambled up the back of the long mound, we discovered that we had a view of the whole clearing; a naturally commanding position.

'This is the place for the OP,' I whispered.

'It's bloody close to the buildings,' said Sparky. 'We're right on top of them. It can't be more than sixty or seventy metres straight across. If we're caught here, we're fucking history.'

'I know. But if we get any farther away, we'll be in the trees, and able to see fuck-all. Listen: I'm going to recce round the back of the buildings. You guys stay here and cover me.

Sparky, rig an aerial and see if you can get a sitrep through to base. Report that we're on Green Four, and find out if they've got any news of the Boat Troop. If it goes noisy, RV back at the dinghy. I just hope to hell these bastards haven't got any dogs.'

I scrambled along the back of the heap, working my way left-handed to the airstrip end. Back on the side of the road I paused, listening, then crossed to the rear corner of the accommodation block. Behind it I found a strip of cleared ground maybe ten metres wide, so that walking up it was easy. There were no windows in the back of the building, which was made of bare concrete blocks, only narrow ventilation slits high in the walls. As I crept along I was thinking, If Luisa and the DA are here, they could be right beside me, the other side of that wall. At the far end of the block I again stood still for two or three minutes, but I heard nothing except the cicadas at a distance, the drumming of the generator close at hand, and the mosquitoes aiming for my neck.

As we had guessed, the second building was the laboratory. It was fifty metres long, and above a shoulder-high wall of blocks it was open to the outside air. Looking over the wall I could see long working surfaces, or possibly vats, and there was a chemical smell in the air. At the far end, a collection of 55-gallon drums stood in one corner, stacked two-high. These would be the ether.

Beyond the laboratory I came to the end of the new building, and beyond that I found myself on the bank of a small river, which ran past the end of the site.

I'd started along the back of the unfinished structure when suddenly I smelled woodsmoke. Somewhere ahead of me there was a fire. Maybe people were camping in the open. Then, within a few feet, I heard a noise that made me freeze: a man snoring. The sound came from head level. There was somebody in a hammock almost within arm's length. Inching backwards, a quarter-step at a time, I retraced my route to the corner of the lab. Earlier, I'd been considering the idea of making my way back along the front of the buildings and getting a look at the doors. Now I decided that any such manoeuvre was out of the question; there were too many people on the site.

By midnight I was back in our OP at the top of the rampart. Sparky had got no joy out of his 319; he'd run an aerial up, but probably it needed to go higher. It wasn't on to go tree-climbing in the dark, so I told him to wait for first light. In the meantime, we needed to get our heads down.

Slinging hammocks at midnight in the jungle was something at which we had had a good deal of practice. If you sleep on the ground, you not only put yourself at the mercy of all the creepy-crawlies on the forest floor; you also advertise your presence by leaving signs – impressions in the earth and dead leaves. The correct procedure is to wrap a length of hessian round the trunk of a tree, so that your support rope doesn't mark the bark, and then lash on.

Soon two of us were swinging gently under our mozzie nets, while the third stayed on stag. I don't think any of us slept.

FIFTEEN

Even by their own swift standards, the Boat Troop had made a fast getaway. The ops officer put out a call at 1715 on Saturday evening, when most of the guys were at home or around the town. The commander, Staff Sergeant Merv Mason, an Aussie famous for his walrus moustache, was in his local Tesco when the bleeper went off in his pocket. Hearing the summons, he cut short his shopping, made a dash for the rapid check-out, and hurtled home to pick up his kit on his way into camp. In under two hours of frantic activity his team had got itself together and lined up the stores and equipment they would need for a drop into the sea and an assault on the *Santa Maria*.

In the background, Merv knew, urgent talks were in progress. The boss was negotiating to get the party aboard an RAF TriStar which was leaving Lyneham that evening. The basic need was to lift the team to Belize with the minimum delay, and have them there ready to deploy as things developed. A Herc plodding round the northern route would be far too slow. After pressure from the Director of the SAS in London, the wing commander in charge of air movements at Lyneham had been prevailed upon to hold the TriStar for two hours, and to throw off a dozen less urgent passengers. In the end a Chinook lifted the team from Hereford to Lyneham, together with their kit, and they flew out at 2200.

Eight hours later, at 0100 local time, they landed in the hot darkness at Airport Camp, Belize. Three four-ton trucks drove out to the aircraft to collect them; leaving the plane before anyone else, they and their kit were whisked away to a holding area in one of the warehouses, where Keith Marshall, their liaison officer, had set up a standby ops room. The rest of the guys got their heads down in transit accommodation, but he was up for the rest of the night, fielding the messages that came in by secure fax from Hereford and Regimental Headquarters in London.

From the faxes Keith could see that diplomatic negotiations had been going on at the highest level. No matter that in North America it was the early hours of Sunday morning; it was Prime-Minister-to-President stuff as Whitehall urgently requested assistance in lifting the Boat Troop to within striking distance of their objective, wherever that might turn out to be.

When the *Santa Maria* sailed from Cartagena at 0830 local time – 1330 in London – an emergency meeting was called at the COBR, the Cabinet Office Briefing Room, underground in Whitehall, which was opened up and manned to act as the control centre. There the SAS Director met senior officials from the Ministry of Defence and the Foreign Office and a representative from the United States Embassy. After an initial conference, as satellite surveillance showed the ship heading north, they stood down the meeting until her destination could be established. When she put into Desierto at 2000 local (0100 in London), the senior officers were routed out of bed by telephone calls, and sleepily reassembled. Later that morning, at the US Embassy in Grosvenor Square, the American Defence Attaché called the duty officer in the Operations Center at the Pentagon and confirmed that help was going to be needed again, this time in the form of a warship to put the Boat Troop within range of their target. 'The British Prime Minister's been talking with the President,' he confirmed. 'The orders are to give every possible assistance.'

None of this background activity concerned Merv Mason and his men in Belize. All they knew was that they had to prepare for Operation Gannet. By midday on Sunday they were ready to parachute into the sea, with their two twenty-five-foot Geminis fully inflated and secured on platforms with all their gear inside them, including the forty-horsepower Mariner engines. The stream of secure faxes, which continued all morning, told them that the Pentagon had agreed to divert a nuclear attack submarine, the USS *Endeavor*, from its exercise in the Caribbean so that it could pick them up and take them covertly into the target area. The planners assumed that the *Santa Maria*, although by no means new, must have effective radar; and this meant that the approach of any large surface vessel or unidentified aircraft would warn the narcos of an impending attack. A submarine was therefore by far the safest option.

Shortly after 2000 on Sunday evening, messages reaching the standby ops room in Belize began to give information about Desierto. The northernmost of a group of small islands which were the tops of extinct volcanoes, it had never been permanently inhabited. Although the others supported small communities of fishermen, Desierto was deserted because it had no reliable fresh water supply. Intelligence routed from the United States Drug Enforcement Agency revealed that in the 1960s a bauxite mining company had built a quay on the shore of a creek on the western side of the island, but that the venture had gone bankrupt and the port had been abandoned. Recently big-time drug-runners had begun to use it again as a safe haven and transit base, cross-decking consignments from one ship to another, and flying small planeloads into Mexico.

In the old days the team commander and signaller at Belize would have spent an anxious hour working out latitudes, longitudes, distances and courses to create a rendezvous between aircraft and submarine in the middle of the Caribbean. Now computers made the calculations in seconds, and then did them again, so that their human operators could feel confident they were right. The upshot was that the Boat Troop boarded a Hercules at 2100 on Sunday evening, for a flight of two hours forty minutes on a bearing of 112 degrees for a rendezvous with USS *Endeavor* thirty miles off the west coast of Desierto.

As the plane droned through the night, Merv looked round his nine men. All were asleep, or nearly so, and certainly none looked worried. A night jump into the sea was routine for them. Gannet was exactly the kind of operation they had spent years training for. Far from being scared, they were positively looking forward to some action. Merv, at thirty-two, was the oldest in the party – although with his short, curly fair hair and pock-marked face he didn't look it. He eased a finger inside the collar of his black wetsuit and settled himself into a more comfortable position.

Once, at about 2230, he went up to the flight-deck for a chat with the captain and a last check of the coordinates. As everyone seemed happy, he moved back down and concentrated his mind on the task ahead. The rendezvous with the sub should be routine; it was the landing on the island which would demand quick assessment and positive decisions. Maps faxed across during the day had given him an idea of the shape of the coast around the creek, but there hadn't been time to send photographs, so a lot would depend on the nature of the shore where they landed.

At 2300 the captain began a gentle descent, easing down from 20,000 feet. Merv plugged in one of the headsets hanging along the sides of the hold and listened in. At 2330 an American voice suddenly came up on the compatible radio channel. 'Alpha Two to X-ray One. How do you read me? Over.'

'X-ray One, loud and clear. Running in on one-one-two. Estimate nine minutes to DZ overhead.'

'Roger. We'll give you a white light buoy on our starboard side, your port.'

'X-ray One. Thanks.'

'Alpha Two. Happy landings, and please not to drop your goddamn boats on top of us.'

Merv knew that to have comms with the aircraft, the sub must have her periscope above the surface. By the time they reached her, she would have surfaced.

'Four minutes to DZ overhead,' the pilot called. 'Stand by.'

The head-loadie held up four fingers. The Herc had levelled off and was flying steadily at 1200 feet. All round the hold guys were adjusting and checking their harnesses. The rest of the hold crew were snapping off the fastenings and removing the nets that had held the boats down. At D minus two the head-loadie hit the button to lower the tailgate ramp.

Warm, fresh air rushed in as the broad platform descended and the back of the plane yawned open to reveal black water glittering below.

The head-loadie held up one finger. Merv counted down the sixty seconds to himself. Then they were into the familiar sequence: 'Red on. Green on. GO!'

First out were the boats. One big shove, and their platforms slid quickly backwards over the steel rollers in the deck until they toppled clear. The team immediately followed, in two sticks of five.

As his chute snapped out, Merv saw the brilliant light shining up out of the sea, and beyond it he made out the long, dark shape of the sub's upper hull. Then he steered for the boats, which were hitting the water with a big double splash three hundred yards away to the east.

Ten minutes later each team was clustered round its boat, still trussed on the platform. Cutting the tie-cords was a dicey business, because if anyone got entangled he could easily go down deep six when the platform fell away. With most of the cords severed, all but two men backed off, and they severed the final bonds in unison.

With both Geminis fully operational, they motored gently towards the long, low hulk of the sub. The crew had already opened up the main hatch above the forward torpedo room – a huge, empty space on the front of the ship – and all the gear went into that; the boats were deflated, rolled up and packed into valises, the engines sealed inside waterproof bags. The guys changed into dry gear and went down into the heart of the ship. The hatches were sealed, buzzers sounded and the crew prepared to dive.

Merv introduced himself as the commander, and met the officer of the watch. He'd been in submarines before, but they had all been small and cramped. This one was mega, with four decks, passages running for a hundred feet or more, and a luxurious amount of space. The whole ship was very quiet, and only the faintest hum of air-conditioning was detectable. It was also spotlessly clean, with fresh pastel colours on the bulkheads. The temperature was a comfortable 68 degrees, the air fresh, and the crew were in shirt-sleeves. The facilities in the enlisted men's mess included a TV screen, a whole library of videos, and a bar at which the visitors were encouraged to make themselves tea and coffee. Their American hosts must have been curious about their mission, but they showed professional restraint. Apart from a few cracks such as, 'What's it like out there?' they asked no questions.

In any case, the visitors were going to be on board for no more than a couple of hours. While the rest of the team relaxed, Merv went along to the CIC, or Combat Information Center, beneath the conning tower, to check details of their approach to Desierto. The island was only thirty miles off, and the sub was closing on it at twelve knots.

For a layman, the CIC was an eerie sight: a circular room, almost dark, full of men monitoring low-lit dials with dark-red figures flickering on them. Since the whole principle of a submarine is that it does not advertise its presence, the *Endeavor* was operating on passive sonar only, sending out no emissions that other vessels could detect. At a bank of complex arrays five men were listening for transmissions at different ranges – distant, medium and close.

'Don't think me a prick,' said Merv to the cheerful first duty officer, 'but if you don't use radar, how do you know where you are?'

'We have very precise inertial navigation systems,' was the answer. 'Gyroscopes – yes? Right now, I can tell you where we are to within a few feet. If we have to, we can put up an aerial now and then to get a fix off a satellite, but most times we're happy to stay down. We can hear a lot, too. Listen in.'

The officer handed Merv a pair of headphones, and he found they were full of mysterious swishing, booming noises.

'Hear that?' said his companion. 'That's a shoal of barracuda giving us the time of day. When we close on this island of yours, we're gonna be hearing the surf on the shore from about four miles out. Now, you call the shots. Just say where you want to go, and we'll squirt you out.'

'Can you give us a sub-surface release?'

'Sure can. In fact, that's all the better for us. If we don't break the surface, we don't break international law. Until we break the surface, we don't become a ship.'

By 0345 they could hear the surf ahead of them. The sub came up to periscope depth and sat there, moving gently forward, five ks off the coast. In the cavernous forward torpedo room the team pulled on their full diving kit and checked each other methodically, then went two at a time into the escape hatch. Merv always found that an unnerving moment: once you're sealed in the hatch in total blackness and the chamber is filling with water, there's no turning back. If anything goes wrong then, you could be written off.

Having released a float with a steel hawser attached, the first pair swam up the cable, popped the air-bottle to inflate the No. 1 boat, and scrambled aboard. Humping the 175-lb engine out of the water and on to the back of the boat was no picnic, but they managed it, and moved away from the buoy. Up came the second team and the second boat. Last to the surface were their bergens full of kit, their weapons and explosives, all done up in Ellison bags. With everyone and everything on board, Merv counted heads, made the total ten, and with a torch flashed a clearing signal to the officer observing them through the periscope.

The time was 0405. The moon had set, leaving the night very dark, and only a gentle wind was blowing from the west, so the sea was calm. The sub had put the boats out west of their target, and they set off on a course of ninety degrees, due eastwards, cruising easily downwind at eight knots.

Soon the coast of the island was showing as a dark line on the horizon ahead. The coxswains reduced speed and continued until, one kilometre out, Merv signalled a halt. With the boats hove to, he and another swimmer slipped over the side and went in alone for a beach reconnaissance. Thirty minutes later they were bobbing in the swell and touching bottom, a few yards offshore, only to find that their navigation had been almost too precise. No more than 300 metres in front of them, a big cargo vessel was moored alongside a jetty, her upperworks showing white in the starlight.

'Too fucking close,' said Merv. 'Let's get round the corner.'

The Int guys at Hereford had faxed him a map of the island. It was only a photocopy, but it gave a reasonable idea of the layout round the port, and Merv had memorized the details. He remembered that the jetty lay along the inner edge of a small bay, and that the bay was sheltered by a hook of headland. He also remembered that the airstrip was inland to the south – about one k away to their right as they faced in from the sea.

Pushing off again, they swam to their right for twelve minutes until they rounded the headland and discovered a second, much smaller bay backed by low cliffs. Coming ashore, they landed on a steep little sandy beach, no more than thirty yards from front to rear. At the back was an overhang of cliff, and centuries of rock-falls had divided up the beach with a series of natural partitions. As a lying-up point, it was ideal. Even in the dark they could tell that it must be out of sight of the jetty, and the combination of overhang and rock-falls would help conceal the boats from any aircraft that might come in. Furthermore, the carry from water to cache-point, was the shortest they were ever likely to get.

Over his covert radio Merv sent the message: 'OK. We've moved 400 metres to the right of our original approach line. Beach clear.' Then he cracked out a cyalume chemical light, placed it in an empty tin can, brought for the purpose, and laid the can horizontally on a rock so that the green glow could be seen by the crews but by nobody on land.

A few minutes later, the boats purred in out of the night. The cache was so close to the water that there was scarcely any need to post sentries to secure their landing-point, but the team went through the drill anyway. They carried the boats the few yards to the base of the cliff, dismantled them under the overhang, and pitched scrim nets over them. Finally they changed out of their diving gear into DPMs and got a brew on.

'Watch the water, guys,' Roger Alton, the second-in-command, warned them. 'It's going to be bloody hot later on, and if anything goes wrong in the jungle we may have to hang around here for a couple of days. So we'll need all we've got. The other thing's sunburn. For Christ's sake keep your heads and arms covered.'

The tide was coming in, and would soon cover the beach. But Roger was taking no chances. He went back to the edge of the water and, working backwards, scuffed away their tracks with a paddle.

'It's like Robinson fucking Crusoe,' he exclaimed. 'I don't reckon anybody's ever landed here before.'

Leaving two sentries to guard the base, the rest climbed warily to the ridge above them. They could see the odd palm tree outlined against the stars, but on the ground there was little vegetation, apart from tussocks of grass.

Everything seemed to be in miniature. The whole island was only about three ks in diameter, and the top level of the headland was no more than thirty metres above sea level. It was still dark when they reached it, but against the paling sky they saw the outline of Mount Desierto, rising to a short, blunt peak ahead of them. The upperworks of the ship showed white against the land opposite; she was moored with her bows to their right, and three or four hundred metres ahead of her, on the inland end of the quay, they could make out a huddle of pale-coloured buildings.

As they lay on the ridge, Merv checked off features he remembered from the map. 'It's a dry creek,' he said, pointing down to the right. 'Comes to a point just below us here. No river. The airstrip's down there, round the corner, and the old bauxite workings are at the back of it. There's a road from the port to the strip, but that's the only one. No other habitation. What we need is cover for an OP.'

Moving along the ridge to their left, they soon found some. A palm-tree had blown over in a gale, bringing up a big plate of earth on its roots, but it was still alive, and its tumble of branches offered excellent shelter, not only from aircraft but also from the sun. When dawn broke they realized that their

OP had one bad feature: the sun came up just to the right of the mountain, in their faces, and they were looking straight into the light. Otherwise, they were ideally placed, not least because the seaward flank of their headland, behind them, was out of sight of the port, and guys could move up and down between OP and base quite freely.

At 0645, as soon as they'd established that the ship was the *Santa Maria*, they got through to Tony in Bogotá on the satcom.

'Blue Team on location,' Merv reported. 'The target's here.'

'Roger. Have you identified the hostage?'

'Not yet. The locals are only just starting to move.'

'OK. Keep me informed. And well done. The Red Team's ready when you are.'

'Roger. We'll let you know.'

Merv established a rota of two men on stag at the top, two at the bottom, and the rest crashed out, cooking or whatever. He and Roger took the first stag, to gauge the strength of the opposition and work out a plan.

One of the first things they realized was that the buildings at the end of the quay were inhabited. Doors started opening while it was still half light, and people went in and out. The watchers saw that a good deal of work had recently been done, both to the buildings and to the quay. Patches of fresh-looking cement showed up on the dock wall, and some of the buildings had had a new coat of paint or whitewash.

Soon the narcos' plan of action was apparent. Machinery started up on board the ship, and the derricks began lifting nets full of bales ashore. The cranes landed each load in the open back of a decrepit four-ton truck, which drove off down the airstrip road, disappearing round the bend of the hill to the OP's right.

'They must have an air-lift going to the mainland,' said Roger – and soon his assessment was proved right by the arrival of a twin-engined Cessna, which came in from the north-west, over their left shoulders, took one sweep to the south, turned back towards them, into the wind, sank out of sight and landed. Half an hour later they heard its engine wind up again for take off, and got themselves well tucked down among the palm leaves, knowing that it would come low overhead. Sure enough, it cleared them by no more than a couple of hundred feet, struggling for height under a heavy load.

'Easy enough to make sure the ship never leaves,' said Roger.

'Swim out and put a charge on the props?'

'Exactly. The trouble is, they'd still have plenty of time to top the Rupert. Somehow, we've got to cut him out first. If that poor bastard's in one of those cabins, he's going to bloody bake when the sun gets up. The ship looks that crappy I bet she hasn't got air-conditioning.'

Two more flights came and left. By then another team had taken over the OP. As Steve was scanning through binoculars, he suddenly said, 'Jesus! There he is!'

Jerry, his companion, whipped up his own pair of glasses and watched as Black emerged from the building they'd christened No. 2, with his hands cuffed together in front of him, followed by a guard wearing DPM fatigues and armed with an MP 5. He'd been ashore all the time. He was wearing a white shirt and dark trousers, but he looked in bad shape: his clothes were filthy, and his face had a dark, puffy appearance.

Steve gave a double tug on the communication cord which ran down to the base of the cliff, and Roger came scrambling up. 'That's him, isn't it?'

Roger, who'd never worked with Black, but had seen him often about the camp at Hereford, gave an exclamation of disgust. 'It's him, all right. But they've been hitting him about. Bastards.'

Black and his escort walked a couple of hundred yards along the airport road, then turned and came back. Exercise time. They went out and back three times, Black walking slowly and awkwardly because of his handcuffs. Then for a few minutes both prisoner and gaoler sat in the sun on a low wall. Two more guards appeared and sat with them. Then all four disappeared into the building.

'OK,' said Roger. 'We know where he is. But why have they got him there, I wonder?'

'The heat, probably,' said Steve. 'In such a sheltered position, the ship must be like an oven.'

'He must have spent the night there – otherwise we'd have seen him come ashore. If they're going to keep him in the same place tonight as well, all the better. Much easier to grab him from there than on board.'

By sundown they had their plan. The prisoner was still inside building No. 2. During the afternoon, guards had come in and out, but Black had stayed put. Everything pointed to a night hit – and there would be no better time than 0300, when everybody concerned should be in the deepest trough of sleep.

At 0130 two men would swim out and place a charge of explosive on one of the ship's propellers, with a timer set to detonate at 0300. At 0230 four men would work their way round right-handed, overland, to cross the road and come in on the buildings, taking with them a couple of made-up door charges in case they had to blast their way into the gaol-house. By 0255 they'd be in position for an assault on the building, but they'd wait for the ship to go up, and then give it a few seconds to see if the explosion would flush anybody from the buildings. If anyone ran out, they'd drop them, and then go in. Having lifted their quarry, they'd make their way back to the boat cache, but one of them would create a diversion by running off along the airfield road and putting down some rounds towards the strip, as if the rescue party were fighting a battle in that direction. Then, with most of the locals distracted by the fire on shipboard, they'd slip out to sea in the Geminis for a rendezvous with the *Endeavor* at pre-arranged coordinates.

At 1730 Merv called Tony on the satcom.

'All set,' he reported. 'We've got it hacked. We'll go in at zero-three-zero-zero local, if that suits.'

'That'll suit just fine,' Tony answered. 'I'll pass the word along.'

'Thanks. And maybe you can ask our cabbies to be at the rendezvous by zero–four–three–zero.'

'Your cabbies?'

'Our cab–drivers.'

'OK. They'll be there. Happy landings.'

SIXTEEN

Down in the jungle we were almost on the equator, so the dawn came up quickly, with none of the long-drawn-out twilight we're used to in the far north. At 0600 we suddenly felt we were under attack from a deafening chorus of insects. It started in the tree canopy with a kind of moaning twang from what we called the stand-to beetle, and spread down to the crickets and other creatures at lower levels. All at once the clearing was bright as day, and we only had a few minutes to settle the details of our OP, as well as get the aerial aloft.

Murdo and I moved a few yards along the top of the rampart until we found a spot where some branches which still carried dying leaves formed a natural screen. Behind them we shifted lumps of wood and kicked away earth to make a comfortable hollow. As soon as we were settled, Sparky went climbing with his wire, aligning it east to west, with the east end ten feet higher. The standing trees gave us overhead cover, and by the time it was full daylight, we were well set. Unless somebody came walking along the top of the mound – which seemed highly unlikely, because the heap of trees and roots was so rough – we'd be perfectly safe. All the same, I reckoned we were too close to the enemy to risk any cooking, so we had a cold breakfast of corned-beef hash and lemonade out of our waterbottles.

As I expected, the locals were up early. Soon after 6 a.m. people came out of the buildings and began moving about. We arranged the stags so that two of us were watching the compound all the time. Most of the earliest activity occurred at the far end; evidently the cookhouse had been set up in the right-hand end of the unfinished block. We soon realized that at least some of the people present were native Indians – tiny, grey-skinned people, wearing nothing but grass skirts. There were also some Colombian guards in DPM fatigues; we couldn't tell the exact number, as they kept disappearing and reappearing, but we guessed there were about ten in all.

It was at 6.30 that a door opened towards our end of the accommodation block and out came a man who was manifestly neither Indian nor Colombian – a carrot-haired, freckled fellow in a dirty white T-shirt and jeans, carrying a towel.

'Jesus!' I whispered to Murdo. 'One of the players.'

Murdo's hair and moustache were dark red, but this guy was practically orange. He slouched off to a door at the far end of the block: the ablutions or shit-house, for sure. As he returned a few minutes later, the door of his room opened again, and out came Farrell.

I went into momentary shock. Somehow I'd made up my mind that he was on board the ship, knocking hell out of Black. Not at all. Here he was, stretching and looking round.

'Don't move,' I breathed. 'This is the fucker I've been after.'

So, for the second time, I had a perfect chance to drop him. My mind flashed back to the scene outside the barn in Ulster. Now, as then, I had only to pull the trigger. But if I fired now, Farrell's mates would surely panic and try to kill their hostages. Even if we dropped all the players, the guards were on hand to carry out whatever orders they'd been given.

Farrell appeared to be looking straight at us, but in fact he was only getting his bearings, and after a moment he too moved off for a piss, with that characteristic dip on the left foot. I let my breath out and turned to Murdo with a shake of my head. Close on Farrell's heels came a third player, shorter than him, also dark-haired. I recognized him immediately from the restaurant in Bogotá. At about seven o'clock all three moved off in a bunch towards the far end of the compound, heading for the cookhouse.

It was Murdo who drew my attention to the end door of the accommodation block, the left-hand one as we looked across. Like the others it was made of metal, but this one was fastened with a hasp and padlock. 'I bet that's where they are,' he whispered. 'It's the only secure room in the place.'

271

Ten minutes later two of the guards came strolling along. They looked a slovenly pair. They carried sub-machine-guns that could have been Uzis, or the American version, Ingrams. At the door one produced a key and undid the padlock while the other covered him. The door opened, and out came a handcuffed man also wearing DPMs. For a few seconds I stared in consternation. Who was this? Had we made a mega cock-up and come chasing after the wrong hostage? Had the toads got their wires crossed? Then I clicked. With a jolt I saw that this scruffy character was the DA. He looked filthy and dishevelled and utterly different from when I'd last seen him.

I felt my temper rising as he was taken off under close escort to the ablution area, and then brought back. Where the hell was Luisa? In some other cell, I supposed. As the DA came back towards us I could see that his face was pale and drawn. He looked as though he'd shed ten kilos.

The subsequent events of that day were few and far between. At 8 a.m. a man brought the DA some food in what looked like a couple of mess-tins. At the same time construction work started up on the new building. Cement mixers began churning, and files of Indians portered stuff around. We could also see action in the laboratory, and a glint of bright blue from the stack of drums confirmed my diagnosis that they contained ether.

Not long after work had started, a single shot cracked out from the jungle near the far end of the compound.

'Jesus!' I said. 'They've topped somebody.' I didn't think it could be one of ours; the DA was certainly inside the gaol-block, and we presumed Luisa was too. We speculated intensely for a few minutes. Could it have been a punishment shooting – the PIRA extending their home methods to the jungle? All was made clear when a commotion broke out in the cookhouse area, and four or five Indians came into view dragging some heavy animal. There was a lot of jabbering and shouting as they pulleyed it up with ropes and hung it on the scaffolding, where they started to skin and butcher it;

272

although we had a fair view of it, we couldn't make out what the hell it was. From its thick brown coat it could have been a bear, but it looked more like a king-sized beaver. Not until we'd left the jungle altogether did I discover that it must have been a capybara, the biggest rodent in the world.

Around nine the PIRA crowd joined forces with some of the guys in DPMs, sorting out weapons and boxes of ammunition, and the whole lot drove off down the track to the airstrip in a decrepit old truck which backfired viciously. Soon we could hear the rattle of small-arms fire in the distance, and it was obvious that the PIRA guys were into training the locals. Their fame as professional terrorists had spread to the jungle, and here they were using the airfield as a range. Then we heard the odd loud *crump* as well, as if demolition instruction was being thrown in.

With them temporarily out of the way, I felt that the air had cleared. This would have been a good moment to launch our attack, if we hadn't been constrained by the need to co-ordinate with the Boat Troop. I almost decided that one of us could slip round through the jungle, scurry across the road, and creep up behind the accommodation block to whisper through the ventilation slits and let the hostages know that help was at hand. Then it seemed better to wait until dark, and until we were organized to strike.

A plan was forming in my mind. One 203 grenade into the store of ether drums would cause a major explosion and put the lab on fire in seconds. But better still, a timed charge of PE; if things began with a big bang from the back corner of the camp, the narco forces might be bluffed into thinking that the attack was coming in from that quarter, rather than from the direction of the airfield. If, during the initial confusion, we blew the bolt of the cell room with another small charge, we could get the DA out. He could tell us where Luisa was, and we should be able to spirit the hostages away down the airfield road without much of a firefight. At least we'd get a start. If we could somehow block or booby-trap the road we might get clear. Then it would be into the dinghy and away upriver with the outboards. If the Islander was still on the field, we'd put

273

enough rounds through it as we went past to make sure it couldn't take off.

Talking quietly, I put the plan to the others.

'The idea of starting it with a bang's good,' said Murdo, 'but we still need more firepower.'

'Well, the other guys will be here this evening.'

'We'll be better off when it's dark, too.'

'Agreed. But let's confirm what's happening on the ship. Sparky, get that fucking radio going.'

Luckily, as Sparky began fiddling his dials, the bulldozer started up. Its noise was so loud we could have yelled at the tops of our voices without being heard, and voice communication became by far the most satisfactory option. In a minute or two we got through to the base at Puerto Pizarro. Johnny Ellis must have been right beside the Colombian signaller, because he came on within seconds of our making contact.

'Green Four,' I told him. 'I confirm one hostage is on site. Second hostage presumed here also. Not the one with blond hair. Three PIRA also on site. Plus maybe ten local guards. On pass to head-shed. Over.'

'Green Three. Roger.' He told us that the Blue team were on their objective. Also, the head-shed had reiterated that any assault we planned must be synchronized with theirs.

'We're ready when they are,' I told him. 'Any time after dark, provided you guys can get here. Is the chopper operational?'

'Green Two, affirmative.'

'Green Four. In that case, we'll expect you this evening. Tell the pilot to fly to the same place as yesterday. You'll need to rope down. But see if you can borrow a chain-saw. There's one tree that prevents the chopper landing. Cut that down if you can, and bring the saw with you. Then launch your dinghy and drift. Don't use the engine. There's no need to paddle, except to steer, because the current's quite fast. Aim to launch at 1800 hours. After one hour forty, watch the right bank for a big clearing. We'll be there to meet you. We'll give you double flashes from a torch. Over.'

274

'Green Three. Roger. We'll see you there.'

'Green Four. Try for a pair of bolt-cutters, also. And inform Green One we're in good order. Anything else? Over.'

'Green Three. Yes. The narcos are demanding a ransom of one billion pesos for the return of the British hostages.'

'Green Four. Billion or million? Over.'

'Green Three. Bravo for billion. Over.'

'Green Four. That's peanuts. Emphasize that recovery is fully possible, and keep the negotiators talking. Out.' I turned to Murdo and said, 'A billion. That's about a million quid.'

'Bollocks to them. They can whistle for it. Pity Johnny can't line up a fucking great tin-opener and bring it with him. Then we'd just carve open the roof of the shed and lift our two out.'

The day seemed to last for ever. By noon, with the sun dead overhead, the heat was overpowering. Back under the jungle canopy it wasn't quite so bad, but out in the open it hit you like a blow over the head. I kept thinking that under the tin roof of the accommodation block it must be fearsome. We still had to go easy with our water; we'd brought two bottles apiece, and could have drunk twice as much. After dark we'd be able to refill them from the river – we had Stereotabs to kill the bugs. I wondered what the narcos were doing about their own supply. Getting it from the small river and boiling it, I supposed.

The shooting party came back and debussed into the cookhouse area for lunch and, we presumed, a siesta. A man brought food and drink to the DA's cell. Construction work stopped, and silence fell on the compound. What with the heat, the mosquitoes, and processions of inch-long ants marching into our OP, we didn't have that comfortable an afternoon.

The highlight was the appearance of a decidedly unwelcome visitor. I was dozing when Murdo suddenly nudged me and said, 'Hey! Look at this!'

I rolled over and peered out through the leaves. Half-way across the open ground was a monstrous snake, slithering

275

towards us from the far side. If I said it was the length of a cricket pitch, I'd be exaggerating. But I'm sure it was twenty feet at least, and a foot in diameter at the thickest point.

'Fucking python!' Murdo whispered.

'No, it's an anaconda.'

'How d'you know?'

'No pythons in South America. I read it somewhere.'

'Whatever it is, it could swallow a bloody goat.'

'And crush you like an egg. Thin out, snake.'

As if it had heard me, the huge reptile hung a right turn and headed away down the approach road, leaving a trail as deep as if a heavy log had been dragged through the dust. With the binoculars I could see its tongue flickering in and out.

Around four o'clock thunder began to rumble in the distance, and the sky darkened as a big storm built up. Back at Santa Rosa somebody had mentioned that the dry season was about to end, so maybe this was the beginning of the rain? The forest birds, which had been screeching away merrily all day, went quiet. Then the trees began to stir in a hot wind, and the storm came steadily closer, the noise growing all the time, until at about five o'clock it burst over us.

Being so close to the enemy, we didn't want to pitch our ponchos, which shine like hell, so we simply had to endure the rain, which came hammering down with such force that in a couple of minutes everything was flooded; cascades started running down the side of our rampart, and every hollow was full of water. When I looked across the compound, I couldn't see the far end for the sheer volume of rain falling. What I could see was that the deluge was raising a kind of brown froth several inches from the ground as the incoming drops beat air into the dust soup. The noise was phenomenal: a background roar of rain as loud as a train in a tunnel, and through it sizzling crackles of lightning, instantly followed by earth-shaking thunderclaps.

Within half an hour the storm had rolled on. It left us soaked through and miserable, but at least it cooled the air by a few degrees, and enabled us to fill our bottles with fresh water: I'd sent Sparky back into the jungle to spread a poncho and use it as a miniature catchment.

As soon as full darkness had fallen, Murdo and I set out to meet the incoming party, leaving Sparky to man the OP. The storm had turned the dust to mud, and we couldn't help leaving tracks, but we kept to the edge of the road to make our trails as inconspicuous as possible. When we reached the airstrip we stopped for ten minutes' observation. The Islander still sat in the same place and, except for the insects and the sound of water dripping, everything was quiet. Skirting the edge of the open area, we made our way to the river bank, identified our cache by the high tree, and came down on to the dinghy first time.

From its mooring among the roots there was no view out over the water, because the outer branches of the trees hung down to the surface, so we cast off and pulled ourselves out until we were in the very fringe, then made fast to the end of a branch to hold ourselves against the current.

By then it was 7.30. 'What do we do?' asked Murdo. 'Start flashing?'

'Yeah. I reckon so. If there's been heavy rain upstream, the river could be running faster. They could be here any minute.'

So we sat in the dark and waited, with Murdo giving a double flash upstream every thirty seconds. There was time to think of a hundred things that could have gone wrong. The helicopter could have gone US again and never taken off. It could have taken off and been forced to turn back. The pilot could have failed to find the rock outcrop. The dinghy could have got punctured. My mind flew to the propaganda tower in Bogotá, and Tony cooped up there on the fourth floor. I imagined wretched Peter Black, sweating in some oven of a cabin on board the *Santa Maria*. I saw Tracy and Tim in England. What time was it there? Two-thirty. They'd just have had lunch. Maybe they were walking in the spinney behind the cottage. I hoped they'd had no more strange phone calls . . .

Suddenly, from out on the water to our right, came a low

whistle, which Murdo returned. Seconds later a black lump with heads sticking up out of it bore down at us out of the dark. Murdo kept the torch on to guide them in, and the second dinghy bounced gently into ours.

'How's that for fucking navigation?' said a Scots voice, which I recognized as Stewart McQuarrie's.

'Shit hot,' I told him. 'Good on yer, Stew. Who's with you?'

'Me,' said Johnny Ellis.

'Me,' said another voice.

'Who's that?'

'Mel. Who else?'

'Great!' I said. 'Welcome to Shitsville.'

'Can't be. We've just come from there.'

'This is another.'

'What's it like?'

'Fucking horrible. But you'll get used to it. Did you bring a power saw?'

'Sure did. We cut down that prick of a tree, too.'

'Brilliant. What about bolt-shears?'

'Nothing doing. None to be had.'

'Too bad. Any news from the north?'

'Yeah. The Boat Troop are still on target. What's the plan, then?'

'The boat guys' operation's going down at 0300. I told Tony we'd go in then too, unless we tell him different.'

'Christ! We'd better shift our arses. What weapons have you got?'

'Only the one 203, and MP 5s. There's supposed to be a load of stuff coming down from Belize, but the Colombian aircraft went US somewhere up country.'

'¡Carajo! What about ammunition?'

'Loads.' Somebody tapped on a metal box.

'Good. Let's get ashore, anyway. Watch yourselves on these tree roots. They're slippery as hell.'

We pulled both dinghies in, secured them deep among the root tangle, and hid the engines about twenty yards along the bank.

Up on the edge of the airstrip I gave a quick briefing to bring the new guys up to speed. It was easier to talk out there in the open, well away from the compound. I had to choose words carefully to give them a good idea of the layout without drawing any diagrams, but they got it well enough. I repeated the outline of my rescue plan.

'How many guys are there on the site?' asked Johnny.

'There's the three PIRA, maybe ten guards – guerrillas, or whatever they are – and some technicians, brewing the coke. Plus a few Indians. The bank we've established the OP on is a natural strongpoint. It commands the whole open area. From there, I'd say we could drop most of the guys on the spot, as they react to the explosions and run out into the compound. Now we've got the saw, we can also fell a tree across the road, so they won't be able to follow by vehicle. If we put rounds into the plane as well, they'll be grounded. Then we motor upriver to the LZ, and have ourselves choppered out.'

'What about their comms?' asked Stew. 'It would be good to knock them out, so they can't report what was happening.'

'We haven't identified any VHF mast or aerial, so we assume they've got satcoms – and the same on the ship. The bastards are probably comparing notes all the time.' I paused, then added: 'The sooner we get out of here, the better.'

Back at the ranch, I settled everyone on the rampart, and in whispers explained the layout again, this time pointing to the various locations. Members of the garrison were on the move, but the centre of activity was the cookhouse.

After the rain, the mozzies were out in force, and even with liberal smearings of repellent, everybody was swatting and cursing.

I decided that Murdo should be the man to hit the stack of ether drums, so, when movement in the compound had died down, I took him with me on a recce beyond the buildings.

This time, as we crept behind the accommodation block, I looked up at the first ventilation slot – a horizontal slatted opening about eight feet off the ground. It was only six feet

279

from the end of the building, so it must go through into the room where the DA was held.

At the far back corner of the lab, I pointed out the stack of drums, and we briefly discussed possible approaches. In fact only one spot was practicable – where we were.

'No problem,' Murdo breathed. 'This'll do just fine.'

As we were returning, I said, 'Listen, I'm going to make contact with the DA. Give me a platform.'

Under the ventilation slot Murdo bent over and braced himself against the wall. With a bit of a jump I was up on his back, my head level with the opening. The stink that came out was anything but reassuring.

'Hey!' I hissed. 'Major Palmer!'

For a moment there was no answer, but I heard movement inside.

'Major Palmer!' I hissed again.

'Who is it?'

'Geordie Sharp. SAS. We've come to get you out.'

The DA gave a kind of grunt. 'Thank God! When?'

'Three o'clock in the morning. Listen – where's Luisa?'

'I don't know. They took her away.'

'When was that?'

'Can't remember. I heard her screaming.'

'Oh. Shit! Are you tied up?'

'Only handcuffs.'

'Not chained to anything?'

'No.'

'OK.'

I tried to think. It wasn't on to stay where we were any longer, I just said, 'All right. I'll tap on the door just before three. It'll start with a big bang from the far end of the compound. A few seconds after that we'll blow the lock on your door. When you hear the first explosion, get your hands over your ears and keep them there until your door comes in – but be prepared for take-off. OK?'

'Yes, yes.'

'Keep away from the door. After I've knocked, keep on the front wall, at the far end from the door. OK?'

'All right.'

'Hang in there, then.'

Back on the mound, we speculated furiously about what had happened to the woman. As far as we could see, there was no other room in which she could be held. Could she have been flown out to some other narco hideaway?

There was no way we could do any more recces. The chances of being compromised were too high. The operation had to go down.

I assigned everyone a role. Whilst Murdo would hit the ether, I would see to the door-charge, and escort the hostages when they came out. Sparky would help me with them; obviously they'd be disorientated and need close supervision. Johnny would be away down the approach road with the chain-saw. The moment the ether went up, he'd start cutting, with the aim of dropping a good-sized tree. Once he had a barrier in position, he'd jettison the saw. Stew and Mel would give covering fire from the top of the rampart for as long as they could, or as long as seemed necessary. As soon as the whole party was on the move, we'd pepperpot our way back to the boats.

'Easy peasy,' said Stew.

SEVENTEEN

We'd synchronized our watches down to the last second. I stood back round the end of the accommodation block. My watch read 0259. One minute till things went noisy. The night had been long. Those of us not on stag had tried to get our heads down for a couple of hours, but sleep had been elusive. The locals had held some form of piss-up round the cookhouse fire, and there'd been a good deal of drunken shouting. We'd seen the three players go into their room at 11.30. At least we knew where they were; but we weren't so certain about the guards. We reckoned that some of them were living in the far end of the accommodation block, but a few must have been sleeping somewhere else. I kept thinking about Farrell and I kept thinking about Luisa.

At midnight Sparky had sent his last sitrep back to our forward mounting base at Puerto Pizarro, confirming that our operation would go down at 0300, and that after it we'd make our way out to the airstrip, then upriver to the LZ.

0259 and everyone in position. Murdo was up at the ether store with a one-pound charge of PE, already made up with a detonator pushed into it, and a thirty-metre length of black Don Ten wire for cracking it off from a distance. I'd already crept along the front of the building and placed a tiny charge no bigger than my little fingernail on the padlock of the DA's door. I'd also given a couple of gentle warning taps.

Now I held the clacker in my left hand, MP 5 in my right. Sparky was with me, to give covering fire and help propel the hostages in the right direction. Johnny was away down the road to a tree that he'd selected in a midnight recce, and the other two were on the rampart, ready to put rounds down if the defenders started to come forward. They'd done useful work up there, clearing out a second position about ten metres along from our OP, so that they could open the firing from there, and then move along if anyone started to shoot back.

Another storm was brewing. Big bangs of thunder were rolling gradually closer, and the darkness was intense. The usual two bulbs were burning in the lab area, and in their glow I saw Murdo slinking up the side of the building. He was moving carefully, with his MP 5 slung over his back and the made-up charge in his hand.

Then I caught my breath. In a sudden flurry of movement a figure rushed out at Murdo from the right. Murdo obviously had his mind on planting the explosive, and was taken by surprise. But the assailant had picked the wrong man; before he could even grapple, Murdo had let go his charge and dropped the attacker with a kick in the groin. Next second he was on top of him, arms round his neck. The man didn't even have time to scream. One of those big, tattooed hands had clamped over his mouth, and with a violent jerk his neck was broken. The whole incident was over so quickly that our timing remained as planned.

I saw Murdo pick up the charge, go forward, place it and move back out of sight. Fifteen seconds to go. If we'd been properly kitted up, with covert comms, I'd have been giving a countdown into the guys' earpieces. In the absence of radios, I was counting to myself. 'Seven, six, five, four.' I closed my eyes. 'Stand by . . . stand by . . . GO!'

BOOM!

I'd been expecting a good bang, but this was mega. It was nuclear. The whole compound twitched and juddered under the shockwave. As I opened my eyes again, a fireball fifty feet wide exploded into the air and continued up in a searing pillar of fire. Suddenly the jungle all round was lit by a ruddy glare. Pieces of debris rained down all over the place.

My heart was pounding, but I forced myself to wait – wait for doors to open, wait for the locals to run away from me towards the fire. There they went: the guards first, then the PIRA. Three guys out of the PIRA room in a flurry of movement. In the dark it was hard to see if they were carrying weapons; they were just ragged silhouettes against the leaping flames.

One more shout wouldn't matter now. 'Block your ears!' I yelled. Then I closed the clacker. *Boof!* went the lock charge. I ran forwards. The door was swinging outwards. I leapt into the room and found the DA standing dazed right inside.

'Come on!' I yelled. I knew he'd be deafened and disorientated, so I grabbed hold of his arm and started dragging him.

'RUN!' I roared. 'RUN! RUN! COME ON!'

In the glare of the fire at the far end of the compound, men were racing all ways. One started to run in our direction, but a burst ripped out from the top of the rampart, stopping him in his tracks and swivelling him round. As he went down, he tried to bring his Uzi to bear, but another short burst nailed him to the floor of the compound, and he lay still.

I could see the DA was in deep shock. He tripped over the door and half-fell – he felt like a sack of suet. I grabbed him tighter and held him up. 'Listen!' I screamed. 'WHERE'S LUISA?'

All he did was shake his head. We had to go. The flames had built up to such an intensity that steam was hissing out of the leaves of the nearest trees, and some of them were catching fire. More rounds rattled off the rampart. Then came another explosion and another. First I thought that isolated drums of ether were going up. Then I realized that either Stew or Mel, or both, were putting 203 grenades into the transport.

In a few seconds we were on the road and under the trees. Sparky was at our heels, turning to put down the odd burst from his MP 5. Murdo appeared from behind the accommodation block, running fast.

'I found her!' he yelled. 'She's dead. Go for it!'

He started to run with us. The other two were still on the rampart. Ahead of us I heard the chain-saw screaming, then a crash as Johnny dropped his tree.

Light from the fire penetrated only a short way down the road; further under the trees the night was intensely black. Now we'd have to be bloody careful not to score own-goals by

284

shooting each other.

'You OK?' I shouted to the DA. He was still so shattered he didn't answer. From the smell I knew he'd shat himself.

'We haven't far to go,' I told him. 'Only to the airstrip.'

We came to Johnny's barrier. He'd seen us approaching, silhouetted against the fire. 'This end,' he called softly. 'It's easier here.'

Our own covering fire had died down. Looking back, we saw Stew and Mel running like hares to join us. I rapped out a warning so that they didn't go arse-over-tit into the felled tree. Just as they reached us, rounds began to crack past and smash their way into the jungle farther down the road. Our guys hit the deck, but the DA just stood there.

'Down!' I snapped. 'For fuck's sake get down.'

I grappled him to the ground. More rounds cracked past overhead.

'Don't fire back!' I called. By shooting back we'd give away our position – and in any case, for the moment no targets were visible.

The compound was a fantastic sight – flames leaping and smoke billowing in a framework of primeval jungle.

'So much for your billion fucking pesos,' Murdo cried.

'We're not out of it yet,' I told him. 'Stew – you and Mel hang on here while we go ahead. If you see anyone coming, drop them, but don't fire without a good target. RV at the dinghies as soon as we can.'

'Fair enough.'

I turned to the DA and said, 'Right – we're off.'

We started down the road at a fast walk. The darkness was such that at the first bend we walked straight off the track and into a patch of undergrowth without seeing it. Suddenly I found myself caught up in those bloody awful thorns known as 'wait-a-while' which dig into you like barbed fish-hooks and rip you to shreds if you try to pull away.

I was struggling to disentangle myself when a sudden, rushing roar ripped past us, instantly followed by a flash and an explosion in the tree canopy beyond. I dropped to the ground, oblivious of the thorns tearing at my arms.

'Fucking hell!' shouted Murdo. 'They've got an RPG.'

I got up again and shouted, 'Keep going!'

No harm to use a torch now. I switched mine on, taking care not to flash it backwards. On we went, more quickly.

Small-arms fire rattled out behind us – our own guys were keeping the enemy pinned in the compound – then we got some incoming rounds cracking past us into the trees. Then another rocket – but this time we weren't so lucky.

The missile must have hit a tree trunk right beside us. All at once I was on the deck, knocked down by the blast and temporarily blinded by the flash. I got up, my ears ringing, and I knew straight away that I wasn't hurt.

'Everyone OK? Murdo?'

'Yeah.'

'Johnny?'

'OK.'

'Sparky?' I waited. 'Sparky?'

I shone the torch towards where I'd last seen him. He was still on the deck, stretched straight out, face down. I ran across. A pool of blood glistened darkly beside his head. I moved the torch closer and saw more blood welling from a hole at the base of his right ear. Instinctively I started struggling out of my bergen to get at the med pack, but before I'd even slipped the straps I knew it was too late. Sparky's eyes were shut. His face was dead white. I'd hardly begun to feel his pulse before I knew the answer: nothing. A piece of shrapnel had driven deep into his head, severing the jugular. Gently I turned his head over. It moved without any resistance in the neck, and I knew the top of the spinal column had been smashed.

'He's gone,' I said. 'We'll have to take him with us.'

Behind us, the firing had died down.

I turned to the DA. 'You all right?'

'Fine.' At last he'd found his voice.

'Can you carry this?' Holding Sparky's torso upright, I disengaged the 319 in its webbing cover and straps, and handed it over. 'It's heavy, but we haven't far to go.'

'I'll manage it.'

286

'Good.'

I took Sparky's bergen and slung it over my left shoulder. The other two were pulling out a hammock, which had handles on the side and could double as a stretcher. They just about had Sparky in it when we heard movement on the road behind us.

'Stew,' I called softly.

'Hello.'

'We've got a casualty.'

'Oh Christ – who is it?'

'Sparky. He copped it from that RPG.'

'Dead?'

'Yep. We've got to get him to the boats.'

'Shit!'

'What's happening back there?'

'We dropped at least six of them. Couldn't tell which. The 203s may have done for more. Ditto the big bang. The survivors are thinking things over. The lab's destroyed, anyway.'

'Come on, then.'

We went on as fast as we could, weaving along the road, with four guys lugging Sparky's body. We reached the airstrip without further harassment. It was a tremendous relief to come out of the claustrophobic blackness of the forest and into the open. Thunder still rumbled in the distance, but the clouds seemed to have lifted and the night was slightly less dark.

The plane was still in the same position. It offered a tempting target – but I didn't feel like making more noise by firing at it. We had enough trouble already.

'Wait one while I whip over and slash its tyres,' I said. 'At least, no, you lot carry on, and I'll meet you above the cache.'

The others picked up their limp burden and continued diagonally across the open strip, heading for the tall single tree. On my own, I ran to the plane, not bothering about the tracks I was making. By the time anybody followed up in daylight, we'd be well away upriver.

It took all of ten seconds to drive the point of my

Commando knife into the side of each tyre, and as I made away the air was still hissing out.

I caught up with the others as Murdo scrambled down to check the dinghies. Then from below came a curse and an exclamation.

'What's the matter?'

'The boats have gone!'

'Don't be stupid.'

'They fucking have.'

In a flash I was down on the edge of the roots beside him. I shone the torch at the bank. There were the blue painters, still tied to branches.

'It's OK,' I said. 'They haven't gone. They've swamped, that's all.'

I pulled on one of the ropes and got a soggy response. When the dinghy at last came to the surface, we were shattered. The rubber skin had been slashed all over, ripped to shreds.

'Fucking crocodiles!' exclaimed Murdo. 'Can you believe it!'

The other dinghy was the same. We had repair kits, but this damage was far beyond anything they could cover. God only knew why the croc had taken exception to the rubber crafts – but he'd torn them to kingdom come.

We didn't look for the engines – there was no point. Back on top of the bank we held a little O-group.

'There's basically two alternatives,' I said. 'Either we make our way to the LZ overland, or we call in help and lie up somewhere close.'

'How far to the LZ?' asked Mel.

'Maybe nine ks.'

'We'll never make it through the jungle.'

It didn't need to be said that, without the extra burden of the hostage and the dead man, we could have done it.

'Let's get on the radio, then. Murdo – you're our signaller now.'

'Where's the 319?'

'The DA's got it. Here.' I moved across, took the radio pack off him, and handed it over.

Murdo began to open it up, but a moment later he said, 'We'll not get many messages out with this thing.'

'Why not?'

'It's fucked.'

He held the set up, shining his torch on it, to show that a piece of shrapnel had blown its guts out.

By 0200 a fresh westerly breeze had sprung up round the island of Desierto.

'That's great,' said Merv as he breathed down his diving gear on the little beach. 'This ripple on the water will suit us fine.'

He and his partner, Terry Llewellyn, checked each other off, pulled on their rebreathing kits, went through their routine against possible oxygen hits, checked again, and slipped into the water. Besides his usual gear Merv was carrying two five-pound charges of plastic explosive in waterproof bags, already made up, with detonators embedded in them. In another bag he had det cord and timers.

The pair swam out round the point of the headland. The sky was overcast, and no lights were showing, either from the ship or from the quay. The chances of being spotted seemed minute, but Merv was not one to take risks. As soon as they came in line of sight of the *Santa Maria* he dived, and swam in at three-metre depth on a bearing of eighty-two degrees, surfacing every three minutes to check his line of advance.

Five lots of three brought him under the stern of the vessel. She was moving gently in the swell, and waves were slapping against her side. He gave Terry's arm four squeezes to indicate that they were on target, then felt his way down the swept-out curve of the hull until his gloved hand bumped gently against one blade of the starboard propeller. Down there, well underneath the ship, they were far out of sight of anyone on deck, so he switched on his helmet lamp, and in less than five minutes he had the first charge in place, tied round the prop-shaft at the point where it disappeared into the hull. Then, paying out the white det cord as he went, he swam down, under the end of the keel, and back up to the other prop. By the time he had the second charge in position and wired up his watch said 0235; so he set the timer for twenty-five minutes and swam quickly away.

Twenty minutes later he and Terry were back on the beach. Freddie Taylor, the single guy on stag at the boats, welcomed them in as they peeled off their kit.

'No problems?' he asked.

'Piece of cake,' Merv answered. 'We'll whip up to watch the fireworks.'

Freddie had the boats fully inflated, ready for the quick carry to the water. Merv and Terry just had time to scramble to the top of the headland ridge.

'Blue One to other Blues,' he said quietly over the covert radio. 'All go at our end.'

He didn't expect, or get, any answer. By then the assault party was at close quarters, and nobody would want to speak. In the event Roger had taken six men with him. One of them was to head out along the airstrip road before things went noisy, so that he'd be well placed to put down diversionary rounds without having to outsprint everyone else.

As the watchers lay on top of the ridge, the wind was coming from behind them, blowing onshore. Through 8 x 56 binoculars the buildings were clearly visible. A Russian-built Gaz jeep was parked outside, a few yards to the left of the objective.

'There!' said Terry suddenly. 'Somebody crossed the front of No. 2. And another. They're on the target, all right.'

'Thirty seconds to go,' said Merv over the radio link. 'Twenty. Stand by, Stand by. Fifteen. Ten. Five. Four, three, two . . .'

Before he could finish, a heavy, dull thump sounded from across the water. A fountain of water and spray flew into the air at the *Santa Maria*'s stern, and the whole ship gave a heave, a kind of slow flip from stern to bow. Then she settled back to her normal attitude, as if nothing had happened.

Lights went on in the ship's accommodation. Men began shouting. Merv and Terry saw people running aft along the cargo decks – but they didn't care too much about what was happening on board, their attention was focused on House No. 2. Now two men were visible outside, backed up against the wall, five or six yards apart, either side of the entrance.

'They're going to blow the door,' said Merv tersely. 'There she goes.'

A flash sparked out from the front of the house, and seconds later the boom of an explosion reached them. White smoke and dust billowed out in a ragged cloud. The assaulters disappeared. Then came two short bursts of automatic fire, the first and loudest in the watchers' earpieces, the second more muffled and through the air.

Suddenly they heard Roger call, 'Bolt-cutters!' A moment later they picked up a *snap*, followed by clinking noises.

At that instant Merv saw a dark figure running up the road from the left.

'Blue One,' he snapped. 'Watch out. One X-ray approaching from direction ship.'

Roger must have had a man outside on stag, because two more bursts rattled out, and the running figure dropped. Immediately afterwards they heard Roger say, 'Let's go. Run!'

Men poured out of the doorway – one, two, three, four, five. A sixth sprinted from the left to join them. Four ran to the right, while two temporarily vanished, having gone down to give covering fire. Then the two were on their feet and running. Hardly had they passed out of sight to the watchers' right when a far louder explosion – the loudest of the night – took House No. 2 apart. In a few seconds the structure was on fire, flames pouring from the roof. More men appeared, running from the ship, but the sight of the blazing house brought them to a halt. The last radio call Merv heard was Roger telling Charlie – his man down the airstrip road – not to stage any diversion, because none was necessary, but to head for base.

The watchers were about to pull back to the beach when Merv took one more look at the *Santa Maria*.

'Jesus!' he cried. 'She's down at the stern. She's sinking.'

'Arse on the bottom, anyway,' Terry agreed. 'Let's go.'

Five minutes later the assault group tumbled on to the

beach, panting but elated. Peter Black still had a shackle and a few links of chain dangling from his left wrist; for the past forty-eight hours he'd been chained to the structure of whatever gaol he'd been in – one night in a safe house used by the narcos in Bogotá, then in a cabin on the ship, then in the island building. He was still in his party gear, or at least the remains of it: the jacket of his suit had disappeared somewhere along the way, and his shirt, once white, was now filthy and torn. But his dark city trousers and black shoes looked ridiculously out of place. He was holding a pistol that Roger had thrust into his hand in case of emergency.

'Good to see you, boss,' Merv said cheerily. 'Had a nice holiday?'

'Charming, thanks. Five-star treatment.'

'Seriously – are you OK?'

'Absolutely. But, Christ, am I glad to see you guys. What a fantastic effort!'

'All part of the service. Now, let's go for a little voyage.'

After a quick sweep to make sure they'd left nothing behind, they fitted the engines, launched the Geminis, and motored out into the wind. As they cleared the headland, well out to sea, they looked back and saw flames rising high above the creek. Merv switched on the satcom and went through to Tony Lopez in Bogotá to report the success of the operation.

Somebody lent Black a sweater, because the night was quite cool, and once he'd got some food and drink down him, he seemed pretty much himself. As the party headed out to sea, they filled him in on their side of the operation, but he seemed desperately eager to find out what had happened to 'the others'.

'Who are they, boss?' Merv asked.

'You don't know?'

'No. We came out so bloody fast, we never got a full briefing. All we knew was that we had to lift you, off the boat or wherever it stopped.'

'Well . . .' Black seemed at a loss for words. 'It was the DA from the embassy, and the . . . woman who runs the comms office.'

'They're at some location in the jungle, and the training

team from D Squadron's gone after them. Their operation was due to go down at the same time as ours.'

'Let's ask the embassy what's happened, then.'

They went through again on the satcom, and Black talked to Tony direct – but all the anchor-man could report was that no news had come up from the south.

'What about the 319?' Black asked Merv. 'Can't we raise them on that?'

'We can try.'

The radio was in the other boat, so they closed on it and called across. But presently the answer came back: no contact.

At 0440 Merv took one last fix with his Magellan and saw that they were almost on their rendezvous, a few minutes early, so both coxswains throttled back their engines and cruised gently forward into the swell. Then a couple of men in each boat dangled their triangle-like signalling devices in the water, fishing for the submarine.

In fact the *Endeavor* had been listening to their engines for the past half-hour, and had been shadowing them. By the time they began to signal, she was almost underneath them. A couple of minutes later they saw her periscope break the surface a hundred metres to their east; next the conning tower hove into view, and finally the long, gleaming whale-like upper body. Within quarter of an hour they, together with all their kit, were safe in the belly of the leviathan.

It can't have been long after that we at last managed to separate the DA's handcuffs. All we had to sever a link of the chain between them was a hacksaw blade I'd been carrying in my ops waistcoat. Taking turns, concentrating so as not to break the blade by exerting too much pressure, we gradually cut through the link.

At the time that seemed a bit of an achievement. Certainly it was better that he could use his hands independently. Apart from having chewed-up wrists, he didn't seem much the worse, but he was exhausted and in shock. At any rate, he was very quiet, and it was only when I asked how he'd been lifted that he at last became articulate.

'My fault entirely,' he said. 'We'd had a few drinks, you remember. I was driving. I stopped outside the door of the restaurant, and we stared in. Then we drove off, came back, and did the same again. The next thing we knew, we were cut out by two cars full of armed men – and that was it.'

'And they brought you and Luisa here?'

'Yes, but we got separated as soon as we arrived.'

'Then what?'

'I'm afraid they gave her a bad time. I could hear her screaming . . .' His voice faltered and stopped.

'It's all right,' I said. 'You needn't go on.'

'I can,' said Murdo. 'Her body was lying on the floor in another room. She was naked, and it looked like she'd been badly beaten.'

I didn't answer, but I was thinking one name only: Farrell. That was his hallmark: rape and torture. Probably he'd been trying to make her divulge what SAS forces there were in the country. Once again my resolution to avoid personal vendettas had been blown to the winds, and I bitterly regretted my failure to take the bastard out while I'd had the chance.

We'd withdrawn into a small open area just inside the jungle at the north end of the airstrip. The rain had held off, but the mosquitoes were a major pain. The DA was still wearing the DPMs that the Colombians had given him, so that at least his arms were covered; but he had no hat, and the only way to protect his head was to drape himself in a little tent of netting.

We sat around miserably in the dark, debating our options. One faction, led by Murdo, was in favour of going back for a second hit on the compound. He argued that surprise would be on our side once again. The narcos and the PIRA – however many were left of them – must think that we'd somehow slipped away downriver, and they wouldn't be expecting a repeat performance.

'Listen,' I said. 'We came to lift the hostages. Now we've got one, and the other's dead, we want to get the hell out. We've lost one guy already. We don't want to risk any more. If any

PIRA have survived, they'll be well into the jungle by now.'

'In that case,' said Murdo, 'for fuck's sake let's get back to the LZ, so that the chopper can pick us up.'

That made good sense – and I didn't think we'd have much difficulty navigating. Our basic need would be to head due north. Obviously we'd have to weave about, taking the easiest route through the jungle, probably along animal tracks. But if ever we seemed in danger of getting lost, we could make our way back to the river and steer by that. The trouble was the physical difficulty of making progress. As I knew from past exercises, the jungle grows thickest along river banks, and our best hope would probably be to keep in the thinner areas, further inland.

Bitter experience, on training and previous operations, had taught us that it was impossible to move through the jungle in the dark. All the same, Murdo insisted on having a try, and he set off in company with Mel, announcing that they would move on a northerly heading. They never made more than a couple of hundred metres. For the next twenty minutes we could hear them cursing quite close to us as they tried to push their way through the undergrowth, and in half an hour they were back, with skin and DPMs ripped into shreds by the wait-a-while thorns. We agreed that we'd start trying to blaze a trail north as soon as it was light. In the meantime, at 0500, we pulled out the pin from one of our TACBE beacons, hoping that the international distress call it put out would be picked up at Puerto Pizarro and alert our rear-party to the fact that we were in the shit.

Thereafter, all we could do was sit and wait for the light. As we were in thick cover, we got a brew on, and that cheered things a bit, but time seemed to be moving at the pace of a constipated snail. I kept looking at the wretched bundle in the hammocks, all that was left of Sparky. You poor bugger, I was thinking. All your money-saving didn't do you much good in the end. Also on my mind was Luisa's naked body, lying on the floor, with flies and ants getting at it.

'Let's hope the Boat Troop have had better luck,' I said, and everyone grunted assent.

Eventually dawn broke, retarded by the fact that the sky was still overcast. Grey light filtered down through the tree canopy, and we were just sorting ourselves out for the off when, to our consternation, we heard an engine splutter and start up out on the strip.

'Jesus!' I cried. 'The plane!'

In twenty seconds we were out on the edge of the cleared ground. The Islander was some 600 metres off, at the other end of the strip and facing away from us, but even in the half-light we could see that both its props were turning.

'They're nuts!' I shouted. 'I fixed the tyres. They'll never get off.'

'If they do, we can drop them,' said Murdo. 'They'll have to take off this way. They'll be right over our heads. Just go on automatic and give the plane plenty of lead.'

I watched, half-hypnotized, as the Islander started to move. Was it possible that someone had come down to the field and changed the wheels during the past couple of hours? Or was the pilot in such a panic that he hadn't checked the tyres before he went aboard?

Slowly the plane turned right-handed and straightened. We heard the pilot winding up his engines. But then we heard something else.

My TACBE, which had been beeping quietly for the past hour, sending out the emergency beacon, suddenly came to life. An English voice was saying, 'Green Four, this is the QRF. Do you read me? Over.'

I seized the set and switched to the voice channel. 'Authenticate!' I shouted. 'Authenticate!'

'Operation Crocodile,' came the answer. 'Op Croc.'

'Green Four, roger. You're loud and clear. Where are you?'

'Estimate zero eight ks from your location. We're airborne towards you.'

'Roger. We're on the north end, repeat north end, of the new airstrip beside the river. There's an Islander trying to take off at this moment. It's the narcos' transport. If it gets airborne, shoot it down.'

'Roger. We have eyes on the river. Turning downstream

now. There's smoke rising from the jungle to the west. Is that you?'

'Negative. That's the laboratory. We hit it during the night. We're one k east of the smoke, right by the river. Repeat. One k east of smoke.'

'Roger. We'll be with you in two minutes. Wait out.'

I put the set down, hardly able to believe my ears.

'Bloody hell!' shouted Murdo. 'Who is it?'

'QRF from the Regiment. For fuck's sake let's not have a blue-on-blue.'

'Green Four,' I called again. 'I confirm, our location is on the northern end of the airstrip, on the edge of the forest.'

'Roger,' called the QRF leader. 'Location coming in sight. We have eyes on the aircraft.'

On the ground the Islander was still teeing itself up, engines screaming at full revs. At last it started forward, towards us, but not accelerating quickly, as it should have been. Rather, it began weaving from side to side in a sluggish, drunken stagger. After no more than a couple of hundred yards of that, it veered off to its left, coming to a halt a few yards from the jungle wall.

As the pilot doused the engines, we became aware of another sound: the heavy thudding of helicopter blades and the scream of turbines. A second later two Hueys swept overhead, with side-gunners sitting in the open doorways. We waved frantically, and one of the pair went into a hover above us. The other carried straight on, to land well beyond the stranded aircraft.

The Islander's door had popped open. Two men jumped to the ground and began to run. One was aiming for the end of the road, the other came our way, heading for the jungle on our right. Instantly the machine-gun overhead opened up with a heavy hammer. A line of bullets flickered across the strip, kicking up puffs of dirt ahead of the farthest runner. No warning could have been clearer: stop or you die. The man continued to run, and within seconds he'd been cut down by another burst.

At the same moment rounds came snapping across the tops

297

of our heads. Belatedly I saw a group of two or three Colombians way down the field. As we returned fire I suddenly realized that the single figure disappearing to our right was running with a limp. Farrell! I swung round and put in a burst from the MP 5 just as he disappeared into the trees.

'Stay with the DA!' I yelled, throwing Murdo my spare magazines. 'Keep them off. I'm going after him.'

Incoming fire was still cracking past, but I was possessed by the realization that this was my last chance, and I gave no thought to the rounds going past. In a few seconds I was on the edge of the jungle at the spot where I'd last seen the fugitive. There, on a big leaf, was a splash of fresh blood. He was wounded, at least. Possibly dead, but anyway wounded.

I dropped on one knee, listening for sounds of movement. Behind me rounds were still going down, and I could hear the choppers landing, but my whole attention was focused on the wall of vegetation ahead. A wounded animal is the most dangerous of all. What weapon was Farrell carrying? I hadn't seen any long, but he could well have a pistol.

There was more blood on a plant ahead. On the forest floor some dead leaves had been turned over. Further on, at the edge of a clearing, I saw threads torn out of a shirt and hanging on the wait-a-while thorns. I guessed he wasn't far in front.

Twenty yards across the clearing, a bush moved. I whipped a burst into the foliage and heard a yell. The branches thrashed about and Farrell half fell into the open. I raised my weapon to engage him again, but when I pulled the trigger, nothing happened. With a sickening lurch of the stomach I knew I was out of rounds – and I'd given Murdo my spare magazines.

Farrell was on all fours, struggling to stand up. I raced straight for him and kicked him full belt in the ribs. The blow sent him flying on to his back. I saw blood all down his right side – one burst had got him in the arm and flank.

Never before in my life had I lost control, but I did then. Holding the MP 5 in both hands, I smashed the butt down on to Farrell's jaw. With his good hand he grabbed my sleeve and tried to drag me down on to him. Caught off-balance, I toppled and landed with all my weight on my left forearm, right on the old break. A stab of pain shot through me, like a shot from my recurring nightmare.

I gave a yell, drew back, kneed him in the bollocks, ripped free and stood up, panting. Blood had started to trickle from his mouth. I kicked him again in the side of the head and knocked him flat sideways – but still he was trying to get up. I was on the point of using the MP 5 on him again when I felt a touch on my arm. I whipped round, and there was Murdo, offering me his weapon.

'Shoot the bastard, Geordie. It's easier.'

I took the MP 5 and levelled it at Farrell's head. Still he was struggling to prop himself on his left elbow. He looked straight at me and spat. Then, in a snarl, he said, 'Don't fucking miss.'

'Go on!' snapped Murdo. 'Top him!'

'No.' I handed the weapon back. The hatred had suddenly drained out of me. 'No,' I repeated, 'the cunt's far more valuable alive.'

Back on the airstrip, the occupants of the plane had given themselves up. Everybody had been searched and lined up in the open. The second Huey had landed; six more armed SAS troops in full combat kit rapidly debussed, and the pilot shut down the engine. Silence fell over the airfield.

Murdo and I propelled our prisoner towards the commander of the QRF, whom I recognized as Billy Bracewell – big, blond, muscular, a staff sergeant with G Squadron.

'Geordie!' he shouted. 'Are you all right?'

'Fine. Let's get the fuck out of here.'

'Who's this?'

'Declan Farrell. One of the key members of the PIRA. He's volunteered to come back with us, to help the police with their inquiries.'

'OK. Hand him over to two of those guys there. What about the hostages?'

'That's the DA. He's all right.' I pointed to our group

behind me. 'But they killed the woman. You'll find her body in the concrete building. Sparky's dead as well. That's him there.' I gestured to a little mound under a poncho.

A minute later, as people were milling around, I got Billy to one side and whispered fiercely: 'Farrell. That's the fucker who killed my wife.' I felt choked. Suddenly I was hit by everything at once: the let-down of tension, lack of sleep, frustration over Farrell, grief over the loss of Sparky. I sat down on the deck with my head in my hands and tried to get myself together.

Presently I felt a hand on my shoulder. There was Murdo, with his moustache drooping fearsomely in the grey dawn light.

'Come on, Geordie,' he said. 'Let's have a proper brew and a bloody great breakfast. Then we'll all feel better.'

300

EIGHTEEN

They couldn't get us out of the country fast enough. It was as if we'd created too much of a disturbance already, and the authorities feared that the narco bosses would order a revenge strike if they could find out where we were. The other worry was that the media would latch on to us and start bringing out wild stories. The big essential was that we kept our heads down, and as a result our feet hardly touched the ground.

Landed back at Puerto Pizarro by the Hueys in the second of two lifts, we found that the prisoners, including Farrell, had been taken on ahead to some holding centre. A Herc was awaiting us, and we flew straight back to Bogotá. We weren't allowed into the embassy, but at least we got a proper shower, a change of clothes and a decent meal at an army barracks outside the city. Also, I managed to phone Tony, and asked him to call Tracy, to say we were on our way home. He filled me in on the success of the Boat Troop's operation, but said that the guys were still on board the *Endeavor*, heading for Florida.

Then, that same night, it was into an RAF VC10, which had come in after dark with a reserve crew on board, and turned straight round as soon as it had refuelled. At the last moment Tony joined us, so that we had plenty to talk about during the flight. He told me he'd been through to Tracy, and she was fine.

Missing out Belize, we went north to Gander, to refuel, then across to Brize, and landed there feeling more dead than alive at 2200, after a total of fourteen hours in transit. As we waited for our baggage to come off, I dialled home, and was puzzled to find the answerphone switched on. Oh well, I thought. The plane was late. Maybe she's come to camp to meet me?

301

All the same, worry began needling me. No, I was thinking, surely she'd never take Tim into camp at ten o'clock at night. There was something odd going on.

Because the operation had turned out a big success, the camp helicopter came up to meet us, and we had an immediate debrief on the aircraft as we flew down. When we reached Hereford, we found everything set for a big celebration. The ops officer was there, the CO, even the Director, who'd come down from London in the middle of the night. They cracked open bottles of champagne, and it was all congratulations and back-slapping until one o'clock in the morning. I tried to enter into the spirit, but I was too wound up to get the party feeling, especially after I'd slipped out, rung home again, and once more got the answerphone.

At last, around 0145, the duty driver took me out to Keeper's Cottage. To someone fresh in from the jungle, the April night air seemed very cold, and I shuddered as I got out of the car outside our door. As far as I could see in the dark, everything was neat and shipshape. The Cavalier was parked on the gravel, and Tim's miniature mountain bike was leaning against the wall. But why were all the windows dark? Why hadn't she left the hall light on for me?

I didn't have a key, and was about to press the door buzzer when I thought, No – she's expecting me, so she'll have left it open.

Sure enough, the door gave when I turned the handle. I switched on the light and looked round. Everything seemed normal. I put down my bergen and holdall and called up the stairs, 'Trace – hi! It's me.'

No answer.

Must be fast asleep, I thought. But a loud alarm was clanging in my head. I ran up the stairs three at a time and switched on the landing light. Our bedroom door stood open. I flipped on the light in there. The bed was made up, un-slept in. I rushed into Tim's room. The same.

Back downstairs I tried the kitchen. There too everything was immaculate, neatly squared away. Panic threatened to choke me. I stood holding the handle of the kitchen door, rooted by fright. Then I shook myself free and went into the living room. As the light flicked on, my eye went straight to an alien object on the rug in front of the wood-burning stove.

I dived and picked it up: a Polaroid colour print, five by three. It showed Tracy, holding Tim on her hip, in front of the fireplace, and, on either side of her, a man in a black balaclava armed with a pistol. They were standing in the mock-heroic attitudes always shown in the IRA murals in Belfast.

I sat down hard on the arm of a chair, breathless with shock. How did they know? I thought desperately. How did they connect her with me? And then in a flash I remembered. That man I'd chatted to so innocently about fishing in the Spanish Galleon, the pub on the coast of County Antrim. The man who'd come round to the cottage next morning. That one contact had been enough.

My hand was shaking. I stared at the photograph, and the expression on Tracy's face. A stranger might have thought she was smiling, but I could see how scared she'd been when the flash went off.

ZERO OPTION

So, for the second time [the Pharisees],
summoned the man who had been blind and said
'Speak the truth before God.
We know this fellow is a sinner.'
'Whether or not he is a sinner, I do not know,'
the man replied.
'All I know is this:
once I was blind and now I can see.'

John IX 24–26
The New English Bible

GLOSSARY

ASU	IRA Active Service Unit
Bergen	Rucksack
BG	Bodyguard (noun or verb)
Blue-on-blue	Accidental strike on own forces
Box	General name for intelligence services
Camp	Stirling Lines, SAS headquarters in Hereford
Casevac	Casualty evacuation
CAT	Counter-attack team/Civil Administration Team: IRA disciplinary unit
Chuckies	Provisional IRA
COBR	Cabinet Office Briefing Room, Whitehall
Comms	Communications
CT	Counter-terrorist
CTR	Close target reconnaissance
Det	Intelligence gathering organisation
DF	Direction finding
Dicker	IRA scout
Director, The	Brigadier commanding Special Forces
DOP	Drop-off point
DPMs	Disruptive pattern material camouflage garments
DZ	Drop zone
EMOE	Explosive method of entry
ERV	Emergency rendezvous
FMB	Forward mounting base
FOB	Forward operating base
GPS	Global positioning system (hand-held navigation aid)

Head-shed	Headquarters
Incoming	Incoming fire
Int	Intelligence
IO	Intelligence officer
Kremlin, The	SAS headquarters
LUP	Lying-up point
LZ	Landing zone
Magellan	Brand-name of GPS
MPI	Mean point of impact
MSR	Main supply route
OP	Observation post
Phys	Physical exercise
PIRA	Provisional IRA
Player	Terrorist
PNGs	Passive night goggles
PUP	Pick-up point
QRF	Quick reaction force
R & R	Rest and recreation
RTU	Return to unit: noun or verb
RUC	Royal Ulster Constabulary
Rupert	Officer
Satcom	Telephone using satellite transmission
SAW	Subversive Action Wing
SB	Special Branch
SEAL	Sea, Air and Land – American Special Forces unit
Shreddies	Army-issue underpants
SOCO	Scene of Crimes Officer
SP	Special Projects
SSM	Squadron Sergeant Major
Stag	Shift/Watch
Tacbe	Emergency radio beacon
Tout	Informer
UCBT	Under-car booby trap
U/S	Unserviceable
VCP	Vehicle control point

WEAPONS

AK-47	Soviet or Chinese made 7.62mm automatic rifle
Barrett	.50 inch American sniper rifle
Browning	9mm pistol
Claymore	Anti-personnel mine throwing ball bearings
Dragunov	Soviet-made 7.62mm sniper rifle
Haskins	.50 inch American sniper rifle
Long	Any rifle
MP 5	9mm sub-machine-gun
RPG 7	Soviet-made rocket launcher
Short	Any pistol
Sig 226	Sigsauer 9mm pistol

ONE

It took me a few moments to get myself together. I sat on the arm of the easy chair, practically paralysed, staring at the polaroid photo, unable to believe that my son and girlfriend – my whole family – had gone. My hand began to tremble so badly that the outline of Tim's little face blurred; I could hardly see Tracy at all. Then a shudder pulsed through my body. It seemed to start at my feet, then rose quickly through my knees, hips and trunk. When it reached my head I suddenly regained power of thought and movement.

I studied the picture again. It had been taken with a flash from a few feet away. Tracy was standing in front of the fireplace holding Tim on her right hip. Her face was twisted into a smile of sorts, but I could see the fear behind it. That grin was one of bravado, defiance. Close on either side of her stood two men in black balaclava ski-masks, brandishing pistols like in those crappy, mock-heroic wall-paintings you see on the walls of buildings in West Belfast. Both were wearing dark sweatshirts. They weren't actually holding her, but you could see that if she'd moved an inch either way they'd have grabbed her.

The picture had been taken horizontally, so that it cut off the grown-ups at waist-level. There must have been three intruders at least: these two, and the guy who held the camera.

Fingerprints, I thought. Don't destroy any. I realised I

shouldn't have touched the photo at all. Without changing my finger-and-thumb grip I stood up, crossed to the bureau, fished out a brown envelope with my left hand and slipped the photo into it. Then I spread a handkerchief over my palm and fingers before picking up the phone and dialling the emergency number in camp.

'Hello,' said the switchboard girl. 'Stirling Lines.'

'Guardroom, please.'

'One moment.'

I waited, glancing at my watch. It was less than half an hour since I'd checked out of camp and said goodnight. Then I heard, 'Guardroom. Sergeant Howard.'

'Chris,' I said. 'It's Geordie.'

'What's up?'

'Listen, they've lifted the pair of them.'

'Who? What are you saying?'

'They've taken Tim and Tracy.'

'*Who*, for Christ's sake? Who are you talking about?'

'It's the PIRA.'

'Don't be daft. How d'you know? Where are you?'

'At home. I found a photo on the floor. Two guys in ski-masks, either side of Tracy and the kid. Nothing else. Chris, what the fuck can I do?'

'Jesus! You'd better head back into camp.'

'OK. But can you get someone out here to keep an eye on the house?'

'Of course. I'll put a guy on his way. Sit tight until he arrives. Then head right in.'

'OK. And listen: get the police to activate their plan to close every main road out of town.'

'Operation Cougar. I'll tell them right away.'

I switched on the outside security lights and stood in the hall, trying to think. How in hell had the IRA found out where I lived? How had they known that I was abroad?

2

Waiting was tough. I started pacing up and down like a lion in a cage, frantic to get some action going. Yet there was nothing positive I could do. Every minute that passed gave the snatch party a better chance to make their getaway. Deep down I knew it was already too late to intercept them anywhere nearby: they'd have had far too long to get clear.

I walked out into the dark and made myself take a few deep breaths, inhaling the soft, damp, earthy smells of England in late April. For a few moments I enjoyed the night, but to somebody fresh from the jungle the air felt cool and I was soon back indoors. I tried thinking back, to see where there could have been a leak. What about the man I'd chatted to in the pub on the coast of County Antrim? The one who'd called at the cottage Tracy and I were staying in while I was out?

My other immediate inclination was to blame Farrell – Declan Farrell, the big PIRA player with whom I'd been feuding for months. But now . . . it could hardly have been him. I and my mates in an SAS hit team had captured him in Colombia only a couple of days before, and the last I'd seen of him he was being hauled off to the nick in Bogotá.

Unless, of course, he'd ordered this operation before he went out to Colombia . . .

Less than forty-eight hours earlier we'd blown the shit out of a cocaine processing laboratory beside a tributary of the Amazon. We'd taken one casualty – Sparky Springer, killed by shrapnel from a rocket – but after a dawn shoot-out we'd wounded Farrell and caught him. So now it was a real kick in the bollocks to find that his pernicious influence had struck on my home territory.

Fighting to keep calm I took another look round, keeping a handkerchief draped over my fingers so that I left no prints. As far as I could see nothing was missing;

I owned very little of any value, but the obvious targets for a gang of thieves – the hi-fi, the TV, the microwave – were all still in place.

Then, in the dishwasher, I made a small find: two plates smeared with tomato sauce, two glasses, and knives and forks in the basket. In the waste-bin was an empty packet that had held two cod steaks. So they'd had tea, probably at about six o'clock.

I went upstairs. Tim's bed was still made up, his pyjamas neatly folded under the pillow; he'd never gone to bed or had his evening read. The idea of the boy being grabbed made me feel sick, but I forced myself to think. The snatch must have taken place between six and eight – seven or eight hours ago. The hostages could be anywhere by now.

I went to the answerphone. The blinking red light was indicating two messages. I ran back the tape and listened, but the calls were the two I'd made myself – one from the airport, one from Camp on my way home.

The scrunch of wheels on gravel whipped me to the front door. Two of the Regiment's duty Range Rovers had pulled up outside, their sidelights still on. I went to the driver's door of the first and saw that the guy at the wheel was Nobby Clarke.

'Thanks for coming,' I said.

'No sweat. I'm to run you back in. We'll leave Les Abbott here.'

'OK.' I nipped across to the second car and said, 'Hi, Les. Back off till you're level with that bush there. You'll be out of sight of anyone approaching, and you can sit in the vehicle to watch the house.'

'Fine. No one's to enter the house until the police arrive. But I'm not to walk around either. There may be footprints, and they don't want them spoilt.'

'Fair enough. Good luck, then.'

4

'Have you locked up?' Nobby asked.

'Just going to.'

I pulled the front door to, then at the last minute I realised I probably wouldn't be back before morning, so I dived inside again and grabbed my day-sack, which contained washing kit. Finally I closed the door and turned the key.

Nobby slung the Range Rover through the lanes, making the tyres scrabble, and we were back at the gates of Stirling Lines in eleven minutes flat. In the guardroom the four guys on fire-picket were watching a porn video with that glazed look that comes over everyone on duty in the small hours.

Chris stood up, slim and trim in his DPM shirt and trousers and blue stable belt with its silver buckle. 'Ah, Geordie,' he said. 'I buzzed up the ops officer and he's come in already. The CID are on their way. You'd better get your arse up to the ops room.'

I never looked forward to meeting the ops officer, Major Alex Macpherson (generally known as 'Mac'). He was efficient enough at his job, but he had a sarcastic manner that pissed the guys off. Having been a troop commander in the eighties, he'd returned to his regiment (the Black Watch) for a spell, and then wanted to come back to the SAS as a squadron commander; but the fact that at the age of thirty-six or thirty-seven he'd only made it to ops officer seemed to sour him. Even at the impromptu party which greeted our return he'd been low-key.

I ran up the stairs of the head-shed building, known to all and sundry as the Kremlin. The door of the ops room stood open and I found Mac, dressed in a dark blue polo shirt and jeans, rubbing the sleep out of his eyes. Serve the bugger right, I thought: normally it was he who routed us out of bed in the middle of the night,

5

and took some pleasure in doing so. His short black hair was standing upright, as if he'd forgotten to brush it when he staggered up. His DPM uniform was thrown over a chair, and his kit – bergen and a pair of boots – stood in a corner.

'Christ, Geordie,' he said. 'That didn't take long.'

'What d'you mean?'

'You've only been back in the UK about five minutes and already you've stirred the shit something wicked.'

'For fuck's sake, Boss. It's nothing *I've* done.'

'No – well . . .' He stopped, looking at me. The edge in my voice must have made him realise what a state I was in.

'This is the picture they left.' I held out the envelope. 'I've touched it once, in the corner, but otherwise it's clean.'

He went to a shelf and brought down a new file-holder with a flap of cellophane over the front. I decanted the photo carefully into it so that the picture was protected but visible, and laid it on a desk.

'Bastards!' he muttered as he looked at it. 'Let's get a brew on, anyway.' His tone had softened. 'We're going to have to do some talking. Sugar in your tea?'

'No, thanks.'

He moved off into the little annexe where there was a kettle and stuff for making hot drinks. I glanced round at the room: desks with computer terminals on them, filing cabinets with combination locks, shelves full of books . . . this could have been an ordinary office but for the fact that on the walls drab grey curtains were drawn over boards which carried details of the Regiment's current secret operations.

I heard the kettle coming to the boil, and after a couple of minutes' fiddling about Mac handed me a mug. As I drank it I could feel my head clearing. The

6

ops room started filling up with people. First came the Intelligence Officer, a thin, bespectacled guy called Jimmy Wells, carrying a hefty, buff-coloured file of papers; then his clerk (or gofer), who'd also been dragged out of bed, and brought a laptop computer with him. Then came Detective Sergeant Ken Bates of the local CID – prematurely grey-haired, sporting a spiky grey moustache – together with a dumpy, fair-haired detective constable called Mary.

When everyone was seated round a table the int officer led off, telling his gofer to record everything I said on the laptop. The police girl was also to take down my statement in shorthand, to save me saying everything twice.

'The trouble is, I know so little about it,' I began. 'I just got home, and they were gone.'

'Wait a minute,' said Bates. 'I need to take your full name.' He had a blunt Northern accent – Manchester, perhaps.

'Sharp,' I told him. 'Geordie Sharp.'

'Army number?'

'24369207.'

'Rank?'

'Sergeant.'

'Age?'

'Thirty-one.'

'Where's home?'

'It's called Keeper's Cottage. Out in the country, quite isolated – six miles from town.'

'What's the village?'

'It's not in any village. It's just off the Leominster road.'

'What time did you get there?'

'Just about two.'

'And where'd you been?'

Jesus! I thought. This guy knows nothing. But then,

7

how *could* he know anything about me? I've got to explain everything from scratch.

So I took a deep breath and said, 'We've been on an operation overseas. I've been away six weeks. We landed back at RAF Brize Norton at ten – that's near Oxford – then we came on here and had a bit of a piss-up to celebrate our success. We must have got into camp about midnight.'

'But you'd tried to phone home earlier,' Mac put in. 'You mentioned that at the party.'

'That's right. I called first about half-ten, from Brize, while we were waiting for our baggage. Then again about half-one when we reached camp. The answerphone was on both times. And listen . . .'

I told them about the plates with tomato sauce on them, the packet in the waste-bin, and Tim's unused bed.

'But your wife could have used the plates at lunchtime,' said Bates.

I tried not to glare at him. 'It's not my wife,' I said evenly. 'My wife was killed by a bomb in Belfast.'

'I'm sorry . . .'

'It's all right. We're talking about my girlfriend, Tracy Jordan. She came to live with me and look after my kid after Kath had been murdered.'

'What about Susan?' asked the int officer. 'Where was she?'

'Susan?'

'Susan Jones, the woman who's been sharing the house with Tracy.'

'God – I'd forgotten all about her. She's away a lot of the time, travelling for a cosmetics firm. She's probably on one of her tours.'

The detective sergeant cleared his throat. 'Can you describe Tim, please?'

'Well, you can see him in the photo.' I swivelled the

8

file cover so that the picture faced the sergeant. 'He's four and a bit. Very fair, fine straight hair, and blue eyes.'

'How tall?'

'Jesus! I don't know. Two foot six? But he's normal for his age.'

'What about his clothes?'

'Like here: green polo shirt, grey jogging pants and trainers. That's his regular gear.'

'And can you describe Tracy?'

'She's tall and slim, with red hair.'

'How tall?'

'Five ten . . . Here, look.' I pointed at the photo. 'She's level with both the PIRA guys, at least.'

'And is her hair the colour it looks here?'

'No, it's not as dark or chestnutty really. It's quite a fiery red. I've got better pictures of her at home.'

'We'll need to see them, then. What else can you say about her?'

'She's got freckles on her face and arms.'

'Anywhere else?'

I looked up sharply. Was Bates trying to take the piss? He read my reaction correctly and said in a flat voice, 'It may be a body we're dealing with.'

I swallowed. 'All right, then. On her shoulders as well.'

'D'you recognise the clothes she's wearing?'

'Yes. That turquoise top is a loose cotton sweater that comes down nearly to her knees. She was probably wearing dark blue jeans and white Reebok trainers. Those big earrings are regular fixtures too. And she always has that gold chain round her neck.'

'Tracy's how old?'

'Twenty-eight.'

'When did you last have contact with her?'

'Oh Christ, I don't know.' My mind spun as I tried

9

to unscramble events in Bogotá and the jungle. 'Several days ago. A week, maybe. But a mate of mine phoned her from Colombia the day we left. That was yesterday – no, two days ago. She was fine then.'

The questions fired on, one after another. What security systems did I have on the house? Only lights outside. Had I ever been followed back from camp? Not that I knew of. Had I or Tracy ever hung out military uniform on the washing line? No, I washed all my kit at the launderette in camp. Did I ever travel home in uniform or a military vehicle? No. Had we ever seen strangers hanging about near the house? No. Had there been any strange phone calls?

'Yes,' I said. 'There was one. When I phoned her from Colombia she told me a man had rung and asked if I was enjoying myself in the sun.'

'When was this?'

'About a week ago. I spoke to her from Bogotá.'

There was a pause as my inquisitors thought things over, and I began to feel desperately tired. Our flight home had stretched out over more than twenty-four hours, with demoralising periods of waiting in between, and we'd gone through several time zones. That would have been an ordeal on its own . . . and now I had all this.

The ops officer knew almost everything about my background, and the int officer knew some of it; but the detective sergeant, because he was starting from scratch, needed filling in on possible motives for the kidnap. Again, I had to make a big mental effort to go back to the start of the trouble.

'Kath was a Belfast girl,' I explained. 'She'd gone home to look after her mum, who'd had an operation. She was killed by an IRA bomb that went off prematurely outside a supermarket.'

Bates nodded and gave a sympathetic grunt.

10

'Some weeks later I got posted to Northern Ireland, and I found out from the RUC who'd been responsible for the explosion. It was one of the leading players in Belfast, a guy called Declan Farrell. Of course I wanted to top him, and I got a chance one night when he came to a weapons hide at a farm. But one of the group was the RUC's best informer, so the head-shed wouldn't let us fire.'

I stopped because I could see Mac's eyeballs rotating. The things I was saying shouldn't have been heard by anyone outside the Regiment; not even the police should know what had gone on across the water.

'Where were you stationed?' Bates asked.

'Classified information!' snapped the ops officer. 'He can't tell you that.'

I looked from one to the other before going on. 'Anyway, that was when I decided to go after Farrell on my own. I thought I could take him out single-handed. I was going to shoot him at the place where he was living. Highly irregular, of course, but it seemed the only way. It turned out that some other security organisation already had him under surveillance, and they picked me up . . .'

'So?' the sergeant prompted.

'I came back to Hereford, never finished my tour. But the Regiment were very good: they could have RTU'd me but they let me off with a caution. I tried to call it a day and forget the whole thing. But then it started again.'

I finished my tea and paused before continuing. 'In November a team of our lads went out from here to train the President of Colombia's bodyguard. I was in command. We were half-way through the course at a military camp down country, everything going well, when we travelled up to the capital one weekend for a bit of R and R. And suddenly there the bastard was:

11

Farrell, can you believe it, in a Colombian restaurant, with a couple of other Paddies and some natives.

'Obviously the PIRA was into drug-running and arms-dealing, big time. Anyway, two of the embassy staff were stupid enough to go down to the restaurant to get a look at them. The next thing was, the pair was lifted, along with one of our ruperts who'd been doing liaison.'

'Ruperts?' Bates frowned.

'Officers. Well, that caused a big panic. We got clearance from DAS – the Colombian secret police – to bust the operation. We followed the kidnappers down into the Amazon jungle, and things ended up with a fire-fight at a coke-manufacturing plant miles from anywhere. Farrell got wounded and captured.'

'So you think this kidnap is a vendetta by Farrell?' Bates asked.

'Not directly. It can't be, because he never knew who it was that had come after him. Before that last moment, when we picked him up, he'd never seen me, hadn't a clue who I was. For all he knew I might have been Colombian. He couldn't have equated me with any problem he'd had in Ulster, and in the jungle he was just shot by some strange soldier and taken into custody. Someone else in the PIRA must have ordered the lift – somebody at this end, when news came back that Farrell had been nicked.'

'Unless he's already escaped,' the sergeant suggested.

Jimmy, the int officer, suddenly came to. 'No. No, he's still inside.' Blinking through his spectacles, he turned back to the most recent sheet of paper in his file and said, 'At least, he was yesterday evening. The British and Colombian governments are negotiating about his extradition.'

'In that case,' the sergeant persisted, 'how did the IRA know who to come after?'

12

'My fault,' I admitted. 'I blew it. After Christmas I took local leave in Ulster. I told my people in the Regiment I'd gone back to the mainland, but in fact I stayed put. I got Tracy across and we took a holiday cottage on the north coast. I'd been told it was a safe area, used by tourists, so one night I went to the pub in the village and got talking to a local about fishing. That was all, but it was enough to give them a line on me.'

'This guy Farrell,' said the ops officer. 'What is he in the PIRA?'

Jimmy flicked through his file. 'At the time of the supermarket bomb incident he was adjutant of the Belfast Brigade. But since then we believe he's taken charge of what they call "international liaison". That means drug-running, arms-dealing – anything that raises funds and weapons from abroad.'

The detective sergeant rubbed his chin, his fingers scratching on the early-morning bristles. 'What sort of a person is he?'

'If that man fell into a pit of shit,' I said bitterly, 'he'd come out smelling like roses. He's got a charmed life. I mean, I ought to have topped him two or three times already, and look what's happened now. He may be in the nick, but that hasn't stopped him.'

Suddenly I remembered the presence of the female constable, scribbling in the background, and felt the colour rise in my cheeks as I turned to her and said, 'Sorry . . .'

Still writing, she gave a quick grin and raised her left hand, and I felt myself warming to her.

'The thing is, he's a well-educated guy,' I blundered on. 'He's got a university degree. He's big, dark, good-looking, he's a bit of a wine buff . . . I don't know what it is that makes him tick.'

A telephone rang. The ops officer swung round, picked up the receiver and listened. After a few seconds

13

he said, 'That's fine. We'll expect you then,' and hung up. Turning back to us he said, 'That was Special Branch. Because of the nature of the incident there's a standby team coming down from London. They'll be here in three hours' time. Geordie, you're looking knackered – you'd better get your head down. Is there anything else, Sergeant?'

'Nothing immediate. We'll want to look at the house first thing in the morning. And Geordie, you'll come with us.'

'Fair enough.'

'I'll take that photo with me. Once Forensic have been over it I'll have it copied, so that we can circulate prints. Then no doubt SB'll want it. By the way . . .' He looked back at Mac. 'No press release of any kind. The last thing we want is for this to get into the papers.'

'Don't worry,' Mac assured him. 'I will personally throttle anyone who talks.'

'All right, then.' Bates turned back to me. 'Seven o'clock at the guardroom?'

'I'll be there.'

14

TWO

I spent the rest of that night in the sergeants' mess, in the room I shared with a mate, Pat Newman. He, being married, lived at home, and normally neither of us slept there, using the place as a store for some of our kit. It was a small, bare room, with little more than a bed, a wardrobe and a washbasin as furnishings. The bed was piled with our gear — bergens, para bags and webbing — so I heaved the lot off into a corner. There was a sheet in the cupboard, I knew, but I couldn't be bothered to make the bed at that stage, so I just kicked off my shoes and got under the top blanket. I felt jaded and filthy. Normally I would at least have washed my face and cleaned my teeth, but such a wave of exhaustion had swamped me that all I wanted was to lie down and pass out.

The next thing I knew I was wide awake. For a few seconds I couldn't think where the hell I was: strange room, narrow bed, unfamiliar window already allowing in the grey dawn light, birds singing outside. Then back it all came with a bang.

My watch said 5.35. Jesus! Special Branch would be here any moment. I jumped up, dug out my sponge-bag and went along to the washroom, where a shave and a shower brought me back to reality. My biological time-clock might have been all to blazes, but the combination of hot water over my face and alarm at my family's predicament soon cleared my brain.

15

By six o'clock I was back at the guardroom, and the Special Branch Rover rolled down to the barrier a few minutes later. The guard commander had been told to take the party to the ops room, so I volunteered to show them the way. The boss figure was Commander John Fraser, a slender, lightly-built guy in his forties with a thin face, sandy hair and a slightly harassed expression: not physically impressive, but with a reassuring manner that quickly inspired confidence. I noticed he had taken trouble over his appearance. He had a slight Cockney accent, but his voice, like his presence, was unobtrusive and comfortable.

With him came a sidekick in the form of a burly detective sergeant called Denis Haynes, wearing a hairy tweed jacket, and a blonde, pale-faced young woman detective constable with looks reminiscent of Barbra Streisand. At the first introduction I missed her name, but it turned out to be Karen Terraine.

In the ops room Mac gave the newcomers a short brief. Fraser's most urgent request was for a room that could act as a control centre for the duration of the incident: somewhere with secure comms in which his own staff and the CID could work alongside each other, with immediate recourse to the military if they needed it. The request presented no problem, because up there, on the first floor of the Kremlin, one room was kept ready for just such an emergency. After a quick look, the commander pronounced it ideal.

Mac realised that the visitors' next most pressing need was to get some food and drink down their necks, so he handed Fraser a print-out of the statement I'd given earlier in the night and despatched us all to the sergeants' mess for breakfast.

As the others started down the stairs I hung back with Mac and asked, 'How much can I tell him, Boss?'

'Anything he wants to know,' he replied. 'With

Special Branch, no problem.'

Until that moment I hadn't felt hungry, but as I led the party through the dining room towards the kitchen counter, the smell of bacon brought my appetite alive, and I got myself a big fry-up: two eggs, bacon, sausages, potatoes, tomatoes – the lot. So did Fraser and his sergeant, but I noticed that the woman DC, who had a cracking figure, stuck to tea and a piece of toast.

For privacy we took over a separate table, and as we sat down I saw Fraser look at me in an appraising but sympathetic way. 'Just in from South America, are you?'

'That's right.'

'Not a very nice homecoming, I'm afraid.'

I suddenly felt choked, so I simply shook my head.

'Not to worry – we'll get the villains sorted. You may not know, but there's a major incident plan permanently in place for just this kind of emergency. Within that framework there are three planned responses – one for airport hijack, one for siege and one for hostage-rescue. In your case, the hostage recovery plan, Operation Beehive, is already under way.'

'Sounds OK. But what does it involve?'

'In this case, surveillance on all flights to Ireland, north and south. Increased surveillance on suspected IRA players resident in this country, and increased surveillance on safe houses used by them. Numerous other checks. We'll be looking to see if certain characters are going about their business as normal, or whether they appear to have taken a sudden holiday. We'll put word out through our touts that special payments are in prospect for the right information. Of course, I can't promise anything – but what I can tell you is that our responses are frequently tested on major exercises, and we're confident they work. Now – wait while I read these notes.'

Nobody spoke while Fraser went through the print-

17

out, eating as he read. Then he brought out a mobile phone, dialled, turned away from us, and had a short conversation, his voice too low for me to hear.

Turning back, he said, 'I just threw three or four names into the frame. What about this fellow Farrell? What was he doing in Colombia?'

I gave him an outline of what had happened: how, after Farrell and his colleagues had lifted our rupert and two diplomats from a restaurant near the British Embassy in Bogotá, our follow-up attempt to rescue them had taken us to a brand-new laboratory built deep in the jungle. Fraser listened carefully as I explained how the woman had been killed and the two men saved, but I sensed that his real interest lay in Ulster.

'When your wife was killed . . . how did you find out who was behind the bomb?'

'Through contacts in the RUC.'

'Who d'you know there?'

'A man called Morrison, mainly – a chief superintendent. He came over to lecture us when we were on the Northern Ireland course.'

'Morrison, Morrison . . . I know him. A good man, that; he'll help us. Are there any of your colleagues I can talk to?'

'About Farrell? Not really. None of our guys saw him in Northern Ireland. The people who do know all about him are the Det – the int boys in Belfast. They've got a big file on him.'

'All right. We'll get anything relevant sent over by secure fax.'

'Can *I* ask *you* something?'

'Of course.'

'What's this kidnap in aid of? I mean, what do they hope to get out of it?'

The reply was what I'd been expecting. 'Simple: they want Farrell back.'

18

'But what can *I* do about that? The man's in the nick in Bogotá. At least, that's where I last heard of him. The Colombians could have topped him by now. They could have moved him somewhere else. I can't get anywhere near him.'

'I know, I know.' Fraser gave a flicker of a smile, quick but friendly. 'But now that these guys have managed to grab a bargaining counter they'll exploit it to the hilt.'

'What d'you expect them to do?'

'They'll wait for a few days. Then they'll come up with a demand for a swap.'

'By phone?'

'Yep. They may call your home or the barracks here. We'll get a tap on your own line – in fact, it's being done already.'

'What if they do come on?'

'Keep them talking as long as possible. The longer they're on, the better the chances we have of tracing the call. They'll try to keep things short, to cut down that possibility, so it's up to you to prevaricate.'

'So I pretend to negotiate – say that we're getting some action over Farrell or whatever . . .?'

'We'll come to that later – but basically, yes, make it sound as though things are moving at your end.'

'They won't ring from an ordinary number, though. If they did, we could get straight on to it.'

'No. They'll use a mobile or a phone fitted with a chip that blocks any attempt to back-track calls.'

'Any idea where they'll be?'

'London, most likely. West London.'

'Why there?'

'Safety in numbers. It's such a vast conurbation, swallows people up. They've got safe houses there in places like Ealing, Acton. One problem is, the players keep shifting their ground. Here today, gone tomorrow.'

19

'Would they move the hostages too?'

'Less likely. There's always a risk someone will see them. Once they've got them somewhere secure, they'll probably keep them there.'

'Are these the people who've been planting the London bombs?'

'Could be.' He gave an enigmatic smile, as if he knew more than he wanted to say. 'The London Active Service Unit's pretty strong. By the way, where's that photograph?'

'The CID guy has it. Why?'

'I'll take possession of it presently. There are various techniques we can use on it – computer enhancement, for instance. I gather the two men are holding weapons?'

'That's right.'

'Well, if we blow the picture up and enhance areas of it with the computer, we may be able to make out numbers or other distinguishing marks on the pistols. It may turn out that one of the weapons has been used in a known crime elsewhere. Equally, there may be a small area of tattoo or a scar showing on a wrist or neck – something that may give us a clue to the identity of the men. You'd be surprised how much information an infinitesimally small piece of evidence can produce. Now . . .' He glanced at his watch. 'I think the CID will be needing you at the scene of the crime.'

The CID Vectra was parked outside the guardroom. Fraser introduced himself and his team, and after a quick discussion it was agreed that while the bosses carried out the site inspection their number twos would stay in camp and get their incident room set up. For a few minutes the whole crowd disappeared into the Kremlin to discuss the layout, then we were off in the Special Branch Rover, with the Streisand lookalike driving and myself calling the turns.

The sun was just up, setting the brick-red soil on fire and illuminating the hedges, now fully out, their new leaves glowing the freshest green. Except for the black cloud looming over my head, it was a perfect Herefordshire spring day.

'This is it,' I announced as the car turned into our lane, and there stood the little brick cottage, snug among its trees, with the peaceful woods and fields rising gently into the distance all round.

'Stop here, please, Karen,' said Fraser. 'We'll walk the last bit. What a place!'

He and Bates spent a minute changing out of their city shoes and into rubber boots. As I waited, I was hit by a blast of remorse. I should never have brought Tracy here, I thought bitterly. I'd imagined that the cottage would be the perfect home for my family, and yet it seemed to have a deadly effect on any woman connected with it: Kath killed, and now Tracy kidnapped. Even on that fine morning the house had lost a good deal of its charm.

It's not the place that's doing it, I told myself. It's you and your problems.

The two coppers set out slowly, side by side, down the last hundred yards of track, scanning every inch. I followed close behind them.

'What vehicles have been down here since last night?' Bates asked.

'The Cavalier that dropped me,' I said, 'and the two Range Rovers that came out when I phoned. Otherwise, there shouldn't have been any.'

'I see.'

The policemen's manner had altered. Both had suddenly become sharper, more concentrated.

'What's this?' Bates stooped and picked up a piece of paper from the grass at the edge of the track. The scrap was blank, but he put it carefully into the folder he was carrying. In one muddy patch he bent down to examine some tyre tracks, but several had been superimposed on each other so that no clear pattern was discernible.

As we reached the gravel sweep in front of the cottage, a figure in DPMs popped out from behind the bushes to our right and advanced aggressively to challenge us. Although Les wasn't actually holding a weapon, his right hand was in the pocket of his smock. His face was pale from lack of sleep, his expression tense, but as soon as he saw me he relaxed.

I walked towards him. 'Hi, Les. Everything OK?'

'Fine. Your only caller's been a bloody great fox – came past the back of the house about an hour ago and left his calling card by that gatepost.'

'I know him,' I said. 'He's always around. Listen, these guys are CID and Special Branch.'

Fraser stuck out a hand and introduced himself briefly. Then he said to me, 'Right. I want you to tell me exactly what you did when you came home.'

'Got out of the car about here.' I pointed to a spot on the gravel in front of us. 'The whole house was dark. Then I went to the front door and in.'

'It wasn't locked?'

'No. I assumed Tracy had left it open for me.'

'Wouldn't she have had it locked earlier?'

'Probably not. We don't bother much out here until we go to bed.'

'So you didn't walk round outside at all?'

'Not a step.'

'Let's have a look, then. Hang on here, please.'

The two set off clockwise round the house: Fraser slim, sandy, lithe, like the fox reported by Les; Bates greyer, heavier, a badger. Foxy Fraser and Badger Bates, hunting in partnership. Until that moment I hadn't been particularly impressed with either of them, but

22

now that I saw how much time they took, how carefully they moved, what attention they paid to every little detail, it was another matter.

They kept a yard or two from the building and advanced a few feet at a time, constantly glancing from ground to house and back. While they disappeared round the back I looked about me and saw that Tracy had cut the grass during the last day or two: the tracks of the mower were still showing clearly. She'd also weeded the flowerbeds against the front wall, the earth now freshly turned over.

'No sign of any attempted break-in,' Bates announced as the two came back into view.

No need for one, I thought. They just walked in.

Fraser looked back up the lane and waved at Karen to drive down. 'We got this,' he said, holding up a spent match. 'Any of your lot smoke?'

I shook my head.

'One footprint, too.' Then he turned to Bates. 'You'll need to take a cast of that. Looks like a trainer.' To me he added, 'It was on a bare patch in the grass, which makes me think they were here in the dark. Nobody would have put a foot down there in daylight.'

I led them inside, trying to remember my every movement. In the hall I said, 'I put my kit down here,' and indicated a spot on the carpet.

Bates took up the questioning. 'What was it?'

'A bergen and a holdall.'

'Made of?'

'Something synthetic – nylon, I suppose. That's the stuff there.' I pointed at the drab olive bundle on a chair at the side of the room.

'OK. And what did you do then?'

'I switched on a light – there – and went upstairs. I tried our bedroom first, then Tim's.'

'You had to open the doors?'

23

'No – ours was open.'

'Then what?'

'I ran back down and into the kitchen, put the lights on in there. Nothing. So I went into the living room, switched on the light, and then I saw the photo on the floor in front of the stove.'

'Yes?'

'I picked it up, finger and thumb, and sat down on that chair.'

'*In* that chair?'

'No, on the arm nearest to us.'

'What were you wearing?'

'Same as now – these jeans and sweater. But a different T-shirt . . .' I broke off, hearing a vehicle draw up outside the open door.

Bates stuck his head out and said, 'Good. The forensic lads. A squad from Birmingham.'

As men began unloading gear from their van, Fraser said he'd seen enough and was heading back to the incident room. That left me and Bates with the forensic boys.

There were four of them, and they kitted themselves up in white overalls, white hoods, white gloves and white overshoes. I knew that the job was going to take some time. All the same, it was a shock to hear their boss announce that it would last all day at least.

To give us somewhere to base ourselves, they cleared the kitchen first. The care they took was amazing. Having carried in lamps and stands, they lit up each room in a blaze dazzling enough for a film production; then they crept and crawled and peered and prodded, dusting for fingerprints and examining every square inch of every surface through magnifying glasses.

As they worked, I looked for a recent photograph of Tracy. The best likeness was a framed photo of her and Tim which stood on the kitchen window-sill. It had been taken just before I'd gone to Colombia, and she must have had it mounted while I was away. It showed her standing behind Tim at the top of one of the big slides at Alton Towers, about to give him a push off. She'd been laughing and joking as I took it, and her coppery hair was cascading down the back of her neck, shown off by a white windcheater. It was a good shot of Tim, too; you could see his fair hair, broad forehead and blue eyes, all picked up from his mother.

'There's your photo,' I said to Bates. 'That's them to a T.'

'Mind if I borrow it?'

'Help yourself – but I'd like to have it back.'

'Of course. I'll get it copied right away.'

'I can dig out some more negatives of the kid as well.'

'That would be grand.'

After little more than an hour the forensic team declared the kitchen clean – it had yielded no evidence, and the indications were that the intruders had never gone in there – and the search moved to the hall and sitting room, allowing us at least to get a brew on in the kitchen.

The CID boss spent much of the time with the specialists, and every now and then I was needed to answer a question; but for the most part there was nothing I could do except sit around and feel anxiety eating into me. Where had Tracy and Tim been taken? Were they being fed properly? Had they got enough clothes? My mind was filled by a horrible image of them stuck in a blacked-out cellar with only a bucket for a toilet, food being thrown down to them, and rats running about the floor. Anger boiled up inside. I'd just love to get my hands on the bastards who'd taken them.

I'd never had any direct evidence that telepathy can work, but at that moment I exerted my will-power in an all-out attempt to send reassuring messages. Hang in

25

there, I was telling them. Don't despair. We're on our way.

It was six o'clock when the team called it a day. Their leader promised a full report in the morning, but for the moment he let on that they had found signs of a struggle on the landing. Fibres from Tracy's pullover suggested that someone had grabbed her there and sat on her to hold her down before hustling her down the stairs. Again I felt anger taking me over; the idea of other men getting their hands on her, bruising her fair skin, made me see red. I imagined Tim trying to scuttle away from the masked intruders but not getting far on his short legs, maybe yelling out as they seized him.

Different fibres they'd found told a more important story. One of the raiders had sat down and leant back in the chair that I'd perched on, resting his elbows on the arms. As soon as this fact reached Bates he lit up, and said that he knew of one well-known IRA player, Danny Aherne, who had a habit of sitting back in chairs to gloat over victims. Immediately the name went back over a secure phone to London.

With the search completed there was no reason why I shouldn't move back into the cottage. But did I want to? For a while I hesitated. It would make sense, obviously – if I was there I'd be able to take any message that came from the PIRA – but the idea of being there alone, with Tim and Tracy gone, seemed too depressing. On the other hand, the thought of spending another night in the mess pissed me off even more. I had to drive back into camp in any case, because I'd left my bergen there, so I decided to have supper in the mess, then head back out.

In the dining-room my luck took a turn for the better. There, eating on his own, sat Tony Lopez, the

American SEAL who'd joined D Squadron for a two-year tour. There was nobody I'd rather have fallen in with. Tony and I had been close ever since we'd been captured by the Iraqis during the Gulf War and spent six weeks together as guests of Saddam Hussein. We hadn't been treated as badly as some other allied prisoners, but our spell in gaol had been tough enough, and it had forged a lasting friendship. On the operation in Colombia Tony had acted as our liaison officer and anchor-man. Being Puerto Rican by birth, and having Spanish as his first language, he'd proved an invaluable link with the natives.

'Hi there, Geordie!' He raised a knife in greeting. 'Any news?'

I shook my head. 'Nothing yet. All right if I come and join you?'

'Go right ahead.'

Thinking of Tony and his penchant for Mexican food, I chose chilli con carne, with a green salad on a separate plate.

'They've searched the house from top to bottom,' I told him as I sat down. 'A couple of small clues, but no fingerprints. They reckon the sods all wore gloves.'

'How many of them?'

'They think there were four. One to grab Tim, one for Tracy, one to take the picture, one to stand guard outside. Very brave of them – the twats.'

'Anything on their vehicle?'

'Nothing. Too many other tyre marks. One print of a trainer in a mud patch behind the house. Otherwise, blank.'

'Geordie, I'm sorry. I wish to hell there was something I could do.'

'Thanks. Listen, why not come back and have a beer? What I need most is company.'

'OK. I'd like that.'

As soon as I'd eaten I checked in at the incident room to see if anything was moving, and found a depressing lack of progress. The place was full of computer terminals, fax machines and newly-installed telephones, but activity had died down for a day and, like me, everybody was waiting – waiting for the word from the other side, waiting for a tip-off from an SB tout.

Tony picked up his car, an ancient red BMW that he had found going cheap in Ross-on-Wye, and followed me out to the cottage. Driving down the lane, seeing the cottage's windows dark, I was hit by a wave of despair. All through our time in the jungle and during the marathon journey back, my expectations had built up: home, bed with Tracy, decent food, family life, picking up my relationship with Tim . . . now all this had turned to ashes.

Once inside the house, we gravitated to the kitchen. For one thing, the Aga was ticking over and making the room warm; but somehow I didn't fancy being in the sitting room where the photo had been taken.

I got a couple of cans of lager out of the fridge and we sat, one either side of the pine table. 'Cheers!' I said. 'And God rot the PIRA.'

'Amen to that.' Tony's dark chestnut eyes were watching me steadily. 'Geordie,' he said, 'you look pretty much washed up.'

'I am. I didn't get my head down till after three. Then I was up at five-thirty. I'll try and get a proper kip tonight.'

When the telephone rang, I jumped a mile. 'Jesus!' I exclaimed. 'This could be them.' I snatched the receiver up and snapped, 'Yes?'

Silence. I was on the point of saying something more when I realised what was happening. I listened a moment longer. Nothing. Then the line clicked and went dead.

'It *was* them,' I said. 'They just wanted to know if I was here. Nuisance calls – that's going to be their game.'

I dialled the incident room in camp. 'I had a call,' I reported. 'I'm sure it was them.'

'If it happens again, take the phone off the hook,' advised the SB officer on duty. 'In the morning we'll get the lines re-routed so that any calls they make come in here.'

'OK, then.'

I sat down again and swallowed a mouthful of beer.

'Couldn't they trace it back?' Tony asked.

'Too brief. The line's tapped anyway, but what we need to do is keep them talking, to give the Special Branch a chance of DF-ing them. The trouble is, the fuckers are probably using a mobile and cruising around in a car.'

We sat in silence for a while. Then Tony said, 'Know what? This reminds me of the first time I came here. Remember? That was a low spot, too.'

Tony knew better than anyone how, in the aftermath of the Gulf War, Kath and I had become estranged, how I'd hit the booze, and how, when she had gone back to her parents in Belfast for a trial separation, I was really bumping along on the bottom. For a few weeks he'd moved into the cottage, partly because it suited him, but also because he knew he could help me just by being around. Apart from any-thing else he was an excellent cook, and with him in residence I'd started eating sensibly again. One way or another, I owed Tony a good deal.

Now he said, 'You just gotta take it easy. I know it sounds stupid if I say "C'mon, relax", but there's nothing else for it. Sooner or later they'll come back on the air with a demand. Or the SB guys will get a lead.'

'Yeah, but what if they're maltreating Tim? He must

be shit-scared, Tony. Poor little bugger – he's not even four and a half.'

'I know.'

'And what if somebody's molesting Tracy? Christ, I'd rip his bloody bollocks off with my bare hands.'

'It's tough,' Tony agreed. 'But you can't do anything about it.'

'Why the fuck didn't I drop Farrell while I had the chance? There's something about that guy, Tony. It's as if there's a superior force protecting him. I'm getting to think he's invincible.'

'Aw, you're imagining things.'

But Tony had never seen Farrell. He'd flown out to Colombia with our training team, but when everything had gone tits-up he'd had to stay behind in Bogotá as our anchor-man, liaising with the British Embassy and the Americans. The result was that, to his great chagrin, he'd missed the fire-fight in the jungle. I'd already described the final showdown to him half a dozen times – how we'd blown up a pile of ether drums in the laboratory with a mega bang and fought our way back to the air-strip; how I'd slashed the tyres of the narcos' Twin Otter so that it couldn't take off; and how, as Farrell had tried to slip away into the forest, I'd wounded him with an MP 5 before running out of ammunition. I'd told Tony about that moment, when I had Farrell on the deck in front of me, when a mate had run up and handed me another sub-machine gun with a full mag on it, shouting, 'Go on, finish him off!' But somehow the hatred had drained out of me, and I'd let my victim get captured . . .

'All we needed to do was throw him in the river,' I said now. 'The crocodiles would have had him in a flash. The water was heaving with them. I didn't even have to kill him; the crocs would have done the job for me. He'd just have disappeared off the face of the earth.'

'Too bad,' Tony agreed. 'But don't let the guy bug you. You'll get even with him in the end.'

Neither of us wanted to make a night of it, so Tony went back to camp soon after ten-thirty, and I locked up all round.

Foxy Fraser and his SB team didn't seem to think that I was under any threat myself; on the contrary, he'd said I was the fulcrum over which the PIRA would try to exert pressure with their lever. In other words, they positively needed me where I was, so I could initiate moves to have Farrell released. All the same, I didn't feel like taking any chances. That was why I'd badgered the storeman in the armoury in camp into letting me take a Sig 226 pistol home overnight.

So, after a soak in a hot bath, I took a few precautions before I went to bed. Ever since my bad experiences in Iraq I'd had a thing about the bedroom door, finding it impossible to sleep unless I locked it. I turned the key and stood a chair against the inside with two saucepans balanced on it, so that even if somebody did get through he couldn't come in without making a hell of a clatter. I put the phone on the floor beside the bed, laid the pistol on the bedside cabinet, and finally turned in.

I must have laid awake for some time, because afterwards I remembered how our resident owl had tuned up in the oak tree outside the window, but in spite of all my anxieties I eventually dropped off. Some time later I became aware of a scratching noise. I rolled over on my back and listened. There it was again: a scrape, followed by a click. I knew the sounds exactly because I'd made them myself, dozens of times – sounds of someone picking a lock.

The noise was coming up from the front of the house and in through the open window. Without being able to see anything, I somehow knew that the men at the door were wearing black balaclavas.

Jesus Christ! The PIRA were back. And this time they'd come for me! Moving my hand carefully I reached down, brought phone and receiver under the bedclothes, and dialled the incident room. All I got was Mac's recorded voice saying, 'Sorry, old boy, we can't deal with your call at the moment, we're rather busy. Call back in half an hour.'

'Twats!' I muttered. 'Fucking useless!' Then I thought: the Sig. Of course, the Sig. What was best? Fire out the window at the intruders, maybe drop one and scare the rest off? Or let them come in and hope to drop the lot?

But it was too late to wonder; they were inside already. I heard a sound on the stairs, a low voice. The door handle of the room turned, and at the same moment there was a different noise outside, the faint clank of my aluminium ladder being stealthily placed in position. Then I became aware of movement at the window and saw a black figure loom up, blotting out the starlight. I was trapped.

I lay dead still on my back, holding my breath. The window was to my left, the door straight ahead. The door began to open. Faint light showed through the crack – a torch. The chair I'd propped against the door fell over and dropped its load with a crash. At that instant I sensed movement in the opposite corner of the room, over my right shoulder. Someone else had got in already, and was coming from that direction. There were men all round me.

I reached for the Sig, felt, groped, snatched in the dark – but the pistol wasn't there. It had gone from the top of the cabinet. Panic. I went to roll out of bed, only to find I couldn't move. A tremendous weight was holding my legs down. I glanced to my left: the black figure was half-way in through the window. I looked straight ahead and saw the man with the torch coming at me from the doorway. Looming bigger and bigger, he was almost on top of me. In spite of the dark I could make out the shape of a pistol in his hand. Within seconds I could see the faint sheen on the muzzle, the ring of death. I was looking straight down the barrel at point-blank range.

BANG! Instantly I was wide awake, shaking and soaked with sweat. The sheets were knotted up around me. Struggling free of them, I felt for the bedside lamp and switched it on. The Sig was still on the cabinet, the phone on the floor where I'd left it. The chair and saucepans stood unmoved against the door. The corner to my right was empty.

I lay back on the pillow, gasping. My watch said 2.45. For a few seconds I glared round the room in disbelief, blinking; then I turned the lamp off again, got up and went to look out of the window, standing well back. By now the moon had risen and the garden was brightly illuminated. I watched for a minute or two and saw that all was peaceful.

I started shuddering. After the Gulf I'd been plagued by terrifying dreams very much like this one. It was those bad nights that started the trouble between me and Kath. My answer to this terror had been alcohol; I'd gone on the booze, and that had made everything far worse. Was all that crap about to start again? And would a Scotch or two be a good idea now?

'No, for Christ's sake,' I told myself. 'The one thing you do *not* need is a drink.' So I went back to bed, sickened by the knowledge that a long, lonely war of nerves lay ahead. I'd just come through one nightmare, but another was beginning, and this one was going to be far worse.

THREE

Even though I was dog-tired I couldn't sleep. I'd got over my fear of an immediate attack, but there was no way I could stop thinking about Tim and Tracy. After a while I went to lie on Tim's bed, imagining the look of his head on the pillow when we came in to check him last thing at night, the way his flaxen hair lay softly on the back of his neck. Even at four and a bit he was still wedded to Billy, his teddy bear, and usually dropped off sucking one of the damn thing's ears. Now Billy sat forlornly on the window-sill, and I knew that Tim, wherever he was, would be all the more miserable because he hadn't got the little bugger with him. What heartless bastards the PIRA were, to lift a kid as young as that.

In time I began to feel cold, and forced myself to accept that lying in his room wouldn't bring him back. So I returned to my own bed and tried to shut my mind down. I heard the clock in the hall strike three, then four – but that was all. I must eventually have nodded off, and the next time I came to it was seven o'clock.

Since I was officially on leave I had no need to hurry into camp. So instead I called the incident room to make sure there had been no developments, then made myself breakfast and spent an hour going through Tracy's things. As usual, her desk was in perfect order: there were a couple of unpaid bills, but otherwise she had everything beautifully squared away. A school

34

exercise book contained a record of her expenses, in her neat writing, and she'd collected the drawings Tim had done at school into a folder. Most of them seemed to have violent subjects – tanks exploding, planes being shot down – and it wouldn't have taken a psychologist long to work out where all that came from. But the tidy way in which Tracy operated nearly choked me, because it made me realise how much she'd done for me.

At the time of Kath's death she'd been working as receptionist in the Camp Medical Centre. A week or two before I got posted to Northern Ireland she and her friend Susan had been thrown out of their lodgings in Hereford, so I had suggested they should occupy Keeper's Cottage while I was abroad. Events then speeded up in a direction I hadn't anticipated: Tracy and I fell for each other, and she had moved into the cottage for good, taking over Tim as though he were her own son. In a few months she had grown up with incredible speed and developed from a lively, knock-about girl into a responsible foster mother. She'd kept on her job for a while, but then, when I went to Colombia, she'd given it up.

Driving away from the cottage wrenched me back to the present. In camp again, I was heading for the Kremlin when I spotted Jimmy Wells, the int officer, coming towards me on a converging path. A scrawny fellow with a narrow face and lank, dark hair brushed sideways over the top of his head, he usually went about with a hunted look, as though he were permanently worried; but his harassed appearance belied him, because he was at heart a cheerful character, always inclined to make the best of things.

'Hi, Geordie,' he called. 'No news yet?'

'Nothing so far.'

'Got time for a natter?'

'Well . . . sure.'

At the top of the stairs I followed him into his office and sat down in front of his desk. As I quickly found out, he was bang up to speed on the kidnap situation, and I realised that he'd invited me in purely to give some friendly support. He was like that; not being a badged officer – not a member of the SAS, but on attachment to us from Intelligence Corps – he had no hang-ups about regimental priorities or feuds and could afford to be himself with everyone, high or low.

'By the way,' he said in a conspiratorial voice after a pause in the conversation, as though letting fall some tit-bit of local scandal, 'Farrell's on his way back to the UK.'

'What?' I was taken aback. 'Already?'

'Well, more or less – I'm jumping the gun a bit. But the Colombian authorities have agreed to extradite him.' He picked up a sheet of fax paper and scanned it briefly. 'It seems they don't want anything to do with him. Don't blame 'em. He'll be flown out by military transport later today. Apparently he's suffering from gun-shot wounds in the right arm and flank. Flesh only – nothing serious. Who shot him? I wonder . . .'

'No idea.'

I saw Jim smiling. He knew what had happened, of course, because he'd covered the Colombian operation from this end.

'If only I'd aimed a bit bloody straighter,' I said. 'But it was still only half light, and the bastard was running like the clappers.'

I stopped, suddenly remembering something I'd read about a British weightlifter at the opening of the Berlin Olympics in 1936. 'I read once about this bloke who found himself standing right next to Hitler in some parade,' I told Jim. 'He realised he could have topped the bugger there and then. And afterwards he said,

"What a hell of a lot of time and trouble I would have saved." I feel like that about Farrell. I could have saved the country millions. What'll they do with him here?'

'Put him in the nick on remand while they sort out a case against him, I imagine.'

'There's any amount of things they can get him for: drugs, kidnapping the rupert, murder . . .'

We'd been chatting for several more minutes when my eye strayed to a photograph in the in-tray: a blown-up black-and-white mug-shot of a man with a moustache wearing a dark beret. Although the picture was upside-down I felt the hair on my neck crawling, because I was certain I recognised the subject.

It wasn't long before Jim noticed my attention was distracted. 'What's the matter?' he asked, following the direction of my eyes. Then he shot out a hand to cover the photo and said, 'Ah. That's strictly need-to-know . . .'

'I know it's none of my business,' I said, 'but could I have a proper shufti?'

'You're not supposed to. Why?'

'I think I know the guy.'

'You can't possibly . . .'

'Let's have a look anyway.'

'Well . . . I'm not showing it you. You haven't seen it.' Watching me curiously, Jim picked up the photo and flicked it across the desk. The moment I saw it straight, all doubt vanished.

'It's him.'

'Who?'

'Shitface. I don't know his name. But this is the bastard that gave us a hard time in Baghdad. An Iraqi, isn't he?'

'That's right.' Now Jim was looking at me in a yet more peculiar way, as if he was seeing a ghost. 'Geordie, are you certain?'

'Absolutely. He came to the gaol three or four times to interrogate us. There was always a big palaver when he arrived – the guards shouting and saluting as though he was some high-ranking officer. It was this fucker who used to hit the plaster cast on my broken arm with his swagger-stick. That was bloody agonising. But it wasn't the pain that got to me, so much as his attitude. He started saying that if I didn't give him the information he wanted, he'd open up the plaster, infect my wounds with bugs, and plaster it over again, so that I'd get gangrene and lose my arm. Sadistic bugger! I'll not forget him in a hurry. Luckily for me, the war ended before he could carry out his threat.'

'He sounds a sweetie,' said Jim.

'He is.' I shuddered as I remembered the screams that came from other parts of the gaol. 'He likes to see prisoners jump. To be more specific, he likes to see them convulsed. He's a specialist at administering electric shocks, and favours giving them through wet sponges, so that the prisoner gets a high charge but isn't left with tell-tale burns. We called him Shitface because he was always frowning, like here. What's his real name?'

'I can't tell you that.'

'So what's his picture doing on your desk?'

'Classified, I'm afraid. But look: this identification's very important. Can you be absolutely sure you know the man?'

'One hundred per cent.' I saw doubt in the int officer's face. 'You don't believe me?'

'Well, a lot may depend on it.'

'I tell you what. There's another guy here in camp who was in that gaol with me: Tony Lopez, the American. He'll remember the sod as well as I do.'

Suddenly Jim was all lit up. 'Where is he now?'

'He's on leave, after Colombia. But he'll be around

the Lines somewhere. I saw him last evening. If you like I'll go find him . . .'

'No. I'll ring round and see where he is.'

A flurry of telephone calls ran Tony to earth in the gym, and he said he'd come right up. As we waited, I saw that Jim was in a state of excitement. I realised why he hadn't let me go looking for the Yank myself: he wanted to confront him with the photograph before I'd had time to give any briefing.

In came Tony, looking big and brawny in his ash-grey tracksuit, sweat still trickling down his temples. 'Apologies for showing up like this,' he began. 'I was half-way through my weights, but this sounded urgent.'

'No sweat,' said the int officer – and then, grinning at the unfortunate pun, 'I'd just like you to answer a simple question.' He flipped over the mug-shot, which he had turned face-down. 'D'you recognise this man?'

'Goddamn it!' Tony cried. 'It's Shitface, the sonofabitch who gave us third degree in Iraq.'

'There you are!' I said. 'What did I tell you?'

'Yeah!' Tony went on, his voice loud with indignation, jabbing a forefinger at the portrait. 'We used to think he looked like Saddam Hussein, with the moustache and the beret. But then, all Iraqi officers do. This one always seemed to be scowling. A big guy, shambling, a bit like a bear. Boy, what wouldn't I do to get my hands on that bastard!'

Jim nodded. 'OK,' he conceded. 'That does it. Now you'd better forget I asked you.'

'Wait a minute,' said Tony. 'What's he got to do with us now?'

'Nothing.' Jim stared straight at me. 'As I say, forget it. And don't mention it outside this office. You never saw the picture, and I never asked you anything.'

Of course we couldn't forget it. Tony and I obeyed

orders and didn't mention the matter to anyone else, but we talked to each other about it at lunch that day, then again in the evening. Obviously the Iraqi was up to something that involved the SAS, but we couldn't figure out what it might be. We guessed Saddam Hussein might be using him to suppress the Kurds in the north of the country; but at that time the Regiment had no presence in Iraq — at least, none that we knew of — and a couple of veiled enquiries drew blank. On the other hand, secret operations were our bread and butter, and when guys got involved in something really hot they were generally tight as gnats' arseholes about it. So it seemed quite possible that some operation was brewing and nobody was talking.

Nor did the day produce any information about Tim and Tracy. Telephone engineers had re-routed the lines so that anyone calling my old number in the cottage went straight through to the incident room, where the phones were manned twenty-four hours a day, and the line was bugged, so any conversation on it would be automatically recorded. Foxy Fraser of Special Branch, who was there in person for much of the time, decreed that the phone must be answered by men only, with instructions to be as non-committal as possible. That way, if the PIRA did come through, they might think it was me on the other end.

For several hours I sat in on the control room, listening to the check calls that came through from Special Branch in London, Birmingham, Holyhead and other places, fervently hoping that one of them would bring news of a positive lead. At first I was on edge, jumping around whenever a phone rang; but after a while boredom began to kill hope and I settled into a resigned torpor, crushed by the realisation that we were probably in for a grinding marathon of a wait.

Hanging around, flicking through old magazines, I

couldn't help being aware of the Streisand lookalike, Karen Terraine, with her swept-back blonde hair and big nose. There she sat, all neat and tidy in a pale blue blouse and grey skirt, taking the odd call, making notes, checking things, going through to the SB central computer for specialised information, and bringing up one list of names after another on her screen. Most of the time she looked totally demure, but twice I caught her giving me the eyeball, and I began to get irritated by her presence.

Fraser saw I was less than chuffed, but he naturally attributed my unease to the general situation and tried to cheer me up by saying, 'Don't worry, Geordie, the touts are out there. The touts are about. They're all hungry, and they're all listening. Our eyes and ears are open.' A search was on in Ulster as well, in case the party had somehow managed to cross the water undetected; but the presumption still was that the hostages had been taken to London.

In the afternoon I went out for an eight-mile run through the lanes, but although I kept pushing myself I couldn't settle into any rhythm. I just had too much on my mind. My anxiety about Tim and Tracy prevented me from concentrating on the exercise. The result was I wasn't looking at the ground properly and I kept stumbling and jarring myself, so that running, instead of being a pleasure, became hard, uncomfortable work.

It was the same when I went to the gym and got on the weights. Nothing would go right. From my own experience – and from watching other guys who were into big lifts – I knew how essential full concentration is; without it, you're at only half strength, and liable to do yourself damage. Now I just couldn't get my timing. After half an hour I thought, Ah, fuck it! and gave up.

As I came into camp next morning – the second day

after the kidnap – I went up to the Squadron Interest Room and found a note in my pigeon-hole. I was on the point of reading it when the clerk forestalled me by saying, 'Hey, Geordie. You're to report to the ops officer, soonest.' I went upstairs wondering what this could be about.

Mac Macpherson was in his usual gracious mood. 'Lucky sod, Geordie,' he said. 'Looks like you're in for more action already.'

'What d'you mean, Boss?'

'You're to report to the OC, SAW – immediately.'

'What's on, then?'

'Don't ask me. Ask him.'

'Christ! This isn't a great moment for me to go away anywhere.'

'See what he says before you start worrying.'

Before I'd even reached the bottom of the stairs I had made the connection: this had to do with the int officer's photo.

The Subversive Action Wing was the most secret part of our organisation, the unit that took on the most sensitive jobs, often working in cahoots with MI5 or MI6. Just as the two Government agencies were known as the 'Firm', so the SAW was known simply as the 'Wing', and its operations were the most highly classified of any the SAS undertook. People trying to be clever described it as the cutting edge of the organisation – and in fact that wasn't a bad description. Because of its connections outside the Regiment, it was almost a national force.

To gain entry to the SAW's area, one had to punch a series of numbers into the pad beside the door. Not knowing the combination, I had to bang on the steel door and wait for someone to let me in.

I found the OC sitting at his desk. In his day Major Yorky Rose had been a fearsome boxer and front-row forward. On his way up through the ranks he'd never bothered to shed his Yorkshire accent or drop his native expressions like 'ee bah gum' and 'you'll not get owt for nowt', and similarly he'd never given a bugger what people thought about his ferocious training regimes. Whenever strange noises were heard emanating from his office, it was said that Yorky was practising walking on all fours: toes and knuckles.

Now in his late thirties, he'd lost most of his dark hair, and kept what was left shaved so short that at first glance you might miss the fuzz on his scalp and think he was totally bald. He had a high, domed forehead that made his head egg-shaped, and his thick, arching eyebrows seemed to accentuate the length of his face. Guys in the Regiment tend to age prematurely, due to the amount of effort they put into life; by the time they're thirty-five, they look like they're pushing fifty. Yorky was no exception: he already had deep lines across his forehead and down his cheeks.

'Well, Geordie,' he began, 'I'm sorry to hear about your kid and Tracy. Any news of them?'

'Not a whisper, Yorky.'

'That's tough. I hope you get sorted soon. Meanwhile, I need your help. Take a seat there a minute.'

I perched on the chair at one side of his desk, pretty certain what his next step would be – and sure enough, he opened a folder, brought out a photograph, and turned it round for me to look at.

'You know this gent, I gather.'

I nodded. 'You're telling me.'

'How would you like to top him?'

'*Top* him?' For a second I was taken aback. But a moment later I said, 'Try and stop me.'

Yorky smiled briefly. 'As I thought.'

'Where is the bastard?'

'Last seen in Piccadilly Circus . . . No, you'll know

soon enough. You've been selected to lead an operation to take him out. We want you to command one of the SAW patrols.'

'Jesus!'

'The timing of it, you mean?'

'Exactly. This isn't a good moment for me to piss off abroad.'

'I know that.' Yorky pushed back his chair and went walkabout, throwing a pencil in the air and catching it as he spoke. 'All the same, it could work out all right. I've talked it through with the CO and the ops officer. Also I had a word with the SB guy, Fraser, about the way he thinks things may go here. I've come to the conclusion that it's on for you.'

Missing a catch, he had to crawl under the desk to retrieve the pencil from the floor. 'The point is,' he continued as he stood again, 'this is going to be a quick job: in and out. You'll not be abroad for more than six days. Two weeks' training here, then less than a week away. To get the hostages back may take a couple of months.'

He saw me grimace, and went on, 'If anything breaks on the hostage front during the training phase you'll be here to deal with it. Your personal problem may well be cracked before the operation goes down. But even if it ain't, we can hold the fort for you while you're out of the country. Besides, you'll have Satcoms as usual, so that you won't ever be out of touch.'

I sat holding my forehead in my hands. My head felt as if it were bursting. Already, with this new deployment barely announced, the stress was piling on. This was going to be a high-risk operation, fraught with danger – could I stand the strain of another episode likely to be as traumatic as the one in the Gulf? Could I handle it on top of my acute personal troubles?

My instinct was to stay home at all costs, to be there

when the PIRA called. I couldn't take the thought of somebody else making a cock-up that might lead to the hostages' death. But I knew perfectly well I had no option but to go; if I refused I'd be kicked out – not only from the Regiment, but out of the Army.

At moments of this kind it's easy to let resentment build up. The Regiment is notorious for pushing its members to the limit, putting them under intense pressure without regard to their mental state. The head-shed simply assumes that all the guys are fit, physically and mentally, all the time, and ready to go.

Now, for a few seconds, I thought, Ah, sod them. Why can't they make a few allowances? Why can't they send someone else to do their dirty work? I looked up at Yorky and said, 'Does it have to be me?'

He stopped pacing and stood beside my chair. 'You know what the Regiment's like, Geordie. They'll talk sympathetically about your family, blah, blah, blah. But in fact they couldn't give a flying monkey's, especially when a job like this comes down from Whitehall. If the Government's ordered it, it's got to happen. It doesn't matter what you do – you can go in and spout Army regulations at the adjutant if you like – but I can tell you, it won't wash. Sorry, old mate, but it's got to be you.' His tone wasn't unkind, just matter of fact.

I took a deep breath and said, 'Fair enough. I suppose it might even take my mind off my home problems, having a fastball job to do.'

'Gradely, lad. And you're not just our number-one choice for the job; you're the *only* choice.'

'Why's that?'

'Because you alone will recognise the target without fail.'

'You could show other guys the mug-shot.' I pointed at the photo. 'They could memorise what he looks like.'

'It's not the same thing. You've seen him several times. You know him.'

'The thing is, this mug-shot's well out of date. Even when I saw him two years ago he'd aged a good bit over what you can see here. His face had got a lot heavier and more lined.'

'All the more reason for you to be in command.'

'OK. But Tony Lopez saw him just as much.'

'I realise that. I'm hoping I can get Tony on the operation with you for that very reason. But the whole thing's so sensitive that we're waiting on clearance from the Pentagon before we can include him in the team.'

'For Christ's sake!' I exclaimed. 'Is the target in fucking Moscow or somewhere?'

'Yer daft bat! Listen, Geordie. This is a black operation. You know what that means. Nobody has heard about it – *nobody*. It's not to be discussed with anyone – not even your closest mates. Outside these walls, it doesn't exist. And when it does go down, it will be completely unattributable: nothing you do must leave any trace to show that the Regiment was involved.'

'Yeah, yeah. OK.' I'd been given all this shit many times before. I knew Yorky had to bring it out, but even so I didn't like having it rammed down my throat.

'There's to be a team briefing here at 1600 hours,' he was saying. 'All will be revealed then.'

In the afternoon, on my way across, I checked into the incident room again. Fraser and Bates were both intent on a computer monitor, which I saw was carrying details of the player called Danny Aherne who liked sitting down to eyeball his victims. He was thirty-two, fair-haired, unemployed, and had a weakness for the drink. He was known to have been active in London earlier in the year, but had recently gone AWOL from

46

his last known place of residence, a bed-and-breakfast room in Acton.

'He's involved,' said Fraser with some conviction. 'I'm damn sure of that. But I don't know why he's shifted. That may mean something or it may not. But those fibres . . . I'll bet my boots he was there.'

In Yorky's den I found five other guys assembled. They'd been on the Wing for some time already, and constituted one of its two standing teams. The only one I knew well was Pat Newman, a big, dark, ruddy-faced lad with snow-white teeth, one of the heaviest eaters in the business, but very quick on his feet and a useful fellow to have around if things got physical. There was an obvious reason for him being on this new job: he'd done a course in Arabic, and spoke enough of the language to communicate about everyday matters.

A lesser acquaintance was Billy Walker, a little Londoner known as 'Whinger' on account of the fact that he was always moaning or making snide remarks in his own debased form of Cockney rhyming slang. He had peculiarly coloured hair – very light brown, like tow – which looked so artificial that strangers suspected him of dyeing it or wearing a wig; but anyone who lived and worked with him knew that it was his own, and never changed. He also had a horrible habit of rolling his own gaspers, which stank out any room he was in. But he was a good operator nevertheless: small, skinny and tough.

Of the other three, the tallest was Fred Parry, a fair-haired beanpole from A Squadron who'd had a great time blowing up fibre-optic comms towers in Iraq during the Gulf War. Then there was Stew Stewart, a gingery fellow from Merseyside who'd come into the Regiment from the Cheshires. Stew, sometimes known as 'Turnip', wasn't exactly a figure of fun, because he was a good, willing lad, but he did take a lot of stick because of the trouble he had keeping girlfriends. With his broad, ruddy face, he looked exactly what he was – a farmer's boy – and he was perpetually worried that his head was the wrong shape, a deficiency which he tried to remedy by resorting to fancy haircuts. That left only Norman Paxford, a stocky, dark Glaswegian whose aim in life seemed to be to talk as little as possible. He might easily have been nicknamed 'Jock' because of his hellish accent, but – maybe because he spoke so rarely – he was known simply as 'Norm'. People said that it was his Mexican-style moustache, neatly clipped into an upside-down U, that clamped his mouth shut and made it difficult for him to utter. But he was never rude, and if you asked him something he'd always answer, only in the fewest possible words. If you said, 'Everything all right, then, Norm?' he'd just go, 'Aye, thanks,' and leave it at that. In spite of his taciturnity he was a terrific worker, and utterly dependable.

We had a couple of minutes' chit-chat, and I noticed that the mug-shot of our Iraqi friend was up on one of the wall-boards, with several lines of writing beneath it. Then the ops officer and Jimmy Wells came in towing a middle-aged guy in a shiny grey suit.

'I know this feller,' said Pat under his breath. 'He's been here before. We all know him – from the Firm. Gilbert the Filbert.'

Before we sat down on the chairs facing Yorky's desk, Mac introduced me briefly to the man from London: 'Geordie, meet Gilbert Dauncey. Gilbert – Geordie Sharp, commander of the team.' Then he led off, cautioning us yet again about the need for total security.

'Operation Ostrich,' he began. 'As you know, this is a black operation. That means there's to be absolutely no word of it outside your own team. If anyone drops the slightest hint about it, he'll be RTU'd immediately. OK?'

I saw Whinger bend his head to the left and flip the fingers of his right hand upwards past the back of his ear. He could have been scratching at an itch or knocking away a fly; he could also have been saying 'Fucking roll on!' in sign language.

The gesture wasn't lost on Mac, who said sharply, 'Don't piss about, anybody. Just listen. The aim of the operation is to take out this man.' He indicated the mug-shot. 'You'll all have a chance to memorise the face. The guy in question is General Mohammed al-Khadduri, a top-ranking Iraqi who's defected to Libya. Our colleague here' – he indicated Gilbert – 'will brief you on his background in a moment.

'First, though, the location. Al-Khadduri is now working from a military camp on the outskirts of Ajdabiya. That's a town about a hundred and fifty kilometres south of Benghazi, the Libyan capital.'

Mac turned to face a map of north-eastern Africa, with the Mediterranean spread across the upper half and the Bay of Sirte taking a shallow scoop out of the Libyan coastline top-centre. 'Here's Benghazi,' he pointed with a broken-off billiard cue, 'at two o'clock on the coast of the bay, and here's Ajdabiya thirty ks inland, at five-thirty on the bay. The military complex is about here, ten ks beyond the southern outskirts of the town on the edge of the desert. All this ground immediately to the east is a training area.

'Cross-border insertion will be by heli from the military airfield at Siwa, just inside Egypt.'

He placed the tip of his pointer to the right of a thick purple line running north to south, which marked the frontier between Egypt and Libya. 'A Chinook will put you down as close as possible to the target, but to avoid any chance of your being compromised the LZ will have to be at least fifty ks short of the camp. The run-in will be by quad bike.

49

'Now . . . timing. We have a strict time-frame, imposed on us by external constraints. The operation has to go down under cover of Exercise Bright Star, which is scheduled for May seventeenth to twenty-second. Bright Star is a major international deployment involving US and NATO forces. The aim is to establish and reinforce a simulated front line at a location in the Egyptian desert, against a threat from baddies to the south. If you like, it's a re-enactment of the start of the Gulf build-up of 1990. The exercise will involve all the NATO airforces as well as the USAF, and a considerable number of army units. That means there'll be a large number of air-movements, many of them from Cyprus, in the middle of which ours will get nicely lost.

'You'll stage through Akrotiri dressed as pathfinders – desert cam clothes, maroon Para berets and belts. As far as Cyprus, anybody who sees you will think you're umpires taking part in the exercise. Then, during the last phase of the flight, you'll change into rough civilian gear. Any questions so far?'

I glanced round the semicircle of faces. Everyone was looking hard at the map, thinking things over, but at that stage nobody had anything to say.

'All right, then. I'll ask for a few words about the target from our colleague from the Firm. Most of you know him anyway: Gilbert Dauncey.'

Gilbert stood up and began talking in a crisp, educated voice, public school but not lah-di-dah. 'General Mohammed al-Khadduri. You've seen his photo, and one of you I know has seen *him*. A big, burly fellow, we guess six feet, and powerfully built. A bit like a bear, but he's going to seed a bit now: we think he's put on a good deal of weight lately.

'His record wouldn't stand him in very good stead at the Court of Human Rights. For several years he was responsible for eliminating the political factions that

50

threatened Saddam Hussein's government – and when I say "eliminating", I mean "eliminating". He didn't disband the dissident parties; he rubbed them out with wholesale executions, families and all. Another feather in his cap: it was he who directed the campaign of extermination against the Kurds in the north during the late eighties. The use of chemical weapons is his speciality, particularly against his own people.

'By the time of the Gulf War, Khadduri had risen to become Saddam's chief of military intelligence. At that time he enjoyed the President's full confidence, and spent much of the run-up to war with him in Baghdad. In the first days of the air-war he had a narrow escape from an incoming Cruise missile, which hit a building when he was in the basement, but he came through the conflict unscathed.

'Afterwards, however, he and his boss fell out. We're not clear what caused the rift, but subsequent events suggest it was a basic disagreement over policy. Saddam wanted to soft-pedal things while he rebuilt his army and kept the Western powers in play, but Khadduri developed more and more extreme right-wing views. It seems that he took Iraq's defeat by the Coalition as a personal insult, and as time went on he became ever more eager to avenge it. Things reached the point at which he was going behind Saddam's back and privately inciting other Arab states to prepare for a joint assault on Israel, as a kind of reprisal. He was for an all-out attack using chemical and biological weapons.

'In the end, of course, word reached Saddam – and that was too much. Early last year, in February, Khadduri was arrested. It looked like he was for the chop, but then he was let out of prison on parole. He did a runner and pitched up with his friend Moammer Gadaffi, President of Libya. There, he's continued to promote the idea of an attack on Israel. In particular, he's tried to win support from Mubarak, President of Egypt, luckily without success. Worse, from our point of view, he's become a red-hot champion of the IRA. He seems to think that by promoting revolution in Northern Ireland he can get his own back for the humiliation the Arabs suffered in the Gulf. Also, the CIA are worried that he's started supporting the fundamentalists behind the bombs on the mainland in the States.'

'Fuckin' 'ell,' muttered Whinger, maybe a bit louder than he meant. 'What an arsehole!'

Gilbert heard him and went on without a flicker: 'Precisely. Indications are that during the past year the amount of money reaching the IRA from Libya has more than doubled. Arms the same. Remember the merchant vessel that ran aground off Cork back in October? The *Sirius*? She was carrying containers that held more than a thousand AK-47s and several million rounds of ammunition. The manifest listed the containers as having been loaded in Amsterdam, but we believe they came all the way from Tripoli, with Khadduri's signature on the docket.

'In other words, this man has become a severe threat to the stability of the Province. He's also a menace in the Middle East as a whole. Now that he has the ear of Gadaffi, there's no telling what he may touch off. Our friends in the CIA agree his time is up.

'Fortunately we have excellent relations with Egypt, and we can use Egyptian territory as a covert staging-post for an operation. Still more fortunate . . .' Gilbert's face softened into the ghost of a smile. 'As of yesterday we discovered that one of you has the big advantage of being personally acquainted with General al-Khadduri.'

I nodded, aware that the other guys were giving me the eyeball. I glanced along the line and thought I'd better explain. 'When I was in the nick in Baghdad, after the patrol got compromised, this bastard used to come along once a week and give us the third degree. I'd recognise him a mile off in thick fog.'

'He's your man, then, Geordie,' chirped Whinger. 'Nice little solo venture. Piece of cake.'

'Fuck off, mate,' I replied equably. Then I asked Gilbert, 'What's he doing, exactly? I mean, has Gadaffi given him a job?'

'Officially he's in charge of officer training. That's why he's based at Ajdabiya, which is Libya's answer to Sandhurst. But signal intercepts show he's using the place for every kind of political and revolutionary activity. I repeat: he's regarded as the most dangerous single operator in the Middle East, Saddam Hussein not excepted.'

There was a short silence. 'Gadaffi!' exclaimed Pat contemptuously. 'That guy's mad as twenty fucking hatters.'

'That's the trouble,' Gilbert agreed.

'Can you give us any personal gen on the target?' Pat went on. 'Any clue about his movements or habits?'

'Not much, I'm afraid. He's married, with a family, and he tends to join them at a house on the coast whenever he has days off. But while he's working he lives in the commandant's quarters on the base. One point that may prove relevant: we know he's a night owl, and sits up all hours working, when everyone else has gone to bed and things have quietened down.'

'How do we know that?' I asked.

Gilbert hesitated, then said, 'You'll find out shortly. Now, for details of the camp layout we're awaiting satellite intelligence from the CIA. A courier should be in London by tomorrow. I'm afraid some or all of you will have to come to London to see what he brings. The office have judged the material too sensitive for it to go outside, even here. Any more questions? No?'

He sat down, and Mac took over. 'Thanks, Gilbert,' he said. Then he turned to us. 'I don't have to emphasise that your hit team will have to be absolutely clean. You'll wear Arab or some sort of civilian clothes, use Soviet or Chinese weapons and ammunition. None of you must carry any trace of any Western organisation. Webbing, bergens, boots – everything's got to be checked for names or labels. If the team suffers a fatality, it will be absolutely imperative to bring the body out with you. If that proves impossible, you'll vaporise the body with a bar mine.'

'You mean we're going to take nice British bar mines with us?' Whinger said.

'No, no,' Mac assured him, 'we've got a few Chinese ones that'll come in handy.'

'How alarming,' went Whinger. 'Bloody charming.'

Mac ignored him and continued. 'Back to timing. As I said, Bright Star runs for six days. That means you've got to be in and out within this time bracket, while the cover lasts. And it commences on the seventeenth, which means you've got less than two weeks in which to get prepped up. OK? Any questions?'

'What about weapons?' Pat asked.

'You'll draw non-attributable AK-47s from the SAW section of the main armoury. They're being delivered from London in the morning. Once you've got them you'll store them here.' He gestured to the lockers at the sides of the room. 'Anything else?'

'Why isn't Tony Lopez in on this?' asked Fred Parry. 'He was in the nick with you, Geordie, wasn't he? He must know the guy.'

'That's right, he does.' Mac answered for me. 'Tony's an obvious candidate with his special knowledge. But because of American political sensitivities we haven't yet got clearance for him to join the team. We're still hoping he'll be able to come in.'

For a final word, Mac turned to me and said, 'If there's anything you want to know, Geordie, these guys will fill you in. They're all genned up on the way the Wing works. And if there's anything you need, don't worry about asking for it. What you may not realise is that the SAW has its own budget: within reason, money's no object, and there are no restrictions on equipment. If you need civilian clothes, for instance, go and buy them. Any bits and pieces of extra kit – the same. You're in a different game now.'

With the ruperts gone, I got the lads to gather round for a minute. 'Right,' I said, 'we start training proper tomorrow morning. But we can begin sorting out our priorities now. First things first: wills. Have you all made out a will?' I glanced round the team. Pat, who was married, gave a nod, but the other four looked blank.

'Well, even if you don't think you've got anything to leave, I suggest you get organised. There's no guarantee that all of us will come back. Correction: there's no guarantee that *any* of us will come back. Jabs the same. Get your arses up to the doc's office: see the clerk in there, and make sure you're up to date. It's no big deal.

'Now – individual responsibilities. I'll be team medic; I've got the training. Fred, you're in charge of explosives. You'll need to check out these Chinese bar mines, make sure you read the instructions. Right?'

Fred nodded.

'Whinger, signals, OK? We're getting in some special non-attributable kit, and there's a rep coming up from the Firm to run you through it.'

'Yeah. I know most of that stuff, but a refresher wouldn't do any harm.'

'Good. Pat, how's your Arabic?'

'Shit hot!'

'Say something.'

'*Aaaarrgh!*' he went, and then gave a kind of hiccup.

'What did that mean?'

'Fuck off.'

'Don't piss about.'

'Honest, that's what I said.'

'You did the Arabic course?'

'Yonks ago.'

'It'll come back to you. Get on the tapes in the language lab and you'll make it.'

'*Allah karim.*'

I turned to Stew Stewart and said, 'You're from Mobility Troop, Stew. Go down and speak to the MTO about the quads. Get a mechanic to take you through anything we might need to know.'

'Fair enough.'

Because Norm Paxford was already a competent signaller, I told him to work with Whinger as his back-up on the radios. 'Take all the sets along to the signals technician and make sure the frequencies are in line,' I said. 'The other thing is, we'll use throat-mikes rather than booms, because booms would pick up the noise of the wind and the engines.

'And wait a minute,' I went on. 'A bell's ringing. Covert Method of Entry. Weren't you posted to the CMOE wing, Norm? Didn't you do the specialist lock-picking course?'

'That's right,' he said. 'All two years of it.'

'Great. You're our CMOE expert, then.'

In a moment of black humour I saw all the members of our team in terms of what they didn't have – the areas where, in military jargon, they'd gone deficient. I'd gone deficient in terms of family; Norm couldn't be bothered to talk; Stew was definitely deficient in the legover stakes; Pat couldn't control his appetite; Fred wasn't overburdened with brains; and Whinger didn't

56

know when to stop cracking jokes. Still, I thought, we've all got our own strengths, and even if we're not fucking perfect we'll make out.

Back in the incident room I found Fraser still in occupation. 'Hey, Geordie,' he said. 'I've got news for you.'

'What's that?'

'Farrell's back.'

'Christ, that was quick!'

'Yep. He landed at Lyneham after lunch. Maximum security all the way.'

'Where's he been taken?'

'Winson Green, Birmingham.'

He picked up a sheet of fax paper and studied it. 'The prisoner's wounds are infected, and he's suffering from septicaemia. He's running quite a high fever, by the look of it.'

'I'm not surprised,' I said, 'the amount of shit there was in that jungle. Some of it's bound to have been sucked into him with the bullets. Does that mean he's in hospital?'

Again Fraser consulted his notes. 'Yep, he's in a single cell in the hospital wing. He's on fifteen-minute watch. That means one of the screws takes a look at him every quarter of an hour.'

'What about visitors?'

'He hasn't had any yet. One guy tried to see him, and a search revealed that he was carrying an escape kit inside a transistor radio. So that was the end of that. Now the Home Secretary's imposed a ban on visitors until further notice.'

'How long can that be maintained?'

'Only a few days. You can bet that a fellow like Farrell will know his rights down to the last letter.'

'And if the ban's lifted?'

'He'll be able to have one fifteen-minute visit a day, but only in a closed environment with prison officers present. That is, if he's graded Category A – which I've no doubt he will be.'

'And who was the guy who tried to visit?'

Fraser checked his notes and said, 'He identified himself with a driving licence in the name of Peter Smithies – but of course it turned out the licence had been stolen.'

'So the PIRA know where Farrell is anyway?'

'Oh yes. They know.'

That evening, for a change, I ran home. It was a good distance – about my usual eight miles – and I'd sussed out a route through the lanes that was almost entirely free of traffic. But again I had trouble with my rhythm. Even more now I was feeling the pressure, and I was so needled by the contradictory thoughts chasing through my head that I couldn't settle to a steady pace.

I was pleased now that Operation Ostrich was going down, as it promised genuine action to distract me, and the chance of doing a hard job well. Besides, I positively looked forward to topping al-Khadduri. At the same time, I was apprehensive about leaving the UK with my own affairs in such a mess. On the one hand it seemed there was nothing to be gained by hanging around at Hereford. If or when the PIRA came on the air there would be plenty of trained negotiators on hand to deal with them; in any case, I was fairly sure that if I did demur about going, the Regiment would order me to. Yorky Rose had admitted as much. On the other hand, Hereford was the last place I'd seen Tim and Tracy, and my natural inclination was to cling to any trace of them that I had. If I went overseas and someone made a cock-up in my absence, I might never see them again; my whole life would go to ratshit. Similarly, if I went under

58

in a foreign country, Tim would never remember his father, we would never get to know each other properly. What sort of a person would he grow up to be without me to guide him? What would Tracy do, left without support?

Trying to think everything through, I realised that although I'd already made a will I might need to make some adjustments. As things stood I'd arranged to leave a small amount of money for Tim, who'd get it when he was eighteen, and the house to Tracy. She and I had talked all this through before, and she'd agreed that if I died she would adopt the boy. But now – to face the worst – there was a chance that she might not outlive me. I decided that in the morning I'd better go into town to visit my solicitor, the owlish Mr Higgins.

As for Farrell – I couldn't help feeling nervous about the situation. At least the bastard hadn't escaped. I'd half expected the Colombians to let him out, through corruption or sheer incompetence. Now he was behind bars in Birmingham, and it sounded as if he was too ill to cause trouble for the time being.

But sooner or later he'd start to agitate, and when he did he'd stir more trouble than all the turds in China.

FOUR

I was at the solicitor's office by nine o'clock. 'Thos C. Higgins & Partners' said the highly-polished brass plate beside the door. I had no appointment, but I knew Higgins kept the first half-hour of the morning free and was confident he'd see me. In fact he walked up to the front door at the same moment as I did, and greeted me like an old pal, spectacles flashing.

His office smelt of lavender furniture polish, and the handsome grandfather clock was ticking away as steadily as ever in a corner. Since he knew my affairs well, there wasn't much explaining to do, and I soon put him in the picture.

'I don't know if it makes any difference,' I said, 'but Tracy's pregnant.'

'*Is* she?' he exclaimed. 'Congratulations!'

'Well, it's only two months so far.'

'You mean you would like to make the child a beneficiary of your will?'

'That's what I was wondering.'

'I think it's hardly possible. I mean, if she were, God forbid, to be killed during the next few weeks, the child could not survive.' He paused for a moment, then said, 'Is there no one else you could name as a residuary legatee?'

I shook my head. 'As you know, I'm an orphan. I don't have anybody.' Then suddenly an idea came to me, and I said, 'I know. Yes. I'd like to nominate a

60

colleague: Tony Lopez.'

'Is that his full name? Tony?'

'No, it's Antonio. He's American, Puerto Rican by origin. If Tracy and I are both written off, I'd like him to get everything. But the most important thing is that I'd like him to be the guardian for Tim.'

'Very well,' replied Mr Higgins cautiously. 'I'm sure that can be arranged. I shall need Mr Lopez to complete certain documents, of course.'

'*Sergeant* Lopez,' I said.

'Sergeant. I'm sorry.'

Mr Lopez! Just thinking about it creased me up. Tony was so much the professional soldier that the very idea of him being a civilian seemed ridiculous; I knew he'd bust his butt (as he would put it) laughing about it.

The morning's highlight was the arrival of the quads. Seven brand-new Honda Big Reds – one for each member of the team, one spare – were decanted from a truck into the tender loving care of the MT section, which at once set about destroying their glamour and making them look as nondescript as possible. By the time our lads went down to take delivery of the bikes their appearance had changed completely. Not only had every trace of scarlet paint been scraped, rubbed or grit-blasted off and replaced by a drab sand-colour, but the engine numbers had also been ground off the crank cases with emery wheels and the serial numbers scraped off the frames. The ignition keys had been stripped of their numbers so that no identification remained, and the engineers had cut different numbers of notches in their rims, one to seven, so that they could still be matched to the right bikes.

As Whinger remarked, such treatment didn't exactly enhance the value of the machines – but then, after the operation had gone down, we weren't planning to

61

auction them off in the main souk in Tripoli.

We'd all ridden quads before, but we got a quick run-down on this latest model from Mike Molloy, the MT officer, a grizzled little terrier of a captain. 'They're fully automatic,' he said, sitting on one to demonstrate. 'No clutch. The gear pedal's this one, by your left foot. As you move off, just keep coming up with your toe – Super Low, One, Two, Three, Four. For reverse, push this red button on the panel between the handlebars, then down with the gear lever. Nothing to it.

'Watch your starts, though. The motor's quite poky, and if you give it too much throttle it can put you on your back. As you'll see from the manual, wheelies are *not* recommended.' To demonstrate his point he started the engine, kicked into gear and revved up sharply. For a second I thought he'd overdone it. The bike seemed to leap into the air. It shot forward, but at the same time the front wheels came high off the ground so that it was almost vertical, and Mike was clinging on like a jockey on the back of a rearing horse. A tiny bit more power and he'd have gone right over backwards, but in fact he came down safely and switched off. 'See what I mean?' he said.

'Another thing to look out for is the tyres. As you realise, they're designed to operate at very low pressures – two point nine p.s.i. – cross-country. If you find you've got to run on tarmac, blow 'em up to at least double that or you'll knacker them.'

We were given basic instruction in maintenance – changing wheels, mending punctures, adjusting brakes, fiddling carburettor jets and so on – but Stew Stewart arranged to come back another day and go through the drills for things like ignition faults and fuel blockages.

Most of the guys ignored the manuals that came with the bikes, but a couple of them gave short, satirical readings from the printed instructions. Whinger started honking off in a pseudo-Japanese voice: '"Always check for obstacles before operating in a new area."' He gave a short, sardonic laugh. 'Thanks, mate. Just send us a load of large-scale maps of eastern Libya, all five thousands sheets! "Always obey local off-road riding laws and regulations." Phone the Libyan Embassy, Geordie, and ask for a copy of the desert off-highway code. "Never go fast over the top of a hill." For fuck's sake! If Gadaffi's nasties come after us I'll be going like shit off a shovel, I can tell you, even if I'm right on the summit of the biggest bloody mountain in North Africa.'

That afternoon we loaded into a four-tonner and drove away to the Brecon Beacons for practice over rough terrain – through mud and water, up, down and across steep grass slopes. For me, this was another psychological hang-up to be overcome. It was a motorbike accident which had led to my getting captured in Iraq: as the squadron had been moving up to a new location in the desert I'd dropped into a hole and smashed my left arm – and then, as an American casevac team was lifting me out along with other wounded, the chopper had been shot down. Now, once again, I was going to be riding a bike behind the lines in enemy territory. Admittedly I'd now have four wheels instead of two, and there wasn't a war on, but all the same the idea was a bit of a hurdle. To be nicked by the Libyans wouldn't be much less unpleasant than being nicked by the Iraqis – especially as our presence in the country would probably be denied by the British authorities and we could easily be left to rot in one of Gadaffi's penitentiaries.

Was it imagination, or did my arm produce a couple of twinges as I powered off up a rough grass track into the hills? For months it hadn't given the slightest trouble, even when I was on the weights in the gym, but now it seemed to be aching.

I set myself to concentrate on balance, and getting the feel of the quad. With two front wheels the steering seemed much firmer than with one, but it was OK once I'd got used to it. The trick was to sit forward on the long saddle when climbing, back on the way down, and lean uphill on the cross-slopes.

Pretty soon I had got the hang of it and started enjoying myself – and in fact everybody came back well chuffed with the machines, which were comfortable, fast, sure-footed and ideal for the job. Of course, we had been riding them with front and rear racks empty, and we realised they'd be a different proposition when loaded with all the kit and stores we were going to need.

While we were out in the hills, a message had reached camp to say that our American contact had flown in from Langley, Virginia, and would brief us on the camp at Ajdabiya in the morning. With this in mind we stopped work and went home early.

First light next day saw us piling into a Puma and whipping up to RAF Northolt on the western outskirts of London. It frustrated me to think that we were heading into the very area where Tim and Tracy might be held, and during the flight I was seized by the fantastic idea that I'd simply look down and see them being taken along a street – whereupon we'd bin our meeting with the Firm, fast-rope down on top of the prisoners' escorts, overpower them, and recover the captives.

The rest of the journey into town – by road – took so long that we reckoned we could have tabbed it faster, and it was nearly ten o'clock by the time our wagon crossed Vauxhall Bridge, slipped in through twin security gates and pulled up in the basement of the Firm's forbidding new head-shed building on the south bank of the Thames. Our friend Gilbert met us in the basement and escorted us up into the heart of the block, punching in combination numbers to open one locked door after another. Security here was so tight that it felt as if we were in a submarine, passing through a series of watertight compartments. We'd been told that this building got swept electronically at least once a day to make sure no listening bugs had been infiltrated, and we had no difficulty believing it.

We were never told the full name of the CIA agent who briefed us; Gilbert brought him into the lecture-room and introduced him merely as Gus. He was a short, stocky fellow in a navy blazer, with a pointed face, heavy suntan, close-cropped grey hair and shiny brown eyes – a combination that reminded me of a squirrel. Before he spoke, Gilbert gave us another dose of warnings about the need for total security – but here, in this alien environment, our guys were on their best behaviour, and Whinger didn't even scratch his ear.

When the American began to talk we were riveted, because the depth of his information was amazing. It took a couple of minutes to get used to his broad southern accent, but soon we were hooked. Not even his habit of saying 'OK?' after every few words could put us off.

Satellite data had been down-loaded into his laptop, some of it enhanced into three-dimensional computer images, which he fired on to a screen, so that what we got was a series of snapshots taken from a variety of overhead angles. As we sat there watching, all the guys were impressed by the lecturer's high-tech apparatus and approach, but at the same time I couldn't help thinking how typical it was that, although the Yanks could see a fly twiddling its legs on the far side of the world, when they wanted guys to go in and shoot somebody unpleasant, it was the Brits whom they got to do the job.

First Gus showed us the extent of the military camp. It was roughly rectangular, with the sides extending about two kilometres and the main approach road coming down to it from the north. Using a propelling pencil as a pointer, he picked out points of interest. 'The perimeter fence is weldmesh,' he told us. 'OK? Ten feet high, with a two-foot extension tilted outwards on top. Four strands of barbed wire – dannart, you call it? – on angle irons. I don't know whether you'll want to go through that or over it – through it, I guess. On the whole, we believe that security on the base is fairly primitive. The locals reckon the camp's protected by its location, with nothing but desert to the south. We can't tell from the satellite imagery whether or not the watch-towers are manned, but we think not.'

'Excuse me,' I broke in. 'Is it all right to make notes?'

'Go right ahead – so long as you don't write down names, or anything that would identify the place to outsiders. OK?'

'Sure.'

'So far as we can see, the fence isn't alarmed. No electric current in it, either – no sensors. Now, I'll just quickly show you the main areas of the camp. These are the accommodation blocks. Cookhouse, here. Mosque here – very important. Parade ground. Headquarter building, with a communications tower above it. Transport compound – you can see all the trucks lined up – and a few armoured vehicles here. Gasoline tanks in circular bunds. Gas filling point here. Two fifty-yard ranges; the main ranges are out in the training areas to the east. Ammunition bunkers way out on their own . . . here. Armoury here. That's one thing about the Arabs: they can't stand having weapons around the camp. Everything has to be locked away – that is, except for the guns carried by the guards. This is the recreational area: football fields, volleyball court. OK?'

'What are all those round things?' Pat asked.

'These?' Gus pointed to two or three small dark blobs. 'Palm trees. Remember, you're looking at them from right overhead. Now, the building you're interested in is this one. Bottom left-hand corner, as God and our satellites see it. On your left if you approach out of the desert from the south.'

The tip of the pencil-shadow trembled slightly as it hovered over an L-shaped structure set a little inside the angle of the perimeter fence. 'This seems to be a combination of office and residential accommodation. OK? It's on two floors, ground and upper, possibly also a basement. Concrete block construction, painted some light colour, buff or cream. Flat roof, double skinned to give some insulation from the sun. Metal window frames. This is where the target lives during his working week.'

'How wide's that gap between the building and the fence?' I asked.

'Maybe a hundred yards, maybe a little more. I'll take you in closer for more detail.'

In the next image the building occupied most of the picture. Two vehicles were parked in front of it, and part of a swimming pool was visible on the left-hand side. 'OK. The main entrance is here, on the southern side. There's another door on the right-hand end, here, and a rear door at the left, here. See this curving row of trees? It looks as though there's some sort of garden been planted in back. The private accommodation is here, around the west end. The room in which the target works nights is this one, on the corner of the upper floor. Two windows, one facing south, one west. Look at this.'

The speaker put up a night-time shot, taken from an oblique angle. Everything was dim and hazy, and needed explanation. 'You're still looking down, but from a little way out front – a slightly different orbit. These are the lights on the perimeter fence . . . and this is the south face of the accommodation building. The main doorway I mentioned is about there.' He pointed at the middle of the south front. 'Now. See the bright spot in this top corner? That's been there on several satellite passes made between one and two a.m. Rest of the building dark, this window lit, OK? That's where we think he'll be.'

'But how do we know it's him?' I asked.

Gus hesitated and turned towards Gilbert, as if uncertain who should answer the question.

'Inside information,' Gilbert quickly explained. 'We have a sleeper who works in the building – a computer maintenance technician. The guy files us reports on a regular basis. The only thing is, he has one hell of a time because the power supply keeps going down. There are back-up generators, but they don't work too well either.'

I was rather impressed. I hadn't realised that the Firm had such a far-flung web of contacts. 'How late does the target stay there?' I asked.

'Typically until two or three in the morning,' Gus replied.

'And where does he sleep?'

'In back of the building, on that same floor.'

'What about guards?'

'Two or three sleep on the premises. There are normally two on duty nights, but that doesn't mean they're going to be awake. You know what Arabs are like.'

Gus paused, thinking. Then he added, 'If you're going in close, one thing in your favour will be the

68

primitive air conditioning. There's no central system. Each room has its own unit set into an outside wall, and the fans are pretty noisy. Whenever the AC's on, there'll be a solid background roar. That'll help mask any sound you make.'

'How far away is the nearest building?'

The CIA man switched to another photo, half-way between the first and second in scale, and measured the space from the house to a neighbouring structure, off to the north. 'Also about a hundred yards, we think. This other thing's some kind of a store, probably uninhabited at night. I don't think it'll worry you.'

For a minute or two we all sat staring, memorising details, and I made a few notes in my book. Then Whinger forgot himself and declared, 'All we need do is take a couple of Uzis with us and accidentally scatter them about the place. That'd put the finger on fucking Israel, all right.'

I saw Gilbert looking rather pained, so I said, 'Not on, mate. We need to keep ourselves clean.'

'Was that a joke?' asked Gus. 'I hope so. Oh, I nearly forgot. I don't want to overburden you guys, but there's a secondary target that would merit your attention.'

He projected yet another image from his laptop and showed us a picture of a satellite receiving station – a thirty-foot steerable dish aerial with a couple of ancillary buildings – in a small compound of its own. 'This is one of the nerve centres of their military communications network,' he said. 'Knock that out and you'd do everyone a good turn. It was built by the Soviets, and with things being as they are now it might not be too easy to replace.'

'Where is it in relation to the accommodation block?' I asked.

'On the other side of camp. The east side. I think you'd see it OK from the perimeter wire.'

'And how far from that gate you showed us?'

'Maybe three hundred yards.'

'RPG,' said Whinger judiciously. 'Slip a rocket up it as we're moving off. No problem.'

'Like I said,' Gus emphasised, 'it's very much a secondary target. Only to be engaged if you've hit Number One. And certainly I wouldn't want you to prejudice the main operation.'

'Got that,' I said. 'Can you fill us in on the surrounding terrain?'

'Sure.'

A wide-angle shot (or maybe one taken from a higher orbit) showed an expanse of desert south of the camp. To our untrained eyes the picture didn't mean much. Apart from a single dirt road coming out from the fence to the south-east and ending at a range, there were a few wadis and stream-beds winding about, but we couldn't identify anything else specific. Yet Gus, armed with notes, gave a useful general description.

During the chopper flight in we would overfly one MSR (main supply route), a metalled road running north-east to south-west, he told us. Once on the ground we'd have to cross another road, a smaller one, and a single large wadi. Down to the south the desert was flat, but as we approached the area of the camp we would come into a belt of dunes a couple of miles across from south to north, the range as a whole lying east and west, the northern edge of which was less than a quarter of a mile from the camp fence. Gus reckoned the dunes were 150 feet high, and should give us an excellent site for an observation post. The elevation was ideal: we'd be looking down slightly. Another picture, taken soon after sunrise, proved his point: strong light coming low from the east caught on the sweeping, curved rims of the dunes, casting pools of shadow hundreds or maybe thousands of yards long.

As I stared at the picture my mind flew back to the Gulf, and the crappy gen we'd been fed in the run-up to the war. For months we had trained in the sand of the United Arab Emirates, firmly believing that the desert plateau in the west of Iraq – where our patrols would be inserted – also consisted of sand. The basis of our belief was US satellite imagery, from which our own int boys had deduced that Iraq was covered with sand from top to bottom. Then, when our patrols had gone in, what did we find? The entire environment was rock and shale, with not a grain of sand in sight. All the kit we'd brought for building OPs was useless, and we were caught with our pants down: you can't build anything out of solid rock.

Were we being given another load of crap now? I didn't want to seem aggressive, but I had to ask – so I put the point as politely as possible. 'Excuse me,' I said, 'but in Iraq we got stuffed because everyone misread the terrain.'

'I know, I know!' Gus grinned in a friendly enough fashion. 'That was real tough. But the fault didn't lie in the imagery. The trouble was, your intelligence guys didn't know how to interpret the data they were getting. Nobody had time to brief them properly and pass information on down the line.'

'So you're confident this environment *is* sand?' I gestured at the screen.

'One hundred per cent. Look at the soft curves on these dunes. They couldn't be made of rock. Apart from anything else, they change shape with the seasons as the winds shift their surface. There's another thing, too: it's the loose texture of the ground that stops the Libyans using this sector for manoeuvres. As I said, they've got enormous infantry training areas, but those are all further north where the desert's harder and more stable.'

71

He paused and added, 'You're going in on ATVs, I think?'

'That's right.'

'They'll be fine. Roll over the sand no problem.'

That reassured me. At least this info was coming straight from a guy who knew what he was talking about, rather than through a range of filters and competing intelligence agencies hundreds of miles apart.

Gus moved on to show us more detail of the terrain on our run-in. The large wadi was almost two miles wide. 'In winter that can be some river,' he told us. 'But right now it's dry, and likely to remain so. Could be the odd pool still lying in the bed, but my bet is you'll cross dry-shod.'

He then gave us a run-down of temperatures at first and last light. Here again I was on my guard, because in Iraq we'd been totally misinformed. Nobody had warned us that on the plateau in winter we would encounter snow, ice and vicious winds, with daytime temperatures barely above freezing, and night-times well below. The result was that we went in with nothing like enough clothes, and two of our guys died from hypothermia. Now in Libya we were promised a night-time minimum of eighteen Celsius and a daytime maximum of thirty-six. From the magic laptop came three-day weather charts giving temperatures, humidity, moon state, and first and last light. When I challenged the temperatures, mentioning our Iraq experience, the answer was, 'Yeah – but that was winter, and on the plateau you were a thousand feet above sea level. This time it's early summer, and even on those goddamn dunes you'll be at sea-level or maybe even below it.'

Again I relaxed.

Gus continued with an analysis of vehicle

movements up and down the approach road to the camp, but these were of less interest to us. I couldn't see us getting up round that side of the establishment at all. We'd come in from the south or south-east, find a lying-up point a kilometre or so short of the fence, and build an OP on one of the dunes. Mine's a steak, as Whinger would say: piece of cake.

Having made sketches and taken some notes, I felt reasonably confident. But one point that still worried me was the sheer number of *jundis* likely to be on site. Gus reckoned that there might be two or three hundred troops on the camp at night. If the alarm went up and that lot got deployed into the desert, they could form a hell of a cordon, through which we'd just have to blast our way.

All the more reason for us to operate discreetly: we'd need to be in and out before anyone became aware of our presence.

Back in Hereford, the knowledge we'd gained focused our training effort. Now we knew that we needed practice at building OPs in a sandy environment, so we loaded the quads into another four-tonner and made away to the dunes near Borth on the Welsh coast. There we had a couple of good days riding the bikes on the loose, steep slopes and making OPs by digging into banks, building walls with bags of sand, and roofing over the hollows we'd made with extending aluminium rods covered with scrim netting and marram grass. The second day turned out fine and warm, so when we'd finished work two of the guys stripped off and rushed into the sea; but the water was so cold that they were out again in short order, cursing wildly and covered in purple-red patches.

After a few hours riding the quads I'd thought of a couple of modifications that might prove useful. One was a bracket mounted above the handlebar panel to hold a Magellan GPS kit, so that we could keep an eye on our little displays while driving with both hands on; the other was a speedometer (as delivered, the bikes had nothing to tell you how fast they were going). So I got the MT Section to give us all Magellan-holders, and to cobble up two of the quads with speedos.

Weapons and weapon-training were another major preoccupation. From the SAW's own closed-off section of the armoury we drew brand-new AK-47s, silenced Browning 9mm pistols, and one Soviet-made Dragunov 7.62 sniper rifle – a semi-automatic, bolt-action weapon fitted with a telescopic sight. The AK-47s were Chinese-made Type 5611s, with skeleton stocks that folded under for easier transportation, and Chinese characters stamped into the metal. It was obvious they'd never been fired because the working parts were still coated in their original grease; they could well have been part of the shipment seized off the Irish coast which Gilbert had mentioned.

After stripping the rifles and giving them a good clean-up, we took them out to an isolated range and began getting to know them. The AK-47 is a primitive beast, coarsely made and finished, but it's a robust enough weapon, and at normal distances reasonably accurate. The safety-catch, on the right-hand side above the pistol-grip, is dead simple – one click down for fully automatic, two down for semi-automatic – and provided rounds don't jam in the magazine you're laughing.

To free up the working parts we loaded magazines fully with thirty rounds apiece, and fired a few initial bursts, four or five rounds at a time. Three of the mags proved sticky, if not downright defective, so we binned them on the spot. Then we got down to zero the rifles, and found that at a hundred yards we could achieve three-inch groups, firing at plain white aiming marks on a buff background. At two hundred the rounds were falling four or five inches, but an adjustment of the battle-sight, half-way up the barrel, soon put the point of impact back in the bull. Nevertheless we decided that our best policy would be to keep the sight in its normal position and, if necessary, aim a bit high.

I never saw the AK-47 as our assassination weapon. It would be our main armament if we got involved in a contact, but it was too crude and cumbersome for the close-quarter job which I envisaged. Our aim was to take Khadduri out with maximum precision and minimum disturbance: a surgical strike at point-blank range, for which a silenced pistol would be ideal. I therefore paid close attention to my 9 mm Browning.

Like the rifles, the Browning is a basic weapon, but this customised version had a thick cylinder of sound-baffle wrapped round the barrel. Another silencing device is the button which locks the top slide of the pistol forward after a shot, keeping most of the noise inside – the penalty being that you have to knock the lever off to re-cock the mechanism. After a few warm-up shots I fired at a Hun's-head target from close range – between ten and twenty feet. Although the pistol was accurate enough I didn't like the trigger-pull, which was too heavy, and I wasn't happy with the sluggish action. So in the afternoon I took the weapon back to the armourer and got him to polish up all its working surfaces, and next time out on the range I found a big improvement. At twelve feet I could put every round not just into the Hun's head but into a two-inch circle in the middle of the forehead.

I knew that, if I could get close enough to the target, I would nail him.

Our joker weapon was the sniper rifle, which proved deadly accurate. We set the telescopic sight at 300 yards, and worked out how much to aim up or down at other ranges without altering the zero. Already a plan of campaign was forming in my mind: when the assault party of two or three went in to penetrate the building and engage the target, the rest of the guys would be on the perimeter fence, ready to put down rounds if anyone came after us. In this last role the Dragunov could prove a big asset; if it dropped a sentry, for example, three or four hundred yards from the real scene of activity, it would create a useful diversion.

As for the secondary target – that would have to take its chance.

Explosives I left mainly to Fred Parry. After some discussion we decided to bin the idea of taking bar mines, Chinese or otherwise, as they weighed about forty pounds each and we already had too much kit to carry. Instead we indented for a supply of Semtex, with which we could blow the fence, a door or a window, or make diversionary booby-traps that would delay any attempt at follow-up. We could also use it to destroy a quad, if one was disabled, or – *in extremis* – to vaporise a body. A further joker in our pack was a clutch of Claymore anti-personnel mines, which are easy to transport. These curious-looking things – like little green bars in the shape of crescents, only an inch and a half thick, with a leg at each end – pack a nasty punch in the form of ball bearings, which fly out like grape-shot when the mine is detonated. American-made Claymores have TOWARDS ENEMY stamped on the business side. Ours, which were Soviet-made, bore no such legend; but as we were all familiar with the weapon, we knew well enough that the outside of the crescent was the face to show the Libyans.

A trickier subject was rations. We were going in on hard routine – no cooking, no fires, no heating of brews, even – and this meant that for three days at least all our food would be cold. That didn't worry the guys, especially as we would be in a hot climate; all the same, it was a drag having to transfer every boil-in-a-bag meal from its silver pack, which had writing on it, into an anonymous, clear plastic bag with a zipper-lock fastener. By the time we'd cut off one end of each pack and squeezed sausage and beans or steak and kidney into another container, the meal was even more featureless and gunged-up than before. Yet nobody cared much: on an operation, people accept that they're not at the Ritz; they eat only to shove the necessary amount of calories down their necks, and look forward to proper meals when they get home. Besides, the plastic bags would have a useful secondary role: after we'd eaten their contents we could crap into them.

You'd be surprised how dangerous body wastes can be. Not only do piss and shit stink, and attract flies and wandering dogs, but one turd may give away a mountain of secrets. Laboratory analysis can show not only what type of food the guy who laid it has been eating, but also his age and the physical state he's in. Whether or not the Libyans had the techniques for that sort of work we couldn't tell, but it was perfectly possible that undisciplined crapping might reveal that we were a bunch of fit young westerners.

We also devoted time to working out our loads. The maximum weights given in the manual were 60lb. for the rear rack on each quad, and 50lb. for the front; but it was clear that such puny limits were no good to us. We decided, for a start, that each of us must take one jerrican of spare petrol and one of water – these two alone would add up to nearly 100lb. – and on top of that we had weapons, ammunition, explosives, cam-nets and poles for OPs, shovels, other tools, food, spare clothes and other personal kit. I told the guys to cut down to the absolute minimum compatible with safety, and everybody kept packing and repacking to see what they could leave out. Another necessity was to ensure that the kit was properly secured to the bikes. I wasn't happy with the straps I already had, so I went down to Meg, the camp seamstress, who ran me up some webbing straps with ratcheted buckles to my own design.

After discussing what we needed and what we didn't in various Chinese parliaments, with all the team sitting round for a general discussion, we decided to take a single trailer, in which a good load of the heavier, bulkier items like jerricans, spare tyres and cam-nets could travel. One of the quads would have to pull it, but we could take turns – and, as somebody pointed out, if we did get a casualty, the wounded man or dead body could be transported in it. So the MT section obtained a trailer, and put it through the same process of removing all its identification marks.

As always in the Regiment, physical fitness was left to individuals. All the guys knew that they had to be in really good nick; if we hit trouble, our lives might depend on our ability to cover big distances at speed in alien conditions, possibly with little food or water. So there was no need for organised runs or training sessions; people just went on with their own fitness routines whenever they had time. It was the same with inoculations. Right at the start I had told everyone to make sure his jabs were up to date, and, if any were missing, to get his arse down to the Med Centre pronto.

The two RAF crews who would be flying us came down to give us briefings and discuss our requirements. Both were dedicated to special forces support, so that they were old friends, and I recognised Pineapple Pete, the Herc captain, from several earlier missions. (Why he was called that history did not relate; I suppose some Petes just *are* pineapples.)

'Off for a nice little drive in the desert, are you Geordie?' he asked. 'Just the job for the time of year.'

'Yeah,' I agreed. 'Spot of sightseeing. Nothing dramatic.'

The Herc crew were on a need-to-know basis. All that mattered was that they took us to Cyprus, and on to Siwa, according to the schedule that the Kremlin had devised. What we were doing was another matter and something about which they didn't even ask. The crew of the Chinook had to have more information: they knew that we were on a non-attributable operation, and they knew to within a few miles the area in which it would take place. But they, too, were in the dark about our target, and Steve Tanner, the skipper, was no more inquisitive than Pete. Of far greater importance to him was the state of the moon on the night we went in, and he was glad to find that it would be three-quarters full.

Together with him, his co-pilot and his head loadie, we worked out distances, timings, weights and so on. But we never breathed a word about our target. At the back of my mind I kept thinking: there's always a chance that the heli will go down in the desert, and if it does, the less the crew know about us, the better – the less they can give away. All the same we had to plan emergency drills with them, in case the chopper's navigation systems went u/s, or it was shot down or forced down by engine failure. There were emergency rendezvous points to be memorised and procedures to be worked out. In the last resort, we might have to destroy the aircraft with explosives to make sure that no Libyans got their hands on it.

The crew also needed a cover story, to account for why they were in Libya at all. We decided they would say that they'd been taking part in Exercise Bright Star, that their navigation systems had gone down, and that they'd flown into Libyan air space by mistake. That might not sound very convincing but it was the best that could be devised.

FIVE

My own trouble was that I couldn't seem to shake off the tension which still built steadily. Normally I find the best answer to mental stress is hard physical exercise, but this time the remedy wasn't working. I was forcing myself to run and work out every day, yet still I was unable to relax, and sometimes I thought my head was going to burst with the pressure.

My days were packed with activity; not so the nights. Back at the cottage I had far too much time to brood. Several times I had asked the SB guys if there was any future in making some initiative on the hostage situation ourselves, trying to put out feelers, but the answer was always, 'No. The PIRA have got to move first. Unless, one of these days, a tout picks something up, or we get an intercept that gives us a line.'

Tired as I was, I found it hard to sleep – and the nightmares started again, similar to the one I'd had after the Gulf. Usually I was travelling fast through the dark, on a strange kind of roller-coaster or maybe a bike, until suddenly something grabbed me by the left arm, so that terrific forces threatened to tear me in half, setting up the most horrendous pain, and I'd wake up in a muck sweat, yelling with fright.

Soon there were only five days left before take-off. So far, everything had gone well. Then we had a set-back which caused aggravation and distress at the time but almost immediately bounced back to our advantage.

We'd gone out into one of our nearby training areas to try the quads fully loaded on rough terrain at night; our aim was to run through the main moves of the operation, using a range-hut as the target building. Having ridden to within walking distance we all tabbed forward to a wire fence. Pat and I then cut our way through, leaving the rest of the guys on the barrier, two to guard the opening we'd made, two to lay diversionary charges four hundred metres to the east, in roughly the position occupied by the south gates of the Libyan camp.

The first stages all went according to plan. Pat and I made a covert approach to the building, broke in through a window, fired a couple of rounds through a Hun's-head target in one of the rooms, and then let off a stun grenade outside to indicate that things had gone noisy. As we were moving back to the fence, a big bang went off down the line, simulating the diversionary explosion, and we all legged it to the spot designated as our ERV.

So far, so good. But by then heavy rain had come on, and as we rode away in the dark the bikes began to slither around like snakes on the greasy grass. We were only using bags of sand as weights, but we'd measured them out and made sure that we had eighty pounds on the front rack and a hundred on the back, well strapped on. The loads certainly pushed the quads down on their suspension and made the steering heavier.

Coming downhill close to the lip of a ravine, Fred Parry, our lanky explosives star, hit a rock and skidded towards the edge. The crust of heathery peat broke away beneath his left-hand rear wheel, and a second later he and the bike were rolling over and over down the steep bank towards the stream.

He might have got away with it if it weren't for the lumps of rock sticking out from the sandy bank. By sheer bad luck the quad came down on him and pinned him against a rock that had no give in it, dealing his left leg a fearsome smack. He finished up face-down in some grass with the machine on top of him and the engine still running, wheels turning.

I'd been riding next in line, and there was just enough light for me to see him go arse over tip down the bank. In a flash I was off my own bike and running down towards the casualty.

Fred was pinned down by a handlebar in the small of his back. His right leg was straight, but my torch-beam showed that his left leg was bent out at a diabolical angle.

I yelled, 'Don't move!' and reached under the handlebar panel to switch off his ignition. The smell of petrol was everywhere. I had visions of a sudden *woof!* and the pair of us on fire.

Fred was just moaning, 'Shit! Shit! Shit! My fucking leg!'

'Keep still,' I told him again. With a big heave I rolled the bike off him, back on to its wheels. At that moment heads appeared against the sky on the rim of the ravine above, and somebody shouted, 'Get up, wanker!'

'Bollocks!' I yelled at them. 'He got a bad break. Get on the mobile for the chopper. Tell them the casualty's got a broken leg, high up. Femur or hip.'

I knelt down beside Fred. His eyes were screwed tightly shut. 'How is it?'

'Fucking horrible.' He tried to move and gave a groan.

'Stay how you are. It'll be better if we don't try to move you. The doc's on his way. He'll be here in twenty minutes.'

The other guys came down and gathered round, making sympathetic noises now. Since we were only training, we had only a limited medical pack to hand, and so couldn't give Fred anything to ease the pain. But we wrapped him in our sweaters to keep him warm and covered him with ponchos to throw the rain off. I stayed with him while the others recced round for a place at which the chopper could put down. The ravine was too narrow for the pilot to hover, and it was obvious we'd have to carry the casualty up on to more level ground; but I reckoned it was better to wait until the doc had put a shot of morphine into him and got the leg splinted.

As I chit-chatted to keep up his morale, the rest tied ropes on to the stranded quad. With one guy steering it and two bikes pulling from above, they heaved it up on to the open hillside. The fuel tank had been punctured on the top, presumably by impact with a rock, but apart from a few dents and scratches the machine still seemed in remarkably good nick. The rest of the guys then got their bikes deployed in a big circle, with their headlamps shining inwards, to make a pool of light on which the chopper could put down.

The recovery went without a hitch. In twenty-two minutes from call-out the standby Puma was overhead and settling towards the lighted patch. In a few more seconds Doc Palmer and his medic were beside the injured man with their bags of tricks. Within five minutes they had him hot to trot, well doped with morphine, his left leg secured in a pneumatic splint blown up like a giant condom, which held the broken limb snugly alongside the good one in the stretcher. While they were working we loaded the bent quad into the Puma and lashed it down. Then four of us carried Fred up out of the ravine and slid him on to the floor of the chopper. The last we saw of him, he was giving a cheerful wave as the helicopter lifted away.

★

On our way back to camp I felt depressed. With four days to go, we were a man down and urgently in need of a replacement. But then, as if Pat had intoned *Allah karim* ('God is good') a few hundred times, I found we had one: that afternoon, clearance had at last come through from Washington for Tony Lopez to join the team.

For me this was a big breakthrough, and it gave my morale a boost. Tony was the guy I wanted more than anyone else – partly because he too would recognise the target and remove any possibility of identification error, and partly because I knew he was a ferociously effective operator, veteran of many hairy operations in Panama and elsewhere. Having spent five weeks in gaol with him, I was absolutely confident that we could rub along together. Besides, he knew more about the Arab world than the rest of us put together, because, a couple of years before the Gulf, he'd run a SEAL team job in Abu Dhabi, instructing the local forces in weapon training and close-quarter battle techniques. Like Pat, he'd done a course in Arabic, and had a smattering of the language.

Until then I'd observed the letter of the law and hadn't given him (or anybody else) the slightest hint about what I was doing. I'd had to tell Fraser that I'd be abroad at the end of the week for six or seven days, but I hadn't said what the operation was or where it would take place.

Now, with the agreement of the ops officer, I was able to put Tony in the picture.

When he heard what the deal was, he leapt up and punched the air with loud whoops of 'Great fuckin' snakes!'

'You're going to have to do the explosives,' I warned him. 'That was poor old Fred's job.'

'No sweat!' he cried. 'I've blown the shit out of more goddamn automobiles, trucks, houses, trashcans,

84

bridges and railway lines than you could ever imagine.'

For a more thorough briefing, we decided that he should come out to the cottage and cook a celebration dinner.

The enemy, however, had other plans. At six-thirty that evening I'd just reached home when the incident room rang to say that the PIRA had called what they thought was my own number. I was to return immediately.

Having scorched back, I listened with a mixture of rage and fascination to the brief tape recording.

'I'll speak to Geordie Sharp,' said a man with a strong Belfast accent.

'I'm sorry,' replied Karen, the Streisand girl, who was on duty, 'he's working at the moment.'

'Can I call him somewhere else?'

'Afraid not,' she said. 'He's out and about.'

'Who are you, then?'

'I'm looking after the house for him. Shall I get him to call you? Who's speaking, please?'

'Nobody he's heard of. What time will he be back?'

'What time is it now? I haven't got a watch.'

'Now? It's twenty-five past six.'

'Well . . . he said seven o'clock.'

'Half an hour, then?'

'That should be fine. Can I give him any message?'

'No. I'll call.'

'What name shall I tell him?'

'No name.'

'No name?'

'You can say Kevin.' And with that the man had switched off.

The call had been made from a mobile. From the way the signal came and went we were pretty sure he'd been in a car, driving around. He'd been on the air only a few seconds; Special Branch would have needed four or five minutes to DF him accurately. But at least there was now a chance of another call coming through for them to work on.

I listened to the tape three times. The twang of the accent – 'nay', almost 'nayee', for 'now' – took me straight back to Northern Ireland and the slimy, sleazy methods of the PIRA. In particular I thought of the night when, lying in a ditch a few yards from an isolated farmhouse, I could have topped Farrell as he stood there bollocking some underlings for failing to go through with a shoot. I remembered how he'd roared 'Cunts!' at them, addressing them as though they were shit. The guy had been barely thirty yards from me. My companion and I could have dropped the whole group of players – but the head-shed had forbidden us to open fire because one of them was then the most valuable tout in business.

This guy on the tape had the same sort of peremptory, domineering manner. The way he'd started in – 'I'll speak to Geordie Sharp' – immediately put a stamp on him. There was no question of 'can I . . .?' or 'please', just arrogance and bluster.

'Christ!' I muttered. 'Just wait till the bastard comes through again. I'll sort him.'

'Take it easy, Geordie,' said Fraser, who'd come flying back into the incident room from the digs he'd taken in town. 'Whatever your feelings, it's no good getting stroppy with these people. They're always hoping to make you lose your rag, and if you do you play into their hands.'

I settled in to wait. The girl had said I'd be back in half an hour. Kevin, whoever he was, should call again around seven. I rang Tony and told him I'd been delayed. 'Why not go on out to the cottage and make yourself at home?' I suggested. 'You know where the key is – on the hook.'

'OK,' he agreed. 'I've been to the supermarket and got the stuff to cook something real good. I'll see you later.'

As I hung around, the SB girl, Karen, began to get on my tits again. I had to admit that she'd handled the call as well as anyone could have – she'd tried to keep the guy on the line, and given nothing away – yet there was something about her that annoyed me, an air of complacency that came over more in the way she looked and acted than in anything she said. She was wearing a track suit of dark-blue velvety material, and she seemed unable to keep still. She was forever looking at her nails, filing one of them for a second or two, bringing a mirror out of her handbag, tweaking at her eyebrows, patting her fair hair into place, all as if she was trying to attract attention. The trouble with her, I decided, is that she's too damned pleased with her looks. I also caught her staring at me a couple of times in a way that was strictly unoperational. I realised that she must have been bored to tears, sitting around day after day on her fanny with nothing happening, living in some dreary bed-and-breakfast dump away from her home, wherever that was. I knew I should have made an effort to chat her up and be friendly, but I just had too much on my mind.

Seven o'clock came and went. Seven-thirty, eight, eight-thirty.

Fraser could see I was getting more and more steamed up. 'Relax, Geordie,' he said. 'This is standard practice. They do it to wind you up. Don't fall for it. Stay cool.'

'It's OK for you,' I said. 'It isn't your kid they've got.'

'I know. But I do have a little girl about Tim's age. I can imagine what you're feeling.'

I'd been so wrapped up in my own problems that I'd never paused to think about Foxy's domestic circumstances. The news that he had a family made him seem suddenly more human. Looking at the lines on his forehead I thought, You must have started late, to have a daughter of four. And he, as if reading my mind, added, 'I didn't get married till I was thirty-seven.'

'Sorry,' I mumbled. 'I didn't mean anything personal.'

He smiled, and as he came past where I was sitting he gave me a bump on the arm with the heel of his hand.

At nine o'clock I rang Tony. 'Listen,' I said. 'The bastards haven't called. They're stringing us along.'

'Aw, shit. I've made a hell of a Mexican bean stew.'

'Go ahead and eat it, then. I don't know when I'll get back.'

'I'll keep some warm for you anyhow.'

'Thanks, Tony.'

It was nearly eleven when the call at last came through. I was sitting by the phone, but not wanting to appear too eager I let it ring five times before I picked up the receiver. Then I just said, 'Yes?'

'Geordie Sharp?'

'Yep.'

'I'm calling about your family.'

Was this the same voice as on the tape? I didn't think so. A Belfast accent, all right, but somehow different. The connection was brilliantly clear, as if the call was short-distance. I looked across at Fraser and raised a thumb.

'Kevin, is it?' I said.

'It is not. A friend of Kevin's.'

'Oh – right.'

'You're wanting them back.'

'Where are they?'

'I said, you're wanting them back. Are you not?'

'Of course.'

'You know what to do, then.'

'What?'

'Get our man out.'

'What man?'

'Declan Farrell.'

'Farrell?' I said. 'Who's he?'

'Look, if you want to see your little boy again, or your girlfriend, you'll not mess about.'

'Wait a minute. I don't know who you're talking about. Who is Farrell?'

'It's the man you were after murdering at Ballyconvil. You know him.'

'Bally-what? I never heard the name before. Where's this guy supposed to be?'

'The Brits have him.'

'What, in Belfast?'

'No, on the mainland.'

'What's happened? Is he in the nick or something?'

'In gaol, so he is.'

'What am I supposed to do about that?'

'Ask around. Find out where he's been put, and spring him.'

'But I'm army, not police. I don't have the contacts. Besides, I'm working. I don't have the time.'

'I said – ask around.'

'All right. Listen, I'll do what I can. Give me a couple of days. Then I'll get back to you.'

'You will not. I'll call you in two days' time. That's Thursday. Seven o'clock.'

'Hello?'

I was going to try and glean some scrap of information about how the hostages were, but the line had gone dead.

'Well done!' said Fraser keenly. 'That was great, the way you kept him on the air. Let's see what the boys have managed.'

A couple of minutes later we learnt that the call had

been traced to a phone box in West Belfast. Of course, by the time the RUC arrived there the caller would have gone, but there was a chance of getting some fingerprints. The fact that the PIRA had rung from Northern Ireland alarmed me, as it seemed to work against Special Branch's theory that London was the most likely place for the hostages to be held. But Fraser remained unruffled, saying that, naturally, their spokesman would phone from Belfast wherever the prisoners were.

The exchange left me screwed up with a seething mixture of anger and frustration. The arrogance of the guy's manner had really pissed me off. That was bad enough, but almost worse was my own helplessness. What the hell could I do? If I'd lost my rag and called him a scumbag he'd merely have laughed. If I'd admitted I knew where Farrell was he'd have gone on saying, 'Get him out, then.'

Did the PIRA realise I'd been in Colombia and had been responsible for Farrell's capture? The caller had given no sign of knowing that, but it made little difference. Somehow the terrorists had established the connection between me and their big player, and little details – like the fact he was in a high-security prison – were not going to worry them.

Screw the nut, I told myself. Like Foxy says: stay cool.

It was midnight by the time I got home. I found Tony asleep on the settee in the sitting room with the TV burbling some crap about fitted wardrobes. Going in quietly I switched it off, got down behind the armchair and let out a loud yell – whereupon he leapt eight feet in the air and came down facing the door in an exaggerated crouch, as if to take on all comers.

'Great sentry you'd make,' I told him, rising into view.

'Boy!' he gasped. 'Did you give me a fright!'

'Have a drink. How about a Scotch?'

'You having one?'

'Sure. I need something after that.' While I poured two drinks I told him about the telephone contact. He brought out the remains of the bean stew he'd cooked with such care, and I ate it at the kitchen table – gratefully enough, though gasping a bit at the chillies – while I filled him in between mouthfuls on what had happened.

'This is driving me crazy,' I told him. 'There's no way we can get at them.'

'What are Special Branch doing?'

'Looking around and listening. Checking the movements of known players, going through their own records on the central computer. That's about all they can do. Tony – d'you think I'm crazy to go on this operation?'

'Not at all. You wouldn't achieve anything if you *didn't* go – except making yourself feel real bad.'

'That's true. But what if I get written off?'

'Might be the best way of getting the hostages released.'

I stared at him. 'You're joking.'

'Nope. I mean it. If you disappeared from the scene the terrorists' emotional blackmail would be at an end. They couldn't exert anywhere near the same pressure through anyone else. They'd probably just turn Tracy and Tim loose somewhere and call it a day.'

'You think so? Do the IRA ever release hostages?'

'Sure, if they've nothing to gain by holding them any longer. I was talking to Fraser about it this morning.'

'But Tracy's seen their people. She knows several faces by now.'

'Nobody important.'

'In that case,' I said, 'next time they come through,

91

maybe the word should be that I'm dead and they've missed the boat. Anyway . . . sod that. Let's talk about the operation.'

I opened out a large-scale map of north-east Africa and spread it on the table. The area for which we were heading was an extension of Egypt's Western Desert, birthplace of the Regiment during the Second World War. It was there that David Stirling had formed his Long-Range Desert Group, from which the SAS had emerged, and created havoc by blowing up aircraft far behind enemy lines. It was there also that Jack Sillito had made the most famous escape in SAS history, tabbing more than a hundred miles through the desert after he had been cut off behind the German forces.

'What the hell did he do for water?' Tony asked.

'Good question. Some people reckon he drank his own piss. Others say he managed on condensation that formed at night in old jerricans. Either way, it was some feat.'

Talk of this and other exploits carried us into the small hours. We also pored over the map to discuss our route to the target. From the Egyptian airfield at Siwa, a Chinook was due to lift us over the border and then due west across 300 kilometres of empty desert. The map showed the single MSR running from Ajdabiya in the north-west to a place called Al Jawf, 800 kilometres out in the Sahara to the south-east. Once we crossed over that we'd be within striking distance of our drop-off point, and the chopper would land us only sixty kilometres short of our objective.

'Funny, having another Al Jawf just there,' I said. 'That was the name of the place where we had our FMB in Saudi.'

'It means "interior",' said Tony. 'It can also mean a hole or depression, but down there I guess it's the interior. I expect there's dozens of Al Jawfs, if you look around. Hell of a place we're going.' He jabbed a forefinger at the map, indicating the vast empty spaces, unmarked by roads, towns or any other sign of civilisation. 'Nothing for hundreds of miles.'

'I know. But you know as well as I do: the biggest hazard's going to be wandering goatherds. If Iraq's anything to go by, the Libyan desert'll be full of the bastards too. They arrive out of nowhere, just when you least want them. And then, if they see you, you're faced with a bad decision. If you let them go they tell someone else there are nasties about; if you top them their friends come looking.'

In the incident room next morning the idea of my disappearing from the scene went down like a lead balloon. Fraser reckoned that if I vanished, the PIRA's response might easily be to knock the hostages off and make the bodies disappear.

'Forget that,' he said. 'What we need is a controlled release of information to keep them in play. Next time they come on the line, tell them a little bit about Farrell. Tell them you've found out that they're right: he *is* in gaol, and you're trying to discover where.

'I see the point,' I agreed. 'But look, as I told you, I'm off abroad on Sunday for a week. What happens while I'm away?'

'I've been thinking about that. I'd like to find someone with a similar accent, and have him stand in for you. We can brief him up on what to say.'

I didn't like the sound of that. Again, it would increase the chances of a cock-up. But I couldn't really hold out against it. 'Well,' I said, 'there's no shortage of Geordies in the Regiment. I can think of two others straight away.'

Then I had an inspiration. 'Listen – I know the man you want: Billy Bracewell, a staff sergeant on G

Squadron. He was in command of the QRF that got us out of the jungle in Colombia. He saw Farrell when we captured him – flew back with him to the forward base, in fact. He can talk about him better than anyone.'

So Billy was roped in to impersonate me if the occasion arose.

But for the whole of Thursday and Friday my mind was in turmoil with a new idea. In the Wing, on the range, in the laundry, in the gym, in town, at the cottage . . . no matter where I was or what I was doing, I could think of nothing else. The first time I'd run up against Farrell, in Ulster, it had proved impossible to top him in legitimate operations, and in the end I had reached the conclusion that the only way to get him was to go after him on my own – which was what I did. Now I'd begun to think that my only hope of recovering Tim and Tracy might lie in another extra-mural effort. I knew Farrell was in Winson Green. If I could discover the routine there – or, better still, find out when the prisoner was going to be moved somewhere, possibly for a court hearing – I and a few of the lads might be able to ambush the police convoy, spring him, and hand him back to the PIRA. We could buy an old banger for a couple of hundred quid cash, or even steal one, and ram the police van with it, then use one of our own cars with phoney licence plates for the getaway. The activity would be criminal, I realised – but when you're growing desperate, as I was, you think up desperate measures.

I didn't want to involve Tony in such a wild scheme, because if anything went wrong it would bring his service with the SAS to an abrupt end. Pat Newman, though, was a different matter. He was eighteen months older than me, and already talking of leaving the Regiment when he'd completed ten years (in a few months' time), so he had less to lose.

That Wednesday evening I waylaid him and suggested we went for a pint at the Crooked Billet, a pub out in the country not much frequented by our lads. There we got stuck into a corner of the public bar, which contained nobody else but one typical old Herefordshire cider-head, with a face as purple as a beetroot and greasy hair half-way down his back.

I started by talking about details of our imminent operation. I noticed Pat giving me the eyeball in a peculiar way, and after a while I stopped. 'What's the matter?' I asked. 'Don't you want to hear all this?'

'Yeah, yeah,' he went. 'It's just that Yorky asked me to keep a close eye on you, make sure you didn't try to run out.'

'For fuck's sake! Who said I was going to run out?'

'Nobody, but he wasn't sure you were really on for Libya. He told me to chat you up about it, keep you on side.'

'Thanks, mate.'

'I didn't, though. Did I?'

'Not a word. Good on yer, Pat. But, Christ, what bastards they are! Always trying to get round your back and put pressure on from behind.'

'Forget it, anyway.'

'All right.' So I switched to talk about my new plan.

Pat's reaction was forthright. He put down his mug, stared at me incredulously, and said, 'Geordie, you're fucking *mad*! The strain of this thing is getting to you. That's the craziest idea I've ever heard. Even if we managed to spring the guy from the convoy we'd all be nicked. There'd only be a few of us against hundreds of coppers. What are we supposed to do? Shoot our way out and leave a trail of corpses? It's not as if we're in bloody Ulster. It might be different if we could mobilise a whole army – but Christ! No: think of it. The thing would end in a pitched fucking battle, a civil war.'

95

'Well, if we did it at night we'd have a better chance of getting away with it.'

Pat shook his head and said, 'They don't take star prisoners to court at dead of night. Forget it, mate. I know they've got you over a barrel, and I'm sorry for you, but this is *not* the way out.'

'For "barrel" read "Farrell",' I said savagely. 'I just hope the bastard's rotting in gaol. I hope his wounds have turned gangrenous. By the sound of it, they have: I hear he's quite sick. He's got a ban on visitors too.'

'Oh? How's that?'

'Foxy Fraser told me. The first guy who went to see him got searched on the way in, like all visitors are, and they found something on him – an escape kit he was trying to smuggle in. That was the end of that.'

'So the feller never made it?'

I shook my head. But for all the cold water that Pat had poured, I couldn't abandon my idea. Maybe if I got together a few guys who'd left the Regiment recently, a few old hands . . . What I needed first was inside information about Winson Green – and as I thought about this problem I had a brainwave. A former member of the SAS, Jim Roberts, whom I'd known, had joined the prison service as some kind of welfare officer. Maybe if I found out where he was, he would give me some leads.

One certain fact was that I didn't have time to get anything going before Operation Ostrich went down. There were only two days left before take-off, and both were hectic with last-minute preparations. I therefore said no more to Pat, except that I told him not to mention my madcap scheme to anyone.

For me, the next hurdle that needed clearing was the second PIRA call, due on Thursday evening. Together with Foxy Fraser I'd worked out more or less what I was going to say. As far as he knew, the ideas I suggested were not an action plan but pure fantasy, designed to keep the PIRA interested; there was no way Foxy could tell that I was seriously considering putting my scheme into practice.

'Excellent!' he said several times when I proposed intercepting a police convoy. 'Capital. I like it.'

It seemed highly unlikely that the PIRA would meet the deadline of seven o'clock, but I got down to the incident room on time, just in case. Once again Karen was on the desk, wearing the same slinky tracksuit, and she gave me one of her flirtatious sideways looks as I came in. Also present was Billy Bracewell, fair-haired and beefy, my alter ego, who'd come to listen in to what was said and tune in to my reactions.

To everyone's amazement, my home line rang at seven-fifteen, barely quarter of an hour late. This time I waited for the caller to speak. There was a pause of several seconds before a man said, 'Hello?'

'Yep,' I went, very curt.

'Is that Geordie Sharp?'

'Yep.'

'What news?'

'You're right. Farrell's in this country.'

'Where?'

'Winson Green.'

'Where's that?'

'Birmingham.'

'Jaysus! What have they put him there for?'

'Don't ask me.'

The way the man had hesitated before asking 'Where's that?' made me certain he already knew where Farrell was. That was why I gave him the true answer: otherwise he might never have trusted me again.

Presently he went, 'Well?'

'Well what?'

'What are you doing about getting him out?'

97

'Listen, Kevin. Kevin, is it?'

'It is. Go on, now.'

'I've been thinking. To spring him from gaol would need a fucking army. I've got a few lads lined up, but we can't muster that strength.'

'So?'

'The way to do it is to wait till he's being moved. Wait till he's outside the gaol, on his way to court or something. He's on remand at the moment, but soon they'll have to take him to court to charge him. Then we may be able to hit the convoy and do a snatch.'

'Good. That sounds better. So when's he going to court?'

'I'm trying to find out. The preliminary hearing's bound to be soon. I can get a question to one of the screws who works in the prison through the father of one of my mates. He's retired, but he used to be a screw as well. He's abroad at the moment, back at the weekend. I'll get news then.'

'Fair enough. Is your contact on the hospital wing?'

'I don't think so. But even if he isn't he'll know the guys who are.'

'All right. But you need to get a move on. Your family's deteriorating.'

'What d'you mean?'

'They're missing you. Listen to this.'

I heard a couple of clicks, then a hissing noise. I realised the guy had turned on a small tape recorder and was holding the mouthpiece to the loudspeaker. Suddenly I heard Tracy's voice, shaky and peculiar: 'Geordie,' she said, 'for God's sake do something to get us out. For God's sake . . .' Then came more hissing, and suddenly Tim's voice: 'Daddy, I don't like it here. I want to come home.'

That was all he said, but it nearly cracked me up. 'Hello!' I called loudly. 'Tim! Hello!'

'Seven o'clock on Monday, then,' said the Belfast voice.

Suddenly everything was too much. '*Hey, cunt!*' I shouted. '*Give me my kid back!*'

The line had gone dead. 'FUCKING ARSE-HOLES!' I yelled. I crashed the receiver down so hard that it split the cradle of the phone clean in half. The whole instrument disintegrated in an explosion of grey plastic. In a surge of frustration I hurled over the table and sent a shower of files cascading to the floor.

Fraser and Bates were standing back against one wall, both looking shocked by the violence of my outburst. Fraser was speaking into another phone, and I heard him saying urgently, 'Mobile, moving around in the Ealing area of West London.'

Bates came forward and laid a hand on my shoulder, muttering, 'Take it easy, Geordie.'

I fought down a wild instinct to belt him one, so furious did I feel. I shook off his hand and said, 'Ah, get away!' Then I took a grip of myself and apologised.

'That's all right,' Bates said gently. 'I know how you feel.'

When I recovered I found SB much encouraged, as though they'd got a breakthrough. The fact that the call had come from the area they'd been predicting raised everyone's hopes.

People filtered away into the room next door, and as I sat there on a kind of bar-stool in front of a counter, still feeling stunned, I became aware that Karen had come up close and was standing right behind me.

'You look creased,' she said quietly. 'Would you like me to come out and cook supper for you? Or you could come to my place . . .'

I tensed myself, unwilling to believe my ears. The woman was making a proposition. I nearly spun round and belted her away with the back of my hand, but I held myself in check and grunted, 'Thanks, but I'm all right.'

'Sure? I'd really like to. You could stay the night if you wanted. There's a spare room. Or, as I said, I could cook supper at the cottage.' As she spoke she leant forward to pick up the telephone, deliberately brushing her breasts against my shoulder blades.

I should have stood up and walked away; I knew what she was after, and wanted nothing to do with her. But I was in such a low state that I sat tight and said, 'All right, then. Maybe I *would* be glad of company. Let's go to the cottage. There's plenty of food in the freezer.'

'I'll get something fresh on the way out of town,' she said. 'Half an hour?'

Everything went fine at first. Karen drove her Fiesta back to her digs and changed into a white frock with blue polka dots on it, which made her look very feminine. Then she dived into the supermarket and came out with a couple of steaks and some stir-fry vegetables. Having showered and changed while she was on the way, I dug out a bottle of red wine from the cupboard under the stairs and sat at the kitchen table chatting while she cooked.

We ate, and it was all harmless enough. She seemed genuinely sympathetic, and when she asked about my family background I found it a relief to describe how, after getting wounded and captured in Iraq, I'd found it impossible to settle back in with Kath, how I'd hit the bottle, and become so difficult to live with that a trial separation seemed the only answer.

'The worst thing of all was that she'd agreed to come back,' I said. 'I was on the up again. When I rang and suggested we got back together it was all she wanted to do. Another week, and she'd have come . . . Then that bastard Farrell sent his young feller with the bomb.'

100

'Tough,' Karen agreed. 'Really tough. But what's so special about Tracy?'

At that point I should have scented danger. But the words weren't said in an aggressive tone, and I took them at face value.

'Well, she was fantastic. She just took over the house and became a foster-mother to Tim.'

'Right away?'

'No . . . after a decent interval.'

'How did you meet her?'

'She'd been around for ages. She was working as one of the receptionists in the Med Centre.'

'Obviously you fancied her.'

'What d'you mean? Everyone fancied her. Guys positively looked forward to reporting sick with some minor ailment, just so they could chat her up.'

'But what *is* it about her?'

I wasn't going to say that her gloriously long legs turned me on, or that she did wild things in bed. I just told her, 'She's a gassy person. Always full of jokes. She's great at making stupid remarks that crack me up.'

'So you're planning to get married?'

'That's on the cards.' I wasn't going to mention the baby to this inquisitive cow.

'You must have made advances,' she said abruptly.

That *did* jar, and I retorted, 'What's that got to do with you?'

Karen didn't answer but stood up, walked across to her handbag and brought out a cigarette, which she lit. That pissed me off as well. I don't like people smoking in my house, especially without asking.

'Is there any more wine?' she asked.

'Sorry, that's it. I just had the one bottle.'

'How about a Scotch, then?'

'You oughtn't to; you've got to drive back.'

'Oh, one won't hurt. Not after all that food.'

101

'Help yourself, then.'

'What about you?'

'No, thanks.'

She moved across to the dresser, took down a glass and the bottle of Haig, and poured herself a measure. I wasn't chuffed with that, either. She did it with her back to me, trying to conceal the amount she was taking, but I sneaked a glimpse and saw that it was three fingers at least. Then she ran some water into the glass and came back to the table.

Instead of livening her up, the spirit made her morose. I tried to draw her out about her own background, but she seemed reluctant to discuss it and, beyond the facts that she was twenty-six and came from Norwich, I learnt practically nothing. It sounded as though she had no steady boyfriend, and never kept one for long. 'My career,' she kept saying. 'It's all down to my career.'

By eleven o'clock she wasn't making much sense, but still she needled away about my relationship with Tracy. I kept my cool and fended her off with non-committal remarks, until suddenly I'd had enough. At that point I stood up and said, 'Look, Karen, thanks for coming. I'm grateful to you for keeping me company, but it's time to break up the party. You can't drive back in that state. You'd better get your head down in Susan's room and go back to town in the morning.'

'Shushan?' she said. 'Who's that?'

'The friend who's been sharing the house with Tracy.'

'Another of these smashing red-heads, I suppose.'

'Don't be stupid. Come on, now.'

'Washing up,' she slurred.

'It can wait. Leave it. I'll find you a towel.'

I ran up the stairs three at a time, and saw her clawing at the banisters as she came up behind me. On the

102

landing I switched on the light in the spare room and said, 'Here you are. The bed's made up. The bathroom's next door – there. It's all yours.'

I half expected her to make a grab at me because she'd previously shown such obvious signs of sexual frustration. But she simply said, 'Good night then, and thanks,' and went into the room, closing the door behind her.

Five minutes later I locked my own bedroom door and crashed out, so exhausted that I went straight to sleep. The next thing I knew, somebody was knocking on the door. For a moment I couldn't think who the hell it was. Then I struggled up on one elbow and called, 'What's the matter?'

'It's me – Karen.'

'What's the problem?'

'There's water dripping.'

'For Christ's sake! Forget it. I expect the roof tank's filling up.'

'No, this is coming through the ceiling somewhere.'

Ah, hell, I thought. But I said, 'OK. Wait one, I'll have a look.'

I pulled on a bath-robe and opened the door. As I went to step out on to the landing I walked straight into Karen. She was standing in the doorway stark naked. In an instant one arm was round my neck and the other hand going for my crotch. Instinctively I brought up a knee and bumped her in the groin, whereupon she gave a scream and threw herself at me like a lunatic. I don't know if you've ever been attacked in the dark by a naked, sex-starved female – but it's quite an experience, I can tell you. Half the time I was trying not to get myself ripped and scratched, and the rest I was trying not to hurt her; but inevitably, as we wrestled, I kept getting a handful of this and that, with the result that she became still more desperate.

On me, the effect was anything but arousing. All I could think of were those terrible women brought into escape and evasion exercises to humiliate students who get captured, stripped and interrogated. When a guy's naked and at his lowest ebb, one of these old slappers comes in and starts insulting him with remarks like, 'Is that an acorn you've got stuck between your legs? I can hardly see it.' That was how I felt when I was pushing Karen around. She had a firm, meaty body, and in easier circumstances might have been a great lay — I could feel that all right — but she turned me on about as much as did the idea of Farrell and the IRA.

Things finished up with me getting her in a double half-Nelson and giving her a couple of slaps on the rump, whereupon she burst into tears.

'For Christ's sake!' I said. 'Go back to bed or go home, I don't care which. If the cops get you on the way, that's your lookout. But just stop bothering me.'

Those were the last words we had. I re-locked my door and eventually fell asleep again, and at about half-past six I heard her car start up outside. When I went to shave and looked at myself in the mirror, I saw I had a couple of scratches down one temple, and straight away I began to think of a way of explaining them to the lads.

SIX

As at the start of any operation, the guys were tense and quiet, exchanging the odd bit of chit-chat while we waited for the off, but thinking all the time of what lay ahead and wondering what they might have failed to pack.

Whinger was dragging on one of his filthy, home-rolled fags. He'd had an amazing haircut that left his head covered with short, tow-coloured fuzz and made him look like a coconut. To everyone's amazement Norm had shaved off his moustache, on the grounds that a Mexican appearance might not do him much good if the Libyans caught him. ('You never know,' said Tony, who'd picked up the vibes of the team very quickly, 'it may loosen his tongue. By the time we make it into the desert he'll be talking his head off.') Stew, also, had had a fancy haircut – a flat-top job, in imitation of Tony – and was taking stick from everyone about his girlfriend.

'Managed to slip her a length, did you?' sneered Whinger.

'Bollocks, mate.'

'You mean she wouldn't have it? Must be your technique that's at fault. Puts the wind up her something chronic.'

'Take her by surprise,' said Norm – and I thought, By God, Tony's right!

'Belay her to the bed-head,' I suggested. 'Then she wouldn't have much option.'

105

Poor Stew had gone red as a beetroot, and I lifted my chin at Whinger to say, 'Hey, leave him alone.' As for me, I kept thinking uneasily of my best-of-three-falls with Karen, and hoping she wouldn't try to take it out on me while I was away. But to have mentioned that episode to the lads would have made my life not worth living, so I kept mum.

Now it was operational details that mattered. I'd already made one last check to ensure that everyone was properly sterilised – that is, not carrying anything, however insignificant, which might betray our origins if any of us was killed or captured. One box of matches, a chocolate-bar wrapper, a bank note or coin, an envelope, a label on a shirt-collar or the tongue of a boot – any of these would be enough to give us away. In keeping with Regimental practice, preparation had been left to individuals, and nobody had done anything so old-fashioned as line the team up for inspection: I'd just asked everyone to make doubly sure he was clean.

As for me, I made yet another mental check of my possessions: AK-47, spare magazines, Browning, spare mags, Semtex, detonators, det cord, clackers, Magellan, covert radio, torch, spare batteries, camera, binos, Commando knife, PNGs, ski goggles, medical kit, water-bottles, food, extra fuel, cam-net, poles, shovel, sand-bags, shamag. My only personal item was a tiny silver St Christopher, given me by Tracy, which I wore on a chain round my neck. Seeing it one evening in the shower, Tony had suggested I'd do well to leave it behind; but I pointed out that no Arab would know what it was, except some kind of good-luck charm, and therefore it wasn't a risk. By then I was really attached to the little figure, which seemed to have protected me in Colombia, and with things being how they were I wanted to preserve any possible connection with Tracy and Tim.

Our departure from Hereford was by no means routine. Except for a few small items in day-sacks, all our kit, including weapons and ammunition, was packed and strapped down on to the quads or in the trailer, and we didn't intend to touch it again until we were over Libya, about to come out of the chopper and start driving towards our target. We were wearing desert DPM fatigues with Parachute Regiment berets, so that as we staged through Cyprus we could pass as umpires taking part in Exercise Bright Star; but we carried no money, no passports, and no means of identification. Our desert clothes had been packed up in one large bundle, and we planned to change into them once we'd taken off from Akrotiri on the last leg of the flight. We all had shamags to wrap around our heads, and our shirts and trousers were the kind of cheap cotton, drab olive or grey or brown, that low-grade Arabs wear to work.

An intelligence update during the past few hours had reduced our window of opportunity to a dangerously narrow span. Some bright int guy had belatedly realised that the Arab weekend consists of Thursday and Friday, rather than Friday and Saturday as our briefing had laid down. This meant that our target might well leave the camp on Wednesday afternoon or evening. Since we weren't going to reach our location until very late on Monday night we'd have only Tuesday night on which to get him.

We'd just taken this news aboard when yet another update came in, emanating from the sleeper-agent within Ajdabiya itself. This last message said that al-Khadduri had a very important visitor coming to see him for secret discussions on Thursday morning, so that he'd definitely be around on the Wednesday night. That evened the score a bit – it gave us two possible chances – but the tightening of our schedule naturally made my adrenalin flow all the faster. And of course, the sooner we got through our business in the desert, the sooner I'd be back to sort out the mess at home.

The quads went on ahead by four-tonner, and a minibus collected us at 1530. For me, leaving camp seemed like an echo of the recurrent dream in which my left arm kept getting caught and dragged backwards; although I was departing in the general direction of North Africa, part of my mind was stuck fast in Hereford, anchored there by the fact that Tim and Tracy were in enemy hands. As we drove off eastwards, I felt as if the knowledge was tearing me apart.

At RAF Lyneham, Hercs were lumbering off the runway every few minutes, and a whole line of them was drawn up on the pan, but one aircraft stood apart from the rest in a distant corner of the field. We drove straight out to it, and found that our bikes had already been loaded. The trailer had been backed in first, and the quads had been strapped down to rings in the steel deck, facing the tail-gate in a zig-zag line so that we could ride them straight out when the time came.

The flight crew greeted us like old pals. Pineapple Pete was his imperturbable self, and Alf the head loadie – a huge guy with arms covered in tattoos – gave me a run-down of all the units taking part in the exercise.

'You lot are never part of it,' he said teasingly.

'Of course we are. Can't miss out on the chance of getting ourselves some decent suntans.'

Although Alf didn't say any more he winked, and I saw that he knew we were up to some special villainy.

In spite of the high level of activity everyone seemed relaxed and happy. Our take-off was scheduled for 1830, and at 1810, as Pete and his co-pilot walked out, I fell in with them.

'Once we're airborne you're welcome up front any time,' Pete said. 'Make yourself at home.'

I thanked him and climbed into the back, where the

lads hadn't waited for any invitation but had been busy slinging para-silk hammocks from the cargo nets on the sides of the fuselage.

Soon the engines were turning and burning, but we could tell at once that something was wrong: one of the motors kept back-firing, and ran so rough that after a while the crew shut all four down. A few minutes later they tried again, but the result was the same: one explosion after another shook the aircraft. Eventually, after a second shut-down, word came over the intercom that we were to abandon ship.

'This fucker's no better than a heap of scrap metal,' said Pete contemptuously as he stood on the tarmac and kicked one of the aircraft's tyres. 'I'm not flying the bastard anywhere, least of all to the middle of bloody Egypt.'

To the consternation of the movements officer he demanded another Herc immediately – and so forcefully did he state the importance of our deployment that after only half an hour he got one taken off the main exercise rota and seconded to us. Naturally that left someone else in the shit, but it was no business of ours.

Then, of course, all the paperwork had to be re-done and the load transferred. Among our own guys there was a good deal of honking as they dismantled their sleeping accommodation and bundled it away – but after a delay of two hours we were at last airborne and on our way.

The noise in the back of a Herc – a high, ringing scream – is so punishing that talking requires a major effort. The result was that nobody bothered to make conversation. Anyone who wanted could pull on one of the head-sets dangling from the sides of the fuselage and listen in to the crew, but that soon palled and we generally preferred to get our heads down, aiming to doze or sleep the seven-hour flight away.

A couple of hours out I started worrying about our late take-off, because our timings on the following night were going to be critical. I suspected that after the long haul to Cyprus the crew would have to have a regulation break. Then there'd be a three-hour flight to Siwa, the Egyptian military base – and we needed to be there by early evening, so that we could do a quick transfer to the chopper and be on the ground within reach of our objective while there were still several hours of darkness ahead.

Sweating about it, I headed for the flight deck to ask the skipper what the drill was. Up there, everything seemed pleasantly relaxed; the atmosphere was less claustrophobic than in the back, the noise level much lower. With the plane on autopilot, Pete and his co-pilot sat chatting over their head-sets, and through the windshield a vast array of stars was visible above us, with the lights of some German town twinkling far below.

'Fear not,' said the skipper when I put my question to him. 'We can fly, and remain on duty, for up to sixteen hours at a stretch. If you want we could take you straight on to your destination with only an hour to refuel. It's up to you.'

'No, no,' I said. 'We're not that pushed. Let's stick to the schedule. I'd rather come into Siwa just on dark, in case there are eyes around the airfield. Christ knows what the security's like on Egyptian bases. As long as we're there by 2100, we'll be fine.'

'OK, then. Our ETA in Akrotiri is now 0330 Zulu. That's 0630 local. Siwa's an hour behind that. If you don't want to be there before dusk we won't need to take off until 2000 local. That'll put us into Siwa at about 2200, by which time it should be good and dark. That suit you?'

'Perfect.'

'In that case, I'll put in for a departure slot at 2000.'

He scribbled a note on his knee-pad.

Reassured, I went back, pulled on some ear-defenders and got my head down like everyone else. The next thing I knew, I heard the engine-note dropping as we began our descent into Akrotiri. After a landing smooth as silk, Pete taxied off to a secure area at one corner of the airfield and we stumbled out into a beautiful dawn. The sky was clear, the air warm but still fresh, with sharp, lemony scents all around.

'Who's for a peach?' said Whinger, giving an almighty yawn.

'Peach?' said Pat. 'What the fuck are you on about?'

'The beach, cunt.'

'To hell with the beach,' Tony told him. 'What about a shower and breakfast?'

Taking our day-sacks, we bussed across to the sergeants' mess, showered, and got ourselves big fry-ups. Then, and all day, we kept close together in a group, discouraging approaches and questions from outsiders. We were given basic accommodation – bare rooms with two bunks in each – and so spent most of the time in or around the mess. Everybody was eager to spruce up their tans, which the English spring had hardly got going, but by mid-morning the sun was seriously hot and I cautioned the guys about getting burnt. Not that they really needed any warning; because they'd all served abroad in hot countries, they knew that if they did go down with sunburn it would be their own fault and they could be put on a charge, just as if they'd got drunk or caught a dose of clap.

Even if we'd wanted to, we couldn't have left the base – partly for security reasons, but mainly because there was always a chance our departure time might be brought forward. So the lads screwed the nut on any idea of looking for amusement, and accepted that this was just a steady day.

We spent much of the morning going through our plans in an informal O-group, sitting on the concrete floor of an unfinished building which had a roof but no walls, so that plenty of air drifted across it. In particular we confirmed the six away-points, or emergency rendezvous – the points in the desert south of Ajdabiya we'd head for if we were forced to split up – which we'd already punched into our Magellan GPS sets. These were designated 'ERV One, ERV Two' and so on. They existed only in our minds, and there were no marks on any of our 1:50,000 maps, but those sets of figures could easily prove life-savers.

We also concentrated on correlating the latitude and longitude readings punched into the Magellans with the old-fashioned grid-system on the maps. The lat–long figures were more accurate, and there was always a chance that the batteries in the GPS sets would fail or that there'd be a shortage of satellites overhead at some critical moment. If either of those things happened, we'd be forced back on to the more primitive navigational system of grid-references and compasses.

Our Herc remained under guard where it had come to rest, and it attracted no attention because the field was dotted with similar planes, landing and taking off all day as they ferried personnel and stores southwards towards Egypt and the exercise. Soon after midday a bowser-truck went across to refuel ours, and when it was clear we walked back to the plane to break out the bundle of desert clothes; but we soon spewed out of the cargo bay cursing horrendously, because with its tail-gate closed the aircraft had heated up like an oven, the inside temperature had soared well into three figures – and we decided the job could wait until we were airborne that evening.

It was at lunchtime that we hit a problem. At the far end of the long mess hall Stew spotted someone he'd known pretty well in his parent regiment, the Cheshires. We realised that they must be acting as marshals on the base for the duration of the exercise, and that this created a serious risk that somebody would recognise him and start asking questions – potentially a major disaster, and a prospect which haunted all members of the SAS on covert operations. All Stew could do was slip away as soon as he'd finished his meal and lie low in the room he'd been allocated until it was time to leave.

For the rest of us, the best feature of the sergeants' mess was the supply of fresh oranges. We reckoned they must have come straight off the trees on the island, because they tasted a hundred times sweeter and fresher than any orange we'd had before. A great big basket of them stood at the end of the counter, and after Pat had eaten four, straight down, I said to him, 'Watch it, mate, or you'll have the runs.'

'Last vitamin C for a week,' he retorted as he put away yet another – and we all pouched a couple to eat during the next leg of the journey.

This time our departure ran smoothly, and within a minute or two of take-off we were heading south-east over the Mediterranean. As soon as we were in level flight we sorted out our civilian clothes and changed into them, bundling up our DPMs for return to Cyprus. Our desert gear smelled musty and unfamiliar – Christ alone knew who had worn the stuff last. Whinger yelled that his shirt stank like an Arab's jock-strap, and Stew shouted back, 'It'll stink of you soon enough.' My own shirt wasn't much better, and I shook myself around inside the drab, buff material to get the feel of it. The shirt, a pair of sand-coloured trousers and a thin grey jersey were all I reckoned I'd need.

Our makeshift hammocks had remained in place, so

we climbed back into them and lay there in the dim light, ear-defenders in place, each thinking his own thoughts. Mine were of Tim and Tracy – and in particular the boy's paintings I'd found in the desk at home. There was one I remembered in detail: a tank blowing up, with a brilliant, jagged flash of flame all round it and some spiky wrecks of shattered trees in the background. Where could a kid of four have picked up such violent images? Only from the TV, or maybe from listening to me talk about the Gulf. I wished he'd get interested in nature and try drawing the things like squirrels and rabbits that he saw every day. Perhaps when he was older.

And right now? I had a sudden, horrible thought that his captors would be trying to indoctrinate him against me, teaching him foul language and filthy ideas. I remembered how kids his age in Belfast shout 'Fucking pigs!' whenever they see a Brit soldier come past, and hoped to hell that the PIRA wouldn't have time to corrupt Tim's mind in that way.

After a while, unable to relax let alone sleep, I went up on the flight deck, and I was there when we crossed the Egyptian coast. Far off to our left a spread of lights was twinkling hazily in the dusk.

'Alexandria,' said the skipper.

Beneath the nose the odd cluster of lights marked smaller towns along the shore, and the occasional flares we saw were from oil wells burning off gas; but beyond them, inland, the desert stretched away black as night, with nothing to break its monotony. At this point our target lay about eight hundred kilometres away to the east. Pity we can't just fly across and drop a bomb on the bastard, I thought – and I was on the point of saying as much to Pete when I remembered that he knew nothing of our operation, and had been too professional to make the smallest enquiry about what we were up to.

So for the time being I returned to my hammock, but half an hour later Pete called me back to the flight deck to say he'd been in touch with an RAF liaison officer in the control tower at Siwa.

'Your Chinook's ready for you,' he said. 'God knows where it's come from, but it's parked on a pan near the western perimeter of the airfield. As soon as we hit the deck they're going to send out a vehicle to lead us to it.'

'That's excellent. Will there be other Hercs on the field?'

'Absolutely. It's just like Akrotiri. The place is heaving with them – all part of Bright Star.'

'That's what the chopper's been on too,' I said. 'Officially it's gone tits-up and been retired sick from the exercise for a few days.'

Full darkness had fallen by the time we began our descent. The loadies helped us unshackle the quads and get ourselves organised. Without head-sets on it was impossible to hear spoken orders, so Big Alf, who was listening in to the flight deck, resorted to his usual system of hand-signals as we were coming in.

At five minutes to touch-down he gave us five fingers outspread, then three two minutes later. With two minutes to go we started our engines and sat there with the quads ticking over, ski goggles on in case grit flew about when we landed. With all the noise it was hard to tell if the individual engines were still running, so I reached down with my right hand to feel my exhaust. Exhaust fumes began to fill the hold, but before they built up to a serious level we were getting one finger. I realised I needed a piss, but told myself it would have to wait.

The top half of the tail-gate rose slowly, letting in a rush of warm, fresh air, and with it an even fiercer engine scream. Through the rectangular opening we could see lights shining from latticed towers and

115

vehicles moving. Then, with a thump, the plane was on the deck and rolling.

The bottom half of the tail-gate began to go down while we were still taxiing. The Herc made a couple of turns, left and right – I guessed it was following a lead vehicle – and we had barely come to a standstill before Alf was waving us off. First down the ramp was Tony, and the rest of us followed swiftly in single file, Stew and his trailer bringing up the rear.

Outside, the first thing that hit me was the smell of an African settlement, the inevitable stink of heat and drains and dust hanging in the hot night air. The Chinook was within fifty metres of us, tail-gate down, rotors whirling. In seconds all six quads were at the bottom of the ramp, and we leapt off to manhandle the trailer backwards up the slope – first on, last off. Then, one after another, with Stew leading, we reversed into the belly of the chopper and parked in another zig-zag alongside the big, black rubber sausage of an extra fuel tank.

Our new head loadie was sitting in the hatchway of the partition that separates the hold from the flight-deck. He twisted round to get a look at us, and the moment I gave him the thumbs-up he hit the button to raise the ramp. He also passed word to the pilot, who immediately revved up his engines, put on pitch and lifted away.

The transfer couldn't have been accomplished any faster. I didn't believe that anyone could have seen us, but even so for the first few minutes the captain headed due south, to confuse anyone who might be watching, and made sure that he was out of sight before he swung on to an easterly heading. When I waved at the cockpit to indicate that I wanted to make contact, the head loadie pointed to a head-set, which I plugged into a socket on the wall.

I had to think for a moment who our new skipper was. Then I remembered him and his crew coming to Hereford. Of course: it was Steve Tanner, another Geordie, a small, dark fellow with sticking-out ears.

'Evening, Steve,' I went. 'Geordie Sharp here.'

'Hi, Geordie,' came the reassuring voice. 'Good to have you aboard. We've crossed the border already. Welcome to sunny Libya.'

'Great! That was a neat pick-up.'

'Not too bad.'

'What's our flight time?'

'We're estimating one hour fifty. There's no wind to speak of, so you should be on your location just after midnight.'

'That'll do well. Can we just make sure we're all agreed about where we're going?'

We spent a few minutes double-checking not only that night's destination, but also the precise location of ERV Six, the spot in the desert from which the Chinook would recover us once the operation had gone down. There seemed to be no problem: the figures tallied, and I was able to relax for the time being. All the same, I stood for a while, peering out of a porthole. The night was clear, the moonlight bright. I knew that the crew's PNGs must be giving them an excellent view ahead – and they needed it, because they were skimming the desert at 150 m.p.h. and at no more than fifty feet, low enough to stay beneath any radar, and seemed confident that no obstructions lay in our path. Rather them than me.

'As far as we know there's nothing whatever between us and the MSR,' Steve said, 'and that's nearly an hour ahead. A hundred and thirty miles of f-all but sand.'

In the back the guys were sorting out their weapons and ammunition and re-lashing the remainder of their kit. I followed suit, loading one full magazine into my AK-47 and sliding four more into the pouches of my belt-kit. These final preparations didn't take up much time, and there was still an uncomfortably long wait ahead. My mouth felt dry, as it used to before football matches at school, so I ate one of my oranges to slake the thirst.

As we flew, Steve kept up an intermittent commentary over the intercom. 'Got a fire to our left,' he said suddenly. 'Looks like a bedouin encampment on our port front. We'll give that some space, I think.'

The heli took a violent heave to the right and climbed, then, a minute later, another to the left as we straightened back on to our true course. Presently Steve said, 'There's the MSR now. Not much moving on it. One set of lights heading north to starboard, and that's all . . . unless some mad bugger of an A-rab is driving without lights – which is quite possible.'

I felt the Chinook climb again, and imagined the thick red line on the map, which ran across our line of advance almost at right-angles. Then, as Steve banked right, I knew he was swinging north to keep away from three small settlements that lay either side of a kink in the road.

'That those villages on the MSR?' I asked.

'Clearing them now.'

A few minutes later he came on for the last time and in his best railway official's poncified tones announced, 'This is your next station stop. All passengers prepare to alight.' Then he reverted to his normal voice and said, 'When we're on the deck, Geordie, I'll wait for sixty seconds to make sure you're OK. Then, if you don't shout, assume there's no drama and we'll be off.'

'Roger,' I answered. 'That's fine.'

'Good luck, then. See you in a couple of days.'

'Thanks,' I said. 'Nice trip.'

Once more we settled ourselves on our quads. I ran over my equipment mentally, also feeling everything I could: AK-47 slung on my back, spare magazines in belt-kit, Browning in waist-holster, knife in sheath, water bottle on belt kit, ski goggles on forehead, PNGs round neck. I tugged at all the straps on my racks, fore and aft, to make sure they were secure. Looking round, I saw that everyone else was doing the same. Tony, who was behind me, gave a wink and a grin, sticking up his right thumb.

At the two-minute signal we started our engines, wound our shamags round our heads and settled ski goggles over our eyes. I switched my radio to the co-pilot's channel and said, 'OK, Gerry. I'll call if there's any problem. If I don't come on in sixty seconds flat, it'll mean we're OK.'

'Roger,' he answered.

At one minute, the Chinook started settling into a hover with the tail-gate descending. A blast of sand and grit came flying into our faces and there was a bump as the wheels touched; out of the corner of my right eye I saw the tail-gate loadie give me a raised thumb, and a second later I was rolling down the ramp.

Our plan was to fan out in an instant bomb-burst. I aimed forty-five degrees to the left through a storm of dust and sand. Tony did the same to the right, Pat at sixty degrees behind me, Whinger behind Tony, and Stew and Norm straight forward with the trailer to a position in the centre of our circle. In that mass of flying shit it was impossible to tell how far I'd gone, but when I reckoned I was seventy metres out I stopped, brought my rifle to the ready and sat facing outwards with the engine ticking over. Out there, I was clear of the dust-ball, but when I looked back, all I could see was a huge cloud seething and heaving in the moonlight.

If there'd been any sort of drama I'd have called the

co-pilot, put a couple of bursts in the direction of the trouble, and driven straight back up the ramp. But after a minute, when no SOS call came, Steve built his revs back to a peak and the aircraft lifted away. In a few seconds the heavy, thudding beat of its rotors had faded into the night, leaving us alone in the desert's tremendous silence.

There was sand beneath me – I could feel it shift under my toes – but it seemed quite firm, as if there was a hard bottom a couple of inches beneath the surface. That augured well for our run in. So did the three-quarter moon, which was on its way down. The air felt warm on my face, and out here, away from civilisation, it smelled completely clean.

My watch was reading eight minutes past midnight. I waited, watching the dust-cloud settle and disperse. Then I switched my radio back to our chatter channel and jabbed the pressel. 'Everyone all right?' I asked. 'Tony?'

'Yeah.'

'Pat?'

'Yep.'

'Whinger?'

'Yep.'

'Norm?'

'Aye.'

'Stew?'

'Fine.'

'OK. Check Magellans.'

I switched mine on and pressed the button for the light that illuminated the little screen. Stuck in its special holder above the handlebar panel the instrument was at easy reading height, but we still had to sit and wait for a satellite to come over the horizon and pass within range. Because the satellites are all in different orbits, they come past at irregular intervals: sometimes you have to wait half an hour, then get three in twenty minutes. We could have moved off right away, and I knew that the guys must be itching to go, but Tony had agreed that it was better to get an accurate fix before we started. With luck, the Chinook should have dropped us right on the spot, but if we were a bit off target we might be all to cock in our navigation.

Five minutes passed. Ten. 'Come on, you sonof-abitch,' Tony muttered over the radio. 'Shift your butt.'

I knew how he felt. We seemed to be very exposed, sitting there in the moonlight with the desert stretching away level all round and not a stitch of cover in sight. I tried to imagine the next satellite, zooming round the earth at 17,500 m.p.h., and smiled at the thought of it shifting its butt in response to Tony's exhortation. Then Whinger came on the net with, 'Oh, for fuck's sake. Let's get going.'

'Chill out,' I told him.

A moment later Tony said, 'There we go. That's number one. It's looking good. We just need two more for a triangle.'

The second and third satellites came up within a couple more minutes. 'OK,' I announced. 'We're on twenty-one East, twenty-four thirty-four. Twenty-eight North, fifty-nine twenty. Everyone agreed?'

Skipper Steve had done us proud. We were within a few yards of the drop-off point chosen in Hereford. Now all we had to do was follow our pre-set course to the location of our lying-up point, about sixty-five kilometres due north – and navigation was dead easy because the displays on our screens showed us if we were on track, or deviating to right or left.

'Right,' I said quietly, 'we've all got the ERVs, if anything happens. Pat, you do lead scout to start with. Go as fast as you can manage comfortably. Probably Stew and the trailer will set the limit at the back. The weight of the stores will make him the slowest – see how it goes. The rest keep in line ahead, at whatever interval we can see at. Try it out. Keep right in each other's tracks if you can. When we get nearer the target, we'll put pickets out.

'On this first leg there shouldn't be anything ahead of us for fifteen ks. Then there'll be a road across our front. After that, nothing till we come in sight of the high-ground feature. Skirt that right-handed, then start looking for the big wadi. Once we're through that it should be only half an hour to the area of the LUP. OK? Let's go.'

Pat led off, with me next and the others following. The combination of moonlight and PNGs gave a good view – I reckoned I could see some detail at nearly three hundred metres – but of course, in those conditions anyone on the move is at a big disadvantage versus anyone stationary. It's always movement that takes the eye, whereas men lying or kneeling on the deck can easily pass for stones . . . until it's too late. Thus we were all well aware that we could ride into an ambush at any moment.

All the same it was great to be moving, the warm air flowing past my face. Riding in second place I had a chance to relax and think while the lead scout carried the biggest load. He had to keep his eyes skinned for dips, hollows and rocks – to say nothing of possible nomad encampments or even Libyan army positions. It was also down to him to hold the right course and keep the speed up. All this put him under heavy stress, and I'd planned in advance to switch the lead every half hour.

Pat looked like a solid black blob bobbing on ahead of me. His wheels raised a small dust-cloud, which a breath of wind from the west was carrying off to our right. At first the going was good: the terrain was flat, with outcrops of rock here and there, and the quads ran easily over the firm sand. I'd taped over all the lights on my handlebar panel, but the needle of the speedometer was still visible, and from its angle I could see that we were maintaining a steady thirty k.p.h. Every now and then I pushed the light button on the Magellan to check our heading, and kept finding that Pat was spot-on.

We were running through shallow sand, and inevitably leaving tracks. Behind the trailer, which was last in line, we'd rigged up a primitive sweeper-rake – some hessian sacks lashed to a cross-bar – to obliterate our individual wheel-marks so that, even if the Libyans did spot the trail during daylight, they wouldn't be able to tell what sort of vehicles had made it. Even so, it would be easy enough for the pilot of a jet or helicopter to follow the trail and see where we'd gone. I just hoped that a strong wind would blast all our traces into eternity – or else that, in the immensity of the desert, nobody would fly over or come past until we had done our business.

Twenty minutes into our first run, Pat came up on the chatter net. 'Geordie, I'm stopping. There's something ahead of us. I can't make it out.'

'All stations stop,' I replied. 'Switch off and wait out. OK, Pat, I'm coming up to have a look.'

I cruised up beside him and shut down my engine. 'There,' he whispered, pointing ahead and to the right. 'Something black. I thought I saw it move.'

Peering through my PNGs I immediately spotted what he meant: a black shape, possibly two hundred metres off, with an irregular outline, its left side low and its right taller and pointed. It could have been two men close together, one kneeling or sitting, the other standing.

'Can't get it,' I murmured.

'It's the right-hand bit that I thought I saw move.'

I pushed the PNGs up on to my forehead and

123

brought out my binoculars, but the ambient light was so faint that they were no help. With the PNGs back on I watched again. It was quite eerie, sitting there in the great silence of the desert, the gentle puffs of wind coming in over our left shoulders and I felt myself getting jumpy.

'Chill out,' I said under my breath. 'You're doing fine.' I knew from past experience that when you're out at night, almost anything will move in the end – or seem to – if you watch it for long enough. Whether your eyes deceive your mind or vice versa I'm not sure, but if your nerves are on edge even rocks appear to take on a life of their own and start shifting stealthily about.

'Anyone back there make it out?' I asked over the net. 'Two o'clock to our line of advance.'

'Thorns,' said Whinger. 'Couple of thorn bushes.'

'You sure?'

'Reckon so. The right-hand one *is* moving. The top of it's blowing in the wind.'

'OK,' I said. 'I think you're right. We'll carry on. Head left, Pat, and give it some room. I'll cover you until we're past.'

I unslung my AK–47 and sat with it at the ready as Pat set off left-handed. Whinger had been right. The clump of thorns waved in the wind as we passed, and we left it to its own devices in the dark.

After another twenty minutes without incident I decided to bring Pat back. I knew he wouldn't want to give up lead scout – being mustard keen, he'd carry on all night if I let him – but I also knew that he'd inevitably get tired, and that the edge would go off his vigilance.

'Thin out,' I told him over the radio. 'Norm, move up front.'

'It's no sweat,' Pat called back. 'I'm fine here. D'you want me to go faster or something?'

'Not at all. You've done a great job. I just want everyone to rotate.'

'OK, then.' As he fell back past me and Norm went forward, I gave them both thumbs up.

Soon the sand seemed to grow deeper; I could feel it dragging at my wheels. The quad started to slew about, the steering grew heavier, and I needed more power to maintain speed. Then Stew, at the back, called to say that he was falling behind; the trailer wheels were digging in, and even on full power he was losing us.

'Ease off, Norm,' I instructed. 'Aim for twenty rather than thirty.'

'Aye, OK,' said Norm. 'I'm throttling back.'

'Good,' I went. 'See if you can hold that, Stew.'

I could feel my adrenalin flowing fast now. At all costs we had to be on target by first light, predicted to be at 0445; by then, we needed to have found a suitable lying-up point and to have built an OP. If we maintained our present speed we'd reach the area of the LUP inside another hour, and we'd be OK. But if we had to start winching our bikes up and down the walls of the wadi our speed of advance could drop from twenty k.p.h. to one, and we could well end up in the shit.

When we'd been running for an hour I called a refuelling halt. I couldn't tell how much petrol we'd used, but it obviously made sense to top up our tanks while nobody was harassing us; also, it took a few kilos off the load on the trailer. Two of the guys assumed defensive positions, twenty-five metres out on either side, while the rest of us tanked up, then two others took over from them while they came in and did the same. Although the desert seemed empty, we couldn't be sure that the Libyans weren't out on night exercises, that a patrol might have heard us coming.

Soon we were rolling again, with Whinger now in the lead, and after only ten minutes we seemed to begin

125

to emerge from the deep-sand belt, the bikes starting to move more easily. But then came a sudden call from the rear.

'Geordie,' said Norm, and from the way he said my name I knew there was something wrong.

'What is it?'

'I've dropped a bollock.'

'How?'

'My fucking Magellan.'

'What's happened to it?'

'I've left it behind.'

'Don't be stupid.'

'I have.'

'Where?'

'At that halt.'

'Bloody hell! All stations stop!' A surge of alarm drove down into my guts. Again and again I'd harped on the importance of not shedding any item of kit, however trivial, in case it betrayed our origins and a Magellan, programmed up with our courses and way-points, was the worst possible object to leave lying in the desert. Norm was usually the most careful member of the whole team. 'What the hell were you doing, taking it off the bike anyway?' I asked.

'I didn't want to risk splashing petrol on it, so I took it out of the holder and put it on the ground while we were gassing up.'

I felt exasperated – but Norm knew he'd screwed up, and I saw no point in mouthing off at him. So I just said, 'You'll have to go back. There's no alternative. We can't risk leaving it. D'you think you can find the place?'

'Dunno. Have to try. How long is it since we restarted?'

'Eight minutes,' said Stew. 'We were rolling for eight minutes exactly.'

'Time yourself back,' I told Norm. 'You should be able to see the marks where we did the refuelling. Whinger, go with him. The rest of us will wait for you here. And take it easy – we're still all right for time.'

So we were, but not by much.

Two of us sat in a hollow, with the other two posted out on either flank. It was reassuring to find that the noise of the quads' engines died away quickly into the night, but tension built up as the minutes ticked by. Feeling restless, I got off my bike and walked away to have a piss.

'Stupid cunt!' Stew muttered as I came back, voicing the anxiety that all of us were feeling.

'Easily done,' I said. 'You might drop the next bollock, Stew. Give him a break.'

Presently in my ear-piece I heard Norm say, 'Back on site.' Then, a moment later, he exclaimed, 'Got the fucker!' and everyone relaxed.

With the party reunited, we rolled forward again to the north until, from in front, Whinger called, 'Stopping, stopping. There's an obstruction ahead.'

'OK,' I answered. 'I'm closing on you. Everyone else, wait out.'

I cruised up beside him.

'See it?' he said quietly. 'Like a wall.'

'It's the road, but it's on an embankment. In the desert they're often built like that, to stop sand drifting over them.'

'Yeah, but there's something this side of it.'

'Wait one.' I reached forward to the top flap of my bergen and undid the straps, feeling for my binoculars. The 10 x 50 lenses, bloomed for light-gathering, instantly revealed the nature of the problem.

'Shit and derision!' I cried. 'It's a fucking pipeline! Two-deck, each pipe about a metre diameter. There's no way we can ride over that.'

127

'How in hell didn't that figure on the briefing?' said Tony. 'Didn't the CIA guy mention it?'

'Not a dicky-bird.'

'Jesus Christ!'

'Let's blow the shit out of it,' said Whinger. 'Make a passage.'

'Brilliant!' I told him. 'And attract every son of the Prophet in Libya straight on to us. They'd send out all choppers in the country to sweep up and down until they found out what happened. No thanks. There's only one thing for it. Scout right and left. There must be a culvert under it somewhere for herdsmen to walk through. Tony, you and Pat go right. Norm, you and Whinger left. Move up a bit closer to it first, then keep heading along parallel with the road till you find an underpass. Stew and I'll hold here until one of you calls.'

The two pairs went off, disappearing into the dark like black dots. Nearly ten minutes had passed – ten minutes of steadily increasing tension – before Tony came back on the air.

'OK, guys. Head right. We've found a tunnel.'

'Roger,' I answered. 'We're coming. Norm, did you get that?'

'Aye. I'll close on you. No luck this way.'

We found Tony and Pat on their feet, wielding their short-handled shovels like lunatics. They'd discovered a culvert, but sand had drifted into the mouth of it and left only eighteen inches of headroom. At first glance the task of clearing a passage looked colossal; but, as Tony had appreciated, the drift tapered off rapidly inside the tunnel, and we only had to lower the first few feet.

Again we lost ten minutes, at the end of which we were all sweating like pigs. When we moved off again the wind felt icy as it cooled the moisture on our bodies. Now we really were up against the clock. It was 0315, and I reckoned we had ninety minutes at most before dawn broke. In that time we had to cross the wadi, find a site for an LUP, ditto for an OP, build the OP and settle down out of sight. I was needled by the multiple uncertainties ahead. The distance we had to travel was relatively small, probably not more than ten kilometres. What mattered was the nature of the terrain ahead. What would we find in the area of the OP? Would we get a good enough view of the camp? Were the Libyans in the habit of coming out into this part of the desert?

Once more we made good progress, and soon Norm called back to say that he could see the feature hill.

'I have Mont Blanc on my left front, where it should be,' he reported. 'It's quite impressive in the moonlight. Steep sides, crags on top. Reminds me of Stirling Castle.'

For Norm that was an epic, the speech of a lifetime. Boy, I thought, the desert must be really turning him on.

Having given the hill a wide berth we got back on to our northerly heading and pressed ahead, now with Tony in the lead. The ground became more and more stony, until we were jolting around over loose shale. In one way I was pleased – on this surface we would leave no tracks at all – but on another level I began to worry: if the terrain was like this close to the camp, we'd be screwed when it came to building our OP, and we might find ourselves in another Iraq-type fiasco.

The desert started to undulate, with small, dry valleys running north-east to south-west across our line of advance. I guessed they were tributaries of the main wadi ahead – and sure enough, Tony presently called back to say that he could see the valley ahead of him.

There we got our first lucky break. It was obvious that over the centuries winter torrents had cut a deep scar through the desert, and in many places the walls of the trench took the form of rocky cliffs, perhaps twenty feet high. But at the point where we arrived the bank had collapsed into a broad tongue of shingle, and, far from having to resort to ropes and winches, we were able to ride straight down it, leaving no trace. Boulders dotted the floor of the dry watercourse, and we wove our way between them easily enough for maybe one kilometre until another sloping bank took us out the far side.

That simple passage boosted morale and put us nearly back on schedule. By 0330 the moon was low on the horizon to our left, but by then I reckoned we were within five or six kilometres of the location for the LUP as one by one the surrounding features fell into place. First we ran off the shale and back on to sand. Then we saw the ground ahead of us rising in dunes.

I called Tony to a halt and put pickets out to ride level with him, right and left.

Less than a minute later Whinger, who was out on the right, called, 'Eh, Geordie. I'm on a road.'

'A road? You can't be.'

'I fucking am. It's brand-new. Just been bulldozed out.'

'Stand by. I'm coming up.'

Whinger was right, of course. I found him parked on a dark-looking strip of track, with the sand scraped off into ridges on either side. The underlying rock felt pretty rough, but it was easily negotiable by vehicles with reasonable clearance.

'This wasn't on the satellite shots,' I said. 'They must have been working on it in the past few days.'

'It's coming down from the north-east,' said Whinger, checking his compass. 'Remember that track the satellite showed, leading out from the camp towards the range? I reckon this is an extension of it.'

'Looks like it. What a bugger!' I sat still for a

moment, considering this new development. It meant that, if things went noisy, the Libyans would in theory be able to drive out behind our temporary positions and cut off our retreat.

'I don't like it,' I told Whinger. 'But we can't stop now.'

By ranging up and down, we found a point where sand gave over to rock and no new banks had been heaped up, and we all crossed the line of the track there, in single file, leaving no trace of our passage. But the mere existence of the road made me uneasy.

On we went, slowly now, into the dune-scape, circling the bases of the hillocks. The sand here was very soft, so that although we were leaving wheel-marks they more or less filled themselves in behind us. Then Norm, who was scouting left, called, 'Watch yourselves, lads. I can smell smoke.'

'Everyone stop,' I went. 'What is it, Norm?'

'It smells oily, like diesel burning. Coming on the wind.'

'Probably some goatherds camping out,' I said. 'They'll be burning old oil in a drum. Can you see anything?'

'Nothing.'

'Pull off, then. Come back this way. Feel your right, everyone. We're going round it.' So we made a detour, and slowly came back on to our heading.

The incident had done nothing to reassure me. I didn't like the idea there were other people besides us out there in the desert.

Soon afterwards Whinger, who was still on the right, went up on to a rise and suddenly called, 'Geordie! Lights ahead.'

I rode over and came up behind him. There was no need for him to point this time. The first thing I noticed, high in the air, was a single bright-red glare,

131

then below it I saw lights burning faintly across our front, some in a line, others in clusters beyond them.

'Got it!' I said. 'That red thing must be the warning light on the comms tower.'

'I reckon so.'

'How far out are we?'

'Hard to tell. Could be one kilometre.'

'We're close enough, anyway. I'd like to put more ground between us and those bastards behind us, whoever they are. But we can't go any nearer the camp than this. Got to find an LUP site around here. That row of lights must be the perimeter fence, with other installations beyond.'

Everyone went lookabout, and within a few minutes Pat called to say he had located a good spot, away to our left. Closing on him, we found him in a gully, with sand underfoot and a vertical rock wall about three metres high along one side. There were fissures in the rock, into which we could drive pegs, and the whole area had a fairly rough texture. I saw straightaway, as he had, that if we parked the bikes nose-to-tail along the wall, and slung cam-nets over them at an angle like a sloping roof, it would make as good a hiding-place as we were likely to find.

The time was 0355, and already I thought I could detect a faint lightening in the eastern sky. We rolled the trailer in backwards, hitched it to Stew's bike again, and manoeuvred the rest of the quads into line ahead of it, ready for a quick take-off. Then we broke out the gear for the OP and prepared to move forward on foot.

'Final check,' I said quietly when I'd gathered the guys round. 'Me and Tony will spend the day in the OP. Depending on what we find, we may decide that the op should go down tomorrow night. If there's any problem, we may have to wait until the night after. Either way, we'll want the support party forward soon after dark tomorrow.'

'Tonight,' Tony interrupted.

'As you were. Tonight. I'm talking about tonight, Tuesday. For Christ's sake – I'm losing track of the days. Cancel all that.'

I pressed the light button on my watch for a check.

'It's now 0400 on Tuesday. If possible, the op will go down tonight. If everything looks OK, we'll call the three of you forward once it's dark.' I jabbed a finger at Pat, Whinger and Norm. 'Stew, you'll be our back-marker. Hold the fort here. OK?'

'Sure.'

'Whinger, get a sitrep back to the Kremlin as soon as you've got an aerial sorted. Tell them we have eyes on the target area and everything's hunky-dory. And *everybody*, go easy on the water. It's going to get hot as hell when the sun rises, and we don't know how long we're going to be here. OK, all?'

Getting no answer except a couple of grunts, I said, 'Right – we're off. Pat and Norm, you help us carry the stuff forward for the OP. Then back here. Let's go.'

We settled our bergens and rifles on our backs, slung the other bundles about us, and began to move off.

'Give 'em hell,' said Whinger.

'I'll wait till you're in the front line with us,' I told him. 'Then you personally can stand up on top of a dune and fire the first shot to start the battle.'

SEVEN

On the side of a dune facing the camp we found a hollow fronted by a couple of scrubby thorns. By cutting a few more bushes elsewhere and bringing them across to reinforce the natural thicket, we made a small enclosure. At the same time we deepened the hollow by digging, and used bags filled with sand to make walls inside the thorns.

A rectangular gap left in the front wall gave us a view forward into the camp, and a cam-net stretched across the top, with more thorn branches scattered on it, completed the basis of our hide. The dune gave us natural protection from the rear, its disadvantage being that we couldn't see anyone coming from that direction. We reckoned, though, that the little hill was in direct line-of-sight from the LUP, so that the back-up party could watch our rear for us.

We'd almost finished building when a sudden noise from the direction of the camp made us freeze. The first blast of it — a kind of screeching groan — lasted such a short time and cut off so abruptly, almost like a dog's bark, that we couldn't make out what had caused it.

'Jesus!' exclaimed Pat. 'What the fuck was that?'

Before anyone could answer the sound came again. This time it kept going for several seconds, and Tony let out a gasp, half relief, half amusement.

'Not Jesus,' he said. 'Allah. It's the *muezzin*, giving the first call to prayer.'

We were at least two hundred metres from the perimeter wire, and the sound was coming from somewhere beyond it; yet the volume of the amplified voice was such that it blasted past us like a gale of wind, and we felt sure the guys in the LUP, a kilometre behind us, must be hearing it too. So it proved: they told us later that the grating, metallic, undulating chant of '*Allah akhbar! Allah akhbar!*' carried way past them and on into the desert to the south.

'Sounds like he's underwater, poor bugger,' said Pat.

'That's just their crummy electronics,' Tony told him. 'The old mullah'll be up a tower someplace. We'll see the mosque as soon as it gets light.'

'Come on, guys,' I interrupted. 'Don't piss about. Never mind the mullah. We need to get tidied up here.'

In the eastern sky the dawn glow was coming up fast. It would have been good to carry on working and perfect our camouflage, but time had run out. From previous stints near the equator I knew how quickly the light would strengthen as the sun rose. The Libyans might have eyes on the desert, and I wasn't going to risk any movement after dawn.

'Away you go,' I told Pat and Stew. 'You don't want to be caught with your pants down.'

'Right then. Good luck.'

'Same to you. We'll see you tonight.'

Off they went, walking backwards round the side of the dune and whisking away their tracks with strips of hessian. A few minutes later they called on the radio to say that they were back in the LUP, and that they had eyes on the back of our mound.

Tony and I settled down for a day of observation. For me, breakfast consisted of cold spaghetti in tomato sauce, washed down by a brew of powdered lemonade. Tony had his favourite corned beef hash and pineapple slices, eaten together. We'd been planning to work

135

alternate shifts – two hours on, two off – but found that, despite the fact that we'd had practically no sleep, neither of us felt tired. Our excitement supercharged us, and we both watched eagerly as dawn revealed the secrets of our objective.

The perimeter fence was just as the CIA man had described it: three metres of weldmesh, topped by an outward-sloping overhang of barbed wire. Every hundred metres there was a floodlight atop a slender pole, but several of the bulbs were out of action, and useful pools of darkness lay between the illuminated stretches. The goon-towers – built into the fences several hundred metres apart – might have been run up for a film about some German prison camp in World War Two: primitive wooden boxes on stilts, once painted white but now peeling, with wide-eaved flat roofs to give shade and the sides open to the air. There was one at the corner of the wire, slightly to our left, and another in the middle of the south fence to our right. This second tower stood beside a wide gate, also made of mesh, and the rough track Gus had indicated ran away from it towards the range in the south-east.

The important thing for us was our discovery that the towers weren't manned. Nor was there any patrol on the wire. With our binoculars we scanned every tower for signs of infra-red lamps or microwave dishes or TV cameras, but saw nothing; the whole system looked too primitive for any such high-tech devices.

'As the guy told us,' I said, 'they're not expecting any threat coming out of the sand.'

We'd positioned ourselves opposite the office cum accommodation block, and our binos gave us a brilliant view of it: a scruffy, off-white building, two storeys tall, with patches of discoloration staining its walls, air-conditioning units under every window, and long, dirty, tapering streaks beneath them where condensation had been dripping down over the years. The front entrance was in the middle of the wall facing us, a flight of five or six semi-circular steps leading up to its plain porch.

The door we became more interested in was at the side, to the left as we looked. Soon after six o'clock it opened from the inside, and some kind of *jingli*, or servant, began going in and out. The guy, who was quite old and had frizzy grey hair, wore a khaki shirt and trousers, but no shoes.

'Could be our best entry point,' said Tony quietly. 'Out of sight of most of the camp. Besides, the perimeter light opposite it is down.'

'Just thinking that. The tradesman's entrance.'

The window of the room in which our target was supposed to work was at the top left of the building. When we had arrived on site the room had been dark – but that was hardly surprising, as it was already four o'clock by then.

As the light strengthened the perimeter lights went out, but the single red lamp on the comms tower continued to glow. Then, at about six-thirty, the sun came over the eastern horizon and low rays blazed across the camp from our right. From the scribbled notes and plans I'd made during our brief in London, I soon identified the compound's main features: the approach road coming in from the north, the guard-room, the headquarter block, the tall mast marking the comms centre, the armoury, wired off in its own secure enclosure inside the perimeter, the fuel station, down near the wire to our right, and the mosque, gleaming white, with an onion dome and huge loud-speakers sprouting from the corners of a balcony round its tower. Far off to the right, in a little compound of its own, we could see the comms facility that Gus had given us as a secondary target. The white dish aerial was pointing nearly straight up.

'That damn thing's farther off than he reckoned,' I said.

'What did he tell you?' Tony asked.

'He said two-fifty metres from the wire. It's got to be three-fifty at least. It's still in range, but not by much. Anyway, it's non-essential. We'll see what happens when the time's ripe.'

As the camp came slowly to life, Tony's earlier tour in Abu Dhabi proved invaluable, because he was able to interpret all the small events we witnessed. Apart from the *jingli*, the earliest arrivals on the scene were bread and milk vans, which pulled up by the guardroom on the far side from us and then, after long delays, drove in to various buildings which were obviously messes.

'What's all the fuss on the barrier about?' I asked.

'Typical,' Tony replied. 'The guys on duty have to assert themselves somehow and show they're superior to the ignorant drivers. So they give them a hard time, even though they see them every day. You watch in a minute, when the rank and file arrive. But, Jesus . . . look at this.'

'What is it?'

'See that long building with the green roof? Look right over the top of it.'

'Got it. Rotor blades.'

'Yep. There's a goddamn chopper parked there.'

'Let's hope it's gone u/s. We don't want that bloody thing overhead.'

Soon after seven o'clock, a stream of ordinary cars and land cruisers began rolling down the approach road and on to a big car park outside the wire. By then a man with a mill-board was scuttling about, trying to reserve the spaces nearest the fence, and evidently taking flak from the drivers he chased away.

'See that?' said Tony. 'The bastards are so idle they won't walk a step if they don't have to.'

138

'Why don't they drive in, though?'

'Against the rules. Bad security. Nobody trusts anybody. I mean, any of these guys might have a bomb in his vehicle and park it next to the headquarter block. One of them might try to top the colonel.'

Within twenty minutes some sort of physical training was taking place. A long straggle of men in shorts and trainers came trotting round the track inside the perimeter, with one instructor leading and another trying in vain to drive on the laggards at the back. The front dozen or so were actually running, but everyone else was walking. A few of the guys were mock-fighting, hitting out and kicking at each other, but most of them were simply chit-chatting as they ambled along.

'What tossers!' I cried. 'What a fucking shower!'

'They are,' Tony agreed. 'But if you quizzed any of them they'd swear they run a marathon every morning.'

At ten past eight, after that virtuoso display, the camp went dead as everyone disappeared indoors for showers and breakfast. By eight-thirty our active night had begun to tell on us. The sun, striking into the OP from our right, was already seriously hot, and, with no action to watch, we both felt tiredness attack.

'Get your head down while there's nothing happening,' I told Tony. 'If any action starts up I'll wake you.'

He shaped to argue but I more or less ordered him to sleep, and in a couple of minutes he was out, lying along our right-hand wall. Looking down at his dark Puerto Rican complexion, I thought that in an emergency he might pass for an Arab, especially at night.

When I squinted up at the sky through our roof of cam-net and thorns, I wished we'd been able to create something more solid in the way of a sun-shade. The best remedy was to tie my sweater horizontally to the underneath of the net, but even in the shade I could feel the sweat going out of me like steam, and I wanted to drink all the time. We'd each brought two belt-bottles full of water, and a gallon can as a back-up, and I knew we were going to need strict discipline to stop us running out.

At nine-twenty people started drifting on to the drill square, apparently for some sort of parade. *Jinglis* carried out armchairs and set them in position on a dais under a pointed wooden roof, and various slovenly-looking characters drifted about.

I was just thinking there was no point in waking Tony until the show began, when suddenly I saw something that grabbed my attention. Out of the front door of the accommodation block came four armed men, obviously guards, who formed up, two either side of the entrance. A moment later a big, heavy fellow in white drill shirt and trousers appeared, carrying a peaked cap in his hand. If he'd had the hat on his head I might not have recognised him. As it was, I gave Tony a kick and cried, 'Eh! Eh! Eh! Look at this!'

He was up beside me in a second, binos glued to his eyes. 'Shitface!' he exclaimed.

'Christ!' I felt my heart pounding with a surge of adrenalin. 'If we had the sniper rifle we could drop him here and now without ever going through the wire.'

'Yeah – but the marathon runners would be out after us.'

'I don't think they'd catch us. But if they got the heli airborne, we'd be deep in the shit.'

We watched fascinated as Khadduri smirked to right and left, apparently making small talk to his bodyguards. Then he settled his cap on his head and set off along the front of the building, heading for the parade.

'Doesn't change, does he?' said Tony. 'Great sense of humour. Remember how he used to laugh when he was hitting you on the arm?'

'Will I forget it?'

Soon the parade had formed up, but we never had a clear view of it because a thick heat-haze had begun to shimmer and shudder above the ground. Through the fuzz we saw the officers take their places in the arm-chairs, with Khadduri in pole position at the right-hand end of the line. In front of them the rank and file sat on the deck in rows, cross-legged; and a tall man in white robes, who could only be the mullah, moved up and down the ranks bellowing into a microphone, his torrent of abuse outrageously magnified by the loudspeakers.

'What's he bollocking them for?' I asked.

'Anything he can think of – being late, not saying their prayers enough . . . Look how they're cringing.'

As the priest advanced on each man, shaking his fist and roaring insults, the guy would bow his head in submission until it touched the ground. It was like an amazingly hammy theatre show, and I was loving every minute of it, when a call on the radio jerked me back to the task in hand.

'Watch yourself, Geordie.' It was Pat.

'What's the problem?'

'Camels. There's a bloody great herd coming across behind you from the left. They're going to pass between you and us.'

'Is there anybody with them?'

'Can't tell yet. They're streamed out over hundreds of metres. We can't see the back of them.'

'What are they doing, running?'

'No, no – just grazing on. Stand by till we see the end of the line.'

I looked at Tony. He was pointing at his bergen, asking with his eyebrows if he should stuff everything into it. I shook my head and whispered, 'Not yet. This must be the lot we passed in the dark, when Whinger smelt that fire.'

141

If we got compromised, all we could do was to leg it back to the LUP, jump on the quads and scoot away into the desert, having called for immediate helicopter evacuation. But that would be a disaster – the end of the operation.

We waited a couple of minutes. I could feel sweat running down my backbone. Then Pat came up with, 'There are two herders, a man and a boy.'

'Have they got a dog?'

'Wait one . . . Yes. There's one dog, like a big grey lurcher.'

'Shit! How close behind us are they going to pass?'

'Maybe two hundred metres.'

'Keep us informed if they start coming any closer.'

'Roger.'

As far as we could tell in our baking hollow, there was no wind at all – not a breath that would carry our scent behind us. Besides, five hours had passed since any of us had crossed the line on which the camels were advancing; I couldn't believe that any dog would pick up any traces from that burning sand.

Presently I heard a shout, then another, from alarmingly close quarters. Over the radio link I asked, 'Pat, for Christ's sake. What are they doing?'

'Chill out,' he replied calmly. 'The lead camels are passing you now. They're just wandering on. Now the leader of all's having the crap of its life. No bother. Sit tight.'

I found I'd unconsciously been holding my breath, so I let it out and inhaled deeply.

'Keeping on,' Pat continued. '*Allah karim*. Half-way across . . . Three-quarters. There must be two hundred altogether. The end of the column's level with you now. Look out, though. The dog's turning in your direction.'

'How far from us?'

142

'Still the two hundred metres. Stand by . . . No – it's OK. The dog's OK. He's only having a piss on a tuft of dead grass. That's all he's about. Now he's carrying on. Herders the same. One herder pissing . . . Now they're clear. They're squared away.'

'Thanks, Pat.'

'You're welcome. By the way, what's that godawful noise?'

'That's the local vicar clearing his throat, having a gargle.'

'Are his congregation bloody deaf or something?' .

'Yeah, I should say they are by now.'

The parade over, everything went dead again, both in the desert and in the camp. The camels vanished into the heat haze, and inside the wire, after their mass bollocking, the inmates dispersed to hangars or classrooms for their morning instruction. I tried to get my head down, but was bothered by the steadily rising temperature. 'What did they predict for us?' I asked fretfully. 'Wasn't it thirty-six? This feels more like fucking forty.'

All the same, I must have dropped off to sleep, because I came to with Tony shaking my elbow and found that two hours had passed.

'Anything doing?'

'The duty officer's been round – a jerk wearing a red sash and carrying a cane under his arm, sticking his nose in everywhere, throwing his weight about. And now they're lining up for the big event of the day, midday prayers.'

From all corners of the camp men were trudging towards the mosque. The wind had got up, blowing into our faces as we watched, and the heat seemed to have eased a fraction. I reckoned that hot air was rising off the desert floor behind us and drawing slightly cooler air down from the north, ultimately from the sea.

At any rate, the breeze had cleared some of the haze, and through our glasses we could see the faithful taking off their boots and socks, which they left neatly set out in a long line before they went in to pray.

'I always wonder how in hell they know whose are which,' said Tony. 'Look at that: three hundred pairs of goddamn boots in a line. Just imagine what a screw-up there'd be if we put a couple of bursts into the tower: they'd be fighting like lunatics to find the right pair.'

But before I could answer another terrible cacophony burst from the loudspeakers as the mullah launched into his chant of '*Allah akhbar! Allah akhbar!*', and the prayers were under way.

At 1230 the personnel fanned out from the mosque and disappeared indoors again, presumably for lunch, and the next we saw of them, an hour later, they were ready for the off, queuing at the guardroom for the duty officer to sign their exit chits.

'They all get searched when they go out,' Tony said. 'Nobody trusts anybody.'

'But what could they possibly nick?'

'Weapons, ammunition. Anything liftable.' Tony looked at his watch and added, 'Know what? This is the beginning of their weekend. They're on their way already.'

'What about Shitface? I hope he's not going to thin out as well.'

'He *is*, though. That's him in the white jeep. Don't worry. He'll be back for that special meeting tomorrow.'

The afternoon slowly dragged itself away. The heat hammered in on us, in spite of the wind, and tiny black biting flies hopped around the sand. We squashed dozens of them as they landed on our bare arms and necks, but every nip from the ones we missed left a red mark and started up an itch. We sweated and drank, sweated and drank, but so great was the rate of evaporation that neither of us wanted a piss all day.

During my stag Tony dropped off again with his shamag spread over his face, and I had a struggle to keep alert. Looking down at his peaceful form, I felt glad that he was with me, yet at the same time wondered if I'd boobed in making legal arrangements for him to become Tim's guardian. If both of us got written off now, my affairs would be in chaos.

At 1530 we heard another call to prayer, but this meeting was poorly attended compared with the morning effort, because most of the faithful had departed in that exodus after lunch. Aside from that there was practically no movement inside the camp, nothing to engage my interest. What kept me awake was the succession of disturbing thoughts that chased each other through my mind.

The idea of killing someone in cold blood isn't a pleasant one. It is true that I had a personal grudge against our target, for the way he had treated me and Tony, and for his callous, cynical attitude in general. Yet that alone didn't justify murdering him. To weight the scales against him I mentally threw in the fact that he was financing and supplying the IRA on a massive scale. It was his support – or, at any rate, the support of people like him – that had led indirectly to Kath's death and, now, to the kidnapping of Tim. The flow of money and weapons from overseas was what kept the IRA going.

And in any case, I told myself, this isn't a personal matter. The fact that I happen to have a personal involvement is coincidental. The operation is one that the Regiment has been tasked to carry out, and fate – or luck, or whatever it is – has decreed that I'm the guy in charge. That's all it is: a job to be done.

Trouble was, I had a far more difficult job to do back in the UK. Now we'd got as far as the OP, the topping of Khadduri seemed relatively simple. I felt sure that Tony and I would hack it, no bother. Infinitely more complex was the problem of recovering my family.

As I wrestled with this prospect, my mind kept harking back to the scheme I'd proposed to Pat – that a gang of our lads should take the law into our own hands, spring Farrell from police custody and hand him back to his mates in Belfast. Once again I heard Pat saying, 'You must be fucking *mad*!' and I realised the plan was probably quite unworkable. Nevertheless, I couldn't banish it from my head – and gradually, as the baking afternoon wore on, it evolved into a new version.

What if I kept the basic idea, but instead of trying to do something unilaterally, I brought the Regiment and the police on side, and got their backing? With the co-operation of the police we'd snatch Farrell while he was being moved between gaols, hold him in some safe house, tell the PIRA he was free, and exchange him for Tim and Tracy. But we'd arrange things so he could be immediately recaptured, possibly by putting a bug into his clothes or the heel of one of his shoes, and having a chopper airborne to follow whatever car he got into.

The scheme seemed so brilliant I felt quite lit up, and ceased to worry about the heat or the sand flies. But would the Regiment wear it? Impossible to say. In fact, I supposed, even if the head-shed agreed, authorisation for any such operation would have to come right from the top, from the Home Office, the Home Secretary or the Prime Minister. As in Operation Ostrich, permission would have to be completely unattributable, and deniable. Yet why shouldn't it be? Here I was, stewing deep inside Libya, about to murder a senior army officer with the direct connivance of the British

146

Government. If Whitehall sanctioned the elimination of dangerous foreigners, why should it baulk at a plan that merely ran rings round the IRA?

I was so chuffed with my idea that I wanted to discuss it with someone immediately. But it didn't seem fair to wake Tony, who was sleeping quietly. I could hardly start honking about the plan over the radio to Pat.

So for the time being I had to bottle it up inside me.

I was still on stag when Khadduri reappeared. It was after six, the sun hanging low over the desert, and the heat had at last started to abate. Tony was getting some food down his neck when I saw the clean, white land-cruiser hurrying down the approach road towards the main entrance. Instead of detaining it, as they had every other vehicle, the guards whipped up the barrier and saluted it past.

'Watch this,' I said. 'It looks like the VIP visitor. I thought the bastard was supposed to come tomorrow. Looks like he's a day early – or our intelligence was out.'

The jeep drove straight through the camp to our corner and pulled up outside the front door of the accommodation block. Out stepped Khadduri with one other guy, both went indoors, and the vehicle drove away.

The sight prompted me to a quick decision. 'Listen, Tony,' I said, 'we're going in tonight. There's nothing to be gained by waiting. Quite the reverse. He might clear off before tomorrow evening, after all. D'you agree?'

'Fine by me. Provided the bird stays on the nest.'

'Right, then.' I held in my pressel switch and called, 'You there, Whinger?'

'Roger. How you doing?'

'Fine. Onpass to head-shed that the bird's on the nest

147

and the operation can go down tonight. Get them to clear that, OK? And ask if there's any update from their end.'

'Roger. I'll call you presently.'

I imagined Whinger going through on the Satcom – a direct, one-to-one call to the comms centre in Hereford: 'Zero Alpha, Zero Alpha, this is Delta Four. Over.' At the other end I could see Yorky and Mac, and probably the CO, sitting round in the ops room while the duty signaller kept an eye on the set. 'This is Zero Alpha,' Mac would answer, 'go ahead.' Whereupon Whinger would pass on what I'd said and ask for permission to proceed. There'd be a slight delay after each person had spoken, but the voices would be crystal clear. There was no question of anyone eavesdropping on the exchanges because speech was automatically encrypted; the snag was that a satellite transmission created a much bigger electronic splash than high-frequency radio, and so was easier for a direction-finder to pick up. Exchanges were therefore kept as short as possible.

I also imagined the Prime Minister taking the closest possible interest in the operation. By my calculation the time in London was four o'clock, and probably the PM was in the House of Commons, fielding questions and giving stick to the Opposition. But at the back of his mind, I told myself, I bet he's thinking of us. I bet he's wondering how we're doing.

In the baking, sandy confines of the OP we waited for an answer, and presently Whinger came back on the air. 'OK,' he said, 'I've been through. I told the head-shed that two guys have eyeballed the bird, and that he's definitely on the nest. They just want to be sure you've seen enough and are confident about going in.'

'Tell 'em we're fine. No problem. We've seen everything we need to. We'll aim to go in at midnight, when the rest of the personnel have thinned out. If all goes according to plan, we'll want the chopper on ERV Six by 0200. Check that with them too. And ask if there's any news on the personal front, please.'

'Will do.'

Again we waited, and soon Whinger relayed confirmation through: no personal news, but the operation was on.

'In that case,' I said, 'we need you three guys up here by 2200. That'll give us plenty of time to brief you on details before we move up to the wire. Make sure Norm has his lock-picking kit. Bring both RPGs and the Dragunov. Don't forget – plenty of Semtex, and a can of fuel for a distraction charge.'

We saw them before we heard them: dark figures moving slowly towards us through the moonlight. When they were thirty metres off I said quietly over the radio, 'OK, lads, we have eyes on you. We're right in front.'

We stood up and let the three come to meet us. Then we led them round the front of the dune to give them a view of our objective.

'There's the building,' I began. 'And there's the lighted window. As in the script. The main entrance is the one facing us, but there's a back door round the corner to the left, in the shadow. Look at the fence. See where the first missing floodlight is? Up that side, fourth from the left-hand corner, more or less behind the building. We aim to cut the wire at that point, in that pool of darkness. Once we're through, Norm – you'll accompany me and Tony to the building, to pick the lock on that back door. When we go in, you'll stay in place to cover the door. All right?'

'Aye.' Norm nodded.

'Whinger, you stay on the fence to secure the gap.

You'll have the Dragunov as well as your AK-47. If any Libyan threatens our withdrawal, you can drop him from there with the sniper rifle. OK?

'Pat, I want you to range right-handed along the front fence.' I swung a hand across. 'Get down as far as the gate beside the tower there and get ready to crack off a distraction charge. If we can, we'll keep everything quiet. But if things go noisy, set a time-fuse and pull back this way. When the charge goes, put a rocket into the satellite dish where those red lights are showing. From the gate, the range should be about three-fifty metres. Is all that clear?'

'What if it doesn't go noisy?' Pat asked.

'We'll call you as soon as we're back through the wire. Once we're together again, you may still get a go at the dish. Then we'll tab off in orderly fashion to the OP. There we pick up our kit, leg it for the LUP, and away. Any more questions?'

'What if you can't find the target?' asked Whinger.

'We'll find him. We know the bastard's in the building. Ten to one he's sitting in that room right now. But if anything goes wrong we'll have to play it by ear. If he gets out of the building, by any mischance, one or other of you fence guys will probably have to drop him.'

The temptation to go in early built steadily. By 2300 the camp had fallen totally quiet. The light burned on in the target room, but nobody else seemed to be stirring. I imagined Khadduri at his computer terminal, working out details of his strategy for a mass Arab attack on Israel. We'd told the head-shed that zero-hour was going to be midnight, and for a while I reckoned we'd better stick to that.

Then, as we sat in the moonlight on the face of a dune opposite the corner of the wire, Stew came on the air with a question that fairly put the wind up us. 'Aye,' he said, 'Are you guys on the move somewhere?'

'No,' I told him. 'We're sitting tight with eyes on the target building. Why?'

'I've just seen three people moving out to my left as I face you.'

'What were they doing?'

'Walking in single file. Apart from that, I couldn't tell. They were right at the limit of visibility.'

'Any weapons?'

'Not that I could see.'

'Roger. It could be the camel herders. We'll carry on regardless.'

I pretended to be cool, but in fact the sighting changed my mind about waiting. If there were people about in the desert, the less we hung around the better. 'Bollocks to it,' I said. 'Let's go in now. There's no point in farting about any longer.'

I called Stew again. 'Tell the Kremlin we've advanced the deadline: we're going in right away, and we'll keep them informed.'

While the others hung back and covered me, I crawled forward seventy metres to the fence at the darkest point and went to work with bolt-cutters. A thick ground-wire ran along the bottom: it felt as if it was under tension, so I left it alone and made an L-shaped incision in the mesh, with sides two feet long. The wire was fairly soft, and the blades made practically no sound as they bit together through each strand.

Having stowed the cutters in my belt-kit, I pulled up the flap of mesh that I'd made, put my AK-47 through and crawled after it. Tony and Norm followed, and all three of us scuttled for the shadow at the back of the accommodation block.

There we waited, each on one knee, facing outward. Close under the wall the noise of the air-conditioning units was considerable: a steady roar which drowned out all other small sounds. From here I saw that, to anyone inside the camp, the lights on the perimeter fence made the desert beyond seem black as a witch's tit. Even for us, it was impossible to detect that our other guys were out there.

'Right, Norm,' I whispered. 'There's your door.'

Tony and I remained on full alert as he set to with his torch and little bag of tricks, ten metres from us. We were both sweating like pigs, partly from the heat, partly from tension. I saw Tony's forehead gleaming in the faint light and beads of moisture trickling down his cheeks.

Inevitably Norm made a few clicks and scrapes – exactly the sounds I'd heard in my nightmare at the cottage – but nothing to compare with the steady background drone that filled the air, and in an incredibly short time he had the door open.

'Rubbish,' he muttered, indicating the lock. 'Just a Yale-type. Opens from the inside with a turn of the knob.'

'Brilliant! We'll see you soon.'

We slung our rifles over our backs to leave our hands free, slipped inside and closed the door gently behind us. Inside was a passage, dimly lit by a single fluorescent tube. A smell of spicy food hung in the air – turmeric or cumin – and I guessed we were in the kitchen area. After the heat outside, the air-conditioned atmosphere bit cold. I began to shudder, and felt the sweat congealing in the small of my back.

Two metres to our left the corridor came to a dead end in a closed door; to the right, it turned a corner. I calculated that our target room was almost directly above our heads.

I peeped round the corner. Another passage, longer, with doors on both sides, almost dark. This one lay parallel with the front of the building. I reckoned it must lead to stairs opposite the front door.

The floor was cement painted with some dark-green compound. Our boots made no sound on it as we tip-toed along. In fifteen paces we were at one side of a small entrance-hall or lobby, bare of furniture. The front door was to our right, and stairs with a metal banister rail and the same dark-green paint on the treads rose to our left. Beyond the reception area the passage carried on through the other half of the building.

Tony put a hand on my arm and pointed. Farther down the corridor, on the left, light was showing through the crack of a partially opened door. The room could have been an office – but equally it could have been the bog. Whatever it was, nobody was moving, and I shook my head to show we should ignore it.

I went up the steps first, the Browning cocked, while Tony covered me from below. At the head of the stairs another corridor ran directly above the one on the ground floor. Dim fluorescent tubes glowed in the ceiling.

Standing on the second-top step, I put my head cautiously round the corner of the passage. From under the last door on the left, at the end, light was showing. Without turning back, I waved my left hand to bring Tony up. A moment later I felt him materialise at my shoulder.

There in the heart of the building the noise of the air conditioners was much reduced, and it was quiet enough for me to hear my heart pounding. This was it. This was the spot we'd come 4,000 miles to reach. All we had to do now was creep forward about twelve metres, open the door and drop the target where he sat.

Suddenly we heard a noise below: a chair had been pushed back or the drawer of a filing-cabinet slid shut. Then door-hinges squeaked, and soft footsteps came towards us along the ground-floor corridor.

In a second we were both round the corner, into the upper passage, backs to the wall, in full view of anyone who came out of the target's room but shielded from the stairs. The footsteps started up the first flight. In ten seconds they'd be level with us.

Without a sound Tony pressed his Browning into my left hand and drew his Commando knife from its sheath on his belt. As the newcomer reached the top step Tony struck so fast round the corner that I saw nothing but a flurry of movement. The man made hardly a sound – just one gargling grunt as the blade drove into the side of his neck. If you rip out a guy's jugular and windpipe with one thrust, he doesn't start shouting. Tony caught him by the shoulder as he crumpled, turning the torso away from himself so that the spurting blood flew wide. The limp body slid bumping down the steps and came to rest on the half landing.

I could feel Tony quivering as I handed him back his pistol. Now, I thought: move, *move*.

Before I'd taken a step the passage lights went off. A second later they flickered back on, pinking and clicking, then went off, came on again, and finally died. With them went the air-conditioning, and the background drone sank away into total silence.

Jesus! A power-cut. The extreme tension made me connect the shut-down with the corpse on the stairs. Had we somehow caused the breakdown? Had the fall of that body triggered some switch? Impossible, surely. It must be a coincidence. Whatever the cause, maybe the blackout would work to our advantage. Maybe it would flush Khadduri out and send him straight towards us.

I felt for my torch, down a slim pocket on my left thigh. 'Get ready,' I breathed. 'This'll bring him out.'

For a moment nothing happened. I was stricken by a fleeting panic that Khadduri wasn't in his lair after all. Then we heard movements inside his room, and I tensed myself for the door to open.

Another wait. What the hell was he doing? Maybe he was frantically trying to save whatever he had in his computer. But then, after another few seconds, came back the power: the fluorescent strips clicked and popped back into life; the air-conditioning units started up again.

With the background noise restored I ducked back on to the staircase, jabbed my pressel switch and said softly, 'Pat, what the fuck's happening to the power?'

'Dunno,' came the instant answer. 'The whole system went down for a few seconds. The entire camp was dark. Back on now.'

'OK. Nobody moving?'

'Not a soul.'

I felt my boot slip on the second step down, and realised the stairs were running with blood. Now I'd be leaving footprints. Too bad. Even our boots were Soviet-made.

I gave Tony a nudge and pointed down the corridor, breathing, 'Let's go.' But we'd taken only a couple of steps when the power went down yet again.

We stood still in the pitch-black corridor. I had the Browning in my right hand, torch in the left. Now he'll come out, I told myself. I reached back, hooked the torch round Tony's elbow and drew him forward with me. We crept on, one step, two, three, until I reckoned we were no more than six or seven feet from the target's door.

Noises came from inside the room: somebody stumbling over furniture. We heard the handle turn, then the hinges squeaked as the door came open. Torch on. There in the beam was al-Khadduri – heavier, greyer

155

than I remembered, hair ruffled up on end, but without the slightest doubt the same man – in an open-necked white shirt, carrying a buff file-holder in his right hand.

His eyes had a startled look and he opened his mouth to say something, but before any word came out my 9mm bullet smacked him in the centre of the forehead. The impact knocked him backwards bodily, and he slumped to the floor. On the deck his head turned sideways, and in an instant I was on top of him, putting a second round through his skull just above the ear. At the second shot the body twitched and jerked as if it had had an electric current shot through it, and the feet, which were encased in some kind of soft shoes, went *slap*, *slap*, *slap* against the wall as the dead man's knees doubled up and straightened violently, up, down, up, down. I saw now there'd been no need for the second round, because the first bullet had blown off the back of his skull and a mess of brains was hanging out. The papers had cascaded out of his file and scattered along the floor. There was blood on his face, his shirt, the floor, the door.

Subconsciously I knew that even the silenced pistol had made two heavy thuds, enough to have alerted anyone on the upper storey, but our immediate need was to snap some pictures of the dead man so that Western intelligence chiefs got absolute proof he'd been eliminated.

For a couple of seconds I sat on Khadduri's legs to stop that mad thrashing. Then, as the nerve-responses faded, I stood up, and in a pre-arranged move Tony holstered his pistol and grabbed the body under the armpits. The hands and arms were still twitching as he dragged it a couple of steps backwards and propped it against the door. By the time he had it in position I'd got my Instamatic camera lined up, the torch beam giving enough light to aim the lens, and I knew the automatic flash would do the rest.

'For Pete's sake get a move on,' Tony gasped. 'The bastard's bleeding all over me. I hope to hell he hasn't got AIDS.'

'Tip his head back a bit,' I hissed. 'Up! Up! Get him by the hair . . . That's it. Wipe the blood off his nose. There – hold him there. Now turn his head sideways for a profile.'

I fired off six frames, three full-face, three profile, then pouched the camera and turned to go. In a couple of seconds we were at the top of the stairs, but shouts and a rush of feet in the lower corridor halted us on the top landing.

Men were yelling '*Misabeeh! Misabeeh!*'

'Lights,' whispered Tony, 'they're shouting for lights.' Then, voicing my own thoughts, he said, 'They'll find the body on the stairs. That'll stop them. Use the window. It's only a ten or twelve foot drop.'

We ran back to Khadduri's door, stepped over his huddled body, turned the handle and went in. On impulse I reached back, felt for a soft, still warm hand, grabbed it, dragged the body into the room and shut the door behind it.

The room was slightly less dark than the corridor, lit by enough moonlight to make out the pieces of furniture. As Tony picked his way through them to the window I felt for the key and turned it in the lock.

Then he hissed, 'Shit!'

'What's the matter?'

'Can't shift the window. Must be locked.'

I knew from our observation during the day that the casements were made of heavy-duty metal. I came up beside Tony, grabbed the lever-handle and heaved downwards. No movement whatever. Bringing out my Browning, I slammed the butt against the glass – but although the pane buckled it didn't break. Against the

157

moonlight I peered closely and saw that it was reinforced with wire mesh.

I whipped back to the door and opened it slightly to listen. They'd found the body on the stairs and were jabbering like monkeys. There was no way we'd get down past them. We were trapped on the upper storey.

I locked the door again and got on the radio. 'All stations. The bird is down. Repeat, the bird is down. But we've been compromised. We need immediate distractions. Pat, are you hearing me?'

'Loud and clear.'

'Get an RPG into the right-hand end of our building. Upper floor, *your* right-hand end. Now. Then fire your distraction charge soonest. After that, if it's still on, have a crack at the satellite dish.

'Whinger?'

'Hello.'

'Once the rocket's gone, get rounds down into the area of the guardroom. Are there any lights on in the camp? Over.'

'No lights, Geordie. The whole system's gone down.'

'OK. Let me know if anything comes on. We're in the bird's nest itself. We're stuck for the moment. But it's no sweat. When we can, we're coming out through the window that was lit.'

In one of the pouches of my belt-kit I had two small demolition charges, ready made up. It took only a few seconds to mould them on to the window fastening. 'I'll wait for the RPG to hit,' I told Tony. 'Then I'll blow it. Block your ears.'

We both lay flat on the floor at the base of the outer wall, heads away from the window, thumbs over ears. Seconds crawled past. I held the clacker between my knees, willing Pat to let drive. Then, without warning, there came a thunderbolt, an immense roar, and a concussion that shook the entire building. In its aftermath, the boom of our little charge was tiny, but still enough to leave our ears ringing.

Tony and I leapt up. The window had swung open. With my shamag in a bundle I swept the sill back and forth to clear any broken glass and went out feet-first. The barrel of my AK-47 caught on the top of the frame, and I had to wriggle my torso violently to free it. Then I hung down, flexed my knees and let go.

The landing was hard but OK. Just as Tony thumped down beside me, a huge sheet of flame split the night from along by the gate, instantly followed by the *boom* of another explosion. Good on yer, Pat, I thought.

On the radio I called, 'Norm, we're out front and coming round the corner towards you. Are you there?'

'Roger. Ready and waiting.'

We scuttled to the corner of the building, felt rather than saw Norm in front of us, and all three headed fast for the gap in the wire. By then rounds were going down in every direction. Short bursts were coming in from Pat and Whinger, but from several points inside the wire tracer was flying out into the desert, most of it in the direction of the gate, where the explosion had started a small fire.

As we reached the wire I heard the *whoosh* of another rocket coming in. Turning, I saw the streak of it heading for the comms dish. Automatically I began counting: one, two, three . . . By four I knew it had missed. Fractionally later came a *boom* as it self-destructed.

Fuck the dish, I thought. We're not risking our lives for that.

We wriggled through the gap in the wire, ran until we were well clear of the fence, and dropped into a hollow. I was panting and sweating in the hot outside air, but on a high, boosted by a mixture of fear and elation. I felt neither tired nor hungry, not even thirsty

– just great. 'Stew,' I called. 'Have you onpassed to the head-shed that the bird is down?'

'Roger. Message passed and acknowledged. The heli's on its way.'

'Brilliant. Let's go.'

We fell in with Whinger easily enough. 'Fucking missed!' he went.

'No sweat,' I told him. 'Where's the launcher?'

'I binned it.'

'OK, let's leave it. We've got problems enough already.'

Little did I know the validity of what I was saying. When we reached the OP – our first ERV – there was no sign of Pat. He should have been there by then.

'Pat,' I called over the radio, 'ERV One, now.'

No answer. I called again, and waited with anxiety mounting fast. Then at last came an answer.

It was Pat all right, but not the jaunty, confident response we were used to hearing. His voice sounded weak and slow. 'Problem,' he slurred, 'I've been hit. Can't move.'

'Jesus!' I cried. 'Where are you?'

'Main gate. Five o'clock, two hundred metres.'

'Hang on there. We're coming.'

We started running in his direction, parallel with the wire, a couple of hundred metres out. Bursts of automatic fire came cracking out over our heads, with the odd red tracer round looping past to show us it wasn't all that high. Whinger kept yelling 'FUCKIN' ARSEHOLES!' like a lunatic. I nearly shouted at him to shut up, but decided he'd pay no attention.

Whether or not the defenders could see us it was impossible to tell, but I guessed not. I reckoned they were just loosing off rounds into the desert to raise their morale. They had plenty to keep them occupied. The blaze started by Pat's distraction charge had died out,

160

but the accommodation block was well alight, with flames spreading along it from the right-hand end. I could see figures running about outside the building, and hear men yelling in high, harsh voices. Vehicles were on the move, headlights sweeping the desert. I tried not to look at the lights or flames because the glare destroyed my night-vision.

The ground was uneven enough to make searching difficult, the hollows containing pools of deeper darkness.

'Spread out,' I called. 'Get a line. It's the only way to find him.'

We fanned out to twenty metres apart in a line end-on to the wire, tripping and falling in the sandy hollows. Whenever headlights swung in our direction, everyone went down and stayed flat until the beams had passed. This made progress erratic, and confused our eyes still more. I was beginning to think we must have gone past Pat when Norm suddenly called, 'Here he is.'

We were round him in a flash. He was lying in a bit of a dip, on his right side, with his left leg curled up but his right leg straight out beneath it. As we huddled round he didn't speak. With my back to the camp I switched on my torch and immediately saw blood gleaming in the sand.

'Right leg,' I said. 'Turn him over.'

He groaned and blasphemed as we got him on his back. With my knife I cut his trousers and slit upwards. One look told me that a bullet had gone right through his leg and caught his femur just above the knee. A splinter of bone was protruding from a bloody opening. I whipped out my shamag and twisted it up into a sausage to make a tourniquet above the wound.

'Get on the radio to Stew,' I ordered. 'Tell him we need the trailer forward, as close behind the OP as he can get it.'

I got the tourniquet in position, broke out two thick wound-dressings from my emergency pack and bound them into place with Norm's shamag, one on either hole. When I shone the torch on Pat's face he looked deathly pale, and his eyes moved slowly. I felt round his neck for the sachet of morphia. It was still in place, so I jerked the cord in half, pulled off the cap and banged the needle into his good thigh.

'He's lost a lot of blood,' I said. 'He needs an IV, fast.'

Suddenly a brighter glare blazed out of the camp, and the beam of a searchlight swept over the desert to our right. 'For fuck's sake!' called Whinger. 'Let's get him into a deeper hole.'

He and Norm took Pat by the arms and began dragging him backwards over the sand, ignoring his protests. I picked up his rifle and went after them. Then I saw the beam of the light swinging fast towards us.

'On the deck!' I snapped. 'Down!'

Down we went, but not quick enough. The light beamed on to us, swung past, then checked and came back. The operator had seen us. A second later rounds came flying down the line of the beam. The air all round my head was suddenly full of vicious snapping and crackling. It was a machine-gun, firing long bursts.

We were pinned down fifty metres short of the dunes and good cover. If we'd all been fit we could maybe have rolled into hollows and got away with it. But Pat couldn't move on his own. To me his body showed up as big as an elephant's, caught in that lethal beam. If anyone had good binos at the other end, they were bound to see it.

There was only one thing to do. I rolled a couple of metres to my left, came up in a firing position and let drive at the light with my AK-47: one, two, three short bursts, raising my point of aim slightly each time. I was aware of someone else firing too, on my right. At my fourth burst the light vanished, but rounds were still snapping close overhead.

'Keep down!' I yelled. 'Give 'em time to lose their point of aim.'

In a few seconds the firing stopped.

'OK,' I called. 'Let's go.'

Whinger got hold of Pat again, but Norm wasn't with him.

'Norm!' I called. 'Where are you? Norm?'

I scuttled four or five steps to where I'd last seen him, and there he was, flat on his front, slumped face-down over his rifle. Feeling desperately exposed, I knelt with my back to the camp and flicked on my torch. Blood was welling from a hole at the base of his neck. A bullet had gone in on the inner end of the collar bone, killing him instantly. The round must have raked through his chest and out through his spine.

I found I was shaking. 'Norm's gone,' I said.

'Want me to carry him?' Tony was lying beside me.

'I'll manage him. You help drag Pat.'

The volume of incoming fire increased again, green tracer now added to the red. There must have been twenty or thirty guys loosing off from various areas of the camp, and now two machine-guns were firing. Praise be, the whole lot was going high. Looking back, I saw that the power had been partially restored: a few lights were showing dimly, as though worked by emergency generators. More sinister was the fact that vehicles were lining up one behind the other, facing the centre gate, as if a sortie was about to be launched into the desert.

With the air full of lead, everyone's instinct was to stay on the deck and crawl into shelter. But you can't crawl in soft sand dragging a heavy weight. Scary as it was, the only thing to do was to stand up. With Tony's help I got Norm over my shoulder in a fireman's lift, his arms hanging down my back. Even though Tony had taken his rifle, he seemed a hell of a weight. I started taking very short steps, but my feet slid in the sand and I made practically no progress.

Then out of the air came Stew's reassuring voice: 'On the move with the trailer. Can you give me a steer?'

I was panting so hard I could hardly speak. 'Stew,' I gasped, 'we're in the shit. Norm's been topped. Thirty seconds, someone'll be on the back of a dune. Give you two flashes, repeated.'

I struggled on a few more steps. I could feel Norm's warm blood dripping down the backs of my legs. The other two were dragging Pat on, drawing ahead. Tracer was still sailing high over us. Somehow we had to make the back of the first big dune, in dead ground from the camp.

No breath left. I had to put Norm down. I got hold of his limp left hand and started trying to drag him, but in the deep sand his weight and the pouches of his belt-kit made it almost impossible.

Dimly I realised that Tony and Whinger had got Pat over the lip and into a temporary refuge. A second later Whinger was back beside me. He grabbed Norm's other hand, and the two of us got the body moving. By the time we had it in dead ground Tony had started giving Stew double flashes. With incredible relief I heard the engine of his quad, purring towards us. In a moment he was alongside.

'What happened?'

'Norm got one smack in the chest,' I said. 'Instantaneous. Pat's got a gunshot wound to the right leg. He's lost a lot of blood.'

I knew we ought to put more ground between us and the enemy before I started work on the casualty. On the other hand, I didn't think Pat could last very long.

'Get the body in the trailer,' I said. 'And Pat. I've got to give him an IV right away.'

While the others lifted Norm and lowered him into the bottom of the trailer, I broke out the med pack and sorted an IV drip. My hands were shaking so much I had trouble with the packaging.

'Watch that fucking gate for me, Whinger,' I said. 'Tell me if the bastards start out.'

I slit away the sleeve of Pat's shirt and got the needle in his arm, but I had nothing to hang the bag of fluid from, so I handed it to Stew and said, 'Hold that a minute.'

'Watch it, Geordie,' called Whinger, who was observing from up on the mound. 'They're at the gate now.'

'Tell me when they've got it open.'

'Wait out.'

We got a minute or so's respite. Then Whinger called, 'They're coming through. Six, seven, eight vehicles.'

'Head for the LUP, then. Gimme the bag, Stew. I'll ride with him.'

But could we move? When Stew went into gear and revved up, his wheels just spun in the sand. The weight in the trailer was too great. I leaped out, preparing to walk beside Pat, holding the IV above him. But still the trailer wouldn't shift.

I pushed as hard as I could with my free hand. Tony was on the other side, heaving like he was in a rugger scrum. Whinger was still up top, observing the enemy. The temptation was to call him down and get him pushing too, but we needed him where he was.

We made maybe fifty yards at a desperately slow speed, before the quad slewed sideways and slid, dropping into a deep, steep-sided hole, with the trailer jack-knifed round against it. The fall had jerked the

165

needle out of Pat's arm, and I was left with it dangling on the end of the tube. At that very instant Whinger called down, 'Watch it, Geordie, they're turning to come in along the new road ahead of us.'

I took an awful decision: we had to ditch Norm, and Pat we must save at all costs.

'Where's your Semtex?' I asked Tony.

'Some here,' he patted his pouches. 'Most of it's in the trailer. Why?'

'I want you to get rid of Norm's body.'

'Aw, shit!'

'I know. But we've got to do it. Those are our orders. If we keep him with us we'll put everyone at risk.'

By then we were in one hell of a mess. Our only hope of getting the trailer out of the hole was to empty it. But Pat was lying on top of the heap, and before we could get Norm clear we had to shift Pat back on to land, causing him horrendous pain.

I broke out a fresh wound-dressing, wrapped the IV needle in it and laid the whole kit on top of my AK-47. Then I went to work. The body was still warm as in life. Holding it under the arms, I hauled it out and dragged it ten yards clear. Tony came with me, carrying his gear.

'What shall I do?' I asked. 'Put him on his side in a foetal position?'

'I guess. I've never done this before.'

'How much Semtex have you got?'

'Twelve pounds.'

'Put five in his midriff, and we'll wrap him round it. Tie his hands behind his knees.'

'What about the fuse?'

'Wait till we've got the trailer sorted. Then give us fifteen minutes.'

'OK.'

'Can you manage?'

166

'I guess so.'

'Sorry, Tony.'

I felt round Norm's neck to make sure he wasn't wearing his ID discs on a chain, then scuttled back to the quad. Stew had already unhitched the empty trailer and pulled it up on to level ground. I broke out a rope and called Whinger down to help pull. With Stew driving and us two heaving, the bike scrabbled its way back on to the flat. All the time I was working, my mind was on Tony and his horrible task.

We were all moving fast and silently, shocked by the realisation that Norm, our taciturn but ever-reliable mate, was about to be blown to eternity. We also knew that we were rapidly being surrounded. Still not speaking, we hitched up again, reloaded Pat and the two spare weapons into the trailer, and tried another start. This time the quad went forward without anyone pushing, and I knew we'd made the critical difference to the load.

I got the IV needle back into Pat's arm and told him to hold the bag up above his head with the other hand. 'Keep it up as long as you can,' I told him. 'Then have a rest, and up again.'

Turning to Tony I called, 'How are you doing?'

'Finishing now. What about the fuse?'

'Start it going.'

Whinger had scrambled back to his lookout post. 'Lights moving out,' he said. 'Coming across our line of retreat.'

'Shit!' I muttered. 'Let's go.'

We reached the LUP without further incident. Stew had already ripped down the cam-netting, so we folded it over into a makeshift blanket, to give Pat some padding from the bumps and insulation from the air. In the distance behind us the Libyans were still filling the air with lead.

'Booby trap both spare quads,' I told Tony. 'Pile most of the Semtex on them, and put a jerrican of petrol underneath. Quick as you can.'

I put my head close to the casualty's and said, 'Pat?'

'Yeah.'

'You hear me all right?'

'Sure.'

'Listen. We've got to motor. Keep the bag up for as long as you can, OK?'

'Right.'

I turned to Tony and said, 'Pat's pulled back a bit already. I reckon he's stable now. How are you doing?'

'Matter of seconds. I'm giving this one fifteen minutes of det cord.'

'How long till Norm goes?'

He shot a quick glance at his watch. 'Eight minutes.'

'Let's get moving then.'

'OK. It's burning.' Tony stood back for a second, then crossed to his own quad and jumped aboard.

At last we were properly under way, heading due south, myself in the lead. Already the sand was firmer, the going faster. With every minute that passed, the noise of firing faded behind us. I uttered a silent prayer of thanks for the Magellans. With the coordinates of ERV Six punched in, the needle on my little illuminated dial was giving me our course, and warning me every time I deviated to right or left.

Yet as the seconds ticked away, I felt terrific tension rising inside me. Norm was about to be vaporised. The idea was disgusting, incredible. I thought of the bomb at Warren Point which had killed nineteen Paras. Two of them had literally disappeared into thin air; no trace of them was ever found.

Lights! Lights ahead of us and below, maybe three hundred metres from us.

'Everyone stop,' I called. 'Standby to see how far

they're going.'

Like the twats they were, the Libyans were driving slowly along the new road with headlights full on. The vehicles were maybe a couple of hundred yards apart, engines and gearboxes grinding in low gear.

'First explosion imminent,' said Tony's voice in my ear – and then, before I had time to agonise any more, it came. A terrific flash split the sky behind us, and a heavy *boom!* buffeted through the air. Norman was gone. I tried to shut my mind to details about which bit of him might have been blown where; I just hoped there was nothing whatever left. Annihilation.

When I tried to swallow, my throat felt desperately dry, and I was shaking with reaction. Concentrate on the job in hand, I told myself.

I looked at the road and realised something was wrong with the picture I could see.

'Whinger,' I called softly, 'you said you counted eight vehicles through the gate?'

'Correct,' he answered. 'There's only six still moving. Two of the bastards have stopped off somewhere.'

'Wait one.' I pulled up my kite-sight and switched it on. Sure enough, I picked up the two delinquents, one a couple of hundred yards to the left of our line of retreat, the other twice that. 'They're putting out a cordon,' I said. 'The next one will stop in a moment . . . There he goes.'

A third vehicle came to a halt and doused its lights. Scanning the ground with the night-sight, I saw that fortune at last was favouring us. From where we were a shallow gully ran down to the new road; rolling down it we would be invisible, and the sides would contain the sound of our engines.

'We'll slip through between them,' I said. 'How long till the next bang, Tony?'

'Four minutes.'

'We'll use that as a diversion. Give us a count-down. All stations get your eyes shut before the flash. As soon as it goes, we roll. Whinger, stay back to cover the rest of us across. Once we're over, we'll stop and cover you.'

'Roger.'

While we waited, I kept scanning with the sight. As I had expected, Gadaffi's fearless warriors preferred to do their soldiering from the safety of their vehicles. Nobody got out and started to walk about.

'One minute,' Tony announced.

I tucked the sight down the front of my shirt and settled my PNGs back over my eyes. At fifteen seconds I closed my eyes – and it was just as well, because the flash and bang came fractionally before Tony called them.

This second explosion, being much closer, sounded far more dramatic. Anyone looking back towards the camp would have got an eyeful. Before the echoes had rolled away we were bobbing down the gully and across the road. I held my breath and kept going steadily until we were well clear, then stopped everyone and turned to cover the crossing while I called Whinger on.

Now we were on the hard ground and up to full speed. We had a much shorter way to go than on the run-in, because our pick-up point was only a couple of kilometres beyond the south bank of the big wadi.

After twenty minutes of steady travel, I called, 'All stations – comms halt now. Close on me.'

With pickets out ahead and behind, Whinger set up his Satcom and started aligning the little dish-aerial. I thought of the big aerial in the camp, still functioning, and tried to put that minor failure behind me. As Whinger fiddled, I took another look at Pat. When I loosened the tourniquet, blood started to seep through the wound-dressings, so I tightened it again and got another IV going. I stayed with him while Whinger was getting through to Hereford, chatting quietly to encourage him, trying not to think about Norm.

'Fucking great bang,' Pat muttered hazily. 'What was that?'

'Tony put your quad into orbit, to stop anyone else getting their hands on it.'

'Shit hot!'

'Going through,' said Whinger.

I passed the IV bag to Tony and took the handset. 'Zero Alpha, Zero Alpha, this is Delta Four. How do you hear me?'

'Zero Alpha. Loud and clear. Over.' It was Mac's voice, his Glasgow accent unmistakable even via the satellite.

'Delta Four. I confirm the bird is down. We're clear of the target area and heading for the pick-up point. ETA there between figures four zero and figures six zero minutes from now. Repeat from four zero to six zero minutes.'

'Zero Alpha. Roger. Your transport is en route to you. Will confirm your timings to Captain Steve. Over.'

'Delta Four. Roger. We have one casualty. Bravo Seven has a serious leg wound. He's stable, but we need a doctor soonest. Best if we can have one on the Herc. Over.'

'Zero Alpha. Roger. We'll do what we can.'

We found a different way down into the wadi and picked out a path across its boulder-strewn floor without difficulty. After a quick run across the gravel plain, we were on the pick-up location well within the window I'd given. The ground there was flat and hard, with a bit of sand on the surface, but no obstructions, so that the heli would be able to land anywhere. Having chosen the best-looking spot, we spread out in all-round defence and listened for the sound of engines.

The night was utterly quiet, with just a breath of wind from the south-east. Looking back to the north, I could see no lights in the sky, no sign of vehicles moving, and I guessed that after a token watch in the desert the Libyans had retreated into camp. I imagined a fire-crew fighting the blaze in the accommodation block. If the whole building had gone up and Khadduri's body had been incinerated, the home team might never realise that he'd been assassinated.

Scanning through my PNGs, I could make out the other quads dotted round in a circle. It was difficult to sit still and wait, so hyped-up did I feel. Every minute or two I had a word with Pat, lying in the trailer beside me. During one of the longer silences, the idea of meeting Norm's next-of-kin began to bug me. Because he came from so far away – Glasgow – and spoke so little, I didn't know much about his family. I had the impression that his father was dead and his mum had married again. What was I going to say to her?

I kept trying to work out when our Chinook would have taken off from Siwa and how long it might take to reach us. As we had no solid information, everything was guesswork. From their pre-briefing, the crew knew that ERV Six was twenty kilometres due south of the camp perimeter, and I was confident they were heading for us.

It was Whinger, with his very sharp ears, who heard the sound first. 'Aircraft engines east,' he announced. I switched my radio to the channel I expected the chopper crew to be using and called, 'Hello Steve, hello Steve, this is Geordie. How d'you read me? Over.'

'Hi, Geordie. You're loud and clear. I'm heading two-six-zero. Estimating six minutes to the LZ. Over.'

'Roger. That's great. Keep coming. We can hear you due east of our position. The deck's clear for you to land. We've got a firefly on now.'

'Roger. Do my guys need any particular instructions for loading your casualty?'

'No, thanks. We've got him laid in the trailer, so he can be driven straight in.'

'Roger. Standby.'

'And . . . Steve?'

'Yes?'

'We've only four quads left. Had to bin the others. So the loadies'll only need to count four in.'

'Roger.'

It was a fantastic relief to know that the chopper was on course. Again I gave thanks for the existence of the Magellan and the pinpoint accuracy it offered us. No doubt the crew of the Chinook would have found us in the end by using old-fashioned methods of navigation, but almost certainly the recovery would have taken longer. Most of my anxieties fell away; now the main worry was Pat.

For three or four minutes the engine hum grew steadily louder.

'We're hearing you stronger,' I called. 'Keep coming.'

'Roger,' Steve called, and then, 'OK, OK. I've got you. We were almost spot on. Turning towards you now. OK, the firefly's on the nose. All clear to land beside it?'

'Perfect. We're standing off.'

'Roger. I'll come straight in.'

I went back on to our chatter net and called to Whinger: 'Pull away from his line of approach or you'll get your bloody head cut off. All stations, start up. He'll be here in under a minute. Stew, you'll be first on with the trailer.'

'Roger.'

Pulling the PNGs down on to my chest, I replaced

them with ordinary ski goggles, started the quad and turned to face into the circle. For a few moments I could hear the noise of my own engine. Then the thudding of rotor blades and the scream of turbines blotted it out, and all at once a great black monster was looming towards us out of the night, practically at ground level, with a dark sand-cloud seething behind it.

Without wasting an instant, Steve hovered, turned in the air and put his arse down right beside the firefly. In the last few seconds the noise became overwhelming. Sand and dust boiled up furiously, and as I drove into the cloud I found the ramp already down, and there were the loadies, beckoning Stew on. In less than a minute all four quads were safely aboard, and we lifted away.

In the dim light of the hold I could see that Tony's face and hands were smeared with dried blood. Khadduri's. My hands were the same, but the blood was Pat's. The blood all down the backs of my legs was Norm's.

For our lads, the relief of being airborne was overwhelming; we felt we were already half-way home, our troubles behind us. For the crew, though, things were different. From their strained faces I could see they were shitting themselves with the possibility of going down in alien territory. Not until we'd cleared the Egyptian border would they be able to relax. Engine failure, or a SAM from a trigger-happy sentry in some Libyan frontier-post – either would spoil the party in a few seconds. In my mind I ran through the emergency drills we'd talked about in Hereford, what we'd do in the event of a forced landing. We still had enough explosive to destroy the Chinook if need be, but that would be the last resort.

As for Pat, I knew the important thing was to make him keep fighting. On other operations I'd seen guys who'd been wounded hold out well until they thought they were in safe hands, and then suddenly slide downhill as they stopped making a positive effort to survive. When that happens, shock can take over.

I went and looked down over the side of the trailer. Pat's eyes were shut, so I gave him a tap on the arm and shouted, 'Stick at it, mate. There's going to be a doctor on the Herc. Only an hour to go.'

The morphine had put him half-under, but he mustered a bit of a smile and muttered, 'Fuck 'em all!'

I raised a thumb, held my fist above his head for a moment, gave him a tap on the shoulder and moved away.

When I called the head-shed on the secure radio link, I was put straight on to the CO. I told him about Norm and Pat, but there was only one subject he seemed interested in: was I sure that the target was dead?

'As fucking mutton, Boss,' I told him. 'He had two rounds through the head, one from the front, one from the side. His brains are spattered half-way across Libya. We've got photos to prove it.'

'Good work,' he conceded. 'And nobody got a good look at you?'

'Only the target. No one else.'

'Brilliant. We'll see you back here presently.'

EIGHT

When I heard that Tracy had been on the phone the night before my heart leapt, but the surge of hope lasted only a few seconds.

'I'm afraid she made the call under duress,' Foxy Fraser told me. 'The message was very downbeat. Listen for yourself.' He switched on a tape deck, and when Tracy's voice came loud and clear out of the speakers it nearly cracked me up. I had to get hold of myself before I could grasp what she was saying. Apart from the emotional shock of hearing her apparently so near, there was something odd about the rhythm of her speech; it didn't sound natural, and I had to run through the tape twice before I realised she'd been reading out a prepared script.

'Geordie, listen,' she said. 'You *have* to come and get us. You *have* to make the arrangement very soon. We can't wait any longer. If you haven't made the arrangement by midday on the first of June they are going to kill Tim. Tim first, then me. Geordie, I love you. You can't let us die. For God's sake send a message through Sinn Fein in Belfast.'

I clenched my fists under the table, took a deep breath and looked across at Fraser.

He twitched his head quickly to one side, chin out and back, as if to say, 'I'm feeling for you, mate.'

'What do we do?' I asked. 'We've got to move now.'

Fraser cleared his throat. 'We had one false alarm,' he

said. 'Not sure what it was – whether the tout was trying to make a quick buck, or what. We got a tip that the hostages were being held in a flat in Earl's Court – not one of the known addresses. We put the place under surveillance immediately. That night three men came out at ten o'clock. Nobody we knew. While they were in the pub a lock-picking specialist slipped in and took a look round.'

'And?'

'Nothing. There was nobody else at home, no sign there ever had been. Our operator left a microphone in the ceiling light, but it's yielded nothing. The men are just Paddies working on building sites. All they talk about is prostitutes and race-horses. It was a bum steer.'

'This call . . .' I gestured at the tape, 'was it a bluff?'

'With the PIRA you can never tell. They're so blasted erratic. Obviously they're trying to crank up the pressure. Somebody in Belfast is probably putting the screws on the London boys. We need to take the threat seriously, whatever.'

'What's this about Sinn Fein?'

'We do sometimes send messages through their office in Belfast.'

'Well, can you do that now?'

'Of course – when we've decided what to say.'

'In that case I'm going to make a move.'

Fraser glanced at me sharply. 'What are you proposing?'

'You know that scheme I told them about the last time?'

'For springing Farrell from a police convoy?'

'Exactly. I'm going ahead with it.'

'Geordie!' Fraser stood up and moved towards me with an anxious expression on his face. 'There are some things you can do, and some things you can't. This is –'

'Listen!' I cut him off. 'It's my kid's life that's at stake.

177

I'm not going to sit around and let him get killed. We've got to get off our arses and act.'

'I wouldn't say we're sitting around, exactly. We've got a big operation going on out there.'

'Yes – and what's it producing? Two thirds of three fifths of fuck-all.' Seeing Fraser colour up, I added, 'I didn't mean that personally. I'm not trying to criticise; I know how cunning these bastards are. But they're not getting away with this one.'

I found I was pacing about the room: something I don't usually do. I made myself sit down again and said, 'I've thought it through, and it's perfectly possible.'

'I don't see it,' Fraser replied. 'Apart from anything else, you'll get yourself kicked out of the Regiment.'

'No, no – I haven't explained properly. I changed my mind. We'll do it *with* the Regiment. Their support will be essential.'

Fraser looked blank. 'I still don't get it. Don't tell me your commanding officer's going to sanction your breaking the law of the land, setting a dangerous criminal free.'

'Maybe he will, maybe he won't. *Everyone's* got to agree, of course.'

'Who's everyone?'

'The Regiment. Yourselves. The prison authorities. The regular police. Then, I suppose, the Home Office and the Home Secretary. Maybe ultimately the Prime Minister.'

'I think you're getting a bit carried away.' Fraser was staring at me as if I'd gone round the twist. 'So what exactly do you propose doing?'

'I'm calling it Plan Zulu. In training or on operations we always start off with Plan A and Plan B – Alpha and Bravo. This is the ultimate plan, the last resort. Therefore it's Plan Z for Zulu.'

I started pacing around again. 'We have a big O-group – collect together all the people I've mentioned, and explain the scheme to them. Then, at an agreed time on an agreed day, the prison authorities move Farrell from Birmingham to somewhere else – it doesn't matter what the destination is supposed to be, as they don't have to tell him. The prisoner'll be in a closed van, and won't know where he's going.'

'He could be going down the road to Long Lartin,' said Fraser.

'Where's that?'

'The nick near Evesham where quite a few IRA prisoners are held.'

I stared at the Special Branch man, amazed that he seemed to be entering into my plan.

'Great!' I went. 'Presumably they don't have any obligation to tell him where he's going.'

'No. When they ship people like that and don't give a destination, it's known as putting them on the ghost train.'

'Got it. So they bring him out. We get guys from the Regiment to drive the police cars and the prison van – the meat wagon, you call it, don't you? – and at a predetermined spot we ambush the convoy, ram the van, force it off the road and stage a realistic battle, with plenty of bangs and rounds going down. We – myself and two or three of the lads – grab Farrell and take him to a safe house. As far as he'll know we're renegades from the army, doing this on our own initiative. I'll tell him I'm so desperate I've taken leave and brought in some civilian friends to help.'

Fraser had his eyebrows raised in a sceptical arch. 'Go on.'

'Then, from the safe house, we'll contact the PIRA and tell them to set a rendezvous for an exchange. But we'll also put a bug into one of Farrell's shoes, or his belt, and make certain that he can be trailed. Then we'll hand him over, do the swap, secure Tim and Tracy, let Farrell think he's got clear, and have the police nab him again.'

'And throw a bridge across the Irish Sea at the same time, just so you can go after him quicker.'

I glared at Fraser. He seemed to have lost heart again. 'Look,' I said, 'you don't appear to realise that all this is shit simple. We're trained to the eyeballs in ambush techniques. We have the cars to do an intercept, we have the weapons to stage a battle, and we can set up a safe house in our sleep. Apart from back-up on the ground, we'll have a helicopter airborne but standing well off out of sight, so that Farrell won't stand a cat in hell's chance of getting away. Nobody else has to do anything except put him in a van and let us drive him a few miles out of Birmingham into the country. All we need is the co-operation of the authorities.'

'And your commanding officer,' Fraser prompted.

'And the CO, of course. I'm due to see him in a minute, for a wash-up on our operation. Once that's over, maybe you and he can get together.'

'You're going to propose Plan Zulu to him, then?'

'Most certainly.'

'Well . . . I wish you luck.'

'Thanks.'

I got up to go, feeling that Fraser was still with me and willing to have a go – but only just. 'By the way, what's become of your assistant? Karen whatever?'

'Oh.' The Commander looked suddenly uncomfortable. 'She's . . . she's gone on a couple of days' leave.'

At the time I didn't challenge his statement, but there was something about Fraser's manner which made me doubt if it was true.

On the flight back from Cyprus Pat had been given priority and put on board a TriStar, so that within an hour of touch-down at Lyneham he was in the operating theatre of the tri-service hospital at RAF Wroughton, south of Swindon. The rest of us had lumbered back in a Herc, but because our departure was delayed we'd come in so late at night that our debrief had to be postponed until the morning.

Now, in Yorky Rose's office in the Subversive Action Wing, members of the head-shed had gathered to welcome us back.

Apart from Yorky himself there was Mac, the ops officer, the int officer, Gilbert the Filbert from the Firm, and above all the CO, Lieutenant Colonel Bob Brampton – commonly known as 'Wingnut', because of his ears, but liked and respected none the less. A fitness fanatic, he was glowing with good health; he looked like he'd been for a ten-mile run (which he probably had) and then had a big breakfast of vitamins.

The lads in our team were well spruced up, shaved and showered, but it wasn't surprising that we all looked a bit hollow-eyed, and yawns were two a penny.

If it hadn't been for the death of Norm, the atmosphere would have been positively euphoric. As it was, the CO was on a kind of muted high. He shook each of us by the hand, exclaiming 'Well done!', 'Great effort!', 'Tremendous!' and suchlike, but behind his laughing and joking sadness hung like a dark cloud.

He addressed us all. 'The Regiment's going to get a lot more work as a result of this. We're going to be run off our feet by the demand for our services.'

I knew that our success would increase his own credit rating as well – he might even end up with a gong – yet I could tell that he was feeling our loss as much as we were.

When the initial hubbub had subsided, the ruperts took a row of chairs behind Yorky's desk and we sat in a semi-circle facing them. The prize exhibits were the mug-shots I'd taken of Khadduri, full-face and profile. (The film had been whipped off me the moment we reached base and developed in the middle of the night.) The photos weren't a pretty sight, but they were technically spot-on, and proved that Tony and I hadn't been exaggerating. You could even see the tattoo of an eagle on the back of Tony's left hand as he held the dead man's head up by the hair, with the blood-spattered door of the office in the background.

The CO led off his formal spiel by saying a few words about Norm. He confirmed that the families officer was going to contact the next of kin, and said he would let us know the date of the funeral. More cheerful news was that Pat had come through his operation fine, and that the surgeons were pleased by the way things had gone.

Then the CO asked me to run through Operation Ostrich, which I did, with the int officer's gofer taking notes on a laptop. As I went along, the ruperts asked quite a few questions, and we took it in turns to answer. Their main concern was whether the defenders had seen any of us well enough to pick us out at an identity parade. To that the answer was 'Definitely not.' I reassured the int officer in particular that, with the exception of Khadduri, we hadn't met anyone face to face; in fact, I doubted whether the Libyans had actually got eyes on any of us. The fact that Norm and Pat had been hit was purely a fluke: first somebody must have seen the flashes as Pat put bursts into the camp, and sprayed rounds randomly in his direction; then we'd got caught in the searchlight.

At the end of the debriefing the CO told us again that we'd done exceptionally well, were a credit to the Regiment, had performed a service to humanity, and sundry crap of that kind. Then he added, 'You'll be glad to hear that Gadaffi's blaming the Israelis – off the

182

record, of course. No public announcement has been made – Khadduri wasn't supposed to be in Libya at all – but in private Gadaffi's claiming that one of his own senior officers has been killed, and saying he has evidence that Mossad carried out the assassination.'

'Maybe somebody dropped something after all,' I said, giving Whinger an exaggerated look.

'What's that?' The CO turned his long, narrow face in my direction, so that I got his sticking-out ears in profile against the light.

'It was just a joke we had. Before the operation went down, Whinger suggested we should scatter a few Uzis around – or anything with "Israel" written on it – to lay a false scent.'

'But you didn't, I hope?'

'Of course not. As far as I know we didn't leave anything behind except a few shreds of anonymous metal and . . . and whatever remained of poor old Norm.'

'What about the body?' asked the CO.

I gestured at Tony.

'I doubled him up on the ground with five pounds of Semtex in his midriff,' he said. 'There can't have been anything left.'

Nobody spoke for a moment. Then the CO cleared his throat and said, 'OK. That was the right thing to do.'

Again there was a moment's silence. Then the CO adroitly changed the subject. 'You'll be glad to hear you have a fan at Number Ten. I found this fax waiting for me when I came in.'

He handed me a sheet of paper, which had 'FROM THE OFFICE OF THE PRIME MINISTER' embossed at the top, and, in the middle, the brief message:

Delighted with your ornithological success.
Congratulations, and my personal thanks.

'Where's the champagne, then?' I demanded as I handed the note on to Tony. 'I thought the bugger would have sent a few bottles in this direction by now.'

'We'll have a drink in the mess tonight,' said the CO. 'Make up for lost time then.'

The atmosphere was so good that I was tempted to press straight on to the subject of my own predicament. With everyone in such a genial mood this seemed the ideal moment to broach the idea of Plan Zulu. But then I thought, No – not in front of this crowd. I'd rather get the CO on his own. So, as the meeting broke up, I said to him, 'Could I grab five minutes with you, Boss?'

'Sure.' He took a quick look at his watch. 'Ten o'clock?'

'Fine.'

I was outside his office a couple of minutes early, bolstered by the knowledge that, for the moment at any rate, the sun seemed to be shining out of my arse. I wasn't naive enough to suppose that our success on Ostrich would warp the Boss's judgement or make him any more inclined to take rash decisions, but the fact that I'd just done a good job would at least encourage him to give me a fair hearing. Apart from anything else, he had two boys of his own, and could hopefully understand how I felt about Tim. Also he had a good sense of humour, and a reputation for taking the occasional risk when he thought it was justified.

Inside, I perched on one of the bog-standard chairs and looked around the room while he closed down his laptop. His bergen sat in one corner, and in another, curled up on a dark-blue bean-bag, lay his black Labrador, Ben, fast asleep as usual. No doubt he'd been on the ten-mile run as well, and that was him settled for the day.

'God's boots!' the Boss exclaimed when I had

outlined my plan. With his elbows on the desk, he put his face between his hands and dug in his thumbs above his ears, as if to squeeze out the craziness of what he'd just heard. 'Pull the other one, Geordie.'

'No, no. I'm dead serious. We're up to our necks in shit, and sinking. We desperately need a new initiative – and I'm convinced Plan Zulu's the one. As I told Fraser – the SB guy – there'd be virtually no risk to anyone. OK, a couple of vehicles would get damaged and the guys in the meat wagon might get rattled around a bit, but that would be all.'

'What about our reputation? Can't you just see it in the tabloids? "SHOCK! TERROR! SAS SINKS TO GANG WARFARE TO FREE IRA CHIEF". You'd drop the whole Regiment in the shit, Geordie.'

'Not if we handled it properly. Nothing need ever get out. It'll be just one more covert operation on the mainland. There's dozens of others going on already, after all. Covert ops are bread and butter to Special Branch, just as they are to us.'

'That's true.' At last the CO looked up, as if seeing some light at the end of a tunnel. 'I have to say, I wouldn't mind if you gave it a go. But how the hell am I going to convince the powers that be? There's the Director, for a start. I can't see *him* sanctioning your scheme. He'll go bananas. Then there's the Home Office and the Home Secretary, if we want the police to be involved at high level. And what about the governor of the gaol? *He'll* throw a major wobbly as well.'

'I don't know,' I said. 'He might be glad to get rid of the bastard. Now that the PIRA know where Farrell is there's a chance that they'll stage a hit on the gaol. The buggers are that mad, you can't tell what they might try.'

'The thing is, they've already got you as a lever.' The

185

CO looked at me steadily before continuing with his list of objections: 'Ultimately, of course, there's the Prime Minister.'

Suddenly I spotted an opening. 'In that case, why not go straight to him?' I suggested. 'It's no business of mine, but we do know he's an old friend of the Regiment. It's not just that we did him a good turn in Libya. He's been on-side for years.' I pointed at a signed, framed photograph hanging on the wall, one of many official portraits presented by Very Important Visitors, among them Prince Charles and Princess Di. 'Remember the time he came down to the Killing House?'

'Of course.' The CO smiled, thinking about the day we'd given the PM and a couple of senior parliamentary colleagues a demonstration of lifting a hostage from a room in the special building used for training the counter-terrorist team. The walls were hung with sheets of thick rubber so that live rounds could be fired inside. As bullets had hammered close past the visitors in the confined space one of the sidekicks had hurled himself to the deck and pissed himself; but the PM had remained super-cool, and came away mightily impressed.

'If *he* OK'd it, that would be all we'd need,' I said. 'What about that fax you've just had, after all?'

I sensed that the CO had become rather taken with my idea, so I continued enthusiastically: 'Word would pass down the chain, and everyone else would have to come on board. With Ostrich having gone down so well he might fancy another unattributable operation.'

'Unattributable!' echoed the CO. 'I should think it bloody well would be. The least attributable operation ever mounted by the Regiment!'

To give himself a moment to think, he started talking about the lack of time. 'According to their last deadline, we've only got until midday on Tuesday,' he said. 'It's Thursday already. Not much room for manoeuvre.'

'Enough,' I said, 'if you can handle the bureaucracy, I guarantee I can manage the logistics.'

I sat back, feeling slightly out of breath, amazed that I was talking to the colonel as if I were of equal rank, planning an operation equally between the two of us. The truth was, we were both caught up in the excitement of the idea.

'Well,' he prevaricated. 'What does Special Branch think of it?'

'The Commander thinks I'm crazy. He doesn't realise how easy it would be, but all the same he's coming round to a position supporting me.'

'Does he reckon the regular police would cooperate?'

'I haven't asked him. I expect the answer's no, but as I said it would be a different matter if word came down from the top.'

'The plan's utterly outrageous, of course. I don't think we've a hope in hell of getting it sanctioned.' The CO looked at his watch. 'I'll play fair with you, though. I'll run the idea through the system. It's now 1035. Give me till lunchtime, OK? Back here at one. Meanwhile, get the bones of your plan on to paper. One of the clerks will do the donkey work for you on a word-processor, but get it all down as briefly as possible in note form. We'll push it up to the Director by secure fax and see what the reaction is.'

I walked out feeling pretty low and extremely tired. I knew the Boss was sympathetic, but he was a realist as well, and it was obvious he didn't think my idea had a chance. I could tell from the look of him that he'd only been humouring me. For a while I walked around outside, trying to clear my head, then I thought, Sod it,

I'll get a plan done anyway. I've nothing to lose by that.

In the adjutant's office I grabbed the services of a clerk called Andy, whose grammar and spelling were streaks ahead of mine, and in twenty minutes we'd hammered out the briefing. Back in the incident room I tried to raise my spirits by saying to Fraser, 'Better get your skates on, Commander. It looks like the wagon's going to roll.'

'You're joking.'

'Not entirely. The Boss is taking Plan Zulu seriously. At least, he's making enquiries at high level.'

'Am I supposed to know about it?'

'He knows I told you my idea, but probably it's better not to say anything until I've been back to him. We're meeting again at one o'clock to see if we can take it farther.'

To fill in time I sought out Tony. I'd spun him the outline of my scheme during our day in the OP, so there was little need for further explanation. 'If this goes down,' I told him, 'I'm going to make bloody sure you're on it with me. In fact, I hope we can keep the Ostrich team together. We understand each other as well as we ever will; I know we can muster the necessary skills between us. Listen, it may be premature, but why don't we get a few things planned?'

We settled ourselves at a table in the incident room with a road atlas and a notebook.

'Plotting the revolution, are you?' Fraser quipped as he came past.

'More or less. You don't mind us being here?'

'Not at all. You're welcome to carry on.'

Out of the blue there had come into my mind an image of the new bypass round Ludlow, the market town in Shropshire. The road was a single-carriageway but fast and open, curving gently in a wide semicircle, with several miles from one roundabout to the next and no side-turnings in between. A perfect setting for an intercept. There was a similar ring-road round Evesham, I knew – and in a way that would be a more appropriate location, since it would fit in with rumours that the prisoner was being moved to Long Lartin – but the country through which it ran was too flat and open, with too many houses in sight. Ludlow presented a wilder and therefore more attractive option.

'This is the place,' I told Tony, indicating the northern end of the bypass. 'If the police block out other vehicles for five minutes before the convoy comes through, the entire system will be empty. We can ram the prison van off the road anywhere here. Plenty of room to stage a mock battle, grab Farrell, and away.'

'How do we stop him seeing too much?'

'He won't see anything at all. First, we'll do it at night. Second, when we hit the meat wagon, our opening move is to fill the back of it with CS gas. That'll disable him and the guards as well.'

'How do we get into it?'

'We whack a hole out of the side. Power-saw with a carbon fibre blade.'

'OK.' Tony scribbled in his notebook. 'I'm making a list. We're gonna need CS, a saw, breathing kit for ourselves . . . What else?'

'Two cars. We'll draw a couple from the training pool at Llangwern – something pretty fast and beefy. Some kind of a hefty van for the intercept itself.'

'How many guys on the team?'

'Two drivers, and at least three others: two to handle Farrell, one spare in case someone gets hurt.'

'How do you pick the team?'

'As I said, I'd like to stick to the Ostrich crowd – if the head-shed will let us. So it's us two, Whinger and Stew. That'll be the core. We need one more really.

189

Maybe Yorky can spare someone.'

Tony got up and walked around. 'How are we going to control Farrell?'

'Handcuffs. We keep him cuffed to one of us all the time.'

'Two pairs,' said Tony as he wrote. 'Whenever you change his guard, you want him linked to the new guy before the old one lets go. And a chain: when you're hitched to a guy, you need room to manoeuvre.'

'OK,' I agreed. 'Two pairs and a chain. Next thing. He'll be cuffed to a screw in the van before we get to him. So we need bolt shears as well. And a hood to put on him.'

'And what happens when we've got him?'

'We drive him to a safe house and get in touch with the PIRA to set up a rendezvous, where we exchange him for the hostages.'

'What safe house?'

'The Regiment owns several – holiday cottages, mostly. Some of them belong to former members. Tucked-away places where a guy can thin out for a while if he has to disappear.'

'Are there any available right now? I mean, it's holiday season. They could all be full.'

'There'll have to be one. We can probably find something in the Welsh mountains.'

'How about bugging Farrell's clothes?'

'He'll be in prison uniform when we get him. So it'll make sense to have a set of civilian clothes for him to change into. We'll get a belt and some shoes doctored up.'

'In that case we need to get his sizes. I'll make a note of that too.'

We tried to plan timings, but it was practically impossible without knowing how the PIRA would react to the news that their man was out of custody – or rather, out of gaol. I reckoned we should stage the exchange of prisoners as soon as possible after we'd lifted Farrell, to cut down the chance of him escaping or anything else going wrong. The best scenario I could see was that we'd get our hands on Farrell on Friday night, pass word to the PIRA immediately, and set up the exchange for Saturday. But that was only *our* programme. Given the way the terrorists were inclined to piss about, there was no guarantee they would get their act together in time.

'I don't know where they'll propose,' I said. 'They'll assume our lift is going to take place somewhere close to Birmingham. But if they're in London, as we think, they'll probably opt for a handover rendezvous somewhere around the capital.'

'Who are we supposed to be? The other members of the team?' Tony asked.

'Friends of mine. The rest can be former members of the Regiment, but you – well, you're just an American pal, over here on holiday. You'll be a positive help in the deception, because Farrell won't connect an American with the SAS.'

'What's my profession, then?'

'Peanut farmer.'

'Thanks, pal. I'll write that down too.'

Tony grinned before going on. 'Our clothes . . .'

'What about them?'

'Got to be civilian.'

'That's right. And no weapons showing. No covert radios or other specialist gear. Whatever back-up we have has got to be well out of sight.'

After a salad in the sergeants' mess I was back at the CO's office for one o'clock – and from the look of suppressed excitement on his face I could see that we were in business.

'Bit of luck,' he began.

'What's happened?'

'I don't know whether you'd call it lateral thinking or lateral influence or what, but outside events seem to be working to our advantage. This came in from Special Branch this morning.' He picked up a sheet of fax paper and held it off the desk with both hands. At first I thought he was going to give it to me, but it seemed that he preferred to paraphrase its contents. 'Through an intercept, SB have got wind of PIRA plans for a high-level political assassination in London. They believe the target's the Prime Minister himself.'

'Charming!' I muttered. 'They're aiming high.'

'They are. The man SB overheard on the phone was talking about a special weapon they've brought over to do the shoot.'

'Not that rifle they were using in Armagh?'

'The very one. A Barrett Light Fifty – at least, we assume that's what it is. A five-oh, anyway.'

'Jesus! One hell of a weapon. That means they're planning a long-range shoot.'

'Exactly,' the CO agreed. 'That puts the police on the spot. They're organised for close-quarter protection, but they can't occupy every building in line of sight every time the Prime Minister goes somewhere.'

'No.' I thought for a moment, then said, 'What's that got to do with us?'

'Nothing directly.' The CO pushed his chair back. 'Except that SB believes the crowd they overheard are the same lot as the ones holding your people – the West London ASU. The thought is that if Plan Zulu goes ahead, you may get in among them and break up the cell.'

'You mean we can go ahead?' I nearly jumped off my chair.

The Boss gave me a beady look and nodded his head. 'You want to watch yourself. The Director is *not* chuffed with you.'

'What's wrong?'

'He's had to spend the morning at an emergency meeting in the COBR, liaising with Downing Street, the Home Office and Scotland Yard. That meant he couldn't clear other things off his desk, and he reckons you've buggered his weekend.'

I thought of the big fat brigadier, huffing and puffing in the Cabinet Office Briefing Room, the underground sanctum in Central London which is activated to deal with major emergencies . . . but I didn't feel too sorry for him.

'Mind you,' the CO added, 'if you smash the West London ASU I think he'll forgive you. The security forces have been trying to bust the organisation for years, and haven't managed it. They've made a number of arrests, but never got the key players.'

'All right then,' I said thoughtfully. 'What we're going to do is set a fucking great trap, and let the PIRA walk into it.'

When I asked Yorky for someone to replace Norm on the team, he promised to have a quick think; but before he came back to me I had an idea of my own. Living in Hereford having recently retired from the Regiment was a guy called 'Doughnut' Dyson, formerly of D Squadron. He'd had a job BG'ing some Arab sheikh, but at the moment he was out of work. I suddenly realised he would be ideal. For one thing, he was older than the rest of us, and looked it; for another, he really *was* ex-SAS, and if necessary could prove it by talking about his BG work. He'd add credibility to my claim that my team was a private army. Further, Doughnut was a hefty guy, and I foresaw that weight and muscle

193

would come in handy when we were dragging Farrell around.

Doughnut was a larger version of Pat – dark, straight hair, rosy cheeks – powerfully built and into weights, but nippy with it. He was quick-minded too: when I rang him at home to brief him he picked up the situation in a flash. Above all he was cheerful, the sort of guy who fits easily into any team and is a pleasure to have around.

His real name was Eric, but he had once made the mistake of appearing for a rugby trial in a cream-coloured jersey with a red blob in the middle. He never wore the damn thing again, but from that moment he was Doughnut.

He possessed one other minor advantage: whereas the rest of us has short, scrubby haircuts, his was fairly long and had a less military appearance.

A full O-group was called for 1700 that evening. But before the forces of law and order could assemble we had a pile of things to do. My first reaction was to collect the lads and put it to them straight.

As Plan Zulu was my benefit number, none of them was obliged to take part; they were officially on leave after Ostrich, and could duck out if they wanted. The fact that nobody did gave me a big boost. Far from trying to slide off, they all came on-side with so much enthusiasm and emotion that it nearly choked me.

By the time we'd cleared the air on that one, we had three hours left before the O-group. A safe house had been found – Laurel Cottage, near Ruardean in the Forest of Dean, less than half an hour to the south-east of Hereford – so we despatched Whinger to suss the place out. Stew and Doughnut shot off down to the Llangwern Army Training Area over the Welsh border to collect a couple of the intercept cars, while Tony and I hammered away to Ludlow to recce the bypass and pick a spot for our interception.

In the MT Section in camp a dark-blue Ford Transit van, bought second-hand for cash an hour before, was being prepared for use as the ramming vehicle. Half a ton of concrete blocks were wired and bolted to the floor in the back, a heavy bar was welded to the front bumper, and an anti-roll cage fitted inside the cab.

Other people pressed ahead with the logistics of the operation, sorting out food and drink for the cottage, finding out Farrell's sizes from the prison authorities and buying civilian clothes for him, and bugging a couple of pairs of shoes.

Before Tony and I set out, I needed to send a message to the PIRA, to gear them up for action. 'How do we do this?' I asked Fraser. 'If anything goes through your channels, they'll smell a rat and realise I'm working with you.'

'That's right. It's got to be a direct call. Make it from your own number, and if they bother to trace it back they'll be happy. Dial 192 and get the Sinn Fein number in Belfast from Directory Enquiries.'

With Fraser's guidance I composed a cryptic message – but when I got through I was disconcerted to find myself connected to an answerphone. I put my hand over the receiver and whispered as much to Fraser, who indicated that I should talk anyway. So off I went:

'This is Geordie Sharp speaking from Keeper's Cottage, Hereford, at 1400 hours on Thursday the twenty-seventh of May. I have a breakthrough as regards your man. He should be with me by midnight tomorrow, Friday the twenty-eighth of May. If he reaches me safely, I'll contact you again immediately to arrange a mutually convenient rendezvous, location to be proposed by you. Leave a number for quick contact. Message ends.'

★

It took us only forty minutes to whip up through Leominster and on along the A49 towards Shrewsbury. The weather had turned thundery with heavy cloud cover, and on that gloomy afternoon there was little traffic moving. As we passed a sign for Kimbolton to our right Tony said, 'Hey, I know that name! It was a USAF base during World War Two. I'm sure it was . . .' but he couldn't remember which squadrons had been stationed there.

Heading north, we came on to the Ludlow bypass from the wrong direction, so to speak, and drove straight to the northern end of it before slowing to check things in detail.

'OK,' I said as we hit the northern roundabout. 'The ring-road starts here. Call this Point Alpha.'

Once again Tony was taking notes and making sketches. 'What d'you call this damn thing? A circle?'

'Roundabout. Don't you have them in the States?'

'We may have, but I don't think I ever saw one.'

'Point Alpha, anyway. I'm going round it again. That other road leading off is the A4113 to Knighton. Get that? OK . . . let's time ourselves from here to the next roundabout. I'll take it steady, simulate the prison convoy.'

I headed back south at 40 m.p.h. We went over the old main road on a bridge, then under a smaller one, and reached the second roundabout in two minutes and twenty seconds. 'Point Bravo,' I told Tony. 'Signed Ludlow to the east, the A4117 to the west. I reckon this next link will be the one for us.'

I continued driving slowly, and after a minute or so we came to a stretch where there was a wide verge on the left with a big, gently sloping grass bank behind it.

'Look at this!' I exclaimed. 'Could have been made for it. One minute twenty after Point B. Got that?'

'Sure.'

Through a cutting in the grass bank on our left, a farm or forestry track ran down a shallow ramp to join the road. Clearly it had been built as a concession to the landowner when the new road went through, to give him access to the highway. Changing down into second, I swung left off the tarmac and eased the Cavalier up the track, gravel scrunching under the tyres. 'Hear that?' I said. 'They went so far as to put down hardcore for our benefit. Even if it's raining, the van'll get up here no bother.'

At the back of the bank, out of sight of the road, we found a small turning-area, with a wooden-rail fence and gate bordering a plantation of young oaks: an ideal LUP for the rammer van.

'All we need do now is measure the distance to the centre of the highway,' I said. 'What is it? Sixty metres?'

'Seventy,' Tony suggested. 'I'll step it out.'

'OK. Stand on the edge of the tarmac, and when there's nobody coming, wave me down for a trial run.'

As he strode off down the ramp, taking deliberately long paces, I turned the car and lined it up five metres back from the lip of the bank. Then, at his signal, I started forward, gently at first, to simulate a laden van, then accelerating, before I braked hard and slewed to a halt on the shoulder of the road.

'Seven seconds,' I reported. 'They'll need to practise with the van itself, but that'll be it, near enough.'

'Sixty-eight metres,' Tony announced as he climbed back aboard. 'What do we call this place?'

'Impact Ramp. It's a nice site for a shoot-out, too. A few bursts into the banks won't hurt anybody.' I pulled off on to the grass again for a moment.

On the other side of the main road the ground fell away into a shallow drainage ditch. 'If we can hit the prison wagon into that it'll be perfect,' I said. 'The van'll probably roll over and we can go in through the roof.'

Driving on again, we took three and a half minutes to reach the third roundabout – Point Charlie – south of Ludlow, where the old main road headed back into the town. Between Bravo and Charlie lay a three-mile stretch of road with no side turnings. That gave us bags of space: even if something went wrong on Impact Ramp, we'd have several minutes clear in which to sort ourselves out.

'We're OK,' I told Tony. 'We've hacked it. Let's head for home.'

The O–Group took place in the main lecture hall, a big room with rows of seats set out in semicircular tiers. There was a full turn-out from the Regimental head-shed, and the outsiders included Gilbert the Filbert from the Firm, a senior representative from Special Branch in London, a leading light from Winson Green prison, and police chiefs from Warwickshire, Shropshire and Herefordshire.

The CO set the pace by announcing that, although Plan Zulu was certainly unorthodox, it had been ordered in the national interest by the highest authority. The immediate aim was to recover the hostages, but the wider strategy was to flush out as many players as possible in the West London ASU, and to break the power of an organisation which was posing a serious threat to the government. He therefore hoped everyone would give of their best in making the plan work.

In fact, most people seemed only too willing to co-operate. The only big-wig who caused any trouble was the guy from the gaol, a frowning superscrew with a pock-marked face, who started in whingeing about his responsibility for the prisoner's health and safety. 'You don't seem to realise that the man is still recovering from gunshot wounds,' he said, when asked for his comments. 'If he gets thrown about in a crash it may lead to serious complications.'

'He'll have to take his chance,' said the CO firmly. 'Your responsibility for him will cease when he leaves Winson Green, so his continuing health won't be your concern.'

That ended the complaints, and by cracking on in such positive fashion the CO got everything squared away within the hour, so that the meeting broke up soon after six.

The arrangement was that the intercept would go down the following night: Friday 28 May. The police would close all three roundabouts on the Ludlow bypass at 2215 and divert traffic, on the grounds that the road had been blocked by an accident. The convoy, consisting of a van with unmarked police cars fore and aft, would reach Point Alpha as close to 2225 as the drivers could manage.

By then our intercept cars would be parked nose-to-nose at an angle across the road half a mile south of Point Bravo, their panic lights flashing as if they'd had a crash. Our rammer van would be waiting in the turning space above the road. When the convoy approached, the lead driver would slow down as he saw the stranded cars ahead and report a blockage over his radio. At that moment our van would start its run down the ramp, aiming to hit the front of the meat wagon . . .

By 1830 I was feeling pretty knackered. It was five nights since I'd had a proper sleep and I was keen to get my head down for more than two or three hours at a stretch. All the same, Whinger and I were determined to call on Pat in hospital, because we knew he'd be fretting about his chances of regaining full fitness, and we reckoned he could do with a bit of moral support. Besides, once Plan Zulu went down, it might be days before we got another chance to see him.

After a quick bite to eat I phoned Pat's wife, Jenny, to see if there was anything she'd like us to take along, but it turned out she wasn't feeling very sympathetic. 'Take him a bottle of arsenic pills,' she said. 'That'll sort him.'

'OK, I get the message.'

I turned to Whinger and said, 'Cow,' then I called the hospital to make sure they'd let us in. There was the usual palaver about 'no visitors', but I bluffed our way with the sister in charge by telling her that we were special mates of Pat's, and got her to agree that we could spend a few minutes with him.

On the M4, Whinger gave me details of the safe house, which sounded pretty good. Laurel Cottage, he said, was made of brick and solidly built. It was small, with three rooms (including the bathroom) downstairs and three above, but it had been modernised recently and had a new kitchen and a Calor-gas hot water and heating system. The windows were adequate if not great – lockable, but not double-glazed. Whinger had been through all the drawers in the kitchen and removed a couple of receipted bills which gave the names of local tradesmen. He'd also checked the immediate area for estate agents' signs with giveaway phone numbers on them. The house was in a secure position, isolated as it was up a lane on the side of a hill, and there was a tumbledown wooden garage about thirty metres from the door. The place wasn't overlooked, and there were no other buildings in sight.

The only slight worry was one other house, which stood beside the lane where it joined the main road; anyone there would be in a good position to monitor comings and goings. But enquiries had revealed that this second building was also let intermittently, and at present unoccupied.

Comms wise, the cottage was well placed – not in a

hole where radios and mobile phones wouldn't function. Whinger had taken along with him a technician from Box, who'd installed a special phone containing an encrypting device and a chip that prevented anyone tracing a call back. Tests had shown that all forms of communication functioned well.

As we drove, I tried to imagine myself in Pat's position. When I got my arm smashed in the Gulf War I'd been in a fairly bad state myself, but I never thought that the wound was serious enough to threaten my career and basic fitness. A shattered femur was something else, and I knew how daunting it must be. At least he was in good hands. I knew that Army and RAF surgeons train to deal with bullet wounds by operating on pigs anaesthetised and shot at the secret defence establishment at Porton Down.

I'd made several visits to Wroughton before, to have my arm checked while the bones were re-knitting, and as we drove up the long approach road to the old airfield on top of the downs I thought once again how strange it was that a service hospital should have so little security. There was no fence, no barrier, no guardroom; anybody could proceed straight to the front entrance. Mind you, you needed to be fit to find the person you were looking for, because the building was about half a mile long, with wards leading off central corridors on its two floors, and it was a fearsome hike from one end to the other.

Hospitals bug me. The gleaming surfaces, the smell of disinfectant, the bright lights, the impersonal passages and doors . . . the whole environment seems alien, exactly the sort of world you spend your life trying to avoid.

After a marathon tab, we eventually came on Pat in one of the high-dependency units – a small side-ward with an RAF police corporal sitting guard outside the door. I'd had the sense to conceal my flask-shaped half-bottle of Johnny Walker against my stomach inside my loose shirt, so we got past the guard and the sister without hassle.

It was a shock to see such a physical guy as Pat laid low, flat on his back, amid a tangle of drips and drains. His left leg was in plaster, with a cage of stainless steel pins coming out through the case above the knee, and drain-tubes leading out of it. The sight of all the gear took me straight back to the hospital in Baghdad, and the Iraqi surgeon who'd threatened to blind me with an anaesthetic syringe before he operated. Of course, I also thought of Bully-boy Khadduri coming to the gaol and hammering on my plaster cast with his swagger stick. At least *he* wouldn't torment any more patients.

As we went in, Pat turned his head and gave a big grin. But although his brain was working fine, his responses were slow, and I could see that he was quite heavily sedated.

'They haven't killed you yet,' I said.

'They keep trying.'

'Lot of pain?'

'Nothing. It's fantastic.' He pointed at a little domed rubber pump, taped to his left arm just above the wrist. 'Whenever I get the gyp I give myself a shot with this thing.'

'What is it?'

'Morphine, I reckon. Got a bag of it up there somewhere. Want to try it?'

'Thanks a lot,' said Whinger. 'Time for a shot.'

'Look.' I brought out the Scotch. 'This is for when you're on the mend.' I laid the bottle at the back of the cupboard in the cabinet beside his bed and put a box of Kleenex in front of it.

'Brilliant!' Pat said. 'Thanks, Geordie.'

We began to chat about his journey home and things

at Hereford, then suddenly he remembered my own problem and said, 'Aye – what about the family?'

'Bit of a breakthrough. The PIRA sent a taped message from Tracy advancing the deadline for us to hand their man over, and we're preparing a response. We may get some action quite soon.' I'd already decided not to pass on details about Plan Zulu, just in case Pat started muttering in his sleep.

As I was talking I saw him get a twinge of pain, and he primed his morphine pump a couple of times. By the time I'd told him a bit about the wash-up after Ostrich I could see him losing concentration; so I was surprised when he suddenly said, quite loud, 'I hope you told them about the priest clearing his throat up his fucking tower.'

'The mullah! I did, Pat. Don't worry. I told them about your diversionary explosion by the gate too, and the RPG blowing shit out of the building – the lot.'

He gave a faint smile, but his eyes were closed, and he drifted off into a doze. I adjusted the position of the Kleenex box slightly, and we slipped out of the room.

In the corridor I saw a doctor whom I recognised from my own visits. It turned out that he had helped with Pat's operation, and he welcomed the pair of us with a friendly mock-salute. I knew word had been put about that Pat's wound had been caused by an accident on the ranges, so I didn't refer to its origin; but the doctor raised one eyebrow and said, 'You fellows are getting a bit trigger-happy, aren't you?'

'Well . . .' I spread my hands. 'These things happen.'

I could see he knew more than he was letting on, so I changed the subject. 'What's the long-term prognosis?'

'Pretty good, we reckon. He's a strong lad. The leg should knit up OK, provided we can keep infection out.'

My mind flashed to Farrell and his septicaemia – but all I said was, 'Back to full mobility?'

'We can't be sure, but there's every chance.'

'He'll be all right,' said Whinger loftily. 'Hot cross bun. This one will run and run.'

NINE

It turned out to be a filthy night of rain and wind – but that made no difference to our plans. By 2145 we were rolling along the bypass towards Impact Ramp, and five minutes later all three vehicles were parked in the turning area. Our main getaway car was a souped-up Audi Quattro that had seen service in Northern Ireland. It had been brought back to the mainland because it had been compromised: after a couple of successful operations the IRA knew it too well, so it had come home for a respray and the issue of new plates.

From the outside it looked the same as any other silver Audi; but lurking beneath its skin it carried potent extra assets. One was the engine, which had been given racing specification during a visit to the workshops at the Donington Park circuit in Leicestershire. The tweaked unit fired the car with fearsome acceleration and a top speed of 150 m.p.h. There were also slices of Kevlar armour in the doors and down the backs of the front seats – and to cope with the extra power and weight, both brakes and suspension had been uprated. The result of all this was that the driver could throw it about the road like a racing-car – which was just what Whinger fancied.

Our other vehicle was an old black Granada – less brutal, but solid, dependable and fast enough for most contingencies. I'd nominated Stew as driver, with Doughnut Dyson as his co-pilot. The rammer van was being driven by two other guys from the Regiment.

Someone had pointed out that, as the police were not going to give chase after the intercept, there was no need for us to use such a high-performance beast as the Audi. I countered with the possibility that other people might get caught up in the operation – accidentally or on purpose – and we might in the end be glad of a genuine getaway car. In any case, it was important that, once we had Farrell on board, we should cover a few miles at seriously high speed, as though the law were truly on our tail.

In our jeans and trainers we looked like any old layabouts, but covert radios and pistols in shoulder holsters under our sweatshirts gave us the teeth we needed. In the boot of the Granada were three MP5s, a box of loaded magazines, and a case of flash-bang stun grenades.

On our vantage point at the top of the Impact Ramp we sat in the dark and waited, the raindrops pearling on the windscreens. The Audi was first in line, with the Granada behind it, and the rammer van last.

The traffic on the bypass below us was spasmodic. For several seconds at a stretch the road would be empty, then a car or truck would come past, its lights glistening on the wet tarmac. The first sign of activity – or rather, lack of it – should come soon after 2215, when the police were due to seal off all approaches to the ring road.

'Does he know what's happening?' asked Tony quietly.

'Who?'

'Farrell.'

'Can't tell. It's possible word's got back to him, but I doubt it. He hasn't seen any outsiders since the ban on visitors was imposed.'

'Where does he think he's going, then?'

'I don't suppose he's got a clue; they don't have to tell prisoners where they're taking them. That's why it's called the ghost train. He may think he's going down to the IRA nick at Evesham. Or there's another one called the Dana at Shrewsbury. That's not far off, either.'

Time dragged. I stared out of the window at the dismal conditions, thankful that at least all the guys on the team knew what our target looked like. Mug-shots of Farrell, full face and profile, taken in the nick, had gone up on the board in the incident room. Seeing them, I had realised that even after months of pursuit I had never had a really good look at him. The night I'd seen him at the barn outside Belfast he'd been thirty or more metres off, standing in poor, flickering light; it was my colleague in the OP, a guy from the Det, who'd recognised him. And when I had chased him into the edge of the Amazon jungle it was in half-darkness, and in any case I'd been nearly blind with rage. The pictures taken in Winson Green showed him looking pretty rough, with hollow cheeks and dark shadows under the eyes.

Something else was niggling at my mind as we waited: a sheet of a telephone transcript which I'd glimpsed on Fraser's desk in the incident room. It was a record of a conversation with the PIRA which had obviously taken place while we were in Libya. Somebody had rung in, demanding to speak to Geordie Sharp, and 'KT' – Karen Terraine – had taken the call. For a while she'd stalled the man with stock answers, but when he had insisted on talking to me, she'd said: 'Well, you can't. He's not in the country. He's gone abroad for a few days.' Beside these words somebody had made a couple of big red crosses with a felt tip, as if to draw attention to a major breach of security. Why, for Christ's sake, had the woman said that I was overseas? Was it just carelessness, or was it spite –

revenge for my giving her the brush-off in that bout of midnight fisticuffs? Either way, I got the impression that Fraser had moved her smartly out of the team working on my problem. He told me she'd gone on leave, but I reckoned she'd been fired. Whatever had happened to her, one potentially dangerous fact was now in enemy hands. To some extent Operation Ostrich had been compromised.

I looked at my watch again and said, 'Now. It's quarter past. The road blocks should be in position.'

For a while we saw no change; the occasional vehicle continued to come past. Then, after one last lorry from the south, the flow from that direction ceased. A couple of minutes later the same thing happened from the north – a single car came down and disappeared southwards trailing a cloud of spray – and then everything went quiet.

'Standby,' I said over our chatter net. 'Engines running.'

Whinger turned the ignition key, and the Audi burbled into life with a deep, throaty grumble. I switched to the police channel, and a moment later heard a voice I recognised as that of Ross Tucker, driver of the lead vehicle in the convoy: 'Point Alpha now.'

Back on our own net I called, 'OK. Take up position.'

Whinger switched on his headlights, which blazed out across the bypass, and rolled the heavy car down the slope. He headed a few yards to the left, so as to leave the rammer van a clear run, and brought the Audi to rest at an angle across the carriageway, its nose pointing south. In a couple of seconds Stew had eased the Granada round ahead of us and backed it up so that its rear-bumper was touching our front mudguard. By the time he'd switched on the alarm flashers and raised the lid of the boot, the two vehicles presented the very picture of an unfortunate shunt.

I nipped to the boot of the Granada, grabbed the power-saw, switched on and gave a couple of pulls on the starter cord to make sure it would run. At the second tug the engine burst into life, and after belching out a cloud of white smoke, revved up smoothly. I switched off and returned the saw to its place. The rest of the team stationed themselves on the south side of the barricade, away from the impact area.

'Standby!' called Tony. 'Lights to the north.'

On the chatter net I called the driver of our rammer van. 'All set, Joe?'

'Turning and burning,' he replied calmly.

'Fine. Listen out for my count-down.'

The lights bore down towards us, at first only one big glare through the drizzling rain, then three distinct pairs of headlamps, with blue police lamps flashing fore and aft. They were less than a quarter of a mile off when Tony's voice suddenly broke into the chatter net. 'Geordie,' he called. 'The cops are saying a rogue vehicle's bust through the cordon. There's a fourth car coming down the road.'

Jesus! I thought. Somehow the PIRA have rumbled us. They've overheard one of our planning conversations. They're coming to join the party.

I had about five seconds in which to make a decision. Abort or carry on? Pointless to abort. If this *was* the PIRA, we were fairly well equipped to take them on here and now. If it was someone else pissing about we could stuff them with the greatest of ease. I said, 'Carry on as planned. Whinger, watch for a fourth fucking vehicle.'

In the distance, beyond the convoy lights, another faint glow was already visible. But I had no more time to worry about it. Ross, driving the lead police car, had seen our obstruction and began to brake. The middle vehicle closed on him a bit, then slowed, increasing its distance again. The little group cruised on towards us at a diminishing pace. I kept mentally calculating the distance they had to run.

'Stand by to roll,' I told Joe. 'Five, four, three, two, one . . . GO!'

We stripped off our covert radios and dumped them in the boot of the Granada. Tony and I pulled on pairs of lightweight goggles. My eyes were glued to the approaching convoy, but my ears were listening for the engine of our van. There it was, running at high revs in second gear.

I flailed my right hand at the oncoming lights, urgently waving them down. The lead car had barely coasted to a halt when the van, its engine screaming, hurtled down on to the carriageway at right-angles and caught the meat wagon broadside. With a huge, crunching crash of metal and a screech of tyres the wagon was hurled sideways. As the wheels caught on the tarmac, the impetus toppled the van on to its right side and sent it powering on, sparks flying from the side that scraped over the road. From close quarters the violence of the impact was shocking. With a sudden stab of alarm I thought that the van was going to catch fire. If Farrell got roasted alive, that would be the end of everything.

It came to rest with the roof vertical, on the edge of the shallow ditch. Then things happened very fast. I dived for the power saw, grabbed it, ran to the ditch, started up and applied the carbon blade to the metal. Tony stood beside me, directing a torch on to the roof. Above the scream of my saw I heard rounds going down in bursts, then the *boom* of flash-bangs.

The saw bit through the thin metal sheeting of the roof as if it were cardboard, and in a few seconds I'd made two big cuts running downwards and outwards from a central point at the top. A hail of fiery red sparks flew in all directions, and I thanked my stars that the fuel I could smell spilling out over the verge was diesel, not petrol. Out of the corner of my eye I saw somebody struggling out through the left-hand door of the cab, which was uppermost. Knowing it was one of our own guys I didn't worry; he'd keep out of the way, or maybe just lie down.

One more cut across the bottom of my triangle and the job was done. As the piece came away, Tony stuck his head in through the hole, swept his torch beam and fired off with a canister of pepper spray in the direction of the tail. Then he scrambled in through the opening and I followed.

The vehicle's lights had gone down in the crash, so the torches were our only illumination. In the beams I saw two figures piled into one back corner, struggling on top of each other, gasping and cursing and rubbing at their eyes. Tony reached them first and lifted the upper man bodily into the air, only to find he was attached to the second by a handcuff and a short chain. Which was which? The top man had fair hair, the bottom one was dark; the minder was uppermost, Farrell on the deck.

Bolt shears out. Snap through the links. Blood shining on the floor of the van – or rather on the wall. Grab Farrell.

He yelled a string of obscenities as I slammed him face-down, wrenched his arms behind him and got a pair of plasticuffs pulled up tight on his wrists. 'Take it easy, Seamus!' he managed between coughs and splutters. 'That fucking gas! It's you, Seamus, is it not? Jaysus, man, get off me! Get me out of this!'

That was all he could manage. He couldn't open his eyes. Blood was frothing out of his mouth, and as the pepper got to him properly he relapsed into incoherent roars. The spray was getting to me as well. My eyes were OK inside the goggles, but my nose, mouth and throat were burning, and I tried not to inhale.

I saw Tony had Farrell under control, so I dived back through the hole into the open and gasped in a few breaths of fresh air. Outside it sounded as though a full-scale battle was in progress: bangs, flashes, rounds clattering down, police sirens screaming. The moment Farrell's head appeared in the opening I grabbed him by the hair and pulled him bodily out. He collapsed on to the ground, bellowing and choking. A second later Tony dived out as well. Between us we hoisted the prisoner to his feet and gave him the bum's rush in the direction of the Audi. To right and left I noticed bodies lying on the ground.

It had originally been my intention to get Farrell in the back seat between Tony and myself. But on impulse I opened the boot, dumped him bodily inside and slammed the lid.

'Let's go,' I yelled.

Whinger loomed up in front of me, thrusting his MP 5 in my direction as he went for the driving seat. I grabbed the weapon, pointed it up in the air and squeezed the trigger, purely to make sure it was unloaded. To my amazement, five or six rounds hammered off into the night before the magazine was empty.

'For fuck's sake, Whinger!' I shouted.

'Get in! Get in!' he yelled. 'Stop pissing about.'

He already had the engine running. I leapt into the passenger seat, Tony into the back and with a squeal of tyres and the engine howling, the Audi shot away down the bypass.

'Those guys on the deck,' I panted. 'What happened to them?'

'Nothing.' Whinger sounded perfectly cool. 'They

212

just lay down when we started firing.'

'What about the extra car?'

'A pale blue Lexus. It went past.'

'How?'

'Scraped round the front of the Granada, on the verge.'

'What was it doing?'

'Not a clue. But it was going like shit off a shovel.'

'*Phworrh!*' I was still choking and spluttering. 'Your fucking pepper, Tony.'

'I know. But it did the trick. I don't reckon our guy saw anything at all.'

In seconds we were nudging 120 m.p.h. Having tried an experimental ride in the boot earlier that day, I knew that Farrell couldn't possibly hear us talking: the noise inside the tin can was diabolical. 'Take it easy,' I told Whinger. 'At this rate Stew'll never keep up.' On the radio I called, 'Zulu One to Zulu Two, what's the score? Over.'

'Zulu Two,' came Stew's voice. 'Mobile towards you. We have you visual.'

Looking back, I saw the Granada's lights in the distance. 'Zulu One to all Papa stations,' I went. 'Clear Point Charlie now. Anticipating Point Charlie figures six-zero seconds, repeat six-zero seconds.'

'Papa Nine,' came the answer. 'Roger.'

Whinger had throttled back to ninety and the lights of the Granada had closed a little. But then ahead of us our own lights picked up the shape of another car parked beside the road.

'Fuckin' 'ell!' cried Whinger. 'It's that bastard Lexus.' He put his foot down again and the Audi surged forward.

'Zulu One to Zulu Two,' I called. 'Watch yourselves. The intruder vehicle's parked up ahead.'

As we hurtled down towards it I had to remind

myself that this was Shropshire, England, not some godforsaken bog outside Belfast. I was so hyped up by the intercept that our best option seemed to be to spray the Lexus with a few busts from the MP 5s as we went past . . . Take it easy, I told myself. You can't do that here. The guys in that car may easily be PIRA. Farrell hoped I was Seamus. Was he *expecting* an intercept? But equally, the Lexus crew could be drunks trying to evade the breathalyser, or joy-riders baiting the police.

By the time we reached the Lexus it was already rolling, gathering speed. I caught a glimpse of three young faces, two in front and one behind. Just after we'd roared past, its lights came on.

'Hey!' I yelled. 'These bastards are after us. Sort them, Whinger. Don't kill 'em, for fuck's sake, but put them out of contention.'

Over the radio I called, 'Zulu One, the intruder's now between us.'

We were rounding a gentle curve. A moment later our speed had carried us out of sight of our tail. From our recce I remembered that there was a picnic site coming up on our left, a pull-up with rustic chairs and tables, screened from the road by conifers.

'There!' I exclaimed. 'Dive in there!'

Whinger had seen the entrance too. He hit the brakes with such a thump that the Audi slewed left and right. With a juddering rush we banged down off the tarmac on to the gravel of the pull-up. Whinger doused his lights and simultaneously switched off the ignition so that the brake-lamps wouldn't light up.

'Slow down, slow down!' I called to Stew. 'Keep back. We've bombed into a lay-by. We're going to hang in here, then take them out.'

In about five seconds the Lexus overshot. Maybe the driver had been confused by the disappearance of his target – at any rate, he seemed to be moving more slowly than before. Whinger watched the lights go past outside the screen of firs, then started the engine again and came out after him.

Like a greyhound after a hare, the Audi surged up behind its prey, showing no lights at first, then with everything blazing. Before the other driver had time to react Whinger was up beside him, still accelerating hard. Then, just as our tail was about to clear the Lexus's front, he braked fiercely and jerked the steering wheel to the left.

The hit was perfectly timed. There was no way the other driver could have avoided us. In a split second he found his car whacked sideways and sent out of control. As Whinger straightened and accelerated away, I saw the Lexus spin through 360 degrees, go half round again, and finally roll over on to its side.

'Brilliant!' I went. On the net I said, 'Zulu One. Problem solved. Continue as per schedule.'

'Roger,' Stew answered.

'That's as far as they'll get tonight,' said Whinger. 'Whoever they were.'

'Dickers, for sure,' I told him.

'You're joking. I reckon they were joy-riders, I bet the car'd been nicked.'

'Maybe.'

'I got to see their faces quite well,' said Tony. 'I shone my torch on them as we came past. All youngish – twenties, I guess.'

'Irish?'

'Coulda been. I don't know. How do you tell?'

'You can't,' I said. 'SB'll show us some mug-shots when we get back. See if you recognise any of them.'

'Ah, come on!' said Whinger. 'You're getting PIRA on the brain. We shook 'em up, anyway.'

After all that things quietened down a bit, and I had a moment to wonder how Farrell had fared during the violent manoeuvring. At Charlie Three, the southern roundabout, there were no police cars in sight. I guessed that some were about, but standing well back, as arranged. We went across unopposed, and sped on southwards past Leominster to a spot where a side-road carried up through some woods. There, on the brow of a hill, we were due to switch from the Audi into a minivan – another precaution laid on to bluff Farrell, who would certainly have the wit to realise that in any real chase the police would radio details of the getaway car ahead, leaving it liable to arrest.

Just before we reached the rendezvous I said quietly to the other two, 'Don't forget – from now on we've all got to *act*.'

They knew what I meant: until then we'd been on our own, but for the next few hours or maybe days we were going to be at close quarters with our man. Everything we did or said in his presence must confirm our claim to be renegades, acting on our own for my personal benefit. No hint must be given that we had the full backing of the Regiment and the security services.

The white van was standing on the designated spot beside a bus-shelter on the outskirts of a village. Although there was nobody in sight, I knew that some guys from the Regiment had the place staked out; they'd be somewhere in the background, eyes on the vehicle. They would pick up the Audi as soon as we were clear, and drive it back to base.

As Whinger pulled in and parked alongside the van, I jumped out and went round to open the boot. My torch beam revealed Farrell lying on his right side, hands cuffed behind him, his knees drawn up to chest.

'Out!' I snapped. 'Get out!'

'Get out yerself, yer fucking twat!' he exploded. 'What in God's name d'you think yer doing, giving me shite treatment like this?'

'Out!' I repeated.

I noticed that his voice had sounded thick and peculiar, but I grabbed him by the upper shoulder and dragged him into a sitting position. 'On your feet.'

'Is Seamus with you?' he spluttered. 'Or is he not?'

'He's not.'

'Who are you, then?'

'You'll find out. Come on.'

His voice definitely sounded odd – thick and lisping. It was something I didn't remember from before. Slowly, painfully, his wrists still tied behind him, Farrell knelt up on the floor of the boot, then lifted one knee over the back of the car so as to lower his foot to the ground. 'Get these fucking cuffs off me,' he gasped. 'They're after killing my hands.'

I ignored the complaint, heaved him upright, dragged a balaclava hood down over his head with the eye-holes at the rear, and propelled him in the direction of the van. He walked unsteadily, and I remembered that the man had a chronic limp, apparently the legacy of a car accident.

'OK,' I told him. 'You're beside the other vehicle now. Get in, to your left, and sit in the middle of the back seat.'

With Tony to his left on the bench seat, me to his right and Whinger back at the wheel, we set off again, heading south. The arrangement was that the Granada, which had stood off while we switched vehicles, would proceed to the cottage independently.

We went by a roundabout route – although, with his eyes full of pepper spray, the hammering in the boot of the Audi and now the hood, I didn't think Farrell had a clue where he was or whether he was facing east, west, north or south. It gave me an odd feeling to be shoulder-to-shoulder with this murdering, torturing pride of the Belfast Brigade. Because of his plasticuffs he

217

had to sit forward awkwardly, and I could see he was in some pain, but I just thought, Ah, stuff the bastard.

Occasionally he asked some question about where we were and where we were going, his voice muffled by the hood, but when none of us answered he gave up. The silence left me time to think. I was trying to work out what he knew and what he didn't. The fact that he thought he'd been lifted by his own guys showed – surely – that he was totally in the dark: maybe the PIRA had been trying to set up a lift, but obviously he hadn't got wind of Plan Zulu, and it dawned on me that he might not even know that Tim and Tracy were being held hostage. After all, we'd captured him in Colombia before they were lifted, and, including the first two days in Bogotá, he'd been in the nick ever since.

Looking back over the interception, I couldn't remember anything we'd done that would give our game away. I started to wonder: did Farrell even know who *I* was? He'd shown no sign of recognising me. Then I remembered that on the only occasion he'd seen me, when we had fought in the Amazon jungle, I'd had my face blacked up for the night operation.

Whinger drove brilliantly, never missing a turn, even when he came to the steep, winding lanes of the Forest of Dean. Admittedly he'd recced the approach to Laurel Cottage the day before, but his route-finding was impressive. Not knowing that part of the country myself, I found the roads thoroughly confusing. On the final stretch I reminded myself *not* to make some stupid remark like 'Is this it?' which would betray the fact that our destination was new to me. In fact, I decided I was going to say as little to Farrell as possible. My aim was to move him on as fast as we could. He surely knew by now that we weren't his own people, and I hoped he'd be in shock for a few hours after the lift, and that the prospect of a quick escape would stop him trying to analyse the situation too deeply.

Eventually we climbed a steep gravel track through a wood, passed a battered white gate that stood open, and pulled up outside a house which was already lit up; Stew and Doughnut, in the Granada, had got there ahead of us. While Whinger went on in, Tony and I got Farrell out of the van and hustled him through the front door into a small hallway and on into the kitchen. Only then did I bring out a pair of regular steel handcuffs. Having locked Farrell's right hand to Tony's left, I cut the plasticuffs away with my Leatherman pliers. And none too soon; because the prisoner had been tugging away at them, the cuffs had ratcheted themselves up tighter and tighter and his hands had started turning blue.

Removal of his hood gave me a shock. He looked a right mess: face pale, eyes red-rimmed and bloodshot from the pepper, dried blood crusted over one cheek, and his upper lip all puffed out with a split down it to the right of centre – I guessed from being thrown against the wall of the meat wagon in the crash. There was blood on his blue and white striped prison shirt as well, and on his regulation-issue brown trousers.

'Better wash your face,' I told him. 'Use the sink there.' It wasn't that I felt sorry for him, just that I didn't fancy looking at such a wreck.

While Tony led him across to the sink and stood beside him as he scrubbed off his face, I took a quick look round the house with Whinger: lounge, bathroom and separate bog on the ground floor, three bedrooms upstairs. Everything was painted white, with terrible, twee little pictures of animals on the walls. A woman laid on by the Regiment had been in to make up the beds and put out towels and suchlike. The place was so small that the idea of spending days there gave me instant claustrophobia.

'Get a brew on, Whinger, for fuck's sake,' I said

quietly. 'We've got some talking to do.'

I found Tony and Farrell side by side on the settee in the lounge.

'He's bitten his tongue,' Tony told me. 'He's got his teeth smacked together in the crash. That's why he's speaking kinda funny.'

'Does it need stitches or anything?'

'No, no. The bleeding's stopped. It'll be fine. He just can't talk any sense.'

The telephone stood on a glass-topped coffee table near Farrell's left hand, so I pushed it towards him and said, 'Right. You'd better get talking.'

The dark-blue eyes glared at me from out of their inflamed rims. 'Talking?' he spat. 'What about?'

I stared back at him. Was he trying to wind me up, or had he really no inkling of what was happening?

'D'you know who I am?' I asked.

'Not a clue.'

'In that case, I'll start from the beginning. My name's Geordie Sharp. I'm in the SAS. Some of your people in the PIRA have lifted my four-year-old, Tim, and his guardian, Tracy. They're holding them hostage, to get you released.'

I watched the information sink in. Farrell's eyes were wary, as if he didn't believe what he was hearing. He said, 'SAS? Like fuck you are. How would the SAS be after attacking a police convoy?' With his split upper lip and swollen tongue, Farrell couldn't get his mouth round the consonants and he was lisping.

'They wouldn't,' I said. 'That wasn't the SAS. That was myself and a few pals – my private army.'

'But you're in the regular army. You just said so.'

'I'm on leave. I've taken time off specially, to sort this out.'

'Who are these other turds, then?'

I gestured towards Tony. 'He's a friend over from

220

the States. He's doing some BG work here.'

'BG? What's that?'

'Bodyguarding. Close protection.'

'All right. And these others?'

'Also friends. Former members of the Regiment, in civvy street now.'

Farrell looked out through the doorway, towards the rest of the guys in the kitchen. Again, he seemed to be weighing up what he was hearing. 'So . . . what's the game?'

'The game's dead simple,' I told him. 'Your people have told me that if we get you out, they'll release my two. We've got you out. As soon as the kid and the woman are in my hands, you can go.'

At that moment Whinger came in with a couple of mugs of tea. 'Will I do one for him as well?' he asked.

I was about to say no, but I changed my mind and told him, 'All right, then. Give him a cup.'

'You can keep yer fucking tea,' Farrell snapped. 'Whisky if you have it, but not fucking tea.'

Ah, sling yourself, I thought, but all I said was: 'Just get on the phone – right? And set up a rendezvous for an exchange.'

He shot me a look of hatred and said, 'Look, I've not been in Belfast for over a month. I don't know where any of the lads are.'

'You'd better find someone, and quickly. Otherwise you may not make it until daylight.'

Farrell reached for the phone, but stopped and withdrew his hand. 'Hey! Sharp! You're the little prat that was after shooting me at Ballyconvil.'

'What if I am?'

'You made a fair cock of that operation, didn't you?'

'Dial!' I told him. 'And get something set up for first thing in the morning.'

At last he moved. Holding the receiver in his left

221

hand, he had to draw Tony's left hand across with his right in order to pick out the buttons. I knew the call would be monitored and recorded, so I didn't bother trying to memorise the numbers, although I did notice the dialling code for Belfast, and guessed he was calling one of those sleazy bars on the Falls Road where IRA players drift in to drink at all hours of the day and night.

The first man he got was evidently pissed out of his mind.

'What are you at?' Farrell snapped after a moment. 'Answer my question, will you?'

'Bollocks!' came the answer, so loud I could hear it across the table.

'Bollocks yourself!' Farrell shouted. 'Pull yourself together, man.'

A bellow of laughter came down the line. Farrell held the receiver away from his ear and I heard a voice say, 'By the powers, we have a right prick on here!'

'Get off the line, twat!' yelled Farrell. 'I'll speak to someone sober . . . Hello?'

The man had gone. Another came on, apparently in little better shape.

'Is Eamonn there?' Farrell demanded.

'What's that?'

'Eamonn! It's Eamonn I want.'

'Eamonn who?'

Getting nowhere, Farrell banged down the receiver and dialled again. This time he found a contact who was making more sense, a man he knew called Charlie.

'Now, Charlie,' he said. 'It's Declan here . . . Yes . . . More or less . . . I don't know – some charming friends . . . What? Of course it's me. It's me fucking tongue, that's all – I bit it in a car smash . . . Yes . . . Certainly not. Not at all . . . Where *am* I? Wait one.' He put a hand over the mouthpiece and looked at me enquiringly. I spread my hands out and down. 'No idea,' he went on. 'About two hours from Birmingham, but God knows where . . . Yes. These fellers are looking to swap me for the woman and kid . . . That's right. Are they with you? . . . Oh, I see . . .'

Talking to this guy, whoever he was, Farrell was fairly polite. Eventually he was given another number and hung up. While he dialled again, although I knew the SB monitors would pick it up, I watched the first four digits and saw that they were 0802 – a mobile.

The moment the call was answered, Farrell's manner changed. He became arrogant and hectoring, just as he had been on the night at the barn outside Belfast. He wasted no time on explanations, just yelled, 'You'll get me out of this shit-hole first thing in the morning. You know that?'

Whatever the other guy said only seemed to enrage him further. 'When I say tomorrow, I mean *tomorrow*!' he shouted. 'Upgrade your fucking ideas, man, or I'll see you regret it! I'll give you quarter of an hour to sort something. Then I'll be back.'

I noticed Farrell was trembling as he hung up. 'Jaysus,' he said, 'the fever is on me again. I thought I had the better of it too . . .'

I put the back of my hand on his forehead, which felt burning hot. 'Your wounds, is it?' I said.

'It is.'

'What happened?'

'Some fucker shot me.'

'Really! Where was that?'

'South America.'

'You get around.'

Farrell's face contorted, as if in sudden pain. 'Listen,' he said. 'I need the bog.'

'Go on, then. Tony'll take you.'

'I'm not going with him. I need some privacy. Take these cuffs off.'

'No way. Tony's watched plenty of guys taking a dump. You can shit in company or not at all.'

Farrell gave in grumbling, and while the two were in the bathroom I said quietly to Whinger, 'Have you got those tablets the Med Centre packed?'

'Sure.'

'Fetch a couple out, then, and a glass of water. We need to get something down the bastard. We can't have him dying on us.' Special Branch had found out from the prison hospital what antibiotics Farrell had been getting, and the Med Centre had made up some of the stuff into plain white pills that looked like Paracetamol. When Farrell reappeared, I gave him two.

His response was predictable. 'What – are you after poisoning me?'

'Don't be daft. Alive you're worth a lot to us; dead, you'd be worth fuck-all. These are just aspirin. Can't do you any harm. And listen – when you get back on to your man in a moment, I want to speak to him myself. That's the only way to get ourselves straight with details of the meeting.'

Farrell took the tablets and drank the water. A few minutes later he put the call through, and while he was talking I quietly asked Tony, '*Did* he want to shit?'

'Sure did!' He held his nose and scrunched up his eyes. 'Boy, has he got the runs.'

'Got to watch him,' I went. 'We don't want him getting too sick to travel.'

After a few exchanges Farrell handed me the phone. I put my palm over the mouthpiece and asked, 'Who is it?'

'Feller called Malcolm.'

'Hi, Malcolm,' I said. 'What's the score?'

'The M25, northbound,' went the Belfast voice. 'Between junctions fourteen and fifteen. One mile north of fourteen there's an emergency phone on a pillar. Be there on the hard shoulder at eight forty-five in the morning – eight forty-five on the dot. Our people will pull up fifty yards behind you. The hostages will walk forward towards you. You'll bring our man back. The exchange will take place when the parties meet in the middle.'

I repeated the details carefully, then had to check something: 'Farrell was saying tomorrow but it's today, Saturday, we're talking about?'

'It is. And no more than two of you in the car.'

'Your man plus two.'

'All right. And no surveillance, either.'

'You're joking!'

'Just so you know.'

'What vehicle will you be in? . . . Hello? . . . Hello?' The man had gone.

'No point in asking,' said Farrell. 'They probably haven't got the wagon yet. They'll nick some old banger in the morning, and come in that.'

TEN

The night wasn't exactly a rest cure. First I'd had to put fresh dressings on Farrell's wounds. A furrow through the flesh on the inside of his upper arm was healing well, but the twin punctures, fore and aft, at the edge of his abdomen just below the bottom rib, didn't look so good. I could see that somebody had made an exploratory incision – presumably to clear out debris drawn in by the bullet – but there was an angry flush round both ends of the wound, and some suppuration coming out through the stitches. Even though medical training had killed the last of my squeamishness, I didn't enjoy patching up this particular patient; I'd rather have stuck a knife through his ribs and be done with it.

For the rest of the night we chained him to one of the iron bedsteads in the double room, wrist and ankle. To make doubly sure he didn't do a Houdini on us, Tony volunteered to sleep in the other bed.

With Farrell safely shackled upstairs I took a walk down the drive with my mobile phone, and called the incident room from the middle of the wood. Ever since the intercept I'd been shitting myself with worry that we might have hurt or even killed somebody, so when I got through to Fraser, my first question was, 'Was everyone OK on the bypass?'

'Fine, fine,' he answered. 'No problems at all.'

'What about the guys in the van? Both vans.'

'A few bruises. A couple of vehicles bent. Otherwise,

nothing.'

'That's great. Who were those guys in the Lexus?'

'We don't know yet. They cleared off on foot into the hinterland. By the time the cops got there they'd gone. The car'd been stolen in Shrewsbury.'

'So we don't know if they were players or joy-riders?'

'The last, we reckon.'

'Well – hell. They gave us a fright and a half. And did you monitor those three calls?'

'We did. We got some numbers to work on. What about your lot?'

'We're all in good shape.'

'Your guest behaving?'

'More or less. But listen, we've set up the exchange for the morning . . .' I confirmed details of the arrangement and asked for back-up, both from SB and from the Regiment.

'Crafty bastards!' Fraser said. 'Typical, to call the RV on a motorway. Especially *there*. At that point the M25's four lanes in each direction, and at that time of the morning it'll be heaving with traffic, even though it's the weekend. Hell of a place to put on surveillance.'

'I know. But for Christ's sake don't do anything obvious. Don't have a car on the hard shoulder anywhere, not even on the opposite side. The slightest thing could put them off.'

'Leave it to us,' said Foxy. 'We'll be watching you. And once you've done the swap, we'll be going for a quick intercept of the PIRA vehicle.'

'OK. Can I speak to Yorky, please?'

Yorky came on, and when I had gone through things with him he echoed Fraser's disgust about the choice of location. 'Bah gum, it's bang under the flight-path out of Heathrow.' He paused. 'We'll have a chopper airborne, but it'll have to stand right off. There's no way

227

it can come overhead around that area.'

'I know,' I said. 'For Christ's sake keep everyone out of sight.'

'Fear not, Geordie. I've been in this business longer than you have.'

'I know. I'm getting jumpy, that's all. Any media leaks anywhere?'

'A reporter from a local paper got on to the police in Ludlow, and they told him there'd been a minor accident, that was all. That choked him off.'

I didn't get to sleep until nearly three o'clock. And all too soon the alarm went and Doughnut came in with a brew. Farrell, he told me, claimed he hadn't slept a wink, but Tony knew this was garbage because he'd heard the man snoring. I was glad to hear that Farrell had made no fuss about putting on the clothes we'd bought for him: black jeans, a white T-shirt and a dark-blue sweat top. Of course, he hadn't much option but to wear them: he couldn't carry on in his prison kit of striped shirt and brown trousers, and his own clothes, such as they were, had been left in a bag inside the police meat wagon. Having discovered from the screws at Winson Green that he had a thirty-six-inch waist, we'd deliberately gone for the next size up so he'd have to winch the trousers in with the belt that had been doctored to contain a tracking chip. When we got him he'd only been wearing a pair of cloth slippers on his feet, and so he also went happily for the new trainers we'd supplied. They looked like brand-new Reeboks, but they'd had a little expert attention around the heels.

By the time I got up, Doughnut already had some porridge on the go, and Farrell surprised me by consenting to get a bowl of it down his neck. His face and tongue had swollen more during the night and he had problems swallowing (he also looked fairly grotesque), but at least his fever seemed to have eased.

Nobody spoke much at breakfast. I think we were all feeling shattered. After a quick nosh we hooded our prisoner again, to make sure he didn't pick up any idea of where the safe house was, and set forth.

We pulled out in the minivan at 0500, Whinger again at the wheel, myself beside him, and Farrell cuffed to Tony in the back. To give each of them slightly more freedom we'd put them on two pairs of cuffs with a short chain linking them. We'd left Doughnut and Stew to look after the cottage, confident that the Regiment would have put plenty of other guys out to OP the rendezvous.

The rain had moved away, leaving the sky clear, but mist still hung in the hollows and made driving tricky until the light was strong.

We headed down through the Forest of Dean to the M4, and by the time we hit the motorway my spirits had really picked up. The thought of seeing Tim and Tracy again in a couple of hours gave me a tremendous lift. The dawn mist had burned off, and the glorious day that was developing exactly matched my mood. The early sun shone in our faces as we headed east, but I welcomed every ray of it.

To help while away the time, I tried to work out how many days had passed since I'd got back from Bogotá. It was twenty-eight or twenty-nine, but with Libya thrown into the middle the time seemed longer. No doubt it was the same for the hostages. With no word from me or anyone on our side, the four weeks must have stretched out like eternity. I worried that Tracy would be blaming me for not making more effort to find her. Well, I thought, it shouldn't be long now.

All went well until we were on our way past Reading. The traffic had been steadily building up, but all three lanes were still moving fast and everything seemed normal. Then, maybe three miles short of Exit 10, where we wanted to turn south for Bracknell and the M3, Whinger let out a curse as he saw brake-lights coming on in front of us. There was no chance of sliding up some slip road; all he could do was stick to the outside lane and wind down to a halt in company with everyone else.

'Shunt,' he said. 'Must be. What do we do?'

'Sit it out,' I told him. 'We've time yet.'

We sat and waited. Five minutes, ten, fifteen . . . and no movement. Twenty minutes, and we couldn't even see any flashing lights in the distance ahead. The block had tailed back for miles behind us.

The irony of the situation was not lost on me. If we'd have been responding to a real emergency we'd have ignored the rules and gone like shit off a shovel up the hard shoulder, prepared to front it out if the police turned snarky. But now, the last thing we could afford was any entanglement with the law. I knew SB would have warned off the force operating in the area of our rendezvous, telling them to keep their hands off a white Renault van with our plates on it, but down here in Berkshire it might be a different story. If coppers caught us with a hooded, cuffed prisoner in the back, our entire deception would be up the spout, Farrell would realise that he was being conned, and the only chance of recovering my family would be gone.

At last the lines of massed cars began to creep forward, only to stop again after a few yards. Whinger kept cursing and muttering under his breath, and presently his impatience started seeping into me. I shifted around in my seat, wondering what we could do.

'What the hell are all these people doing, heading into town on a Saturday?' I said irritably.

Nobody answered. Our covert radios were on board, but bundled up inside a bag. Because, we couldn't afford to let Farrell see or hear us using them. What we *could* use, though, was the mobile phone.

I turned round and said to Farrell, 'Here – we're in the shit with this traffic. You'd better call your contact in London on my mobile. Say we've got held up and may be late.'

'Jaysus,' he mumbled through his hood. 'I don't have the number. I left it in the house.'

'Call Belfast then, get the number again.'

'Get this fucking hood off of me first.'

'Not likely, mate. You can keep it on and talk through it. What's the number over there?'

Before Farrell could give it there was a sudden movement in the traffic ahead, and we began making ground again, reaching a reasonable speed. 'Cancel that,' I said. 'Hold on a minute. Looks like we're going now. I don't think you need call after all.'

Then, inevitably, everything slowed down. This time, before we came to a halt, I spotted a break in the central barrier. A section of the heavy rail had been removed, maybe for repair, and the gap was blocked only by plastic cones. The traffic coming the other way was light.

To alter the RV time would be the final resort. Anything rather than that . . .

'Through there, Whinger!' I said on impulse, pointing at the cones. 'Whip through and turn round. We'll go some other way.'

Whinger wasn't the sort to query a decision like that. He watched for a gap in the oncoming traffic, made the U-turn in a second and joined the stream flowing west. Some officious turd hooted in protest, but as I looked back in the wing-mirror I saw one or two other cars following our example.

'If any self-righteous bastard reports us, I'll murder him,' I said. 'Now for a bit of map-reading.'

Heading west, we came off the motorway at the next exit, and immediately entered a nightmare of sub-urbanised villages and towns: Spencer's Wood, Swallowfield, Finchampstead, Crowthorne, Bagshot, all crawling with pottering weekenders. As I called the turns, Whinger went as fast as the van, the road and its competing users would let him, and eventually we battled our way through to Junction 3 of the M3. From there I calculated it was sixteen miles to our RV: sixteen minutes if we kept to sixty m.p.h. and met no more hang-ups. Since we had four minutes in hand, I told Whinger to pull into the forecourt of a garage, keeping well away from the pumps and the office.

'Where are we?' Farrell wanted to know.

'In some godforsaken arsehole of a lay-by,' I told him. 'We're going on in a minute.'

'I need a piss,' he said.

'You're not getting one here, with that hood on or without it. There are too many people passing. The cops have probably put out mug-shots of you all over the country. They've probably had pictures on the TV news. It only needs one person to see you and that's it.'

Four minutes later we slipped on to the M3 and stuck with the inside lane, which was moving at just about sixty. I felt my adrenalin coming up. Our target area was practically in sight, yet still there were umpteen things that could go wrong. I kept thinking of Tim, seeing the boy so clearly that I was pretty much talking to him. Tracy, too: I was getting the feel and smell of her again.

We reached the junction with the M25 in eight minutes – exactly what I'd reckoned. Eight more minutes to go. On our side of the big ring-road a solid river of traffic was flowing northwards, four lanes abreast. Again we kept in the slow lane, reaching Junction 13 in four minutes. As Yorky had predicted, the traffic there was yet more dense, all four lanes jam-packed with vehicles, nose to tail.

Three minutes to Exit 14, then a minute more. I looked at my watch, at Tony, at the hooded figure of Farrell. Jesus, I thought, the trouble this guy's caused me.

'Fourteen,' announced Whinger coolly, pointing up as we passed under the blue and white board. 'Sixty seconds to run. There's the phone, up ahead now.'

'Just pull in gently, as if we've got engine problems. There – go over now.'

Whinger put on his left indicator and cruised in. All we need now, I thought, is an AA or RAC van on patrol, coming to rescue us without being asked.

I checked my watch. We were thirty seconds early. As yet the RV was empty.

As Whinger came to a halt and switched on his panic lights, I said to Farrell, 'OK. We're on site. Stand by to transfer. The drill is going to be this: they'll park fifty metres behind us, one guy will walk towards us with the hostages, Tony will go back with you. In the middle of the gap, once my people are past him, he'll release you. Are you with me?'

'I am.'

'And don't fuck about. Don't start pulling or trying to run before he unlocks you, OK?'

Farrell nodded. Through the hood I could hear him breathing fast. I knew he was hot – we all were – but was sure this panting was caused by adrenalin.

'Pull the bonnet catch,' I told Whinger. As soon as I heard the click, I jumped out of the passenger door and whipped round the front of the van. There in the open the traffic roar was horrendous, and a wide-bodied jet, labouring up off the runway at Heathrow, added its scream to the general clamour. When I dialled the incident room on my mobile, I could hardly hear the voice on the other end.

'*Zulu One on RV now!*' I yelled, and I just made out a man's voice say, 'Roger.'

At least I'd confirmed that we were in position, and word would fly out over the radio to the guys deployed around us. The head-shed's intention was to go for a hard arrest on the PIRA wagon as soon after the exchange as possible. As I looked round I wondered where the hell anyone could have established an OP in this urban jungle. All about me were asphalt, brickwork, concrete walls, the blank ends of buildings, electric wires, pylons, roaring lines of traffic. Yet doubtless the guys were deployed in there somewhere, watching me.

I raised the bonnet of the van and propped it with the stay, pretending to tinker with the engine. A British Airways 747 came roaring over, drowning out even the traffic. I wondered where it was heading. America, maybe. I thought of the passengers settling themselves for a long flight, the stewardesses putting on their aprons to start serving breakfast.

My watch said 0847. Already the opposition were late. Typical PIRA. I felt sure that at any moment some of their dickers would pass in some vehicle of their own – maybe two separate lots of them – and send word back over their CB radio links: 'Yeah, yeah, they're there. It looks OK. It's clear. It's on.' I tried not to stare at the drivers as they whipped past, for fear of putting the wind up one of the scouts.

Back round the passenger side of the van, I stuck my head in through the window. The noise was less deafening inside.

'Late!' I yelled at Farrell. 'We made it on time. Your bloody people are late.'

'Don't worry,' he shouted. 'They'll be here.'

Yet his composure was only skin-deep. When another minute had gone by with no sign of action, he

234

began to fidget and curse. I stood by the passenger door, gazing back at the unending flood of vehicles pouring up from the south. Another jet screamed out of the airport. It looked like the control tower was launching a plane every two minutes.

At five minutes past H-hour, Farrell started effing and blinding, abusing the underlings in the PIRA for their incompetence. 'They're swine,' he went. 'They get pissed out of their minds at night, and can't get up in the morning for wallowing in their own shite.'

His tirade was getting on my nerves. 'Swine yourself!' I shouted. 'It was you who got us into this mess in the first place.'

At that instant Tony snapped, 'Look out! What's this?'

Through the small rear windows he'd seen another vehicle pulling up behind us. The first sight of it made my heart jump. It was an old banger of an estate car, beige-coloured, scruffy, decrepit, lop-sided, with patches of rust showing along the bottoms of the doors; exactly what I'd expect the PIRA to be driving. But a second later I realised there was something wrong. The arrangement was that the PIRA would pull up fifty yards short of us, not five. Besides, this wagon was going down fast. Steam and smoke were pouring out through the radiator grille and from the sides of the bonnet.

The smouldering wreck wobbled to a halt about four feet from our rear bumper. The driver's door opened, and a stout, middle-aged Indian, a Sikh with a grey beard and white turban, eased himself out on to the hard shoulder. He took one despairing look at the smoke and steam, then waddled towards me.

Shit, shit, shit! I thought. Of all the world's disasters, this is the worst that can befall us. With that thing there, nothing on earth will make the PIRA stop.

The Sikh came lurching up. 'Sir, I am apologising most profoundly,' he began. 'Car is overheating. You help me with rope? Yes?'

It flashed through my mind to say, 'Do the fucking rope trick yourself, mate, car and all,' but it wasn't the moment for jokes, and I didn't want to be rude. What could I tell the poor bugger? Even if I'd drawn my pistol and ordered him to get his jalopy away from me it would have been impossible for him to obey.

All I said was, 'Sorry, no rope.' I spread my hands, and fervently hoped that was it. But the brute had spied the mobile sprouting from my pocket.

'Make call, please,' he went, pointing at it.

'Sorry, it's not working. No batteries.'

'Sir – you are very kind gentleman. You are giving me lift to garage.'

I felt frantic. I glanced at my watch. Six minutes past the deadline. Through the open window of our van I could hear Tony relaying events to Farrell.

'Sorry,' I said. 'I'm broken down as well.' I pointed at the raised bonnet. 'That's why I stopped by this phone.' Then I had a brainwave. 'There's a service station a couple of miles ahead,' I said, inventing the place on the spur of the moment. 'If you go on slowly, you'll make it.'

It was a shameless lie; I knew there was no service station for miles.

As I stood looking at the stranded Indian, my face twisted into a grimace of totally false goodwill, some sixth sense made me glance out into the passing traffic – and there, right beside me, was a small, grey van, old and dirty. The vehicle had slowed down, causing others to concertina behind it. Somebody clapped a hand on his horn, and others responded. For a second I had direct eye contact with the driver and front-seat passenger. Both were staring sideways at me, two pale young faces concentrating in a way that could mean only one thing: this was the PIRA wagon.

By the time I'd made the connection it was past. For a few yards it wavered in and out, as if the driver was about to pull on to the hard shoulder, but he never did. A few seconds later the van straightened and carried on to the north.

I stared after it, suddenly out of breath. Jesus, I thought: Tim was in that thing. Tracy was in it. My family had gone by within inches of me. I felt a terrific pull, as if that vehicle had been a powerful magnet.

Ignoring the Indian, I leapt back in front of our own wagon. Using the raised bonnet as a shield to make sure Farrell couldn't hear, I redialled the incident room. When I heard a voice answer, I said loudly, 'Zulu One. The PIRA wagon's gone past the RV. Heading north. Didn't stop. It's a grey Morris Thousand van with some black logo on the side.'

Again I heard, 'Roger,' and that was about all.

I slammed the bonnet shut. The Indian was still hovering, a hurt look on his face. I brushed past him, jumped aboard, closed the door and said to Whinger, 'Let's go!'

Whinger started the engine and we eased back into the slow lane.

'See 'em?' I asked.

'Yep.' Whinger nodded. 'The grey van.'

'That's the one. Get after it! Oh, Jesus!'

'What happened?' Farrell snarled from behind us.

I told him in words of one syllable: 'Why the hell did they not stop?'

'How could they, with another fucking vehicle up your arse? It might have been full of coppers or anything.'

'It was full of big, fat Indian women in headscarves,'

237

I told him. 'They could have seen that. What the fuck did they think they were doing? And what'll they do now? Will they wait up ahead or come back on another run?'

'Not a chance,' said Farrell. 'That's it for the day. One run, and that's it. They'll never try again at the same place.'

'In that case, we won't either.'

Using hand-signs I indicated that Whinger was to ignore the M4 west, our natural route for base, which was coming up fast, and carry on clockwise towards the M40.

As he drove I was struggling to make a mental readjustment. The let-down was colossal. In spite of my attempts not to, I'd been counting chickens prematurely. I'd assumed that in about five minutes the whole drama was going to be over, that we'd be rid of Farrell and I'd have my loved ones back, that we'd all be able to go home in peace and get on with our normal lives.

Now everything had ended in fiasco, and we were faced with the task of setting up another meeting somewhere else. The prospect was so appalling that for a few minutes my mind went blank. All I could focus on was the fact that Farrell knew the precise location of the RV. Therefore he knew we were on the M25. Therefore we needed to confuse him about the route we were taking home. My own priority was to confer with the incident room, and with Stew and Doughnut back at the cottage – but to do that I had to get out of Farrell's earshot.

First of all we needed a pit-stop so that everyone could relieve themselves; Farrell wasn't the only one bursting for a piss. A service station would be out of the question – we couldn't march a manacled prisoner into the bog without attracting attention – so the only alternative was open country. We took the M40 west and came off at Junction 2. From there we headed south until we were in some dense woods. At last, when he'd made sure there were no giveaway signs in sight, Whinger pulled off on to a cart-track, and we all thinned out into bushes to do our business. Once again the guy who had the worst of it was Tony, chained as he was to Farrell.

While they were busy I got in another call to the incident room, to say that we were returning to base. I told Fraser what had happened, and asked him to pass word to the cottage. His only news was that the grey van had been found abandoned within two miles of where I'd reported it. The PIRA must have had another vehicle coming along behind, and transferred personnel only a couple of minutes after the van had passed the RV. Sure enough, Fraser told me it had been stolen earlier that morning in North London. There were some old cushions on the floor in the back, and forensic examination might reveal whether or not the hostages had been on board, but for the time being there was no indication. Our guys had established an OP in a factory overlooking the motorway, and although they'd watched the RV for a further hour, no other vehicle had stopped there.

As we set off for base my mind was reeling with disappointment. But at the same time I couldn't stop thinking about the wretched Indian, who was probably still where we'd abandoned him. The incident must have convinced him that all Englishmen are heartless bastards, racist to the roots of their hair, and treacherous to boot.

ELEVEN

'Get on the phone,' I told Farrell the moment we were back in the cottage, 'find out what the hell happened, and fix another RV for this evening. But keep it short: we don't want anyone tracing calls to this number.'

With ill grace he started dialling his contacts in Belfast. I'd already discovered from Fraser that one of the numbers was the Rock Bar, a drinking den on the Falls Road, which stayed open twenty-four hours a day and was frequented by most of the leading players in the Belfast Brigade. The RUC naturally had eyes on the place, and filmed all the comings and goings, but the PIRA men were so arrogant and sure of themselves that they patronised it regardless. The Falls Road was their territory, and they weren't going to stand for any interruption of their favourite routines.

On our way back Farrell had thrown me by identifying a piece of classical music that had blasted out of the radio as Whinger was jumping stations. We only got a few seconds of it, but our prisoner suddenly woke up and cried, 'Beethoven! *Leonora* number three.' The music sounded pretty dire to me, and the rest of us looked at each other with expressions of alarm, but I could see that on Farrell's part it was a spontaneous reaction, not designed to impress us. Once again I thought it very strange that a man with his record of crime and thuggery could also have genuine cultural interests.

Back at base, the only two guys on our team still

functioning properly were Doughnut and Stew, who'd got their heads down while we were on the road, managing to catch up on a bit of lost sleep. The rest of us were edgy with hunger and exhaustion – and I knew that sheer tiredness could lead to somebody making a fatal mistake. Farrell himself seemed almost comatose, but still we were aware that one careless remark from any of us might arouse his suspicion. I had therefore asked Doughnut to take over as warder-nanny so as to give Tony a break, and I stood over them as they swapped the handcuffs.

Stew had had the brilliant idea of putting some potatoes to bake in the oven, and the cottage was full of the smell of them, good and crusty. I told the others to get on and eat – breakfast or lunch or whatever it was – and said I'd join them as soon as we'd set up another meeting.

Farrell finished his call to Belfast, then dialled the mobile number, which SB had traced to West London.

'Mother of Mary!' he exclaimed after talking for a minute. 'Why ever didn't they stop?' He listened for a few more seconds then said, 'That's no way to carry on. He'll have to be reported . . . What? . . . Of course I was. Bursting for a run-out as well.'

I grabbed the receiver from him and said, 'Hello. This is Geordie Sharp. Stop pissing about and fix a rendezvous tonight.'

'It was yous fellers that fucked it up,' retorted the voice.

'Bollocks, mate. We were there ahead of schedule.'

'But you never had our man with you.'

'What d'you mean? He was there in the back of the van. He just told you.'

'Why wouldn't you let us see him, then?'

'You would have seen him if you'd stopped.'

'And a second vehicle up your arse-end as well.'

241

'That was nothing to do with us. The guy's engine had overheated, that was all. He arrived at the last minute. If you'd bloody well been on time he wouldn't have been there.'

There was a sick laugh at the other end of the line, and the man said, 'You fucking wee bastards! That's all you are if you expected anyone to stop with that circus parked there.'

'Listen,' I said, struggling to keep my temper, 'insults aren't going to get your man back. Like I said, name another time and place for an exchange. We'll call you again in fifteen minutes.' With that I slammed the receiver down.

'Come on,' I told Farrell. 'We've got to get something down our necks.'

At about 11.30 we had a peculiar brunch of fried cod steaks and baked spuds with plenty of butter in them, and tea to drink. It bugged me to have Farrell slurping and spluttering alongside the rest of us in the kitchen – I would have liked to see the bastard starve – but I knew it was in my interest to keep him in reasonable health. Again he surprised me, this time with the way he ate. Considering that one hand was cuffed, his table manners were immaculate. We didn't give him a knife, but he held his fork properly, and when he'd finished he laid it down neatly on his plate. He didn't stuff his mouth full of food and swill tea down through it; he ate first and drank afterwards. It was only his swollen tongue and lip that made him clumsy. At least, while he was eating, he didn't try to make conversation.

With food inside me, my mind came back to life. I urgently needed to confer with the head-shed, but reckoned I'd do best to wait until we had the second RV lined up.

'This time,' I told Farrell, 'I'm talking to your man myself.'

'Please yourself. You've got the number.'

When I dialled, the phone was answered instantly, as if the guy had been waiting for the call.

'All right,' I began. 'Where's it to be?'

'No exchange,' went the voice.

'No exchange? Why not?'

'We're not satisfied with the identity of your hostage.'

'What the hell d'you mean? You know bloody well who he is.'

'We know who you *say* he is. But we've no proof that it's him.'

'Jesus!' I took a deep breath and put my hand over the mouthpiece. 'They don't believe it's you,' I told Farrell. He flipped his left hand up and back in a gesture of disgust, and I talked into the phone again. 'He's spoken to people he knows in Belfast. They must have recognised his voice.'

'That's the point, exactly. They said it didn't sound like him at all.'

'He's got a split tongue and lip, that's why. He hit his face when we rammed the prison van and got his teeth smacked together. He can't use his tongue properly. That's why he sounds peculiar.'

'We need to get a proper look at him. We need to see it's himself.'

'Ah, bollocks! Like I said, you *would* have seen him if you'd been on time this morning.'

'We need to see him, or there's no deal.'

The way the man kept repeating himself, like a zombie, really got to me. I put my hand over the mouthpiece again and exclaimed. 'This is shite!' Opening up again, I said, 'Wait one.'

With my hand back in position I asked Farrell, 'D'you know this guy?'

'Not at all.'

243

'Well, speak to him anyway. He doesn't believe you're you.'

'Holy fucking Jaysus!' Farrell grabbed the phone and blasted off, bollocking the fellow to kingdom come. But for all his obscenities he made little progress; the man at the other end was like a brick wall. In the end Farrell yelled, 'All right, then! I'm going to call one or two of my friends in West Belfast and get them to put a fucking bomb under you.' He would have rung off if I hadn't signalled him urgently to give me back the phone.

'So what are you proposing?' I asked.

'Come to the Great Western marshalling yard at Swindon at eleven tonight.'

'Wait one, I need to write this down.'

I looked round for a pen and paper, but it took a hell of a search before we dug out a pencil from a drawer. The only thing we could find to write on was the opened-out packet which had held the cod steaks. At last I was ready. 'Carry on,' I said.

'Go down Brunel Road to the bottom, past the station . . .'

'Brunel,' I repeated, 'OK.'

'At the bottom, don't turn left where the main road swings round, but carry straight on through a gateway. There's wire mesh gates across it. They may be closed, but even if they are they aren't locked, you can push them open. Are you with me?'

'I am.'

'There's two brick pillars at the entrance, holding the gates. Pass between them and you're in the old yard.'

'Got it. Eleven o'clock, you said?'

'Eleven, so it is. Farrell and two. No more.'

'Three,' I said. 'One to drive and two to look after your man.'

'All right. Three. In that case there'll be three of us as well.'

The line went dead.

Farrell's face was dark with anger. 'What a shower of cunts!' he snapped. 'They've got some bloody cheek, demanding to see me. Wait now while I get the bastards sorted.' He started to dial Belfast numbers again, but things quickly went yet further downhill. One after another, his cronies gave him the brush-off. Either they refused to speak to him and let their side-kicks take the call, or they told him to get stuffed and stick to the plan already made. With every call I could see him growing more rattled; it was clear that he couldn't understand why the players in Belfast were behaving as they were. It didn't make sense to him. Something had changed.

Gradually his bluster abated, and by the end of his calls he was looking really scared.

'What's the problem?' I asked. 'They don't sound very happy.'

'Fucked if I know.' He shook his head in a mixture of disbelief and alarm, muttering, 'They've all gone round the twist.'

I tried to draw him out, but he wouldn't say any more – and as I knew the telephone conversation had been recorded I didn't press very hard. We could check it out later.

As if to change the subject, Farrell suddenly said, 'I need a shower.'

Since he was smelling like the ferrets my Uncle Phil used to keep at the bottom of the garden I said, 'Good idea,' and suggested that after he'd had a clean-up we should all get our heads down.

We'd taken the precaution of screwing the bathroom window shut, so that it presented no security risk, and I reckoned it was safe to unshackle Farrell while he washed, provided there were two of us present when he came out again.

'You can let him go,' I told Doughnut. 'But he's to

245

get undressed in the passage and leave his clothes outside.'

The ablutions went according to plan. When Farrell stripped off, I saw that he was indeed well built, with powerful shoulders, but running to fat around the midriff. When he went into the shower I stepped outside and walked round the back of the cottage to keep an eye on the bathroom window, just in case he tried anything funny. For a few minutes I stood there, enjoying the sunshine, listening to the birds, and fervently wishing that we could bring this horrible nightmare to an end, so that life could return to normal.

We'd bought Farrell shaving kit, toothbrush and so on before the intercept, and when he emerged ten minutes later, he was looking a lot more spruce. The wound dressings had got wet, so I peeled them off and put new ones on. The inflammation seemed to have gone down a bit, but as a precaution I made Farrell take a couple more of the white tablets. As soon as we had him shackled to the bed again, wrist and ankle, everyone felt more relaxed.

I was all for getting my head down as well, but first I had to take another walk into the wood. Half-way down the hill a grey squirrel ran across the track in front of me and raced up the beech tree I was proposing to stand under. For a moment it sat on a horizontal branch with its tail fluffed up behind it, but when it saw me coming in close to the trunk, it whipped up into the greenery above. Saucy little bastard, I thought. It's all right for you. You don't have much to worry about.

'We're OK so far,' I told Yorky over the mobile. 'Did you pick all that up – the details of our rendezvous for tonight?' I confirmed the arrangements, such as they were, and asked him to get surveillance on the site as soon as possible. 'The PIRA are bound to send in dickers,' I said. 'But probably they won't turn up until evening. It would be great if we could get eyes in there first.'

'No problem,' Yorky replied. 'There's two guys on their way already. I sent them off as soon as I heard the plan. The other thing we need to do is stick a tracking device on the PIRA car. This should give us a great chance. As soon as we've got an idea of the topography, we'll work something out – the optimum placing of your vehicle and all.'

'Thanks, Yorky. We're going to need some back-up, too. It's possible the PIRA will try to lift Farrell. We could do with a QRF somewhere close.'

'That's no problem either. Again, we'll suss out the site and make arrangements. Geordie, you sound tired.'

'I am. I'm fucking knackered. We've been on the go since five this morning. Didn't get much sleep, either.'

'Why not get your head down, then?'

'I'm going to. There's not a lot we can do between now and then. Er . . . Yorky?'

'What's that?'

'Any more news about PIRA safe houses? Any news at all?'

'Yes. They're concentrating on two flats in Acton. Our Red Team's moved up to Hounslow Barracks. They're on standby there. Twenty guys, all their vehicles and kit. The police have a team from SO19 standing by as well. In fact, the commander of SO19 has just been here, going through various options with the head-shed.'

'So there is some movement?'

'Definitely.'

'Thanks, Yorky. That sounds great.'

'Don't worry, lad. Everything's in hand at this end. Listen – your prisoner doesn't sound a very nice guy.'

'What d'you mean?'

'The RUC faxed us his dossier. The things he's been

suspected of but never got for: three murders, GBH, arson, extortion.'

'Didn't I tell you?'

'You did,' Yorky admitted. 'But when you see it written down . . . Keep a good grip on him, anyway.'

'Will do. But the bastard doesn't seem very happy. Something in those last calls pissed him off.'

'I know,' Yorky suddenly sounded quite chuffed. 'I've been listening to the tapes. His people seem to have turned against him, for whatever reason. They were giving him two fingers. One of them was talking about putting a CAT team on to investigate him.'

'No wonder he's shitting himself, then. I don't know what he's done, but obviously he's dropped a bollock somewhere. Since those last conversations he's really gone down.'

'That's right.'

'The sooner the miserable sod's off my hands, the better,' I said. 'Listen, Yorky, I'll call in again at four o'clock to check the form. OK?'

Now I understood why Farrell had become so agitated. The Civil Administration Teams are the PIRA's notorious means of enforcing discipline within the ranks. If someone gets a call saying, 'We need to come round and have a talk,' he knows he's for it – at the very least a few cold baths and some beatings to make him produce information, at worst a kneecapping or even an execution.

For three and a half hours I was dead to the world, and I awoke with the unpleasant but familiar sensation of not knowing where I was. Staggering up, I found Tony in the kitchen, heating up some soup.

'Get to sleep?' he asked.

'Yeah. How about you?'

'Sure did. Couple of hours. I feel a whole heap

248

better. Like some soup?'

'Great. In a minute, though. I'm just going to put in a call.'

Again I slipped out, down the track and into the wood.

'Yer daft bat,' said Yorky straight away. 'Where've you been?'

'Kipping it deadly,' I told him.

'Well done, lad. I was hoping you'd come on. We have two guys in an old railway wagon right alongside the RV site – Andy Peake and Terry Mason, from the SP team.'

'Fabulous,' I said. 'What wagon is it?'

'It's a closed freight car with the serial number zero nine two painted in big white numbers on the side. The sides are fairly intact, but part of the floor's gone, so they've got easy access to the track. They've a good view of the yard, and they're pretty sure no PIRA have shown yet.'

'All right. So what do we do?'

'You'll need to decoy the PIRA car as close to that wagon as you can. Then, while the players are concentrating on you and Farrell, somebody will slip out from between the wheels with a little goodwill package . . .' Yorky explained that the yard was a couple of hundred metres long but only fifty wide. Our best tactic, he said, would be to drive in along the left-hand side, close to the rails, and then at the end do a U turn, so that we came to rest facing back towards the entrance gate, with our left-hand doors close to the high wall that bounded the yard on the road side. Parked there we'd be opposite the occupied railway wagon, and the logical place for the PIRA to pull up would be right beside it, across the yard from us.

'Sounds good,' I said. 'What about back-up?'

'There'll be two cars, each with four, in the road

above. There's a pub up there, the Railway Arms, so there should be enough people coming and going to create a bit of a distraction. But our guys won't do anything or show themselves unless the PIRA start messing about. They'll only intervene if there's an attempt at a snatch.'

'Fair enough. Will you brief the police to stand off?'

'Of course. What vehicle will you be in?'

'The Granada. And I'm not taking any chances on this one. We're going to be there early.'

We set out in good time, with Farrell blindfolded once again. To give Whinger and Tony a break I had left them to house-sit, taking Stew to drive and Doughnut to act as principal minder. Another belt of wet weather had moved up from the south-west, and a soft rain was falling – no bad thing, as it would reduce visibility at the RV site. In another conversation with Yorky and Fraser I'd learned that, sure enough, two young fellows with every appearance of being PIRA dickers had appeared outside the Railway Arms at about half-past four and walked along the road that ran above the marshalling yard. They'd made one pass out and another back, and were presumably based in a car parked up there on the high ground. Without doubt they'd report our arrival to colleagues over a mobile phone or CB radio.

Whether or not Farrell had any inkling about where the safe house was, I couldn't be sure. On our way out to the rendezvous in the morning we'd made one diversionary detour off the M4 and driven through a few of the roundabouts on the outskirts of Swindon, purely to confuse him and give the impression that we weren't doing a sustained motorway run. Next, back on the M4, we'd come on the block at Reading and had to turn round, which providentially added to his disorientation. Then on the way home we'd come via the M40 and Oxford, so that once again there hadn't been any long stretch at high speed. All in all, it seemed to me that he'd have to be a bloody genius to work out the location of the cottage.

This time, as a further variation, we went north-about through Gloucester and across country to Cirencester, so that we came into Swindon from the north-west. By the time we hit the outskirts it was almost fully dark, and under the sodium lamps the streets were glistening with rain.

It may be that some other town in Britain has more roundabouts per square kilometre, but if it does I don't know where it is. We went through dozens of the bastards, some single, some double, and many of them practically touching each other.

'The town planners went fucking mad here,' I said as we missed a turn and had to circle yet again to pick up the right road.

'Too right,' Doughnut agreed.

We found Brunel Road with fifteen minutes in hand, so we decided on a drive-past.

'There's the entrance,' I said as we came towards the left-hand bend. The big mesh gates were shut, as predicted, and we only caught glimpses of the yard beyond.

'Pretty damn dark in there,' said Stew.

'Yep,' I agreed. 'But that's to our advantage.'

Again we were caught up in an insane network of roundabouts and one-way streets, with the result that it was nearly 2255 by the time we made our second run. This time I jumped out, slid back a bar-catch and pushed the right-hand gate open. Its base scraped over a rough surface – earth or cinders – but I forced it back, left it wide open and nipped into the car again.

'Now,' I said. 'Just take a swing round and park. Anywhere will do.'

Stew knew that my last remarks were cover. I'd briefed him on the exact procedure that Yorky and I had worked out.

There were the old railway wagons, on a line right beside the yard. They looked very tall, because there was no raised platform at that point and we were down on the same level as the tracks. Farrell was still hooded, so as we came level with number 092 I pointed at it silently, and Stew nodded. He drove past, then swung right-handed into a U-turn, brought the Granada to rest about three feet from the high wall, switched off the engine and doused the lights.

'OK.' I turned to Farrell. 'We're there. Now it's up to them.'

He only grunted in reply. I think he felt as nervous as we did, and I don't blame him. If anyone did attempt a snatch a fire-fight would erupt within seconds, and he'd be in the middle of it.

The only light in the yard was a feeble spill-over from street-lamps along the road above. Under the wall, we were in deep shadow. The floor was uneven and pock-marked with holes. I presumed it must once have been covered with railway tracks, and now pools of water glistened in the depressions left behind where the sleepers had been ripped out. The whole place looked black as coal, and whenever a train went by on the main line, only a few yards away, the noise sent my mind back to the steam engine which used to pull a few tourist carriages up and down a branch line near where I was brought up, in the north.

I wished to hell we could use our covert radios. I was a good friend of Andy Peake, one of the guys hidden in 092, and I longed to chat him up. Had he seen the dickers any more? Had they come down and sussed out the yard? Had any other car made an approach? Were our own guys in position up top? Andy would be

252

listening in on the net, and would know the score exactly. All *we* could do was hope that the lads had everything under control.

Once again the deadline came and went. To cover my anxiety, I began mentally rehearsing possible moves.

'When they arrive,' I told Farrell, 'you're going to stay put. You're not getting out. If they want a good look at you, they'll have to come up close and take a shufti through the window.'

'We'll see,' he said. 'I can't vouch for what cunts like that may do.'

Suddenly I found myself thinking of the hot, clear nights in the Libyan desert, a world away from this soft English rain. I thought of the moment when Norm had found he'd left his Magellan behind, and the crazy, blaring crackle of the *muezzin*'s first call to prayer as dawn was about to break. Once again I saw our target in his death throes, and heard his slippered feet going *slap, slap, slap* against the wall.

'Watch yourselves!' Stew's voice jerked me back to the present. 'There's a car trying to turn in at the gate.'

The driver had his right-hand indicator on, waiting for a couple of oncoming vehicles to pass. But when the road cleared, all he did was drive into the yard, swing straight round and out again.

'Lost,' said Stew. 'Can't blame him. There must be hundreds like him in this bloody maze.'

Five more minutes crawled past. Already the PIRA were ten minutes late.

None of us had anything to say. With the windows of the Granada open, we could hear sounds of revelry from the distant pub: drunken shouts and outbursts of song. I began to think the opposition had succumbed to temptation and gone in there. I'd known it happen in Ulster. Bombers or shooters, on their way to a hit, would stop off for a quick pint to steady their nerves, and end up drinking six or seven, so that they'd be out of their minds and the operation would have to be aborted. But this was only a harmless meeting, without danger, so, surely . . .

'Here we are!' said Stew.

This time a pair of lights swept through the gate without hesitation and blazed in our faces. In retaliation Stew snapped his headlights on to full beam and lit up an elderly-looking red Peugeot, cruising gingerly over the potholes. I held my breath, willing the driver to keep straight on along the line of the tracks.

Our psychological reading of the site must have been spot-on, because he did just that, and came to rest within a few inches of where we wanted him. Then he doused his lights and sat waiting.

I let half a minute tick by before declaring, 'If they're not coming, I'm going.'

I got out and walked round the front of the Granada. By then I'd un-zipped my jacket so that I had quick access to my shoulder holster, but as I strolled across I deliberately kept my hands well away from my hips. Out there in mid-yard I felt cold and exposed. I knew Andy was in the wagon straight ahead of me, beyond the Peugeot, and I was confident that I had more support behind me, up above, but if one of the players lost his nerve and opened fire, I'd be the first to get it.

A yard from the driver's window I stopped. The face inside the rain-spattered glass was still a blur. The flash of a torch in the fellow's eyes might be taken as a provocation, so I waited till he wound the window down by hand.

'Come to see someone?' I went.

'Where is he?'

'In the car.' I jerked my head backwards.

'Bring him over, then.'

'Not a chance. You can come and look.'

254

'Not fucking likely. You bring him here.'

In line of sight over the roof of the car, not ten feet away, I detected movement down among the wheels of truck 092. Jesus! I thought. Andy's not waiting. He's crawling out with his tracking device. Whatever might happen later, I had to keep the PIRA fully occupied for the next few seconds.

'Listen,' I said. 'Are you the guys who came up the M25 this morning?' As I spoke I leant forward and rested my hands on the edge of the roof, deliberately making the car rock in the hope that the movement would help cover any slight disturbance that Andy might create.

'Get yer hands off!' snapped the driver.

'I was only asking.'

'Get off anyway!'

'Was it you, then?' I stood up, letting the Peugeot rock back.

'What difference does it make?'

'You fucked up, that's all.'

Now I thought, I'm getting him well stropped up. I'll switch on the torch anyway.

The effect was excellent. The driver twisted in his seat, rocking the car again. 'Get that thing off!' he hissed.

But I'd already recognised him. He'd been the passenger in the grey minivan that morning, the guy with whom I'd had that flash of eye-contact. His companion in the passenger seat was an older man with stiff grey hair cut short, definitely not the driver on the M25. He was the one, I guessed: the player who'd come to make the identification.

I flashed my torch round the inside of the car, partly to make sure there was nobody else on board, partly to dazzle the occupants. Both of them twisted about in their seats, shielding their faces from the beam.

'I said, get that thing off,' said the driver.

'You told me there'd be three of you.'

'No, only two.'

'What happened to your mate?'

'He couldn't make it in time.'

'All right, then.' As if climbing down, I switched off the torch and said, 'Well, I'll make a compromise. We'll bring him half-way across. But that's all.'

Another main-line train trundled past, shaking the ground and filling the yard with the scream of big diesel engines as it picked up speed out of the station. Once again I caught a hint of movement under the railway wagon, and reckoned what I saw was Andy's heels going back into cover, his job done. He'd certainly had time to place a magnetic device on the petrol tank and crawl away to shelter. Stepping back ostentatiously, I turned round and walked towards the Granada.

'Get him out after all,' I told Doughnut. 'We'll take him half-way over.'

I opened the door and stood back, expecting Farrell to start creating. But he said nothing as Doughnut wriggled out crab-wise, and he followed him into the open without fuss. When the pair were on their feet I took off Farrell's blindfold and said, 'Right. We'll go twenty steps and stop.'

We walked forward three abreast to the middle of the yard, Doughnut on the right, Farrell in the middle, myself on the left. I was stepping on the tips of my toes. If any attempt at a snatch was going to be made, this was when it would come. And no snatch *would* take place, because if they tried anything, Doughnut and I would drop the pair of them.

For a few seconds there was no movement from the Peugeot. Then the passenger door opened, on the side away from us, and I knew it must be the grey-haired guy getting out.

256

As he advanced towards us I muttered to my two, 'Keep still. Your arms particularly.'

Behind us I heard a click, and I knew that Stew was opening the boot of the Granada so that he had immediate access to the loaded MP 5s. I could just make out that the PIRA man was carrying some light-coloured object in his left hand, but it looked harmless, like a big envelope. He stopped a yard from us, and I spotted his right hand coming up. In a split second I had my torch beam on him, and saw that he too was holding a flashlight, which he switched on and shone into our faces, first mine, then Doughnut's, then Farrell's. There the beam stopped.

'So it *is* you, yer fuckin' wee cuntie,' he muttered in a quiet, menacing voice. 'Even better looking than usual, with that pout on yer.'

If Farrell had been free, I'm sure he'd have hit the guy. As it was, he just said, 'Holy Mary! It's Marty Malone.'

There was a moment's silence, as if both men were getting over the shock of seeing each other. Then Farrell said, 'Jaysus, but I never thought I'd see you this side of the water.'

'Maybe you didn't. But you've seen me now. Which of these turds is Geordie Sharp?'

'I am,' I said, 'and watch yourself.'

'I'm watching, and I don't like what I'm seeing. So it's the mighty assassin I have before me, is it? Here.' He held out the manila envelope. 'Take this. It contains your orders.'

'Orders for what?'

'You'll see. If you go murdering our allies overseas, it's only fair you do something for us in return.'

A shiver of alarm ran up my back, but I had the presence of mind to come straight out with, 'I'm not with you. What are you on about?'

'Come on! We know you've been abroad.'

'What d'you mean? I've been nowhere.'

'Oh no? Not even to north Africa.'

I shook my head.

'Libya?' queried the man in a horrible, taunting voice. 'Ajdabiya camp?'

'Sorry, mate. Your wires are crossed somewhere. Those names mean nothing to me.'

The temptation to drop the guy was fearsome. From Farrell's reaction I knew he must be some big player. We could smack him and his driver in about five seconds. But if we did, that would be the end of Tim and Tracy.

The man shone his torch in my face again and said, 'You wouldn't be lying to me, would you, Sergeant?'

'Listen, I told you. I've never heard those names. I don't know what the hell you're on about.'

'General al-Khadduri was very important to us. We didn't like losing him.'

'General who?'

'The man you shot.'

'Look,' I said, 'piss off, and stop all this rubbish. Now that you've seen your man, you'd better get going before the law arrives to break up the party.' I made a half-turn to the right and said to my lot, 'OK. Let's go.'

As we walked away, the PIRA guy stood looking after us until we were nearly at the car. Then he too turned and went back to his vehicle.

'Let them thin out first,' I told Stew. Internally, I was seething. Jesus Christ! an inner voice was shouting. How in God's name did they find out about Libya? Or *do* they really know about it? Are they just guessing that the SAS was involved? Then suddenly I realised: it was Karen, that bitch of a policewoman, telling them I was abroad when they called. *That's* what they'd cottoned on to. They can't have any proof, I told myself, they've simply put two and two together . . . and made about ten.

The worst thing was that I couldn't utter a syllable of these violent thoughts, or Farrell would have been on to it in a flash. I just sat there in the dark with my mind racing as we waited for the opposition to clear. After a minute it became clear that they were doing just the same, and I said to Stew, 'Ah, fuck it, let's go. Fast, as well.'

Our back tyres spun on the cinders as he put in a scorching take-off. In a second we were through the gate and burning up the hill. Behind us I saw lights come on as the Peugeot also got going. From its speed down the yard, I reckoned the party was going to try and tail us.

'Take the first left you can!' I snapped. 'They're going to play funny buggers.'

Though not quite in the Whinger class, Stew was no slouch as a driver. Before the Peugeot had even gained the top of the hill and come into sight, he'd dived left-handed into a residential street, pulled into the kerb between two parked cars and doused his lights. Looking out through the rear window, we saw the Peugeot hurtle past along the main drag.

'Great!' I said. 'Now we can take it easy. Give it a minute, and we'll slide out the way we came.' Then, as though it were a casual afterthought, I added, 'What the hell was that guy on about – Libya and all that?'

'Ask me another,' said Stew.

'Any idea, Doughnut?'

'Not a clue.'

'Nor me. Sounds as if they lost a key player or something. Some Arab, by the name . . . whatever it was. Tell you what, I could do with something to eat.'

'Me too,' said Stew. 'There's a good few takeaways about. I was eye-balling them on the way in.'

My mind was very much on the contents of the buff envelope, but instinct told me to play that down as well. So for the time being I left the package on the floor behind my feet. Five minutes later, with no further manifestation of the red Peugeot, we drove back on to the highway, and at the fifty-seventh roundabout (or thereabouts) we found a Chinese takeaway still open. Chicken and chips all round put us back in good heart; we ate sitting in a lay-by, and didn't hood Farrell up until we were ready to set off for home.

Then, as Stew pulled out on to the Cirencester road, I picked up the envelope and switched on the map-reading light to examine its contents. The first thing I saw was an Ordnance Survey map, a sheet of the 1:25,000 series, two and a half inches to the mile, covering part of the Chiltern Hills. Next I came on a page of what looked like instructions, typed in short, numbered paragraphs. Only when I unfolded it and looked at the head of the page did I realise that it was addressed to me. And when I read it, my breath seemed to lock up in my chest.

With the motion of the car and the feeble light, I couldn't take in every word. But the gist of the document was all too clear. Because I had been personally responsible for the murder of a leading financial supporter, it said, I was now ordered to carry out an operation for the IRA. To secure the release of my family, I not only had to hand Farrell over, I was also required to shoot the Prime Minister on the terrace of Chequers, his official country house in Buckinghamshire, on the morning of Thursday 2 June – two days' time. If I failed, the hostages would be killed and their weighted bodies would be dropped into the Thames.

I think we were nearly in Cirencester, a dozen miles down the road, before I fully took in what I was reading. The idea was so outrageous that at first I thought it was some grisly joke. Assassinate the Prime Minister? They couldn't be serious. Then I saw the notes that somebody had made after a recce of the park at Chequers, with bearings and distances, and details of the security arrangements protecting the house, and I realised that the plan was in deadly earnest.

Stew must have seen that I was shaken, because he glanced sideways at me and said, 'Everything OK, Geordie?'

'Yeah, yeah.' I switched off the map light and tried to sound flippant. 'Just the usual bloody nonsense. We'll sort it out when we get back.' But everything was far from OK. I felt the whole world was coming down on top of me.

TWELVE

During the journey back nobody spoke much: Doughnut kept the music going on the radio, and when Farrell
asked me some question I pretended to have dozed off.
I knew Andy would have reported direct from the
railway wagon, so that the SB guys in the incident room
would already know that our meeting had taken place.
All the same, they'd be panting to hear our version of
the story; but with Farrell in the car I wasn't going to
start honking off about it while we were on the road.

It was after one when we reached the cottage.
Whinger and Tony had sat up waiting for us, and they
got a brew on as soon as we arrived. Of course they
wanted to know how things had gone, so I described
the meeting a bit and said that everything had been OK.
I told them that Farrell's identity had definitely been
confirmed, but I didn't mention the PIRA orders.
When Farrell started asking about them, I said they
were a load of shit and we'd deal with them in the
morning. Then, after we'd all had a cup of tea, I asked
Tony to put the man to bed.

'It's like looking after a goddamn baby!' he protested.
'The next thing I'll have to do is wipe his butt for him.'

'I know. But someone's got to do the job. And
anyway, our baby's special. When this is all over, I'll see
you're issued with a diploma, so that you can get a job
as a nanny.'

As for me – I couldn't imagine going to sleep. I

needed to call the incident room, but first I wanted to talk things through with the other lads. So, with Farrell safely shackled to the bed and out of earshot upstairs, we settled into a Chinese parliament in the living room.

At first the others were as incredulous about the orders as I'd been. The scheme was so monstrous they couldn't believe it. But as we went through the PIRA reports, we could see how thorough the terrorists had been in their reconnaissance and research. The documents were semi-literate in places, but neatly laid out by a word processor, and full of information.

'Listen to this,' I said, and I read out a paragraph labelled 'Political Background':

A conference for Commonwealth Heads of State will take place at Chequers on 2 and 3 June. The first of the foreign dignitaries is due to arrive there at 1100 hours on 2 June. The first full session of the meeting will start at 1430 that day.

> The Prime Minister will travel down from London by car the night before, 1 June. When in the country during the summer months it is his habit to walk out into the garden before breakfast, and before any guests are up. He is a very early bird. Often out by 0630. Being a rose freak, he likes particularly to go round the rose garden on the south terrace. There is every chance that on the morning of 2 June he will be attacking the greenfly by 0700 am at the latest. This will present a sniper at Point D with an ideal opportunity . . .

I picked up another sheet of paper and said, 'There's no doubt they've been and cased the joint.' I read them some more:

The range from Point D to the retaining wall at

the front of the south terrace is 580 yards. The security screen round the house extends no more than 200 yards. Therefore Point D lies well beyond the reach of cameras and other security devices.

'Sounds as though their intelligence is shit-hot,' I added. 'They must have people all over the place. I mean, we know they've got men in London, but it looks like they've got Swindon sewn up, they've spent a lot of time at Chequers . . . They can put guys in wherever they need them. The question is, how the hell do we respond?'

'We can't handle this on our own,' said Whinger. 'Got to tell the incident room and the head-shed.'

'We'll call them in a minute,' I agreed. 'Fraser's going to do his nut. He's been wittering on about a shoot in London – but wait till he hears this.'

Tony, practical as ever, asked, 'What weapon are they proposing for the shoot?'

'There's something here . . .' I flipped back a couple of pages and read out: ' "The sniper weapon will be collected from a transit hide, details later." '

'Gotta be some weapon, to be effective at the range they're talking about.'

'Wait a minute,' said Whinger. 'It's not that fucking great five-oh they had in Ulster, is it?'

'Could be,' I told him. 'Could easily be. SB had wind that some big cannon was being brought over, or maybe *had* been brought over already.'

'A five-oh!' Tony whistled. 'That's something else.'

'We're jumping to conclusions,' I said. 'But that's what it sounds like.'

Everyone in the Regiment who'd served in Ulster knew about the fearsome rifle with which members of the security forces had been taken out in the late eighties and early nineties. It was so accurate that it could hit a man at a thousand yards, so powerful that a round would go straight through a flak-jacket and blow the wearer away. The guy using the weapon had become such a menace that the SAS had twice tried to get him. They'd set up special patrols that appeared to be from the green army, in the hope of luring the sniper to take a shot and give his position away, but by a combination of luck and guile he'd always evaded them and had never been accounted for.

'If they're talking about a range of six hundred yards,' said Tony, 'that's peanuts for a weapon of that calibre.'

'All right,' I said. Somehow, thinking about the big rifle had suddenly cleared my mind. A flash of intuition had shown me the way ahead. But all I said for now was, 'What are we going to suggest?'

'Suggest?' Whinger looked baffled. 'Who to?'

'The head-shed and Special Branch.'

'Isn't it up to *them* to suggest something?'

'I mean, are we going to have a crack at this or not?'

'At what? Sorry, Geordie, I'm not with you.'

'The shoot. Why don't we go through with it? Keep the charade going. Tell the PIRA we're on-side with them for the big hit.'

The others leant back in their seats with expressions of amazement on their faces. Stew said, 'You have to be joking.'

'The bastards have me over a barrel. The only thing we can do is play for time, right up to the last second. We know the search for the hostages is closing in, but we're not at the end of it yet. It's the only option I have. It's the zero option.'

'Take it easy, Geordie,' said Tony. 'Don't tell me you're going through with this?'

'Of course I'm not. But I might as well pretend I'm on, just to play the PIRA along.'

This time nobody spoke. They all stared at me in silence as if I'd flipped completely.

'Listen,' I continued, 'everything's gone brilliantly so far. The whole idea of the intercept was outrageous, but we hacked it. Nobody got hurt. No security leak. Nobody any the wiser. One van wrecked, but so what? We've had fantastic back-up from the Regiment and the police. And from the politicians, come to that. *And* the Prime Minister. If we just stay cool, we can carry the process one stage farther.'

Whinger shook his head. 'I still don't get it. Unless you *do* drop the guy, how are you going to make the PIRA hand your family over?'

'It's all a question of timing. We buy more time by shaping to go through with the shoot. In the two days between now and the second of June, SB may crack the puzzle.'

'Time . . .' Doughnut said suddenly. 'Did Andy get a device on the PIRA car, I wonder? If he did, Special Branch may have a breakthrough already. The car may have led them to the hostage location.'

'Possible,' I agreed. 'Look. I'm going down to camp.'

'Now?' said Whinger. 'It's two o'clock on Sunday morning.'

'The incident room will be manned. They need to know about this soonest. After all, this is a national emergency – or about to become one. And the head-shed need to know that Ostrich is blown.'

'Ostrich!' exclaimed Whinger. 'What a fuck-up!'

'You didn't leave the Libyans a little present after all?' I went. 'Like a copy of the head-shed's secret telephone directory?'

'Piss off, mate.'

For a few seconds silence prevailed. Then Stew said, 'The powers that be will never sanction a phoney shoot. It's too dicey. They'll tell you to screw the nut on that

266

one.'

'Why?' I challenged him. 'Hitting a guy at six hundred yards *does* take a bit of doing. But missing him – that's a piece of cake. If I'm holding that rifle, I can tell you, the man'll be as safe as houses.'

'Sorry, Geordie.' Whinger shook his head. 'I still don't see how this is going to work.'

I cleared my throat and started again. 'We show Farrell these orders, right? We tell him we're prepared to go ahead. But he has to come with us on the shoot, so he can see for himself what's happening. You with me?'

'More or less.'

'Also we tell him that, immediately after the shot, things have got to happen fucking quick, or we'll be nicked in the park at Chequers. That means that he's got to give the word for the release of the hostages the moment the shoot goes down.'

'So?' Whinger still looked highly sceptical.

'The head-shed briefs the Prime Minister. On the morning he's to take a wander out on to his terrace, as per normal. By then we're in an OP, watching the house. We fire a single shot, close past him. At the crack, he drops and lies still. As soon as Farrell sees he's down, he gives the order for the hostages to be handed over at a prearranged RV.'

'How's he supposed to communicate?'

'Over my mobile.'

'And how does he think he's going to get his own arse away out of the park?'

'We'll tell him to have his guys lay on a chopper. They can hire one to come in and pick us up. We'll fly out together. Then, later, we ditch him. I need to think that bit through . . .'

Whinger shook his head again. 'They'll never buy it.'

'Who won't?'

'The police, for one. Can you imagine them letting

a leading IRA player creep up on the Prime Minister with a bloody great five-oh rifle? The very idea'll send them fucking ballistic.' He broke off and screwed up his face in his efforts to imitate a plod on the beat: ' "Hexcuse me, sah. Before you pull that triggah, may I hinspect your firearms certificate, please?" For fuck's sake!'

'Farrell won't have the rifle,' I insisted. 'I'll have it. That's the point. There'll be two of us with him, one to mind him, one to shoot.

'In general, if we seem to be co-operating with the PIRA, we'll keep the lid on the whole thing. There'll be no risk to anyone. On the contrary, by agreeing to go through with the shoot, we'll bring a serious threat under control. We'll take possession of a dangerous weapon, and with any luck we'll bust the London ASU in the process.'

I looked round the tired faces, and thought I saw a couple wavering. 'What if we *refuse* to co-operate?' I persisted. 'Number one: I don't get the hostages back; the PIRA will kill them and dump them in the river. Number two: we're stuck with Farrell. Number three: the PIRA still have the rifle; the shoot will go down anyway, probably at some later date. The security forces will be left with the same problem. The threat may be deferred, but it'll still exist. The London ASU will remain intact, and they may easily get the Prime Minister in the end.'

'Well, whatever,' Tony began cautiously, 'you better move pretty damn fast. There's less than two days to get organised. If we pick up the weapon at all, we've got to test-fire it someplace. Farrell will insist on that. Otherwise, how in hell are we supposed to know where it's shooting?'

'Good point. That's why I'm heading for camp right now.'

'Want me to come with you?' asked Whinger.

'Thanks, Whinge, but I'll be OK. You might be needed here. I'll probably get my head down in the sergeants' mess for a couple of hours, then come back first thing in the morning.'

'What if Farrell starts asking where you are?' Stew asked.

'Tell him I'm asleep,' I said. 'Or just don't tell him anything.'

For a quiet take-off, I rolled the Granada down the hill and started the engine by letting out the clutch in third gear when I reached the gate at the bottom of the drive. Then, as soon as I was under way, I called the incident room on the mobile and got a duty officer strange to me.

'Geordie Sharp,' I said. 'I'm coming in. There's been a big development. I'll need to speak to Commander Fraser. Can you get hold of him?'

'Not to worry,' came the answer. 'He's here already. I'll put him on.'

'Geordie?' came Fraser's voice. 'Where are you?'

'Heading your way. I'll be there in half an hour.'

'What's new?'

'Can't tell you from here. Any luck with that car?'

'Yes and no. Tell you when I see you.'

'OK . . . and listen.'

'Yes?'

'I need an urgent meeting with the ops officer. Yorky Rose as well. Can you alert them?'

'Right away?'

'Afraid so.'

Rolling into camp at three in the morning made me feel I was back at the start of the whole drama, back to the night we had got in from Bogotá and I found my family gone. That now seemed as though it had been light-years ago. The last two days and nights alone had been so full that I felt I hadn't seen Stirling Lines in months.

By the time I ran up the stairs to the incident room a full reception committee was there to meet me: not only the SB team, but Mac Macpherson, Yorky, and the CO. The only man anywhere near correctly dressed was Fraser, in a shirt, tie and pullover; the others had track suits or sweat tops over what looked suspiciously like pyjamas. As always, there was a brew on the go.

We had no banter or pissing about, but went straight into an informal O-group – and you could have heard a mouse fart in the next county while I explained what had happened.

When I started to outline the programme for the Chequers shoot I was seriously worried Yorky might explode; he turned red in the face and his eyeballs rotated at high revs. In fact, such a proportion of what I said was so utterly outrageous that all of them, one after the other, soon looked close to apoplexy. I don't know who was most agitated – Fraser, when he heard that we'd met Marty Malone in the railway yard, or the CO when I told him that Operation Ostrich had been blown.

Fraser muttered, 'Marty Malone!' in a voice he might have used if he'd won a million on the pools. 'This is the guy who's been masterminding the bombing campaign on the mainland. But so far he's always operated out of West Belfast, never dared cross the water. I'll bet my trousers it was him who brought the big rifle across.'

He took a deep breath and added, 'If all this resulted in our nicking Marty Malone – boy, would that be something! He's one of the most evil pigs in the whole organisation.'

Remembering the lean, drawn look of the older man's face in the marshalling yard, I said, 'Maybe it was him who was down to do the shoot.'

'Possible,' Fraser agreed. 'In fact, more than possible. The fact he's here at all means there's something really big in the offing.'

The Boss cried, 'God's boots!' Then, turning to Mac, he said, 'You haven't had wind of any leak on Libya?'

'Nothing at all.'

'Get on to the Firm immediately,' said the CO. 'See if they've heard anything.'

As Mac went next door to make the call, the Boss muttered, 'I don't believe there *has* been a leak. I believe the buggers are guessing, trying to bluff their way.'

'I tell you what,' I said to Fraser. 'It was that miserable girl of yours. It was her that dropped us in the shit on this one.'

'Well,' he went, 'it may have been. But I tend to agree with your commanding officer. All the PIRA heard was that you'd gone abroad for a few days. You could have been anywhere in the world.'

'That's right,' said Yorky. 'They can make what they like out of what the woman said, but I'll lay a hundred pounds to a penny they haven't got a scrap of evidence to back it.'

'These PIRA orders,' said the CO. 'Where are they?'

'Here.' I opened the manila envelope and began to pull out the documents.

'Wait!' Fraser snapped. 'Prints.'

'I've handled the papers already.'

'Never mind. Forensic can try. Give them to Sergeant Alden. He'll photocopy them while we're talking.'

I handed the package over, and the tall duty sergeant took it out of the room. On the way he passed Mac, who came back in shaking his head. 'Nothing known to the Firm on Ostrich. Not the slightest suggestion of a leak. The Libyans are still blaming Mossad, and Egypt's

271

denying all knowledge of the operation. But I've asked Gilbert to call first thing in the morning.'

'All right,' said the CO. 'We'd better ring round to make sure everybody's ready with their denials – the FO for one.'

'I reckon you're right about the PIRA trying to bluff us, Boss,' I said. 'But even if you are, it doesn't make much difference. No matter how much or how little they know about Libya, they still have me over a barrel. So what I propose is this . . .'

I launched into my spiel again – and the reception was much the same as in the cottage: a mixture of alarm and incredulity. At first the ruperts couldn't believe I was being serious. Yorky really thought I'd gone round the bend. He walked up and down at one hell of a pace, exclaiming, 'Eh, lad, you're in it now,' throwing up a pencil and, as often as not, missing it when it fell. His movements became so distracting that the CO told him for Christ's sake to sit down.

'As for Chequers,' I went on, 'the PIRA have really done their homework. You remember that fuss a few years back about getting a footpath diverted, so that it wouldn't pass so close to the front of the house? Well, that got done. But still the path is only five or six hundred metres from the terrace, and the PIRA have it all sussed out for a shoot from there. Everything's in those papers – distances, elevations, bearings, routes in and out, prevailing winds, security arrangements . . .'

As the logic of what I was saying got through to them, they all began to calm down a bit. The CO was the first to crack. 'In purely operational terms it's feasible,' he admitted. 'I can see that. I'd trust you to handle the shoot, Geordie. But we're going to have the devil's own problem selling it to Whitehall.'

'The point is, the situation hasn't changed from when we started,' I said. 'Except that now the person directly threatened is the Prime Minister himself. That makes it all the more important to go straight to the top. He's the one at risk. It's him who'll benefit if we get these bastards sorted. If we take on the shoot ourselves, it'll increase our chances of busting the ASU.' I started going through the benefits of proceeding, as I had with the lads in the safe house: that we would hijack the PIRA's plan for the shoot, get the weapon, and so on.

'Geordie!' The CO scratched his head. 'I have to give it to you. You make everything sound dead simple.'

Now it was he who got up and went walkabout. 'What you're going to have to do is present an appreciation, in the normal way.'

'No time, Boss. If we're going to pick up the rifle, we've got to do it tomorrow night – tonight, I mean.'

'OK. That leaves the morning. I vote we all get our heads down for a couple of hours. Sleep on the problem, then have another brief. How about that, Commander?'

'Fine by me,' said Fraser. 'Just bear in mind that none of this caper may be necessary. There's a chance that we'll get to the hostages first. That car your fellows bugged has narrowed the field a bit.'

'Oh, great!' I said. 'Where did it go?'

'We followed it to Earl's Court. It's there now, parked in a stack off Oldbury Road. We've put round-the-clock surveillance on it. Unfortunately we couldn't keep tabs on the occupants, but as soon as they come back we'll get a tail on them.'

'You mean you lost them?' Suddenly I saw red. 'For fuck's sake! How did you manage that?'

'Take it easy, Geordie. It wasn't that simple.'

'Bloody hell, though! After we'd been to all that trouble to get a device on the car . . .'

'I know. But listen: the guy in the passenger seat got

273

out and jumped straight on to a bus a couple of blocks short of the park. Then, at the barrier on the entrance to the stack, the driver swapped places with someone else, who put the car away.'

'Couldn't your guys keep on him, though?'

'He was gone like a rat down a bloody drain.'

'Ah, hell!'

I saw Fraser giving me a wary look and half getting up from his chair, as if he expected me to throw another track and start smashing the place up again.

'Chill out, Geordie,' Yorky said. 'Everyone's doing their best.'

As I felt the rush of anger draining away, I let out a deep breath and said, 'Sorry I shouted. All this is getting to me.'

'No sweat,' Fraser replied evenly. 'They're cunning bastards, they really are. All the hints we've been picking up from intercepts have suggested an assassination attempt was being planned for July, and in London – when Clinton's due to visit. Now it looks as though all that was cover, a blind.'

'Typical,' I said. 'At least we know what the real plan is. But we've got to budget for the worst. These telephone calls Farrell's making – aren't they leading anywhere?'

'We tried following up the last mobile number, but it's gone off the air. They're using quite a few different phones.'

The sergeant reappeared with a sheaf of photostats, and the ruperts started passing them round. The detail in the papers made them gripe and groan, and had the effect of reinforcing my presentation.

'Curses!' went the CO. 'I see what you mean. You'd better leave the originals with the Commander, for the forensic boys.'

'That's fine. Copies will do for Farrell. He doesn't

even know what the envelope contained. What about the map, though?'

'We'll get another in the morning.'

The meeting was about to break up when Fraser said, 'This Farrell – what's he like?'

'A pain in the arse. We're keeping him cuffed to one or other of us all the time. It's like having a bloody bear or something in the house.'

'Has he tried to do a runner?'

'No. Physically, he's in fairly poor shape. The bullet wound in his flank hasn't healed properly. He's on antibiotics, and that's dragging him down a bit. The brush-off he got from his pals in Belfast knocked him back a bit too. But we're not taking any chances.'

'Quite right,' said Fraser. 'We picked up some good stuff in an intercept yesterday. The boyos are after him for laundering funds from Colombia. They think he's filtered out seven or eight million dollars.'

'Ah – so *that's* what it is.' Suddenly those peculiar reactions made sense. If Farrell had been creaming off cocaine money, and had been rumbled, no wonder he was getting nervous. 'Maybe, in the end, they won't want him back,' I said.

'On the contrary,' said Fraser. 'They'll want him all the more, so they can give him a going-over. Also to stop him spilling any secrets.'

'Perhaps he won't want to go, then . . . On the other hand, he's arrogant enough to think he can talk himself out of it.'

'It can't be very comfortable, being cooped up with him,' suggested the CO.

'Could be worse. I'm having as little to do with him as I can. I don't want to get drawn into conversation, in case I give anything away. I tell you one thing, though.'

'What's that?'

'He's into classical music. Beethoven.'

'How d'you know?'

I told them about the episode with the music on the car radio, and when I said the piece was something called *Leonora* number three the Boss got it immediately.

'I know,' he said. 'Beethoven wrote three different overtures for his opera *Fidelio*. Couldn't decide which to use. There's one called *Leonora* number three. Great stuff. Come on, now. If the guy's into that, he can't be all bad.'

'He is,' I insisted. 'He's shit from head to toe.'

It's surprising what three hours' sleep can do for you, especially if you're running on adrenalin. When I finally got my head down in my room in the sergeants' mess it was nearly four o'clock, and once again I felt I was back at the beginning of the nightmare, on the first night after the kidnap.

But come seven o'clock, and a good breakfast, I felt a new man.

By 0745 the cast from the night before had reassembled in the incident room. The CO kicked off with, 'Right then, Geordie, what have you got for us?'

I'd already jotted down a few headings in my notebook, in the hope of making things reasonably clear, but I was glad to find that one of the int office's gofers was present with his laptop to make a proper written record.

'Mission,' I began. 'The mission is obviously to recover the hostages held by the Provisional IRA. To give Special Branch and the other security forces more time, we propose to simulate our willingness to carry out a shoot on the Prime Minister at Chequers . . .'

I ran through place, date and time as if this were a normal operation, and then listed the steps that I expected to take:

1. Contact PIRA, agree to carry out shoot.
2. Receive instructions for collecting weapon.
3. Collect weapon.
4. Move up to Forward Mounting Base in vicinity of target location.
5. Test-fire and zero weapon.
6. Negotiate with PIRA to set final RV site for exchange of Farrell and hostages. Deal will be that Farrell will authorise release of hostages by mobile phone soon as he sees the target is down.
7. Make Farrell arrange escape from RV site: helicopter to be hired by PIRA.
8. Carry out early-morning shoot as detailed, in Farrell's presence.
9. Fly out of target area. Land at intermediate RV, switch to vehicle, drive to final RV.
10. Exchange prisoners.
11. Security forces follow up tracking devices, recapture Farrell and accomplices.

The CO was at his sharpest, challenging each point as I brought it up, probing for weaknesses in the plan and scouting for problems.

'What have you got in mind for an FMB?' he demanded.

'We need another holiday cottage. The one we're in now has been perfect for down here, but it's going to be too far from the job. We need something on the edge of the Chilterns, within a few miles of Chequers. Not too close.'

'Not so easy up there,' he said. 'We don't have any tame house-owners in that area.'

After a pause he asked, 'What's the point of zeroing the rifle, if you're not trying to hit the target anyway?'

'Farrell will insist on it. He'll want to come with us when we do it – he's that sort of guy, very practical.'

'Where will you do it, then?'

'Depends where our safe house is. When we know where we've landed, we can pick an out-of-the-way spot in the country and go out there with a target at first light. I've been looking at the map: there are plenty of big, deserted valleys up there.'

The CO had adopted his favourite thinking attitude, forehead in hands, ears sticking out well to either side, and elbows on the desk. 'The PIRA will know when the shoot's going to take place,' he said. 'On the morning, they may send dickers to stake out the park.'

'I thought of that. We're going to need back-up on site. There's a farm just behind Point D. Here.' I twisted the map round so that the Boss could see it right way up. 'Brockwell Farm. It would be ideal if we could get some of the lads in there under cover of darkness the night before. Then, if Farrell did try to do a runner, or if anyone tried to lift him, we'd still be covered . . .'

Mac, the ops officer, was his usual sarcastic self. 'Of course, all this may be so much moonshine,' he said. 'If SB find the hostages first you can forget all this fancy caper.'

'Christ!' I exclaimed. 'If that happened, nobody would be happier than me. I'd be over the bloody moon. If I never saw Farrell again – if I didn't have to go back and meet the bastard again now – I'd be chuffed to bollocks.'

So it went on. The CO was pretty sceptical at first, but, as usual, he fancied having a go at something outrageous. When I left camp at 0830, I had his permission to carry on planning for the time being, and the promise that once again he would take things to the highest level in Whitehall.

Back at the cottage, I gave Farrell short shrift. When he asked where I'd been I told him to mind his own business. Then I brought out the PIRA orders. While I read out the main points, he listened with a variety of expressions passing across his face. Sometimes he looked amused, sometimes contemptuous, sometimes interested – but he never seemed particularly surprised.

'Last night you told me this was all shit,' he said.

'At first I thought it was.'

'But now you'll go along with it?'

'Have to,' I replied. 'I don't see I've any alternative. I've drawn the zero option.'

'The boyos have changed their minds, then.'

'What about?'

'The plan for the shoot. They were going to have it in London. This looks more like business. Better than trying to drop a mortar into the garden of Number Ten Downing Street, anyway.'

'What have you fellows got against the Prime Minister?' I demanded. 'He seems a harmless enough guy to me.'

'Harmless!' Farrell nearly shouted. 'Harmless, begod! He's the head of the British Government, is he not? It's him who's the architect of repression in Northern Ireland. The number of murders that fucker's got on his hands – Holy Mary, they can never be avenged. A bullet's too good for him!'

'If we hack this,' I said, 'and the shoot goes down, I don't want your people crowing about how they got an SAS man to do their dirty work for them. You get me?'

Farrell nodded.

'The Regiment would deny it anyway,' I told him. 'They'd rubbish any story that came out. But publicity's the last thing I want.'

'Don't kid yourself,' said Farrell scornfully. 'If the job gets done, the PIRA will claim a major success. They're not going to give the credit to some prat in the Brit forces.'

'All right, then. Find out our RV for collecting the weapon. We need to go for that tonight.'

Using my mobile, he went through to Belfast and started one of his usual hectoring exchanges. The prospect of action seemed to have put new life into him; he was half-way back to his former aggressive self, as though he were taking charge of the whole operation. The upshot of the conversation was that we would get our instructions for the pick-up through an intermediary in Ulster. We were not to call the PIRA on the mainland any more – we were only to ring Belfast.

'They're getting jumpy,' I said to Whinger when we were alone in the kitchen.

'Don't blame them,' he answered. 'I am too.'

'This fucker Farrell,' I said. 'He's starting to give me the shits. I've got a horrible feeling that he's invincible, and that somehow he'll get the better of us in the end.'

'Come on, Geordie,' said Whinger. 'Pigs might fly.'

From exposure to countless previous Whingerisms I knew that meant 'Never say die', so I just said, 'Good on yer, mate,' and put an extra spoonful of sugar into my tea.

As I sipped the piping-hot drink, I couldn't stop thinking about an account I'd read in a magazine of the murder of Grigory Rasputin, the peasant monk who bewitched the Russian royal family in the years before revolution. Rasputin had an amazing hold over the Empress, Alexandra. Some people said he was secretly screwing her, others that he was the only person who could comfort her son Alexei, who was mortally ill. Anyway, when the army officers tried to murder the monk they found they couldn't do it. First they gave him enough potassium cyanide to kill an elephant, and it had practically no effect. Then they shot him through the heart with a revolver from point-blank range, and still the bastard wouldn't die. One moment he was stretched out on the flag-stones of the palace like a corpse, the next he was up, roaring, and attacking them with his hands, so violently that he tore an epaulette off one of their tunics. When he staggered to his feet and ran out through the courtyard towards the street, they couldn't believe it. Again they gunned him down, and finally they dumped his trussed body into the river through a hole in the ice. But the performance had left them shattered. They thought their victim was the devil incarnate, and they were terrified he'd return to haunt them.

Stupid as it sounds, I was beginning to feel that Farrell was another Rasputin, an evil and indestructible force. The magazine article had carried pictures of the peasant, with his wild black beard and staring eyes. I started to think I could see likenesses in Farrell's swarthy features, and I felt I was in the grip of some malign influence, which was driving events forward in a way I couldn't control. It was easy to believe that, whatever I did, I would never get the better of him . . .

Deep down, of course, I knew I was suffering from cumulative lack of sleep and letting my imagination run away with me. And the best way to control my anxieties was to concentrate on the practical details of the task ahead.

When we went back through to Belfast I took over the call myself, so that I could make sure I understood everything properly. With a man dictating and myself checking back, I wrote down a grid reference for the transit hide somewhere in Oxfordshire, and a series of detailed instructions: a road junction, a lane, woods, fields, paths, a clearing on the edge of the forest, an old well with a cast-iron water pump. On paper, the notes meant practically nothing, and I could only hope they'd relate accurately to features on the ground.

At the end the contact said, 'That's all. The weapon is there, and can be collected any time after dark tonight.'

THIRTEEN

Tony and I set out at two o'clock, leaving the rest of the team to guard Farrell, close down the cottage and move up-country to whatever FMB the head-shed managed to arrange. As we drove off in the Granada, I felt a terrific relief at being away from the grotty presence of our prisoner. The man had wanted to come with us to collect the weapon, sure enough, but I told him we could manage the pick-up on our own.

As we headed east, my mind spun with conflicting possibilities, and in an attempt to clear my head I bounced some of them off Tony.

'I'm trying to puzzle out what the PIRA's state of mind is,' I began. 'They're so bloody devious, you can never be sure what they're up to.

'One thing we do know is that they want the Prime Minister dead. That's obvious. Also obvious: they want us to do their dirty work for them. But what do they reckon *my* intentions are? I suppose they think I'm so shit-scared of losing Tim that I'm simply going to do the shoot on their behalf. But what do they imagine I'll do after it's gone down? Bugger off? Disappear? Perhaps they think I'll just be able to keep my head down and nobody will find out who did it.'

'Maybe you should tell Farrell you've got a passage booked back to Colombia,' Tony suggested. 'Let him know you've fixed yourself up with a slot there, and give the impression you're going to quit Britain immediately, taking the family with you.'

'Thanks a lot! It's still possible the PIRA have no intention of handing over the hostages, whatever we do. Maybe they don't intend I should get away at all. If they stake out Point D at Chequers, they could drop us immediately after the shoot.'

'Possible,' Tony agreed. 'But unlikely. They've been to the place. They've seen it. They know it's heaving with security. You let one round off there and the park will be like an anthill. They'd never make it out. The thought should keep them away.'

'Yeah – but if they lay on the chopper, like we've suggested . . .'

I drove in silence for a few minutes, then said, 'They must trust me to some extent. After all, they're letting us get our hands on one of their most valuable weapons.'

'We haven't got the damn thing yet. They could be staking out the pick-up site right now, planning to hit us when we show up.'

'I know.' I turned and grinned at him. 'That's why we've got the MP 5s.'

I drove on, heading up the M4 for Reading. The site of the transit hide had been described as the side of a wood, up in the hill country near the village of Nettlebed, maybe fifteen miles overland from Chequers. The PIRA guy had described the cache as an old well on the site of a former cottage. I was tempted to do a daylight drive-past, get a feel for the area – but I ruled it out on the grounds that if any dickers were about a passing car would be bound to alert them.

In Reading our first port of call was a general bookshop, where we bought a copy of the local 1:25,000 map. That showed some detail, but what we really needed was the relevant sheet of the six-inches-to-the-mile Ordnance Survey, and we ran one to ground in a specialist map shop in London Road. Thus armed, we stoked up with some good spaghetti in an Italian restaurant, and pored over the maps while we drank our coffee.

'Roman coin hoard found here, 1953,' Tony read out, twisting the map at an angle.

'Is that right? Near where we're heading?'

'Not far off.'

'They'll have to add another line to the next edition,' I said. 'Barrett Fifty sniper rifle found here, 2002.'

The site of the transit hide was easy enough to identify within a hundred yards or so, even though we couldn't pinpoint it. The PIRA guy had said the old well was on the southern edge of a small, triangular wood called Kate's Copse, which had its apex pointing north and its base running east and west. We found the wood all right, but we couldn't tell how far along the half-mile base the well would be.

The route given us by the PIRA would bring us in along a lane which ran one field away from the northern point of the wood. If we took that road we could park within a couple of hundred yards of our objective. I checked the route through, turn by turn, against the map, and saw that the description was painstakingly accurate: go south off the main drag on unsigned side road, three cottages on corner; 500 yards, farm on right; 500 yards, sewage works on right, ninety-degree turn left; 700 yards straight, then deciduous wood on right; 200 yards on, grass ride on right. Leave car here . . .

The more I looked at it, the less I fancied it. If dickers were out that was where they'd be: watching that lane, anywhere between the main road and the site. With the motivation of the PIRA so uncertain, my instinct was to keep well clear.

'Look at this,' I said. 'Kate's Copse is on the brow of the hill. But there's another track here, to the south of it, along the bottom of this valley. We can park down here and walk up over. Then, if anyone's watching the top lane, they'll miss us.'

'I'm with you,' Tony agreed. 'It's not much farther. Better all round.'

Back in the car, I called Whinger's mobile. The first time it didn't connect, and I assumed that he was on the move in some low-lying area. When I tried again five minutes later he came on, patchily, but clear enough to say that they were on their way to a new safe house 'with ten miles of target', with an ETA of 2000 hours. I didn't want to ask the place's precise location because I knew Farrell would be listening to the conversation, so I told Whinger I'd call again when they'd arrived.

The evening was dim and murky. No rain was falling but there was heavy cloud cover, and I could see that darkness was going to fall early. All the same, we had an hour in hand, and I'd been planning to stop in a quiet lane so that we could get in a few minutes' kip. But by the time we cleared the northern outskirts of Reading the old adrenalin was running again, and I felt too hepped up to be sleepy.

'Tell you what,' I said, 'I don't want to count any chickens, but we've got time to recce a site for the test-shoot tomorrow. Let's take another look.'

I pulled off the road on to a patch of earth under some big beeches, and we'd hardly started scrutinising the map again when Tony pointed with his forefinger and said, 'Hey! Whaddaya know? A genuine rifle range, all ready for us.'

Sure enough, in a remote, wooded valley a few miles east of our site, the 1:25,000 map showed a narrow rectangular opening in the forest, nearly half a mile long, marked white among the green, and bearing the legend 'Rifle Range'.

'I don't believe it,' I said. 'If it's like the map shows, it's got everything: six or seven hundred yard sight-line and a remote location, no houses for miles. Let's go for it. You drive, though. Those little roads could be private tracks; if we get stopped, you do the talking. We'll be American tourists, lost in the great British jungle.'

'What do I do?' said Tony in mock alarm. 'Act dumb?'

'Act yourself,' I told him, 'and that'll fool anybody.'

He gave me a look as we changed places.

Twenty minutes later, we left the main road and dived down a spectacularly steep lane. At the bottom the ground flattened out, but soon the road swung left-handed into the beginning of the secluded valley. We passed a pair of cottages on our right, then a farm on our left. Beyond the farm the surface suddenly deteriorated from tarmac into pitted gravel, and a hand-painted notice, black on white, proclaimed it a PRIVATE ROAD.

'Thought so,' I said. 'Keep going.'

We crawled on, lurching through potholes, with steep grass fields lifting away on either hand. A few minutes later we passed the remains of some ancient building on our left, walls smothered with ivy, standing back from the road.

'Jesus!' Tony exclaimed. 'It's the ruins of a church. This place is getting spooky.'

Soon we were into the woods, which turned out to be dense beech, with branches hanging over the lane and turning it into a tunnel. In there the light was already so dim that I instinctively glanced at my watch to make sure we weren't running out of time. In fact we were fine, and I could see from the map that we were almost at our objective.

'Round this next corner, it'll be on our right,' I said. 'I'll believe it when we see it.'

But see it we did. Tony swung left, and after a couple

of hundred yards we came upon an opening in the trees on our right, with a red and white barrier pole across it. We pulled off the track, got out of the car, dodged under the pole and walked through the gap, to find ourselves, sure enough, on a rifle range. A long, narrow strip of rough-mown grass sliced through the forest along the contours at the foot of the hill, and ended in a natural butt away to our right. There was a firing point every hundred yards, and although the place had an amateurish, partially-kept air about it, the range was clearly in use. Tyre-marks in the mud showed that quite a few vehicles came and went, the grass had been cut lately, and a couple of poles for flying danger flags had recently been repainted white.

'Incredible!' I said quietly. 'It must be the TA who use it. There's not even a range hut. They must bring everything with them when they do a shoot. But what a place! We've even got the distances marked out for us: no need to step them out.' We'd come out at the 200-yard mark, and away to our left we could see five more firing-points stretching away, giving 700 yards in all.

'That big rifle's going to make one hell of a noise down in here,' said Tony, looking up at the sides of the valley all round. 'It'll sound like a cannon.'

'Won't matter. We'll just take a couple of shots and slip away. I don't fancy driving in along this bottom track, though. We could easily get trapped. There must be some way we can come in on foot.'

Recourse to the map showed another track running steeply uphill to the north, past the far end of the range, towards a main road on the next ridge. We took it, but soon saw we'd made a mistake: rainwater had carved deep channels out of the mud, and even a four-wheel-drive vehicle would have had problems negotiating the track. Seeing that the Granada wasn't going to make it, Tony eased off and backed carefully down.

'That's our way in for tomorrow, all the same,' I said. 'Park at the top, walk down, shoot, and away on foot. If anyone turns up we can disappear into the trees. Let's get round there now for a shufti — back the way we came, out along the valley, then up and over. All we need is to find a place where we can park in the morning.'

As I'd forecast, night came early while we were driving towards the transit hide. Full darkness had fallen by the time we reached the lane I'd earmarked. Again we parked under trees, and we hadn't gone fifty metres from the Granada before the car had vanished from sight. Our walk-in to the site was relatively short — about a mile — and as we were in no hurry, I took it at a snail's pace. For camouflage purposes we'd pulled on DPM smocks over our civilian gear; we both had pistols in shoulder holsters, and each of us carried an MP 5 with spare magazines. From camp, I'd also brought a night-sight of the kind we'd used in Iraq — an image intensifier that gives really good vision in the dark. I had it slung round my neck on para-cord so that I could bring it up with a single movement. And for the first time since the intercept at Ludlow, we were wearing our covert radios.

Tony and I kept about ten metres apart as we walked uphill over a grass field beside an overgrown hedge, myself leading. Even with my eyes accustomed to the dark I could see very little — but memorised details of our route were printed in my mind.

There was practically no wind, and what there was — a breath from the west — was coming from our left, through the hedge.

After four hundred metres, another hedge led off across the hill to the right at ninety degrees to the one we were following. Luckily cattle had pushed their way through it, creating gaps, so that we were able to slip through with scarcely a sound. Another five minutes brought us to the point on the brow of the hill where our guiding row of bushes came to an end. A barbed wire fence ran across our line of advance, just visible on the horizon against the cloudy sky. I beckoned Tony forward and held the top strand down taut while he went over it, to prevent the wire twanging. Then he did the same for me, and we crept on silently over the big field beyond, the last before our target wood.

Still the breeze was steady on my left cheek. I stopped. Ahead and to our left, something pale was showing. The night sight revealed it as a sheep, outlier of a large flock. Hearing Tony move up close behind me, I whispered, 'Sheep. We'll detour right so we don't panic them.'

On we went. Frequent checks with the sight showed that the sheep were aware of our presence – they had their heads up and were looking in our direction – but by skirting round them we persuaded them that we weren't a threat, and they stayed where they were.

Now the southern face of the wood loomed ahead of us like a black wall. We were coming in towards its right-hand corner. About a hundred yards out I stopped and went down on one knee for a thorough scan. The sight revealed fence posts and tree-trunks, but nothing sinister. Thinking back, I remembered the PIRA's instructions about a clearing and a disused chalk-pit. The old well, they said, was just inside the wood, close to the fence, but the clearing and the pit were behind it. Therefore, I reckoned, I should see some sort of opening in the trees.

'Got it,' I breathed. 'I can see an open space. OK. We're on course.'

Heading slightly left, we approached the straight boundary of the wood at an angle. Our feet were making no sound on the sheep-mown grass, and the night was so dark that anyone without special equipment would be practically blind. Nevertheless, something made me stop twenty yards out from the trees.

When I went down flat, Tony did the same a few feet behind me. For a minute we lay listening. Nothing. Then on the wind I caught a very faint whiff: cigarette smoke. A shiver went up my back as I thought of the moment in the Libyan desert when Whinger had smelt smoke, just as we were about to establish our LUP.

Reaching round, I snapped finger and thumb quietly, and I heard faint rustling as Tony wormed up beside me.

'Cigarette smoke,' I whispered. 'There's someone out to our left.' I raised the night sight and scanned again. 'There he is,' I said quietly. 'A man, on the corner of the wood.'

'What's he doing?'

'Standing there. He's got binoculars. Looking round.'

'He'll never pick us out – too dark.'

'No, but let's get into cover.'

We crawled forward, belly to the ground, and in a few seconds were under the bottom strand of another barbed wire fence. Inside it, out of sheep-reach, longer grass and shrubs were growing.

Leaning outwards, I took one more look at the corner. The man hadn't moved. 'You stay here,' I breathed. 'Get your arse backed into the undergrowth while I go and look for the hide. Take the sight and keep an eye on our friend. If he heads this way, warn me, and we'll lie low till he's gone past.' I lifted the cord over my head and handed the sight over.

'OK,' Tony whispered. 'Good hunting.'

In the cover of the woodland edge, it was safe to

stand up, so I got to my feet and shuffled carefully forward. My mind was moving far faster than my body. The guy on the corner could be a gamekeeper, on the look-out for poachers, but at this time of the year that seemed unlikely. More probably it was a dicker – and if it was, what was his brief? What the hell was he doing here? Was he supposed to intercept us as we came to the hide? Or pretend he'd caught us stealing the weapon, and drop us in possession of it? Did he have a colleague on the hide itself?

My sixth sense told me that the answer to the last question was no. Already I was on the edge of the clearing and very close to the hide, yet I had no feeling that anybody was near me.

I moved on, pushing each foot gently through the long grass. At the south-western edge of the clearing – according to my brief – there should be an old iron hand-pump mounted on a brick base . . . I nearly bumped into it before I saw it, standing shoulder-high in front of me. This was the means by which people living in the cottage had once brought their water up out of the ground. I reached out and touched the rounded top of the pump. From the rough feel, I could tell that the cast iron was pitted with the rust of ages.

The opening of the well had been described as six feet out from the base of the pump. I dropped on to hands and knees. The temptation to use a torch was strong, but I resisted it – better to operate by feel. I was looking, or groping, for a circular wooden cover covered by sods of turf. Pulling my Commando knife from its sheath, I began jabbing the blade vertically into the ground, and after four or five soft touches I suddenly hit something hard, which gave out a quite different sound. I reached out farther and jabbed again. This time I got a definite hollow thump.

A moment later I had located the two wooden

handles. Steady, I told myself. This could be booby-trapped to blow when someone moves it.

Feeling carefully about in the surrounding mulch, I picked out the perimeter of the cover and ran my fingers round it. When I came on no wires or catches, I reckoned all was well, and lifted the cover clear.

For a moment I sat back on my heels and held down the pressel switch of my radio. 'Tony,' I said quietly. 'I'm on site. Found the hide. What's our guy doing?'

'Hasn't moved.'

'Nobody at the other corner?'

'Nope.'

'OK, then. I'll get the weapon up.'

Below ground level it was safe to use the torch, so I reached down into the cavity and switched on. The beam lit up a blue nylon rope, anchored at the top to an iron ring set into the neck of the well, and dropping ten feet into the old, brick-lined cistern. On the dry mud floor at the bottom lay a fat grey cylinder about five feet long.

Quickly I switched off, pocketed the torch and began hauling the rope up. The tube was a fair old weight – thirty pounds, I guessed – but it came up hanging at an angle, so that I was able to bring it through the neck of the well without it touching the sides.

Just as I laid it in the grass Tony's voice suddenly came in my ear. 'Watch it, Geordie. The guy on the corner's heading this way. Fifty yards . . . forty . . . thirty. Ah, Jesus!'

I wriggled the MP 5 off my back and knelt silently with the weapon at the ready, watching, waiting. I kept thinking, if this were Northern Ireland we'd simply grab the guy, hand him over to the police and have him whipped away.

When nothing happened I asked, very low, 'What's he doing?'

No answer. That could only mean the man was extremely close. 'Is he within ten yards?' I went.

Back came one brief *psssch*, as Tony gave his pressel a single nudge. That meant yes.

'Is he within five yards?'

Psssch.

Bloody hell! I concentrated intently on keeping still, and counted seconds to give myself an idea of how much time was passing. I'd gone past 180 – three minutes which seemed like thirty – when at last I got another beep in the earpiece.

'Moving off?' I asked.

Psssch, psssch.

'Great. Tell me when he's clear.'

I waited another whole minute. Then Tony came up with, 'OK. He's down at the other corner.'

'I'm coming out then.'

Hurrying now, I brought out my knife again, cut the cradle of rope round the container, dropped the severed ends down the well, replaced the circular lid, swept the grass back and forth a couple of times to mask the edge of the cover, picked up the pipe by the webbing cradle round it, and nipped back to the fence.

Seconds later Tony and I were away across the middle of the field at a fast walk; but only when we got back to our marker hedge, out of sight and hearing of the wood, did he burst out with, 'Boy, was that a close one! The bastard was standing with his heels three feet from my head!'

We ran the other lads to ground at the new safe house not far from Great Missenden. Whinger guided us in on the phone, calling the turns, until finally we pulled round the back of a farmyard to find a hideous modern bungalow built alongside the biggest heap of shit in Buckinghamshire – or so it seemed: there was a mountain of old straw and manure piled up right in front of the turn-around, and the air was full of the stink of cows.

'What have they done to us?' I yelled as I walked in. 'What a shower!'

'Close the door, for fuck's sake,' said Whinger. 'The only hope is to keep the smell outside.'

Cowshit apart, the place was nothing like as good for us as the cottage in the Dean. For one thing it was too close to the main road and to the farmyard; for another, it had big plate-glass windows, so that anyone passing could see in. A third defect was that the internal walls were paper-thin, so people could hear what was going on in the room next-door. And to make matters worse the telephone was insecure; there hadn't been time to instal a new one.

'Oh, well,' I said. 'At least it's in the right area, and we're not going to be here long. Nothing new from Fraser, I suppose?'

Whinger shook his head. 'All quiet on the western front, I'm afraid.'

'All right, then. Let's suss out this damned rifle.'

In the past I'd done quite a bit of sniper work, and at one stage I'd worked as commander of the sniper detachment on the Regiment's SP team. Stew, also, had been on the team. But for that work we'd used 7.62 calibre PM rifles – far smaller, lighter weapons. The only one of us with experience of a .50 was Tony, who'd trained on it in the States.

The carrying case for this one was home-made but practical: a tube of rigid grey polythene, like a length of outsized drainpipe, with a cap on each end carefully sealed with parcel tape. Inside, we found the rifle cocooned in a jacket of bubble-wrap. As I drew it out on to the kitchen table, everyone crowded round, including Farrell, who was now cuffed to Stew.

'Are those curtains good enough?' I gestured at the window behind me. 'They look bloody thin to me.'

'No, no. They're OK,' said Whinger. 'I've checked from outside and you can't see through.'

Afterwards, I wished I'd been watching Farrell's face when the wrappings came off the weapon. As it was, I kept my eyes on the job in hand, but when the angular grey metal frame appeared, he gave a low whistle.

'What the hell is it?' I said. 'Not a Barrett at all. No woodwork.'

'No,' said Farrell. 'It's a Haskins. I know that feller.'

'You mean you know this actual rifle?'

'Ah . . . I mean, no. It's the type. I've seen the *type* before.'

Even in the excitement of unveiling the fearsome beast I had noticed that odd hesitation, but I carried on peeling off the layers of bubble film until the weapon lay revealed. The rifle comprised a long, thick barrel with a sound-deflector at the muzzle, a skeletal action, a bipod hinged under the fore-end, a high-grade telescopic sight on top, and, strangest of all, a short metal stock joined to the action by twin hydraulic shock-absorbers, clearly designed to soak up some of the recoil. The rifle had seen service – its metalwork was scratched here and there – but it looked beautifully clean, and when I drew the heavy bolt back it moved sweetly in its oiled bed. I noticed that there was no magazine: single shots only.

Also in the pack were two short belts of rounds, twelve in each, every cartridge six or seven inches long, as big and menacing as an anti-tank shell.

'Bloody hell!' said Whinger. 'That thing would kill a fucking elephant.'

'So it would,' said Farrell. 'And leave a big hole in the bastard, too.'

I picked the rifle up – it weighed at least twenty

pounds – and flicked down the legs of the bipod to set the weapon up on the floor. Then I lay down behind it, brought the stock into my shoulder and shuffled myself into an easy position. Of course I couldn't see much through the sight, because it was out of focus, pointing straight at a wall about five feet away, but I liked the look of the reticle: crossed bars, thick at the edges, thin in the middle. I imagined it centred on the distant figure of a man, probably wearing a loose, woolly jumper. Altogether the rifle felt comfortable and solid. I opened and closed the bolt to cock the mechanism and applied the first pressure on the trigger. At the second pressure it went off crisp and clean, giving a loud click, with a pull I estimated to be four pounds.

When Tony also got down for a trial, I told him, 'Don't touch the sight. It's suppose to be set at six hundred yards, which is just right. We'll try it in the morning.'

'No sweat,' he grunted. He too took a couple of dry pulls on the trigger and said, 'Yeah – it feels quite nice. I could hit something with that.'

I lifted the rifle back on to the table, and over a brew we all got talking about long-range shoots, not least the effect of wind on the bullet.

'The thing is,' said Tony, 'even if there's no wind at the firing point, there can be some farther out. You need to watch for that – anything like leaves or grass moving near the target.'

'Yes,' Farrell said, 'and you have to look out for mirage, too.'

'Mirage?' said Whinger. 'What the hell's that?'

'You know when you get a heat-haze, and see the air kind of boiling? If there's no wind the air will be rising vertically, and you get what's known as a boiling mirage. Lateral movement – what you might call drift – looks like a stream of clear water rippling over a bed of pebbles. That can affect the bullet quite badly, so you've to learn how to judge it.'

'OK,' I said, 'but we're not going to get that in the early morning, are we?'

'Probably not,' Farrell agreed. 'But then temperature's going to be a factor. A high temperature will increase your muzzle velocity and throw your bullet high.'

'Yeah. But again, early morning's likely to be cool.'

'Sure, so you may need to aim fractionally high. Humidity's another thing. If you get a mist, that means the air's more dense. Your bullet meets greater resistance and drops – so again, you need to give it more elevation.'

'Light,' said Tony. 'That's important. If it's dull and cloudy like today, you're liable to shoot high. Dunno why, but that's how it seems to work.'

'It probably will be like that at seven in the morning,' I said. 'Anyway, we can try it tomorrow.'

'Have you got somewhere lined up for a practice shoot?' Whinger asked.

'Yep. We found a place.' Because Farrell was with us I didn't describe the little range in the woods. I turned to him. 'It's amazing how your people find the sites for hides. I mean, the one where we collected the rifle – it was miles from anywhere. How the hell would they know about a place like that?'

'Easy,' Farrell replied. 'Some Paddy gets a job working on the farm. Maybe he does a bit of pigeon-shooting or something. Gets to know the woods, finds the old well. Next thing he's in the pub, blathering about it, and there's a man listening. Or maybe the Paddy falls out with the farmer. Maybe he gets the sack and thinks, I'll fuck this fellow up a bit. Use his property without him knowing.'

'Is that how guys get drawn into the organisation? As

297

simple as that?'

'Sometimes, yes.'

I stared at our prisoner, with his heavy but still handsome face and his thick, wiry black hair. The swelling on his lip had gone down, and his eyes were back to normal, so that he looked quite presentable again.

'Don't you ever feel guilty about some of the things you do?' I asked.

'Guilty?' He gave a kind of snort. 'What about? It was those stupid fuckers of ancient Greeks who invented the idea of guilt. They thought there were creatures called the Furies who came after you if you did something bad. They called them the Eumenides, the Kindly Ones, to try and make them seem less frightening. It was all a load of bollocks, of course – but people have been foolish enough to go on believing it ever since.'

'Some people call it conscience,' Tony said drily.

It was on the tip of my tongue to ask why the dickers had been out, watching the approaches to the hide, but instead I said, 'How does someone like you get into the PIRA? I mean, you went to university. You're an educated guy. You could have a good job and a settled life. If you'd gone straight you could be making a good living by now.'

'Making a living!' Again Farrell gave that derisive snort. 'What d'you think *you'd* be like if *you'd* been brought up in Belfast? You'd be the worst fucking killer of the lot. I know. That's all you army fellers are, anyway – trained killers. Are you not? A tribe of murdering bastards.'

As Farrell glared at me and I glared back at him, I suddenly realised that we'd all started chatting over the weapon and listening to his advice as if he were one of us. The way he'd been talking, he could have been a sniper instructor. Obviously he was hot on the subject; but not only that – it had sounded as if he'd had training from Americans. Some of the phrases he'd used were out of American text books.

In a flash it occurred to me that maybe it was he who had done all that damage in Ulster. Maybe he was the mysterious long-range assassin who'd harassed the security forces so badly. To my disgust I realised I'd been drawn into discussion with him in a way I'd vowed I would avoid. It was bad enough that for a few minutes I'd been treating him as an ordinary human being; far worse was the fact that I'd talked things over as though speaking with an acknowledged expert.

Once again I felt that he was casting some sort of spell over me. To break it I stood up and said, 'There's one thing certain. Once this is over, if I ever come across you again, make no mistake, you'll be going down.'

'The same yourself,' Farrell spat back. 'If you ever set eyes on me again you'll need to start saying your prayers.'

I took a deep breath and moved away. 'Let's spruce up the barrel,' I said. 'We need a target, too.'

The PIRA had included a cleaning kit within the tube: a springy steel rod with a jag on the end, and a roll of white flannel four inches wide, marked off by red lines every two inches. For smaller calibres, like 7.62mm or 9mm, a single piece of four-by-two is enough to make a tight fit in the barrel; but for this cannon I cut a double piece, a four-by-four, and wrapped it round the jag. Even that lump went through the barrel without too much friction, and when it came out at the other end it was perfectly clean. With the bolt out, I held the rifle up and looked straight through the barrel towards a lamp. The swirl of the rifling gleamed in the light, and I could see that the PIRA had taken good care of their prized weapon. I also had a close look at the telescopic sight, a high-quality optic with magnification variable up to the power of nine.

While I worked, watched by Farrell, Doughnut and Tony sorted out a target. The best option was a shallow cardboard box, eighteen inches wide and three feet long, in which some groceries had come up from the cottage. The bottom of the box was unmarked, and in the middle of it they stuck a piece of white paper six inches square, using paste made out of flour and water as glue. The result was a good aiming-mark in the middle of a target about the width of a man's torso. For zeroing purposes we could have done with a broader background. Although above and below the bull there was at least a foot to spare, if the first shot went more than nine or ten inches wide of centre we'd probably never see its point of impact.

Once again we were in for a short night. It was close to one in the morning before we stopped fiddling about, and I'd already set reveille for 0500.

'What about you?' I said to Farrell as Tony was about to chain him to his bed. 'You coming with us in the morning?'

'Sure I am. I need to know the rifle's in order. I wouldn't want to rely on what you fellers might tell me.'

'OK, then. Five o'clock it is.'

I'd known the answer to those questions before I asked them. Tony's prediction about Farrell wanting to witness the practice shoot was spot-on. Even though we seemed to have conned the bastard properly about our intentions, he wanted proof that we'd be able to hit the target.

'He's fired this thing himself,' I said quietly to Tony when we were alone again. 'This actual rifle. I'm sure he has.'

FOURTEEN

In the morning we used our covert radios openly for the first time. I told Farrell we'd been out and bought them specially, as they'd be the only means of co-ordinating our operations efficiently during the Chequers shoot. 'Bloody ruinous they were, too,' I added.

'How much?' he asked.

'I wouldn't like to say.'

Rather than take the Granada, which somebody might have spotted the night before, we drove the dark-blue Opel Rekord in which the lads had come up-country. As far as our prisoner knew it belonged to Stew, but in fact it had come from the pool at Llangwern. We'd given Farrell a DPM smock to wear over his sweatshirt, and because the grass would be soaked with dew we all wore rubber boots. The Haskins was in the boot, cradled in bubble-wrap alongside our makeshift target, and I'd brought one belt of twelve rounds.

We pulled out of the stinking farmyard soon after five-thirty, and by six, after a twisting, up-and-down drive across the hills, we were on the ridge above the range. It was another dull, murky morning and the light was late in coming, but my intention was that we'd get our rounds off the moment we could see properly, and clear out before any locals came looking to find out what was causing the disturbance.

I planned to walk in down the muddy track which

301

had defeated the Granada the afternoon before, and on the map we'd pinpointed the spot at which the path came up to join the road. As we arrived I did a drive-past, to make sure nobody was hanging about.

Half a mile down the road we found a single, enormous old beech tree standing out from the upper edge of the forest, and the moment I saw it I said, 'OK, if anything happens, that's our ERV.' With that established, I went back and parked the car out of sight of the road, in the neck of the muddy lane.

The Haskins was an awkward bastard to carry. The easiest way seemed to be to grasp it near the muzzle and hold it with the barrel slung back over my shoulder and the rest of the weapon hanging behind me. So we set off down the steep hill, Tony cuffed to Farrell and holding the target in his spare hand.

Down among the trees in the valley the light was even worse than I'd expected, but it improved marginally as we came out on to the 700-yard firing point. As I looked up the long corridor of grass with my binoculars, I saw some small brown animal standing out in the open.

'What's that?' I asked, handing Tony the glasses.

He watched for a moment and said, 'Some kind of deer. Now there are two of them.'

'Can't be deer, surely.' I took the binos back. 'They're too small. Wait a minute, though. You're right. They're muntjac. Barking deer.'

Tony began asking what in hell a barking deer was when suddenly Farrell exclaimed, 'Shoot one of the fuckers!'

'Why?'

'It's a perfect target! Four hundred yards. If you can hit that it'll show the rifle's bang on. Get down, man! Shoot!'

I almost agreed. Then my mind skipped back to an

episode on an exercise in Africa, when one of our lads had shot some small animal and the local Bushmen had gone ballistic, saying he'd angered the spirits of the mountain. Next day an SAS guy fell off the rocks while climbing and was killed, and the whole troop got so badly spooked that we couldn't get our arses out of that place fast enough.

No, I thought. I'm not going to run a risk by killing something needlessly. In any case, if we shot one of the deer we'd have a body to dispose of. Luckily, before I could argue, both animals moved off into cover and the chance was gone.

Farrell didn't hide his disappointment. 'You'd a great chance there,' he griped. 'You were too slow by far.'

Ignoring him, I asked Tony to take the target down-range. 'In fact,' I added, peering at the butt in the far distance, 'in this light, our spotter scope's not going to be a lot of use. See if you can tuck yourselves into a niche that's safe, somewhere close to the target. Then call the shots back to me on the radio.'

'Sure,' Tony agreed, then turned to Farrell. 'Come on, Danny Boy.'

As the two figures moved away side by side, I followed in their wake as far as the next firing-point. At the edge of the sloped bank a little white-painted marker post had '600' cut into it.

I made myself comfortable. As I'd expected, the grass was wet, but I paid no attention as I settled the angular stock of the Haskins into my shoulder and looked through the sight. The heavy rifle sat rock-steady on its bipod, and the light-gathering capacity of the scope was excellent. Through the lens the prospect looked far brighter, and with the magnification set on six the men came up a good size in the scope. Wait though, I told myself, they're still only half-way to the target area. I moved the sight off Farrell's back and tried the trigger

303

with a dry pull. *Click!* went the action, and once again it felt good.

Through my binos I watched the pair move up towards the target bank. In the trees around me the wood pigeons were cooing – a soft, heavy sound that suited the dull morning. Not a breath of breeze stirred the forest, so wind was not a factor. Poor light tends to make you shoot high, I remembered; on the other hand, moisture in the air tends to make the bullet drop. So today, I guessed, one circumstance should cancel the other out, and I decided to fire right at the centre of the aiming mark.

Now the men were on the bank. I saw Tony looking round for something to steady the box. He must have found a flint or a clod of earth, because in a moment he had the target standing upright.

His voice in my earpiece asked, 'See that OK, Geordie?'

'Fine, thanks.'

'OK. There's a kind of a cave cut into the side of the hill about thirty yards back. We'll get a great view from there. I'll tell you when we're in.'

'That's good. I'm ready when you are.'

The whole point of long-range shooting is to be relaxed. The worst thing, for a sniper, is to have to react suddenly to a command like 'Standby, standby . . . GO!' Far better if he can take his own time and think himself into the right frame of mind. Now, with nothing to pressure me, I concentrated on lying tight, elbows and wrists tucked in, and settling my breathing down into a steady rhythm. My technique has always been to take the shot so gently that, when it goes off, it comes almost as a surprise.

When Tony called that he was in place, I acknowledged briefly. Then I loaded one massive round into the breech, breathed down again, took up the first pressure on the trigger, and at the end of an out-breath squeezed the shot off.

BOOM!

The noise was colossal, and the report thundered away into the wooded valley; but the recoil was less than I'd expected. Although the heavy weapon pumped back into my shoulder all right, the twin shock-absorber arms had taken the meat out of the jolt.

All at once the sky above the range was full of pigeons – black shapes going like the clappers in every direction. My ears were still ringing from the explosion, but I could tell that the chorus of cooing had come to an abrupt end.

'Great shot!' Tony was reporting. 'It's dead central, twelve o'clock, two inches above the top of the white.'

'OK,' I said, 'I'll try another. Same point of aim.'

I loaded a second round and went through the same sequence: tuck in, breathe down into a rhythm, try not to blink or flinch . . . take up first trigger pressure . . . breathe out . . .

BOOM!

'Same again,' came Tony's voice. 'Dead centre, two inches above your first shot. Perfect grouping.'

'I'm aiming at the centre of the white. So the MPI's six inches high. Is that right?'

'Exactly.'

'OK, then. I'm going to put the sight down three clicks and fire again. Standby.'

It took me a couple of minutes to make the adjustment with the little turret on top of the scope. Then I told Tony I was ready, settled again and touched off a third round.

'Dead on,' he called. 'Now you're in the white, an inch below the top edge. You're not going to do better than that.'

I was on the point of saying we'd call it a day when

Tony came back on the air with, 'Watch it, Geordie. Some goddamn vehicle's pulled up by that barrier. It's a Land Rover. Two guys.'

Instinctively I collapsed the legs of the rifle to lower its profile, and wriggled backwards down the slope of the firing point. Then I realised that two empty cartridge cases were lying there in the grass. Leaving the weapon, I wormed forward again to grab them just in time to see two figures appear at the entrance we'd come to the previous day. They popped into view as if they'd been running, and looked wildly up and down the range. Then, spotting the target, they ran towards that.

'Tony,' I said, 'I'm going to fire a diversionary shot. Then I'm heading for the vehicle. Get out of there when you see a chance. Make your own way up and RV at the tree as soon as you can.'

'Roger,' he called.

I got my binos and the empty cases into the pockets of my smock, loaded a fourth round, moved into the bushes at the side of the grass, took a good grip of the rifle and fired it into the ground from a standing position. This time the recoil nearly blew me over backwards, but I kept on my feet, pushed through the cover to regain the path and started up the earth track.

For the first hundred yards or so I ran. Then lack of breath forced me down to a fast walk. Over the past few days I hadn't been able to do any training, and now the effects were coming through. What with the gradient and the weight of the rifle, I was soon gasping like a pair of bellows. All the same, I kept going fast to the crest of the hill, and when I reached the edge of the wood I paused to get my breath back.

As soon as I'd recovered I tried to call Tony, but got no answer. From the angle of the hill, I knew he must be out of my line-of-sight, and probably wouldn't come back on the net until he too had climbed out of the valley.

The Rekord was where we'd left it, with nobody in sight. In a couple of seconds I had the rifle rolled back into its protective wrapping and laid under an old blanket in the boot. I also pulled off my DPM smock and threw that in. Already I was thinking, Shit! I can't stay here now. Those guys in the Land Rover might power up to the ridge at any moment.

Rather than risk a confrontation, I started the engine and drove away northwards, back towards base. As long as nobody associated the car with the shots, it wouldn't attract attention. My plan was to turn round after a couple of minutes, make a reverse run past the big tree, and keep talking until Tony came back on the air.

But I'd only been going about thirty seconds when a police car appeared, travelling fast in the opposite direction. Even though the two guys in it hardly looked at me as they hurtled past, I didn't like the speed at which they were moving. It looked as though they were responding to a call-out.

I drove on slowly, trying to read the local map as I went. Finding I couldn't see it properly, I pulled into a lay-by and took a steady look. That reassured me.

A car following the main road, as the police were, would have to go six or seven miles on a roundabout route before it could reach the rifle range. That would give Tony and Farrell at least ten minutes to get clear. 'Chill out,' I told myself. 'They'll make it, no bother.'

I got out of the car and raised the bonnet as if I had engine problems. An old banger of a white pick-up truck came from the south and went by without slowing. As the minutes passed I began to sweat. Calls on the radio produced no answer. What the hell could the other two be doing? The worst scenario was that they'd got captured. The idea was horrendous. If Farrell fell into the hands of the police at this stage, our entire plan would be scuppered. I tried to put that possibility out of my head.

More likely, I told myself, they were stuck in the thicket above the range. During our recce the night before I'd noticed that there were few big trees on that side of the hill. It looked as though a fire or a storm had taken out the main crop, and all that was left was hawthorn, brambles and other scrub which had grown up in the vacuum. One man, crawling on hands and knees, could probably push his way along tunnels made by deer; but for two, cuffed to each other, progress would be a nightmare. I thought of the wait-a-while thorns which had torn us to pieces in the Colombian jungle, and of Farrell collapsing at the edge of the forest.

Ten minutes after seeing the police car, I turned round and made a run past the big tree, calling all the way on the radio. Nothing. Driving on, I found the road twisted downhill through another big wood, then emerged into open farmland as it dropped into a valley. I followed it right down to a T-junction at the bottom, and there turned to come back.

Another drive-past, more calls. Still nothing.

Back at my lay-by, I pulled in again and called Whinger on the mobile.

'Bit of a fuck-up,' I went.

'Been compromised?'

'Yes and no.'

I told him what had happened. 'Anything doing your end?'

'All quiet in the shit-house, but things are moving outside.'

'How?'

'I don't know exactly. You'll have to ask Fraser. But apparently the PIRA are getting nervous. I don't know what they've seen, but they're starting to feel pressure

308

coming on them. There's been some talk about moving the hostages.'

'Oh, God! I'll call the incident room. And listen . . . Whinger?'

'Yes?'

'I'll be back there just as soon as Tony and Farrell emerge from this fucking jungle.'

'OK, mate. We'll be waiting for you.'

I restarted, turned and headed south again. 'Hello, Tony, hello, Tony, are you reading me? Over.'

Still nothing.

At the bottom of the hill I stopped and called the incident room. Fraser was off duty, but Yorky was there. 'Yes,' he confirmed. 'SB have got it down to three locations. One's a semi in Sudbury, next to Wembley. One's a block of flats in Greenford, and the third's a house in Ealing. They're all under round-the-clock surveillance, but we desperately need confirmation.'

'Can't we hit all three at once?'

'It's not on, Geordie. We're not certain of any of them. Until we *are* sure, it's not worth the risk. If it turned out we were wrong and the hostages were somewhere else, they'd certainly get topped.'

'What's this about the PIRA moving them?'

'It's only talk so far. Nothing's happened yet.'

'Where's our team now?'

'Still on standby in Hounslow Barracks. They couldn't be better placed – only a few minutes from all three locations.'

I took a deep breath and asked, 'What's the position on approval for the shoot?'

'Nothing confirmed yet.'

'Ah, shit!'

'How are you doing, Geordie?' Yorky sounded quite concerned, like some old uncle.

'Slight local difficulty. But basically, we've got the weapon and done the practice shoot. Once we're out of here, we're going ahead with the recce of the park itself.'

'You'd better carry on, then. As soon as we hear anything, we'll pass it to your safe house.'

'Roger, Yorky . . . and thanks.'

I was about to switch off when I heard him say, 'Hello?'

'Yes?'

'The Commander's just come back in. I'll put him on.'

I waited a moment, then heard Fraser's cheerful voice. 'Geordie? How's it going?'

'So so.' I filled him in on what I'd told Yorky, and got back the same stuff about the three locations. But then Fraser added, 'From what we're hearing, the PIRA aren't very happy with your man.'

'Don't they want him back, then?'

'Oh yes, they want him all right. But now their aim is to top him.'

'Delightful!'

'It is,' Fraser agreed. 'Does he realise that?'

'He knows he's in the shit. But he's that arrogant, he probably thinks he can talk his way out of it. At least, that's how we read him.'

I switched off feeling very low. This thing seemed never-ending. It had dragged on so long already that I couldn't imagine it coming to any definite conclusion. I tried to galvanise myself with the thought that it was going to *have* to come to a conclusion within twenty-four hours – by this time tomorrow. Either the shoot would go down as the Prime Minister walked out into his rose garden before breakfast, or the PIRA's patience would run out.

Yet again I turned, drove up the hill and past the big

tree. No answer on the radio. It could still be that the curve of the hill was blocking us, even if Tony had climbed clear of the range and was struggling up through the scrub. He, if anyone, would get Farrell out of the mess safely. I trusted Tony at least as much as I trusted any of my British mates, not only for his physical strength and capability, but for his level-headedness.

Back at the lay-by, I pulled in for the third time and sat looking at the map. I'd just tried the radio yet again when I looked in the mirror and saw a car coming up from behind.

Police. Pulling in behind me, too. Jesus! I sat tight, watching, while the two men got out and advanced on the Rekord. I just had time to scramble the earpiece and throat-mike out of sight before they drew level.

I wound down the window and said, 'Good morning.'

They returned the greeting civilly enough, but immediately began to ask questions. The boss figure was a sergeant – beefy, red-faced, with a big belly, like a rugger player gone to seed.

'Can I ask what you're doing here?'

'On my way up to Great Missenden. Had a bit of time in hand.'

'You came the other way just now.'

'That's right. I was delivering a parcel.'

'Where to?'

'An address in Stonor.'

'Do much delivering, do you?'

I was uncomfortably aware that the second copper was walking round behind the car, giving it the close eyeball. Probably they thought I was a poacher, and had a deer in the back. Probably they were scanning for traces of blood.

'Look,' I said. 'What's the matter?'

'Nothing,' went the sergeant. 'May I have a look in

311

the boot of your car?'

I got out and faced the guy, to find that he was a couple of inches taller than me. 'You'd much better not,' I said.

'What's in there, then?'

'Nothing to do with you.'

'We haven't been poaching, have we?'

'Certainly not.'

'So why all the secrecy?'

'I can't explain.'

The radio in the sergeant's breast pocket began honking off, and he was distracted for a moment as he dealt with the call. What could I do? It was possible that the police in the Chequers area had already been squared away and told to stand off, but the guys down here would know nothing about our operation. If I did a runner I'd be chased, and the car would be traced, and Tony would be stranded. If I refused to open up, I might be arrested for obstructing the police.

Before I could take a decision the sergeant said, 'I'm afraid I require you to open the boot.'

'Listen . . .' I stood between him and the back of the car. 'I'm a member of special forces, on a classified operation. Will you please get on the phone to my control room?'

Without answering, the sergeant lumbered forward and jabbed his thumb on the boot catch. Short of knocking him out of the way, there was nothing I could do to stop him. Up came the lid. With the movement of the car through the bends, the rifle had rolled over once, partially unwrapping itself, and the barrel lay there plain to see.

'What the hell . . .?' began the sergeant. His beefy face suddenly turned even redder as a surge of adrenalin flushed up through him until I thought he was on for vertical take-off. Reaching down, he pulled away the bubble-wrap and exposed the main body of the weapon. 'What the devil is this?'

'It's a Haskins five-oh sniper rifle,' I told him in the most casual voice I could muster.

A second later I saw him reaching for his radio in a kind of automatic twitch.

'NO!' I said sharply. 'Don't put through any report. Not until you've spoken to my control. Here.'

I pulled out my mobile, dialled the incident room, and providentially got straight through to Fraser. 'John,' I said. 'Geordie. I have a problem. I'm with a police sergeant. He's seen I've got a big rifle in my possession, and I need you to explain what we're at.'

'All right.' Fraser sounded imperturbable as ever. 'Where are you?'

'Out in the Chilterns, above the range I told you about.'

'Has he caught you with the weapon?'

'Yes.'

'OK, I'll speak to him.'

I handed the phone over and stood back, watching the sergeant's face go through every conceivable expression: shock, incredulity, alarm, bewilderment. It took several minutes, but I could tell Fraser was winning the battle, because after a while the sergeant began giving details of his own head of station, along with the telephone number. In the end he said, 'Very good, sir,' and handed the phone back to me.

'Is he going to speak to your boss?' I asked.

'That's right.'

'Great. I'm sure they'll sort it out between them.'

The sergeant looked shattered. 'Never heard anything like it,' he went. 'Never seen a weapon like that out here. Buggered if I have.'

'You live and learn.'

I didn't know what Fraser had told him, and I wasn't

313

going to ask; but now that our practice shoot was partially blown, I reckoned I might as well resuscitate my covert radio.

'I got separated from a colleague,' I explained. 'I'll just see if I can raise him.'

This time the first call produced an answer.

'We're on the RV,' Tony confirmed.

'Has anyone seen or followed you?'

'No.'

'Standby, then. I'll collect you in a few minutes.'

A moment later the sergeant's radio came to life again, and he got a stream of instructions to thin out. From the way he kept repeating, 'Yes sir, no sir, very good sir,' I knew it must be his boss. At the end he said to me, 'Well, that's it. I'm to leave you alone.'

'Thanks,' I said. 'And you won't talk about this, either?'

I made it sound like a question, but it was more or less an order – and when he said, 'no' he almost added 'sir' again.

'Cheers, then.' Without more ado I closed the boot, got back in the car, swung round and set off for the ERV.

Not knowing quite what the plods had heard, I didn't want them to see Tony come out of the undergrowth with Farrell cuffed to him, so I went back down the road at a fair bat and scorched to a halt under the big tree. Almost at once Tony emerged from the bushes behind it. Even though I was expecting him, he gave me quite a shock, because his face was covered in blood, with sweat-streaks coming down through it. Farrell's was the same.

'Get in, get in!' I snapped, holding a back door open. Then, when we were rolling, I asked, 'What happened?'

'Goddamn thorns!' Tony exclaimed. 'We're ripped

314

to bits by the bastards. We got bushed in that thicket. Jesus Christ – I never knew you had jungle like that over here.'

Back at the shit-house, it took us a good hour to sort ourselves out and get some breakfast down our necks. After they'd had showers, Tony and Farrell didn't look too bad. Their faces were scratched, but only superficially, as if they'd been caught on the job by their girlfriends. As I'd anticipated, they'd had a miserable time forcing their way uphill along animal tunnels under hawthorn bushes and through brambles, while the gamekeepers, decoyed by my distraction shot, charged around in the valley below.

As if to confirm my earlier suspicions, Tony told me that Farrell had gone over the moon about the rifle. When he had seen the bullet holes opening up in the white he nearly pissed himself with delight. 'I'll tell you one thing,' Tony added. 'Boy, do those rounds make a racket! It's a supersonic crack like nothing on earth. If the Prime Minister gets one of them go close past him he's going to jump a mile.'

'No he isn't,' I said. 'He's going to drop down like a sack of potatoes.'

As soon as I'd got myself together, I called the incident room again.

'I hear you've been advertising your presence throughout the Home Counties,' said Yorky.

'Bollocks,' I told him. 'We couldn't help it. We did land up in a tight corner, though.'

'Not to worry. The Commander's got it sorted. And you've got your permission.'

'What? For the shoot?'

'Yes. A secure fax from Number Ten came in a few minutes ago.'

315

'Jesus!'

'The Prime Minister has OK'd it. In fact, he's definitely in favour.'

'He must have balls, then.'

'He has. But he's been listening to what Special Branch had to say. They advised him that he's in a dangerously vulnerable position. The threat from the PIRA has intensified, and they can't guarantee to contain it. In other words, they were saying there's a good chance he's going to get bloody shot sooner or later. This operation you've hatched is seen as the best means of defusing the situation.'

'Got it.'

'By gum, you'd better get yourself sorted,' Yorky went on. 'If this goes wrong, it could bring the government down.'

The PM's reaction was what I'd been expecting – what I'd been wanting, really: anything to get me out of this mess. But when the go-ahead finally came through it was a shock all the same.

Yorky hadn't finished. 'So – you're on. But you still may be saved the trouble. The SP team are going ahead with plans to assault the hostage location, just as soon as we've got it pinpointed.'

'What's the latest on that?'

'I'll hand you over to the Commander. He'll fill you in.'

'Geordie?' It was Fraser.

'Hello.'

'I got your local copper straightened out.'

'Thanks. Sorry to come at you out of the blue like that.'

'Don't worry. You shouldn't get any more hassle from the law. Now, listen. As for the hostages: we're concentrating on our second alternative. The flat. It's number fifty-seven Cumberland House, on the fifth floor of a block in Ellerton Road, Greenford.'

'Oh, God! You think they're there?'

'There's a good chance. It's a two-bedroomed flat. Quite an old block, built in the sixties. Your guys are going to do an outside recce, and meanwhile we're trying to trace the owners of the apartment. Also, we need to get the original architect's plans, so that we know the exact internal layout. The trouble is, the flats aren't standardised – quite a lot of variation from one to another. One minute . . .'

He paused, as if he was looking through his notes, and then continued: 'Various owners have carried out alterations, as well. The firm that designed the block has been taken over, but we're hoping to find the plans with their successors. Also, we're hoping to occupy number fifty-eight next door, to do a bit of through-the-wall surveillance.'

All at once I felt choked, and couldn't speak. The fact that so many people, all highly skilled, were working away on my behalf, doing their utmost to save Tim and Tracy . . . Suddenly it seemed too much.

'Geordie? Are you there?'

I got hold of myself and said, 'Yep.'

'Take it easy, lad. You'll be all right. Call again when you're back.'

'Will do.'

'Here's Yorky again.'

'OK.'

'What are your plans now, Geordie?'

'Tony and I are off to recce the park. I don't trust the PIRA measurements and details. I need to see for myself.'

'Fair enough. But as soon as you get back, we need a detailed breakdown of your projected movements and timings. OK?'

'Sure.'

Farrell had predictably tried to muscle in on the recce, but I told him there was no way Tony and I would take him with us. 'Walk around the park of the Prime Minister's official country residence with you cuffed to one of us?' I had said. 'Pull the other one. You'd be back in the nick within minutes – and we'd be there with you. You're not walking round on your own, either.'

A few minutes' drive northward through the lanes had brought us within reach of Chequers. It was now 2.30 pm. The day had heated up a good deal but the sky remained overcast, and the air was muggy. I was still high on adrenalin, feeling tense and brittle, both exhausted and hyper-alert at the same time. I'd deliberately left behind the PIRA notes and instructions, but I carried them word-for-word in my mind.

Once again, in an attempt to clear my head, I was bouncing theories off Tony. 'If Fraser's squared things away properly with the local cops, I presume he's done the same with the security force at the house,' I said. 'So we shouldn't get any aggro, either today or tomorrow morning.'

'I guess not,' Tony agreed. 'But presumably normal security will be operating. If the home troops see anybody acting suspiciously, they'll challenge them. I mean, they may see us walking round, but they won't know who we are.'

'That's right. We could be a couple of PIRA dickers. But we've got to get a good look at the place. Good enough to be able to convince Farrell that we've done a proper recce.'

'Sure. Take it easy now. Only a mile to go.'

We were driving northwards along the bottom of a broad valley, farmland rising on either slope, and woods high above us to right and left. I slowed down, and a moment later Tony pointed right, saying, 'Dirtywood Farm. Hell of a name for a house. In a minute we'll see the lodge and the park gates of Chequers right in front of us.'

There it was. The lodge turned out to be a substantial building made of brick, with pillars supporting wrought iron gates. Beyond the formal entrance the drive ran straight along an avenue of trees towards the main house, which was visible in the distance. Here the main road swung hard right, and we followed it round to the east. Three or four hundred yards on we came to another sharp bend, a left-hander this time, with a rough parking-place on the outside of it. A couple of cars were already standing there, at the point where a long-distance footpath crossed the road. Obviously it was a favourite take-off point for walkers setting out on a hike.

I pulled in on to the sandy verge. 'This'll do,' I said. 'We can tab it from here.'

We'd dressed as casually as possible, in check shirts and jeans, to make ourselves look like run-of-the-mill hikers. Our binos could be just a sign of our interest in birds.

There were already a couple of other people ahead of us on the footpath, so we set off after them, through an iron kissing-gate and across a big open field of young corn. Now we were heading west, back towards the drive and the entrance lodge, with the house sitting in its shallow valley away to our right. Immediately features began to chime in with the PIRA descriptions I'd committed to memory: the back drive coming in to the house at right angles from our right, the clumps of trees, the memorial obelisk high on a hill in the distance.

Soon we came to the avenue and the main drive.

'One camera here,' said Tony quietly.

'Got it.'

A closed-circuit camera, flanked by an infra-red light, was mounted on a pole so that it could scan the outer stretch of the approach road which lay in dead ground from the house. Without looking at it overtly, we gave it a quick inspection as we went past. Then, carrying on across the drive and up the gentle slope beyond, we followed the footpath to the corner of Maple Wood.

'Point D,' we both said simultaneously.

Whoever the PIRA scout had been, he was obviously right. This was the place from which to take the shot. By now we had gained a bit of height, so that we were looking down across a wide-open field towards the south front of the house. At our back was a dense beech wood – immediate cover if we needed to disappear. Our binos could pick up any amount of detail around the house itself: a brick wall across the front of the terrace; a little brick summerhouse with a pointed roof at each corner; low, neatly-clipped box hedges, rose beds, a big, ugly conservatory to the left, and behind it all the tall, stately building of soft red brick, with mullioned windows, high chimneys, and numerous sharply-peaked gables.

But it wasn't the architecture that grabbed our attention.

'There's a camera on a post just to the left of those two little trees,' said Tony.

'Got it. And another alongside the wall, mounted on a pole. Go further left, and you'll see three more.'

'I have them. There's also an electronic device of some kind on the third pillar along from the summerhouse. It could be a microwave, covering the walls.'

'That summerhouse,' I said. 'Go to the bottom left-hand corner of the window. There's some other device

320

there. That looks like a microwave as well. I bet it's pushing out across this field to pick up any movement. Jesus! They've got the place really sewn up. You couldn't get much closer than this without being detected.'

'They must have a massive array of TV monitors somewhere,' Tony said. 'Banks of them in a control room, and a large number of guys keeping an eye on them. Watch yourself, Geordie. There's someone in an upstairs window.'

'Where?'

'See the main door? Go up to the top floor and right. There – the curtains moved again.'

'OK. Probably a cleaner.'

I looked to my left and saw a young couple walking towards us along the footpath. I wanted to stay where we were for a bit longer, so I sat down on the grass, took off my right boot, and pretended to feel inside it for an offending nail until the hikers had passed.

As I retied the laces, I said, 'Even first thing in the morning there are liable to be people coming past here. We can't hang around in the open waiting to do the shoot.'

'Lie up in back there, maybe,' said Tony, pointing into the wood.

'Yep. That's the answer. Then come down into the open at the last moment.'

Under the old beeches the forest floor was fairly clear. There were straggling elder and hazel bushes and patches of bramble, but plenty of open spaces between them.

'We'd have better elevation from up one of the trees,' I said.

'Yeah, but with that rifle you need the bipod on the ground. If there was the slightest movement in the branches you'd be all over the place. What's the range?'

'What they told us – six hundred. I'd say that's spot on . . . I've just noticed something else as well.'

'Oh yeah?'

'Those evergreen shrubs – the clipped ones on the terrace. What I'll do is put the bullet into one of them. If we hit one of the walls, shit and corruption would fly in all directions. But that bush of box – or whatever it is – will conceal the strike. From this range, nobody will be able to see the real point of impact.'

'Good thinking. And here's something else.' Tony pointed at some muddy, well-rolled wheel-marks which passed close in front of us, following the edge of the wood and parallel to the footpath. 'There's a regular vehicle patrol along here. Another reason to keep back in cover.'

As we walked on, Tony said, 'Know what? *Any*body who can shoot a rifle could take out the Prime Minister from here. People talk about the special skills you'd need, blah, blah, blah – it's all baloney. Just lie down and fire one careful shot.'

'OK,' I agreed. 'But number one: you'd need a special weapon. Number two: you'd need to know when the target's going to be around. Number three: you'd need a means of getting out – unless it's a kamikaze mission. And number four: you've got to be fanatical enough, or crazy enough, to want to do it in the first place. It's just unfortunate the PIRA's organised in all departments.'

Our next focal point was at grid reference 834055, the spot at which the PIRA had told the incoming helicopter to land for the pick-up. Again we confirmed it as a good choice because it was in a different field, behind another wood, out of sight of the house, and could be approached by a chopper coming low out of dead ground to the west, where the land fell away in a succession of steep valleys.

Back on the main path we carried on our clockwise circuit, swinging right-handed through a belt of trees and across the track beaten down by the vehicle patrol. On either side of the official footpath were frequent notices, white on green, saying PRIVATE – KEEP OUT, shutting off side-tracks and blocks of woodland. For a while we respected them, but when we saw the mast of what was obviously a small re-broadcasting station on the bare summit of a hill, we let curiosity get the better of us. Our instinct, in any case, was to check out all the high ground near the house in the hope we could find a better vantage-point for the shoot – but a rebro station: that definitely needed investigation.

Having climbed a barbed-wire fence, we scrambled up some steep, sheep-mown turf alongside a stand of box and emerged on to a rounded summit, to find that the relay station was dug well into the ground. A flight of concrete steps led down to a steel door in a brick surround, and the short mast was anchored by guy-wires.

'This must be part of the security set-up,' I said. 'It'll be a booster station, giving radios a wider coverage.'

Closer to the house, maybe a hundred yards away, was another small summit on which young trees had been planted within a ring of fence.

We'd just come up to it, and found that the view of the terrace was blocked from that angle, when Tony snapped, 'Keep down!'

I ducked instinctively. 'What is it?'

'A Land Rover Discovery heading this way on that track outside the wood, where we've just come from. Looks like the cops. Let's get out of here.'

We quickly backed off the skyline and slithered down the steep turf. We were half-way down the edge of the box thicket when the Land Rover came back into sight, heading straight for us. Without a word we both plunged backwards into the tightly-packed stems. Luckily for us, box has no thorns, but the intense dark-green smell of the leaves made me think of churchyards and tombstones. A couple of yards inside the thicket we were completely hidden, and we heard the vehicle come grinding uphill in low gear. Assuming the guys on board had seen us from a distance and had come out to chase us off, we lay low where we were for ten minutes or so. Then, from above us, came noises of men at work: hammering, and an electric drill screaming, as if some kind of maintenance was in progress.

We wriggled our way back into the open and slipped downhill to rejoin the footpath. 'Better stop messing about,' I said. 'There's nothing for us round this side. Point D's the place.'

Our next task was to recce the drop-off point that we'd already selected on the map, and to walk the route in that we'd use in the morning. That meant back-tracking round our circuit and returning to the car. On the way, we could see the Discovery still at the rebro station, and the figures of a couple of workmen on the skyline.

As we passed Point D, we lingered once again to get the feel of the position. I brought out my compass and took a quick bearing on the centre of the house: 11 mils.

'What if the worst occurs and there's pea-soup fog?' I said.

'Might not be the worst,' Tony replied. 'Might be the best. You'd have a cast-iron excuse for not carrying out the shoot, and your own guys would have that much more time to find the PIRA hide-out and hit it.'

'Yes, but the bastards might go ahead with their threat.'

Tony looked steadily at me, as if to say, 'They won't.' Then he studied the map again and said, 'Know what? Right now, we'd do better to hike from here to the drop-off point and then walk back in, rather than go round by car.'

'All right. We'd better keep inside the wood, though. We don't want to walk up the field and get spotted by any more damned gamekeepers.'

Instead of heading back eastwards across the park and the main drive, we cut away to the west, along the southern edge of Maple Wood. Outside the trees, on our left, a long, narrow field ran up between the blocks of forest, and towards the far side of it stood Brockwell Farm.

'That's where our QRF wants to be, or part of it,' I said as we passed the huddle of buildings. 'We'll confirm that when we get back.'

At the head of the field we came across a well-used bridleway running through the wood across our front, and we turned left along it, heading gently down a shoulder. Just after we'd joined the path two fair-haired teenage girls came cantering uphill on glossy ponies, and the leader shouted 'Thanks!' as we stood out of the way to let them pass. How happy they looked, I thought, how healthy, how normal, how carefree. What a difference between them – an ordinary, harmless part of the country scene – and ourselves, creeping furtively about with our minds full of death and deception.

The sight of them nearly choked me again, and I knew my mental reserves were running down. When Tony said, 'Nice piece of ass, that first one,' all I could do was give him a sickly grin.

Fifteen minutes' steady tab brought us to the point where the track ran out on to a metalled lane, and there we found a muddy lay-by, big enough for a car to pull off the road, the spot conveniently marked by a sign of a rider on horseback.

'This is it, then,' I said. 'We drive in to here. Quick

drop off, Doughnut carries on northwards. We walk in. No problem.'

Our return journey took almost exactly the same time: fifteen and a half minutes to Point D. Given that in the morning one of us would be carrying the Haskins and the other would have Farrell hitched to him, I reckoned we should allow twenty minutes to get ourselves into position.

Back on the corner of Maple Wood, we took one more scan with the binos across the park to the house. Now there were a couple of men working in the terrace garden. Although the top of the retaining wall obscured their legs from the knees down, the upper parts of their bodies were in full view. With the brilliant green of the young corn, the trees in full leaf and the mellow brickwork of the old building, the scene looked as peaceful as could be.

'It just shows how much tourists miss,' I said with a touch of bitterness. 'Thousands of them must walk along this path every year. They come and gawp at the place and think how beautiful it all is. But they only see the surface, and they haven't the first fucking clue about what's going on underneath.'

At 1700 I walked out of the shit-house and round the back of the farm to call Fraser on the mobile.

His first words were, 'We've taken possession of number fifty-eight Cumberland House.'

'Oh – great! Any luck?'

'Yes. We've got echo-phones on the walls, and we can hear next door fairly well. They've got the telly on a lot of the time, probably to mask voices, but we're listening. SO19 will be there any minute now with a drill. We're going to bore through the party wall and see if we can get a fibre-optic probe in place.'

He paused, then said, 'That's the good news. The

bad is that the PIRA have put in another death threat. The final one, they call it.'

I said nothing, waiting in dread for him to go on.

'If the shoot on the Prime Minister doesn't go through, or if the Prime Minister escapes, they say they'll kill the hostages at nine tomorrow morning.'

'Oh, Jesus! Can't you hit them before that?'

'We're trying to, of course. But as things stand, we're not hopeful of going in before ten, at the earliest.'

'In that case, it's just as well we've got this mock shoot lined up. Can you put me on to Yorky, please?'

'With pleasure.'

A moment later Yorky came on, and I said, 'Listen, this is what I've fixed with Farrell.'

'Fire away.'

'Our sniper party will be dropped off at 0530. The drop-off point's at 838045, where the bridleway leaves the lane. We'll proceed on foot to the PIRA's Point D, 839052. I estimate the walk in will take twenty minutes. So we'll be in position before 0600. We'll conceal ourselves in the wood and wait for the PM to appear, presumably any time after six-thirty.'

'Roger,' said Yorky. He was obviously looking at the 1:25,000 map, because he said, 'Which side of that narrow field will you go down?'

'North side,' I told him.

'OK. Part of our QRF will be in that farm – Brockwell Farm. They'll probably see you go by. Just so they know what to expect, how many of you will there be?'

'Four. Myself with the rifle, Tony with Farrell, and Whinger for back-up. Doughnut's going to drive the Granada, and Stew will bring the Rekord in later.'

'OK. And what about after the shoot?'

'If the target goes down, Farrell will use my mobile to phone through the authorisation for the hostages to be released. He guarantees they'll be driven to our final RV point, on the M25 between Junctions fourteen and fifteen.'

'That was where you had the aborted RV the other day, wasn't it?'

'Yep, but that was northbound. This one's heading south. The first emergency phone past Junction fifteen.'

'Trust those bastards to hold it somewhere we can't have a chopper overhead.'

'I know. But we'll make sure Farrell's wearing his magic shoes. Also, as soon as the handover's been done I can put the make and number of the PIRA vehicle out over the radio.'

'OK. Go back a bit, though. How do you get out of the park at Chequers?'

'The chopper's laid on to be standing by from 0630. The idea is that the pilot will put down somewhere out of sight a mile or so to the west. The moment Farrell calls him, he'll come straight in to pick us up from 834055. That's in a field west of Whorley Wood.'

'Got it. Looks as if it's out of sight of the house.'

'It is.'

'Then what?'

'We fly south for two or three minutes, then west, and put down in a field, just east of Junction Six on the M40. Doughnut will be waiting there with the Granada. We pile into that, and away towards London. Off at the next exit, number five, where Stew's waiting with the Rekord. Switch into that, and on to the M25.'

'Right, right. Got all that. I'll go back through it with you.' Yorky ticked off the points, one by one, then said, 'What if there are more PIRA on board the aircraft? What if they try something funny?'

'They can't. A Jet-Ranger can only take four passengers. There'll be me, Farrell, Tony and Whinger. That's it. Anyway, we'll all have pistols and knives.'

'All right.' Yorky paused. 'Now – d'you want to hear my side of it?'

'Of course.'

'So. We've established a forward control room in Chequers itself. I'm heading up there myself in half an hour, to direct operations from now on.'

'Great!' I said. 'That's really good.'

'We're putting a comms centre into the house as well. Did you see the rebro station on the hill to the west of the house?'

'Yeah, we went up and had a look at it.'

'Our signallers stuck up an auxiliary mast this afternoon. That'll give us secure comms over the whole area.'

'Wait a minute!' Suddenly I had twigged the identity of the vehicle which gave us such a fright. 'Was that them in a police Land Rover? About four o'clock?'

'Sounds like it.'

'Christ! They scared the shit out of us. We were up there when they started heading for the site.'

'That was your bloody fault, for pissing about. The net's up and running, anyway. The signallers have stayed put, and we're bringing up a team of medics. The QRF will consist of three four-man teams: one in the farm, one in a vehicle, standing back, and the third in a chopper, ditto. Their call-signs will be Black One, Black Two and Black Three – in that order. Got that?'

'Sure.'

'You'll be Green One, the Granada Green Two, the Rekord Green Three. Our local head-shed will be Zero Charlie. Got all that?'

'Yeah, yeah. I'm making notes. It sounds as if half the Regiment's getting seconded to this operation.'

'It is. And of course we're liaising with the Prime Minister's own close protection squad. So you'd better not drop a bollock, Geordie.'

'No way. I'm going to play it straight down the line. I take it the Prime Minister's been briefed on the shoot itself?'

'Absolutely.'

'You'd better warn him about the noise. According to Tony, the sound of a five-oh round going past is like the crack of fucking doom.'

'OK. I'll see he's told that. Now . . . what's the time? I should be up there for half-eleven. D'you want to call me again then for an update?'

'Sure. What's the number?'

Yorky gave it, and I rang off feeling relieved that at least the situation in the country would be well contained. As for London – I could only hope. I kept saying to myself, 'Find them! Find them!'

The whole evening seemed to consist of briefing sessions. No sooner had I finished with Yorky than I had to run through everything again with Farrell. Of course, many of the points were the same – our drop-off, walk in, and selection of firing position – and I had to be careful not to say anything that would betray the fact I'd just been in touch with the security forces.

'Let's get things straight,' I said. 'If the shoot goes down, you'll use my phone to give the codeword for releasing the hostages. Right?'

'I will.'

'What *is* the codeword?'

'You'll hear soon enough.'

'So we make for the helicopter pick-up point.'

'We do.'

'And the chopper lands us here, by junction six on the M40.'

'Agreed,' said Farrell. 'He's going to fly south first and disappear through the valleys, to confuse anyone who might see us take off. Then he'll turn east and head for the motorway.'

'Fair enough. Then, at the pick-up point, Doughnut's waiting with the Granada. By the way, you'll need to put your spare kit into the car before we start in the morning: dry socks and shoes and so on. Wear wellies for the shoot. The grass'll be full of dew. Keep the trainers for later . . . As I say, Doughnut collects us and drives us to the next exit. Stew's there with the Rekord. We switch cars and carry on to the final RV on the M25.'

'Correct.'

'What about the rifle?' I asked. 'What d'you want done with that?'

'Jaysus, man. That's coming with me. I wouldn't be leaving such an asset behind, would I?'

'OK. You take it. And the spare ammunition. Next, how do we correlate timings? I mean, where will your lot be coming from?'

'They've a shorter distance to travel than we have,' said Farrell cryptically. 'Once we're on the road, we'll call them to set a time.'

'Well . . .' I pretended to measure distances on the map, although I'd thought them through already. 'They'll have to shift, because it won't take us long. From our pick-up point to the motorway interchange is only twenty miles. Say twenty minutes if we take it easy, twenty-five including the switch from one car to the other. But when we hit the M25 it may be a different matter.'

'What d'you mean?'

'It's going to be the rush-hour. Any time between about seven and nine-thirty the motorway can seize solid along that section.'

'It's no problem. We'll be in touch with the boyos on the mobiles. If we get late, we'll tell them to hold back a bit.'

'All right,' I said, 'but this time I don't want any fuck-up at the RV.'

'And neither do I. I'm wanting out, I tell you. I've had enough of being chained to some stinking turd of a Brit or a Yank day and night.'

'It's OK for you.' I glared at him, deliberately not rising to the insult. 'If anything goes wrong, the worst that can happen to you is that you land back in the nick. For me, it's a matter of life and death.'

'Come on, now. Nobody's threatening you.'

'Not me, but they're threatening my family. What's going to happen if we can't carry out the shoot for any reason? What if the Prime Minister doesn't appear?'

'He'll appear,' said Farrell heavily. 'He's always at his filthy roses.'

'He might not come out tomorrow. He might feel under the weather or something. He might just be late. How long do we wait, for God's sake? If it gets to mid-morning and we haven't seen him . . .'

'So what?' said Farrell calmly.

'There'll be people about by then. Hikers all over the place, coming along that footpath. We saw quite a few today.'

'They'll not bother us. We'll keep back inside the wood until the right moment, so we will.'

'And the chopper. What about him? He can't sit around half the day in somebody's field.'

'I can always call him up and tell him to pull off until I give him a new deadline. Ach, don't bother yourself. We'll be away and gone by seven o'clock, I'm certain of it.'

Farrell sounded confident enough, but I could sense that under his veneer of calm he was nearly as tense as I was. Thank God, he seemed to have no inkling that a huge net was being spread to capture him and the leading lights of the London ASU.

At least, so I thought, until he started talking again.

'And yourself, now. What are you going to do if you get your people back?'

'Collapse with relief, I should think.'

'Yes, but on the ground – in the flesh, I mean.'

'Drive home, I suppose. I've hardly dared think about it yet.'

'Yes, but your unit . . .'

'The Regiment? What about them?'

'How will you account for the hostages being let go?'

'I won't know anything about the reason. I'll only know there's been a phone call telling me to get to the RV.'

'How will the Regiment contact you to pass on the details?'

'They've got my mobile number.'

'Where do they think you are now?'

'They don't know. I could be anywhere. I'm on leave – they haven't been in touch for days.'

Farrell gave a non-committal grunt. 'And afterwards?'

'As long as your chopper pilot performs properly, we'll make a clean getaway. The murder will be put down to the PIRA, and that'll be that. There'll be nothing to connect it with me. After all, I don't happen to own a five-oh rifle.'

'This house, though . . . and the other one.'

'We took them in false names, and paid cash.'

'The cars?'

'We changed the plates for the duration of the exercise.'

'All right, so you've done well.'

For the first time in my life I saw Farrell smile. But when he put in a final check-call to one of his mobile numbers, the temperature fell sharply once more.

'They're suspicious,' he said, holding his palm over the receiver. 'They think you're acting in concert with the security forces, and with the military.'

'Ah, bollocks!' I went. 'If the Regiment knew what I'm doing, they'd kill me. I've told you, these guys are just friends. Let me speak to him.'

I reached for the phone, but Farrell lifted it back to his ear. 'Sharp wants to talk to you . . . No? Fair enough.' He covered the mouthpiece again and said, 'He'll speak to another one. Not yourself.'

'All right, then. Tony. You talk to him.'

'Not Tony,' Farrell snapped. 'They know about the Yank.'

'Doughnut, then,' I said. 'For fuck's sake, tell him what you do.'

Doughnut was brilliant, very cool and laconic. He'd been waiting for this. 'Yeah, yeah,' he went. 'BGing . . . Yeah. Bodyguarding . . . An Arab sheikh . . . No, I'm not allowed to say which . . . Only when he's in London . . . Now? He's in South Africa, on holiday. That lets me out . . . He comes here on business, but that's in quotes. It's really to procure women. Bloody amazing they are, too: Zanzibar, Morocco – you name it, he has them . . .' On he went, mainly about the colossal amounts of money the Arabs threw around. When he said that the sheikh had twenty-four cars – including three Rollers and a pre-war Lagonda – in his London garage, the guy on the other end capitulated.

'There you are,' I said to Farrell. 'What did I tell you? Now, for God's sake, let's all go to bed.'

FIFTEEN

When Doughnut shook my shoulder and brought me a mug of tea at 0500, I couldn't believe I'd ever been asleep. I seemed to have been twisting back and forth all night in spasms of anxiety about things that might go wrong. The worst was that the PIRA would take fright and murder the hostages prematurely; the next worst, that the Prime Minister would get killed by mistake; the third worst – but still unfaceable – was that we'd go through the whole charade, and then for some reason the RV would fail once more.

I had learned that at 58 Cumberland House specialist technicians from SO19 had completed one penetration of the party wall and successfully introduced a fibre-optic probe into the flat next door. They'd gone through the wall low down – so that there would be less risk of plaster-crumbs making a noise tumbling to the floor when the tip of the drill emerged – and by sheer bad luck it had come out behind a piece of furniture, a sideboard or a free-standing cupboard, moved there since the owner of the apartment had gone abroad. The result was that we still had no positive identification. So the technicians had begun drilling all over again.

This I'd been told by Yorky, when I had last spoken to him just after midnight. By then he was established in the new control centre, designated Zero Charlie, inside Chequers itself, and sounding well in command of the situation.

After that, with Farrell out of the way in the end bedroom, we'd held one last briefing session in the kitchen, squaring away final details: we'd run through everybody's roles, verified map references and timings, cleaned our pistols, checked magazines and made sure that our radios and mobile phones had fully-charged batteries. 'During the shoot,' I told the lads, 'the overriding factor we've got to bear in mind is this: *we* know we're going to be acting out a charade, but to Farrell every detail has got to seem credible.'

Eventually, at half-one, we'd gone to get our heads down – but I, for one, couldn't drop off. Every minute that had gone by I was hoping for a call from Yorky to say that the assault on the flat had gone in, the hostages had been safely recovered, and we could stand down our whole crazy plan. The Greenford operation, I knew, had been named 'Fruit Salad', and the codeword for a successful recovery was 'Bananas'. That would mean both Tim and Tracy were safe.

For hour after hour – or so it seemed – I had lain there thinking of a man patiently drilling through the wall of a room using an old-fashioned bit-and-brace, giving it just half a turn at a time, to make certain no sound would be heard in the flat next door. The process I had envisaged was agonisingly slow – half a turn . . . wait . . . half a turn . . . wait – the wire-thin bit going in a millimetre or two at a time, the microphones listening all the time for reaction on the far side . . .

All night I had lain hoping that the three magic syllables – ba-na-nas – would bring our manoeuvring to an abrupt end. If that happened, we'd drive Farrell straight to the back door of Chequers, hand him over to the resident security force, and call Doughnut and Stew back to base. The only faint amusement I had got was from the thought of the PIRA helicopter pilot, sitting in some farmer's field at 0600, waiting endlessly for instructions that would never come. Farrell had let on that the operator of the Jet-Ranger they'd hired had charged them £5,000 in cash, paid in advance, for the morning's run. It was clear that the man had realised they were up to no good, because the price was exorbitant. But since the money probably came from Libya in the first place, I couldn't care less.

Now we had a bare half-hour in which to prepare for take-off. I had a wash, got a bowl of raw porridge and milk down my neck, drank a second cup of tea and sorted my kit. Stew was in charge of Farrell at that stage, and when the brute began effing and blinding about being hassled I yelled at him to get hold of himself. 'Ah, sling yourself!' I snapped. 'You can cut that out now. Once we're in the open I don't want to hear a fucking sound out of you. Otherwise you'll screw up the whole bloody operation.' I could see he was suffering from nerves, like the rest of us, but that didn't make me feel any more charitable towards him.

Outside, my spirits lifted a fraction when I saw that at last the weather had changed. The clouds had gone, leaving the sky brilliantly clear, and high over our heads a jet had spewed out a slim, white trail that reached far to the north. When I moved out of range of the dung-heap the air smelt fresh and clean, and there wasn't a breath of wind. If a fine day was to be taken as a sign of hope, we'd got one.

Our short drive to the drop-off point went without incident. We saw no other vehicle, and after just ten minutes all four of us were standing in the dark lay-by watching the tail-lights of the Granada disappear up the lane and into the distance.

After waiting for my eyes to acclimatise to the half light I set off along the bridleway carrying the Haskins over my shoulder. Behind me came Tony and Farrell, cuffed together by a short length of chain, and Whinger bringing up the rear. Though the sky was already bright, inside the wood the darkness hung on. Just like our morning at the range, the trees seemed to be full of wood pigeons, cooing all round us. I knew the noise should have been soothing, but somehow it annoyed me, and whenever a bird flew out from above us, disturbed by alien creatures passing underneath, its wings made a terrific, give-away clatter.

When we reached the top of the long, narrow field, I told the others to hold on while I did a quick recce to make sure the coast was clear. 'Stay here while I check the field,' I whispered. 'I'll be back in a moment.'

'OK,' said Tony. 'Take it easy.'

With exaggerated stealth I crept out into the open and went on fifty metres or so until I knew I was out of earshot. With Farrell left at a safe distance, I held down the pressel switch of my covert radio and said, 'Hello Zero Charlie, this is Green One.'

'Green One, send,' came the immediate answer. Yorky's voice.

'On course and on schedule,' I told him.

'Zero Charlie. Roger.'

If there had been any dramatic news from London, Yorky would have told me. His brief, professional response meant simply that we had to carry on.

I retraced my steps to the others and whispered, 'Can't see anything. But we'll keep right in to the side of the wood, in the lee of the trees.'

So we went steadily on, the light growing all the time but remnants of gloomy darkness lurking along the fringes of the wood. As we passed Brockwell Farm I thought of the QRF, skulking about the barns or hay-lofts, and bet myself they had eyes on us. Sure enough, up into my earpiece came a Welsh voice saying, 'Black One. Geordie and his team are passing us now,' followed by Yorky's quick, 'Zero Charlie. Roger.'

At the corner of the wood, fifty metres short of Point D, an extraordinary sight confronted us. Away in the distance the house was dark, but the lower half of the field between it and us was covered by mist lying in a dense white blanket. The effect was ghostly and unreal, as if Chequers had been constructed on the far shore of a milky lake.

'If that lot rises up a few feet we're buggered,' I whispered.

'It won't,' Farrell replied. 'It'll fall away and disperse as the air warms up. This often happens on a fine morning.'

'You'd better be right.'

'Watch it!' said Tony. 'There's something moving out in the middle.'

We stepped back into the trees to watch. Binos revealed the dark object as the head of a deer, which had popped up out of the fog. I realised the animal must have been grazing with its head down, and that the top of the fog-blanket was just over the level of its back. As we stood looking, another head came up beyond the first, and the two began moving to our left.

'You hang on here,' I whispered to Whinger. 'Stay back in the wood, but keep eyes on the lodge and the drive. If you see any movement, let us know.'

'Roger,' he said softly, and we left him there.

At Point D we moved into the recess among the bushes which we'd identified during the recce. When we raised our heads we could see out over the field to our front, but if we kept down the screen of shrubs shielded us from the footpath. My plan was to stay in cover until our target appeared on the terrace, then to nip forward on to the mossy bank at the very edge of the trees and take the shot from there.

The drawback of our lying-up place was that it had no view along the footpath to right or left, and it was possible that somebody could approach without our seeing him. I therefore decided to leave the other two where they were, with the weapon, and position myself farther forward.

I pulled down the legs of the Haskins's bipod and set it on the deck, keeping the belt of ammunition in the right-hand pocket of my smock.

'What effect will the mist have on the flight of the bullet?' I asked quietly.

'Negligible,' Tony said. 'No wind, either. No lateral allowance needed. The only thing is, in half an hour the light will be pretty bright. That could cause you to shoot a touch high.'

'Agree with that?' I looked at Farrell, who nodded.

'OK. I'll bear it in mind. Sit tight here while I take a look up the footpath.'

I went back to the edge and took a scan with the binos. The two deer were clear of the mist and walking up towards the wood on my left. A light had come on in one of the first-floor windows of the house. Maybe the guy's up even earlier than usual, I thought. Taking advantage of a lovely morning. I looked at my watch: 0610.

I walked slowly along the edge of the wood, in the shadow of the trees, until I was seventy or eighty metres from the others. Away to the east, my right, the sun was still below the ridge, but only just, and the sky was glowing. Even as I watched I saw the fog blanket beginning to thin and break up into patches.

I was fizzing with tension, electrified. I'd already taken one dump, back at the farmhouse, but excitement brought on another, and I withdrew into the trees to deal with it. When I came out again the deer had gone, and most of the mist had vanished. Only a few wraiths still trailed across the young corn.

Suddenly Yorky's voice was in my ear again: 'Zero

Charlie for Green One. Fruit Salad going down at figures zero six three zero.'

'Roger,' I answered automatically. Then the meaning of the message struck me. Jesus! It meant the guys in the Greenford operation had definitely found the hostages. It meant they were going in – and in less than fifteen minutes' time! A hit on a single-floor flat couldn't last more than one or two minutes. In less than half an hour from now, the whole thing should be over.

I felt my heartbeat speed up still faster with the news. I wanted to run out into the field yelling with elation. Thank God I kept my head, because I became aware of a noise to my left, and saw a jogger in a harlequin track suit pounding along the footpath towards me. Easing deeper into the trees as he went by, I passed a quick call along to Tony and Whinger, warning them to keep their heads down.

Now time really crawled, second by slow-moving second. Behind me the pigeons cooed relentlessly. The sun hauled itself over the eastern ridge and sent rays flashing low and long across the park. The last traces of mist vanished.

Then Whinger called, 'Discovery coming up from the right,' and the peace of the morning was spoiled by the grinding diesel engine as a routine security patrol went past. There were two coppers in the front seats, but – no doubt following orders – they were looking away from us and towards the house, rather than into the wood.

At 0626, with the Fruit Salad assault deadline four minutes off, I finally persuaded myself that we weren't going to have to fire a shot. For a moment I allowed myself the luxury of imagining the look on Farrell's face when I told him the score, and the language he would let fly. Then my little day-dream was shattered.

'Zero Charlie for Green One,' said Yorky again.

'Fruit Salad postponed. Technical problem.'

Cumberland House is a seven-storey block of flats on the south side of Ellerton Road, in the West London suburb of Greenford. There are nine flats on every floor, with each of their front doors giving on to a corridor that runs the length of the building. The rooms on that side of the block – kitchens and bathrooms – are dark and gloomy because their windows give on to those internal passages.

Access to the block is by two doors, one at either end; there are two lifts, also one at either end, and two staircases, east and west, as well as an external metal fire-escape on each end wall. The numbers of the apartments start from one in the east and rise to nine in the west, and incorporate the floor number as the first digit, so no. 57 is the seventh flat from the eastern end on the fifth floor.

Behind the building, on the south side, lies a scruffy, narrow open space which passes for a garden. This is bounded on its long side by a six-foot brick wall, separating it from the next street to the south, Longfield Drive, and at the eastern end an alleyway that provides a short-cut between Ellerton Road and Longfield.

(Although I wasn't present during the raid, I got the following details from Fraser and from the guys who took part. Because I'd been on similar operations as a member of the SP team, I could piece together the sequence of events in what I hope is an accurate reconstruction.)

By the afternoon of Wednesday 2 June, while Tony and I were doing our recce at Chequers, SB sources had assembled a fat file of information on the suspect flat. The freehold belonged to an oil engineer, Ernest Wilson, but he'd gone off to work in Venezuela the previous October, letting the apartment fully furnished for a year to a man called Bingham. Suspicion about the tenants had hardened when a Special Branch investigator discovered that the monthly rent of £400 was being paid into the local branch of Lloyds Bank in cash, and in irregular amounts (in November £1,200 had arrived – the first payment in more than two months).

Because of the layout of the building it was impossible to maintain a continuous close-in watch on individual apartments. Surveillance had to be maintained mostly from outside, from vans or other buildings, because any stranger lurking about the corridors or on the stairs would immediately have attracted attention. One known IRA player, thirty-year-old Danny Aherne, described as a travelling salesman, had been seen to enter the building several times during the last days of May. He always went in through the eastern entrance, took the lift to the seventh floor, and disappeared into no. 72, where he had an apparently legitimate arrangement renting a bed-sit from the family that lived there. Yet the mere fact that he was resident in Cumberland House focused the police attention sharply on the block.

When the DF vans had begun tracing PIRA mobile phone calls to the area, the janitor, Stan, had unfortunately fallen ill with a viral infection and was replaced by an SB stand-in called Tom. By dallying with his mop and bucket on the top floor corridor, the new man discovered that Aherne often left no. 72 a few minutes after arriving home from a shopping trip still carrying his supermarket bag, nipped down the stairs to the fifth floor, and slipped into no. 57.

In the early evening of 1 June, with the PIRA deadline approaching, SB decided that it was essential to evacuate the occupants of no. 58 and take the flat over for their own purposes. Fortunately the only person at

343

home was Edith Treadgold, an elderly spinster addicted to detective novels, of which she had hundreds arranged in glass-fronted bookcases. Normally she lived there with a companion, but that day the friend had gone to stay with relations. When Miss Treadgold suddenly found herself called on by a woman detective sergeant she was at first horrified, but then openly thrilled to be caught up in a real-life drama. She needed little persuasion to pack a few things into an overnight bag, surrender her keys, go down in the lift and take the waiting taxi, which bore her off to a comfortable hotel room for the night.

One by one, a team of specialists filtered into the block, using both entrances and taking the lifts to different floors before working their way up or down to no. 58. They were surprised to find that Miss Treadgold had another addiction besides Dorothy Sayers and Agatha Christie: when they pulled back a sofa into the middle of the room to get at the party wall, they exposed a sizeable collection of magazines dedicated to bondage and flagellation.

By chasing up the owner of the flat through Interpol contacts, the SB had established a clear picture of the layout of no. 57. Inside the front door was a central lobby, with the kitchen off it to the left, and the bathroom and a separate toilet to the right. Beyond the bathroom, having a common wall with no. 58, was the main bedroom, which had a window on the south face of the block. Next to it was a smaller bedroom, also with a south-facing window, and next to that the sitting room and dining area, which abutted the kitchen at its inner end.

The windows were old-fashioned and made of wood, and the doors of the bedrooms opened inwards, away from the central lobby. Monitoring of the water and electricity supplies had suggested that at least four people were living in the flat, even though none had been seen to come out, and the only known visitor was Aherne. The regular telephone line remained unused; during the past week not a single call had gone in or out.

At first the listening devices were frustrated by television sound, but at one point the eavesdroppers picked up the noise of a child crying and a woman shouting at him or her to be quiet. The sounds caught by the microphones strongly suggested that the hostages were being held in the main bedroom, so it was into that wall that the drill had started to bite.

Meanwhile two six-man teams, Red and Blue, from the Regiment's counter-terrorist unit, were standing by in their holding base at Hounslow Barracks, a few minutes' drive to the south. As always in emergencies of this kind, control remained in the hands of the police, and would do so until the final moment before an assault went in. But during the evening the CO and the ops officer flew up from Hereford by chopper to take overall command of the military element of the operation, installing themselves in a control room established in Police Headquarters at Hendon.

Further up the chain, an open-ended meeting was in progress at COBR, the Cabinet Office Briefing Room underground in Whitehall, where the director of the SAS, a brigadier, was liaising with senior representatives of the Metropolitan Police, the Home Office and the Prime Minister's personal staff.

In no. 58 drilling continued all night. As Yorky reported to me, the first probe, which went through at 2315, proved ineffective because its view was blocked by furniture. The second, higher up, penetrated the wall of the main bedroom by 0320, near the corner with the outer wall, but by then the room was dark and for the time being nothing could be seen. It was only at 0405, when one of the occupants got up to go to the

345

lavatory, that a light was switched on.

For the top brass, listening in to commentary from the front line, events suddenly became gripping.

'There's a bumping noise,' said the Scots voice of the fibre-optic operator. 'They're moving the furniture around. There's a bed across the door – they have to move it to get out . . .'

The pitch of the voice rose sharply as the man said, 'The light's on. The kid is there! It's definitely him. He's in a camp bed. He's woken up. He's sat up and looking round. Seems to have a black eye. Right eye swollen.

'The woman's gone to the bathroom. Wearing white pyjamas . . . now she's coming back. Two women. One's small, stocky and fair. The other's tall and slim. Not a redhead, though. Wait till I get a look at her face. Yes, it's Tracy all right. But her hair's very dark. Black. Could by dyed. Could be a wig . . . No – she wouldn't wear a wig at night. Her hair's been dyed. Pass that to the teams. Don't be looking for a redhead. We don't want any identities mistaken. The guard isn't much over five foot. You can't confuse the two.'

The news precipitated immediate action. In the control room at Hendon the assault plan was finally ratified. Details were confirmed over the secure net to the Red and Blue teams, and to the assault commander, Captain Terry Morris, who, along with Staff Sergeant Bill Brassey, had set up a forward command post in another commandeered flat, across the street from the north front of Cumberland House. It was from there that the main surveillance had been conducted for the past three days; now closed-circuit television cameras were watching both entrances.

By 0515 both teams had been bussed to the site. One by one they infiltrated via the garden passage. The six guys in Red crept up the fire escape, taking care not to let their MP 5s, axes or other equipment clank against the steel guide-rails. Out on the roof, among the dish aerials and ventilation shafts, they sought anchor-points for their ropes, so that they could abseil down and come in through the windows of no. 57. Simultaneously the six guys in Blue went quietly up the eastern staircase to the sixth floor, moved along the corridor and back down to level five, where they slipped silently into no. 58.

Farther out, two snipers crawled on to the roof of a warehouse which commanded a view of Cumberland House's south front. Their primary role was to report any movement in the hostage flat's windows, which had been numbered One (the main bedroom), Two (the second bedroom) and Three (the sitting room). A secondary task was to watch the windows of no. 72 for any change. When the raid went down, the snipers would also act as cover and take out any terrorist who tried to escape from that side of the building. Also waiting nearby, hidden in the drive of a private house, was the hostage reception van, with another six guys from the Regiment on board. Their job would be to scorch in and whisk everyone away from the scene – hostages and soldiers alike – the moment the assault was complete.

From all these sources quick reports flowed in over the secure net. 'Sierra One,' called the lead sniper. 'We're on. In position. All curtains drawn. No lights showing.'

'Zero Bravo. Wait out,' Local Control replied.

The Blue Team had few preparations to make, and soon the leader reported, 'Blue One in position and ready to go.'

Again Control answered, 'Roger. Wait out.'

It was the Red Team who needed most time to prepare. There were no easy anchor-points for their ropes, and as the light came up the guys felt very exposed on the bare, flat roof. 'Red One,' called Fred Daniels, their leader. 'We need to get a shift on or we're going to get compromised up here. There's people on the move in the streets already.'

'Zero Bravo. Roger,' responded Terry Morris. 'Wait out.'

As the minutes ticked past tension mounted. Danger lay in the fact that the security forces were not certain how many terrorists the flat contained. The aim, in situations of that kind, is to work out the position of every X-ray in advance, so that the teams can be certain precisely where their targets will be before they go in. But in this case it had proven impossible. Thanks to the fibre-optic probe it was known for sure that Tracy, Tim and one PIRA woman were in the main bedroom. The pattern of mobile telephone calls had suggested that there were also two men in the flat – but whether both were sleeping in the second bedroom, or one there and one in the sitting room, nobody knew. The only option was to hit the apartment from both sides simultaneously – Red through the windows, Blue through the door.

The intention all along had been that the assault should go in before 0630, to forestall any need for the shoot at Chequers. But permission had to come down from COBR, and then at the forward control room Terry had to sign an order from the senior police officer present, taking over command of the incident.

While these formalities were being prepared, the Red Team lay flat on the roof beside their coiled ropes, to keep out of sight of passers-by or people in other buildings. By 0625 everything was in place, and Terry was about to sign the hand-over order when a man appeared, walking fast along Ellerton Road with a plastic shopping bag in his right hand. One of the cameras picked him up as he went into the eastern

348

entrance of Cumberland House, and he was immediately identified as Danny Aherne, the tenant of no. 72.

Where had he come from? What was he doing, heading back to his lodgings at that time of the morning? What was he carrying in the bag?

'Zero Bravo for Tango One,' said Terry, calling the reserve team into action. 'A suspect X-ray has entered the building. Move to seal both entrances immediately.'

'Tango One. Moving now,' came the answer, and then from Terry: 'All other stations, this is Zero Bravo. Hold, hold, hold.'

Crouching at the edge of the wood I felt like I'd had a kick in the crotch, and it took me a couple of minutes to recover. I felt physically sick at the thought that something had gone wrong. At that stage I didn't know what had happened. I'd only heard Yorky's message, but surely the security guys couldn't have mistaken the identity of the people in no. 57. Surely they'd got the right flat . . .

Fighting down the disappointment, I made my way back through the trees to rejoin the others. From the way Tony looked at me I could tell that he knew how I was feeling. Through his covert earpiece he too had heard Yorky give me the bad news, and he was suffering along with me. I was grateful for that.

But all he said was, 'It's such a hell of a morning, the target may come out early. Hadn't we better get ready?'

'We *are* ready,' I replied. 'We just have to whip forward and fire.' All the same, I withdrew the bolt from the Haskins and looked through the barrel to make sure it was clear. Then I gave the lenses of the telescopic sight their hundredth polish. I was half-way through getting up from behind the rifle when Tony, who was watching the house through binoculars, said,

'Look out! A door's been opened.'

I had my own binos up in a flash. Yes, there was movement at the back of the terrace. A man in a white shirt and black trousers had come out and was shaking something pale – maybe a rug or a tablecloth.

'It's a butler or some similar jerk,' I breathed. 'At least it shows the household's on the move.'

All three of us were kneeling in a line, Tony on the right, then Farrell, then myself. I glanced sideways at Farrell and saw that his eyes were gleaming, his lips drawn slightly back from his teeth. Watch yourself, twat, I silently told him, you're in for a nasty surprise in a moment.

The butler figure disappeared inside again and the door closed. Now waiting became even harder. The hands on my watch barely seemed to move. By the time they had crawled to 0635 it felt like midday at least.

Temporary relief came with a short, sharp, sudden rushing noise. There, right in front of us, a buzzard was pulling out of a steep dive just above the ground. Whether the bird had swooped at a rat or mouse and missed, I couldn't tell. After a moment he soared up again, talons still extended, his wings working furiously, and the roar of air through his pinions took me straight back to parachuting and free-falling.

All at once I was thinking of the first two training jumps I made, at Weston-on-the-Green. I remembered how somebody went past me, falling after my chute had broken out, with a load, hoarse roar, like that buzzard, only bigger . . .

More movement on the terrace jerked me back to the present.

Jesus, I thought. This is it.

The same door had opened again but a different man had come out. The binos clearly picked out the familiar figure: smooth grey hair, slightly long; pale face, spectacles glinting. He wore a big, sloppy, light-coloured sweater nearly down to his knees, and he was carrying something in his right hand – a small canister, no doubt to blitz the bugs on the roses.

'Begod! It's himself!' Farrell exclaimed.

'Come on then!' I snatched a glance at my watch: 0645. No hope of a reprieve from London now.

I snatched up the rifle and started forward, asking quietly over the radio, 'All clear your end, Whinge?'

'All clear,' came the answer.

I reached the bank and set the Haskins down. The target was moving slowly out into the terrace garden, turning back and forth as he peered at the rosebeds. I looked through the sight and saw that, although the scope was good, it wasn't like a pair of binoculars: it gave a clear general picture but not close details.

'Now!' I stood up and faced Farrell. 'There's a slight change of plan. It's you to shoot, not me.'

'What the fuck!' His face turned deathly white. Then a red flush of anger came up from the neck. 'What's this?' he croaked incredulously. 'What the fuck is this?'

'Get down and shoot,' I told him, 'or the chance will be gone.'

'Treacherous cunt!' he said out loud, and then, almost shouting: 'Fucking treacherous *bastard*!'

If his right wrist hadn't been cuffed to Tony's left I'm sure he'd have taken a swing at me. Then he saw the Sig levelled at his chest and stumbled backwards, heaving for breath.

'You're the shooter here,' he gasped. 'That's the deal.'

'You have the choice,' I said. 'Shoot or die. Simple as that. There'll be few enough questions asked afterwards.'

'I can't shoot that thing.' He flicked his right foot in the direction of the rifle. 'Holy Mary, I never saw a weapon like that in my life. I couldn't hit the house, let alone the target.'

'Bollocks! It was you who shot the British soldier with it at Crossmaglen last August. It was you who killed the man long-range on the border in February. It was this very rifle, and yourself firing it. I don't know how many murders you've got on your slate, but one more's not going to make much difference.'

From the way Farrell flinched I knew I was right. 'Get down and shoot,' I repeated.

'Never,' he said. 'If you're wanting your family released it's you to shoot, and that's all.'

'I'll give you ten seconds,' I said.

He took a step towards me and made a sudden movement with his free left hand, but Tony jerked him backwards so violently that he fell over and landed on his arse. 'Unless I give the codeword they'll never be let go,' he warned. 'They'll be dead by noon.'

'I'll take a chance on that,' I said. 'I'm counting now. Ten, nine, eight . . .'

At six he made a gesture with his right hand, which I took to be one of capitulation.

'Christ Almighty!' he cried. 'How will I shoot trussed up like this?'

'You'll manage. Tony'll get down alongside you. Now shift yourself, or the target'll be gone.'

Through all this Tony had waited impassively, poised for action. I'd told him beforehand what I was planning, and he'd agreed not to intervene unless he had to.

The rifle was already in a perfect position, its bipod sunk into the moss on top of the little bank. Farrell was shaking violently as he positioned himself behind it, and the ferret stink wafted all around us. Tony went down beside him, extending his left arm to give the rifleman freedom of movement at the end of the short chain.

Farrell gave one more curse – a long-drawn-out

groan of 'Ah, you bastards!' – then gathered his concentration, settled his elbows into the leaf-mould on the forest floor, aimed through the scope, opened and closed the bolt, and clicked off one dry shot. The practised ease of his movements made it plain he knew the weapon well.

The target was still meandering about the terrace, but by now he'd moved nearly to the front of it, close to the right-hand summerhouse. In the clear early light his pale sweater showed up a treat.

'Let's have a bullet, then,' Farrell snapped.

I leant over between the two men and laid one of the six-inch rounds in the breech. As Farrell slammed the bolt forward I gave three consecutive double jabs on my pressel switch to warn Yorky that the shot was imminent.

Farrell had the rifle up and aligned, but the target was moving, walking slowly across to our right.

'Wait, man, wait!' I hissed. 'Let him stop. Now! No! Wait again.'

Once more the target had ambled on. But at last he came to a standstill with his back to us, right in front of one of the trimmed box bushes.

'There!' I said. 'Take him now!'

I put my hands flat over my ears and held my breath. *BOOM!*

I saw the big bullet go. At least, I saw the grey streak of disturbance in the air along its path. I was aware of movement at my feet as the recoil jolted Farrell backwards, but I tried to keep my binos on the target. For what seemed an age he remained standing. Then suddenly his arms flew half up, away from his sides, as if his hands had been lifted on strings, and he pitched forward away from us in a flat dead-man's dive. Once down, he was out of sight behind the box hedges, and we could see no further movement.

'Fantastic!' I yelled.

'Bejaysus, I got the fucker!' cried Farrell. 'I nailed him! I fucking dropped him!' In his excitement he forgot he was linked to Tony, and tried to jump up, only to be dragged down again.

'That's his lot,' I said. 'The bullet lifted him right off his feet. Now – send that fucking codeword and we'll get out of here. Quick, they're on the move.' As Farrell stood up I handed him the mobile phone.

The shot had sent pigeons clattering out over the field; dozens of them flashed blue-grey and white in the low rays of the sun as they fled from the clap of thunder. Away in the distance, figures were pouring out of the house. People were running back and forth, and clustering round the spot where the target had gone down. More doors opened, windows too. From somewhere to the right a police siren began to wail.

'I'll call the chopper first,' said Farrell. He punched numbers into the phone, listened and said, 'Yes. Come in now. Pick-up immediately.' As he was doing that I called Whinger to close on us. Then Farrell ended the first call and dialled again. This time his face creased into a frown. He muttered something, switched off, switched on again and punched once more. When he moved the receiver away from his ear I could hear the metallic, electronic voice saying, 'I'm sorry. It has not been possible to connect your call. Please try later.'

'What the fuck are they doing?' he cried. 'The bastards have switched off. Holy Jaysus! They know the timing. They should be on the ball and waiting.'

'Come on!' I shouted. 'We can't wait. Run!'

In Greenford a breathless wait ensued as Aherne disappeared into the building. In less than a minute the reserve team had secured both entrances and fire-escapes, but there was no sign of the player. By then SP

354

technicians had replaced the fish-eye peephole in Miss Treadgold's front door with another fibre-optic lens, which gave them a wide view down the corridor, and enabled them to keep watch on the entrance to no. 57. Everyone expected Aherne to show up there, but minutes passed without anyone getting eyes on him. Had he gone up to his own flat? Was he skulking on the staircase or in the lift? If he was at large somewhere, there was a chance he might appear just as the Blue guys were taping their charge to the front door to blow it in.

'Zero Bravo for Sierra One,' called Control. 'Any change in the windows on the top floor?'

'Negative,' came the answer. 'All the same.'

At last the suspect came back into view. 'Blue One,' the Blue leader reported. 'He's walking along our corridor, west to east . . . He's left a shopping bag against the wall outside the door of fifty-seven. Now he's gone on to the far end.'

Again he vanished. In forward control, Terry was left with a difficult decision. The bag might contain a bomb. More likely it held supplies for the people in the flat. Should he ignore it? Should he get Blue to remove it? Should he wait or go?

At 0644 the sniper leader called, 'Sierra One, movement in window figures two. The curtains have been opened.'

'Zero Bravo,' Control answered. 'What about the others?'

'No change.'

'Roger. Wait out.'

'Red One,' came a call from the leader on the roof. 'We've definitely been compromised. There's a crowd gathering in the street out the back. They've got us marked down.'

'Zero Bravo. Roger. All stations remain on listening watch.' Then a minute later came, 'All right. Ignore the bag. We're going in. I'm being handed control. All stations into position.'

The Blue leader slid out into the passage and silently taped a length of det cord down the line of the hinges on the front door of no. 57. At the same time all six members of the Red team came down the south wall on their ropes, squeezing the handles of their pretzels to descend, and then letting go so that the devices locked up when their feet were just above the fifth-floor windows. Down in the street the crowd was swelling rapidly, but it was too late for anybody there to intervene.

Both leaders reported themselves ready. Then Terry called, 'All stations, wait out . . . I have control . . . Standby, standby . . . GO! GO! GO!'

The Blue leader, hanging back in the open entrance to no. 58, closed the clacker in his left hand. *BOOM!* The door of no. 57 burst inwards and disintegrated. Smoke and dust filled the corridor. The Blue team piled through the opening.

In the same couple of seconds the Red team dropped the final few feet, smashed all three windows with fire axes and piled into the rooms. The two into the main bedroom, Geoff Hope and John Ryle, instantly identified Tracy in a single bed against the left-hand wall, and Tim in the camp bed at its foot. Another bed had been pulled across the door, blocking it. As the female terrorist sat up in it, reaching for a cabinet beside her, a quick double-tap in the head put her flat on her back. Blood flew out over the pillows and ran down the pale wall.

While Geoff went down on one knee to give cover, John dragged the bed away so that the door would open. 'Get down! Get down!' he yelled at Tracy.

Geoff yanked her roughly out of bed, forced her on to the carpet and knelt with a knee in her back. 'Don't

356

look over there!' he yelled. 'Look that way!' With his other hand he grabbed Tim and flattened him on the floor as well.

Before the door was open, two more double-taps cracked off in the other bedroom. When John burst into the hall he found it full of smoke, with his two black-clad mates from Red team down on one knee, covering the guys from Blue. Two terrorists lay dead in the small bedroom, one on the floor, one sprawled across a bed. It took just seconds more for the lads to rip open the cupboards, turn over the beds and sofa and case the bathroom and kitchen to make sure there were no more PIRA in residence.

'Zero Bravo for all stations,' called Control. 'Secure?'

'Blue One,' replied the Blue leader. 'We have three dead X-rays on the location. Two men, one woman. The flat is now secure.'

'Red One,' said Fred Daniels. 'Confirm flat secure.'

'Tango One,' said the boss of the reserve team. 'One suspected X-ray detained in hard arrest. He tried to do a runner when he heard the explosion. We got him on the stairs.'

'Zero Alpha. Roger,' replied the main Control, cutting in. 'All stations, evacuate the building.'

John set Tim on his feet, seized a blanket, rolled him in it and picked him up in his arms. 'Come on, love,' he said to Tracy. 'We've got to go.'

Later he told me she'd gone into shock at this point and didn't seem able to move. When Geoff had lifted her to her feet she nearly fell straight back over, so rigid had she become. Then she appeared to wake up; still without making a sound, she snatched up a dressing gown, stepped into a pair of slippers and ran out on to the landing, with John and Tim following close behind her.

Already the corridor was full of people from the

other flats, some excited, most angry, demanding to know what in God's name was going on. The assault had been so swift that no policeman had yet reached the fifth floor.

One of the Blue team had grabbed the lift and was holding the door open. While John, Tim and Tracy rode down, the rest took the stairs at a run. At ground level the hostage reception wagon was already outside the door. Within seconds, rescued and rescuers were packed into it with all their equipment, and heading clear of the scene.

Running with the Haskins was no joke. The rifle was not only heavy, but awkward too. Farrell was in no shape to run far, either – and being cuffed to Tony didn't help him. Whinger caught up with us after a hundred yards and offered to take the rifle, but I panted that I was OK. Nevertheless, the temptation to head out on to the edge of the open field was strong – the going would be far better along the footpath. But it would strike an obvious false note with Farrell if we revealed ourselves prematurely, and to keep our RV and complete the exchange we positively needed to get away.

We struggled on as best we could, dodging between trees, scrambling over fallen trunks, ripping through brambles, until at last we reached the northern point of the wood. Now we had no option but to break cover; we were on the edge of the field in which the chopper was due to put down. As we paused to recover our breath I could hear the thudding beat of its rotor in the distance.

By now several sirens were wailing from the direction of the house, and my earpiece was full of rapid exchanges, most of them calls for the police to seal off the surrounding roads.

I pushed out through the screen of leaves and

scanned up the sloping grass field that rose gently to our left. The ground was clear. The chopper was still out of sight behind the nearest hill, but the sound of its engine was growing rapidly.

'You two carry on,' I said to Tony. 'We'll cover you till the chopper's in. Go for it!'

I launched the pair with a flick of the hand and watched them run out awkwardly, Farrell dipping on his lame left leg. I'd intended that Whinger and I should follow them after a few seconds, but at the moment I scrambled to my feet I realised that I was getting something different in my earpiece.

'Zero Charlie for Green One,' Yorky was saying. 'Bananas. I say again – bananas.'

Of course it was what I'd been dying to hear. But I'd been so engrossed in our own scenario that my mind was entirely at Chequers.

The message made me stop dead. I hit my pressel and said, 'Green One. Confirm that.'

'Zero Charlie,' Yorky repeated. 'Bananas. All good.'

I let out an almighty yell – no words, just a continuous noise so loud that it made Whinger jump. Tony heard it, too. He looked round for an instant and stumbled.

Before I could get myself back together I heard the abrupt reports of small-arms fire. Jesus Christ! Rounds were going down across the field in front of me. The helicopter was in sight now, a blue-and-white Jet-Ranger, lifting over the skyline and heading our way. But also in sight a little posse of men had appeared suddenly out of a dip, and were running towards our pair. I saw by their irregular DPM overalls and lack of headgear that they were PIRA. The one in the lead was carrying a pistol; the other two had sub-machine guns and were firing from the hip as they ran. They were already within thirty or forty yards of their target.

Instantly I hit my pressel and called, 'Green One. Three armed X-rays on helicopter pick-up point. Request immediate back-up.'

As I spoke, Tony and Farrell suddenly went down. They didn't just fall over, they were hammered to the ground, and one of them let out an almighty roar. Jesus! Had Tony been shot? I yelled out, but it was not enough to distract the leading PIRA guy, who bore down on the struggling heap, obviously intent on finishing off the man he'd wounded.

There wasn't time to get the cumbersome Haskins loaded and aligned. As an instant deterrent I whipped out my Sig and began spraying rounds at the leader. But the action was taking place more than a hundred yards off, and at that distance the shots were all over the place. In any case I had to keep high, for fear of hitting one of my own men. The leader ducked but continued towards the two on the deck, using them as cover. Whinger was firing now, but the guy kept advancing. By the time my magazine ran out he was within a few feet of the fallen couple. He stopped and deliberately extended his right arm, the pistol canted downwards at point-blank range.

By then I'd thrown myself down on the turf outside the wood and got a fresh round into the breech of the Haskins. Feverishly I flicked the bipod into position. The range was barely a hundred metres. Aim low, aim low! I told myself. But before I could bring the sight to bear I heard two shots from the PIRA man's pistol crack out, and with a surge of dismay I thought I'd lost my closest, staunchest friend.

The PIRA gunman was still rooted a couple of yards from the fallen pair. Holding my breath, I brought the cross-hairs of the sight on to his torso and, without waiting another instant, fired. I didn't even notice the recoil.

But – Jesus! I'd missed. Then instantly I remembered: I'd fiddled the sight to make certain Farrell couldn't hit the Prime Minister.

Amazingly, the PIRA guy was standing on the same spot, now looking my way. In a second I had another round up the spout and aimed one body's width to his left. This time the five-oh bullet blew the man away. The impact lifted him backwards off his feet and threw his body on to the ground as if it were made of rags and cardboard.

His mates checked and looked around for a moment, uncertain where the shots had come from. Then the threat of that fearsome firepower evidently became too much for them, and they turned tail and began running back across the field. I loaded a third round, swivelled to my left and touched off another shot at the higher of the two. A burst of chalk and flint chips exploded from the ground above his right shoulder. A second later, before I could load again, he'd vanished into dead ground over a ridge.

The Jet-Ranger had been in a hover – the pilot evidently not fancying what was going on below him – and when he saw the contact erupt he had started to climb. By the time I'd fired my last shot he'd banked hard and was pulling off to a safe distance. I was getting so carried away that I almost loaded another round and let drive at him too. I was sure the Haskins was capable of bringing the chopper down. But within seconds another helicopter was on the scene – a Puma, drab military olive in colour, which swept over the wood from our left, swung round to the far side of the hilly field, hovering just beyond the skyline, and disgorged a shower of black-clad guys who fast-roped down out of our sight. The ensuing crackle of small-arms fire told me they'd caught the two fleeing PIRA operatives in the open. Moments later a voice came on the net saying, 'Black Three. Two X-rays dead in vicinity of pick-up point. Area secure.'

By now I'd loaded a full magazine into my pistol. I left the Haskins on the edge of the wood and sprinted forward to the tangle of bodies in the middle of the field. Both were lying face down. Expecting the worst, I pulled Tony over first. He gave a groan. He was very much alive.

It was Farrell who'd got a double-tap through the temple. As I rolled him on to his back I saw that the whole left-hand side of his skull had been opened up. The mess of blood and brains took me straight back to the corridor in Libya.

Farrell – dead! I could hardly take it in.

Tony was pale and in severe pain. It was he who'd gone down first, with a bullet through the left upper arm. Once both of them were on the deck, Farrell, struggling to break free of his shackle, had yanked the wounded limb all over the place. There was a lot of blood sprayed about the grass. My first action was to get a tourniquet on to Tony's arm above the wound.

Then I called over the radio for urgent casevac. 'Green One. We have two more dead X-rays on the same field, with me. No live X-rays seen. One of our guys is wounded. Get that Puma here soonest. We're only about four hundred metres east of where the QRF landed.'

'Let's have these fucking cuffs off you,' I said to Tony. 'Where's the key?'

Without speaking he patted the breast pocket of his smock with his right hand. I felt inside, brought the key out, unlocked the cuffs and gently took them off his wrist. I knew I shouldn't move Farrell's body before the scene of crimes officer arrived to make his assessment, but I couldn't help straightening out the cuffed arm.

'Better,' Tony muttered, with an attempt at a smile.

'What happened? Did the guy try to top you and hit Farrell by mistake?'

'No way. He went straight for Farrell like a lunatic. Put the muzzle of the pistol right on him.'

'What a bunch of arseholes!' I said. 'Only death can stop them feuding. OK, Tony. Hang on. That chopper will be here any second. Stay with him, Whinger.'

I stood up unsteadily and moved a couple of steps to look at the other dead terrorist. Immediately I recognised the short, grizzled grey hair. 'Christ! It's that bugger from the railway yard. Marty Malone. Old Foxy'll be chuffed to bollocks. This was the one he wanted most.'

The man was wearing a DPM smock. The huge round had gone straight through his right arm and on through his torso, and his pistol had fallen to the ground. Instinctively I bent to pick it up, but then thought, No, the SOCO will want it left where it fell. Looking at the far side of the body I saw that the exit wound was as big as a saucer. The left back ribs gaped open, and blood, scraps of lung and pieces of bone had been sprayed ten metres on to the grass beyond.

In my earpiece Yorky was saying, 'Zero Charlie for Green One. Geordie, the med team's on its way to you. Who's hurt?'

'It's Tony. Bullet through the upper arm. I've contained the bleeding. He could be worse.'

'OK. The guys will be with you in seconds. What's happened to Farrell? Is he still with you?'

'Affirmative. But he's dead.'

I looked down at Tony and said, 'Hear that? The chopper's on its way.'

His eyes were shut, but he nodded.

I knelt beside him, feeling stunned now that the situation was over. When I turned my head sideways I realised that the sun was shining on my cheek. The warmth seemed to bring me back to reality.

'Yorky,' I called. 'Is the Prime Minister OK?'

'The Prime Minister's in roaring form. He's ordered champagne for breakfast, and he's invited you to join him.'

'Don't be stupid.'

'He has. I mean it.'

'Christ, I can't. I've got to see Tim.'

'I know. We've said as much, and he understands. I'm sure he'll ask you again.'

'He put on a bloody good act, anyway.'

'Come on, lad!' Yorky sounded delighted. 'You didn't think that was him, did you?'

'Who was it, then?'

'Scrubber Jenkins, wearing a poncy wig and two flak jackets, one on top of the other. He was shitting himself too.'

'Why?'

'You might have hit him by mistake.'

'It wasn't me on the rifle, Yorky. It was Farrell.'

'Farrell! Jesus! How the heck did that come about?'

'I told him he had to do the shoot or I'd top him.'

'God almighty! Yer daft bat! He might have killed the PM.'

'Not a chance. I twisted the sight off twenty clicks to the right during the night.'

'Jesus, Geordie . . . I didn't hear that. Never mention it again or you'll be up to your neck in shit.' And with that Yorky went off the air.

The seconds ticked slowly past. My mind was full of puzzles, and after another minute I called in again.

'It was another PIRA guy who topped Farrell,' I said. 'What the hell were they up to?'

'Drug money, as we thought,' Yorky replied. 'I heard Fraser talking about a bank account the Firm discovered in the Cayman Islands. Farrell had eight million dollars in it.'

'Eight million!'

'Yeah. He'd been creaming off coke deals for years. If he'd escaped today he'd have done a runner.'

'Where to?'

'Three guesses.'

'Colombia?'

'You got it. He was planning to cut out and make a fresh start there.'

'So the PIRA never really wanted him back?'

'Only to top him.'

'In that case, I've been a pawn to their game all the way through.'

'More or less.'

'Fucking hell! The devious, twisting bastards.'

'Never mind, Geordie. If you're talking chess, it's checkmate to you. You've cleared the bloody board. King, queen, bishops – the lot.'

SIXTEEN

After a hit like that, all the lads are supposed to head straight back to camp. There, they sit down and calm down, and with a solicitor each one goes through every event that's occurred, every move made, every shot fired. The point of this routine is to prevent anybody talking to the police while they're still fired up with adrenalin and might say something out of place. As soon as the police get a chance they quiz you like there's been a murder, and you need to be careful.

So usually the first evening is spent having a monster piss-up, and everyone gets mongolised; and then, next morning, there is a proper debrief.

But in my case all that went out of the window. Because of the special circumstances an exception was made, and I was given permission to see my family straight away.

'Take the chopper,' Yorky told me. 'Go with the casualty. They're taking him straight to Hendon Hospital, and that's where the hostages are anyway.'

'What's happened to them?' I was so hyped up that I immediately became suspicious. 'Did they get injured in the recovery?'

'No, no. Relax. It's just that Tracy's exhausted. She's had more than enough for the time being.'

'OK, Yorky. Thanks. Have you called Doughnut and Stew back in?'

'Done that. They're on their way.'

'Great. I'll leave Whinger here on the ground to deal with the SOCO.'

'Fair enough. One more thing. You can't walk into the hospital in your DPMs – too high profile. There's a pair of plain police overalls on board the chopper. Slip them over the top during the flight.'

'Will do.'

I was still kneeling in the middle of the field, trying to chill out, unable yet to believe the nightmare was over.

'The Haskins is still on the edge of the wood, Whinge. You'll need to collect it and take it with you.'

'No bother. I'll get it now.'

Away he went. As I looked for the last time at Farrell's body, my mind took off on a fast re-run of all the aggravation he'd caused me: Kath's death, the night he'd appeared at the farm outside Belfast, my own attempts to top him, the firefight in the Colombian jungle – and now all this. My loathing for him still burned, but for the hundredth time I wondered how people like him and Marty Malone could let their whole lives be shaped – and cut short – by an irrational hatred of people they don't know, people they haven't even seen. How could anyone be so twisted by religion and history?

Tony gave a grunt, trying to sit up, but I made him lie down again, saying, 'You lost a lot of blood. Just wait for the chopper.'

'Geordie?' he murmured.

'I'm here.'

'Have you got Tim back?'

'Not yet. But he's safe.'

'Tracy?'

'Safe as well.'

'Thank God!'

Unable to speak, I gave him a gentle thump on his

367

good shoulder. Luckily Whinger chose that moment to return with the Haskins and launch one of his rhyming summations. 'Bacon and eggs,' he said.

'Where?'

'The dregs.' He pointed at the bodies. Despite the gore around us, the mention of food had suddenly made me feel starving.

'Talking of eggs, I could eat four easily,' I said. 'Maybe six.'

'Me too. And a few slices of ham with them. And a few pints of Stella along with it.'

The PIRA helicopter had vanished, but I could still hear an aircraft engine, and a minute later the QRF Puma lifted over the horizon, heading for us. As it came in to land a few yards away I crouched down beside Tony to shield him from the blast of the down-draught. I could see several of our guys in the cabin, and they stayed put, giving thumbs-up signs, while two medics whipped out with a stretcher. The nature of Tony's wound was pretty obvious, from the tourniquet and the blood on his DPMs, so I didn't try to tell them what to do, and in a few moments they had him expertly trussed, ready to be loaded. As soon as the stretcher was safely in I gave Whinger a wave and followed aboard.

The flight lasted only fifteen minutes. I slipped into the overalls somebody handed me, and looked down at the sunlit scene below. The time as still barely 0730, and on the motorways the morning rush hour was building up. As we skimmed over thousands of houses and roads jammed with crawling cars, I thanked my stars that I wasn't in the Granada, with Farrell very much alive and kicking, on our way to a doubtful rendezvous under the flightpath out of Heathrow. One more near-miss on the M25 and I'd have gone round the twist.

The Puma was too big to land on the hospital's helipad, so it put down on a playing field, where an ambulance was waiting. I rode in the back with Tony the few yards to the casualty entrance, and suddenly there we were, back in the world of stainless steel, green gowns, starched white caps and smells of disinfectant. I found myself thinking of Pat, with all the pins sticking through his thigh. I realised I hadn't given him a thought in days, and now I resolved to check he was doing all right. Almost certainly Tony would end up alongside him in Wroughton.

They took Tony straight into theatre, and for a minute I was left alone in a waiting room. Then a nurse, a pretty blonde woman, appeared and said, 'Sergeant Sharp?'

'That's me. Where are they?'

'I'll take you up.'

She led the way up a short flight of steps and along a corridor. I followed, uncomfortably aware that in those ultra-hygienic surroundings I cut a peculiar figure. My boots were smeared with mud, and it was three days since I'd shaved. Thank God they couldn't see the Sig in its holster under my arm.

The nurse walked so fast that I almost had to run to keep up with her. 'Are they all right?' I asked.

'Well, they've had a pretty bad time.'

I didn't like the sound of that, but I asked no more questions.

We went through some swing-doors into what looked like a private ward, with single rooms leading off it to either side. A uniformed copper was hovering, and out of an office came a woman in a smart, dark-blue uniform. Dimly I realised that this was the matron – but one hell of a matron: young, chic, and with a dazzling smile.

'Your wife's there, in number one,' she said, pointing at the nearest door.

I ignored the mistake and said, 'Is she OK?'

369

Before the matron could answer, a terrible noise burst through the door – half a scream, half a hoarse roar, inarticulate, but unmistakably Tracy's voice.

I was through the door like a rocket. A doctor in a white coat was standing in the middle of the room with his back to me. Facing him, perched on the edge of the bed in white pyjamas and robe, was Tracy. Her appearance gave me a terrible jolt. Her hair had gone black – of course, no one had warned me of that – and her face was as white as her pyjamas, and screwed up with tension. She looked ten years older, the ghost of the girl I knew.

I came to a halt, rooted by shock. Then she saw me. With another awful cry she sprang off the bed, knocked the doctor spinning, rushed at me and flung her arms round my neck. When I hugged her to me she felt like a sackful of bones.

Hardly had we come together when she went slack in my arms and started sinking to the floor.

'She's fainted again,' said the doctor calmly. 'She's done that twice already. Put her on the bed.'

I did as he said and stood back, breathless with dismay, and with a dreadful fear that the ordeal had sent her mad.

'What's the matter with her?' I gasped.

'Delayed shock. She'll be all right, but she's having a rough ride for the moment.'

I glanced at the doctor and saw he was only about my age, ruddy and fit-looking. He gave me a sympathetic look and explained, 'When she arrived she was on a terrific high. But it only lasted about quarter of an hour. She was laughing and joking all over the place, then suddenly she went right down. And this is the result.'

'What's the answer?'

'The best thing is to sedate her for twenty-four hours.'

'Can't I take her home?'

'Not really – it could be dangerous. She might become violent or do something crazy. She ought to remain under observation. Besides, Special Branch want to interview her as soon as she's stable.'

'You don't think her mind's impaired?'

'Oh, no. Give her time and she'll be fine.'

'Where's Tim?'

'A doctor's looking at his eye. He got a blow on it some days ago.'

'Is he as bad as this – mentally, I mean?'

'Not as bad. Of course, I don't know what he's like normally, but he seems very withdrawn. There – she's coming round now.'

Tracy stirred and opened her eyes. I dragged a chair up to the side of the bed and sat down, holding her hand, my face close to hers.

'It's OK, Trace,' I said gently. 'It's me, Geordie.'

She turned her head and looked at me, but not with any affection. On the contrary, she gave me a hard stare, then turned away again, as if she equated me with the enemy and wanted nothing to do with me. She closed her eyes tight and began to gasp and shake. A shudder coursed down her body, head to toe, so that her whole body frame began quivering on the bed. I realised that the devils were coming out of her, but the violence of it was dreadful to see. Then out burst another terrifying hoarse roar, a noise so ugly I couldn't believe she was making it.

I held on to her hand tighter, feeling my own tears coming, until gradually she quietened. I heard the door close behind me and turned and blinked at it. The doctor had gone. I held on, letting time pass.

The doctor was right. This wasn't something that I could handle. At least Tracy's fingers were clutching mine. Perhaps some contact was getting through.

Presently her shakes subsided completely. I stroked her gaunt cheek with the back of my hand and whispered, 'Stop worrying, Trace. You're safe now. It's all over.'

At last she turned to look at me properly and said, 'Where were you, Geordie? Why did you take so long to come?'

'Sweetheart, I was trying. I was nearly killing myself trying to find you. You can't imagine what's been happening. As soon as you've had a rest, I'll tell you.'

She kept on looking at me, and in her eyes I caught a glimpse of the person I loved.

'Listen,' I said. 'Are you all right? I mean, did they . . . they didn't . . . molest you?'

She shook her head slowly.

'Is the baby OK?'

For a terrible moment she stared at me silently, her eyes like stones. Then, very low, she muttered, 'No. I lost it.'

'Oh Jesus!' I grabbed her hand, but not quickly enough. Again she was off into those dreadful animal roars, doubling her knees up to her chest and writhing all over the bed. To stop her falling off and hurting herself I got her by the shoulders and held her down until the shudders died away and she fell back exhausted, the tears pouring down her cheeks.

When I leant forward and kissed her on the temple, she gave a wan smile and said, 'You need a shave.'

Somebody knocked on the door. The fair-haired nurse came in carrying a plastic beaker in one hand, a shallow dish in the other.

'Take these, dear,' she said. 'They'll make you feel better.'

Tracy looked at me in a questioning way, so I nodded, and watched her swallow the two white tablets. Then I said, 'Back in a minute,' and followed the nurse into the corridor. I was meaning to ask the matron how long Tracy would have to stay in when I saw another nurse coming towards me, holding the hand of a small, fair-haired boy.

'Tim!' I let his name out louder than I had meant to, and my voice echoed down the passage. As the pair approached I rushed forward, bent down and scooped him up in my arms. But at the very moment I touched him, I felt his body go rigid inside the grey track suit, and when I went to kiss him on the cheek he twisted his head away.

Then he said, loud and clear, in a passable Belfast accent, 'Yer fucking wee murderer, yer.'

The nurse took a step backwards. Her mouth fell open, and her face coloured to the roots of her hair. As for me, I was so amazed I didn't know what to feel. I didn't know whether to laugh, cry, curse, smack Tim or what. All I could do was hold him tight and take a deep breath.

'It's those filthy people who've been keeping him,' I said, by way of excuse and explanation. 'They've had a month to brainwash him.'

'That's right,' the nurse replied, recovering her composure. 'It'll wear off soon enough.'

'What about his eye?' Even with Tim's head twisted away I could see that his right eye was swollen and discoloured.

'It'll go down in a day or two,' the nurse replied. 'It seems he got a belt from the woman in charge of him. But Dr Best has had a look at it and apparently there's no damage to the eye itself.'

'Hear that, Tim?' I hefted him up and down. 'You're all right. Come on, now. You've got to help me look after Tracy.'

Still he wouldn't face me, and in desperation I suddenly remembered Billy, his teddy bear. 'Tell you

373

what,' I said. 'We've got to go and find Billy. He's at home, and he's really been missing you.'

Even that produced no reaction. I turned back to the nurse and said, 'Thanks. I'll take him now,' and I carried him back into Tracy's room, stiff as a board. When I put him down on the floor, he stood like a zombie, not moving.

At least Tracy seemed more relaxed. The sedative was taking immediate effect, and some of the strain had gone out of her face. But as I thumped down on the bedside chair I reflected bitterly on how different this was from the homecoming I'd imagined. Over the past four weeks, whenever I had allowed my hopes to rise a degree or two, I'd seen us all back at the cottage, in high summer, out in the garden, a happy family, doing our own things.

Now, in this bleak hospital room, I felt incredibly exhausted. I looked at the frozen boy and the horizontal woman, and thought, 'It isn't one life that I've got to rebuild. It's three.'

THE ONE THAT GOT AWAY
by Chris Ryan

**The number one bestseller that has now
become a classic from the true hero of the
Bravo Two Zero mission**

The SAS mission conducted behind Iraqi lines is one of
the most famous stories of courage and survival in
modern warfare. Of the eight members of the SAS
regiment who set off, only one escaped capture. This is
his story.

The One That Got Away is a breathtaking story of
extraordinary courage under fire, of hairbreadth
escapes, of the best trained soldiers in the world fighting
against the most adverse conditions, and, above all, of
one man's courageous refusal to lie down and die.

'You have personally made SAS history.'
General Sir Peter de la Billière

'It's a thrill-a-minute story of terror, hardship, heroism,
bravery and sheer guts.'   *Sun*

'Raw and brutal.'   *Daily Express*

ZERO OPTION

by Chris Ryan

SAS Sergeant Geordie Sharp, locked in a desperate private battle with the IRA, is required to undertake two top-secret missions, in the full knowledge that, if they go wrong, the authorities will deny all involvement.

In the first operation he serves as commander of a hit team on a Black or 100 per cent non-attributable task assigned to the SAW, the Regiment's ultra-secret Subversive Action Wing. The target is an Iraqi who defected to Libya after the Gulf War. The aim is to kill him and leave no clue as to the identity or origin of the assassins. The hit team will have to be absolutely clean - wear Arab clothes, use Soviet weapons and ammunition, and bear no trace of any Western organization. If anyone is killed, the body will have to be recovered or vaporised with explosives . . .

Returning to base, Sharp finds he must also carry out a high-level political assassination in mainland Britain. If he fails, his four-year old son will die at the hands of the IRA. Trapped between opposing forces in a fight to the death, he twists and turns through a nightmare maze, desperately seeking some way of averting tragedy. Who will be hit hardest - Geordie Sharp or the British government?